A GATHERING OF STRANGERS

SECOND EDITION

DARK SAVIOR SERIES
BOOK 3

JIM CLOUGHERTY

NOTE TO READER

If you enjoy *A Gathering of Strangers*, join the newsletter and receive free side stories set in the Dark Savior Series world! You'll get all side stories released up to this point, including *Slaying the Beast*, *Ground Into Dust*, and *The Seer's Game*. As more are released, you will receive those for free as well!

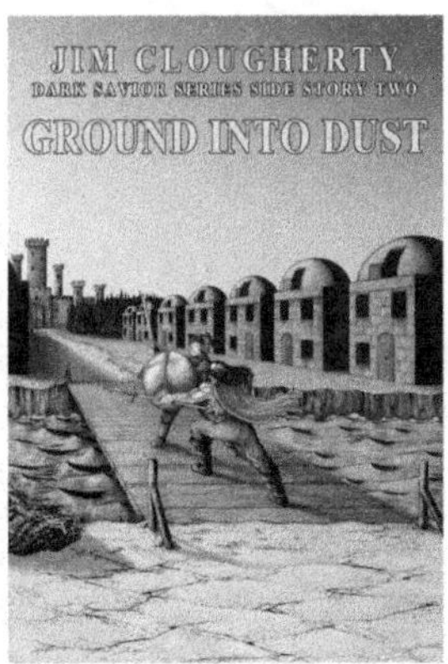

https://www.jimclougherty.com/subscribe-fantasy

For William F. L.

Endoshire
Docks
N
NW
NE
W
E
SW
SE
S
Wealthy District
City Center
Poor Shops

To Blacksmith
Sampson's Shipyard
Wealthy Shops
Church
Fields
To Farms
Bridge
Slums
Outskirts

SYNOPSIS

This is the third story in the Dark Savior Series.

In the second story, *Seven Seals*, Aldous the Wizard intercepted a letter written by Drake Danvers, Village Elder of Faiwell and mastermind of the Mt. Couture disaster a year prior.

The letter detailed how Drake and the mysterious Dark Wizard were building a team to destroy more monoliths of the Dark Savior: The Famine seal, located in Thironas, Mithika; and the Degenerate seal, found in the sewers of Endoshire, Sigraveld. Aldous, on probation for his failures a year prior, chose to forego the Wizard Council's restrictions and tasked his mute cohort Joel with gathering their friends to counter Drake's team.

Upon visiting renowned warrior Dalton Rayleigh and his student Lucia De Vesci at their home, Joel found out that Conrad Mercer had departed Faiwell, only leaving Lucia a letter that he requested not be opened unless he'd been gone for three months or more.

After Dalton opened the letter early, the group discovered that their friend had traveled to Bosfueras, Gentorgul to gather intelligence on a Dark Wizard; one that Conrad had believed to be in his presence during the Mt. Couture disaster.

With that revelation, the group split and agreed to meet back up in Endoshire once their tasks were completed. Dalton and Lucia boarded a ship to cross the sea northeast. Aldous and Joel traveled on a different vessel southeast to Currencolt, where they picked up Alistair

MacRae; much to his overprotective family's chagrin. They traveled south with haste, hoping to beat Drake's team to the Famine monolith in Thironas and protect it from harm.

After working his way through Gentorgul for months, Conrad finally reached the territory of Bosfueras. There, he encountered a strange farming community filled with unresponsive, unfriendly, and red-eyed people. The townsfolk began attacking, forcing him to kill the aggressors. The worst of his troubles came in the form of a monster known as Mr. Willoughby, who tirelessly hunted him all around town and seemed impossible to kill.

In his desperation, Conrad was tricked by Brice Garin, leader of the hooligans from the Mt. Couture expedition. He had gained the ability to change his appearance and lulled the strategist into a false sense of security before knocking him out with newfound strength.

Conrad awoke to a black mass, where the Dark Wizard committed multiple atrocities upon the townsfolk of Bosfueras, further indoctrinating them into his cult-like collective. He did so by injecting *dark essence* into his targets; a liquid that Conrad came to find out coursed through his own veins and had healed his injuries. However, when he refused the Dark Wizard's offer to study under him, the essence was removed, causing his old wounds to return. He was then thrown into a dungeon, where his injuries could fester.

In that time, Aldous, Joel, and Alistair reached the famine-torn city of Thironas. They approached Lord Roland, who agreed to take them to Ometos, the protector of the land. Aldous split up from them, electing to travel down a river leading to Lake Teras, the location of the monolith.

Alistair and Joel were introduced to Ometos, who revealed himself to be the mute's adoptive brother and friend from the distant past, Pierce Thaeon. Like Joel and some other luxians, he had been frozen in time to take on duties as Keeper of the Key someday. He'd made sure to schedule his awakening in the same period as Joel.

Long ago, Joel's adoptive parents had flown into a Gold Fever-induced rage, forcing him to kill them in order to save himself and his brother. Pierce had never forgiven him and vowed revenge. After an inconclusive battle, Angus Grouchet revealed himself as a member of Drake's team and further unveiled that Pierce had been working with him to infiltrate the location of the Famine seal in exchange for food to combat the famine. However, when Angus demanded Pierce's monolith key, the deal was called off. Angus and his new dark essence-enhanced abilities overwhelmed Joel and the others. He stole the key and then flew away with an enhanced avian named Mur'del.

After the arrival of his lover, Greta, it was revealed that Pierce had two personalities: one who hated Joel, and another who cherished him. The nicer personality had come through when Greta arrived, and all regrouped, hoping to think up a plan to stop Drake's team from destroying the Famine seal.

Meanwhile, Aldous cleared a path to the center of Lake Teras, where the Wizard King Zamarim and the monolith resided. Along the way, a group of bandits joined in, posing as starving peasants of Thironas in search of treasure to reverse their fortunes. The Lake Watcher, Guardian of the monolith, attacked and killed several bandits in gruesome fashion. Aldous came to the rescue with his water magic and brought them along to the island. At the island's center, Aldous, the bandits, and Angus fell under the spell of the Psychic Zamarim, placing them in a deep sleep.

In Endoshire, Drake Danvers struck deals and made connections with several influential folk around the city to help further spread the Dark Wizard's tainted brand of black gold. The most notable of these deals was with a slaver named Sampson, who ran a trade under the guise of a shipwright group. Drake purchased a young sex slave named Rose from him, but rather than force her into servitude, he offered to make her queen of his envisioned new world. Despite her initial reservations, Rose didn't want to return to destitution and accepted his offer.

After discovering that their ship's crew were actually timid pirates, Dalton and Lucia were greeted by projectiles from catapults on the shores of Bosfueras. Several rocks struck and sunk the ship, but all on board survived. Dalton paid Captain Auber and his two crewmates to steal an empty vessel and await their return with Conrad.

As the pair snuck through Bosfueras, Conrad was taunted and tortured within his cell at the hands of Brice and his hooligan cohorts, Barret and Powell. He managed to escape his prison, but he was pursued by Mr. Willoughby throughout the dungeon and attacked by the bottom-dwelling hooligan, Daniel.

In that time, Lucia and Dalton set fire to some shacks as a distraction, but they were caught by Brice and Powell, and a battle unfolded. Thanks to a distraction from Dalton, Lucia was able to escape the fight and broke into the dungeon where Conrad was being held. She encountered Barret, who was undergoing a gruesome transformation into a humanoid fly. After some monstrous changes, he fled into the passageways where Conrad had escaped.

A struggle between monsters broke out, which resulted in Willoughby killing Daniel. The beast then vomited dark liquid down a helpless Conrad's throat, mysteriously healing his injuries. Lucia rescued him by setting the monster ablaze. The resulting explosion killed Mr. Willoughby and gave the pair ample time to escape from a mutating Barret.

They met up with Dalton on the beach, where the stolen ship and pirates awaited them. The group narrowly escaped a pursuing mob, watching as the fires of Bosfueras raged in their rearview.

Back in Thironas, Joel and the others infiltrated Lake Teras thanks to the authority of a visiting Princess Ella, and with the help of the Wizard Scout Thurick, crossed the lake. However, before reaching the center island that housed Famine's seal, the Lake Watcher attacked, killing Thurick in the process. The others narrowly escaped thanks to Pierce and his charmed dagger.

In the cave at the island's center, Angus sprung his trap on a tired Zamarim, knocking him unconscious thanks to the Dark Savior's influence, and taking the opportunity to pass through the trials of Teras unopposed. The bandits, who had been contracted by the giant, followed along. All aside from Giles Courci were convinced by Angus that Aldous was out to kill them. Giles had been thankful for Aldous saving him from the lake watcher, and secretly pledged to aid him in defending the Famine monolith.

Aldous confronted Angus in Zamarim's chamber, where the Famine seal resided. Joel and the others rushed through the tunnels, but along the way, Pierce's personality shifted, and a duel between the luxians began. The battle went poorly for an already-injured Joel, but before striking the final blow, Pierce's calm side took control and stopped himself.

The battle for the monolith concluded when Angus destroyed it with his bone club, despite Aldous and Pierce's best efforts. Zamarim awoke from his slumber in a rage and nearly killed the giant, but he had been weakened from the attack on his mind and depleted Anima. Out of desperation, the Wizard King used a Summoner Rune to open a portal, but Angus couldn't be forced in by the weakened duo. To the surprise of all, Alistair tapped into a wind Rune to blast the giant away, banishing him to the middle of the sea.

Despite their victory over Angus, Famine had still been unleashed, and he killed two of the bandits before the Guardian arrived to fight him back into the Cold World. The would-be defenders of the seal had failed, and with that difficult loss in mind, Joel, Aldous, Alistair, and Giles departed for Endoshire, hoping to meet up with their allies and succeed in defending the Degenerate monolith.

What difficulties lie ahead for the brave group opposing Drake and the Dark Wizard? After two seals breaking, would the Wizard's Council finally step in and take the matter seriously? What effect, if any, would the dark essence within Conrad have? After suffering numerous defeats, how will Joel and the others respond to the next threat in Endoshire?

Some bonds can shatter steel…

CHAPTER 1
THE STORM

On the snow-covered landscape of Mt. Couture, a violent storm raged on. Lightning crashed into the mountainside, thunder beat on the sky like a drum, the wind howled, and hail smashed into the grand castle of the Mountain King with the ferocity of swarming hornets.

Olivier, King Wizard of the Greed monolith, sat upon a golden throne with his chiseled arms crossed. He sported a long, white beard that was crossed by a mustache resembling bomb fuses. His hair too was white and long, and atop it sat a gold-plated crown. He snorted grumpily as green balls of light shot out of the finely-crafted luxmortite chalice at his side. In the shadows of the throne room, behind grand marble columns and surrounded by weapons, treasures, and murals, appeared the Mountain King's soul slaves: men and women who had perished in his domain and were forever his *guests*.

Among the soul-enslaved was Henic Foreman, the farmer-turned-miner who had died at the hands of the Gold Fever-infected brute, Wolfgang, over a year prior. He had become accustomed to the same routine over the past year: Wizards would infiltrate the Mountain King's castle, he and the other soul slaves would be summoned, they would let out battle cries to intimidate their approaching intruders, and then attack at their master's signal. Of course, none of the soul-enslaved stood a chance against the high-ranked Wizards sent to dispose of Olivier. As Henic had it figured, they were little more than distractions.

Fighting alongside Henic were the other miners who'd fallen at the battle in the throne room a year prior. When they had been reborn as soul slaves, the men who'd previously been infected with Gold Fever lost the yellow glint in their eyes, and their sound minds returned. With their recovered sanity, however, came bewilderment. To Henic's surprise, none of them had the faintest idea of what was going on; few of the soul-enslaved did. From what he could gather, Greed had escaped from his prison in the Cold World, and for this failure, the Wizard's Council looked to remove the King Wizard from his throne and replace him. Henic had understood that much from rare conversations between the invading Wizards and Olivier before he inevitably defeated them.

Henic hadn't a clue about the ultimate fate of his friends, his family, or if Greed had been contained. The Wizards who challenged the Mountain King never brought other subjects up; they were all about business. He had come to adopt the same mentality; it was the only way to keep his sanity. The immaterial world was a quiet, yet haunting place. Henic was able to speak with the Mountain King or any of the other soul-enslaved while not taking a material form, but drawing attention to himself was ill-advised, as he had come to find out early on in his enslavement. As long as he left the Mountain King alone, and didn't speak out against him, he was left to his own devices.

The soul-enslaved miners stuck together as a group when battling on behalf of the Wizard King. Much like the outside world, everyone stayed with their own: The trolls didn't much care for humans, and neither did the one avian or knocker dressed up as a jester. The other humans included slavers, chainmail-clad men, hikers, cloaked assailants, primitive men in fur garb, and provocatively-dressed women. They had segregated themselves into separate groups since being from different eras and places meant that they had little in common with one another. The provocative maidens were the exception, however. They had become close with the Mountain King over the years, and he valued them more than the other soul slaves. Henic believed that they would be the key to ending his bondage, but they were fiercely loyal to the King Wizard; he would have to carefully form an alliance with them over time.

"Begin the battle cry!" the Mountain King commanded.

Shah!

Shah!
Shah!
After a few moments passed, Olivier said, "Again!"
Shah!
Shah!
Shah!
"Again!"
SHAH!
SHAH!
SHAH!
The Wizard King pointed at his servants, this time.
SHAH!
SHAH!
SHAH!
SH-
Olivier held his hand up, and all fell silent as his grand door creaked open. A cold draft flooded the room, but no one entered. Tension-filled silence overcame the throne room until a *whoosh* drew everyone's attention. A single arrow shot into the chamber, aimed at the Mountain King's head. Olivier reached out and caught the projectile without difficulty. It was gilded in gold.

"Such fine craftsmanship..." he trailed off before clenching down on the arrow and snapping it in half.

Henic looked to the doorway to see an armored man with a puffy gray beard. From the bottom of his chest plate and down, he wore the remnants of a white robe that was lined by various glowing symbols. The old, yet buff man extended his arm toward Olivier, and a dagger materialized. It flew faster than Henic's eyes could see, but he was able to make out its peculiar glow just before the launch.

Olivier pointed a finger upward, and before him sprouted a steel-plated wall. A loud *crack* made Henic's shoulders shoot up to his ears as the dagger pierced through but got stuck at its hand guard. The glow of the dagger faded, and the Mountain King laughed.

"They sent a Conjurer and an Augmenter this time, eh?" he called out before pointing at the steel wall, dispersing it.

Banter during the Mountain King's battle with Aldous was still fresh in Henic's mind. He recalled them mentioning that there were different types of Wizards. He knew that Olivier was a Conjurer who could materialize things that he had a strong knowledge of, but he was unsure what it meant to be an Augmenter. Throughout the year, plenty of invading Wizards had been called 'Augmenter' by the Mountain King, yet they had all displayed different abilities before their defeat.

He looked on from the shadows to see the armored Wizard, accompanied by another old man who wore a brown beret with a feather tucked into it. Poufy clothes and a golden harp in hand granted him an air of nobility, yet the twirling of his long mustache with his other hand made him seem simple-minded, in a way. The pair stopped before the Mountain King's throne, smiling and frowning up at him, respectively.

Olivier snickered at the two old men. "Well? Are you going to introduce yourselves?"

"We are members of the Wizard's Council," the armored Wizard said. His voice was as sturdy as his armor appeared to be.

"I am aware," the Mountain King replied with contempt. "Your names. Tell me something about the lives I'll be taking today."

"I am Galin," he replied with apparent pride.

"And you may call me Oratore," the other said while continuing to play with his mustache. He sounded much like an eccentric and playful old man; one who had seen enough in his life to take little seriously.

"I will call you whatever I please!" Olivier boomed as he slammed his fist into the arm of his chair. Small bolts of lightning danced around the throne. Neither of the opposing Wizards flinched at the furious display.

Galin gazed into the shadows of the throne room. Henic knew that he was supposed to be flashing a menacing grin, but it was difficult to overpower the dread in his heart. This confrontation was already playing out like many of the others had.

"So, the rumors are true. You have partaken in dark magic; you've brought shame upon the Council!"

"Hah! A Council that sentenced me to a slow, forsaken death!" the Wizard King shot back. "Tell me, did they offer you my title as a reward?"

"Perhaps..." Oratore trailed off in a playful tone. "It matters little. You have lost control of yourself, and so your title has been stripped."

The Mountain King grinned. "Oh no, it is not stripped until you *take it from me.*"

"We shall do just that today," Galin said as a large claymore materialized in his hands. He staggered his stance and held the great blade up and outward.

Olivier cackled as his two provocative soul servants approached the throne from behind. They grabbed onto each of his arms and began massaging.

"Kill them!" he commanded. The soul-enslaved charged from out of the shadows.

Henic followed along with the others, knowing that if he didn't obey, the Mountain King would force him to act and then punish him later. In the end, it mattered little. He had never, in dozens of battles, been able to land a single blow on a Wizard.

Oratore chuckled as some trolls and chainmail-clad men approached with weapons, just seconds from striking him all at once. He plucked the strings of his harp and an unbearable noise reverberated about the room. The Mountain King and all others covered their ears in desperation until the tune finally ceased. While others had been bothered by the sound, the trolls and chainmail men writhed in agony on the floor and bled from their ears.

The eccentric Wizard twirled his mustache as he crouched and touched the chest of a troll crying out in pain on the ground. The troll then gasped for air before bursting into green light and shooting back into the Wizard King's chalice. Oratore repeated the process for the other troll and the chainmail men.

Once again, Henic was confused as to what an Augmenter could truly do. At first, he reasoned that the Wizard had amplified the sound of his harp to make their ears bleed, but how could he have killed those trolls and men by merely touching their chests?

He had little time to think on the matter, however, as he noticed Galin charging out of the corner of his eye. Henic and the other miners readied their pickaxes for close combat, but they were taken aback when the armor-clad Wizard swung his blade horizontally well before reaching them. With little time to comprehend what was going on, dozens of daggers materialized along with the slash of the blade and flew into the group of miners at near-imperceptible speeds.

Many of the soul-enslaved men burst into green light and returned to the chalice, but Henic and a few other miners weren't as lucky. He felt the searing pain of blades gouging into his lungs and legs while wheezing on the floor. Now, all he could do was watch as Galin mowed down another group of nearby soul-servants.

After a short time, the armored Wizard approached Henic and the other survivors on the floor. He was taken aback by the sheer size of

Galin's blade up close; it made Lucia's oversized claymore from a year prior look like a butter knife.

"I must apologize…" Galin said as he thrust the giant blade into one of the struggling miner's backs. Like the others before, he exploded into green light and flew back into the chalice. "None of you deserve to experience death this many times over. No matter what sins you have committed in the past, God never intended for your souls to be captured by this treacherous dark magic."

The armored Wizard brought his massive blade down on the miner next to Henic and the green flashes of light stung his eyes. As the spots in his vision faded, his attacker loomed over him to deal the final blow.

"But fear not," Galin said as Henic looked up at him with a smirk, for he knew what was to come next. This was far from the first time he'd been promised freedom by a Wizard invading the Mountain King's castle. All of them had failed. "We shall free you!"

Henic felt that familiar sting of blade on his flesh, this time at his neck, and his head rolled before he burst into green light and returned to the immaterial world.

~

IN SHORT ORDER, most of the soul servants had been defeated by the duo of Wizards. Only the provocative maidens, the avian, and the knocker remained. While Galin was distracted, the avian swooped down and barrel-rolled in mid-air while releasing a couple of knives. One of the knives *clanked* off of the armored Wizard's shoulder plate, and he responded by pointing a free hand at the avian. Several daggers sliced through the air, but the bird-man evaded them with ease.

As Galin chased the avian around, he turned to see one of the maidens approaching him. She wore light blue silk with little else underneath, had long, black hair, and a pair of brown eyes that looked to be full of life despite her bondage.

"Move!" Galin said, stopping in his tracks. Instead, she ran up and hugged him.

"Please! I can't take it, anymore! Save me!" She began crying into his shoulder armor.

He sighed. "There, there… I will personally ensure that you are-"

A weak gasp escaped Galin's lips as he felt the fiery sting of a blade in his lower right back. The soul servant looked up at him and smiled with malice; she had found an open spot in his armor and stabbed him.

"Fool! Get off of me!" he shouted, but much of the energy had been drained from him by the stab wound. She clenched onto him with both arms and wrapped her legs around his torso.

Galin looked up in horror to see the Mountain King leaping through the air. He landed in front of the pair with two hands extended outward. Olivier touched the back of the provocative woman and lightning that seemed to encompass all of the throne room erupted, dulling all of Galin's senses and scrambling his mind.

By the time Galin recovered his senses, the steaming aftermath had already begun fading. Now, only the soul servant and he were emitting vapor from their charred bodies. With a puff of smoke seeping from both her mouth and nose, she fell to the floor.

"Well done, my dear," Olivier said with pride on his tongue. She merely smiled back before collapsing into a green light and returning to the luxmortite chalice, like the others before her.

With that, Galin felt the full effects of the attack: His whole body was smoldering and he was bleeding out of his nose and ears. His legs buckled, and he stumbled back until falling onto his bottom. Long, dry breaths dominated his movements as the Wizard King approached.

"You… sacrificed her…" he muttered, wide-eyed.

"Just as we have done in the past," Olivier replied with a smirk. "She would do anything for me. Such is the bond that I have with my *guests*."

"Bond? I see no bonds here! They are your slaves!" the armored Wizard burst out before he was interrupted by his own blood-filled coughs.

"You fear dark magic that much?" he asked with a venomous grin. "Then again, it's natural to fear the dark, at first."

The Wizard King held his arm back, and using a small lightning bolt, magnetized his luxmortite chalice until it reached his grip. He bit his thumb and then let the blood drip into the dark blue cup.

"I can tell that you are a Conjuring Wizard who creates fine weapons and armor… I too was a *mere Conjurer*, once. Then, I discovered the miracle of dark magic. I came to understand that Dark Conjuration has no limits," the Mountain King said as he knelt and placed his hand over Galin's armor. "Aninam vitriu tranbeo! Venar an satam!"

Olivier stood with a devious grin plastered on his face. Galin looked down at his armor to see it growing long, metal spikes all over.

"Wh-what have you done?" he choked out.

"Over time, I discovered that souls are flexible. They don't have to inhabit a *living thing*. I can give life to *anything*, in other words, with these souls that I have obtained," he replied while pointing down at the armor. A set of sad, metallic eyes formed in the middle of the chest plate.

"It can't be!" Galin cried as the armor groaned and moaned in pain.

"Help me…" the armor screeched. "Please… release me…"

"You know what to do, then," the Wizard King said with a nod to the living chest armor.

The metal spikes of the living armor shot inward and pierced Galin's body. Dozens of holes riddled his torso as he felt the unbearable grinding of metal on his ribs and spine to go along with the searing pain of his tearing flesh. The armored Wizard cried out before vomiting blood, and then he lay on the ground, his body refusing to move and his breaths becoming short. As his consciousness faded, he saw that familiar green light leave his armor and return to the chalice.

Just as Oratore had finished dispatching the avian and the other soul slave woman, he noticed a knocker leaping toward him out of the corner of his eye. *Little bugger*, he thought while turning and catching the mischievous creature by the throat. With but a moment of intense concentration, his augmenting magic got to work: He felt a clot of blood travel through the neck veins and up to the knocker's head. In mere seconds, the jester fell limp and then exploded into green light.

With that, he turned to see his Wizard cohort lying out on the ground. With a sudden urgency, he plucked the strings on his harp in the direction of the Mountain King.

Olivier saw the attack coming, however, and hopped back to his throne before the sounds could reach him.

"Your underhanded tricks won't work on me," Oratore said while twirling his mustache. "You know, the Council asked us to take you alive. But I can feel it: Your Anima is too far gone. You're a true Dark Wizard, now; one who must be destroyed."

"Hah! Only one of you remains. Your chances at winning were already a drop of water in the sea when there were two of you, but now? Death knocks upon your doorstep!"

"Oh… him?" Oratore asked, pointing at Galin. "He'll be alright."

The Mountain King burst out laughing. "What nonsense! He is mortally wounded."

"Yes," the eccentric Wizard replied before clearing his throat. "But he wouldn't be if a *certain someone* would show themselves in these chambers…"

Olivier tilted his head as an old woman wearing an elegant blue robe strolled into the throne room. She had white hair done up in a bun, but some strands fell forward and over her forehead. Her face appeared radiant and cheerful, and she wore oddly shaped rings on each of her ring fingers.

"Took you long enough," Oratore said with a snort.

"You didn't give me the correct signal; the one we agreed upon, earlier. You were supposed to pluck two certain strings of the harp in succession," she replied.

"Ah, my apologies. I thought that the bloody cries of Galin would have been enough," he replied with a roll of his eyes. The old woman walked past and approached the armored Wizard instead of responding.

The Mountain King snickered. "You!"

She stopped and turned to face him with a warm smile. "Yes?"

"State your name."

"Eniba. And what is your name?"

"You already know his name!" Oratore interjected. "You were briefed just like the rest of us. Go and heal Galin before he dies."

"I was only being polite," Eniba replied.

"You are an Augmenting Healer, then?" the Mountain King asked. Amusement crept onto his expression.

"That's right," Eniba said before resuming her walk toward Galin.

Olivier grimaced and clenched his right fist. Little bolts of lightning surged around his body.

"It is unwise to turn your back to the Mountain King!" he shouted, pointing in her direction. The lightning streaked out and then exploded on impact in the near-instant it took to reach her. As much as he didn't want to take his eyes off such a dangerous foe, Oratore had no choice but to shield them against such intense light.

As the dust settled, the Wizard King gasped to see that the bolt had not truly reached Eniba. She held her right hand out, gesturing with her ring finger, and before her stood a translucent red barrier. Bright red lettering glowed on the ring like embers in a fire pit.

"That is… ancient luxian lettering. Could it be a charmed ring?" Olivier asked.

"Not just any charmed ring," Oratore said, wagging his index finger. In the meantime, Eniba knelt, with the barrier still protecting her, and she placed her free hand on Galin's chest. "There are certain items, formerly charmed by the Ancient Ones millennia ago, that became *cursed*."

"I know of cursed objects, you insufferable know-it-all," the Mountain King shot back as he looked over to see Galin sitting up. "Since charmed objects were built off of the anguish and emotions of the luxians, attempting to destroy them will bring upon a curse that increases their power tenfold. But that power comes at a high cost. A cursed object is supposed to drain the user's life. How can she wield such an item and still draw breath?"

"To put it bluntly, she's a bit of a dullard, but her magical prowess cannot be denied," Oratore said while twirling his mustache and admiring the healing process from afar. "To counteract the ring's curse, Eniba constantly heals herself while also being able to heal others."

The Mountain King grinned. "So, it seems that the Council has finally decided to take me seriously. To send a talented batch of Wizards such as you! I welcome the challenge!"

"This time, you will lose," the eccentric Wizard said.

Eniba helped Galin to his feet. The armored Wizard nodded and placed a hand on her shoulder. "Thank you."

"Think nothing of it, my friend," she replied with a smile that quickly turned sour. "I fear that it will not be the last time today, unfortunately."

"I was merely caught off-guard."

"You are not the problem," Eniba said as she nudged her head toward the Mountain King. "It's *him*."

"Well, of course. We're here to solve that issue," Galin said with confusion in his voice.

"No, no. What I mean is that we don't even begin to compare to him."

"How can you be so sure?"

"Out of hundreds of impacts over the years, this is the first time that my cursed barrier has ever wavered..." she replied before letting out a stuttered breath. The translucent shield cracked and then shattered. Galin's eyes widened as Eniba fell to a knee. Her head felt light as a feather and her body was heavier than lead.

"Perhaps we should call *him* in, then."

Eniba let out a long breath through her nose, fluttering the stray hairs on her forehead. She turned to Oratore. "Play the three-note signal."

The eccentric Wizard cocked his head and scoffed. "Nonsense! We don't need anyone else. The three of us will do just fine."

"There are even more? I welcome you to bring as many Wizards as you need. Your heads will make fine decorations for my torture chamber," the Mountain King said with a haughty laugh.

Galin shook his head. "She's right. Play the notes."

Oratore's brow twitched for but a moment before he shrugged in defeat. "You two are overreacting, but since we are a team, and I am being overruled…"

The eccentric Wizard plucked three strings of his harp, and after the notes faded, he joined his cohorts in the corner. A tense silence came over the throne room. Only the hail clunking off the castle exterior remained to comfort Eniba's ears. She had gone into this mission with the utmost confidence in her abilities, yet that one attack was all it had taken to shake her to her very core.

After a short time of all remaining still and quiet, Olivier snickered and crossed his arms. "Well? Where is this backup of yours? Perhaps they understood that all who enter this chamber die at my hand, and they fled? I couldn't blame them for that!"

As if to answer him, a new noise echoed off in the distance: The sound of wood clanking off the floor, out in the hall. The Mountain King remained silent as the noise grew closer and closer, until finally, the throne room door creaked open.

Through the grand entrance walked Aldous the Wizard, sporting an old blue tunic, a long, gray beard, and a walking stick in hand.

"Well, isn't this a surprise?" Olivier said in an amused tone. "I thought that you'd never work up the nerve to show your face around here again. Have you finally decided to join me?"

"My apologies, old friend, but I am here to stop you," Aldous replied as he *clanked* his walking stick off the floor with authority. "But first, I wish to speak with you on a few matters."

"Hah! Why don't you talk to your old friend? Henic, I believe his name was. I must admit, it's hard to keep track of my newer *guests*," Olivier said as he held a hand out and the soul-enslaved miner appeared before the group. "Well? Have you anything to say? It has been well over a year, which is so long to pitiful humans."

"A-Aldous?" Henic asked, his mouth falling agape. "You came back for us! I knew that you would! How are Joel, Conrad, and the others? Is my family survivin' without me?"

The old Wizard returned a bewildered expression. "Oho! Let's talk about that after we have put a stop to the Mountain King's madness!"

"Yes, well-" Henic cut himself off. "Say, did you get a new 'walky-do'?"

"Eh? Pardon me?"

"Y'know, yer walkin' stick. You were always callin' it yer 'walky-do'. It looks different, now."

"Feh! Who do you think you're fooling with that act?" Olivier said as he clenched a fist and lightning barbed around him angrily. A chill ran down Eniba's spine. At any moment, he might unleash a second volley of deadly lightning, and she was unsure if she had enough strength remaining to block. "There is no way that the Wizard's Council would allow Aldous to return here. In fact, they would put him on probation and try to lay the blame on him for Greed's unsealing. And of course, knowing Aldous' stubborn way, he wouldn't want to help you, either. He would go off on his own. Furthermore, his walking stick is his artifact. The fact that your walking stick is different is a *dead giveaway*! That leaves me with one question: Who are you, really?"

"Given away already, eh?" Aldous asked in a different tone; though it was calming and soothing all at once.

Henic gasped. "Your voice..."

"Ah, well... I blame myself. There is no excuse for my sloppiness."

Aldous slowly transformed into a dark-skinned man with a well-trimmed, white beard. He had warm, welcoming brown eyes and wore a traditional Wizard's robe in a dark blue shade.

"Zequim..." Olivier muttered with wide eyes that quickly turned fiery with rage. "You dare to show yourself in my chamber? After sending dozens of assassins to dispatch me? Of all leaders in the Wizard Council's storied history, you are by far the worst!"

"That's not true. We sent Wizards here to take you back peacefully. After all, you have served as Wizard King for such a long time. It was the least we could do. But with all of the Wizards maimed and slain at your hand, the situation has gotten out of control," Zequim replied.

"And what will you do to get things under control?" the Mountain King asked with a menacing grin. Lightning began dancing around him once more.

"Prepare yourselves. If these two start fighting, we'll have to make a run for it, so we don't get caught in the crossfire…" Oratore whispered to his cohorts, who nodded in agreement.

Despite their plan to flee, an odd mixture of excitement and nerves overcame Eniba. She knew that staying behind would mean her death, but she was curious to see what a battle between two of the world's strongest would be like; even if only for a moment.

"I am only here to talk. Are you willing to speak with me?" the Council leader asked.

The Mountain King let out a vain chuckle. "The fact that you are here can only mean one thing: Another of the seals has been broken."

"Indeed. A few days ago, the Famine seal in Thironas was destroyed," Zequim replied.

"And the key?"

"Missing."

"That settles it, then," Olivier said while shaking his head. "It is inevitable. The Dark Savior will rise once again."

"Let me worry about that," Zequim said before clearing his throat. "More to the point, did you feel the presence of a Dark Wizard on the day that the Greed seal was broken?"

"Of course!" he said with raised eyebrows and a joyous smile. Zequim leaned in with interest. "After all, *I* am now a Dark Wizard, am I not?"

"You know what I meant." The disappointment in his tone was overwhelming.

"Hm… I do seem to recall someone suspicious among that group of miners. A dark Anima that one of my roaming eyes picked up on…" Olivier said with a smirk.

"Which one was it? Describe him to me, please."

"Ah! I can't seem to remember all of the details. Perhaps you could jog my memory!" the Mountain King bellowed as he reached back, formed a thunderbolt in his hand, and threw it at the Council leader like a javelin.

The bolt struck Zequim and the greatest eruption of lightning yet enveloped half of the throne room. A twinge of guilt overcame Eniba as she dove to the floor and ducked for cover along with her teammates. Even over the intense crackles and sizzles all around, she heard the harrowing cries of Henic as he was blown away by the blast.

While the dust was settling, Eniba looked up from the ground to see an open portal. Before her was a tall, bald Wizard who was dark as the night and calculating in his expression.

"Axar…" she muttered.

"Time to leave," he said, motioning the trio to enter through the portal. "They're about to get hostile, and this castle won't survive. Neither will you, if you don't hurry."

"Bah! It would have been a pleasure to see Zequim put that arrogant Mountain King in his place," Oratore complained as he stood and walked through the portal.

Galin rose next and gave Axar a nod as he walked through. Eniba stood last and turned her gaze to the settling vapor cloud. Her heart skipped a beat when, out of the smoke emerged Zequim, but not as she was used to seeing him. He had transformed himself into a majestic, quadruped creature with lion-like paws, golden wings, a swishing tail, and the face of a great eagle.

"I-is that a gryphon? I have never seen one up close. Only in paintings… incredible…" she trailed off.

"Admire any longer and you won't make it out alive," Axar said.

Eniba took a step toward the portal before stopping and looking back on the scene in wonder, one last time. Then, with a long breath through her nose, she entered the swirling, dark vortex. As badly as she wished to witness the fight, she knew that she'd only get in the way of what promised to be a bloody, destructive battle.

CHAPTER 2
WHEN A STRANGER KNOCKS

On the outskirts of Endoshire, a beautiful wooded area not yet tainted by the masses, a carriage jolted along a dirt path. In the coach were Aldous the Wizard, Joel the luxian mute, the blustering brave-heart Alistair MacRae and the mild-mannered Giles Courci. It had been sprinkling rain, so drops plopped onto the path from the branches and leaves of trees to make the road muddy. Wildlife was common: Anything from deer to squirrel showed no fear of the carriage as it squeaked by them. The woods were as green as could be; opposite to the barren lands that Thironas, Mithika had exposed them to.

Despite the woods' natural beauty, the narrow, tree-lined path filled Alistair with worry. The big redhead constantly looked to both sides of the carriage, ready for some animal or monster to attack, but nothing save for docile critters approached them. Perhaps he was looking for an excuse to talk, he thought. The journey to Endoshire had been long and quiet; filled with solemn and dreadful thoughts.

After failing to stop Angus from breaking the Famine monolith in Thironas, the group had used the portal Rune to flee the scene before drawing the eye of the Wizard's Council. They then hobbled back to their horses and carriage and used that same Rune again to reach Currencolt's seaport, Garradh-Shoit. The limitation of the portal Rune, and all summoning, was that the user had to know the location well or at least have been to the destination recently. One small mistake would send them hurdling through space and time to their deaths. And so, Aldous had elected not to risk teleporting directly to Endoshire. Instead, they traveled north by ship across the Sigrian Channel.

The trip by sea had been a somber one: Joel stayed quiet while his battered shin healed, and Aldous was doubly silent and contemplative, but at least the big man had Giles to speak with. The former bandit had many similarities to Joel, including his lighthearted nature and even how he looked. It had been easy to strike up a conversation with someone who felt familiar. The 10 days at sea were otherwise difficult on the group, as failure hung over their heads.

Any time Alistair had thought to speak with the others, Aldous' haunting words echoed in his mind:

The beginning of the end…

Was it true? Had their failure in Thironas put them on the path to destruction? Such questions made him contemplate his usefulness in the fight to protect the seven seals, and it was not a happy subject for him to dwell on.

As they continued through the woods, Aldous eyed the big redhead with a smirk. His big, round face was frowning, much like a child about to be scolded by his parents. "You sure have been quiet, lately. Is something troubling you?"

Alistair's jaw nearly hit the floor as Joel nodded in agreement. "Are ya pullin' me leg? It's *you two* who've been somber! I was too nervous ta speak!"

"Yeh," Giles chimed in. "I haven't heard a peep from anyone besides Alistair since we left."

"Oho! Joel can't exactly talk, y'know!" the old Wizard replied in a jovial tone. "But I admit my spirits were down for a while, there."

"Then, why are ya in a better mood all of a sudden?"

"When you've lived as long as I have, you learn to turn the page onward, to the next chapter. There is no use in sulking, especially when we have a job to do," Aldous said.

"So, ya think there's still hope?" Alistair asked with cautious optimism.

Aldous sighed and scratched at his long, gray beard. "Not much, my friend. Not much…"

Joel made hand signals in response. His face, which had been beaten up in the duel with Pierce's *other side* 10 days prior, had finally shrunk back down, though it was still bruised. Beneath the black and blue, a boyish face with curiosity written all over it was apparent.

The old Wizard nodded. "But that doesn't mean we can't try. Knowing that the world is in danger, we cannot sit back and allow its destruction to unfold. The four of us now have a duty: We fight to stop the Dark Savior from resurfacing at all costs."

"YEAH!" Alistair bellowed with a raised fist. Joel raised his smaller fist alongside him, but in silence, as per usual. Giles joined in on the cheer with great enthusiasm, despite not having a full grip of the situation.

Alistair raised an eyebrow, then turned to face the mute. "By the way, lad… how's the leg?"

Joel flexed and gave his shin a light pat, to which he winced.

"Still not there yet, eh?"

"That's alright," Aldous said with a smile. He clanked his walking stick off the carriage floor with a free hand while eyeing Joel's swollen leg. "He will have some more time to heal, methinks. We will wait for Dalton, Lucia, and Conrad before we try anything in Endoshire."

"But what if Drake is goin' through with his plan already?" asked Alistair.

"It's a risk I'm willing to take," he replied with an assured nod. "You got a taste of Endoshire's sheer size when we rode through. It is one of the biggest cities in the world, after all! Now, imagine a maze the same size as the city. That's what Drake is dealing with if he wants to find the Degenerate monolith."

"So, we have time," Giles said.

"Indeed. Charging in head-on may have been our downfall with the Famine seal, but now time is on our side."

"Wait, how do we know tha others will make it back? Bosfueras is supposed ta be a nasty place, ain't it? Combine that with black gold, and…"

Joel smiled and sent some signals to the big man.

"Well, I'm glad *you* have faith in 'em," Alistair replied. Joel smirked and made more signals.

"Oh no, I have faith in Dalton and Conrad. It's tha lass I have my doubts about! If I were there, it wouldn't be a problem at all, though!" he said before giving Joel a hard slap on the shoulder and laughing.

"You still have a rivalry with Lucia? I thought the two of you were on better terms, these days?" Aldous asked with amusement in his tone.

"Oh, we'll be on good terms… when she admits *I'm* tha superior warrior!" Alistair proclaimed, proudly. The mute signed back at him.

"WHAT? She's been trainin' with Dalton all o' this time? That ain't fair! I only got a month with 'im!"

"So, there are more warriors among yer group? That's good, I'm not much of a fighter," Giles said, looking down. "Mayhap they can teach me... I don't wanna be dragging you lot down in the heat of battle..."

"Don' be worryin' 'bout that, lad!" Alistair replied as he slapped his knee and chuckled. "I already told ya back on tha ship that I was takin' ya under me wing, remember? Ya don' need that weak-minded lass as a teacher! And Dalton will be too busy teachin' *me* things! We gotta make up fer lost time!"

Joel made more hand signals before an inaudible laugh escaped his lips.

"It ain't my fault I got deported! Them Village Elders wanted ta sweep me under the rug like a dust bunny! But I'm more like a *dust bear*! If she's gotten so much better from the privilege of livin' with Faiwell's best swordsman, I'll work extra hard to get my due! And if the lass has a problem with that, I'll shove me big boot up her-"

"Looks like we're here!" Aldous interrupted as he snapped the reins and the horses came to a stop.

Joel, Giles, and Alistair peered outside the carriage to see a house on their right. It was built around the trees and looked closest to a tree-house, except on the ground instead of suspended in the air. The trees acted as supports, and to the big man's surprise, they appeared sturdy.

"Shall we?" Aldous asked as he hopped out of the coach.

THE GROUP WALKED UP to the two-story home and wasted little time in knocking at a front door that sported a small metal latch at eye level. At first, nobody answered. Joel and Aldous exchanged knowing glances. Silently, they agreed to wait, hoping not to anger another resident, as they had Alistair's brother, Triston, back in Currencolt.

"Oi! Anyone home?" Alistair shouted as he banged on the door. Joel and Giles held their hands up and pleaded with him to quiet down. Their pleas fell on blind eyes and deaf ears, however. "Come on! We ain't got all day! It's rude ta keep us waitin'!"

After more pounding on the door, the metal latch opened and a pair of brown eyes peered out at the group. Although Joel had expected an angry expression, he was surprised to see a rather calm set of eyes staring back at them.

"Can I help you with somethin'?" a laid-back and deliberate voice asked from behind the door. Once again, Joel was caught off-guard by his reaction, especially given the urgency of Alistair.

"'Bout time ya showed up!" the big man said, crossing his great, hairy arms.

Aldous frowned at him before clearing his throat and looking through the slot of the door with a grandfatherly smile. "Erm, yes… we are cohorts of Dalton Rayleigh. He said that you would have a place for us to stay during our time here."

"Oh?" the voice called back casually. "I don't see Dalton among you. Where is he?"

"UGH! Just let us in, already!" Alistair complained. Joel tried not to laugh as he and Giles held the big man back.

"We are supposed to meet him here. He's coming from a different country. I suppose the old boy is running late," Aldous replied with a nervous chuckle.

"What country?" the man asked. Joel raised an eyebrow. It wasn't an accusatory question, but one of curiosity; as if he were having a regular conversation and catching up with someone he knew.

"Gentorgul."

"Whoa, really? Why would he go to a place like that?"

"Well, it's a long story, y'see…" Aldous trailed off.

"I've got time," the man replied.

"Hey, who's dat at da door?" another voice asked from within the house.

"Shut up, I'm handling it," the man at the door whispered harshly, looking back. He then returned his attention to Aldous. "Anyway, tell me the story. I'm interested."

"Could we perhaps come in and discuss it over tea?"

"We could… but how do I know you ain't approaching me with ill intent?" he asked. There was a long pause before he continued, "If Dalton told you to come here, then surely he would have told you the secret password."

The group looked at each other with worry as Joel combed his mind, trying to think of when Dalton might have told them such a thing. Could it have been at the tavern of Port City? He'd had a lot of drinks that night, and his memory of it all was-

"What? We don't got a password!" the other voice called from within the house.

"Damn it, Rolf! You idiot!"

The group once again eyed each other, this time in visible disbelief.

"What's da problem? Even if dey mean us harm, we can take a sorry lot like dat any day!"

"That's not the point. You're always ruining my fun."

Aldous cleared his throat, and the same pair of calm, brown eyes returned to the opening. "I assure you that we are trustworthy, and here on important business."

"Oh yeah? What kinda business? How do I know I can trust you?" the man asked. Once again, he wasn't asking with malice, but curiosity, to Joel's ears.

"Would you trust a Wizard?"

"Oooo! A Wizard?" Rolf squealed from behind the door.

"Shaddup!" the other man called back while turning to scold him. Moments later, he returned to the door slit. "Prove you are a Wizard."

Aldous smiled back at Joel, then held a hand out. It was fortunate that there was drizzle and mist in the air today. The small drops gathered above his hand until it turned into a floating ball of water. It swirled so fast that it sounded like it was sizzling, and for dramatic effect, Aldous added some mud to the mix.

"Whoa!" Rolf called from inside.

"Neva gets old!" Alistair said with a smile.

"And that's nothin' compared to what he can really do," Giles added with a confident nod.

"Will you let us in, now?" Aldous asked.

"That is impressive…" the man behind the door trailed off. "But how do I know you aren't a *Dark Wizard*?"

"WILL YA JUST LET US IN? SHEESH!" Alistair shouted.

"Yeah! Just let dem in, already!" Rolf repeated.

"It is unwise to let some stranger inside. Remember what I told you about the last time someone came knocking?" the man asked as he turned back to his friend.

"Oh, yeah…"

"We don't need any more odd fellas causin' trouble around here."

"How much do you know about Dark Wizards?" Aldous asked. "Did you meet one?"

"Maybe," he replied. "Let's just say that he took a very *unnerving* form, and made me a doubly unnerving offer; one that I don't think an ordinary Wizard could pull off."

Alistair scoffed. "Well? What could he have offered ya that was so bad?"

"I'm not of liberty to say. But I will tell you this much: He knew that Dalton was on his way here, just like the four of you…"

"Well, I don't really know Dal-" Alistair slapped his hand over Giles' mouth to keep him quiet.

A chill ran down Joel's spine. If he referred to the same Dark Wizard from the Mt. Couture disaster, then just how much did he and Drake know of their plans? The mute signed to the man behind the door. There were a few awkward moments of silence afterward.

"You're lucky I know USL," he said.

"Well, he knew that already. Dalton mentioned that all in the Federland army were required to learn it. The two of you fought in many battles together, didn't you?" Aldous said as he turned his hand and let the watery mud ball drop to the ground.

"That's right…" the man trailed off. He closed the latch, and after a few moments, opened the door.

Before the group stood a stocky yet well-built man with short, dark-brown hair. As Joel had noticed before, he had a calm, laid-back look to his eyes, and he wore the clothing of a huntsman: Leathery armor covered most of his body. Behind him stood a tall young man; Joel estimated him to be around his own age. He had a boyish, mischievous face to go along with a chiseled jaw that didn't quite match the rest of his lanky appearance. He too had dark hair, but it was a bit longer and messier. The young man wore a brown tunic and a weathered pair of dark pants. He was holding a wood axe, but not defensively; the axe head rested on the floor.

"Sorry for the distrust," the stocky man said. "You never can be too careful, these days."

"We understand," Aldous replied, in high spirits. "Especially if you had the displeasure of encountering a Dark Wizard."

"Still rude…" Alistair attempted to mutter, but true to form, it came out at normal volume.

"Well, I said sorry. Deal with it, big fella," the stocky man replied before sticking out a hand. "The name's Kabel."

"Alistair." He went to shake his hand but gasped when the stocky man grabbed his forearm tightly instead, and he gingerly did the same. "Tha hell kinda handshake was that?"

"That's how *real men* shake."

"But it ain't a handshake! It's… an arm shake…"

"Call it whatever you please. It's the way we shake 'round here," Kabel said before approaching Joel.

The mute did his best arm shake and then Giles and Aldous followed suit.

"I'm Giles. I appreciate you takin' us in."

"Yer Mithikan, right?" Kabel asked. Giles nodded. "Thought so. Tan skin, dark hair, and brown eyes… my wife's family is from that country. They were forced to flee."

"I don't blame 'em…" he muttered, looking down.

"I'm Aldous, and that's Joel," the old Wizard said, nudging his head toward the mute. "He doesn't speak; that's why he was using signy-dos."

The group followed Kabel into the house, where they were greeted by the lanky young man.

"The name's Rolf," he said, shaking everyone's hand normally, drawing a notable glare from Kabel.

The interior of the house was beautiful: well-made and almost entirely wooden, in addition to feeling big and open. One could feel a certain pride in the craftsmanship alone. The trunks of trees sprouted out of the floor here and there, acting as support beams, and the condition was immaculate. Outside of his home in ancient Stellinam, Joel had never been inside such a clean house before.

They sat at a table and were handed small cups of tea, which coincidentally, had been boiling over the fireplace before they came in. Joel, Giles, and Aldous accepted the drinks, but Alistair refused.

"No thank you! I ain't in the mood! Right now, a fine ale would hit tha spot, if ya got it!" the big man said.

"Not here, but I know a good place," Kabel replied with a smirk. "Let's save that for later. First, what are y'all doing here in Endoshire?"

Aldous sighed. "Since you're a friend of Dalton's, and the situation is growing more desperate by the day, I will tell you… but it may be hard for you to believe."

"Try us!" Rolf said. "We've been dealin' with some strange happenings, too." He sat at the table and so too did Kabel.

"Very well…" Aldous trailed off, pointing at the fireplace across from the table. The flames erupted to the shock of Giles, Kabel, and Rolf; but Joel and Alistair only smiled knowingly. "It all started with a mining expedition…"

The old Wizard told the harrowing tale of the Mt. Couture Disaster and the incident at Lake Teras. He then went on to explain the origins of the monoliths and the living embodiment of oppression that they sealed: The seven spawns of Stalmoz, the Dark Savior.

After a period of thought, Kabel looked up and asked, "Which monolith does Endoshire harbor?"

"Degenerate," said Aldous.

"Dat explains a lot," Rolf said.

"How do ya mean?" Alistair asked.

"Before we talk about that, I think there's somethin' you lot should see. Up for taking a trip into the city?" Kabel replied.

"What's that got ta do with anythin'?" the big redhead asked, raising an eyebrow.

"You'll see..." the stocky man said with a cool smile. "Besides, I thought you wanted some fine ales?"

"Yer damn right, I do!"

Joel wasn't ready to leave quite yet, though. He had questions, and the longer they went unanswered, the less at ease he would be. He began signing to Kabel.

"Well, let's go-"

Kabel held his tongue when his eyes caught onto Joel's hand signals.

"What'd he say?" Rolf asked.

"He wants to know about the Dark Wizard that visited us..."

"Oh, that's right! How'd ya survive an encounter with one of 'em?" Alistair asked.

For Joel, the question had been more than a curiosity. He was concerned that someone with dark intentions had gotten to and corrupted Kabel and Rolf before they arrived. For all he knew, they were working for Drake and the Dark Wizard. He at least needed to hear what had happened.

"You'd better tell us everything. It could very well have been the same Dark Wizard trying to break the seven seals," Aldous said.

"One rainy night, a week or two ago, we got a knock at the door. I always answer by opening the latch, just in case..." Kabel trailed off, looking down. He had broken out in a light sweat. "When I looked out the latch, I saw my friend."

"What's wrong with that?" Giles asked.

"This man had been dead for years. He died at war," he replied with fright in his normally calm eyes. "But there he was, right at my doorstep. It looked just like him, but when he spoke… how can I say this? It was his voice, but *it wasn't him*. Something about his mannerisms or tone… I ain't sure, but it instead felt like a very convincing imitation; a puppet come to life."

"Dat's creepy…" Rolf added. "Glad I didn't answer da door."

"I have spoken with some performers in the city; those who can do tricks. Maybe they ain't truly Wizards, but they know magic. From what I understand, a Shapeshifter Wizard could change his form to look like my old friend, but he would have to know and study him up close, would he not?" Kabel asked, his frightened gaze turning to Aldous.

"That is correct," he replied while holding up his cup of tea. "But if it were a *Dark Shapeshifter*…"

"They would be able to break the rules, right? He could take any form he wanted?" Kabel asked.

"He would be limited only by his imagination. However, imagination and reality don't often line up. If it was a near-perfect imitation of your friend, voice included, then this Dark Wizard would have known him well before his death," Aldous said. "But there are other possibilities. For instance, a *Dark Conjurer* could create a functioning human, but they would have to provide it with a soul."

Joel flashed back to their battle with the Mountain King and his soul slaves. That must have been how he had pulled it off, he thought: Capturing souls and putting them back in the bodies he recreated for them.

"At any rate, I quickly realized that I was dealing with some sorta dark force. I decided to accuse him of being a fake, and he didn't deny it. Instead, he made me an offer…" Kabel trailed off. The calm in his eyes still hadn't returned, and now the sweat was streaming down his cheeks.

"What did he offer you?" Aldous asked.

"To bring my parents back from the dead. Y'see, they were killed by squawks-"

"Tha hell're 'squawks'?" Alistair interrupted.

"An unkind way of referring to the avian," the old Wizard replied.

"Call it whatcha want, but dey killed his parents, right in front of his eyes. He's entitled to hate dem!" Rolf argued.

"He's entitled to hate the avian who killed his parents, yes, but the *entire species*?" Aldous asked, raising an eyebrow.

"That's beside the point," Kabel said with crossed arms. "The point is that my parents have been dead for a while, and it was the whole reason I joined the Federland army, even when I wasn't old enough... nobody would know that aside from my closest comrades, my wife, and now the people in this room."

"And you are certain that this friend of yours truly died at war?" Aldous asked. "Amidst all the chaos in battle, stranger things can happen. Sometimes, men go missing, but do not perish."

"There was no doubt. You can even ask Dalton when he gets here. Poor bastard witnessed it happen himself."

"In that case, the only reasonable explanation is that it was a Dark Wizard with the ability to not only Shapeshift or mayhap Conjure, but read your mind, as well. That's the only way they could have mimicked your friend's form and voice while also knowing about your parents..." Aldous trailed off. There was a marked nervousness in his voice. "Dark Wizardry allows the user to bend certain rules. An Elemental like me, for instance, cannot just branch out to Shapeshifter; it's simply not who I am and it would never work... unless I were a Dark Wizard. Dark magic provides the user with several odd abilities n' such, but also allows them to perform their own tainted version of the other magic categories."

"How do ya mean?" Alistair asked.

"There are seven types of mage: Elemental, Conjurer, Shapeshifter, Summoner, Nature, Augmenter, and Dark. A proficient Dark Wizard would be able to branch out into one of the other six categories, but it wouldn't be quite the same. It is the nature of dark magic to come out twisted in some way and require a sacrifice, usually involving pain or even death. The few Dark Wizards that live long enough to become powerful can sometimes branch out into two other categories... the strongest in history, as far as the Wizard's Council is concerned, was able to branch out into three additional categories."

"In other words, it's possible I was visited by one of the most powerful?" Kabel asked.

"I can only speculate, but it is a troubling development, to say the least," Aldous replied before sharpening his eyes. "You didn't take his offer, did you?"

Kabel shook his head firmly. "Of course not. Being in his presence made me sick to my stomach."

"Fair enough," Aldous said, putting his hands up. "I only wished to ensure that you didn't get mixed up in anything bad, is all!" He let out a chuckle, but Kabel looked down. It seemed to Joel like something was still bothering him.

"Wait, wait… if this was some powerful Dark Wizard, why are ya still around ta tell the tale? Ain't they supposed ta be ruthless killers?" Alistair interjected.

"I'm not sure why, but he never raised a finger to harm me. He only told me that he'd be in the city if I ever changed my mind… I haven't seen him since," Kabel replied, his voice cracking. "I can't quite describe how disturbing it was to see my dead friend standing before me. Then, just when I'm certain that he is an imitation, he brings up my dead parents… I have been on edge, ever since."

Aldous sipped his tea. "You were wise to avoid him. The primal fear that struck you was your gut instinct warning of danger, no doubt."

Joel nodded and then made hand signals. Kabel leaned in and tilted his head.

"Is this true?" he asked, looking to the old Wizard.

"Yes, Joel is correct. Even if the Dark Wizard were telling the truth, your parents would not have come back the same, and you would have regretted your decision. Have you ever heard that old folk tale about the rabbit's foot?" Aldous asked.

"Naw, never heard of it," Kabel said.

"I have!" Rolf said excitedly.

"Shaddup, Rolf!" the stocky man shot back.

"But I *have* heard of it! It's da story about a rabbit's foot dat grants wishes. A father makes da wish to bring his dead daughter back to life, and she returns, but somethin's wrong with her, see? She ends up going on a killing spree and he has to kill her all over again," he explained.

"Right, and I can tell you now that while only a story, it is based on some true events. Usually, when someone dies, their soul flies away to the *Great Beyond*. To bring someone back from the dead, not only does their body have to be resurrected, but their soul needs to be obtained from the Great Beyond, too. If not, they will come back as a lifeless shell. Bringing a human being back to life and dragging their soul into the body is called *Necromancy*," Aldous said in a malaise-inducing tone. All in the room remained silent, at the edge of their seats. "There has never, and I mean *never*, been a case where the soul hasn't been damaged on its way back from the Great Beyond. A tainted soul means that person will lose the part of themselves that stopped them from doing evil, primal things. An innocent soul that is tainted can become a murderer or some other sort of filth that the world does not need."

"Glad I didn't accept the offer, then," Kabel said.

"Yes, never be tempted by the idea of bringing back others from the dead. It can only result in disaster," Aldous said, looking around the room. "That goes for the rest of you, too."

Everyone nodded in agreement.

"Be at ease, old man. I learned to live with my parents' deaths long ago," Kabel said with a smile. "Now, how about we go down to the pub and-"

The stocky man was interrupted by the front door creaking open.

"Who goes there?" Alistair roared, hopping to his feet.

Everyone else stood and became defensive. Joel brought a hand to his sword's hilt. He hadn't forgotten his new vow to prevent needless death with swift action. However, with a shin injury and unease plaguing his mind, he wasn't sure if he was ready to act.

A small woman wearing a blue hood stood in the doorway.

Kabel laughed. "Don't worry fellas, she won't bite."

The woman stepped into the house with a basket of bread in hand. She was dripping from the shower of rain outside.

"This is my wife, Mirabel," Kabel said. Everyone in the room let out a sigh of relief. "Mira, these are some friends of Dalton's. You remember? My old friend from the war?"

"Dalton, you say?" she asked before looking around the room with a frown.

"Erm... Dalton ain't here... yet..." the stocky man said with a nervous chuckle.

"That explains why you're not both spending the night at the pub," Mira replied with hands to hips and an eyebrow raised.

"No need to worry," Kabel said with a reassuring smile. "I've grown up much since the last time he stopped by. We won't be doin' that again. These are friends of his, and I can assure you that they are good company."

"How does he know that?" Giles whispered, to which Joel and Alistair chuckled.

"In that case..." Mirabel muttered as cheer overtook her expression. "It is a pleasure to meet you all."

There was a radiance to her that attracted the attention of the entire room. With bronze skin, dark hair, and a petite figure, she looked every bit as Mithikan as Kabel had claimed her to be. Something about her smile made Joel feel welcome, despite not even knowing her.

"Are y'all staying for dinner? I'll start making something," Mira suggested.

"Actually… erm…" Kabel trailed off. Joel and Alistair exchanged smirks. "I *may* have told 'em they could stay as long as needed."

"We're taking in more people?" she asked. Even so, her tone wasn't angry, but more curious. In that regard, she was much like her husband, Joel noticed. "Well, I suppose it couldn't hurt to have more hands around the house. Maybe they can help me with dinner."

"*Actually…*" Kabel trailed off as he took a deep breath. "I *may* have promised to show 'em a good time at the pub tonight…"

A tense silence filled the air, except in the case of Alistair, who was failing miserably at choking back his chuckles.

"Could I speak to you in the other room, dear?" Mira asked.

"Sure," Kabel said before turning back to all at the table. "Just gotta talk with the missus and then we'll get goin' to the pub, alright?"

All at the table nodded as the husband and wife walked off into another room. While they argued, Joel found himself distracted. If a Dark Wizard could simply imitate anyone, what was to stop him from disguising himself as one of their own? He was also curious as to what Kabel wanted to show them in the city. Perhaps it was all of the doom and gloom they had just discussed, but the mute had a bad feeling.

CHAPTER 3
DEGENERACY

"Hah! Yer wife sure did put ya in yer place back there, lad!" Alistair said as the group walked to their horses.

"We made it outta the house, didn't we?" Kabel asked with a wink.

"Sorry to be a bother," Giles said.

"Worry not, little fella," the stocky man said. "All is well. Mira just wants to make sure I don't go wild, like in my younger days. Once she gets to know y'all, she'll treat you like family."

"*You* barely know us!" Alistair said before laughing.

"Why do you think we're headed to the pub?" Kabel asked as the group reached their horses.

"Y'see, Mira was worried that I'd made a drunken mistake when we took *this fool* in, too," he continued, pointing to Rolf. "But over time, she came to love him like an idiotic son, or somethin' like that. She's just a lil' more cautious than I am. Assuming you lot ain't the greatest swindlers this side of a troll merchant, she'll come to understand your important undertaking in due time."

Joel, Giles, Aldous, and Alistair boarded their carriage and got the horses ready, while Kabel and Rolf rode their own steeds. The group once again traveled through the lush woods, which were wet and muddy as ever, and eventually reached the slums of Endoshire, where the poor residents lived in their shacks or on the streets.

After passing through the slums, they reached the beginnings of the city center, where the group found a stable to leave their horses and carriage. The rain had finally stopped, but the sun was beginning to set. The streets were narrow and filled with litter. It made for a cramped environment when combined with some of the taller buildings, and it made Alistair anxious. He looked up to the odd bridges crossing from building to building overhead. There, several shadowy figures were laughing and exchanging goods. With curious folk up, down, and all around him, Alistair found himself missing the spacious paths of Ghobmor. Of all things to feel in such dire times, he hadn't expected it to be homesick.

"Not used to the big city, eh?" Kabel asked.

"No, I like havin' space ta move around," Alistair said as a passerby bumped into him. "Oi! Watch where yer goin'! That's rude!"

Rolf laughed. "Dey don't care. Dey'll continue on about deir business without even noticing you. Best not to hold a grudge."

"I expected a city of such prestige to be nicer..." Giles trailed off as he looked around. "This isn't much better than Thironas' upper district."

"Thironas, eh? That's not too far from where my wife's family fled from. A terrible famine drove them away. It must have been spread from Thironas. I still can't believe that one man was the cause of it all," Kabel replied.

"Let me be clear: The Dark Savior is not a man. Or any other conventional species found in this world. He is from a different world entirely," Aldous corrected.

Kabel chuckled. "Whatever you wanna call him is fine with me, old man. Just keep him away from *our world*."

Aldous only returned a half-hearted smile, and those same haunting words echoed in Alistair's mind: *The beginning of the end.*

~

After brushing through some large crowds, Kabel led the group into a pub that was hustling and bustling with music and dancing. Many men were laughing aloud, arm wrestling, or threatening one another drunkenly. Alistair groaned.

"Ain't there ever a time when ya *don't* get swarmed by people 'round here?" he asked.

"You'll get used to it," Kabel replied, waving him off.

The six of them found a small, round table and some stools to sit on. It wasn't long before they got to drinking. Alistair guzzled his first pint down before anyone else was even halfway finished.

"What do you think?" Kabel asked, raising his glass toward him.

"It ain't bad, I suppose… nothin' compared to a good ole' ale from Ghobmor, though!" the big man said before belching. He then got up and made his way for the bar top. "I don' feel like waitin' fer another…"

While he was gone, Joel made hand signals to Kabel and Rolf. The lanky young man tilted his head.

"I never know what da hell he's sayin'!" Rolf said with a chuckle, then slapped Kabel on the back. The stocky man's drink-filled cheeks flared out and desperately tried to contain the ale, but some of it still managed to dribble from his lips. After swallowing what remained, he glared at his cohort. "Can you translate for me?"

"He wants to know how we met and why you're livin' with me, free-loader." Kabel scowled at first, but then he started to giggle.

"Hey! I'm not a free-loader!" Rolf said as he slammed down his glass.

"Ahhh, alright, I suppose you do earn your keep…" he trailed off before returning his gaze to Joel. "I met Rolf in this very pub, believe it or not. He didn't have a home to go back to, so I took him home with me."

The mute tilted his head and signed some more.

"He wants to know why you didn't have a home. You wanna tell him?" Kabel asked, looking back to his friend.

"I was born a slave," he replied, rolling up his sleeve to reveal a branding tattoo.

"But, how?" Aldous asked, raising an eyebrow. "It's supposed to be outlawed around these parts."

"Officially? Yeh, it is. But off the record…" Kabel muttered.

"I see…" he trailed off. "How naïve of me. Of course there would be an underground trade. That's what happens when *anything* is banned."

"Well, ain't there a way to stop it?" Giles added as Alistair sat down with a new drink in hand.

"We've tried a few things. But the cold, hard reality is that the Sigrian Kingdom doesn't care. It wouldn't surprise me if they took part in it," Kabel said.

"If we could just get da slaves to rebel, we could topple da whole trade," Rolf said. "Dere's more of dem dan owners, easily."

"As a matter of fact, there's only one fella in this whole city who runs a trade," Kabel added between sips of his drink.

"Who? I could get the Wizard's Council to-" Aldous cut himself off with a sigh. "Never mind. They won't even lift a figure when the world is at stake. I'm sure they wouldn't help one city, either."

"Y'know, I was taught ta believe that Wizards were legendary; tha best of us all, but you make it sound like they're all a buncha no-good knobs!" Alistair said, firmly pressing his glass onto the table and letting out a satisfied sigh. He had finished another drink.

"Da guy's name is Sampson. He may be a fat lil' man, but don't underestimate him. He's dangerous and has powerful connections all around da land. He usually has slaves workin' on his ships, or leases 'em out to work on other dings," Rolf said.

"But that's enough of the sad talk!" Kabel said. "We're here for a good time!"

THE GROUP of six continued to drink until nightfall came and the crowd began to wind down. The singing, dancing, and general noise shrank to mere whispers. Some men had even fallen asleep, and the wenches had begun to clean the place up.

"I think I'll have a few more!" Alistair shouted with glee.

"How da hell can you drink so much and still be alive?" Rolf asked.

"It's all in tha bloodline, lad!" he said while slapping him hard off the back.

The redhead walked up to the bartender and asked for another drink. The barkeep was a slim man wearing a nice white shirt with rolled-up sleeves and suspenders going over his shoulders. It was obvious that the night had been long: There were heavy bags under his eyes, and his slicked-back, blond hair was starting to look disheveled.

"Haven't ye had enough?" the bartender asked. "Ye've been up here no less than a dozen times, or so I'd say!"

"Only a dozen?" Alistair asked while slamming his fist on the bar top and laughing obnoxiously.

"Cole, just let him have one more," Kabel said, smoothly.

"Yer a friend o' Kabel's, then? I suppose ye can have one more," the barkeep replied, then got to filling up the big man's glass.

After handing the glass back to Alistair, Cole eyed Kabel and said, "And I suppose yer here tonight fer the fun?"

Kabel chuckled and said, "Yeh, somethin' like that…"

"I can't figure out why ye keep stayin' after closin' time, 'cept that yer right crazy in the head, but it never hurts havin' ye here as protection, so I won't complain."

"'Protection'?" Aldous asked, raising an eyebrow. "And why would he need protection?"

"See, that's the interesting thing I wanted to show y'all. Just wait a little longer, and you'll see…"

~

THE GROUP CONTINUED their festivities late into the night until all other patrons and wenches left. All that remained were the group of six and Cole, who looked to be closing up. Most had forgotten that they were there for anything but a good time until they heard a loud crash outside.

"Right on time…" Kabel muttered while standing.

He walked over to one of the pub's front windows and then motioned the others over to join him. The remaining five lumbered to the window and peered over his shoulders.

Out on the street, several people in dark, hooded clothing had gathered in a circle. It started with them chattering amongst themselves, but quickly, they turned violent. Simple shoves turned to punches, and then they drew weapons: Daggers, swords, and axes gleamed in the moonlight as Kabel and the others watched on.

However, instead of turning the weapons on themselves, they began swinging them at buildings and objects around them. They danced and pranced with joy while senselessly destroying whatever was nearby. Across the street, a few of the hooded folk swung swords and axes alike at a window until it shattered. A locked crate lying on the street was hacked to bits by an axe-wielding man, but he chose not to steal any of its contents.

"Tha hell are they doin' out there? What a buncha tosspots!" Alistair said, loudly.

Rolf turned back and held a finger up to his lips. He whispered, "Dey'll hear you…"

Sinister laughter filled the air as the senseless destruction continued. One of the men brought down his hood and then turned a dagger to his own face. He carved a line straight down his cheek and laughed as the blood dripped to the ground. Joel squirmed to see his expression: pure, unadulterated bliss.

"Something is horribly wrong with these people..." Aldous mumbled.

"I coulda told ya that," Alistair tried to whisper, but it came out at normal volume. Kabel turned and shushed him in response. The big man put his hands up and said no more.

Outside, they could hear a commotion coming from down the street. The hooded men and women stopped their acts of destruction and turned their attention to the crashing and shouting.

"Get him!"

"Cut him!"

"Kill him!"

They shouted aloud with glee, then ran down the street.

"Where are they going?" Giles asked.

"They probably spotted some unfortunate soul to attack," Kabel whispered. "They always do this. On their own, it is possible to handle these knobs, but in a group? They swarm you like an angry hornet's nest. I pity whoever they have targeted."

"We have to do somethin'!" Alistair said while drawing his dagger. He had left his battle axe in the carriage at the horse stable. Joel couldn't help but notice that he had also forgotten the wind Rune gifted to him by Zamarim.

This time, the mute was sure he would have to take action. It was sooner than he wanted, but such wild folk targeting someone likely meant a pointless death could be prevented with the aid of his luxmortite sword. Joel drew his dark blue blade, and next to him, Giles called upon a steel sword. The trio made their way for the front door.

"Hold up," Kabel said. The three stopped in their tracks and looked back. Alistair wore a great frown on his round face. "It ain't worth it to go out there."

"Are ya mad, lad?" Alistair asked, putting hands to hips. "I bet you'd want our help if it were *you* out there!"

"True, but I can assure you..." the stocky man trailed off as he pulled his collar down to reveal a long, red scar. "You won't make it out unscathed."

"We're talking about another man's life, here," Aldous said as he joined Joel, Giles, and Alistair.

"Dey have traps ready for anything," Rolf said before pointing to an alleyway at the corner of the window. "Look."

The four gazed into the alley, and sure enough, several cloaked figures were waiting in the shadows that they hadn't noticed before. All had a yellow glint in their eyes.

Aldous gasped. "Yellow eyes…"

"Does that mean something to you, old man?" Kabel asked.

"Back at Mt. Couture, yellow eyes were a sign that-"

"Help!" a voice shouted from outside. It sounded familiar.

"Hold up…" Alistair muttered.

"Oof! Let go of me, ya filthy maggots!" the man cried out.

"That's Triston!" the big man said, dashing for the front door.

"I'm telling ya, it's not worth it!" Kabel said.

"That's me big brother! I ain't gonna leave 'im out there ta die at the hands of them knobs just 'cause tha perfect stranger tells me not ta go!" Alistair shot back.

"Maybe we don't know each other well, but don't forget that I gave you a place to stay. And I can tell you right now, they only intend to intimidate and rough up their targets. I've not heard of them killing anyone before."

"I ain't leavin' 'im behind, and that's that," Alistair said as he grasped the door handle. Joel followed close behind, and so too did Giles and Aldous.

"Hold it!" Cole called out from the back. "If yer a right idjit an' plan on goin' out thar anyway… take this with ye."

The barkeep searched behind his counter for a few moments before retrieving a sheathed claymore. He tossed it, and the big man caught it with a single hand.

"That wee knife ye got thar won't do much to help. Just make sure ye bring it back clean of blood," Cole said.

"I appreciate it, mistah barkeep," Alistair replied with a grin. He then leaned over and nudged Joel. "This is a chance to prove me'self ta Triston. He thinks I'm a wimp, but when I rescue his sorry arse, he'll think differently."

The mute smiled at his excited friend half-heartedly. He knew what needed to be done and was confident in his abilities, but he had a bad feeling.

Even still, Joel followed Alistair and Giles outside, and Aldous accompanied them. A group of seven men had mobbed and dog-piled Triston further down the street.

～

Alistair charged down the road like a raging bull and laid a heavy shoulder tackle on two of the hooded men, whose backs were turned to him. Like lined-up dominoes, all crashed to the ground, one after the other.

Without wasting any time, the big man picked one of the cloaked men up and threw him aside like a hunk of meat. From there, he began pushing and rolling the others away with urgent grunts. After clearing the pile, Alistair looked upon his brother, whose eyes were so wide that they looked ready to pop out of their sockets. He had the same red hair as Alistair, but a normal-sized head. Though not quite as large as his younger brother, he was still an imposing, hulking figure compared to the average man. His face was battered and bruised from the mob attack.

"Ali? What're ya doin' here?" Triston's blood-filled lips flapped as he took his brother's hand to be hoisted up.

"I should be askin' *you* that question!" Alistair replied as another cloaked man attempted to tackle him. He sidestepped the attack while bringing down the butt end of the claymore onto his neck. The hooded man crashed to the ground and after squirming briefly, fell motionless.

"More trash!" one of the crazed men cried.

"Skin 'em alive!"

Another of the hooded men came at Alistair with a club. The big redhead swung his newly acquired claymore at him horizontally in response. The hooded man jumped back to evade, and as the blade was swinging, one of his cohorts lunged out with a knife.

Alistair used the momentum of his swing to bring the claymore around for a decisive blow, but he was too slow. The hooded man plunged the knife into his hand, loosening his grip enough for the claymore to slip. He looked down in horror as blood spurted from his hand and the claymore *clanked* off the ground, several paces away.

"I just *love* the taste of pork!" said the crazed man before licking the blood off of his knife. Alistair's brow twitched in disgust. "I can't wait ta carve up that fat face of yers!"

Alistair backpedaled as the man took several wild swings at him with the knife. At the same time, Triston scrambled for the claymore on the ground. By the time he retrieved it, however, the other degenerates had recovered from Alistair's surprise attack and attacked him with a violent flurry of kicks and punches.

"Damn it, Ali! I told ya that ya weren't fit ta fight!" Triston called out as he covered up his face in desperation. The barrage of kicks continued.

"I just ain't used to a sword, is all! If I had me axe, these here waifs would be dead!"

"What's an axe got ta do with it?"

"It's a man's weapon, of course!"

As he was avoiding his pursuer, Alistair caught wind of a surprise attack to his right, but there was no time to react. Four of the crazed, hooded folk tackled him to the ground and began peppering him with punches, kicks, and shoves. The light of the moon was blotted out by their dog-piling, and even more than the strikes to his body, the feeling that darkness had swallowed him up filled him with far more dread. Once again, he had failed to impress his brother in combat, and this time, it may cost him more than his pride.

~

"I NEED BACKUP! Joel! Aldous! Giles! Where tha hell are ya?"

Alistair's powerful voice carried down the street, where the afore-mentioned group faced down over a dozen hooded men and women.

The mute's heart raced as he glanced at Aldous, who had surprisingly built up a great sweat on his brow. He had almost forgotten that his Wizard cohort was likely going through an internal struggle of his own. A Wizard attacking humans was expressly forbidden unless they were granted special permission, or ranked high enough to make such a decision. Even fighting against Angus back in Thironas had likely been grounds for expulsion from the Council, among his other transgressions. Still, he pointed his walking stick at the cloaked folk, ready to attack.

The hooded figures cackled as Alistair's desperate cries for help echoed off the stone buildings further down the street.

"We shall cleanse this city!" one woman said, hysterically.

"You stand between us and our truth!"

"Burn it all down!"

"Imperialist scum!"

The vitriol of the crowd grew with each of its members' delirious shouts, and within seconds of that rage rearing its ugly head, the cloaked villains began marching onward, like a battalion at the start of a war.

Joel readied his blade and eyed Aldous once more. He returned a reassuring nod and clanked his walking stick off the ground. This was the point of no return.

His thoughts were distracted when a hooded man lunged out and swung a sword in his direction. Joel took a step back and held his blade out for the easy block, but it also broke his stance. The crazed man howled with laughter and went for a follow-up stab. The mute sidestepped and then knocked his attacker's sword away with a sideswipe.

A loud *crack* brought relief to his heart. His foe's blade splintered from the impact of his superior luxmortite, and now he could force a surrender. With a burst of energy, Joel whirled his blade around, aimed at where the neck and collarbone met. Exercising the ultimate restraint and ignoring all of his natural reflexes, he halted the blade just before impact, and let it rest on its target. The hooded man remained still as the night and locked eyes with where Joel had stopped the sword.

Yet, a surrender never came. *How odd,* Joel thought, inspecting the yellow glow in his eyes. One of the Gold Fever-infected would have at least moved away, but this man refused to give ground. In fact, he could swear that he was *pushing the blade into his neck.*

The mute gasped and withdrew his sword at the first sign of blood. He took a step back and wiped a profuse sweat from his brow. The man before him either held no regard for his own life or had simply called his bluff. A difficult realization hit: Joel's threats were the only way he could fight without killing, yet those threats were *empty.* His posture slumping and his blade lowering, Joel felt all fighting spirit spill out of him. He could disarm these opponents all he wanted, but they could not be reasoned with; they would still press forward.

The hooded man approached with a trembling frown. "You… disgust me…"

"What are ye doin'? Defend yourself!" Giles' voice bounced around Joel's mind, but it was distracted by too many other thoughts, both dark and depressing, to truly comprehend the words.

Joel took another step back, then winced from a wave of pain that shot up his leg. He fell to a knee and grasped at the burning fire emanating from his swollen shin. That distraction was all the hooded man needed: He raised his cracked sword overhead with a ghastly cry, and the mute could do nothing but look up with wide eyes.

Just when all seemed lost, an arrow flew into the crazed man's neck, and then another into his midsection. Stutter-breathed, he looked down at the growing puddle of red in his tunic and then smiled with malice at Joel while toppling over. As if springing awake from a terrible nightmare, the mute shot up and looked around in a panic. At his feet lay the degenerate, a growing pool of red seeping out from under his corpse.

"You alright?" The clapping of his shoulder made a jittery Joel recoil, but he quickly calmed himself when he saw that it was only Giles. He pointed to the pub windows with his other hand, where both Kabel and Rolf were aiming their bows and arrows. "Seems like they've got our backs, after all."

～

"Your aim is pitiful, as always," Kabel said, nudging his lanky friend.

"It's not bad, I've just had too much to drink!" Rolf replied.

"Are ye dorbels finished bickerin'? Ye've attracted their attention!" Cole said, half-ducking behind his bar top. He was only visible from his eyes and up.

Kabel waved him off. "Calm yourself. The greatest archer there ever was watches over your pub, tonight."

"Yeh, well, I don' wanna test ye on that! I got a business ta run, ye right gobermouch!"

Kabel turned back to see a hooded man armed with a club approaching the window. He started to load up a new arrow and then shouted at Rolf, "Shoot him!"

The lanky young man unleashed an arrow, but it narrowly missed. Kabel then shot an arrow toward the head, but to his surprise, his target ducked below it. Now that he was visible to the enemy, his aim could easily be predicted.

"Close the windows!" he said. Rolf quickly shut the one he'd been aiming out of, and so too did Kabel. They locked the latches and watched with steady hands on their bows as the hooded man approached.

Rather than using his club to break the window, however, the hooded man simply stood there, staring through it with a rotten smile. Kabel gripped the sword hilt at his hip in anticipation.

"They're rowdier than usual!" he called back to Cole without taking his eyes off the man outside.

"That's 'cause yer crazy friends riled 'em up!" the barkeep shot back.

"Actually, I barely know them..." Kabel muttered, then chuckled.

39

He narrowed his eyes at the man outside, whose grin seemed to grow a little larger with each passing second. "What're you lookin' at, handsome?"

The crazed man head-butted the window, and it cracked. Blood trickled down his forehead, but the same dreadful smile remained. Kabel gripped the hilt of his sword tighter.

"Ain't ye gonna stop 'im?" Cole asked. The stocky man held his hand up to silence the barkeep.

With hysterical laughter, the crazed man smashed his head into the window once more. This time, it splintered so much that he could barely be seen anymore. Kabel could only make out his piercing yellow eyes, fittingly distorted in many directions by the webs of glass before him.

"That glass was expensive! Stop 'im!" Cole pleaded.

Before Kabel could respond, the man smashed his face through and shattered the window. The stocky man took a step back and shielded his face from the flying debris. Then, not wanting to leave himself open to attack, Kabel dropped the bow and drew his sword. The hooded man had donned a crimson mask, which made his bulging eyes and blissful smile all the more noticeable. Instead of trying to climb in, however, he grabbed a loose shard of glass.

"You want handsome?" he asked, pulling the side of his lip out. The crazed man giggled as he pulled the glass shard from the side of his mouth down to the bottom of his jawline. More blood spilled out from the gaping wound like an overflowing dam.

"Now, I ahm hambsum." Blood spewed from his slit mouth as he spoke, and Kabel grimaced while pulling his blade back for a stab. The crazed man held up the dripping glass shard and reached into the window. "Do yhou wanna be hambsum, too?"

With a growl, Kabel lunged out and plunged the blade into his chest. A brief gasp was all he could muster before slumping over the window sill and falling limp.

Kabel pushed him off and back to the outside. He turned to Cole and said, "I'll pay for the window."

He looked back out onto the street to see that Joel and Giles had been swarmed by yet more of the cloaked marauders. They peppered the pair with swings of blunt instruments, blades, punches, and kicks. The first to fall was Giles. Within a second of hitting the ground, several men and women dog-piled him; laying devastating body blows and leaving him completely helpless. Joel turned to help, but he grimaced and grabbed at his shin, instead. That was all the time that the rest of the mob needed, and he, too, was tackled to the ground.

"Damn it all…" Kabel muttered, feeling the scar just below his collarbone. "I didn't think they would react like this. What a crazy lot!"

"I say we help dem," Rolf said.

The stocky man sighed and then nodded. "Let's go."

FURTHER UP THE STREET, Aldous snorted as he fended off the crazed horde with nothing save his walking stick. Since it was his Wizard's artifact and stronger than steel, the stick made for an excellent blunt weapon. However, thus far, he'd only used it to keep his foes at bay. A Wizard directly attacking humans might draw the eye of the Council, and that was the last thing he needed right now.

As he batted away the most recent attack from a crazed woman, he felt a drop of rain hit his head. *Perfect*, he thought. His defensive battle against the mob continued, and over time, the odd drops became a drizzle, and Aldous smiled. As a master water Elemental, controlling even the tiniest specs of water was but a trifle. The raindrops bent and swerved as they fell, but instead of striking the ground, they held in place between the old Wizard and the horde.

In short order, a wall of floating water separated Aldous and the hooded folk. With confused grunts, their attacks subsided, and they began staring at the marvel before them.

"Unfortunate timing for you all," Aldous said as thunder roared, and the sky lit up just long enough that he was sure they could see his confident grin.

Aldous swung his walking stick forward and a great wave of water took the shape of galloping horses, charging at the group. In just seconds, the crazed men and women were washed away while crying and lashing out. Many were violently flung into buildings or obstacles like boxes and stands on the road, incapacitating them immediately. The less fortunate of them continued to be carried by the intense current down the road until they were out of sight.

The old Wizard turned to face the hooded folk swarming Giles and Joel. Kabel and Rolf were on their way to intercept, but they stopped when a great torrent in the shape of an arm came between them and the attackers. The duo stood in silence, mouths agape, as the arm swung at the cloaked men and women, knocking them away as if a powerful geyser had just hit them. All were either flung down the street or into stone buildings, knocking them unconscious.

Joel and Giles rose, bloody and bruised, but in no further danger. The trio let out sighs of relief in unison.

"What happened to you, back there?" Giles asked, looking at Joel. The mute raised an eyebrow. "Are you alright? It seemed like you froze…"

Looking down and letting out an inaudible sigh, Joel signed to Aldous in response.

"He says that his shin injury acted up… it seems we asked you to fight a wee bit too early, eh Joel?" Aldous chuckled while clanking his walking stick off the stone.

Giles only frowned in response. The old Wizard could sense a growing unease within him, but he decided to leave the topic alone for now. He turned to where Alistair and Triston were laid out while tightening his grip on the walking stick. He had a little more work to do.

CHAPTER 4
THE PLAN

Aldous' overwhelming water magic had proven effective in washing all of the hooded fiends away, and as the night went on, it only became easier to subdue them thanks to the pouring rain. Despite their obvious disadvantage, the hooded men and women had been like ravenous attack dogs until light began creeping into the city; and then, they ran off with tails between their legs. It was a marvel to look upon the destruction left by the attackers: Even the veritable river that Aldous had unleashed on the streets could not entirely cleanse them of broken glass, splintered wood, and trails of blood.

After the final attacker departed, everyone took refuge in Cole's bar. All were exhausted, and most were nursing minor wounds.

"So… what did you think?" Kabel asked the group with hands to his hips and a cheeky smile.

"*That* was what ya wanted ta show us? *That* is what ya call interestin'?" Alistair asked as he plopped down on a chair. He rubbed the welt under his left eye. It had quadrupled in size since Aldous rescued him and his brother. Blood leaked through the cloth that was wrapped around his hand, and cuts and bruises painted his body.

"Well, it *was* interesting, wasn't it?"

"It was pure chaos, lad!" the big man replied. Triston sat next to him.

"Tha hell was wrong with those knobs, anyway? All I did was cross paths with 'em on the street, an' next thing I knew, I was blindsided!

They kept talkin' aboot how they wanted ta cut me up!" Triston said. A blood-soaked cloth covered his swollen nose. In fact, his entire face had swollen so much that it made his head seem nearly as big as Alistair's.

"They only come out at night, and they always attack in packs, like wild animals," Kabel said with crossed arms. "We don't know who they are or what their goal is. All I know is that a year or two ago, I started to notice 'em roaming the streets. At first, they would do funny things like piss on buildings or smash objects over their own heads. We all laughed at them and their idiotic behavior, as their numbers grew and they became more aggressive..."

"Den, dey started attackin' people in da streets," Rolf added, sitting at a stool by the bar top. "De authorities stopped 'em at first, but eventually, dey turned a blind eye to deir attacks, just like de slave trade."

Kabel snorted. "These people are resistant to pain, but only because they care so much for disfigurement and destruction. Their targets can be anything from other people to property, or even themselves."

"I hate ta imagine what they woulda done ta me!" Triston added.

"You might have lived." Kabel pulled down his collar to reveal a scar. "They would have maimed or scarred you, but I've never seen 'em kill before."

"That don't make any sense!" Alistair blurted out.

"At first, I could not understand it, either," Kabel said, turning his calm gaze to Aldous. Despite no outward damage, he appeared to be the most exhausted of the group. "But your harrowing tale of the black gold and its effects gave me an important clue."

"Ah, it seems we had similar thoughts," he replied with a weak smile. "But after doing battle with them, I do not think the black gold has anything to do with their behavior."

Kabel nodded and opened his mouth to speak.

"But you said dat Endoshire houses Degenerate," Rolf blurted out, drawing a frown from the stocky man. "If Greed can make man act upon deir worst desires, den Degenerate can turn 'em to decadence, right?"

"I was getting to that..." Kabel muttered.

Joel signed at the group, pointing out that Famine had possessed a couple of the bandits and turned their eyes yellow, too.

"Both of you are correct," Aldous said, nodding along. "I don't believe we are dealing with Gold Fever-infected, but instead a pack of degenerates."

"We know that Greed uses the black gold and that Famine uses them odd fruits at Lake Teras' center island… but how does Degenerate do it?" Giles asked before hacking away into his elbow. Joel felt a twinge of guilt. His hesitation earlier had consequences, including all of the body blows his new friend had taken in the brawl.

"A fair question, m'boy," Aldous said. He leaned back and stroked his long, gray beard. "We must be on the lookout for anything out of the ordinary; things that appeared around the time that these degenerates came to prominence."

"By the way," Kabel said, eyeing the old Wizard. "You never told me. Where is the Degenerate monolith located?"

"Somewhere in the city sewers."

The stocky man chuckled and shook his head.

"Tha hell's so funny about that?" Alistair asked.

"A lil' while ago, my curiosity got the better of me and I followed some of those crazed folk around until dawn. I found out that their gathering spot is near the eastern sewer entrance," he replied, rubbing at the upper section of his chest, where the scar lay. "I didn't get much further than that before they found and ambushed me. I barely managed to escape."

"It's da sewage causin' deir madness, den?" Rolf asked.

"Perhaps," Aldous said, letting out a long breath through his nose and clanking his walking stick off the floor. "But I say we investigate further once the others arrive. It could be *anything*."

"You wanna walk right into the lion's den? Are you mad?" Kabel asked.

"Oho! Worry not. I am a master water Elemental, m'boy!" Aldous replied with a grandfatherly smile. "As I recall, a river flows into Endoshire's sewer. I can wash the deranged folk away with such a supply, easily."

"That's all well an' good," Triston said as he stood, both groaning and wincing at once. "But me an' Ali won't be havin' any part of that! In fact, we'll be takin' our leave-"

"Like hell, I'm leavin'! I'm just as big a part of this as they are!" Alistair shot back.

"Brother…" Triston trailed off, placing his bear-paw-sized hand on his shoulder. "I know ya mean well, but think of how poorly ya fought out there…"

"I saved yer hide!"

"And I appreciate that. But the only reason I got captured in the first place was because I came here to save *yer* sorry hide. I overheard you and yer pals talkin' about Endoshire the night before you disappeared. Ya really need ta learn how ta lower yer voice…" Triston said in a somber tone. Joel and Aldous exchanged knowing glances and held in chuckles. The elder MacRae was *much louder* than Alistair, somehow. "And look at that! My intuition was right! You coulda been killed! It's time ta face facts: The battlefield is no place fer you, lil' brother."

"If you would just give me a chance-"

"You've had plenty!" Triston interrupted. "And now, it's time ta go home!"

"Wait a moment," Aldous said, holding up a steady hand. "You mean to say that you aren't the least bit curious about the ones who tried to mutilate you?"

"Not even a lil'!"

"What about stopping a third seal from breaking?" Giles asked.

"Look here, lil' fella! I don't know nothin' about no seals, but it's none of me business, anyway! And it ain't my brother's, either. He's comin' back with me, and that's final!" Triston bellowed back.

Joel shot a series of hand signals to Alistair for him to translate. The more that the big man saw, the more his previously frowning face lit up.

"Oi! Yer forgettin' somethin'!" Alistair said, his smile growing by the second. "If things keep goin' tha way they've been goin', they'll just send more of these crazed knobs ta Currencolt! They'll travel further an' further south, an' then…"

Triston's face turned pale and his eyes became sharp enough to cut through steel. "Don' say it…"

"They'll eventually send 'em ta Ghobmor!"

The elder MacRae slammed his mighty fist onto the table, rattling it to the core and causing most in the pub to flinch. "Boggin midden Sigraveld! Always makin' life difficult fer the rest of us!"

"We can stop it, Triston; especially with you and your brother helping," Aldous said, glancing at Joel and smiling. He'd caught on to the idea.

"Ya know that mum is gonna have our heads fer this, right?" he asked while snorting in Alistair's direction. The big man smiled and clenched his fists, and so too did his older brother. "But ta hell with tha consequences! I wanna get some payback against the knobs responsible fer all this mess, anyway!"

"YEAH!" Alistair cried, slamming his fists into the table so hard that it nearly buckled, and the wrapping around his gouged hand reddened even more. "That's tha spirit!"

Triston let out a long breath and then crossed his arms. "The only question is: What do we do, now?"

"We wait," Aldous said.

"What? But why?"

"There are three more people who have yet to join up with our little group. We will need all the help n' such we can get," he replied.

"Ah, right… Dalton. I owe him a smack in the arse for offering out my house to complete strangers!" Kabel said. All in the pub erupted with laughter aside from Cole, who groaned while rubbing his forehead. "How long do you think he'll be?"

"Based on the fact that he was traveling to Gentorgul, and then here, I would guess no more than another week, unless their mission went horribly wrong," Aldous replied.

"What if dey never show up? We can't wait around forever," Rolf said.

"True, but we will cross that bridge if we come to it. For now, I feel it is better to rest and wait for the others. Then, we can come up with a plan," the old Wizard said. "Agreed?"

All nodded along.

"Good," Cole said, breaking his long silence. "Now, do ye mind gettin' the hell outta here? I've got enough trouble sleepin' as it is!"

"Thanks for having us!" Kabel said as he motioned the others to leave. "See you later tonight, Cole?" he asked to a few laughs.

"I oughta ban ye from this establishment! But ye owe me a window, first!" Cole said as he shook his fist at the stocky man on his way out the door.

Kabel looked over to Rolf with a nervous smile. "You don't think Mira will mind taking in another stranger, do you?"

"Yer gonna be sleeping outside at dis rate," Rolf said. They both laughed.

The group of seven retrieved their horses from the stable and began making their way for the cozy house in the woods.

～

Later that morning, a giant of a man with a stone face and long, blond hair emerged from a ship of frightened men. Angus Grouchet walked up the dock, alive and well after being expelled from the Wizard King Zamarim's chamber in Thironas. He was eager to visit his boss, Drake Danvers.

The giant had been left in the middle of the sea to drown, but as luck would have it, he had come across a ship. Upon boarding, he displayed his superhuman abilities and quickly took command. He had one simple demand: To set sail for Endoshire, Sigraveld.

Angus plowed through the crowds of people by the docks, often pushing the smaller folk out of his way. After all, most of them were only human. Now, he was above them; both in ability and status. There was no time to trouble himself with peons.

Beyond the docks and at the north end of the city lay the wealthy district, where Drake was staying. The stone building was several stories tall and adorned with fanciful balconies and windows. At the roof, he could vaguely make out some straw. Probably a nest made for the enhanced avian, Mur'del, he thought.

After barging through the main entrance and walking up a few flights of stairs, Angus reached the door to Drake's quarters. He banged on the door, and after a few moments, a large, hooded figure answered.

"And who are you?" he asked. There was no response. "I won't ask again. Answer me unless you want your head bashed in. I am in no mood for games."

"You don't recognize him?" a smooth voice called from behind. The hooded man stepped aside to reveal Drake Danvers, arms behind his back and flashing that same impenetrable smile that Angus could never seem to read. With a shrug, the giant entered his quarters. "That is Ned Prescott, one of my assistants."

The giant eyed his boss, who looked ornate as ever in a fancy, red tunic. True to form, his blond hair was slicked back and there was not a single wrinkle on his gleaming face; somehow managing to appear 20 years younger than he truly was.

"I see… so, he has been given the dark essence, then?" Angus asked as Drake pulled out a chair for him at a table off to the right. There were some grapes set out on a plate, and the giant began mindlessly gobbling them down. It had been days since his last meal.

"Correct. Both he and Hector are now part of our team. A team that I am entrusting you to lead… assuming you were able to destroy the Famine seal?" he asked, leaning in and folding his hands.

"It is done. I trust Mur'del delivered the key to you?"

"Indeed, she has. Well done in breaking the seal. We are closer than ever to our goal, my friend," Drake said. He leaned back in his chair, and Angus felt a little more at ease. Still, there was *some* bad news to deliver.

"Yes, but I should tell you that the two Wizards likely survived the confrontation… unless Famine got to them."

"I see…" Drake trailed off, crossing his legs and nodding along. "I had figured the situation to be something like that when Mur'del returned alone. What happened?"

"Aldous interfered, just as you predicted…"

"But the Dark Wizard explained to me that the Famine monolith was an ideal place to isolate him. Without the proper elements to control, he shouldn't have been a match for you," Drake said. There was a certain judgment to his green eyes that stilled Angus' mindless chomping and filled him with newfound unease.

"He was stronger and craftier than expected, but the true problem ended up being the Wizard King of the Famine seal. He used a Rune stone to banish me; it ended up dumping me into the sea," Angus explained.

Drake let out a vain chuckle. "So then, they were unable to handle you in a direct confrontation. I suppose it makes sense that they would simply send you away."

"Something like that…" Angus refocused on the grapes. He'd decided to leave out the part where Zamarim had nearly caved in his head.

"I'm disappointed that you weren't able to fully complete the objective," Drake said while playing with a grape between his fingers. "But in the grand scheme of things, it could play into our hands."

"You think so?" Angus asked. He was genuinely surprised at Drake's cool demeanor. He had gotten angrier over far less, in the past.

"I do. Aldous is a radical; that is what we have learned. He will undoubtedly come here if he hasn't already, and it will cause more internal chaos within the Wizard's Council," Drake replied, spreading his arms in a grand gesture. "More chaos in the Council means a weaker Council; and when they are weak enough, *that* is when we shall obtain our prizes."

Angus was privy to the plan: Breaking all seven seals to the split identities of the Dark Savior would put so much strain on the Council that its collapse would be guaranteed. Human suffering at the hands of destructive entities like Famine and Degenerate, in combination with severe hits to their collective Anima, would see several Wizards dying; or they'd at least have their hands full. And that was when they would strike for real. The Dark Wizard laid claim to a magic that would grant them Stalmoz' inordinate power for themselves.

"I wonder which spawn of the Savior I should take under my control…" Drake trailed off.

"As long as Edith gets Greed," Angus replied.

"But of course. She needs him, after all."

The giant didn't fully trust his word on the matter. After all, his betrayal was what had rendered her all but helpless in the first place. Yet, any time he searched for hints of a lie in his expression, he simply stared back at him with that cool, confident smile. It was impossible to read him.

"Don't worry," Drake continued with a smirk. "While we wait for the right opportunity, my daughter is getting all that she needs to be kept alive."

Angus thought back to the moment he'd seen her limp body on the ground back in the Gold Pit of Mt. Couture. Such a sight had shattered him worse than Joel had shattered his arm. His future queen, his soul mate, had been taken from him. But even more so, he remembered the immense relief that flowed through his pained body when she spoke and asked him to pick her up.

The process of fusing with the monster Greed had shredded her spine completely, however, and after their escape, Angus saw no choice but to go to Drake for help. The blonde beauty shouted, cried, and complained at the idea, but as far as he was concerned, it was the best option.

Upon returning to Faiwell, Drake had sent them into hiding and got the Dark Wizard to check on her. He had concluded that Edith was slowly transforming into a slave of Greed and that the only way to keep her alive was the black gold. The Dark Wizard had performed experiments on others to see if his dark essence could heal her, but he concluded that it would only prolong her transformation and temporarily allow her to move. To make matters more delicate, the experiments found that too much of the essence would turn her into a mindless monster, like Mr. Willoughby.

The only way Edith could truly be saved was to have her absorb Greed himself through a powerful and forbidden spell. Angus had at first worried about the idea, but upon finding out that both Drake and the Dark Wizard were planning to do the same thing themselves, he became more confident that he could bring her back, more powerful than ever. Then, they could rule over the masses as husband and wife.

Angus' thoughts were interrupted by a young woman that he caught out of the corner of his eye. She had beautiful olive skin, long, dark hair, and wore a fancy robe that appeared too big for her; probably one of Drake's, he thought. She stood in the doorway of Drake's room as if awaiting orders.

"You like?" Drake asked with a cool smile. "Her name's Rose. Beautiful, isn't she?"

"Very much so."

"She is to bare my next child; to be my queen in our new world," he said. "I found her in this city, being sold for sex."

"She was a slave?" Angus cocked his head.

Drake held a finger up and shook it. "No, no. Slavery is 'outlawed' in these parts. But off the record?" His mysterious green eyes focused on Rose, who returned a timid smile. "I am getting into a certain business. Not slavery, though. Indentured servitude."

"I see. So, you mean to get around the anti-slavery laws in Federland this way?" Angus asked.

"I always knew you had an eye for the bigger picture," Drake said before leaning in and folding his hands. "This is a market completely untapped. It's legal; there are no provisions under our laws about indentured servants. We simply buy them as slaves, and then the owners sign the servitude contract for them."

"To know such a thing about our laws... the perks of being a Village Elder, right?"

"Indeed. I have access to everything I need to game the system. And I must be honest, it's *all too easy*," he replied with a grin.

"This is why I wanted to join up with you. I cannot stand the fools who go about their everyday lives like they don't have a mind. But you... you are *never* satisfied," Angus said as he slammed his fist onto the table excitedly. "And neither am I."

"Yes, and with these new connections, we'll be able to spread the black gold all the easier. The early rounds of distribution are underway as we speak. The filthy, mindless masses will soon be under our control, and the best part is that few will have the brain power to resist or complain; their grubby little mouths will be shut *for good*."

"So then, what is the next phase of the plan? How will we go about destroying the Degenerate monolith?" asked Angus.

"For now, we wait," Drake said to a raised eyebrow from Angus.

"The Dark Wizard is bringing many of his villagers to Endoshire. I imagine they will be here in a few days or so. They are trailing that Mercer boy, the mercenary from Luneria, and Dalton Rayleigh… you remember them, don't you?"

"All too well," Angus said, clenching a fist. It cracked so loud that the echoes made Rose flinch from across the room.

"I'm told that they won't be able to catch their ship, but they appear to be headed straight for us, interestingly enough."

"Is that so? Mayhap I should wait at the docks to give them a *warm welcome*."

"Not necessary. I have a contact who said he'd see to their deaths personally. He and his men work at the docks, so this way you can rest up," Drake said, pointing at Angus' neck. An old wound had opened up and blood oozed from it. "It appears you need more dark essence, to keep you strong. Thankfully, the Dark Wizard is bringing a fresh supply to the city. I'll need you at your best to lead the team."

"I won't disappoint you," the giant said.

"See to it that you don't," Drake replied in an ominous tone as he stood. "With that said, the dark essence is such a large presence that our Wizard friend is unable to summon it to us. So, I'm afraid you'll be stuck with that nagging wound in the meantime. But worry not, I have plenty of wine to take your mind off the pain. Would you care for some now?"

Angus paused for a moment. Even for him, an opportunity to mingle with one of the elites was a rare occurrence. "I'd love some."

CHAPTER 5
INTERCEPTED

The trip from Bosfueras harbor to the port of Endoshire had taken Dalton Rayleigh, Lucia de Vesci, Conrad Mercer, and the Auber pirates about 15 days. Over that time, the booze-filled celebrations of Conrad's rescue had tapered off into quiet days out at sea.

Dalton and Captain Geoffrey Auber had spent much of their time discussing treasures and potential business for when they reached Endoshire. Ebbie and Franco stuck closely to their duties as first mate and navigator, respectively. Lucia and Conrad had spent the bulk of the trip alone and together, to Dalton's excitement. Unlike before, however, he was correct in assuming that they had formed more than just a friendship. His tendency to barge into rooms without knocking had seen him walking in on them a couple of times.

The group arrived at the docks on a chilled, foggy morning. The port felt abandoned as Captain Auber anchored down the ship and gazed out onto the docks. It was an eerily still and quiet scene: No movement was apparent in the thick of the mist, and only the calm waters slapping against the docks and rocks were there to comfort their ears.

"Guess we brought the fog with us, eh?" he asked, looking back to Dalton.

"Keep your eyes open. We can't be sure of what to expect," Dalton replied while brushing back his dark, mid-length hair.

Scratching at his scruffy brown beard, the captain asked, "Are ye tryin' ta scare me, or what? I thought ye had friends here?"

"I do, but this is a big city, and... just be on the lookout, alright?" Dalton said. Auber took in a big gulp before nodding.

The warrior next entered Conrad and Lucia's quarters to see them sitting up in bed, only half-dressed. Lucia didn't even bother to cover up this time, and Conrad was leaning up against her with an arm wrapped around her shoulder. They were obviously relaxed, and he couldn't help but be happy for them, short-lived as it was sure to be.

"Sorry to interrupt you love birds, but we've arrived. Get dressed. We'll want to depart as soon as possible," Dalton said.

"You look uneasy," Lucia replied as she tied her dark hair up in a ponytail. "Is something wrong?"

"A bad feeling."

"About?"

"We just burned our enemy's home to the ground," Conrad added while stretching his arms. "There will be a response."

Lucia gasped and the red crescent-shaped tattoo around her right eye expanded along with her shock. Dalton caught Conrad smiling at the display as she turned to face him. "You said that the Dark Wizard could go wherever he wanted in an instant, didn't you?"

"That's right. With Summoner magic, he can transport himself to a location that he is familiar with."

"This is a marked Gentish vessel. It will be easy to identify us. There could be an entire horde of angry Bosfueras villagers waiting for us to get off the ship," Dalton said.

Conrad held up a finger and said, "I wouldn't be sure of that. From all that I have gathered, there are limitations to what he can do. I noticed that he needs to perform a sacrifice of some sort; usually involving pain. If I had to guess, I'd say that the bigger the task, the bigger the sacrifice. Transporting an entire village to Endoshire would take an unprecedented sacrifice, I wager."

"Still, the Dark Wizard could have come here and let Drake know to intercept us."

"Agreed," said Conrad. "And you both mentioned that he had helped put together some sort of team, didn't you?"

"That was why we split up, to begin with. Joel, Aldous, and Alistair were to head off Drake's team in Thironas, Mithika; while we went to Bosfueras for you," Lucia replied.

"There is no time to waste," the warrior said as he turned to leave. "Be sure to pack light."

~

After Dalton left, Lucia stood and began to dress. She was tall and fit, with long and powerful legs that seemed built for combat. There were burns all about the front and back of her torso; something that she had been hiding prior to Bosfueras. However, in recent weeks, she'd learned to think of them as a lesson and not a failure. That, combined with her growing comfort in bearing them before Conrad, saw her thinking about it less and less, even when they became irritated.

As she fitted her skirt around the waist, Conrad tugged her back into the bed and she let out a gasping laugh. Lucia landed on top of him and straddled his legs, then brushed his blond hair back as they kissed.

She sat back up and studied Conrad. Since recovering him from the clutches of Brice and the Dark Wizard, there was something different about him, she thought. Was it his appearance? He stared back up at her with striking blue eyes and an overgrown, blond beard. Even his normally well-kept hair seemed out of sorts.

"I have officially decided," Lucia said, crossing her arms and nodding. "That I like you with a beard."

"Is that so?" he asked, scratching at it. "I can't wait to cut it off."

"Well then, you should get dressed. The sooner we depart, the sooner you can chop it all off," Lucia said as she got up and started for the other end of the room, where her leather torso armor lay.

She was stopped, however, by a tug of her skirt. It wasn't only his appearance, she thought while looking back at Conrad. He held onto the fabric and smiled up at her. Recently, he'd been more impulsive; spontaneous, even. When he first kissed her, it was one of her happiest moments in recent memory, but looking back, it felt out-of-character for a strategist like him to make his move so bluntly. And since that first kiss, it was as if he hadn't looked back. Every move he made or word he spoke irradiated poise with a hint of aggression that she couldn't deny excited her.

"Are you sure we have to leave so soon? We should enjoy our time together, while we can."

"You don't think we can enjoy each other's company outside the confines of this ship?" she replied with an eye roll.

"The moment we step onto those docks, we'll be entering a battle-field. Don't forget that we are up against some of the world's most ruthless people," said Conrad, his smile fading.

"True, but-"

"You gave me a valuable piece of advice back at Mt. Couture. Do you remember?" the strategist asked. Lucia cocked her head. She could only seem to recall her vitriol for Edith on that expedition, and that thought alone brought out a snorting chuckle. "When someone shows that they want to kill you, believe them, and offer no mercy."

"Ah, right. Good words to live by," she replied. Where was he going with this?

"Against our enemy, there will be no time for enjoyment or fun. Letting our guard down for even a moment could be disastrous. I learned that the hard way back in Bosfueras. This time, we will strike them down before they can harm us."

"I'm confident that we'll find time for each other." Lucia placed a hand on his cheek and smiled down at him before turning away once more to fetch her torso armor. "Besides, when Dalton says it's time to go, he's usually right."

She heard him groaning from behind as she adorned her leathery getup. *Yes*, she thought with a twinge of worry. There most certainly was something different about Conrad, of late.

EBBIE CLEANED off his hands and let out a satisfied breath. He had just finished tying the ship down with rope. As first mate of the Auber Pirates, he took to his duties with pride and joy. Still, he thought while looking down at his ragged naval garb and baggy pants, it was diffi-cult to take pride as a pirate in such a miserable outfit. His bandana, which covered a wild head of brown hair, was his only article of pirate-like clothing. He hoped that Dalton's promises to set the crew up with a business partner would lead to riches, and more importantly, better uniforms.

The first mate raised an eyebrow as a man appeared out of the fog on the dock. He wore typical sailor's clothing: Long stockings and a baggy pair of pants with a coat, but he was missing the hat. He walked up to the top of the plank but did not board the ship.

"'Ello," Ebbie said, wide-eyed. "Can I help ye with somethin'?"

"Just ensuring that you've been granted access to the country, sir," the man replied while holding out a hand. "Papers, please."

"Papers? What papers?"

"Official permission from the Sigrian Kingdom, of course. It would have His Majesty's signature on it."

"Isn't Endoshire an exception to that rule?" a familiar voice asked.

Ebbie looked over his shoulder to see his tall, thin crewmate, Franco. Even if he was the navigator and spent most of his time in his quarters, his well-fitted tunic was unbefitting for a pirate or even a sailor. Just another reason that they needed a dress code and better uniforms, he thought.

"Not anymore. His Majesty has changed the rules."

Captain Auber next approached. "Look here, fella… we're sailors from the Lunerian Kingdom. Here ta drop off supplies. Let's not cause any problems, eh?"

"I am happy to let you in if you provide the papers," the man said.

"So, yer gonna send me back to the Lunerian king with these important supplies undelivered? Yer gonna anger a king over some dumb *rule*?" Auber asked, putting hands to hips.

Instead of responding right away, the man looked up and then cocked his head. "Isn't that the Gentish flag you're flying?"

"Oh… erm…" the captain mumbled.

"This is a ship that we commandeered from Bosfueras pirates. A bunch of savages, that lot," Franco quickly added.

"I see. So, it is not officially yours…"

"It is by way of them attackin' us an' losin'!" Ebbie said with unexplainable excitement building up in his chest.

"But I tell ye what. Let us in without any trouble, and the boat is yers for free!" Auber said with a smile that was obviously forced.

The man remained silent; long enough for the sweat to accumulate amongst the pirates. Finally, he smiled, and replied, "Yes, I suppose that would be fine."

He then turned and walked back to the docks, vanishing into the mist as mysteriously as he had appeared.

"Were you just speaking with someone?" Dalton asked, approaching the pirates from the cabin.

"Oh yeh, some idiot tellin' us we needed a document to get in the country. He noticed that our ship was Gentish, but I convinced him to let us alone in exchange fer the ship itself," Auber explained with pride.

Dalton slapped a palm into his forehead.

"What's the problem?"

"You didn't think it suspicious that he would just leave us alone after bribing him? He could be hanged for accepting bribes!" Dalton said.

"Well, er… he seemed a trustworthy fella…" the captain muttered.

"Grab your belongings. We have to get out of here. *Now.*" The warrior's fearsome words sent the pirates running to their quarters with tails tucked between their legs.

AFTER A SHORT TIME, Lucia and Conrad emerged from the cabin. Lucia wore her usual leather torso armor and skirt combination and came equipped with a long sword and bow. Conrad wore his tattered farming clothes from the Bosfueras trip and appeared to carry no weapons, but Dalton was sure that he had stashed a dagger in one of his boots, as was his tendency.

"Ready to go?" Dalton asked with urgency on his tongue.

"What's wrong?" Lucia replied.

"Someone approached the ship and took a bribe from the captain when he pointed out that this was a Gentish vessel."

"How suspicious."

"Precisely," Dalton said as he attached the sheath of his long sword to the waist of his worn-out pants. He had also found a bow and a small quiver of arrows on the ship, and attached them to his other hip and back, respectively. "We may have company, soon."

"Ready ta go!" Captain Auber called from his quarters. His crew followed close behind.

"Good. Now, listen closely. In case we get split up, the rendezvous point is to the southeast of the city. There is a path that leads into the wooded outskirts, and after traveling some distance, my friend's house should be on your right. It is built around the trees and hard to miss," Dalton said.

"And your friend's name?" Franco asked.

"Kabel," he replied, then turned to the ship's plank. "Is everyone clear?"

All nodded along, and soon, they descended from the plank and onto the dock. The stubborn fog remained, making for an eerie journey along the old wood, groaning with each step. After walking to nearly the end of the dock, Dalton stopped and held a hand up; the group behind him halted. A figure appeared off in the distance, but the mist made it impossible to tell who it was. After a tense moment, the figure disappeared, and the pirates let out a sigh of relief.

"Now, I'm suspicious o' everyone..." Captain Auber murmured. "But nothin's really gonna happen, right? We'll be fine, right?"

Before anyone could respond, there was a great *whoosh* through the air, parting the fog before them at an alarming rate. In one swift motion, Dalton drew his sword and slashed diagonally upward. With a great *clang* of metal striking metal, a fluttering arrow passed over the gasping pirates' heads and landed harmlessly behind them.

"Stay with me, and you *might* survive," he said, looking over his shoulder and smirking.

He returned his focus forward to find many figures appearing off in the distance of the fog. Slowly but surely, over a dozen showed themselves at the end of the docks. All of them lumbered in their direction like lions about to pounce on prey.

"Methinks it's safe to say that they didn't take the bribe," Dalton said with a snort. He looked to his left, then his right. There were ships on each side, and they appeared to be vacant. The warrior turned back to Lucia and nudged his head toward the left ship. She nodded in response and then dashed for the vessel with Conrad in tow. Meanwhile, Dalton tugged at the pirates to join him on the boat to the right.

Both groups rushed onto their respective vessels. Dalton and the pirates peered over the railing of their ship to see Conrad and Lucia doing the same, directly across from them. In short order, a group of men adorned in grimy sailor clothing reached a point in the dock nestled between both ships. All of them had their weapons drawn. There were a few archers, but most held sabers at the ready.

In the midst of the pack, Dalton's eyes picked up on someone who looked different: He was short, fat, and wore a fancy fur coat. There was a wide smile on his even wider face, and the others seemed to be waiting on his order. No doubt, he was the leader, Dalton thought. Next, the light glimmer of armor caught his eye. It was another man who stood out: Plated armor covered all but his head, and he stood tall with the pride and nobility one might expect from royalty.

"Ah, shit..." Dalton muttered.

"What is it?" Auber asked, but the warrior only nudged him and then shushed him in response.

With his smile growing into a grin, the ring leader of the men said, "Search the boats, and kill 'em on sight! I want their heads!"

The men grumbled and made for the two vessels. Some of them also wandered down to the ship that Dalton and the others had arrived in. The fat man waited in the middle of the dock with a couple of armed men flanking him.

Dalton and the pirates broke into the ship cabin and made way for the main quarters. The warrior practically begged them not to hide in the same place as him, but they did anyway, much to his annoyance. To make matters worse, the trio constantly bickered as they hid under the bed. Dalton chose to stand along the wall where the door would open. He figured it to be the best spot for an ambush.

"Will ye move over? It's cramped under here," Auber complained to his men.

"Don't look at me. I'm the thin one," Franco said.

"Are ye callin' me fat?" Ebbie asked, loudly.

"Yes," Franco replied.

"Will you three shaddup? You're gonna get us caught!" Dalton said in a harsh whisper.

"Yer the one who's talkin' loud. I mean, come on! Look how little room I gots under here," the captain complained once more. He held his arms out for dramatic effect.

Dalton held a finger up, then pointed it at them. "I don't wanna hear another peep from you three."

That was when he heard it: a creaking noise. *The door*, he thought. Dalton's instincts kicked in and he drew his long sword. However, when he turned to look, the door hadn't moved. The warrior tilted his head, and then a smell crossed his nose. It was like a thick fog; inescapable and all-powerful. It reminded him of rotten eggs.

"Alright, which one of you knobs did that?" Dalton asked with narrowed eyes.

"The captain can really rip 'em when he gets nervous," Franco said.

Auber turned to his navigator and frowned. "Why do ye always think it's me?"

"It was me!" Ebbie proclaimed with overwhelming pride. The captain turned over and shoved him.

"Quiet down, ye blitherin' buffoon!"

"What? I ain't ashamed! I'd do it again too-"

Ebbie was interrupted by another creak, and this time it *was* the cabin door. All fell silent in the room as the door crept open. Dalton prepared his blade for a surprise attack as one of the men in sailor garb entered with his saber at the ready. The man pushed harder on the door, and it bumped into him.

"Show yerself!"

Dalton jumped out of the shadows and swung his sword horizontally. The man hopped back to avoid, and his sword smashed into the door, shutting it. Though it had missed, the warrior's attack carried with it ulterior purposes: He had gauged his opponent's reflexive speed and quickly understood that the room's size would limit both of their options for future strikes.

He pivoted sideways so that his right shoulder faced his opponent, while his sword pointed in the opposite direction. Dalton then bent his left knee and extended the right to complete his long tail stance: a defensive form that was useful in tight areas.

The man across the room cocked his head, which told Dalton all he needed to know. He smiled as the man charged across and lunged out with his saber. Dalton brought his sword forward and up in a roundabout motion, deflecting the thrusting saber and throwing the attacker off balance. The warrior followed up by pivoting while sticking his hip out and grabbing the man's blade-wielding hand. Finally, he brought his leading foot up and extended the hip further to send his opponent tumbling to the floor. Within a split second of the impact, Dalton's sword was in his chest. The attacker let out a surprised gasp as he pulled his blade out.

"Sorry," he said, then plunged the sword into his heart. "My aim was off… heat of the moment, n' all of that."

Quickly, the attacker ceased breathing, and Dalton motioned for the pirates to leave their hiding spot under the bed.

"B-but shouldn't we keep hidin'?" Auber asked with a marked nervousness in his voice.

"That is not an option anymore," Dalton replied while pointing at the dead man on the floor. "If someone comes in here and finds the body, they will alert the others. It's time to go on the attack."

"That's more like it!" Ebbie said with vigor as he hopped up from under the bed. Franco followed, and then Auber gingerly stood.

"I dunno about this… they look tough…" the captain muttered.

"Quit whining, Auber. This is a life-or-death situation, understand?" Dalton asked. Auber took in a nervous gulp and then nodded. "Now... which of you would be best with a saber?"

"Ain't that thing dangerous? Someone could get hurt!" Captain Auber replied. Dalton could only groan.

"I suppose I could... seems like an elegant enough weapon..." Franco trailed off.

"Gimme! I'll hack them waifs down faster than ye've ever seen!" Ebbie said, his fists clenching with uncontainable excitement.

"You've got some backbone, at least... good enough for me," Dalton said, pointing at the saber in the corpse's hand. "Take it."

Ebbie walked over and cautiously retrieved the saber. The warrior could tell that the trio hadn't been around many dead bodies in their day.

"Now, which of you has good aim?" Dalton asked while retrieving his bow.

∼

MEANWHILE, Conrad and Lucia hid in the dark bowels of the ship on the left. They could hear the creaks and stomps of the men searching the decks above, but Lucia had hope that they wouldn't be found. Taking refuge behind one of many shipping chests, she believed that they would give up searching quickly, given how messy and filled-in the area was.

She couldn't tell if their pursuers were formally trained, except for the man in plated armor. He was likely a Sigrian knight, she thought. In that case, they would be at a great disadvantage, lacking armor themselves. Still, she couldn't help but wonder how she compared to him. It had been a pleasant surprise to dispatch her armored opponent so quickly back in Bosfueras, but knights of Sigraveld were held in the highest regard. Either way, it mattered little. A confrontation with the knight would not be a friendly duel. The other pursuers would join in, and so a cautious approach was the only way forward-

Lucia's thoughts were interrupted when she felt a hand riding up her crouched thigh. She turned and shot an icy glare at Conrad.

"Now is *not* the time," she said in a harsh whisper. "The ship is swarming with enemies."

"Sorry," Conrad replied. "I just need to get my hands on a better weapon, and then we can take them out together."

He retrieved a dagger that she had sheathed on the upper part of her leg, under the skirt.

"Oh…" Lucia muttered and then let out a relieved chuckle.

"What happened to hiding it in your boot?" Conrad whispered with a smirk. "I noticed when you got dressed, earlier."

"The boot sheath didn't fit into my plated armor. Remember? The armor I used to save your hide?"

"I do appreciate that…" the strategist trailed off. He bent awkwardly and then drew the dagger from his boot, so he was dual-wielding. "Now, allow me to return the favor. Let's fight side-by-side, and show them who should be running from whom."

"Don't you think we should approach with more caution?"

"It is as I said earlier: Our enemy is ruthless. We must be equally as ruthless, and strike them down before they even know what hit them. If we only hide, they will eventually find us."

Lucia shook her head. "There may be a Sigrian knight among them, and with so many others searching at once-"

"That is why we'll take them out stealthily, one at a time," Conrad replied.

"I'd be more comfortable using that as our last option."

"And *I'd* be more comfortable if the people who want us dead were dead themselves," he said with a furrowed brow. Lucia cocked her head as he took her hand. "No mercy for the merciless, remember? One way or another, I'm not waiting for these people to find and kill us. I'm going on the offensive, and I'd feel much more confident with you by my side…"

She leaned in with confusion all over her face. "What are you saying? This doesn't sound like you at all. Are you sure that the dark liquid-"

Lucia interrupted herself when she heard creaking footsteps from across the room. She peered over their hiding spot to see an armed man weaving in and out of the supply chests and climbing over piles of garbage.

When she crouched back down, Conrad nudged her and then nodded toward the intruder. With wide eyes, she shook her head. Was he going to attack? That might create too much noise and alert the others, she thought. They needed to be thinking about an escape route.

"Don't worry," he mouthed with a reassuring smile.

As Lucia tilted her head in confusion, Conrad sprung up and threw her dagger at the unsuspecting man. It landed in his throat, and the intruder grasped at his neck hopelessly as he fell to the floor, choking on an endless stream of blood.

The strategist stood over the dying man with cold eyes, then ripped the dagger out of his neck. He cleaned the blood off of the blade with the man's shirt and then handed it back to a stunned Lucia.

Had his horrific experiences in Bosfueras changed him *that much*? Lucia recalled how shaken Conrad had been after killing Wolfgang, even after all of the horrible things he'd done. Yet, he had just slain a man with the same lack of care as squishing an annoying bug. Now, he was stripping the corpse of its saber, pushing and shoving it to retrieve the weapon and its sheath. As she watched the cold and calculated display, something caught her eye.

"This man..." she trailed off while holding up the corpse's wrist. There was a brand ingrained into it, and it nearly took her breath away. "He was a slave."

"That can't be right," Conrad said, inspecting for himself. His eyes widened. "It's true. I've read that slaves are often branded like this. But why would he be attacking us?"

"I cannot say for certain, but I *do* know from experience that a slave's friends and family are often used against them. These people don't want to kill us, Conrad. They *have to*. I will see no more slaves fall before me. From here on, we must use stealth," Lucia replied.

"Fair enough, but if it comes down to it, I'd rather slay a stranger than see harm come to you..."

"I appreciate that, but you are starting to worry me."

"How so?"

"I have never seen you as aggressive, violent, or passionate as you have been these past couple of weeks. Are you sure you're alright?" Lucia asked.

"I'm fine," Conrad insisted as he moved ahead, toward the exit of the ship bowels. He stopped near the door and looked back. "Are you coming?"

With a nod and deep breath, Lucia followed him out the door. Whereas before, his change in attitude had filled her with excitement and a bit of worry; those feelings were now reversed.

CHAPTER 6
THE CHASE

Dalton dashed for a man standing guard near the hallway's exit. He was in the midst of turning to face him, but in that time, the warrior had already clasped a hand over his mouth. Before the guard could even make a sound, the long sword sliced across his throat. The panicked, bloody struggle lasted only a few seconds before the man slumped over, and Dalton let the corpse down, gently.

After wiping his bloodstained hands on the corpse's sailor outfit, Dalton looked over his shoulder. Auber and Franco had gone pale, but Ebbie appeared more excited than ever. They needed to get used to this sort of ruthlessness if they wanted to survive, he thought.

With tepid steps, the group of four exited to the upper deck. Two more men patrolled the main deck below, but they were on the other side, and Dalton was able to avoid detection by ducking behind a railing where the overhang ended. He walked along his camouflage, and so too did the pirates. Eventually, they reached a set of stairs and the railing edge of the ship.

Dalton peeked over the edge to see the portly leader of their pursuers still waiting on the dock with two of his men standing guard next to him. His arms were crossed and he was tapping his feet with impatience. *No good*, he thought. More blood needed spilling before they could escape. The warrior looked back at the pirates and nudged his head toward the stairs.

As they crept down the steps, Dalton's eyes picked up on that same glimmer from earlier: The well-armored man roamed about, searching behind some crates near the mast. He appeared tall and sturdy, similar in build to Dalton himself; though his hair was dirty blond and short, and his face clean-shaven. If this man was a Sigrian knight as he suspected, then it added a whole new layer of problems to their current predicament. Thankfully, the group of four evaded notice, and hid behind some barrels of water near the stairs.

"Alright, here's the plan," Dalton whispered. "Some men are still waiting down on the dock, so we can't sneak around anymore. We must take out the two men on this deck if we are to avoid being flanked after escaping the ship. That man in plated armor is probably a knight, so I'll have my hands full while fighting him. I need one of you to bring down the other fella, so they don't team up on me. Can any of you handle that responsibility?"

"I could strike him from afar with an arrow," Franco said.

"A fine idea," said a nodding Dalton.

"Aw, but I wanted ta face someone in combat..." Ebbie muttered, his lowering posture and tone reflecting disappointment.

"Don't worry. I suspect this attack is merely a prelude to what our enemies have in store. You will have plenty of opportunities to fight," the warrior assured him before turning to Franco and pointing at the furthest man patrolling, near the ship's front. "Think you can hit him?"

"I can try."

"Trying isn't good enough. *Do it*," Dalton said while lightly jabbing his shoulder. He then crept off into position, on the right.

After waiting a short while, the armored man approached the barrels to inspect them, and Dalton sprung out to attack. The warrior swung his sword horizontally, aiming for the head, but to his surprise, the knight ducked him, then jumped back and drew his long sword.

"Found one!" he called out with a smirk. The man from across the deck began walking over.

Dalton groaned and muttered, "I hope Franco's aim is true..."

"Have you no honor?" the knight asked while pointing his sword at him. "Or mayhap you are wise to my abilities? That underhanded attack was your only chance at besting me."

"Is that so? Well, if I have no chance at winning, perhaps you could fill me in on who sent you before slaying me," Dalton retorted.

"I don't care to say, quite frankly."

"The least you could do is introduce yourself before our friendly duel."

The knight let out a vain laugh and said, "Most 'friendly duels' end with a sword in my foe's neck. You will be no different. But until then, you may call me Sir Job. When I am not tending to my duties as an honorable knight of the kingdom, I enjoy stamping out scoundrels like you for easy money."

"And I am… erm… Sir Dalton!" he replied triumphantly.

Job minced no further words and charged in with his blade at the ready. In a split second, their swords clashed, signaling the beginning of what promised to be an intense battle.

THE OTHER PATROLLING man's walk turned into a sprint as the *clang* of clashing blades rang out atop the misty deck. Franco took aim with his newly-acquired bow, but his arms were rickety with apparent nerves, and he held his fire.

"What are ye waitin' for? Shoot 'im!" Captain Auber commanded. Franco groaned and let the arrow fly.

It shot off-course and missed by a few paces to the left. The charging man halted and gazed down at the arrow stuck in the deck with wide eyes. He next looked in the pirates' direction, now alert to their presence, and started running toward them, instead.

"Oh, great! Now look what ye've done!" Auber said with a potent mix of fear and anger on his tongue.

"But I-"

"Gimme that!" the captain said as he swiped the bow from him. "Lemme see this thing…"

Auber fiddled with an arrow and then drew it back on the bow string while setting sights on the charging man. The captain felt an odd sense of calm, despite the situation. He heard the latest clashing of blades further ahead, and that was the signal to let the arrow go.

He released the arrow, and his face lit up as it traveled ahead. Such a magnificent sight to see it piercing through the mist, he thought; like a shooting star parting the clouds. There was no way it could miss.

The arrow spun out in midair and fluttered to the deck like a stick that had been clumsily thrown.

"Oh, balls…" he muttered, a pit encompassing his stomach. The arrow had flown no more than a few meters ahead.

"Well done, *sir*," Franco said with barbs of sarcasm.

"Shaddup! If I could just take another shot…" Auber trailed off as he fiddled with another arrow. The charging man was at close range.

"I've seen enough! The time fer hidin' is over!" Ebbie shouted as he leaped over the barrel before him to confront the charging man. The two men crossed blades as Franco and Auber looked at each other with mouths agape.

∽

JOB KEPT Dalton on the defensive with a flurry of downward and diagonal slashes. Rather than returning blows, the warrior let his blade lightly touch the swinging sword and backpedaled with each slash attempt. That way, he could get a feel for the speed and precision of Job's attacks.

Dalton raised an eyebrow as his back touched the ship railing. Job continued the onslaught by bringing his sword down for a decisive blow, but Dalton blocked this time by holding his blade up and horizontally. Then, with a forceful kick against his armor, he pushed the knight back. After regaining his footing, neither combatant made a move, but they held their blades steady.

"There can be no glory in your death with such a pathetic effort!" Job said, shaking his head. "Surely, you can at least leave a scratch on my armor, can you not?"

"What glory is there to face one who is only good for pillaging and murder?" Dalton replied. Job's brow twitched, but he remained silent. "I am a warrior from Federland. Unlike you, we are held to account when we act afoul. We don't have a kingdom to cover for our misdeeds."

"Ah… so, you hail from the west. I've not had the pleasure of battling men from your lands before. But if I may be so bold, I'd like to offer some advice," he replied. Dalton cocked his head. "It is a mistake to believe that you hold the power of righteous judgment over me. You are a foreigner who dishonored an esteemed official of these lands by bribing him. Do you realize what danger you have put him in by even extending such a crooked offer?"

"Not my idea…" Dalton muttered with narrow eyes.

"And on top of that, *you* attacked *me*. You presume me to be a blood-thirsty animal, but the truth is that we are both out for blood, aren't we?"

The warrior nodded. "A fair assessment. With that said, I know what it means to slay a Sigrian knight, and that is not my goal. What do you say we both walk away? I can guarantee that I will cause you no further trouble."

"I'd see my own head roll before backing away in dishonor! Prepare yourself, Sir Dalton!" Job declared as he swung his sword toward the warrior's feet.

Dalton hopped left to dodge the blow while simultaneously swinging for his head in response. Job gasped and stepped back to avoid the tip of the blade as he followed through, and with an opponent on his heels, the warrior decided it was time to go on the attack. His follow-up cut was upward and diagonal with blinding speed. The knight managed to block, but Dalton continued the upward momentum of his swing, and both swords were lifted out of defensive position. He followed up with a swift kick to Job's gut. The knight stumbled back, but once again, his chest plate had protected him. He showed no sign of damage or even discomfort.

"Your armor hardly makes this a fair fight," Dalton said with a snort.

Job spit and then snarled at him. "The blame lies with you for an obvious lack of battle preparation. If you are half the warrior you claim to be, then you must always be ready! Or you will be struck down! That, Sir Dalton, is what separates a knight from a *mere warrior*. It is not a dearth of skill or strength, but a lack of preparation, that see most of my foolish opponents slain."

"That much is apparent. Most of your opponents probably fell to that quick flurry of slashes you tried on me, earlier. You are capable, but I doubt you've ever had to deal with anyone much further than that," Dalton replied as he took a crouched stance.

The knight scoffed and opened his mouth to speak, but Dalton had already begun his next attack: He unleashed a volley of stab attempts, each aiming at the joints in his armor. Job avoided and deflected each lunge, all while maintaining his form.

Dalton's eyes widened as Job swatted his most recent stab attempt away, and returned several horizontal swings, all at different points, making them difficult to predict. The warrior had no choice but to block each attempt on reflex alone. Just as he was becoming accustomed to the pace, however, his eyes picked up on the knight arcing his most recent swing just enough that it got past his defense; Dalton felt the blade cut a split end of his hair as he flung himself backward and to the deck. He looked up to see Job pointing his sword at him, a victorious smirk on his face.

"You were so busy trying to read my past that you failed to match up with me in the present," he said.

Dalton growled and sideswiped with his sword, knocking Job's blade away just long enough for him to hop up and assume a new stance. Job, too, readjusted his form, and the duelists circled one another at a light pace to measure up.

"I must admit that you've impressed me, Sir Job. Are all Sigrian knights of such a high quality?" Dalton asked as he feigned a horizontal slash. Job responded in kind by raising his sword to where the slice would have gone, and then returned to his defensive position. "Or are you in a class of your own?"

"It matters little to a dead man!" Job shouted as he lunged out for a stab.

Dalton directed the knight's blade down to the wooden floor, where it got stuck. In that moment, the warrior stepped down on the blade to keep it wedged, and then brought his sword around for a decisive blow, aiming for the joint in the armor where his elbow and forearm met.

Suddenly, Dalton heard and felt a *whoosh* shoot past his head, stilling his blade. Next came the shrill cry of someone from the dock behind. Both the knight and warrior's attention diverted from their fight: Dalton looked ahead to see that Auber had shot the arrow, and a split-second later, Job gazed over the railing to see what the commotion was on the dock.

The slight difference in what the combatants had reacted to gave Dalton enough time to strike Job in the head with the butt of his sword. The knight's eyes rolled back as he crashed to the floor with a *thud*.

"Speaking of preparation… you shoulda worn your helm!" Dalton said. He turned his gaze back to Auber, who remained still as the night behind the barrels. "What kinda aim was that?"

"S-sorry…" the captain mumbled.

The warrior held a hand up and turned to the ship railing. Upon looking over, he saw the fat leader of their pursuers lying on the dock, grasping his leg. His underlings were hovering over him, and an arrow was sticking out of his thigh. Dalton turned back to Auber and smiled.

"Never mind what I said. Hell of a shot, Auber. Hell of a shot," he said with a nod. The captain let out a relieved breath and wiped a profuse sweat from his brow.

Meanwhile, Ebbie clashed with the other pursuer on the boat. He let out excited grunts with each swing of his saber as he pushed his opponent back with vigor.

Ebbie lunged at him with a stab, which was narrowly sidestepped. He then swung wildly in a diagonal motion on each side of his body. The pursuer gritted his teeth more and more with each block, while the first mate seemed to gain confidence with successive attacks.

Knowing that there was little time to spare, Dalton charged into the heat of battle and pierced his blade through the pursuer's chest. The man looked down with the same shocked expression as Ebbie, and then the sword ripped out, sending him to the floor in a bloody heap. The warrior finished him off with a stab to the heart for a quick death.

"Aw, why'd ye go an' do somethin' like that?" Ebbie asked, putting hands to hips. "I was about ta win!"

"For what it's worth, you did seem to have the upper hand, but there was no guarantee of a quick win, and we don't have time to wait around," Dalton replied. Ebbie sulked, but the warrior placed a sure hand on his shoulder. "Still, good work. If that man had teamed up with the knight, I'd have been skewered for sure."

Ebbie's spirits picked back up as Captain Auber and Franco approached from the barrels.

"Now, what?" Auber asked.

"Now, it is time to run, while we still have a chance," Dalton replied, nudging his head toward the ship plank. "We have been fortunate so far. Out in the open, though, it could be even more dangerous. We don't know how many men the hefty fella commands."

"You think there are more enemies?" Franco asked, tilting his head.

"It is certainly possible. This man has enough pull to command a Sigrian knight. Believe me when I say that they don't come cheap. And to make matters worse..." he trailed off while kneeling next to the corpse and lifting his wrist. Upon rolling up his sleeve, a branding became visible. "He's using slaves to do his bidding."

"What? Ain't slavery supposed to be outlawed 'round these parts?" the captain asked.

"Isn't *piracy* supposed to be outlawed around these parts?" Dalton asked with a smirk. Auber only blushed at the stupidity of his observation. "But that's enough talk. We need to go."

"Should I finish off the knight, sir?" Ebbie asked, pointing at an unconscious Job with his saber.

"Hey! Yer only supposed ta be callin' *me* 'sir'," Auber complained.

"No, leave him," Dalton said as the captain let out a groan that no one acknowledged. "The death of a Sigrian knight will attract unwanted attention."

"What could be more unwanted than the attention we are receiving now?" Franco retorted.

"If the kingdom were to discover that outsiders killed one of their knights, they would start a manhunt for us all. We'll have our hands full moving forward as it is. We don't need Sigraveld taking notice of us."

The warrior walked toward the plank, but at the ship's edge, he stopped and let out a gasp.

"What's wrong, sir?" Ebbie asked, peering over the railing.

"Will ye *stop that*?" Auber pleaded, to which Franco chuckled.

All four looked on as the two underlings draped the leader over their shoulders and disappeared into the fog at the end of the dock. Dalton started walking down the plank. "I had hoped to use him as a hostage…"

"Perhaps we could catch up with them," Franco said, trailing him.

"Doubtful," Dalton replied as the group set foot on the dock. "Be ready to run, and remember, the road to my friend's home is on the other side of the city. Take the path that leads into the woods."

All nodded as they crept forward into the unknown. While walking, Dalton felt a tap on his shoulder. He looked back to see Auber nudging his head toward the ship that Lucia and Conrad had hidden on.

"What about them?" the captain whispered.

"They know the plan. We'll meet them at the rendezvous."

"I don' think I like leavin' 'em behind like this…"

Dalton cracked a knowing smile. "Be at ease, my friend. Those two have survived far worse than this measly onslaught."

The thick mist made for a haunting journey to the end of the dock. Each of the pirates broke out in a nervous sweat; their backs were hunched with shoulders up to their ears as they took careful steps forward. Even Dalton had some hint of worry in his heart. It felt like another surprise arrow could fly through the fog at any time. However, no attack came. They reached the end of the dock and there was not a soul in sight.

A sign to their right read:

DOCK 4

Dalton narrowed his eyes to see the many tall, stone buildings of Endoshire across the road from him. He also saw that the path perpendicular to him curving either left or right. From what he remembered, choosing left would bring them further into the docking area, eventually granting the group access to a main road that crossed through the city center. It was the quickest path, but in his estimation, the most dangerous. It would bring them through the wealthy district of the north, where someone like Drake or the mysterious leader of their attackers probably resided. He was certain that traps would be laid out on such a path. On the other hand, taking a right on the road would bring them around the western coast of the city. It would be twice as long of a trip, but undoubtedly safer.

With the pirates' lack of combat experience in mind, Dalton took a right onto the road, and the others followed.

MEANWHILE, Conrad and Lucia stood with their backs against the wall in the captain's quarters of their vessel. They had made their way up from the bowels of the ship, but at least three men were patrolling the decks. Stealth had become their preference, as Lucia was adamant that they not harm any more slaves.

Outside of the captain's quarters, they could hear the footsteps of a man patrolling the hallway. Before hiding, Lucia had noticed that the hall forked into two paths: One that led to more quarters, and another that exited to the deck. Based on the pattern that the man patrolling the halls had been following, there was only about a five-second window to reach the main deck without being spotted.

After waiting for the patrolling man's footsteps to become faint, Conrad took the initiative and bolted down the hall to his left. Lucia was shocked because they hadn't agreed on when to go, but she followed him with long, silent strides all the same.

On the main deck, the duo dashed to their right and left respectively, on each side of the open doorframe, and pressed their backs against the outside cabin wall. Lucia's eyes quickly caught onto a man further up the deck with his back turned to them. She ran forward and crouched behind some crates, and Conrad followed suit.

It was obvious that they couldn't stay in their current location for long. The man patrolling the halls usually came to the doorway, and would easily spot them if they didn't make a move, soon. On the other hand, the man further up the deck could have turned around and been heading back toward them by now.

Conrad nudged his head toward the steps going up his side of the ship. They would bring them to an upper deck, where there didn't appear to be anyone patrolling. Like before, without warning, he dashed for the stairs before Lucia could even nod back. There was little time to express her annoyance, so she made a run for the stairs, and upon reaching them, looked back to the main deck. She let out a quiet breath of relief to see that the man was still turned away from them, looking out to sea. Up on the second deck, they hid behind the railing.

"We are further away from escaping..." Conrad murmured before nudging her. "It would be easier to fight. You and I could take them down."

"No. As I said, we will not kill another slave. There is no argument to be had."

"Who said anything about killing? We could always incapacitate them."

"Let's just focus on-"

"I found 'em!" a voice called out from behind.

The duo turned in horror to see a slave armed with a saber and approaching from the upper cabin hallway.

"This way!" she said while running for the stairs they had previously climbed.

Along the way, Conrad said, "We've been caught. We must stand and fight!"

Lucia stopped at the railing of the ship and looked down at the water. She could hear grumblings from the men on the deck below, along with the heavy strides of the slave who had found them.

She looked back at Conrad and sighed. "It appears we have no choice."

"That's more like it," he replied as they both drew their weapons and turned to face their attacker.

While the slave charged at the pair, however, Lucia turned to Conrad and pushed him as hard as she could. The strategist stumbled backward, hit the railing, and tumbled off the ship and into the water with a loud splash.

Lucia turned back, just in time to see the slave slashing diagonally at her with his saber. She blocked with her long sword, causing the blades to snag for a moment, and then pushed him back with all of her might. With that brief distraction, Lucia hopped onto the railing as arrows flew past her, and then plunged into the water below.

She was greeted in the sea by Conrad, who frowned at her.

"What was that all about?"

"I made a snap judgment."

"You didn't have to trick me. Aren't we supposed to be a team?" he asked.

"My apologies, but lately, you've been much more aggressive, and I knew you would argue against running away. We don't have time for that," Lucia said as she began swimming ahead. She heard Conrad's strokes close behind.

"I must admit that it's disappointing... you would decline... fighting side-by-side with me..." he muttered between breaths.

"As much as I would... love to do battle by your side... you are beginning to worry me..." she trailed off while recalling Conrad's words before they had left Bosfueras. "Do you remember... how you told me... that the *dark essence*... was forced down your throat?"

"Of course... it's the only reason... that I'm alive," Conrad replied with a chuckle. "My sustained injuries... and infections... would have killed me... if not for its healing properties."

"What if it's changing you?"

"Nonsense."

"I mean it," Lucia insisted as she took another breath. "You said that... it made Brice and the others more deranged... didn't you?"

"I feel fine. They were already deranged... and it affects everyone differently... or so I'm told. I must have been... given a weaker dose... because I'm not physically changing... as they did," Conrad said.

"I think-"

"They're in the water! Shoot 'em!" one of the men called out from the ship.

Both dunked underwater as the noise of arrows parting the air filled their ears. Lucia could hear muted shouts as they traveled beneath the waves. After resurfacing, they swam with more vigor than ever along the port, looking for a way to reach land while avoiding further detection.

~

DALTON and the Auber pirates walked along the western coast of Endoshire as the fog began to lift. They could see more stone buildings to their left with the increased visibility, and with that, the crowds up ahead became apparent. Dalton could immediately detect the pirates' nervousness.

He looked back at them and said, "Try to blend in."

"But what if someone from the crowd attacks us? Anyone could be under *that man's* employ," Franco said.

"We stick to the plan. If the situation calls for it, we'll split up. It will be more difficult for them to track us, that way," Dalton replied without looking back.

Many had gathered on the path to make lines for fish markets, but there was also an abundance of men and women trading with each other in the streets. Gypsies and Magicians performed simple tricks for the passersby, and some horses and carriages carrying rich folk parted the commoners as if brushing by weeds in a field.

When the group got caught up in the crowd, there was an overwhelming sensation of danger that encompassed them all, but over time, they started to relax. The pirates began pointing out the odds and ends of the folk they encountered. From the majestic avian flocks soaring above to great, green troll merchants badgering potential customers with terrible deals, Dalton couldn't help but smile as Auber and his crew soaked up the rich scenery.

"Ah, look at that," Franco said, pointing to a man who sat before a small barrel made of straw. He pressed his lips up to the opening of the piper in his hands. "Isn't that a snake charmer? I wish we had time to stop and watch the show."

Dalton's eyes widened as he realized that the charmer was pointing his piper at them.

"Blow dart!" he cried before tackling the pirates to the cobblestone ground. Even with the gasping crowd around them, Dalton heard the stunning *slit* of the needle soar overhead.

The warrior hopped to his feet and charged at the snake charmer as the crowd grew restless. He swung his blade at the shocked performer and cut the piper in half, then nailed him in the jaw with an uppercut. Blood and a few teeth flew through the air as the charmer toppled over. The crowd began shouting at the commotion and drawing of a weapon.

That was when Dalton started to notice his enemies hiding in plain sight; while some of them were disguised, they all bore the same wrist branding as the slave he had killed back on the ship. He counted at least a dozen armed men closing around him and the pirates.

"What do we do?" Auber asked with panic in his voice.

"Split up!" Dalton commanded as he made a run for his left, toward the alleyways of the dense stone buildings. Auber and Franco ran straight ahead on the western path, while Ebbie elected to head east, back toward the docks.

As the warrior ran, he noticed two men standing between him and the alley. Both enemies drew sabers, and Dalton brought out his weapon as he continued his sprint.

When within reach, he held his blade out to block the swing of one enemy, then turned his run into a slide to evade the other swing. With his momentum continuing, Dalton hopped up from the slide and continued his run into the alleyway.

"After him!" a voice called out from behind.

Dalton sheathed the sword and put his head down while pushing his legs to reach top speed. At that time, he heard a *whoosh* pass his ear, and then the sound of a different arrow striking the ground near his feet. The arrowhead was stuck in the dirt, and his most recent stride had caught on it. With a surprised grunt, Dalton crashed to the ground, rolling and scraping his arms and legs along the way.

Numerous and heavy footsteps kept Dalton alert, however. Within seconds of falling, he emerged out of the roll by planting his hands and pushing up before resuming his run. With at least five men following in his estimation, he took a sharp left between some tall buildings that housed interconnecting bridges on their roofs, and he could see shadowy figures gazing down on him from there. Whether they were enemies or simply onlookers, it made him all the more nervous and pushed him to move even faster, until taking a right between the next set of buildings. At the end of this alleyway was the main road, and it filled his tired lungs with relief.

Upon reaching the main road, Dalton crashed into a group of scruffy peasants who were carrying a basket of fruits. The fruits flew up into the air as all involved in the collision fell to the ground. The sting of cobblestone ripping his skin and the many gasps of passersby in the streets were not enough to keep the warrior still, though.

"Sorry…" he mumbled as the peasants yelled and threw fruit at him.

The warrior grabbed an apple as he stood, then turned and threw it at one of his pursuer's faces. The stunned man grunted as he recoiled and tripped over his own feet, bringing down one of his allies as he fell. Dalton readied his weapon in anticipation of facing the other three men, but they were nowhere to be found. His battle instincts kicking in, Dalton looked behind to see a blade swinging toward his face. The warrior barely managed a block and stumbled back until he tripped over the two downed men. As he fell, Dalton's wide eyes picked up on an arrow flying just above his head.

After scrambling to his feet, the warrior looked back to see that an additional six men had joined in on the pursuit, and two of them were armed with bows and arrows. Now, with so many enemies after him, he knew that his only chance of escape would be to weave in and out of the crowds.

He bolted down the main road, certain that it would take him to the city center. He could hear the pitter-patter of steps close behind him, and that was when Dalton saw a pack of trolls ahead, with their backs to him. A devious smile crossed his face as he took a deep breath and sprinted toward the giant, green folk. They each wore a singlet and carried clubs.

Dalton purposely slowed down as he neared the trolls so that his pursuers would close in on him. As he reached one of the green folk, he stretched out one arm, wound up, and swung as hard as he could at the troll's buttock. The magnitude of the slap echoed off all the buildings as the men trailing Dalton stopped in their sheer shock and looked on. The warrior, in the meantime, ran around in the opposite direction that the trolls turned, so that they never even saw him.

"W-wait!" Dalton one of the men cried as he ran off. Moments later, he heard the roar of the trolls, the screams of desperate men, and the splintering of wood.

The warrior turned down an alleyway and stopped to catch his breath as he chuckled at his pursuers' misfortunes. Dalton knew that he was close to the city center, so he weaved in and out of the alleys until reaching the area, then purchased a cloak with some of his remaining gold coins.

After buying the disguise, Dalton walked southeast for a while through the city and slums, until finally reaching the beginning of the woods. Out of concern, he decided to wait for the pirates. He was certain that they would take some time to reach the rendezvous if they could make it at all. Aside from that nagging concern, he felt great relief to know that he was within reach of his old friend's home. It had been a rough start to the day, and if anyone would start drinking early with him, he knew it'd be Kabel.

CHAPTER 7
THE LONG WAY

After running along the western coast of Endoshire as fast as they could, Captain Auber and Franco took a left into an alleyway tucked between stone buildings to catch their breaths. They did not detect any of the attackers from earlier and reasoned that most had followed Dalton and Ebbie when they split up.

"How… long… do ye suppose we ran for?" Auber asked between labored breaths. He was hunched over and pale; as if ready to vomit.

Franco took a deep breath and replied, "Not for very long, sir…"

The captain groaned, took another long breath, and then stood upright. "Right, then. We oughta stick to the plan. Let's keep movin'."

"Are you sure?" the navigator asked as Auber took wobbly steps forward. "You don't look well."

"Nonsense, I just need ta get me land legs!" he replied before stumbling sideways and then catching himself against the stone building to his right.

"'Land legs', sir?"

"Ye know… like 'sea legs' but for the land? I have such dedication to piracy that I'm only used to bein' at sea!" Auber said with a confident laugh, then stumbled once more. He was unable to catch himself this time, however, and fell to a knee. Eventually, he gave up on his efforts to stand and plopped onto his bottom.

"It is only you and I, sir…" Franco trailed off with an eye roll. "You don't have to impress anyone. I know you are only tired."

Auber narrowed his eyes. "Right… well, er, I didn't get a chance ta eat breakfast either, so that must be why I'm tired."

The navigator sat on the ground next to his captain. "I'm feeling exhausted, myself. Will you stay and rest for my sake?"

"Aye, I suppose we could do that."

~

LUCIA AND CONRAD continued their swim along the docks. The ships and their berths had made for good cover from their pursuers, and since the initial volley of arrows, they had encountered no further opposition. Eventually, they swam at a more casual pace, searching for a place to exit the water.

At a sizable gap between docks, Lucia stopped and shielded her nose. "Ugh! What is that putrid smell?"

Conrad looked ahead with focused eyes. Along the coastline, there was a large sewer pipe dumping muddy water out into the ocean. He turned to face Lucia and smiled.

"It's the smell of land."

With slower strokes, the pair approached the sewer. The rotten smell intensified and made Conrad want to gag, but his exhaustion from swimming for so long and anxiousness to reach land overpowered his disgust. Along the edge of the pipe, they came upon a ladder. As both climbed, Conrad heard a loud splash below. He looked down to see that Lucia had stopped climbing.

"Did you see that?" she asked. The strategist shook his head. "It looked to be a giant snake, slithering into the sewers…"

"How odd," he replied. "I wonder how a snake could live in a sewer. Doesn't seem like there'd be much food, or sanitation, for that matter."

The pair's desire to reach land overruled their curiosity, and they resumed their climb. At the top, they found themselves on a cobblestone street across from a density of tall, stone buildings; wedged between them was another street that harbored well-dressed folk who rode the finest steeds and carriages.

Lucia pointed ahead. "I believe this to be the path that cuts through the wealthy district, then the city center. It is the quickest route to the woods from here."

"True," Conrad said as he looked up and down the tall buildings. He could see shadowy figures lurking within many of the windows, and also atop the odd bridges going from roof to roof. "But I worry that our enemies will be watching, particularly their leader. A man who commands so many others; and indeed, a Sigrian knight, is bound to mingle with the rich nobles of this land. What if his base of operations is in the wealthy district? We could be walking into the lion's den."

"Many of those men wore sailor garb," Lucia replied while shaking her head. "Their base of operations is probably near or at the docks. The sooner we get away from here, the better."

"Wouldn't we have come across them while swimming, then?"

Lucia looked further down the coastline, and so did Conrad. Many more docks stretched to the horizon.

"I don't know about that…"

"Let's compromise, then. To get away from here and stay clear of the wealthy district, we can cut through the alleyways," he said.

"I'd prefer to blend in with the crowds."

Conrad put hands to hips and chuckled. "Only one problem with that: We don't blend in. You tend to stand head and shoulders above a crowd, and my raggedy farmer's clothes will draw the attention of elites who surely roam the wealthy district streets."

"It would seem we aren't agreeing on much, today," she said with a huff.

"Do you think the dark essence is to blame for that, too?" he asked.

Such a question predictably drew a frown out of Lucia and did little to ease their growing tension. Yet, for some reason, he couldn't help but tease her about her concerns. After all, he would know if the dark essence was changing him. There'd be obvious signs, like with Barret and Powell's hideous transformations back at Bosfueras; or at the very least, his eyes would be turning red.

"Very well," Lucia said while gesturing to the alleyway, left of the main road. "Shall we?"

"After y-" Conrad cut himself off when a hand grasped his shoulder from behind. The strategist's reflexes took over, and he simultaneously drew his saber while spinning in place.

As he swung the blade with killing intent, Conrad's eyes picked up on his target, and he stopped just short of Ebbie's throat. The first mate panted like a dog as Conrad stared into his eyes with fire. After a tense moment, he lowered the saber.

"What were you thinking?" Conrad asked in a harsh whisper while sheathing his weapon. "You could have been killed."

"Erm, sorry…" Ebbie muttered after letting out a relieved breath. "I was only happy to have found an ally, an' got caught up in my excitement!"

"Where are the others?" Lucia asked. The trio walked toward an alleyway near the main street.

"We got separated. Dalton wanted ta play it safe, so we walked along the coast, to the west. But it didn't work out. Them blokes set a trap fer us," Ebbie said.

"Just as we feared," Conrad said as they entered the alley. It was filled with litter, but no people. He looked back at Ebbie as they walked. "Did you see how many there were?"

"I'd say at least a dozen."

"Then, I suppose we'll soon find out how much influence the leader of those slaves, and by extension Drake, have over the city," Lucia said as the group reached the end of the alley. She peered out the edge of it and looked both ways. The right led back to the main road of the wealthy district. The left would lead them down more alleys. She turned to face Conrad. "Are you sure you don't wish to blend in on the streets?"

Conrad snickered and then nudged his head to the left. Lucia shrugged and then led the others further into the alleys.

"Where are we headed, anyway?" Ebbie asked.

"I believe we're headed east," she replied while shooting an icy glare back at Conrad.

"And the outskirts are southeast, are they not?" the strategist asked.

Lucia remained silent and increased her pace as Ebbie rubbed his head and looked at Conrad with confusion in his eyes. "Lover's quarrel?"

Conrad let out a snorting chuckle. "A minor disagreement."

The trio weaved in and out through a series of alleyways toward the east until reaching another road, where many carriages carrying well-dressed folk traveled. Men in fancy armor rode steeds, and some were looking at fine clothing and armor displays outside of the shops.

"Still the wealthy district…" Lucia trailed off, then looked back at Conrad with narrowed eyes. "Any other ideas?"

"Simple," he said, pointing across the street to another alley between shops. "We can stick to the alleyways."

"Your strategy isn't working. We need to head south."

"And we will, once we reach the next alley."

Lucia shrugged and then led the group into the street. While walking, Conrad spotted a horse halting out of the corner of his eye. The trio turned and shielded themselves as the steed whinnied and reared, a mere arm's length away from them.

"Whoa, thar!" a knight sitting atop the horse commanded. All breath in Conrad's lungs escaped as it became clear that he was the same armored man from the docks. He looked down upon the trio with an understanding smile. "Now, what are three commoners like you doing in a place like this?"

"Just passing through, sir," Conrad replied with a bow.

"You are travelers, I take it?"

"My friend here got us lost," Lucia said, then pointed back to the strategist, who did his best not to smirk. "Do you know the best way to the city center?"

The knight pointed past the trio and down the street. "The city center is south of here. Of course, you'll need to be careful. There are ruffians wandering around the city and attacking innocents today."

"We shall be on our guard, sir, thank you," Conrad said as he and the others turned to leave.

"Ah, before you go…" the knight trailed off. The trio looked back at him, over their shoulders. "Allow me to impart you with a description of these troublemakers: One is a warrior from Federland called Sir Dalton. He has brown hair and a beard…"

"'*Sir Dalton*'?" Lucia snickered.

"He was accompanied by a stubby man dressed in sailor garb," he added, casting a steely gaze down at Ebbie from his steed.

Conrad and Lucia looked at the first mate with narrow eyes.

"O-oh… right…" Ebbie stuttered between nervous chuckles. "I s'pose he saw me, back then."

The duo let out exasperated sighs, then drew weapons and turned to face the knight. He merely held up a finger and chuckled at them.

"Tsk, tsk. It is illegal to bear arms in the streets of Endoshire-"

"Ah, so we are safe," Ebbie added with a sigh of relief.

"-with the exception of knights!" he finished, drawing upon his long sword. "Your heads will roll at the feet of me, Sir Job! For these streets are not to be tainted by dishonorable cretins like you!"

"To the alleys!" Conrad cried. The trio ran to their left at top speed and heard the early gallops of Job's steed close behind.

"There is no escape!" the knight shouted.

The strategist adjusted the angle of his run to point him and the others in the direction of a fruit stand just in front of the alleyway. When close enough, both he and Lucia slid under the stand. Behind, he heard a loud crashing noise, followed closely by *splats* of the fruit and the splintering of wood; and then came a series of gasps. He looked back to see that Ebbie had plowed through and toppled over the stand.

Job's horse reared and let out a ferocious neigh in front of the destroyed farm stand. The trio dashed through the alley as they heard the knight calling out.

"They are in the alleyways! Bring them down!"

Lucia gasped as an arrow brushed past her skirt while running. Then, from a connecting alley, two men in sailor attire appeared with ropes in each of their hands.

"You sure… we can't kill them?" Conrad asked between breaths as they approached. Both men began to lasso their ropes.

She merely shook her head and then burst ahead with long, speedy strides. Before the slave could toss the rope, she threw an elbow that smashed into his nose and stunned him enough that knocking him over was a trifle. Conrad and Ebbie, meanwhile, tackled the other slave, and the strategist followed up by nailing him in the head with the butt of his saber.

When they returned to running, however, Conrad heard a grunt from Ebbie, just behind him.

"I'm hit!" he cried while stumbling forward. Conrad took him under his shoulder, and the pair hobbled along through the alleys behind Lucia.

A volley of arrows continued to shoot past and around the lingering trio, so Lucia took a right down the next alleyway she could find. The *clinks* and *clangs* of arrowheads bouncing off of stone echoed from the previous alley.

As the group passed by another alley to their left, a chain flew out and wrapped around Lucia's legs, and she tripped over them before crashing to the ground. Her arms filled with fresh cuts and blemishes from the fall, she reached down to untie herself, but she failed to notice the slave on her left, who had tripped her up in the first place.

Conrad threw Ebbie to the ground as the slave raised a saber over-head to deliver a killing blow on her. As the blade came down, the strategist jumped in and swung his saber upward, deflecting it away when mere inches from striking her. Lucia ceased her struggles and looked up at the two men, wide-eyed.

The slave carried the momentum of his parried blow and swung back diagonally and upward. Conrad stepped back, let his saber slide off, and then responded with a downward chop that connected with the side of the slave's torso. The man cried out as blood spilled onto a motionless and stutter-breathed Lucia. He writhed on the ground for a few seconds before his breaths became short and wheezy. His death was all but assured, now.

Lucia hopped to her feet and then shoved Conrad. "What are you playing at? We agreed not to kill them!"

"It was him or you. There was no other choice," he replied before turning to help Ebbie up. "I didn't take pleasure in doing the deed, but when the enemy looks to destroy someone that I care for, their lives are forfeit, as far as I'm concerned."

Lucia kept her eyes on the fast-fading slave while attempting to wipe some of the blood off of her clothes in vain. She had gone nearly as pale as the blood-starved man on the ground. Conrad could tell that something had stirred within her, but he couldn't be sure if the cause was her needless worries about him, or something else.

Then, out of the corner of his eye, Conrad spotted movement. He looked back to see more men chasing them from down the alleyway. "There is no time to mourn, I'm afraid! Let's move."

A single nod was all Lucia could spare before moving on from the now-departed slave. The strategist could spare even less and considered spitting on his corpse for daring to attack someone he cherished. Instead, he took Ebbie under his shoulder once more and followed Lucia's lead.

The trio passed in and out of the alleys, seemingly at random, to throw their pursuers off. Ebbie's breaths grew hoarse and short. While Conrad could not find compassion for the attacker whom he'd just slain, he was quite worried for the first mate's health. His condition had worsened in such short order that panicked thoughts of the arrow taking his life swirled around in his mind like an inescapable whirlpool.

Soon, they exited the alleys and came upon a church that sat atop a small hill on their left. The large, stone buildings and their odd rooftop bridges had become less prevalent, and now they could see more trees and fields off in the distance. They had certainly left the wealthy district, Conrad thought; but it didn't seem like a city center to him, either. There was hardly anyone traversing this road.

"Perhaps we can seek asylum in thar..." Ebbie muttered, pointing at the church with a rickety finger.

"Are you alright? Lucia asked, slowing her jog to a walk. The others fell in step with her soon after. "Your enthusiasm seems to have vanished."

"Just a wee bit tired, is all," he replied, rubbing his eyes. "Me leg is sore."

"Yes, perhaps in the church, we'll be able to find you some medical treatment," Conrad said.

While ascending stone steps that were flanked by sections of a grassy hill, Conrad took in the church and its features. Its grand door, carved from fine wood, reminded him of the entrance to the Mountain King's throne room. All around, he found signs of a former glory: While it sported many murals and a grand structure, the church appeared in dire need of repairs, with broken wood and holes littering the second floor especially.

When the trio entered the church, they were surprised to find no one inside. The red carpet leading up to the stage was old and ragged. The splinter-ridden benches meant for prayer also looked to be in need of some care. Instead of looking around for anyone, however, they sat Ebbie down on a bench to treat his arrow wound themselves. The first mate howled in pain as they ripped the arrowhead out, and Lucia wrapped it up tight with a piece of fabric.

Ebbie let out a sigh of relief, then leaned back on the bench and closed his eyes. "What do ye say we take a lil' rest here?"

"That would be for the best," Conrad said, plopping down next to him. "We can rest up and throw them off our trail in here."

"Agreed," Lucia said before electing to sit on the other side of Ebbie. Conrad raised an eyebrow as she put hands behind her head and leaned back. "Let us take this time to clear our heads."

⁓

On the northwest side of Endoshire, Captain Auber awoke to the clearing of a throat.

"W-wha?" His eyes burst open and he looked both ways in a panic. "Have they found us?"

"No, sir," Franco said, then stood and dusted himself off. "We've been here for over an hour, I'd say, and I've not seen a single one of those men that tried to kill us, earlier."

"Heh! We must'a scared 'em off, then!" the captain boasted with a cocky grin. He, too, rose and wiped the dust from his clothes.

"Or we simply weren't important enough to chase," Franco said.

Auber waved him off. "Nonsense! We're pirates, Franco. We'd make fer a great catch if they had the skill."

"If you say so…"

The captain looked back out the alleyway and onto the main road. Many different folk walked the path, both ways. Peasant families in ragged clothing scurried along, keeping their collective heads down. Wealthy nobles carried by steeds or pulled by carriage parted all others like worthless litter on the street. Aside from them, Auber noticed the half-man, half-horse centaurs parting the sea of people, too; though they traveled together in a pack of over a dozen. On the other hand, he observed the large and green troll folk dragging man-sized clubs or carrying products of questionable repute, often badgering others for deals and driving them away. Even more different still, he looked up to see flocks of the bird-like avian gliding over the buildings. He thought that maybe he saw one or two of them striding through the crowds, too, but their smaller stature lent well to blending in.

"Yer sure that none of them passed by?" Auber asked.

"Indeed. I kept watch as you slept. If an assassin passed us, they were well-disguised," Franco replied.

"Very well. Let's get back to the main road, then."

"Sir? You aren't worried about traveling out in the open?"

"It does worry me, but I hate bein' lost even more. At least on the coastal path, we'll know where to go," the captain said.

Franco chuckled as the pair walked onto the main road and took a left. They continued along the western coast path, admiring the clearing fog on the horizon and accompanying blue waters that beautifully reflected the morning sun. Yet, nothing was more captivating to Auber than the many ships coming and going from the port. *Oh, to be a stowaway again*, he thought with a smile. He could only imagine what each ship's goal was as they approached with a crisp wind backing them from the west.

In the blink of an eye, an hour passed, and the duo reached an intersection. Here, they had the option to take a left back into the city or to continue straight along the rocky coast.

"I believe that this road will take us east," Franco said, pointing left, down the wide path. Auber noted a great density of buildings and people off in the distance.

"I say we continue ta follow this path," Auber said, then pointed down the coastal road.

The navigator smirked. "You just want to watch more ships, don't you?"

"Naturally," he replied with a hearty nod. "What kinda pirate would I be if I didn't appreciate such fine craftsmanship? Besides, the crowds are smaller on this road. It's safer."

"Sir, we must eventually head east to reach our destination…"

"Yeh, we'll do that after we've traveled further south."

"But we don't-" Franco cut himself off by gagging and sticking his tongue out. He then began sniffing around. "What is that *ghastly* smell?"

Auber picked up on the smell, too, and it truly was as awful as Franco had claimed. He turned to the coastline and walked up to it. Upon gazing over the rocky ledge, he spotted a sewage drain below. The captain gasped, not only at the smell, but because a man was climbing up from it.

The duo stepped back as the man reached land and stood before them. He wore a dirtied red tunic, had long, brown hair tied up in a ponytail, and gazed with eyes so relaxed that he looked ready to fall asleep. Though he was somewhat small, his sleek form suggested to Auber that he hid some muscle beneath his clothing.

"Good day, gentlemen," the man said, brushing himself off.

"Erm, good day…" Auber replied with a pinched nose.

The man raised an eyebrow before letting out a chuckle and nudging his head back toward the sewer. "My apologies for the smell. It's a dirty job, but someone's gotta do it."

"So ye clean up down thar? What a cruddy way ta make a livin'!" the captain said.

"I'm sure it is essential to the public," Franco added.

"It is *quite essential*, indeed! Are you two from out of town?"

"Yeh, we're pirates," Auber said with a prideful smile.

Without another word, the smelly man drew a dark blue blade from his hip, both shocking and impressing the captain all at once. He'd never seen anything like it.

Franco desperately waved him off. "We're friendly. We have no intentions of robbing you."

"How about you prove it, then?"

"And how would we do that?"

"Visit my shop and buy some fine items," the smelly man said. Auber and Franco looked at each other and shrugged.

"We've got gold to spend. I s'pose we could buy a few odds n' ends," the captain said. The smelly man pointed his dark blue blade at him, the tip mere inches from his face.

"Plundered gold from the innocent?" he asked with contempt.

Auber put his hands up and let out a nervous chuckle. "N-no! It was given to us."

"You expect me to believe that?"

"It's the truth," Franco added.

"Y'see, we were given the gold 'cause we agreed ta rescue some chaps from the wretched lands of Bosfueras. Not only are we pirates, but we're bloody heroes, too!" Captain Auber bragged. He chose to ignore Franco's quiet groan that followed.

The smelly man shrugged and then sheathed his blade. "To be honest, you don't seem like an intimidating duo…"

"What? We're intimidatin'! But we're also nice! That's the difference between us and other pirates," said the captain.

"If you say so." The smelly man walked past the pair, whistling a tune along the coastal path.

"Oi! Wait up!" Auber cried. He and Franco followed.

After a bizarre quarter-hour where the man pretended that the pirates weren't even there, he finally stopped whistling. Without turning back, he asked, "What are your names?"

"I'm Auber, captain of the Auber Pirates."

"And I am Franco, navigator of the Auber Pirates."

"My name is Amis. It's a pleasure to meet you both."

"The pleasure is all ours, besides the smell!" the captain said, waving a hand in front of his nose.

"Are there really only two of you? Where is the rest of your crew?"

"There is one more crew member, but we got separated from him. We're supposed to meet on the outskirts of the city. Could you lead us there?" Franco replied.

"I'll take you as far as my shop. All you have to do from there is follow a single path, though, and you'll be at the outskirts," Amis said.

"We appreciate yer generosity," Auber said before leaning toward Franco and whispering. "See? I told ye this way would be safer."

"And why are you worried about safety?" Amis asked. Captain Auber let out a nervous stutter as the smelly man pointed to the sky, behind them. "Is it because of that great winged creature following us?"

The pirates looked up to see a large, black bird circling above, as a shark would its next meal.

Auber gasped. "Whoa! That's a mighty big raven!"

"I don't think it's a raven..." Franco trailed off with narrow eyes and a flat hand at his brow. "It looks to be wearing clothes. An avian, perhaps?"

"I believe so," Amis said as he turned forward once more. "Whoever they are, they have been following me for days, now."

"Don't take this the wrong way, but why would anyone follow you?" Franco asked.

The smelly man looked back and smiled. "I can think of a few reasons."

"Is it that blue sword of yers?" I have'ta say, that if I wasn't such a nice guy, I'd wanna steal it from ye me'self!" the captain said with an obnoxious laugh.

"Hm... It could be the sword, I suppose."

"How much do ye want fer it? I'll pay ye right now," Auber said, rubbing his hands together.

Amis snorted. "Sorry, not for sale."

Auber groaned and muttered, "I would rather have a red sword, anyway..."

The group continued their walk for a short while before taking a left into a poorer section of the city. The left side of this road was filled with small houses and shops, while the right side had many broken-down shacks, tents, and farm stands that barely remained standing. One standout on the right side of the road was a tall, pointy monument that was fenced off. Of course, the sign describing what it was had long since been defaced, but curiously, the monument itself remained pristine, leaving Auber all the more curious about it. As they delved further and further into the slum area, the avian turned back and left the group alone.

After an hour of walking through, Amis took a left into an alleyway and then opened the door to a small shop. Inside was a counter filled with small odds and ends: herbal medicines, door handles, knives, and many other knick-knacks. The smelly man peered into a backroom while Auber and Franco looked around.

"Dhogron?" Amis called out, disappearing into the room. "Dhogron! Where'd you go off to?"

He exited the backroom with frustration written all over his face.

"Something wrong?" Franco asked.

"My friend, Dhogron... the bastard up and left my shop unattended!"

"I can understand your frustration. Without anyone to watch over the place, who would protect the..." Franco trailed off, picked up a handle, and then narrowed his eyes. "Door handles?"

"Laugh if you wish, but I have some valuable items for sale, here," Amis insisted.

"Well, what can we buy?" Captain Auber asked.

"I was thinking about that on the way here," Amis said while rummaging behind the counter. He retrieved a small, brown sack. "Have a look at these."

Auber reached out, grabbed the sack, and then opened it. He and Franco looked in to see its contents: an assortment of berries.

"Could we not pick berries ourselves?" the navigator asked with a raised eyebrow.

"Ah, but these are not truly berries," Amis replied, wagging his finger. "I call them beige berries."

"But they ain't beige," Auber replied.

"That's because I soaked them in various dyes."

"What? Ye mean... like killin' someone?" the captain asked, bewildered.

Franco laughed. "No. Dye is used to color some foods. It is common in eastern countries. I'm surprised to see it in practice here, though."

"You are well-cultured to know such a thing," Amis said, wringing his hands and nodding along. "But your enemies? They likely won't know about the true nature of these berries. I seem to remember you worrying about the dangers of Endoshire. I don't know who you have angered, but give these 'berries' to a foe, and they will be incapacitated for some time."

"Are they poisoned?" Franco asked.

"In a small dose. It won't kill anyone, but it will make them vomit, or..."

"Mess in thar pants?" Auber asked with a laugh. "I'll take 'em! How much fer the bag?"

"A gold coin oughta be enough," Amis said.

The captain reached into his pocket and paid the smelly man in exchange for the sack. After shaking hands, Amis led the pirates out of his store and back into the streets.

"Follow this path for a while, and you'll reach the outskirts," he said, pointing forward. "Stop by again sometime, if you need anything else!"

Auber and Franco waved goodbye and began journeying down the litter-filled street. Many peasants, mostly women and children, were coming and going, but none made eye contact. In some strange way, despite the location's unfriendly demeanor, Auber felt safer.

~

CONRAD OPENED his eyes gingerly to see a man in a white robe standing over him in the dim-lit church. Flashing back to his horrid experience at the black mass in Bosfueras, he reflexively reached for the saber at his hip but stopped when he saw that the man put his hands up to show he came in peace.

"No need for that, young one," the robed man said with a warm smile, belying a jaw that looked to be made of iron. Upon truly taking in his appearance, he was at ease. His hair, blacker than night, made him wonder why he'd just called him 'young one'. He didn't appear to be much older than his 30s.

"Are you the priest of this church?" Conrad asked. Both Ebbie and Lucia had awakened, as well.

"That I am. Around these parts, I am called Father Vega."

"A pleasure to meet you, sir. My name is Conrad."

"I am Lucia."

"The name's Ebbie…" the pirate muttered while grasping at his leg and wincing.

Father Vega gazed upon the injury with his emerald green eyes, but his smile did not waver. "Would it be fair to assume that you entered this church to seek asylum?"

Conrad and Lucia looked at each other with worry. Eventually, Lucia cleared her throat, and said, "Yes. We were chased through the city by assassins, and our friend got hurt."

"I thought as much," the priest said with a chuckle. "It's not every day that a knight demands entry into this church so that he might search these hallowed grounds."

A frantic pit took hold of Conrad's stomach as he looked around. What was he thinking, trusting a complete stranger? He put a hand on the hilt of his saber while scanning the area. However, he couldn't spot another soul in the old, rickety building.

"You need not worry," Father Vega said, holding a hand up. "I turned his mob away and convinced them that you weren't here. For now, you are safe."

"We appreciate the help, but… why?" Lucia asked.

"When I first laid eyes on you three, your injuries and desperation were apparent. It seemed to me that you were a group in need. It is my duty to help people like you," the priest said, now standing over Ebbie. "So then, how about we fix up that leg? Would you stand for me?"

The first mate stood gingerly and turned around. Vega inspected the blood pouring out from the back of his leg through the makeshift wrapping.

"It is fortunate that you happened upon this church today," he said while reaching a hand out. Conrad gasped at the subtle golden light around the priest's fingers. "This wound could have become a terrible infection."

Vega touched the back of Ebbie's leg, and while at first, he winced in pain, as if snapping out of a trance or nightmare, his tensed posture relaxed. The blood beneath the bandages dried, and then the priest stood back upright.

"Better?"

Ebbie flexed his leg with care at first, then smiled and flexed it some more. "I don' believe it! You healed me!"

"Happy to be of service," the priest said with a nod. "I can perform miracles, now and then."

"That was Augmenting magic, wasn't it?" Conrad asked.

The priest raised both eyebrows. "It is not often I come across a man who can spot true magic. Most in the city believe it to be parlor tricks. I suppose too many of them have been conned out of their money by performers who are only pretending. But of course, some can perform the real thing with enough good deeds under their belt."

"You are referring to Anima, correct?"

"That's right," Father Vega said. Now, his eyes were wide. "Tell me, are you acquainted with a Wizard, or a Warlock, perhaps?"

"A Wizard. He explained to me some basics of magic, but I still have much to pry from him," Conrad replied with a sly smile.

The priest chuckled. "Good luck! Wizards are cryptic by nature. But I shall not be discrete in telling you that obtaining such power is nearly impossible. One bad action can lower your Anima, and the standard for performing miracles is quite high. It takes a certain dedication that few are willing to put forth."

"I have many questions," Conrad said before Lucia stood between him and the priest.

"As interesting as I'm sure that conversation would be, we must be on our way," she said. Conrad frowned. "Do you know the best way to reach the city outskirts from here?"

"Yes. They are south of this church. After you leave, head down the hill and take a left onto the main road. Then, take your next right. That road will take you over a large river. Keep following that path south and you will reach the outskirts."

The group thanked the priest for his generosity, and as they were leaving, he pulled Conrad aside and said, "I sense that determination within you, by the way."

Conrad smiled in return. He was indeed determined to learn more.

"But I also sense a darkness within. You will have to conquer your demons before walking the correct path," Father Vega said before turning to the others. "I encourage you to visit again soon, whether it be for help, prayer, or company."

THE TRIO MADE their way down the hill and took a left onto the main road, as Vega had instructed. The streets had become busier since they stowed away in the house of worship, and in Lucia's mind, it was to their advantage. She was certain that the tenacious Sigrian knight would still be looking for them, but dense crowds would make for good cover.

After walking for some time, the group came to a fork in the road. The left path continued north, where they could see many fields and shacks. The right led to a large bridge that appeared to go over a river, off in the distance. Once again following the priest's directions, the trio took a right.

As they traversed the bridge, Conrad looked over the railing to see the great river up close.

"Should we be worried?" he asked as Lucia and Ebbie gazed over the railing for themselves. Below, there was a walkway leading to a great sewer pipe, sticking out from the city's foundation. Several cloaked people were coming and going from the sewers.

Lucia thought back to what Aldous had told the group before they split up, back in Federland. The sewer was like a city-sized maze. But even still, she worried that these people might have been with Drake's team, and were well on their way to finding the monolith of Degenerate. Had they arrived in Endoshire too late?

CHAPTER 8
REUNION

As midday approached, Dalton, Conrad, Lucia, and the pirates arrived at Kabel's abode in the woods. To the right, there was a small horse stable in between towering trees, and parked in front was a clean carriage that looked to have had some work done on it recently. The warrior smiled back at his student.

"It appears we lost the race to Endoshire."

"Let's hope they arrived bearing good news in regards to the Famine seal," Lucia replied.

The group walked up to the house built around trees, and all gazed upon it in apparent wonder as Dalton knocked at the front door with excitement building in his chest. After all, this would be a reunion on two fronts. A small, metal latch opened to reveal a set of calm eyes. The warrior's smile grew even larger, for there was no mistaking that the gaze belonged to his old friend, Kabel.

"It's been a while," Dalton said.

"Password?"

Raising an eyebrow, Dalton stared back through the latch, looking for any sign that he was joking. Kabel's calm expression remained, however.

"Erm… we don't have a password, last I checked."

"The *real* Dalton would know the password."

"And what is that supposed to mean? Did you meet someone who looks like me? Or have the filthy streets of the city rotted your mind?" Dalton asked with a laugh.

"I'll have you know that a Dark Wizard has been impersonating old friends of mine, lately," Kabel said before looking past him. "And this sorry lot you've brought along seem shady; like thieves from the slums."

Lucia stepped forward, her brow twitching. "Now, listen here-"

Dalton held a hand up, and that was enough to silence her.

"How can we prove ourselves, then?" he asked.

"At the side of the house, there lay a bucket filled with unicorn's blood. That would nullify any dark magic, according to my new Wizard friend," Kabel said.

"You're talkin' about Aldous, right?" Dalton asked, pointing back to the horse stable with a thumb. "I thought that might have been his horse carriage, back there. He is quite particular about their upkeep and cleanliness, y'see; and that one is immaculate, despite the dreary weather around these parts."

"I cannot confirm or deny the Wizard's identity," the stocky man said as the group outside groaned. "Douse yourselves in the unicorn's blood, and I'll let you in."

Dalton scratched his head before shrugging. He walked around the house and retrieved the bucket, frowning as he returned to the front door.

"*This* bucket?" Dalton asked.

"That's the one."

"It smells..." he muttered with disgust on his tongue. He could hear muffled giggles coming from inside the house.

"Enough of your excuses. If you're not a Dark Wizard, then you will pour it over your head!" Kabel said.

"Just one problem," Dalton replied, swishing the liquid around in the bucket. "This ain't unicorn blood. It's piss!"

With a sudden jerk of his hand, Dalton splashed the urine out of the bucket and at the door. Kabel closed the latch just in time to block it from entering the house. After a few moments, the stocky man opened the door and stared at Dalton with contempt.

"Cheeky as ever, I see."

"Me?" Dalton asked, both eyebrows raised and pointing at himself. His look of surprise then turned to a smile. "I'm glad to see that your reflexes haven't dulled, much."

The two men met up close and grasped forearms, rather than

exchange a traditional handshake. Dalton turned back to his friends and said, "This is my old friend from the war, Kabel."

"A pleasure to meet you all," he said.

"So, is this the feller ye were talkin' about?" Auber asked, looking at Dalton.

"One of 'em."

Kabel eyed Dalton. "What did you tell him?"

The warrior wrapped an arm around his friend's shoulder, then pointed to the pirate. "This here is Captain Auber. He and his crewmates, Ebbie and Franco, helped us escape from that hellhole, Bosfueras."

"Alright, but what does that have to do with me?"

"I *might* have told them that you'd be interested in pirated supplies..." Dalton trailed off. Kabel raised an eyebrow. "Are you still in the game?"

"Haven't been for a few years."

"What about Thomas?"

"He's gone," the stocky man said in a somber tone.

Dalton gasped. "Dead?"

"I don't know... he was caught by the authorities, but instead of being hung at the gallows, he struck some kind of deal with the king himself and received knighthood," Kabel said.

"Did he sell you out?"

"No. I have'ta admit, that much surprised me. I haven't seen him around. He must be somewhere else in Sigraveld. It's a better life than what we had, anyway."

"Well..." Dalton trailed off as he rubbed the back of his head and flashed the pirates a half-hearted smile.

"We're outta luck, ain't we?" Auber asked with hands to hips.

"Don't be so sure," Kabel said, wagging a finger. "I may have use for you. We can talk more about it later."

JOEL, Aldous, and Alistair's faces lit up as Kabel led Dalton and the others to the dining room table. The mute was relieved to see them all in good health, and they seemed to have met some new allies along the way, even. It was becoming clearer by the day that they would need all the help they could get.

"Oho! About time you showed up!" Aldous said, raising a steaming cup at them and nodding.

"We had quite the trip," Conrad replied while smiling up at Lucia.

"Methinks we gots a lotta catchin' up ta do!" Alistair said as he slammed his fist on the table with excitement.

"Yeh! I NEED ta be filled in!" Triston echoed. "All's I been doin' is choppin' wood fer the last week! I need ta know what tha plan is, movin' forward!"

Lucia narrowed her eyes. "Oh lord, there are two of them, now…"

"AND JUST WHAT IS THAT SUPPOSED TA MEAN?" the elder MacRae bellowed as he stood, spilling his drink in the process. Joel rushed to wipe up the mess while Alistair laughed and grabbed his brother's shoulders from behind, plopping him back down on the chair.

"Relax, brother! The lass just feels intimidated in the presence of true warriors!" the big redhead said with a smirk in Lucia's direction.

A vain chuckle escaped her lips. "Only my ears are intimidated by the foul noises that leave your big mouth."

"WHY, YOU-" This time, Triston held Alistair back.

Conrad walked over to Joel and smiled, then nudged his head at the arguing MacRae brothers and Lucia. "It appears that rivalry is alive and well, eh?"

The mute smiled and signed back to his friend.

"Good to see you, too. It feels like *years*, not months, since we last spoke, doesn't it?"

Joel made hand signals back, asking what he had found in Bosfueras. Aldous slid his chair over and leaned in with obvious interest.

"There *is* a Dark Wizard pulling the strings," Conrad said. All chatter in the room fell silent. Everyone's attention turned to the strategist. "He is creating his own black gold in Bosfueras. Enough to brainwash an entire town."

Aldous gasped. "That would take a deep knowledge of dark magic. The Mountain King created his own black gold too, but only one bar…"

"It was his unique brand, though," Conrad clarified. "I don't think it was as powerful as what we encountered at Mt. Couture. They tested the Dark Wizard's black gold, and then the Dark Savior's brand, on me. The original black gold won the battle for my mind with ease."

"That black gold in Bosfueras seemed like it had different effects than the Gold Fever we first encountered one year ago," Dalton added with crossed arms. "Those townsfolk were resistant to pain and single-minded in their focus. When we set the town ablaze, the people paid us no mind. They went straight to the fire and put it out."

"It's bad enough that this Dark Wizard can concoct a substance that enhances his allies, but even his own black gold?" Aldous asked aloud, the disbelief in his words coming through like a clear summer sky.

"So, you encountered people who took in the *dark essence*?" Conrad asked.

"Yeh, down in Thironas. That big jerk Angus was thar, tryin' ta destroy tha monolith!" Alistair said.

"If he survived, then that means Edith…" Lucia trailed off. "And the key to Greed's seal; he must have been the one that stole it."

Joel nodded to confirm her suspicions.

"And were you able to stop him from destroying the Famine seal in Thironas?" Dalton asked.

Aldous shook his head. "I'm afraid not. And to make matters worse, he managed to steal the key to Famine's prison, too."

"But at least that Zamarim fella' sent him away ta the ocean! I bet he drowned, or the marinians got 'im!" Alistair said with a snort.

"I wouldn't be so sure of that," Aldous said, looking down at the table. "He won't be easy to kill. We will surely have to deal with him once more while protecting the Degenerate monolith."

"Not just him," Conrad added. "Brice and the hooligans were in Bosfueras, too. The Dark Wizard experimented to enhance their abilities. Some died in the process, and others died in the fires when we escaped, but I'm certain that Brice is still alive."

"Hold up," Triston interrupted. All in the room looked upon him in silence. "Did I hear ya correctly? Ya set tha enemy's home ablaze?"

"That's right," Conrad said.

"If that were me an' tha boys, we'd travel far and wide lookin' for ya, to exact revenge! What's ta say that these crazed folk won't do tha same?" he asked.

"I fear that the oaf is correct," Lucia said, looking down.

"HEY!" Triston cried.

"When we arrived at the docks, a group of slaves attacked us."

Kabel raised an eyebrow. "Did you happen to see a short, fat man among them? He probably would have been wearing a fancy fur coat."

"Yes, he was there," Lucia said. "Who is he, exactly? How could he have so many enslaved men at his disposal?"

He looked at Dalton and frowned. "You *really* got me into some shite, this time."

Dalton shrugged. "Should we be worried? He took an arrow from Auber and had to be hauled off."

"Our captain is an expert marksman!" Ebbie bragged.

"Oh yes, he just *rains* arrows down upon our enemies," Franco said with a chuckle.

"This is no laughing matter…" Kabel trailed off. The natural calm of his eyes had been replaced with an intense nervousness. "The man you shot goes by the name Sampson. He is the most powerful and connected man in Endoshire."

"In other words, he is yet another enemy that we've made," Conrad said with a frown.

"We woulda had ta fight 'im eventually, anyway!" Alistair said, slamming his fist into the table. Blood began seeping through the bandage on his hand, and Joel internally groaned. The wound had come close to fully healing, but his excitement had obviously opened it back up. "He attacked ya at the docks, and that ain't no coincidence. He must be connected ta Drake and that knob of a Dark Wizard, somehow!"

"I agree. Powerful as he may be, today's attack cannot be overlooked as bad luck. We eventually would have had to face him," Dalton said.

"You don't understand. Sampson has connections to the Sigrian Kingdom. To go against him is to go against the kingdom… unofficially, he commands even more power than the lord of Endoshire," Kabel replied.

"That would explain the Sigrian knight aiding him," the warrior said.

"Oho! It's said that the Sigrian knights are the most vicious in the world. To command even them… we really have our hands full, this time," Aldous said.

"It's worse than that. Sampson has eyes and ears throughout the city. Meaning that this house may no longer be safe," Kabel said as the front door opened.

"What isn't safe?" Mirabel, his wife, asked. She carried some basic supplies, and behind her were Giles and Rolf, carrying the heavier loads.

"Mira! It's been too long!" Dalton called out, happily.

"Dalton…" she replied in a cold tone, nodding at him.

"We may need to abandon this house," Kabel said.

"Why? We worked so hard to make this our home," Mira said.

"There is a very real possibility that Sampson is after us."

Mirabel dropped her supplies, then put a hand over her mouth, attempting to hold back the sobs and failing. After taking a moment to recompose herself, she nodded and said, "Alright, let's get packed up."

Joel sent hand signals to Kabel, asking why Mira had cried.

"You may remember that I mentioned her parents fled Mithika, to start a new life here. Sampson kidnapped and enslaved them, as he often does to confused foreigners. She hasn't seen them since, and was lucky to even escape with her own freedom..." Kabel explained, then let out a sigh. "For that reason, it would probably be safest to move out of here, in case any of his men tailed you. I have a place that we could stay."

"Mayhap we don't need to make such hasty decisions," Aldous said, tapping his walking stick on the floor. "Endoshire is a large city, and this is a lovely home. It would be a shame to abandon it."

"If he did manage to track you, he wouldn't confront us face-to-face," Kabel said, shaking his head. "He would probably come and set the house ablaze at night while we sleep."

"Then, we will guard the house in shifts," Dalton said.

"I-it's risky..." Mira was shivering, now.

"Oho! Don't forget that you have a Wizard on your side! I won't let anything happen to this place," Aldous said with a reassuring smile.

"Your control of water washed those degenerates away with ease, and I could have sworn you even grabbed hold of the lightning one time, but on a day like today, none of that matters. You won't have those things at your disposal," the stocky man said.

"True, but there is one more element I can control..."

"Da fire!" Rolf cried with balled fists.

"The hell are you talkin' about? How would you know that?" Kabel asked, frowning at his lanky friend.

"When he told us dat story about da Dark Savior last week, he was able to move da flames around in da fireplace," Rolf said. Aldous nodded in approval.

Kabel's eyes widened. "Right... that could work. A bit dangerous for the woods, sure, but if we set up a bonfire outside, perhaps you could use those flames to scare Sampson's men away."

"Could you put out any fires accidentally started in the woods?" Conrad asked.

"Within reason," Aldous said. "It would be much easier, of course, if it were raining or I had a nearby water supply. With my abilities, though, I should be able to extinguish any fires as long as I am made aware early enough and it doesn't spread."

"And we only have to worry about that if Sampson's men tracked us here," Lucia said, then looked to Dalton, Auber, and Franco. "I don't know about the rest of you, but we avoided detection after taking shelter in the church."

"I tricked some trolls into clobbering my pursuers," Dalton said, his cheeks flaring out.

"Erm…" Captain Auber trailed off.

"Auber…" the warrior said in an accusatory tone.

"Well…"

"Aw, hell… you told us that you weren't followed!"

"See, we weren't followed *the whole way*," the captain said with a shrug. "There was this big ole raven, y'see-"

"I don't think it was a raven, sir," Franco interrupted. "It was a large, black avian. They were wearing clothes."

Joel raised an eyebrow. He quickly made hand signals to Alistair.

"Oi! That's right! We saw the same giant buzzard-"

"It's an avian, fool. Don't you listen?" Lucia asked with a smirk. "I suppose dullness runs in the family."

"Yeh Ali, get tha wax outta yer ears!" Triston said with a hard slap to his back and an obnoxious laugh.

"You gonna let her bad-mouth our family like that?" the big redhead asked his brother, whose brow furrowed in realization.

"HEY!" Triston glared at her.

"Let's stay on topic," Aldous interjected, turning to the pirates. "There was a large, black avian aiding Drake's team down in Thironas. This may be the same avian. How far did they follow you?"

"I don' know nothin' about this Drake feller, but the avian followed us along the west coast, then turned back after we reached the city slums," Auber replied.

"That makes sense. In the slums, archers will sometimes attempt to shoot down birds for food. Avian who are familiar with the city tend to steer clear," Mirabel added.

"Aren't you forgetting someone else?" Franco asked Auber with narrowed eyes.

"Oh, erm, right. There was this other fella who showed us into the slums. He worked in the sewers… he was real swell, besides the smell."

"But he only took us to his shop in the slums. He pointed us in the direction of the outskirts from there," Franco said.

"So, unless that man was one of Sampson's spies, we should be in the clear, right?" Giles asked.

"All of Sampson's spies tried to kill us, even in crowds," Dalton said, pointing to Auber and Franco. "These two would be dead if the fella who led them into the slums was with Sampson."

"Even so, it couldn't hurt to be cautious," Aldous said, his eyes wandering back to Kabel. "I'm happy to stand guard tonight while you all sleep soundly."

"And I appreciate that," Kabel said with a smile. "But first, we need to fetch lots of material. I intend to give you plenty of fire to work with."

"We can help out with that," Dalton said.

"You better earn your keep, this time," Mira said with cold eyes. The warrior pointed to himself in apparent confusion. "In your last stay, you and my husband sat around drinking all week."

Dalton looked to his old friend, and the two smiled at each other. "Right… well, I'm here on more official business this time."

"That's right. There are a lotta problems in this city and it's well past time we corrected 'em," Kabel said, looking around at all in the room like a general would his soldiers. "Many of you may be strangers to me, but if yer friends of Dalton, that's good enough for me. I say we all band together and fight against the threats that Drake, Sampson, and the Dark Wizard impose."

Joel, Aldous, Alistair, Lucia, Dalton, Conrad, and Rolf all nodded in agreement. Meanwhile, the Auber pirates, Giles, Triston, and Mira all shrugged; they did not seem to fully comprehend what was going on, but in the excitement of such a team-up, all in the house let out cheers of happiness.

Finally, Joel thought, things were starting to look up. All of his friends had gathered in one spot, and they had gained new allies. Even if the odds were stacked against them, he felt better to know that there were more friends in his corner than ever before.

CHAPTER 9
RELEVANT INFORMATION

After agreeing to team up against the dark forces that plagued Endoshire, the new group of allies split up to handle chores: Dalton, Kabel, Rolf, and Ebbie ventured deep into the woods to pick berries. Conrad, Aldous, and Triston were sent to fetch water at the riverbank to the east. Joel, Alistair, Giles, and Auber were tasked with obtaining firewood near the house. Lucia had insisted on staying with Mirabell to help her prepare a feast, mentioning that taking turns at cooking with Dalton over the past year had dulled her culinary skills. Franco had also elected to stay behind with them. In addition to navigation, he had also stood in as the Auber Pirates' cook and showed interest in preparing a meal that didn't involve fish.

Dalton cocked his head as he followed Kabel, who turned left into the thick of the woods, off of the beaten path. Mildew from the high grass scraped off of Ebbie's pant legs and seeped through more and more with each step. He could see that everyone else's legs were becoming damp, too.

"You tryin' to get us lost?" Dalton asked.

"I know these woods like the back of my hand. You *can* handle some wilderness, can't you?" Kabel replied with a chuckle.

Dalton scoffed. "If only you knew what I went through last year."

"Oh, right. Aldous told me all about Mt. Couture. As usual, your luck is pitiful… and it would seem that it has stuck with you like a bad stench," Kabel said with a snort.

"And what about you? I thought you wanted to clean up this city. It seems to have gotten *worse*."

"I've been working on it," Kabel said as the four men stepped over a downed tree. "It is difficult getting folk around here to take up a cause. The wealthy wish to stay wealthy, and the poor are too busy surviving to care. As you know, most people in this city come from different walks of life, and don't care much for one another."

"I see you've at least picked up *one ally* since I last visited," the warrior said while looking back at Rolf.

"Yeh, he's an idiot, but a loveable idiot."

"Hey! Dat was uncalled for!" Rolf complained.

"Fine," Kabel said, smirking back at his lanky friend. "Just an idiot, then."

Dalton laughed as Rolf groaned. Ebbie, meanwhile, focused on the lanky young man's wrist and pointed to it.

"Say… I remember that tattoo. The slaves who attacked us at the docks had 'em, too," he said. Dalton looked back, his eyes wide.

"Dat's right. I was once a slave to Sampson. De only reason I'm free is because Kabel took me in."

Kabel leaned in and crossed his arms, "My idea was to create a slave uprising, but it is damn near impossible to infiltrate Sampson's slave trade without incurring his wrath. I was lucky to find Rolf. He just happened to wander into the pub while I was there. We've been looking for escaped slaves ever since, but Sampson usually doesn't let 'em stray far before maiming or killing 'em."

Ebbie took in a long breath. Before departing, Auber had gotten him and Franco together for a brief meeting. The captain had said that the focus should be on making connections with Kabel and Rolf. Without the guise of being a Lunerian trading vessel, or having any ship at all, the crew had no purpose. Kabel appeared to have something in mind for the trio of pirates, but in the meantime, Ebbie and Franco had been instructed to act the part of reliable and fearsome travelers of the sea, to make a good impression.

"This Sampson feller seems like a lotta trouble. Why don' we just find 'im and kill 'im?" Ebbie asked with pride and a snarl in his voice.

Dalton looked back at him with sharp eyes, and Ebbie felt himself shrink down to the size of a gnat. "What the hell are you on about? Didn't you hear what they said back at the house? He is even higher up in the Sigrian ranks than the lord of Endoshire. Can you imagine yourself killing a lord without any consequences?"

"Oh… uhh…." Ebbie stuttered, a sweat already building on his brow. His mind had been wandering when they all first met up. Much of the information hadn't seemed relevant to him at the time.

"No. It would only bring the full force of the kingdom down on us. All of us, and everyone we've ever known or loved, would be killed; and not quickly, either," Kabel said, looking down.

Rolf smiled at Ebbie and said, "We've dought about dat before, too. Now just isn't da right time."

The four men stopped at a small clearing where several bushes filled with ripened berries awaited them. Even from far off, their fresh scent filled Ebbie's nose and brought a smile to his face. They walked closer to see that there was a near-infinite supply of blueberries in the lush, green bushes.

"See? What'd I tell y'all? Like the back of my hand," Kabel said with a smirk.

The group got to picking berries and placing them in baskets. Ebbie badly wanted to bring up the hilarity of the beige berries that Captain Auber had purchased, but it didn't seem appropriate, given that they were going to eat the blueberries. More importantly, such a topic was not 'pirate-like', so he held his tongue.

"So…" Kabel leaned in and clapped his old friend on the back. "Who is your new lady-friend? Y'know, I always thought you preferred the delicate, sweet types. But it makes sense that you would go for a feisty fightin' type, too."

Dalton raised an eyebrow and let out a snorting chuckle. "Lucia is not a 'lady-friend'. She is my student."

Kabel gasped. "The same student you were lookin' for the last time you visited? Adrian's daughter?"

"Yeh, that's her."

"Incredible that she found her way back to you. I should have noticed the similarity to her father, earlier. I suppose that red lunar mark around her eye means she was hiding in Luneria, back then?"

Dalton nodded. "In her five years away from me, she became a mercenary for the Lunalian King."

"You mean, 'Lunerian', right?" Rolf asked.

"Yeh, that's what I said."

"No, it ain't."

"Maturity eludes you all these years later, eh? How many times did you purposely mispronounce 'Endoshire' last time you were here?" Kabel asked while shaking his head and smiling.

"Well, *you* thought it was funny, from the sound of things."

"Foolish is more like it," he replied with an eye roll. "But anyway, how is your student with a weapon? Does she take after her father?"

Dalton threw a batch of blueberries into his mouth. Between chews, he said, "Since resuming our training, Lucia has improved by leaps and bounds. She is determined to beat me just as we wished to surpass Adrian while studying under him, back then. And just like back then, the student has unknowingly pushed the teacher to reach new heights of his own. So, having her back under my wing has been good for us both. I hate to say it, but within the next year, I'll have nothing left to teach her."

"Ah, trying to defeat Adrian in those practice duels brings back some folly-filled memories, to be sure," Kabel said while rubbing his shoulder and chuckling. "That reminds me: There's somethin' important I need to talk to you about. Whadda you say we discuss over drinks tonight?" Kabel asked.

"I like the sound of that, but will Mira approve?"

"What Mira don't know, won't hurt her."

As the two old friends giggled like excited children, Ebbie said, "Aw, I wanna go out fer drinks…"

"You ain't missin' much," Rolf chimed in. "Dey'll probably reminisce about da old days like a couple'a geezers."

Kabel suddenly ceased his laughter and glared at him. "Could an old geezer do *this* to you?"

The stocky man charged ahead with his fist cocked and ready to punch. However, with his long strides, Rolf dashed away with the speed of a steed and avoided his pursuer.

Dalton leaned in and whispered, "He runs about as fast as an old man, doesn't he?"

Ebbie and Dalton laughed as Kabel chased Rolf around the clearing, shouting obscenities and making threats along the way.

～

CONRAD, Aldous, and Triston exited the green, comfy confines of the woods to be greeted by the drab, oppressive slums of Endoshire. While the two men carried poles with buckets on each end over their shoulders, Aldous only gripped his walking stick, clanking with every other step, as always.

"Now, let's see," Aldous said, pointing further ahead to a path on the right. "The river is this way, correct?"

"That's right. It's where we saw those odd cloaked folk, too," Conrad said.

Triston growled like the angriest of dragons. "Those bastards blind-sided me! I say we pay 'em a lil' visit and rip 'em a new arse!"

"Let's not be rash," Aldous said as he continued down the dirt road, eyeing the branching path to the right. "We are here to gather water, and nothing more. Starting a commotion with those degenerates may draw unwanted attention."

"About that…" Conrad smirked. "I understand that you will be the most efficient at transporting water thanks to your abilities, but wouldn't carrying a whole building's-worth of water overhead draw 'unwanted attention'?"

"Still ever curious, I see," the old Wizard said, beaming him a smile. "As a master water Elemental, my control over it is quite good. I can separate the water into individual drops, so it won't be noticeable in the least. At worst, it will look like rain is floating above us."

"Whoa! Ali wasn't kiddin' when he said you could perform miracles, mistah Wizard!" Triston said with palpable excitement.

"It is hardly a miracle when you consider the amount of work that needs to be put in. I can only imagine how long you had to study before you could perform such a feat," Conrad said.

"Indeed, such lengthy and intense studies are why we Wizards need longer lifespans. I'd say it takes 50-100 years to master a magical art, depending on the subject. A true genius, like the Mountain King, could probably master something within 10-30 years," Aldous said.

"And how fast can a Dark Wizard learn?"

Aldous raised an eyebrow "Why do you ask?"

"Back in Bosfueras, the Dark Wizard captured me and offered his tutelage in the ways of dark magic, but I saw what he was doing to those townsfolk… I couldn't bring myself to say yes, even though I regretted my answer while rotting in his dungeon," Conrad said with wide eyes. Mr. Willoughby's glowing, red gaze had long since burned into his mind. It haunted him nearly as much as its stuttered mockery of breathing.

"You were right to reject his offer," Aldous replied while placing a sure hand on his shoulder. "Usually, the correct answer is the more difficult path."

"Right." Conrad's tone fluttered away like a moth hopelessly searching for flame.

"Do you remember what the Dark Wizard looked like?" the old Wizard asked.

"Yes, but therein lies the problem," Conrad said, his gaze falling to the dirt path at his feet. "He took multiple forms: First, it was a large man with long, black hair and a goatee. His face reminded me of a demon's, and his dark robe was covered in odd symbols. Then, he transformed into your friend, Utrix."

Aldous' expression turned grim and the sound of tightening skin against his walking stick caught Conrad's attention. "So then, for all of those months, I may have been speaking with the Dark Wizard himself, and not my friend. Right under my nose…"

"I know the feeling," Conrad said with a chuckle, but his jovial tone quickly fell more serious. "Does this mean that the *real* Utrix is dead?"

"Most likely," Aldous said before rubbing his eyes and letting out a heavy breath. "Do you remember him displaying any other magical abilities n'such, aside from Shapeshifting?"

"Besides controlling that dark essence and creating his version of the black gold? He called upon a curious pair of skeleton arms, through which he fired a green beam of light that temporarily blinded all in attendance. When my vision returned, I found that the blast had punched a hole through a man who'd refused to fall in line with his collective, and also through several walls of the cathedral."

"We call those 'Dark Hands'. It was the signature spell of *the Oppressor*, way back when," Aldous said with a frown. "But in more recent times, others have taken it as their own. The Mountain King used it against me, back when we fought a year ago."

"You mentioned this 'Oppressor' back at Mt. Couture. Do you suspect that he is the one we are dealing with?" Conrad asked.

Aldous stroked his long, gray beard. "I *did* suspect that, but some things don't add up. For one, the dark presence that I felt at Mt. Couture wasn't nearly as strong or vile as the Oppressor when I fought him all of those years ago. Furthermore, there are no records of anyone escaping his eternal prison, *the Great Chasm*. When someone is banished there, as he was, magic cannot be used. In addition, it is believed that one cannot die; it is much like an *eternal hell*, down there. Wilhelm the Oppressor always came back from the dead, using magic still not understood to this day, but the chasm should have nullified any possibility of that."

"So, we're dealing with someone new," Conrad said.

"Most likely. He may not be as much of a threat as Wilhelm was, but he should not be taken lightly. Dark Wizards are rare because the Council often hunts them down before they can become powerful. How did this one avoid their eyes for long enough to gain such might and influence?" Aldous asked aloud.

"Perhaps it is best not to ask how it happened, but rather, how we can deal with him," the strategist said. "Could we not expose him to the Wizard's Council now? Considering we burned his home down and killed several of his men, I would not be surprised to find him in Endoshire, soon."

"The Council won't believe anything I say. In fact, they will likely excommunicate me before this month is through."

"Why would they do that?"

"As a Wizard Scout on probation, I am not to interfere in Wizardly affairs until they have convened and deliberated on my punishment, if any, for failing to contain Greed in his prison," Aldous said as the group took a right onto the branching path, toward the river. "They may have been planning on an excommunication anyway, but if they find out that I was in Thironas when Famine escaped, that will seal it for me."

"And what happens then? Do ya lose yer powers or somethin'?" Triston asked.

The old Wizard chuckled. "No, no, nothing like that. I will be classified either a Warlock or a Dark Wizard by them."

"But that doesn't make sense. You don't have a dark Anima, so surely you cannot be a Dark Wizard." Conrad objected.

"Yeh, and ain't Warlocks supposed ta be bad, too?" Triston added.

"The Council decides who is and isn't a Dark Wizard. They invented that term for mages deemed too dangerous to let roam free. That is why they are hunted down," Aldous said to Conrad before eyeing Triston with a smile. "And not all Warlocks are bad. In fact, I know a few of the good ones. Think of Warlocks as mages who have achieved a higher being through magic, but aren't part of the Wizard's Council. They are not a group, nor do they have a stated goal. So, they can be good or bad."

Conrad laughed. "You continue to drop fascinating nuggets of information when we talk. Someday, I hope you write a book."

"If I have the time, dear boy, I'll do just that," he said while winking. However, his cheery expression switched to one of concern, to which Conrad cocked his head.

"What is it?"

"I sense something within you…" Aldous trailed off with horror in his eyes. "It reminds me of Angus Grouchet, back in Thironas. Did you take in the dark essence during your time in Bosfueras?"

"I was wondering if you would be able to feel it. After all, you could tell when a dark presence was nearby back at Mt. Couture," Conrad said while shrugging. Aldous raised an eyebrow. "But don't worry, I'm fine. I want to stop the Dark Savior from rising just as badly as you do."

"Even still," Aldous began with a marked nervousness in his tone. "Mayhap we should err on the side of caution. Perhaps this darkness that I feel within you needs to be activated, and it simply hasn't, yet. I know an Exorcist, and he could expel it-"

"That won't be necessary," Conrad said while waving him off. "All of Drake's flunkies were rotten to begin with. I believe that the dark essence amplified those bad aspects of their character. Furthermore, they took in a concentrated dose stored in a well; while a monster injected it into me."

"That don't sound any better ta me!" Triston said.

"He's right, m'boy. Please, think of what this could do to you. For all we know, the Dark Wizard could take control of your mind," Aldous said.

Conrad shook his head and let loose a dismissive chuckle. "Really, I'm fine. All it did was heal my wounds, which were in the process of killing me, by the way. I fear that if the dark essence were removed from my body, it would end my life. You wouldn't want to kill me, would you?"

There was a long pause to the conversation that Conrad knew should have made him uncomfortable, but for some reason, it did not. Instead, it seemed that only his cohorts were stressed. Still, he had only spoken the truth. Why was it his fault if it made others nervous?

"Yes, I suppose you're right," Aldous said with a tepid nod. "But you *will* let us know if you feel unwell, I trust?"

"Of course," Conrad said, forcing a half-hearted smile. Somehow, he knew that this wouldn't be the end of the old Wizard's worries.

～

Joel, Alistair, Giles, and Captain Auber had been chopping down smaller trees for firewood. Much to Joel's obvious chagrin, the others had stopped to take a break after only a half hour or so of work.

"He's… got… some good land legs…" Auber said, looking at Joel. He wondered how such a little fellow could have so much energy.

"What're ya talkin' about, 'land legs'?" Alistair asked as he wiped the sweat from his brow.

Auber snorted and drops of sweat flew away from the tip of his nose. "Ye know… land legs! Don't ye know anythin' about the sea?"

"Are you talkin' about 'sea legs'?" Giles asked.

"I dunno what that is, either," the big man said with a chuckle.

"Awright, I'll explain it to ye, since ye ain't experienced farers of the sea, like me," Auber said with great pride. "Sea legs are how quickly ye get adjusted to bein' out at sea. Y'know, not gettin' seasick, navigatin' the deck like a top naval officer… that sorta thing. As a pirate captain, I, of course, get me sea legs in mere moments from steppin' foot on a vessel."

"Whoa, really? I was barfin' up a storm on tha first day out at sea when we crossed the Sigrian Channel," Alistair said.

"Hm, that means ye get yer sea legs at about the same speed as most landlubbers," Auber said as the big redhead sulked. "Land legs are the other way 'round. It's how quickly men of the sea get used ta bein' on land. I've been out plunderin' the open waters since I was a wee lad, so it takes me some time ta get used to land. Normally, I could chop down wood all day without a break. But sadly, I haven't gotten me land legs, yet!"

Alistair and Giles looked at each other, then back at him; each wearing child-like smiles.

"That's amazin', mistah pirate! Tell us some stories about yer days out at sea! Ya must have had many-a-treacherous battle!" Alistair said with balled fists of raging excitement.

"Yeh, I've always wanted to be a pirate. I bet you've seen the whole world," Giles added.

"Stories? Erm… yes… well, as much as I'd like to tell ye all about my adventures at sea, I'm still a lil' woozy, tryin' to get me land legs. Maybe later," Auber said.

"Fine, but ya gotta tell us somethin' at dinner," Alistair said. Giles nodded along. "You'll feel better by then, right?"

"Perhaps…" the captain trailed off as a nervous pit took hold in his stomach. He would have to think up some stories by the end of the day, he thought, or his plan to look like a fearsome pirate would backfire.

"Well, mistah pirate, even if you have come upon some incredible sights, I wager that I can show ya somethin' that you've never seen," Alistair said while nodding and crossing his arms.

"Oh, yeh? And what's that?"

"Oi! Joel! Will ya come over here fer a moment?"

Joel chopped into the tree one more time before turning, smiling, and then walking over to the resting group.

"You and me both know that a wood-axe don't cut nearly as well as yer luxmortite blade. Show us how it's *really* done!" Alistair said while placing a small log on the ground so that it was standing.

"Hold up," Giles said, raising a hand. "Isn't your shin still injured, Joel?"

Auber cocked his head, and so too did Auber. To his eyes, the quiet little fellow hadn't missed a beat while swinging that wood-axe.

"Ah, that's right!" Alistair slapped his forehead and laughed. "I completely fergot about yer injuries. Ya should'a spoken up, lad!"

"You say that as if he could do such a thing…" Giles muttered. His eyes remained fixed on Joel's leg, much to Auber's confusion. It almost seemed like an accusatory glare. Was the lad faking his injury? The captain took in a nervous gulp. It seemed like these people could sniff out a lie from leagues away, and in that case, they might catch his white lies, too.

Instead of replying, Joel only smiled while waving them off. He drew a dark blue blade, and Auber's eyes widened. It looked similar to the one that Amis had refused to sell him earlier in the day. One-handed, Joel let the sword drop, and it cut clean through the log, vertically, like a hot knife through butter.

Giles and Auber gasped, although the captain quickly returned to his cool demeanor. Joel withdrew and sheathed the luxmortite sword, then nodded at the group with confidence in spades.

The suspicion in Giles' eyes was replaced with amazement. "Between the destruction of Norman's sword back at Lake Teras and the degenerate's cracked blade last week… I thought that perhaps their weapons had merely been brittle, but it was the strength of your sword this whole time, wasn't it?"

"That's right!" Alistair said with pride on his tongue. "That happens to be one of the rarest, strongest blades around! What did ya think, mistah pirate?"

Auber's mind raced in circles. Surely, they would not believe that he had seen a blade like that *today*. Instead, he thought of a different way to word it.

"It is an impressive sword, to say the least!" Auber said with a haughty smile. "I once encountered a landlubber who wielded a similar blade. I nearly defeated him and took the sword as my prize, but he managed to escape!"

Alistair and Giles gasped like children being told an epic tale around a campfire, while Joel tilted his head.

"But of course, retreat is the best option when yer in battle with Captain Auber!" he said with a grizzled laugh.

"I knew that you were a force ta be reckoned with!" Alistair shouted, then slapped him hard on the back. "After all, only someone with yer abilities could have shot his arrow at Sampson, the most powerful man in this city, and lived ta tell tha tale!"

Oh shit, Auber thought. He had forgotten all about Sampson.

"That's right," Giles jumped in. "I'd hate to have a feller like *that* after me. He'd probably enslave you for the rest of your days if he ever got his hands on you."

Auber's face went pale as the nervous pit in his stomach turned to nausea. Within moments, he turned around and vomited.

The trio came to his side out of apparent concern, but the captain waved them off while mixing in coughs with his confident laughter. "Sorry 'bout that, lads! Still don't got me land legs! I need ta rest a while longer!"

"You rest up, Cap'n! The three of us can handle it! We'll need ya at top strength for the upcoming battle, I'm sure," Alistair said as he motioned the others to come along with him back to chopping wood.

Joel remained behind for but a moment, and Auber worried that he had questions for him; questions that he'd have to make up the answers to on the fly. Instead, the quiet lad gave him a nod before turning to join the others in chopping the remainder of needed wood.

～

As THE MEN slowly returned from their chores, they were greeted by the sweet smells of a roasted pig; one that Lucia had hunted down and Mirabel had cooked. Franco, meanwhile, had been crafting tasteful side dishes that included the picked berries, bread, and other greens that had been lying around the house.

Aldous, Conrad, and Triston came back with far more water than needed or could be stored, so the biggest of the men dug a hole to dump most of the water in. Although Mira had sent them out to fetch drinking water, the old Wizard had other ideas in mind when he brought the great mass of it back with him. Not only would he have fire at his disposal while guarding the house that night, but water, as well.

After much preparation, a grand feast began for the newly-formed group of allies. There was much chewing, chomping, laughing, and singing throughout the night, as old friends caught up with each other and new bonds took hold.

When the night began to wind down, it became apparent that at some point during the festivities, Kabel and Dalton had disappeared. Rolf explained that they had probably taken a trip to Cole's pub in the city. This was much to Mira's annoyance; she reminded all in the house that this was what they had done the last time they were together. Every night, they had gone out, gotten drunk, and then lazed around while nursing hangovers the next day. She made all in the house promise that they wouldn't be the same.

While most went to bed, Aldous, Joel, and Lucia elected to sit outside around the bonfire. Its blaze was so great that a blanket of orange covered Kabel's tree-built home and all the way up to the horse stable. Despite her steadfast commitment to defending the home from potential assassins sent by Sampson, Lucia was the first of the three to falter, dosing off midway through the night. Soon after, Captain Auber came out to accompany the group.

"Hope ye don' mind if I join ye. I was sick earlier and had a lotta rest, so now I ain't tired," he said with a chuckle.

"I mind that you woke me up," Lucia chimed in, grumpily.

"It's no trouble at all, Captain," Aldous said with a warm smile. "We are simply enjoying the night while awaiting Kabel and Dalton's return… or for enemies to arrive."

The old Wizard chuckled as Joel made hand signals. Auber cocked his head and began counting fingers, as if doing math.

"My friend here speaks with signy-do's… USL. He's a mute, y'see," Aldous said.

"Ah… I thought he was just naturally quiet," Auber said with nervous laughter.

"He wants to-" Aldous paused, then signed back to the mute, who replied quickly with more hand signals. "Erm… he wants to know if you got your 'land legs' back, I believe? I may be mistranslating."

"Oh no, ye got it right," the captain replied, his cheeks turning rosy. "Tell Joel that I am feelin' much better, thanks."

Lucia snickered. "He is mute, not deaf."

"Oh… uhh, right."

Joel laughed inaudibly before signing some more to Aldous.

"Oho! Is this true?" Aldous asked, looking to the captain with eyes alight. "You've done battle with a foe who wielded a luxmortite blade?"

Lucia leaned in and glared at Auber. The captain began to sweat. He eyed everyone around the campfire with a nervous energy that was easy for Aldous to notice, though he was unsure of why he would act in such a way.

"Joel would like to know how recently you battled this foe, and where it happened. We're lookin' for folk who wield such weapons," Aldous explained.

With a twitch of her nose and a deep inhale, it almost looked as if Lucia was about to yell at the pirate captain, but he did not give her a chance to say anything.

"In that case, let me tell ye about someone I met *today*," Auber said, a nervous smile stretching that silly, patchy beard of his. Lucia had closed her mouth, and all leaned in with apparent interest. "Remember how I mentioned earlier today that we met up with a fella who worked in the sewers? He wielded a blade that looked just like yers."

Auber pointed at Joel, whose eyes grew wide.

"Don't you think that this was relevant information we could have used earlier?" Lucia asked with contempt on her tongue.

"Erm… well, sorry, but how was I supposed ta know that ye were all lookin' fer these bizarre blue swords?" the captain asked with a shrug.

"It is not the sword, but the one wielding it, who interests us," Aldous said before letting out a strained breath. Auber returned little save pure bewilderment on his face. "It's a long story… but let's just say that finding this man would be a great leap in the right direction for us. What did you say his name was, again?"

"Amis."

Aldous looked to Joel and asked, "Do you recall speaking with anyone named Amis in the past?"

The mute shook his head.

"I see. In that case, I feel your sword will gain his trust, as it did Lord Roland's back in Thironas," Aldous said with a smile, then turned back to the captain. "Will you lead us to his shop tomorrow morning?"

"Shouldn't be a problem," Auber said, rubbing the back of his head.

"Next time, tell us *everything*, down to the last detail," Lucia said, spitting nearly as much fire as the blaze before them and sending Auber's shoulders up to his ears.

"Oho! There is little use in lamenting, now. The best we can do is pay him a visit tomorrow morning," Aldous said, then smiled at the pirate. "Now, how about a story? Tell me, Captain, are you familiar with a village called Faiwell?"

CHAPTER 10
TRICKSTER

The next morning, Aldous, Joel, Auber, and Franco journeyed out of the woods and into the slums of Endoshire. More of the allies had wished to accompany them, but it was agreed upon that traveling in too large of a group would be risky. The others stayed back to do morning chores in preparation for breakfast; aside from Dalton and Kabel, who could not be awakened through reasonable means after a long night out at the pub.

Captain Auber and Franco led the way down a path that branched left into the dreary slums of Endoshire. It felt largely empty since most of the peasants had gone out to the fields; as evidenced by a strong wind that reeked of fertilizer. All who remained were some raggedy-clothed children playing in the streets, and the elderly, who tended to avert their eyes whenever crossing paths with them.

After over an hour of walking, the group found themselves in a section of the slums that housed many run-down shops. The items were of such little apparent worth that many of the stores had been left unattended. The captain led them through several alleyways, and wandered in circles, as if lost, until finally reaching a door where a sign hung. Auber groaned while stepping aside to reveal what it said:

CLOSED

"Aw, come on! We walked all this way fer nothin'?" he whined, kicking the door.

All gasped as the door creaked open.

"Hello? Is anyone here?" Franco said. Only the echo of his elegant, steady voice replied.

They peered into the shop to find it in complete disarray. All of the knick-knacks and items had been knocked to the floor. Some chairs had been broken, and all of the amateurish paintings had taken a tumble down from the walls.

"Is this how the shop was before?" Aldous asked.

"It was messy, but not *this* messy," Franco replied.

"Looks to me like-" Auber gasped as an arrow flew at his face and struck him right between the eyes. "Gah!"

The captain crashed to the dusty floor dramatically as the arrow fluttered down harmlessly along with him.

Joel tilted his head, crouched, and picked up the arrow. He gasped inaudibly when it crinkled in his hand. It was made entirely of paper. He handed it to Aldous, who inspected it for himself.

"How odd..."

"Aren't any of ye gonna ask if I'm alright?" Auber asked with the sting of betrayal on his tongue.

Aldous chuckled. "I daresay you're fine, m'boy, considering the arrow was made of paper, n'such."

Franco sighed. "Are you alright, sir?"

"No, as a matter of fact, I am *not* alright!" Auber sat up and rubbed his brow. He grimaced at a faint trace of blood on his fingers. "First of all, that scared the hell outta me! Second of all, it gave me a paper cut!"

Joel sent hand signals to Aldous, who cocked his head for a moment, then turned to Auber. "He wants to know if you have gained your land legs, yet... why does he keep asking about that?"

"Why, indeed?" Franco asked aloud with a smirk.

"Erm..." Auber mumbled as he got to his feet and dusted himself off. "It was a surprise attack. It woulda hit anyone. I was simply unlucky. But more importantly..." the captain looked around as a fire in his eyes grew. "Amis! What is the meanin' of this? Don't ye remember me from yesterday?"

After a moment of silence, a man slowly rose from behind the sales counter. He wore a turban with a shiny green jewel tucked in the middle, and dusty, white clothes that looked fit for desert travel. The rosiness of his fat cheeks shined through his dark skin, and he wore the expression of an experienced troublemaker who had been caught in a misdeed.

"You are friends of Amis?" he asked.

"We only met him yesterday, but I suppose he was a nice enough fellow to call 'friend'," Franco said.

"That sounds more like an acquaintance to me..." the man in the turban trailed off. "What brings you to the shop?"

"We might ask you the same question," Aldous jumped in. "A struggle clearly took place here. What has happened to Amis?"

"I don't know. When I arrived to open up, the shop was already like this."

"Oh?" the old Wizard mused with a clank of his walking stick. He then turned to the pirates. "Are you certain that Amis owns this shop?"

"He does! This here fella is lyin'!" Auber said while pointing at him like a child tattling on his older sibling.

"And who are you to tell me what I do and do not own? You don't look like a lord to me," he replied with arms crossed.

"Hold up," Franco said. The palpable tension in the shop calmed. "Would your name happen to be Dhogron?"

The man in the turban cocked his head and said, "Yes, how did you know?"

"Yesterday, Amis mentioned that you were supposed to be watching the shop. When we arrived, he called out to you, but you weren't around."

"Perhaps I was out to lunch," Dhogron said with a shrug.

"I apologize for being so forward, but we must get in contact with Amis as soon as possible. Do you truly not know of his whereabouts?" Aldous asked.

"I'm afraid not. I have never seen the shop so disheveled. It looks to me like he was attacked."

Joel made hand signals to the group, to which Dhogron raised an eyebrow.

"Sign language?" he asked.

"Indeed," Aldous said, nodding at his mute friend. "He was just pointing out what I already suspected: You are a Wizard, are you not?"

Shock passed over Dhogron's face for a mere moment before he returned to a mischievous expression. "Yes... and you must be the magic presence that I am sensing among your group. It is always nice to meet a fellow Wizard."

"Oho! We have more in common than you know. Would I be correct in assuming that you are the Wizard Scout of the Degenerate monolith?" Aldous asked.

"I am not allowed to discuss such things, and if you truly are a Wizard Scout, then what are you doing here? You should be guarding your own monolith, should you not?" Dhogron asked, straightening his arm out. From his spacious sleeve shot out a sword, which he caught, and then pointed at the group. "State your true business here. Are you the attackers? Are you here to finish me off?"

Auber put up his hands in defense. "Whoa, thar! We just came to check on Amis! I ain't got no problems with a Wizard. Don' mind me-"

A gust of wind blew through the window and bent Dhogron's sword like a flimsy piece of grass. An awkward silence came over the room as Dhogron frowned.

"Y-yer sword's broken..." Auber muttered, pointing to the bent blade.

Aldous chuckled and thudded his walking stick off of one of his boots. "It is made out of paper, just like the arrow-majigger from before, right?"

"So what if it is?"

"You have nothing to fear from us," the old Wizard said while clapping Joel on the back. "Perhaps my friend here will quell your fears."

Joel drew his luxmortite blade and held it out before Dhogron, who gasped.

"A Keeper of the Key?" he asked, to which the mute nodded with a smile. The Wizard in the turban turned his gaze back to Aldous. "My apologies for the distrust. I am a bit on edge since happening upon this mess."

"Think nothing of it. In fact, we are here to help."

"You know where Amis went to?" Dhogron asked.

"I don't know his location, but I *do* know who would benefit from attacking him," Aldous said.

"Was it that raven?" Auber asked.

"Avian, sir," Franco whispered.

"Err... yeh, I meant ta say avian. It followed us as we walked into the slums, but turned back well before we reached this shop," the captain clarified.

Dhogron snorted. "Amis did mention an avian following him, but he has always been a paranoid fellow, and so I did not take his claims as seriously as I should have. As I'm sure you've seen, many avian come and go in the city. It *always* looks as if creatures from the sky are following."

Aldous let out a sigh, his brow furrowing. "If only that were the case. I'm afraid that this particular avian serves a powerful master; one who wishes to destroy the Degenerate monolith. We have encountered them before, you see: Back in Thironas, at the Famine monolith."

"Were you able to ward them off?" Dhogron asked. The old Wizard shook his head, solemnly. "So, then... one of the seals has been broken."

Joel shook his head and held up two fingers.

"T-two seals? Broken? How? How were we not notified by the Council?" Dhogron asked aloud.

"The Council is in denial, I'm afraid. It has been so long since the Dark Savior posed a threat to this world, that they do not believe the current attack on the monoliths to be of concern," Aldous said.

"I... I don't know what to do. We're in some *real* trouble..." Dhogron said, staring blankly at the floor. "I'm not ready... not ready to handle this burden..."

"As I said," the old Wizard began, clanking his walking stick off the ground with a hollow *thunk*. The Wizard in the turban looked up with sheepish eyes. "We are here to help."

"No, you don't understand," Dhogron said to cocked heads from all in the shop. "If what you say is true, then Amis wasn't just attacked. He was probably kidnapped."

"Kidnapped? But why?" Aldous asked.

"I'm sure you already know that the Degenerate seal is in the sewers under this city. But it is like a maze, and there are few in the entire world who could easily navigate it. For that reason, we have a map."

"Oh, dear..." Aldous' brow gleamed with sweat.

"I should say that Amis and I each have our own maps. It is a failsafe, in case of an emergency when we are separated. I have no idea where he keeps his, so this enemy could be torturing him for that information, and there is nothing I can do about it," Dhogron said with frustration in his voice. "I have only been here for a few years, and it turns out my first test as a Scout is nearly insurmountable."

"What is the duty of a Wizard Scout?" Aldous asked. Joel looked at him in surprise. After all of his complaints about the Council, why use them as an example? "They report to the Wizard King. Surely, he could help us?"

The Wizard in the turban scoffed. "You've never met Olius, have you?"

"Can't say that I have."

"He works alone, at all times. Amis and I have worked well together, but he has kept us in the dark ever since I started here. I have only spoken with him a few times."

"It would seem that stubbornness is a common trait amongst the Wizard Kings!" Aldous said before snorting.

Joel agreed; all Wizard Kings that he'd met so far had been arrogant to the point where it harmed their original mission: protecting the monolith. Perhaps it came with the territory, he thought. After all, the standard of power and wisdom to gain such a title was high enough to reach the heavens.

"Perhaps, then, we could work together," the old Wizard suggested. "I realize this doesn't follow the conventional rules of a Scout, but if you think that Olius won't lift a finger to help…"

"He won't," Dhogron confirmed. "He will allow Amis to be tortured, and then deal with any intruders of the sewer himself. From his perspective, Scouts and Key Keepers are expendable."

"So then, the key is finding Amis before the enemy can get the information that they need from him. How will we do that?" Franco asked.

"Yes, and I'm curious who this 'enemy' is that you speak of. Who has been destroying the seals?" Dhogron added.

"A Village Elder from the land of Faiwell, Federland. His name is Drake Danvers. He has been aided by a Dark Wizard, supplying him with information on each monolith and how to destroy them. The Dark Wizard has even managed to harness the power of the Dark Savior, in some ways. He has enhanced his allies' abilities thanks to the black gold produced by Greed," Aldous said, the grim situation reflecting well in his blue eyes. "That avian following Amis around, for instance, is much larger and faster than a typical avian. More concerning still, is that Drake appears to have influence over Sampson."

A horror-filled gasp escaped Dhogron's trembling lips. "Th-the slave trader?"

Everyone else in the shop nodded.

"I don't like these odds," he said, looking down. "Sampson practically controls Endoshire. To defy him is to defy the kingdom, and doing such would bring a hellish wrath not only on us, but all people of this city."

"Not all is lost. Not yet," Aldous assured him, then held his hand out to be shaken. "Will you go beyond your regular duties and help us fight off this great threat, which remains unseen to the common man? Will you help us in our thankless cause, if it means the salvation of this great city?"

With a deep breath, Dhogron approached the old Wizard and shook his hand. As the hands shook, Aldous' mouth fell agape, and Joel's eyes immediately picked up on why: Under Aldous' grip, Dhogron's hand had been crushed to the point where it had caved in.

"B'wahh!" Aldous cried, jumping back as the hand fell to the floor, crumpled up like a piece of paper.

Upon closer inspection, Joel realized that it *was* paper, just in the dark skin tone of the Wizard in the turban and perfectly shaped like a hand. All looked to Dhogron, wide-eyed. He merely giggled as his true hand popped out of his sleeve.

Auber howled with laughter and said, "Nice one! Ye got 'im real good!"

Aldous let out a sigh of relief as Franco snickered and said, "Just like he got you 'real good' with the arrow earlier, sir?"

"Oh yeh, I fergot about that..." the captain said as he gingerly felt the paper cut on his brow. Joel narrowed his eyes at him. Had he exaggerated his abilities, yesterday? Auber turned to Dhogron and said, "Yer a real tricky fella, ain't ye?"

He smiled. "Why, yes, I am. As a matter of fact, I am known as *Dhogron the Trickster* amongst the Council. I prefer using magic to deceive or distract, rather than fight."

"There is no shame in that. It is best to avoid conflict, if possible. I get the sense that you are young, too. Mayhap inexperienced in battle?" Aldous suggested.

"Indeed. I am only 127 years old."

"But that *is* old!" Auber said.

"Not for a Wizard," Aldous said with a chuckle. "I'm 516, y'know!"

"And you are *still* a Scout?" Dhogron asked with a raised eyebrow.

"That is a long story; one for another time, methinks."

"From what I gather, the Scout sounds like a highly important position. Why wouldn't they send the most experienced of Wizards to guard such an important artifact that ensures our safety?" Franco asked.

"That would be a Wizard King's job, m'boy," Aldous explained. "The Scout's main duty is to inform the Wizard King of any potential threats to the seal. It has nothing to do with power, and everything to do with how simply they can communicate with their superiors. Back in Faiwell, if I ever wished to meet up with my King Wizard, he would only need to conjure up a storm, and then I could ride the lightning to him in mere moments."

"What good does paper do in a sewer, then?" Franco asked.

Dhogron held his hands out, and in his palms appeared a small paper boat. "Even though Olius prefers to work alone, we *did* have a system set up to warn him of possible threats, just in case. I could leave a message on one of these paper boats, and let it float into the sewers. It was a good way to avoid being eaten by the horrid Guardian Beast; a fate that befell my predecessor, sadly. That method won't work anymore, though."

"Why not?" asked Aldous.

"There is a river that flows into the sewers at the east end of the city. That is where I used to let the paper boats go because all other entrances have the current flowing out of them," Dhogron said, then crumbled the boat in his trembling hands. "But now, Degenerate's influence has spread so far that it is beginning to infect residents of the city. They have used that eastern sewer entrance as a base of sorts, and I can't get anywhere near there without being attacked. Even if the Council *didn't* forbid us Wizards from bringing harm to humans, there are simply too many of them to fight off, and so we haven't communicated with Olius in about a year, now."

"We encountered them last week. A dangerous lot of degenerates for sure, but if you want to try and send a message to Olius, I can help with that. My command over the water washed them away when we last fought, and with the river as a source, it'd be even easier for me, this time," Aldous said.

"Wait, why don' we just go into the sewers ourselves?" Auber asked with a snort, then looked to Dhogron. "Ye got a map, right? If the maze is so big, I'm sure we could avoid this 'Guardian Beast' who killed the other guy, can't we?"

Joel nodded, then signed to Aldous.

"They make a good point. We were able to avoid our Guardian Beast back at Mt. Couture. Surely, in such a big area, we could do the same here," the old Wizard said.

Dhogron shook his head. "No, it wouldn't be that easy. It would, perhaps, be more accurate to say that there are *several* guardians of the sewers."

Aldous leaned in. "But how? Most monoliths are guarded by one beast from the Cold World. It has been that way for millennia."

"That much is true, but Olius keeps… other pets, shall we say? They may not be as fierce as the Guardian Beast, but they can rip their prey to shreds all the same. Other monsters guard the western and northern entrances. We had some trouble with them surfacing from the sewers when they got hungry, so Amis would go in there to leave them food," the trickster Wizard said.

"That must have been why we met him coming from the sewer on the west coast," Franco said, stroking his chin.

"Alright, then. With what we know, I feel that it would be best to get that warning to Olius via one of your paper boats, immediately," Aldous said, to which Dhogron nodded. "After that, we can come up with a strategy to find Amis. I had wanted to plan our defense out slowly, but Drake is forcing our hand. It seems likely that we'll have to mount our own attack; to rescue the Keeper of the Key before they can obtain that map from him."

Dhogron fidgeted his mouth. "I don't know about 'mounting an attack', as you say, when there are so many humans opposing us. Still, for now, let's be on our way to the east, where the river flows."

Joel had nearly forgotten just how much Aldous had been disobeying the Wizard's Council, of late. If they somehow caught wind that they were in Endoshire and clashing with humans; regardless of the intention, there would almost certainly be hell to pay.

AFTER AN HOUR of traveling southeast through the slums, the group reached the outskirts. From there, they headed further east to the river-bank, where Aldous had gathered water yesterday. Within another hour's time, they had traveled far up the river's stream, where the degenerates were completely out of sight. The bank was spacious and few people roamed the area, save leery peasants coming and going from their work in the fields.

"Do you have a pen quill to write your message?" Aldous asked Dhogron.

With a confident smile, Dhogron held his hands out, and in his palms appeared a little paper boat. This time, however, there was writing inscribed on it. "No need."

"Ah, I see. You are quite talented to visualize your message and conjure it on the paper like that."

"And what about you?" Dhogron asked as he handed the paper boat over. "How will you get it past the degenerates? With a large wave?"

"No, that would alert them to our presence. For now, I feel that stealth is the best option," Aldous said, gesturing at the stream with a thrust of his palm. A bubble formed atop the water's surface, and the old Wizard threw the paper boat into it as it drifted downstream.

The bubble then sank under the water, and with it went the boat. Aldous held a steady hand out as it floated downstream. He closed his eyes and focused on the section of river carrying the boat as if becoming one with it. Every intricacy of the stream, from the flora on the riverbed to the rocks deflecting water became a part of his conscious mind; a second nature. Guiding the boat was as simple as taking steps on a stroll for a master water Elemental. It was only a matter of time before he snuck the boat past those degenerates, and though said time flowed quickly for him, the old Wizard could tell that some others were growing impatient.

Auber groaned from behind. "How long is this gonna take?"

"Patience, sir." The dry sarcasm in Franco's tone almost made Aldous laugh and lose concentration. Those two were almost like a bickering married couple, he thought.

After what he figured to be less than a half hour, Aldous opened his eyes and beamed a pleasant smile at the others. "It is done."

"They didn't notice?" Dhogron asked.

"No. I would have felt if there was any contact with the air bubble," Aldous said while stretching his stiff limbs. "Can you be certain that it will reach Olius?"

"Yes. He won't lend us a helping hand, but at least he will know of the impending attack on the seal."

"Well then, shall we make a plan to rescue Amis, next?" Aldous asked.

"Yes, but where do we even begin? We have no idea where he is…"

"I'd like you to come along with us to the outskirts of the city. More allies await us there. Then, we can make a plan."

"There are more of you?" Dhogron asked, wide-eyed.

"The Dark Savior's negative influence reaches farther than you can imagine, even when he is sealed away. I'm sure there are many more allies to come, in this fight," Aldous said.

The group walked southwest along the river, headed back to the outskirts. Along the way, Aldous couldn't help but ponder the weight of his own words. Could they recruit more members to their group? With Drake, a Dark Wizard, the town of Bosfueras, the degenerates, and Sampson all opposing them, it seemed that they would need all the help that they could get.

CHAPTER 11
THE ARRIVAL

Drake Danvers walked into his room with a stern stride and impatience building up in his chest. His sharp, green eyes locked on to Rose, who had just finished fitting herself into an underdress. Their gazes met for but a brief moment before she darted her eyes to the floor.

"Well?" he asked. Rose opened her mouth, but nothing aside from a nervous stutter came out. "What is the result?"

"I-I… I'm sorry…"

"Bah!" Drake shouted before smashing his fist onto the top of his dresser, rattling both it and Rose in the process. He breathed heavily for a few moments before gathering himself and turning back to her. She was cowering like a puppy; making her too pitiable to stay angry for long. "When I offered to make you my queen, my bride; part of the deal was that you bear a child for me."

"We can try again," Rose said, her spirits picking up.

"Oh?" Drake asked while approaching her with an aggressive posture. The bride-to-be's breaths stilled, and her normally olive skin fell pale as he grasped some strands of her dark, luscious hair. "Do you think that you are in a position to give *me* orders?"

Rose closed her eyes and strained them as Drake pulled on the hair strands a little harder. Some nervous, undignified breaths came from her nose, and she muttered, "N-no…"

He pulled on her hair some more, but slowly, so as not to rip any of it out. She squeaked like a mouse. "I decide what we do. Understand?"

Rose nodded as tears rolled out from her brown eyes, now wide open with fear.

"I'll have none of that, either," the Village Elder said as he released the hair strands and wiped the tears from her cheeks. She flinched in response, but he could tell that she was trying to stay still as night. The poor thing didn't have it in her, though. He had maybe instilled a little too much fear in her. Drake let out a sigh. "I suppose we could try one more time."

"Thank you," Rose said, looking up at him and placing a trembling hand on his chest before resting her head up against it. "I won't let you down."

"See to it that you don't. I'd hate for you to end up like Edith."

Rose lifted her head and looked up at him with confused eyes, still teary. "Who is Edith?"

Drake let loose a despicable grin. *"Precisely."*

Rose gasped as he pushed her onto the large bed behind, covered in many flower petals that plumed out upon her impact. The sweet fragrance reached Drake's nose and intoxicated him; and Rose lay there, ready for him to take her once more. Despite the invite to pleasure before him, his smile fell to a mere smirk. If she did not bear a child this time, then he would have to take more extreme measures.

Out in the dining room of Drake's living quarters sat Angus, feasting on roasted chicken like a ravenous wolf. No matter how much he ate or rested, though, the wound between his neck and shoulder only seemed to worsen. Heavily bandaged as it was, he could still feel the blood seeping through. This morning, he had woken up to blotches of red on his pillow. With his regenerative capabilities having slowed to a halt, he needed the Dark Wizard to impart him with more dark essence. Each day he waited, he felt more and more helpless; more human. His reversion to such a lesser state disgusted him.

Drake's bodyguards, Hector Brix and Ned Prescott, stood at each corner of the room, staring at Angus in their tall, cloaked forms. The giant snarled at them.

"What're you lookin' at?" he asked between grouchy chomps of his meal.

Both remained silent; though, Ned did point past Angus at the grand window. He turned to see that perched on the sill was the enhanced avian, Mur'del. Her ragged, ill-fitting clothes fluttered in the gentle breeze along with a dark ponytail that sported a mixture of hair and feather.

"Any news?" Angus asked.

"They will arrive within the hour," she replied with a nod. "The Lord of Darkness has brought *hundreds* of villagers with him."

"Excellent," Angus said while clenching his fist. He felt a twinge of disappointment when it failed to crack under his faltering grip strength. "They will serve as fine distractions in the coming sewer raid. But more importantly, we'll have everyone together."

"Ah, but I wonder how Brice will take the news that *you're* leading the team." A sly smile crossed Mur'del's mouth, pushing up a beak-like nose that was long, sharp, and dark.

"It matters not. He can fall in line or be struck down. The choice is his," he replied while cracking a smile of his own.

"Is that your way of threatening me?" she asked.

Angus let out a snorting chuckle. "Of course not. We make a good team."

"Forgive me if I take little stock in human loyalty," Mur'del said with a snicker.

"How many times must I tell you? We have progressed beyond our respective species. Comparing me to a mere man is like comparing a dragon to a fly."

"Is that right? You certainly *bleed* like a man," she retorted, nodding at the bandages seeped in red. The giant let out an annoyed huff. "Let's face the truth: We need our benefactors to supply us with dark essence so we can remain this way. We have broken the shackles of our weaker species, only to find that we remain trapped behind bars."

"It will get the job done, for now," Angus said.

"You should think further ahead," Mur'del said, her voice lowering to a chirp-like whisper. "We are expendable. I recommend a backup plan for if you are betrayed. I've already got one."

Angus scoffed. "I plan to rule over a country with my queen when we emerge victorious. If I can't make that a reality, then I'd rather be dead, anyway."

"For your sake, I hope this 'queen' is worth the trouble."

"Oh, she is." Angus forced the stone foundations of his face into a grand smile.

"I have my doubts. She seemed like a whiny brat when I met her," Mur'del said.

"You have a true talent for getting under the skin," Angus said, pressing his fists together. He had expected the crack of his knuckles to fill the room, but it came out weak; decidedly *human*. Despite his disappointment, his confident smile remained. "But I will gladly accept your apology after we've won and become rulers of our own territories."

"Ever the dreamer, aren't you?"

Angus took one last bite of chicken, then stood. "My dream comes closer to reality with each seal destroyed. On that note, how about we take a trip to the docks to greet our Wizard friend?"

"Shouldn't we inform Drake?" Mur'del asked.

He glanced back at the Village Elder's closed door, and with a brief moment of silence, muffled grunts and labored breaths could be heard. "It appears he is busy, at the moment."

Mur'del narrowed her dark eyes and asked, "How many more times will they try to fruitlessly conceive a child before realizing the folly in it all?"

"Considering his age, you may indeed be correct. Unfortunately for the girl, though, he seems to blame his inadequacies on her," Angus said.

"How childish," Mur'del replied with a tweet. She nudged her head to the outside of the window. "Shall we depart, then?"

"I'm going to fit myself into some new clothes. I'll meet you outside," he replied before walking past the bodyguards and into his room.

～

IN SHORT ORDER, Angus and Hector met Mur'del outside of Drake's building. Day was winding down into night, and fog began to set in. The streets were still packed with folk coming and going; and since they were in the wealthy district, most of them were pleasant to look at. As opposed to the unruly trolls and ragged peasants often found in the city center, beautiful women and powerful men sat in fanciful carriages and atop well-dressed steeds. These were the people that Angus was happy to be around, and they quickly lightened his dour mood.

"Shall we notify Sampson?" Mur'del asked.

"We have time. It would be best if he got acquainted with our Wizard friend sooner rather than later," Angus replied.

The trio ventured out of the wealthy district and into the docking area, where the fog intensified. The *clicks* and *clacks* of trotting horses echoed, and crowds of chattering people could be heard, but not seen.

"Such a dreary city," Mur'del remarked.

"I'm surprised to see you walking around with the rest of us," Angus said with a chuckle. "I believe you said something about not wanting to dirty your talons on these streets?"

"Flying draws too much attention to me, these days," she replied with a chirp. "When I fly too low, it creates a gust of wind. And aside from that, I couldn't slow myself down enough to stay at this walking pace."

"Yes, yes, you're 'as fast as a dragon', I know," Angus said with an eye roll. "Just hope that you don't have to *prove it*, someday."

The enhanced avian cawed with amusement. "And you say *I* get under the skin?"

"For you, let's call it a ruffling of feathers."

Hiss-like laughter erupted behind them, and they both turned back, eyes wide, to see that it had been none other than Hector who had appreciated the joke.

"So, you *do* make noise," Mur'del said.

The trio walked to Sampson's headquarters at dock 15. It was a long, rectangular, and wooden building, with multiple floors and openings at the sides for ships to come and go. Many workers were wandering about the dock, but Angus knew them to be slaves in disguise. It was an unspoken truth known to many in the city. The trio entered to see some burly men standing behind a desk that was covered in stacked papers.

"Can we help ye?" one of them asked.

"We are here to see Sampson," Angus said.

"He ain't takin' visitors at this time. Is there somethin' *we* can help ye with?" the man insisted.

"Bring him to me," the giant said, glaring with murderous intent.

"Hold up," one of the men jumped in. He was hairy and had his arm wrapped up in a sling. He looked at Hector with nervous eyes. "Are ye here on behalf of Mr. Danvers?"

"Indeed," Angus said, his voice so monotone that it made him drowsy.

"Come with me," the man said with a forced smile. The trio

followed him through the innards of the headquarters, a series of finely-crafted wooden hallways. "Master Sampson ain't able to move much since his injury, y'see. So, I gotta bring you to him."

"It's no trouble," Angus assured the man, who took another nervous look back at Hector.

After going up a set of stairs, they were led to a grand door. The man with his arm in a sling knocked, gently.

"What is it? I thought I told ye no visitors!" an angry voice thundered.

"My apologies, Master. Cohorts of Mr. Danvers have come to visit," he replied.

A weak sigh made its way through the door. "Let them in."

The door creaked open to reveal a grand room overlooking the docks. The red, patterned rugs matched well with the silk drapes adorning the windows, and several portraits hung from the walls, all notably making Sampson seem more handsome than he was. Right-ward, the man in question lay in a bed with room enough for four, if not five. His foot was propped up on several pillows, and if his three heavy blankets weren't enough to keep him warm, then the legion of crumbs and food discards surely would be.

"Hello. I am Angus, leader of Drake's team," the giant said before looking back at his two partners. "This is Mur'del, and I believe you have met Hector before."

"A pleasure to meet you," Sampson replied with a grunt. Even upper body gestures seemed to pain his leg.

"That looks to be a nasty injury you have, there."

"Courtesy of those miscreants that we tried to head off, yesterday," the slaver replied through gritting teeth. "I swear, when I find the bastard who shot me…"

"In due time," Angus said, holding a hand up. "But for now, how would you like that leg of yours to be fixed up in an instant?"

"You can do such things?"

"Not me," he said while pointing to the bandaged wound on his neck. "But a powerful ally of ours can. And he is arriving within the hour."

Sampson sat up. "Is this the Dark Wizard that Drake mentioned? The man who controls territory in Gentorgul?"

"The very same. One of his many talents is that he can instantly heal what ails us; make us stronger," Angus said with a clenched fist.

"Would you like to come along with us to greet him? The sooner you meet him, the less you will suffer through your injury."

The slaver smiled. "I'll have my men wheel me there."

Preparations were made for Sampson, and a makeshift wheelbarrow was set up to be pushed along by two of his men. The group made their way further down the docks and waited in anticipation of the Dark Wizard's arrival. However, the fog made it difficult to see much of the sea.

"What does his ship look like?" Sampson asked Mur'del.

"It is probably the largest vessel I've ever seen, with eight sails, some the size of ships themselves," she replied. Angus detected an odd hint of pride in her voice. "It is the darkest of blacks, save a few carved-out designs at its side and the decks themselves."

"Sounds like even in this fog, it will be easy to spot," Angus said.

The group waited a little longer until the ship finally appeared, bursting from the fog in a black mass of death. It towered above what Angus could have ever expected and appeared large enough to house hundreds or perhaps even a thousand.

"Impressive..." he muttered. Sampson and the others remained speechless.

Soon, however, it became apparent that the great black ship was veering to the left and making a sweep along the coast.

"What're they doin'? We made plenty of space for 'em here. Even with that massive ship of theirs!" Sampson said.

Angus widened his eyes for a brief moment, then returned to his usual stone expression. "They are searching for the stolen ship; the one that you attempted to intercept. Perhaps they wish to reclaim it?"

He looked to Mur'del, then gave her a nod. The enhanced avian nodded back before taking flight, much to the disturbance of Sampson and his men; the gust from her takeoff nearly toppled them over.

"Where's she goin'?" the slaver asked.

"To greet the Dark Wizard ahead of us. Shall we venture to the dock where those scoundrels dropped anchor? It was dock four, correct?" Angus asked.

Sampson nodded, and with that, they traveled west along the docks. As they did, however, a large commotion broke out: First, an explosion rocked the harbor, and the mist all around them turned a demonic shade of red and orange. Then, the howls and shouts of frightened men and women reached them, and it was music to Angus' ears. It wasn't long before the panicked crowds ran past them like a flock of frightened birds. The giant laughed in the chaos of it all, while Sampson and his men struggled to maintain balance of the wheelbarrow and nearly toppled over.

When they finally reached dock four, the haze had changed from orange and red to dark gray, and the crisp smell of burning wood filled the air. They walked down the dock just in time to see the ship sinking and aflame. The mighty black vessel loomed behind, with hundreds of the Bosfueras townsfolk watching on, their red eyes gleaming through the smoke and fog.

Sampson remained silent; but Angus could see it in his wide eyes: While most would rightfully be fearful of what they had just witnessed, he saw potential. That was precisely why Drake had wished to ally with him, aside from the obvious influence and power that he wielded.

The slaver looked over his shoulder, to his men. "Inform the captains that we will be moving their ships."

"But Master… we have made room at another dock."

"Did I stutter?" Sampson asked with a fiery glare. "Inform them, then get some workers over here. Quickly!"

"S-sorry, Master. Right away."

Angus crossed his arms and cracked a smile. "Impressed already? Wait 'till you see what he is *truly* capable of."

IN THE BOWELS of the great black ship, Brice Garin was strung up in chains, being whipped by one of the brainwashed Bosfueras men. His short stature ensured that he could only reach the grimy floor when on his tip-toes, and his aching arms, which had borne the weight of his body for most of the trip, had become so pale and lifeless that he began to wonder if they might fall off, soon. He could feel that the back of his shirt was in tatters, and underneath were wounds and scars that refused to heal. He had sustained so much damage in his fight with Powell and over the course of this trip, that his reserve of dark essence had run dry.

The brainwashed man cracked the whip against Brice once more, but the pain had dulled in the past few days. He began to wonder what the point of it all was until remembering that this was punishment for allowing Conrad and the others to escape. Even worse, half of

Bosfueras had burned down, and many of those that the Dark Wizard had enhanced with dark essence had died in the attack.

For someone with his abilities, escaping and killing the peons who'd been tasked with whipping him would have been a trifle. However, Brice was allowing the punishment to happen. He still had hopes, however small, of leading Drake's team. This was merely a show of solidarity to the Dark Wizard; his plea to remain a top contender for the position.

Brice raised an eyebrow and looked over his shoulder as he heard the groaning of a door across the room. Someone new had entered, and she held a candle. In the dim light provided, he could see her waving off the man who had been whipping him. After a few moments of chatting in Old Gentish, the man left, and then the woman released Brice from his chains.

He let out a sigh of relief while crashing to the floor in a sad heap. While still on his bottom, he turned and looked up to see who had freed him.

"Catalina…" Brice trailed off. Her long, dark hair and bronzed skin reflected the flame of the candle beautifully. She wore a hastily-crafted dress that sported some rather unpleasant designs; so much, in fact, that the dry bloodstains all over it were a welcome addition. "Why have ye released me? I told ye before that I will accept this punishment to the fullest extent."

"I remember. This time, it was not I who called for your release," she replied, playing with the dark stitches that stuck sloppily out of her neck. "This is a direct order from the Dark Lord himself."

"So, he has forgiven me?" Brice asked with hope creeping into his voice.

Catalina flashed a half-hearted smile. "I suspect that it will take more to get back in his good graces. But I can help you with that."

"Ye should worry about yerself. If he ever found out that ye defied orders and didn't whip me, it would be *ye* up in those chains," Brice said, letting out a giant snort from an equally giant nose.

"And would you whip me, if he commanded it?" she asked.

Brice paused and looked at her with tired, brown eyes. "Without question."

Catalina smiled down at him. "You hesitated. I am confident that if the roles were reversed, you would help me, too. That is why I want *you* leading the team when the time comes."

"Hmph. Yer sorely mistaken. Half the village burned down 'cause of my poor leadership. Many of my friends and subordinates died, too," he said while looking to the floor. "Just do what he says from now on, alright?"

Instead of responding, the Gentish woman held her hand out. Brice shook his head, then, under the waning strength of his trembling arms and legs, reached his feet.

"You can barely stand. Let me help you," Catalina said.

"I don' need it. Why do ye wanna help me, anyway?" he snapped back.

"Because you need a friend. I need one, too. We have more in common than you think…"

Brice scoffed. "The only friend I got left is a giant fly who makes stupid buzzin' noises when he tries to speak. We don't live a life where it's beneficial to have friends. Stick to yer own, and I'll stick to mine."

"You are stubborn," Catalina said as she slipped down and under Brice's arm with inhuman speed. She then straightened to prop him up and began dragging him through the dark ship bowels as if he were weightless. "But so am I."

He opened his mouth to retort, but could already feel himself nodding off. It had been an exhausting trip, and so, for this one time, he would begrudgingly accept her shoulder as one to lean on.

❧

ON THE THIRD deck of the great, black vessel, Sampson hobbled his way up to the Dark Wizard. The large, hooded man sat on a throne that was flanked by two tall candlesticks, both with flames that glowed unnaturally green. The lining of his robe adorned many symbols with dark connotations that Angus couldn't help but wonder about. It was as if some dark, all-powerful God had created the garments himself. Hector stood by his side, watchful and quiet as always.

"My Lord," Angus said, stepping aside and gesturing a bear paw-like hand toward the slaver. "I present to you Sampson, our newest partner. He commands the greatest influence in all of Endoshire."

"So I've heard," the Dark Wizard said with great bass, his dark goatee bobbing from the hood smoothly with each syllable formed. "Drake has told me much about you already. He mentioned your high-class hospitality. I must say that so far, you don't disappoint. I appreciate the accommodations of our private dock."

"Yes, well, I reserve only the best fer my top business partners; and

I know a powerful ally when I see one. I felt it with Drake, and I can certainly see it in you. To make such a fiery entrance impressed me," Sampson said.

The Dark Wizard let out a low-pitched chuckle. "I hope you'll excuse the brief mess. That ship was stolen by some rodents who dared attack my territory. Just in case they get the foolish notion that escape will be possible, I wanted to bring their ship down in the most public way possible."

"Oh, believe me, I have no love fer those bastards." Sampson rubbed the wound on his leg and winced.

"Yes… they are a dangerous lot, too. But worry not. We will draw them out, soon enough," the Dark Wizard said as he stood, looming over all in attendance, and motioned with his head to the cabin behind. "For now, come with me. I have something that will heal your injury."

Sampson grinned as he hobbled behind the Dark Lord. He looked about the size of a child next to the likes of Angus and Hector, but even more so when standing near the Dark Wizard. The pair entered the third deck quarters and then closed the door behind them.

Mur'del, who Angus noticed had been perched upon one of the crow's nests and listening in, dropped to the third deck, lessening the impact with a powerful flap of her wings that forced Hector to hold his hood upright.

"I wonder if he'll give him the concentrated dark essence, or the basic blend?" she asked aloud.

"A fine question," Angus said while rubbing his eyes. Her landing gust had kicked up a building's-worth of dust. "Both would be beneficial for different reasons. It would be nice to have a man with Sampson's influence under our complete control. On the other hand, it may be wise to give such a valuable partner the ability to protect himself."

"What do you think, oh quiet one?" the enhanced avian asked Hector before chirping. As was expected, the cloaked figure did not respond.

In short order, Sampson emerged from the cabin, walking as normal. His appearance had not changed, and neither had his demeanor. There was an air of awe about the slaver, and Angus could hardly blame him. Today was likely the first time he had experienced magic outside of a street performer's parlor tricks; let alone the formidable force that was *dark magic*.

"I see you are in need of repairs, Angus," the Dark Wizard said, waving him over. "I shall fix you, next."

The giant nodded, then followed him into his quarters. Next to a bed sat two cauldrons with dark essence in them. Both began to bubble as the Dark Wizard approached, reacting to the sheer power of his presence.

"Drake informed me of your success in Thironas. Congratulations. To achieve your goal and survive against the likes of Zamarim and Aldous is no small feat. You will make a fine leader for our team."

"Much of my success was thanks to the careful preparations and planning that you and Drake undertook. I faced both Wizards at their weakest," Angus said.

"That much is true; Aldous will present far more difficulties in the sewers than he did in Zamarim's domain. We'll need to concentrate on keeping him outside, or at least away from the team," the Dark Wizard said as he held a hand out and hummed so deeply that it sounded like buzzing. "Resnu domin altigh… etus perios doam laitem… teig dorchae accadh tu… etus imverte isteam doam nearem."

As he spoke in his twisted tongue, some dark essence emerged from the cauldron on the right. It floated in midair, yet did not make so much as a splash or pulse; as if it were frozen in time.

"Remove your bandages."

Angus obeyed, and then, like an unstoppable magnetic force, the dark liquid poured into the wound with great vigor. The giant felt that familiar rush of his body healing and strengthening as his bones cracked with equal excitement.

After taking a few heavy breaths, Angus smirked at the Dark Lord. "I daresay you gave me more, this time."

"Perhaps. It is difficult to pinpoint the correct amount of dark essence that one can take in. The goal is to keep you strong and self-sufficient."

"Does that mean you gave me too little, last time?" he asked, pointing to where the previous wound had been on his neck.

"Not necessarily. Your abilities have limits. You weren't meant to stand up to the stresses of a Wizard King attacking you," the Dark Wizard explained. "Giving you too much is more dangerous. That is how Willoughby became a single-minded beast. Of course, if you wish for such a transformation, it can be arranged…"

A shiver slithered down Angus' spine. "My apologies. I did not mean to seem ungrateful. I'm happy with what you have given me. And thankful."

The robed man let out a deep chuckle that simmered into a grin. "I don't need gratitude. It is *competence* that I seek. If the coming mission fails, the Wizard's Council will likely sweep in with only two seals broken, and our plans will need to be reworked on a large scale. And believe me when I say that the punishment Brice has endured will pale in comparison to what awaits those who fail me this time around."

A bead of sweat rolled down Angus' cheek. The Dark Wizard wasn't *threatening* him; he was simply stating a fact. He decided to change the subject, out of his uncharacteristic nervousness. "So, Brice came along after all? I thought you would have killed him for allowing Bosfueras to burn."

"Since you are a leader of the team, I suppose there is no harm in telling you how this dark magic of mine works. I need *sacrifice* to perform the feats you have seen. Usually, that means some sort of pain or death. Since we departed, Brice has been strung up in the bowels of the ship, being whipped as punishment. His pain fueled your rejuvenation," the Dark Wizard said with a venomous smile. "So, perhaps you should thank him. The scars upon his back have made you powerful. But be careful, for you may find yourself in the same situation someday, for *much* longer. Brice is merely fortunate to have a useful ability."

"I'll be sure to thank him, my Lord," Angus said with uncertainty, then motioned toward the door. "Shall we depart for Drake's quarters? We have captured the Keeper of the Key for this seal, and are working to obtain a precise location of the monolith as we speak."

"Yes… it is time to finalize our plans. Soon, Degenerate will be released from his prison," the Dark Wizard said with a cackle that struck Angus like a bolt of lightning.

CHAPTER 12
POWER STRUGGLE

Drake sipped some wine at his dining table as the Dark Wizard entered his quarters. Angus, Mur'del, Hector, and Sampson followed close behind.

"Good evening," Drake said with a sly smile. "I trust that you had a safe trip?"

"Uneventful," said the Lord of Darkness.

"'Uneventful'? You burned down a ship like it was nothin'!" Sampson said with an obnoxious laugh.

Drake's cheery eyes wandered over to the slaver. "I see that your leg is feeling better."

"This fella can work some real miracles!" Sampson said while bending his legs vigorously.

"You've only gotten a small taste of what he can do, my friend," Drake said. He then looked to all the others in the room. "Would you excuse us for a moment? You'll find there are accommodations for you on the lower floors. Perhaps you could discuss strategies for our upcoming infiltration of the sewers, Angus?"

"Yes, sir," he replied before motioning all others in the room to leave.

Most of the upper floor emptied, save Hector and Ned, who stayed behind to guard their master, Rose remained quiet in the bedroom.

After everyone left, Drake's relaxed expression became sharper than a knife. "That Mercer boy and his friends have already proven to be a thorn in my side. You should have killed him when you had the chance."

"So quick to lay blame when a difficult situation arises… I thought, given your history, that you would welcome the challenge," the Dark Wizard said.

"There is rising to the challenge, and then there is *creating* that challenge to sabotage yourself."

The robed man snarled before sitting across the table from him. "What nonsense. We are closer than ever to the goal. Another seal will soon be broken, and the black gold should be taking its effect in our testing grounds."

"Yes, about that…" Drake trailed off, swishing his wine around in the glass. "Early results have shown that there are still some who can resist."

"That happened in Bosfueras, too," the Dark Wizard said, clenching a fist. "The only answer is to curb the population who disobey."

"Why bother with the black gold if we are going to rule by fear? The goal is for them to *obey us willingly.*"

"Because it makes seizing control easier. Eventually, only those who obey will be left."

"I feel that there is a better solution," Drake said.

The Dark Wizard tilted his head. "*You*, who sit in your tower as a mere spectator, know better than *me*, the creator of the black gold we are using?"

"Calm yourself," Drake said as he poured a glass of wine and handed it to him. "It is my observation that these people are resisting because the demands are too harsh."

"How so?"

"Men are individual by nature; they like to *own things*, however useless those things might be. You are demanding that the unwashed masses change themselves in a way that their weak minds cannot handle. What if we lessen that burden?" the Village Elder asked.

"What do you propose?"

"Allow their ownership of property and worthless knick-knacks to continue; just for now. Everything else can remain the same," Drake said.

"Unacceptable!" he shot back, slamming a fist onto the table. For a brief moment, Drake let slip a face expressing worry, but he quickly recovered and returned to his cool demeanor. "Ownership creates conflict. They will not remain subservient or productive if they have conflict."

"Hear me out," Drake said, holding a hand up. "Early testing shows that the most common resistance to the black gold has to do with simpler things: Property and hobbies. But that doesn't mean we can't plant the seeds for a way of life where they hold no value in such things."

"A slow-burn approach?"

"Hardly. It is only that one thing that causes them to resist. Petty squabbles over property have ignited an untold number of wars, my friend. That instinct cannot be undone so easily."

The Dark Wizard hissed. "You presume to know much about a material that you have not handled yourself. My black gold can suppress feelings of love, guilt, sadness... it should be able to curb their selfish desires, too."

"I'm afraid we disagree about its effects," Drake said with a shrug. "It amplifies a sense of togetherness, more than anything; unites people under one common cause. Give it some time, and eventually, they will shed their desire for material things and care only about the cause."

"I will consider it," the Dark Wizard said between sips of wine. "But for now, we stay the course."

"You'll come to see things my way, soon enough," he replied with a smirk.

"Such arrogance. Remember that this is a partnership, and we each have our roles to play. You'd do well to remember that I don't *need* you, Drake. I have other reserves on hand. You are simply my first choice. A venomous aura irradiated from the Lord of Darkness, so vile that it made Drake want to wretch.

He knew that the Dark Wizard could easily kill him, so lately, he'd been challenging him to see what his breaking point was. So far, he hadn't reached it, and he knew for a fact that the aforementioned 'reserves' were infinitely less appealing options than him.

"I meant no offense, of course." The Village Elder gave a dismissive wave to dispel their petty argument. "Did Angus inform you that we have captured the Keeper of the Key?"

"He did. That was an important first step. We need to obtain a map of the sewers to find the Degenerate seal. I would guess that the Key Keeper, Wizard Scout, and Wizard King all have their own copies. I don't suppose you have obtained the map, have you?" the Dark Wizard asked.

"No luck so far," Drake replied, shaking his head. "The luxian's name is Amis. He insists that there *is* no map, but did offer to show us the monolith's location himself."

The Dark Wizard snickered. "An obvious trap. He'd lead us to the King Wizard or the Guardian Beast."

"I figured as much."

"Did you at least obtain his key?"

"He didn't have it on his person and has remained tight-lipped on the subject. I'm sure we can pry the information out of him, though," the Village Elder said.

"If your torture methods are insufficient, perhaps *I* can *convince* him," the Dark Wizard said with a low-pitched chuckle. Drake let out an amused breath. "You don't think that I can?"

"Can I make a suggestion?"

"You are pushing your luck today," he replied with a grunt. "Go ahead."

"I am a problem-solver. And the way I see it, we have two major problems: One is that we don't know how to reach the monolith in that maze of a sewer. The other is that meddling old fool Aldous and his band of misfits, who will undoubtedly try to stop us," Drake said as the Dark Wizard drank some wine. "What if I told you that we could solve both of those problems in one fell swoop?"

The robed man leaned in. "Go on…"

With a confident smile, Drake finished his glass of wine, ready to detail a plan that would crush his enemies, and enshrine *him* as the true mastermind of the partnership to break the seals.

DOWNSTAIRS, Angus and Sampson feasted on roasted pork while Mur'del picked at her food like a pigeon would their scraps. Although not as nice as Drake's quarters, the room was still luxurious; teeming with fine paintings, a lovely view of the city, and expensive furniture.

Angus eyed Sampson between chomps. "Will your men worry if you don't return soon?"

"Let 'em worry! This food is great!" he replied with infectious enthusiasm. He had just finished gobbling down another slice of pork.

The giant searched Sampson's eyes for any hint of which type of dark essence he had taken in. He could see that they were a light tint of red, but that meant nothing. Anyone who received the black liquid, concentrated or not, had at least a hint of red in their eyes, depending on their mood. Otherwise, the effects varied by subject. Angus would have to wait and see. If the slaver became sluggish and began desiring black gold, then it meant he had taken in the basic blend. It would be more difficult to tell, however, if he had taken in the concentrated doses. In that case, he would display some sort of unnatural ability related to his human weaknesses. It was also possible that the Dark Wizard had only given him a small dose of the basic blend, making the results unobvious.

"Why're ye lookin' at me like that?" Sampson asked as he gulped down another slice of pork. He was hardly even chewing, now.

"No reason," Angus replied with a shrug.

"The way you humans eat is repugnant," Mur'del said, her deep, dark eyes reflecting scorn and judgment. "Could you chew with some elegance?"

Angus and Sampson looked at each other and then burst out laughing. Food flew from both of their mouths as they did so, and Angus could hear his enhanced avian cohort cawing in disdain beneath the veil of their cackles that echoed around the room.

"Perhaps we should discuss the plan moving forward," the giant said, his laughs finally tapering off.

Mur'del tweeted at him mockingly. "Why bother? The fact that they are upstairs and we are down here should tell us who the *true* planners are."

"You think so?" Sampson asked, cleaning off the slop on his cheeks with a handkerchief. "I admit to not having played a big role in Drake's plans, thus far… hell, I don' even know the full extent of his plans. All I know is that he's seekin' a map to some treasure hidden in the sewers, and I want in. Especially if we're workin' with that Wizard fella."

The avian let a chirp slip, and Angus shot her a glare. Sampson obviously didn't know what he was getting himself into, but it was not their place to tell him. That would be up to either Drake or the Dark Lord.

"Please excuse Mur'del. She has a habit of being overly negative," Angus said with crossed arms. "We still have important roles to play, even if we are not the masterminds."

"Whatever you say," she replied with a scoff. "What did you have in mind for a plan, then?"

"Well, I-"

Angus was drowned out by the door barging open. Through the entryway appeared Brice, carried over the shoulder of a young, dark-haired woman in a bloodstained dress. Though the big-nosed man was small-statured, it was still surprising to see how weightless he appeared to her. She was dragging him around like a fancy article of clothing. Such strength meant she had almost certainly taken in a concentrated dose of dark essence, Angus thought.

More surprising still was who entered the room after them. Angus had been informed of Barret's transformation, but he was still not quite prepared to see what a monstrosity he had become. He now took the form of a giant, humanoid fly. Aside from the fact that he stood upright and wore ill-fitting clothes, there was no sign left of his humanity. His wings flickered and he let out a buzz as the trio walked in. His giant, fly-head looked greasy, hairy, and disgusting. Suddenly, the giant had lost his appetite. Even Sampson's ravenous chewing had ceased.

"So, what'd I miss?" Brice asked, letting out a weak mixture of coughing and chuckles as the woman placed him on a chair across the table.

"Are you awright, fella? It looks like a bear mauled you!" Sampson said, the food leaking out of his mouth between words. Angus detected some sort of amusement in his tone, and it was contagious, considering whose expense it was at.

"The Dark Wizard will not tolerate failure," Angus said, a smile cracking on his stone face. "Brice here endured a week of whipping for his inability to stop the enemy."

Brice scoffed and then grinned at him. "Ye oughta know what that's like! After all, ye used ta be Wolfgang's whippin' boy!"

"Unlike that *deranged man,* I will lead us to victory," Angus said. "Perhaps I can teach you a thing or two about leading a team. Your gang of hooligans appears to be depleted."

"Shut yer damn mouth, Angus!" Brice roared back, nearly falling forward in his chair. The woman at his side caught him, but he pushed her away while sitting back upright. "Ye have no right to order me around!"

"That is where you are mistaken," Mur'del interjected. Brice darted his eyes at her, as if he hadn't even noticed her presence until now. "Drake has named Angus as leader of our group."

"*What?*"

"That's right. *We* succeeded in Thironas, while *you* failed in Bosfueras. I'm sure it was an easy decision after that," the enhanced avian said.

Brice sighed and seemed to lose all of his fiery energy. "I was hopin' to get back in their good graces before they chose a leader…"

"What's done is done," Angus said as he held a hand out to shake. "Will you work under me to finish our mission?"

The big-nosed man grasped the giant's hand, and as they shook, he said, "I'll work *with* ye to finish the mission. But remember this: *I'll* be the true leader of this team, soon enough."

Mur'del let out an amused tweet. "Bold words coming from a broken man."

Angus held a hand up and said, "Let's move on to the plan, shall we?"

"I'm all for discussin' a plan…" Sampson trailed off before pointing at Brice's two cohorts. "But who's the lady? And that… big fly monster? What the hell am I lookin' at?"

"This here is Barret," Brice said, pointing to the humanoid fly. Mur'del let out a confused caw and cocked her head. "He was bitten by a fly before takin' in the dark essence. I suppose that's why he looks this way, now."

"Whoa, whoa. I took in that dark substance, too! I don' wanna become a fly!" Sampson said with panic written all over his fat face. Barret let out a series of buzzes, his fly mouth squirming.

"Relax," Angus said with a cool smile. "I don't think you were given a concentrated dose, as he was. And besides, sometimes you get desirable results. For instance, I had a broken arm at my time of receiving dark essence…"

With a flex of his massive arm, a bone blade protruded from out of his skin, sharp as any knife, and several times as hard. He swung it around in a beautiful, white blur that fluttered the blond hair on his shoulders. Sampson's eyes became wide with wonder, and it was clear that his nervousness had faded.

"Mur'del must have been too slow when she was but a *mere avian*, so the dark essence made her 'as fast as a dragon'," he continued with barbs of sarcasm.

"Well, it's *true*," she replied, putting wings to hips.

"And as for Brice…" Angus' cold, blue eyes fell on him. His breaths were long and heavy; as if he were sick. "I was led to believe that you had many abilities, including faster regeneration than the rest of us. But that doesn't look to be the case."

"The Dark Lord laid a beating into me so badly that I haven't been able to regenerate, of late…" he replied. "These wounds on my back may never heal."

"I'm sure he'll give you some more dark essence for the coming battle," Angus said, then looked to the young woman. Now that he was really looking at her, the sloppy stitches on her neck became apparent, and so did her bronzed skin. Almost certainly a Gentish woman who'd been cut open, and then restored by the dark essence, he thought. "And that leaves this young lady, here. Who might you be?"

"My name is Catalina. It is a pleasure to meet you all," she said with a bow.

"It is interesting that the Dark Wizard chose to empower more people. Is it to replace the fallen hooligans?" Mur'del asked.

"I don't think so," Brice said, smiling at the Gentish woman. "She was a 'rebirth' at one of his ceremonies. I think he wanted to see if she could take in the enhanced dark essence after the basic blend."

"Yes, I recall the Dark Wizard experimenting on others with that idea. The results that I bore witness to were quite gruesome," Angus said as he cracked a smile at Catalina. "But luck smiled upon you, m'lady. You appear to have been one of the earliest successes in receiving both kinds of dark essence."

"In other words, she's a rat that got experimented on. What good is she, anyway?" Mur'del replied with a series of tweets.

"And *yer* just an oversized pigeon. What of it?" Brice shot back. Catalina smiled at him as the enhanced avian turned up her beak-like nose at them. "She is a part of this team, now. Deal with it."

"That is not your decision to make," Angus butted in. Brice snarled and slammed his fists into the table, but stood down when the giant held up a finger. "But given that the Lord of Darkness has seen fit she become enhanced, I suppose the decision has already been made."

Upon that confirmation, Brice let out a huff and leaned back in his seat. Catalina and Barret pulled chairs up next to him and sat. Angus folded his hands and placed his chin on them.

"Now, then… about our plan moving forward…"

~

"I MUST SAY that sometimes I wish to choke the life out of you... but you have your moments," the Dark Wizard said, raising his glass of newly filled wine.

Drake raised his glass in kind and they clanked them off of each other. "I accept the compliment. But there is one other matter I'd like to discuss."

"What is it?"

"I mentioned to you before that I had found a woman to be my queen of the new world. She is to bear an heir for me, as well."

"Yes, I recall. What of her?" the Dark Wizard asked.

"You see... we've been trying to bear a child, but the poor thing appears to be infertile..." Drake trailed off with uncharacteristic hesitance. "Do you think that the dark essence could help her?"

The robed man cocked his head. "Are you certain that *she* is to blame?"

"Yes," the Village Elder replied, his tongue drenched in contempt.

With a smirk, the Dark Wizard said, "I may be able to help her. Are you willing to subject your future queen to one of my ceremonies?"

"Of course. I don't want you giving her the concentrated dark essence, though. She is only to receive a small amount of the basic blend, and remain under my command," Drake said.

"That can easily be arranged. I only bring up the ceremony because what I have in mind will be painful to the highest possible degree. To alter her fertility, I will need to slice open the midsection and then forcefully guide the dark essence through her womb. Be certain that this is what you want for your future bride. After I start, there is no turning back."

Drake hesitated for a moment. "I've made up my mind. It must be done. I will have my heir."

"And so you will," the Dark Wizard said as he nudged his head toward the bedroom.

Rose was peering out through a crack in the door. He fired an intense look her way; scaring the bride-to-be enough that she gasped and then closed the door.

"You may have to do some convincing." The Dark Lord chuckled.

"She won't have a choice," Drake said with a scowl. "Speaking of ceremonies, which dark essence did you supply Sampson with?"

"Just a bit of the basic blend," he replied with a sip of wine. "I can always give him more if we wish to fully control him."

"Good thinking. We may need to keep him in check," Drake said, now standing. "Well then, why don't we join the others to see what they've come up with? Then, we can unveil *our plans* to them."

"Very well."

As the Lord of Darkness made lengthy strides for the exit, he caught Rose peering through a crack in the doorway once more. He smiled at her but suspected that his hood hid it well, for she did not react. There would be much pain in her future, he thought; but it would be worth the misery, in the end.

CHAPTER 13
TRAINING DAY

Dalton gasped as some clothing and boots dropped onto his stomach, awakening him from a peaceful slumber. The groggy warrior looked up with squinted eyes to find Kabel standing over him, grinning. He held a wooden baton in hand.

"Training day?" he asked, his spirits higher than the heavens.

"I was havin' a good dream, y'know…" Dalton muttered before turning over in a vain attempt to go back to sleep.

Kabel shoved his friend and said, "Having more dreams about that wench you got settled up with last night? Hilda, wasn't it?"

"Somethin' like that."

"If only she could see you now! She might mistake you for an old-timer, getting hit this hard by one night of drinking!"

"That was *two nights in a row.* Come back when it's not the arse crack of dawn," Dalton said, shooing him away and then burying his face in a pillow.

Kabel giggled like a mischievous child as he wound up with the baton. With careful aim and enough force to bring down a bear, he struck Dalton in the buttocks. A great slap reverberated about the room, and it turned his giggle into uncontrollable laughter.

"Gah!" Dalton cried as he flailed in his bed like a fish out of water.

"Come out and take your revenge!" he called while dashing out of the room.

Sun poked its way through the legions of branches, striking Kabel in the face as he burst out the door of his tree-built home. Awaiting him were Joel, Rolf, Lucia, Conrad, Alistair, Triston, Giles, Franco, and Ebbie. They had all gathered in a circle, and the stocky man came to its center to address them all.

"The reason I woke y'all up so early is because, the way I see it, we need to learn how to work as a team. I'm willing to bet that the dark forces fixin' to break the Degenerate seal will function as one unit. We must also be mindful of the degenerates if we take to the streets at night," he said, crossing his arms. "To start, I figure we can see who our best fighters are."

"Shouldn't we come up with a plan, first?" Conrad asked.

"He's more of a 'strike first, ask questions later' kinda guy," Dalton called out from the back. Kabel stood on tiptoes to see him stumbling out of the house with little in the way of grace and eyes half-open.

"We can come up with a plan later! I wanna get some fightin' in!" Ebbie cried with enthusiasm.

"YEAH!" Alistair shouted, raising his baton in triumph. His eyes then widened, and he looked to the first mate. "By tha way, where is Cap'n Auber? He promised ta show me a few moves."

"Oh, erm… he was feeling a might bit under the weather this morning," Franco said.

Ebbie shrugged. "I dunno what moves *he* could show ye, anyway…"

The big redhead raised an eyebrow, then smiled. "Ohhh, I get it. Ya don' think I'm at a high enough level ta learn from 'im? I'll show ya what I'm made of, then!"

"That's tha spirit!" Triston said as he gave his little brother a hard slap on the back, then pointed to Lucia with his baton. "I'll challenge *you*, then!"

She smiled and twirled her wooden sword while nodding in reply.

With those two matchups set in stone, Kabel cleared his throat and said, "The rest of you, pair up! Body shots are worth three points, and limbs are worth one. No headshots allowed, or you lose! The first to ten points wins!"

As the stocky man finished speaking, Dalton jumped in with a vertical thrust downward. Kabel hopped back to avoid the hit, then adjusted his guard to a staggered, upright position.

"A bit jumpy, are we?"

"I woke up on the wrong side of the bed," he replied while swinging vertically, one-handed, and upward. Kabel redirected the attempt further up, then swiftly tagged his friend with a stab where the chest and shoulder met.

"That's three for me," Kabel said. Dalton groaned. "Are you getting slow in your old age?"

~

FURTHER INTO THE thick of the woods, Conrad watched as Giles went on the offensive against Joel. The strategist was taken aback at how much the pair were alike. Both were somewhat small and boyish in appearance, and with similarly meek mannerisms, too. Conrad had found himself the odd man out of the pairings, and so he decided to face the winner of the duel playing out before him.

Each attack by Giles was flawlessly thwarted with well-placed blocks by the mute, though Conrad noticed that he was putting less pressure on one leg than the other. An injury, perhaps? Or just another artifact of his hesitation to fight back? As the frustration grew in Giles' strikes, the strategist felt a similar frustration building in his chest.

"That is far too soft, Joel! Drake's team will take advantage of your intentionally weak attacks!" Conrad called out with crossed arms. "And Giles will be unprepared for our ruthless enemies if you continue to go easy on him!"

The mute glanced at his friend with curious brown eyes, and at that moment, Giles took the opportunity to attempt a decisive downward strike. He gasped, however, when Joel blocked him without even looking.

Giles took a step back and then lowered his baton. "Are my moves truly so obvious?"

"While your inexperience is apparent, you shouldn't feel too bad," Conrad said, cracking a smirk. "I think that we might find Joel to be the greatest swordsman among us if only he'd stop holding back."

Joel shook his head and made hand signals.

"This is only practice. No one is in danger, here," Conrad said with an affirming nod. "Why not show Giles that same acrobatic style of swordplay that you used against Greed, back at Mt. Couture? Perhaps we could learn something from you."

The mute lowered his baton and Conrad groaned. If only he could make him understand the folly of his merciful ways against their ruthless opponents, he thought.

"How about the two of you face each other, then?" Giles asked with a shrug. "It's obvious that I cannot win, so I surrender."

Conrad drew his baton and smiled. "Alright, Joel. Let's see if I can draw out some of your skill..."

~

AT THE BACKSIDE of the house, Lucia and Triston engaged in an intense struggle. Lucia had first thought that the elder MacRae would lack skill, as Alistair did, but that assumption was shot down when he landed two body blows early on for a six-to-zero advantage. However, after that initial flurry, she'd made the adjustments to properly defend herself and was in the process of a comeback. After tagging Triston on the shin, she had gotten her score up to eight while only allowing one additional body blow to her torso, giving Triston nine.

"Bah!" he cried out while jumping back, huffing and puffing. "Not bad!"

Lucia stretched her arms as far as they could go and staggered her stance, with the back leg also outstretched to complete the long guard.

"You've put up a decent fight... but I'll complete the comeback here," she said while inching closer, her baton at the ready.

Triston staggered his stance, much like Lucia's, but instead of holding the sword up and outward, he pointed it down. It didn't matter, she thought. The reach advantage belonged to her, and if she was careful, it would win her the duel.

Lucia lunged forward, hoping to tag the big man's wrist, but Triston brought his sword up to knock hers further upward. He followed up with a downward and diagonal slash at her front ankle. She met his baton with her own just in time to avoid impact, and with great urgency, pushed him back.

Triston, however, was not finished with his attack. He returned to his lowered sword position before leaping forward and raising his baton. Lucia's heart skipped a beat as she realized what he was trying to do: he was aiming for her chest. With lightning-like speed, she swung her sword at full force to the right and directed his baton just past her shoulder. Once again, she pushed him away, and the pair remained still for a brief moment.

"That guard of yers... is a real pain in tha arse!" Triston complained between breaths.

Lucia snickered. If this were a true battle, she might have just lost in that previous exchange. The flex of a true sword would have gone around her parry and struck her in the chest, as he'd intended.

Not wanting to give him precious recovery time, she dashed forward with the wooden sword outreached, and Triston did the same. They clashed once more, and the sound of hollow wood smashing together echoed off the trees.

～

Aldous and Dhogron exited the small horse stable across the front yard of Kabel's home and sat in a couple of wooden chairs to watch the ongoing duels. They had been performing maintenance on the carriage and tending to the horses, respectively.

"Should we be insulted that they didn't invite us to play?" Dhogron asked with a smirk.

"I daresay they were wise not to," Aldous replied with a chuckle.

"I'm glad to be allied with such a lively bunch. It gives me hope that we can rescue Amis," the trickster Wizard said, his smile falling along with his eyes.

Aldous placed a hand on his shoulder and said, "You mustn't blame yourself for his disappearance. If you had also been taken, then all hope would be lost."

"Still, to find out that two seals had already been broken, and the Council hasn't said a word to us… I can't help but feel that all hope *is* lost."

"True enough. Black, stormy clouds await us on the horizon. But as long as we can fight, we must, even if it is not the fashionable thing to do," Aldous said.

"Even if we succeed, what is the end game?" Dhogron asked, rubbing the jewel centering his turban with a finger. "Degenerate's influence is spreading as we speak, and from what you told me, that was also the case for Greed and Famine. We cannot go on like this."

"I've been thinkin' about that," he replied, tapping his walking stick on the ground. "What if we moved the monolith to a location where it cannot harm anyone?"

"That sounds nigh impossible, or at least improbable," the trickster Wizard said. "Olius is violently protective of the seal and the Council would have our heads before we ever had the chance to move such a massive slab of stone."

"I'm sure you are correct about both of those things, but still… if we can stop the dark forces this time, it is worth considering. I have some ideas for how we could pull off such a feat," Aldous said.

~

IN FRONT OF THE HOUSE, Kabel nailed Dalton in the knee with a baton strike, and the two backed off from one another with swords at their sides.

"I can't tell if I got better, or you got worse! That's eight for me and zero for you!" Kabel said with a smug smile.

"Indeed… you have made a fool of me… thus far…" the warrior said between labored breaths. "Perhaps I should start trying."

There was a tense silence about the air as Dalton suddenly ceased his heavy breathing and smiled.

"You smug little-"

"Victory is so much sweeter against the prideful," he said while adjusting his stance to a stagger, and then brought his baton down and back at his right side. "I have seen through your strategy. You rely too much on thrusts. I'll recommend that you don't do so again."

"Your mind games won't work on me," Kabel said with a chuckle. He too staggered his stance but held his sword upright and angled toward him.

"Very well!" Dalton called out as Kabel charged in.

The stocky man brought his baton forward, as had been the case in their previous exchanges. His strategy had indeed focused on thrusting, but most deceptive of all was that the thrust was performed after a clash of the weapons, which had worked to bypass the warrior's defenses.

This time, however, Dalton brought his sword up from an arced motion and knocked Kabel's baton back, breaking his stance. From there, he easily tagged him with a stab to the stomach. The stocky man wheezed from the blow before jumping back, wide-eyed.

"That makes three for me, eight for you," Dalton said, returning to his previous guard.

"Damn…" Kabel muttered through gritting teeth.

~

CLOSER TO THE HOUSE, Alistair finished off Ebbie with a strike to the ankle. The final score was 10-to-two. Ebbie fell to his bottom and let out a defeated laugh between heavy breathing.

"Yer… battle instinct… is keen… ye know that?"

"Thanks, lad… I hope ta someday be a fierce warrior… like my brother or Cap'n Auber…" Alistair said with some deep breaths of his own. Ebbie wiped the profuse sweat from his brow before cocking his head.

Though curious of why Ebbie was such a novice when he was first mate to someone like Auber, the other ongoing battles had him more curious, still. The big redhead turned to see Rolf and Franco continuing their duel. The navigator had been backed into a tree, and Rolf took advantage with downward and diagonal slashes in quick succession.

After many blocks, one of the swings finally tagged Franco on the side of the arm, a loud *slap* ringing out in the woods.

"Dat's… another one fer me… eight-to-dree…" Rolf said, his eyes twitching from a sweat that refused to relent. "You've got good stamina, you know dat?"

"I appreciate the compliment. But still, the outcome is obvious. Why continue?" Franco asked.

Rolf scoffed. "You've got good footwork, a sturdy defense, and a well of energy to tap into, but y'know what yer problem is?"

Franco raised an eyebrow. "What?"

"Effort. You don' seem to wanna try. Our enemy won't let you get away with dat," Rolf said as he lowered his baton. "But for now… I'm tired! I accept yer concession!"

Both men laughed and then sat in the grass to rest as Alistair and Ebbie approached them with big smiles on their faces. Something about the heat of battle had them all in a sporting mood.

IN THE THICK of the woods, Joel fended off several stab attempts from Conrad by deflecting them to different sides of his body. Giles watched on from the sideline, surprised to see that Conrad was using the wooden sword more like a rapier than the long sword it was meant to mimic.

As the battle continued, his eyes fell to the mute's footwork. Every once in a while, Conrad made stab attempts at his shin or ankle. Giles didn't feel it was sporting of the strategist to attack a friend's weak point, but there was something about the exchange that bothered him far more.

"Hold up!" he called out. Both lowered their weapons and looked at him. "I've been watchin' closely. Joel, yer injury is healed, isn't it?"

The mute's eyes widened for a moment before he let out an inaudible sigh and nodded. As Giles had suspected, Joel's hesitations in battle appeared to be the result of something mental, not physical.

Conrad narrowed his eyes. "Alright, Joel, I didn't want this to be anything more than a friendly bout, but it is clear to me that your urgency is in a deep sleep. Time to awaken!"

He rushed in on Joel, who was now on his heels and scrambling to get into position. This time, Conrad led off with a vertical slash downward; a radical change in strategy from his stab-only offense of earlier. Joel managed a block, but in that time, Conrad allowed the baton to bounce off, turning the momentum into a downward and diagonal swing toward the legs.

Once again, Joel managed a block, but even more narrowly than the time before. Conrad followed up with a roundabout swing at the head. Joel's eyes widened, and but a moment later he brought his sword up to deflect the swing. After the batons met, Conrad closed in, ripped the sword from his hands, and laid a shoulder into the mute that sent him tumbling to the ground.

Joel fell into a coughing fit before looking up to see Conrad's sword pointed at his face. Giles approached the pair before shoving Conrad, who backpedaled away. "Maybe Joel ain't puttin' his heart into it, but you *cheated*. No headshots allowed, remember?"

"The point wasn't to win the game," Conrad said with a glint of red in his eyes. "You cannot continue on like this. We are soon to face opponents who wish to do us *real harm*. If you can't even put effort into a practice match, you'll be putting yourself, and others, at great risk when we confront Drake's team."

"He managed to save *me* back in Thironas," Giles argued, placing hands to hips. "Yer bein' too harsh."

Conrad sighed. "I wasn't there, so of course I don't know what exactly happened. But our current enemies cannot be reasoned with. They cannot be talked to. They don't care if you are peaceful or violent. They have already justified harming you, in their minds. There is only one way to deal with them."

Joel stood and made hand signals, frowning as he did. Giles, of course, had no idea what he was saying, and especially now, it was frustrating.

"Did you, though?" Conrad asked, to which the mute cocked his head. "How many more miners would be alive today if you had acted sooner, back then? You waited until our last moments on that cursed mountain to reveal your sword and truly fight."

Joel huffed and then signed some more at a furious pace. Then, his posture relaxed a bit, and the signs slowed down.

"So, Aldous told you?" Conrad asked with a marked coldness in his tone. "You are both mistaken. The essence hasn't changed me. It actually saved me from death. Try being mobbed by dozens of violent people who can't be reasoned with. Or better yet, try rotting in a cell with festering wounds for 'doing the right thing'. It tends to change your mind on some matters."

"You have that dark essence within you? The very same substance that made Angus so powerful?" Giles asked, flashing back to the giant's bone-based abilities.

"It's not the same. I'm fine." Conrad waved him off.

Joel signed some more, and Giles' mind began to wander. He found himself torn on the matter. There was no denying that Joel was hesitating; and it wasn't only in friendly practice duels, but against their enemies, too. He felt the remnants of a bruise on his ribs; a reminder of the beating he'd taken from the degenerates after Joel had hesitated in finishing one of them off.

Yet, Giles could also not deny that he'd been useless in that battle. What position was he in to tell Joel to carry his weight, when he hadn't managed to protect anyone, let alone himself? That familiar feeling of helplessness crept into his chest, and then up to his throat in the form of a lump. The harrowing screams of his family as he lay in bed, trembling, echoed through his mind and saw him grinding his teeth.

"Let me ask you something," Conrad said, snapping Giles out of his depressing stupor. Both participants in the argument were looking at him, now. "If you had the opportunity to kill the man who was causing all of this trouble, would you?"

"Yeh, I would. The famine is what ruined Thironas, and it was responsible fer my family's death. I got no love fer anyone tryin' to exploit it."

"And what about you?" Conrad asked, turning to Joel.

The mute froze and became pale. His mouth opened, but Giles was certain that even if he could speak, he'd be stuttering, not giving a sure answer.

"I suggest finding your answer before we confront Drake's team," Conrad said, turning to leave the confines of the woods. "Think about it."

Joel looked down with sheepish eyes as the strategist strode away from view. More out of pity than anything, Giles approached and put a hand on his shoulder.

"We both have improvements to make," he said with a sure nod. "At least in your case, the wall is mental. Speed, skill, strength... you've got 'em. But me? I'm no good like this. There is much work to be done if I do not wish to drag the team down."

"Alistair," Joel mouthed, flashing him a weak smile and nudging his head back toward Kabel's house.

"Ah, you think I should watch his duels?"

The mute held up a finger before flexing his arm and clapping a hand onto it. His way of miming strength, perhaps?

Giles smiled, half-heartedly. "Right. He has talked a great deal about taking me under his wing, lately. You think I should take him up on the offer?"

With an emphatic nod, Joel mouthed, "Fighting spirit."

That much was true, Giles thought, rubbing his chin. While he may not have possessed the skill of some of the others, he arguably had the spirit of five battle-hungry men, and more importantly, the strength of an ox.

"Shall we head back to the house, then? I wonder how the other duels have progressed..."

While venturing toward the duel between Lucia and Triston, Conrad looked over his shoulder to see both Joel and Giles exiting the woods. They branched off in the yard, where Joel walked toward Dhogron and Aldous; and Giles approached Alistair and Ebbie. The strategist frowned. He'd hoped Joel would take his words to heart, but something told him that he would need more convincing. Giles, on the other hand, needed far more practice if he was to stand even a small chance of surviving their coming opponents.

Hollow *thunks* of wood echoed in quick succession, bringing

Conrad's attention back to the grueling battle between Lucia and Triston.

The elder MacRae, panting and sweating up a storm, lunged out for a careless one-handed stab. As Lucia sidestepped, excitement built in Conrad's chest; certain that she would land a body blow. However, instead of attacking, Lucia brought her baton to the left, knocking Triston's sword further along, and in one swift motion, swung her sword horizontally, to the right.

In a last-ditch effort, Triston twirled to avoid, dropping his baton in the process and falling to the ground. He then looked up to see Lucia's sword pointed at him.

The big man scowled, but quickly changed his expression to a smile. "Good work, lass. Now, finish tha job!"

Lucia wound up, as if ready to chop down a tree, but slowed her swing so it only tapped him in the chest.

"That's 11-to-nine," she said, reaching out her hand. Triston took it and she helped him up.

"Impressive…" Triston choked out between labored breaths. It wasn't long before those breaths became steady, though. "Ya got some otherworldly endurance, lass! But next time, I'll get ya fer sure!"

"I look forward to the challenge," she said before turning and flashing a brief expression of surprise to find Conrad waiting for her, smiling.

That sequence had demonstrated why he would trust Lucia with his life over Joel. She had finished off her opponent, as she would have in a true fight. Joel, on the other hand, wouldn't have. Before striking the final blow, there was a key detail that Lucia may not have even noticed: As he spoke, Triston had slowly been reaching for his baton. Had she not struck him right away, he may very well have landed a surprise attack and claimed the victory for himself.

"Well done," Conrad said as she approached. He got on his tip-toes and kissed her on the cheek, but groaned internally upon realizing that she *still* had to lean down for him to reach.

"What was that for?" she asked, holding up a hand to that same cheek and smiling. He could see the early remnants of a blush.

"Let's just say that you are far less frustrating to watch in battle than Joel."

Lucia chuckled. "From what I saw of him at Mt. Couture, I'm sure he is difficult to beat."

"Not if you exploit his glaring weakness: He doesn't want to fight,"

Conrad said, crossing his arms. "I just can't help but think, 'What if Joel had acted sooner back at Mt. Couture?' Would Henic still be alive? Or what about Bronrar? Both were killed by a madman, who I think Joel could have soundly defeated if he wished to. Even your burns-"

"*Don't* try to use me in your flawed judgment," Lucia interrupted with an icy glare. "You forget that he and Aldous stuck their necks out for us in the first place. If it hadn't been for their intervention, we'd all be dead; or worse, brainwashed servants of the Dark Savior."

"Maybe I'm out of line..." Conrad trailed off, to which her expression softened. "But let me ask you this: If Drake stood before you, cowering and defenseless, would you kill him?"

"Without question."

"It *is* a question in Joel's mind. Ask him for yourself."

"It won't come to that. You are making up a scenario to rationalize your unjust anger," Lucia said, placing a hand on his shoulder. "How many times must I say this? That dark essence... it is affecting your mind. You *never* would have said these things before."

"Not out loud..." he muttered, trying and failing to suppress his contempt for the topic. "How can you be so convinced that a *mere liquid* has changed me for the worse?"

"This coming from a man who has seen hundreds turn into crazed attack dogs by holding a *mere ore* in their hands?"

"You don't get it. I've been taken by the Gold Fever; both the Dark Savior and the Dark Wizard's brands of black gold have influenced me before. If I was experiencing it, I would know. The truth is, I learned some harsh lessons this past year; and they are lessons that will stick with me forever. That is the only thing different about me today." Conrad brushed her hand from his shoulder and began walking away.

"We still haven't faced each other in combat after all of this time." The implications of Lucia's words stilled him.

He looked over his shoulder. "What of it? I have no desire to fight you. I only wish to fight alongside you."

"The feeling is mutual, actually," she said with a snort.

Conrad turned to see that she had drawn her baton. "Then, why?"

"We need to settle this once and for all. It must get tiresome, listening to me scold you about something I do not entirely know the nature of. Yet, I am certain that it's affecting your mind. If we keep going like this, it will only hurt us both in the long run," Lucia said.

"Alright, so whoever wins gets their way?" Conrad asked as he brought out his wooden sword and whirled it around, the *whooshes* of it gracefully massaging his ears.

"That's right. Aldous told me of an Exorcist that could help you. If I win, you go to see that Exorcist. If you win, I will drop the subject for good. Same rules as earlier."

The strategist held his blade upward, to object. "I have one condition: Hits to the head are allowed."

Lucia's brow twitched, but it was quickly washed over with a well-rehearsed calm. "Fine."

The duo circled one another with batons outreached, ready to strike at the first sign of an opening.

～

DALTON COMPLETED his comeback by striking Kabel in the midsection with his baton. The stocky man fell over, feigning injury, then rolled around as if he were dying.

"Oooo! The pain!" he cried aloud as the others watching laughed. After a few moments, he sat up, smiling at his friend. "That was cruel, what you did. I thought for sure that I had you."

Dalton shrugged. "You shouldn't have woken me up like that. My head feels like a rock got dropped on it last night."

"Nothing some tea won't fix," Kabel replied as he took Dalton's hand and was hoisted up. "Y'know, I think you're an even better swordsman now than you were during the war."

"I've got experience on my side, these days," he said while dropping the baton and rubbing his head. "The tradeoff is that mayhap we can't go out drinking *every night*, anymore."

The stocky man let out a snorting chuckle. "My memory may be hazy, but I'd guess that you could finally give Adrian a good challenge if he were still around."

"I'd give anything to bring him back and find out," Dalton said with a half-hearted smile.

"That reminds me. I keep meaning to tell you when we're out for drinks, but-"

Kabel was interrupted by the sound of wood smacking off of human flesh. It echoed throughout the woods and caused many nearby heads to turn. Off in the distance, he found the source of the noise; the only battle still going: Conrad vs. Lucia.

The strategist held his baton straight, its tip near Lucia's stomach.

They circled each other, and Conrad kept that same fencing-like form the whole time. It quickly became apparent to Kabel that he was using it as a means to keep her on the defensive and at a distance. After all, she had the reach advantage, and the pressure might keep her from making full use of it.

Next to catch Kabel's eye was blood. It trickled down from a welt on Lucia's leg that stuck out like a sore thumb, even from such a distance.

Lucia swatted at the baton with her sword, but after it was knocked away, Conrad replied by swinging for her head. She managed to duck the vicious slash and responded with a leftward horizontal swing at his ribs, to which Conrad hopped away, just barely avoiding the blow. Though the attack had finally seen him relenting on his pressure, it was only a short reprieve. True to his aggressive strategy, Conrad jumped right back in with another swing aimed at her head while she was adjusting her long guard.

As a snappy, crisp, *thunk* echoed from their clashing batons, Kabel looked at his friend with concern in his normally calm eyes. "He is breaking the rules by aiming for her head like that. Ain't you gonna say anything to him? He's endangering *your student*, after all."

"I'm sure it's a rule that they agreed to ignore, knowing those two. Besides, Lucia can handle herself just fine. There's nothin' to worry about," Dalton said with a shrug as he walked toward the house. "Now, let's get some tea. I need somethin' for my head…"

Kabel's worried gaze wandered over to the duel one more time before shrugging and following his friend to the house. He didn't understand why Dalton was so lax on the matter, especially since Lucia was his fallen mentor's daughter.

～

Conrad continued his furious onslaught with a series of stab attempts, straining Lucia's eyes, which she dared not blink. Her arms, too, were tiring; they had taken over on reflex alone. She panted harder with each dodge or parry, but the burning in her throat and the mere welt on her leg were nothing; more than worth it if she could manage a win. The filth within Conrad needed to be exorcised.

An exhausted Lucia pushed his baton upward and to the right, then brought her sword down for a thrust. Conrad had no choice but to sidestep instead of parry, due to the short range of motion required for her attack. With that sidestep, however, came a new opening: Lucia turned the stab into a leftward swing that tagged him in the ribs.

That made the score six-to-three, she thought with a heavy breath. Just a couple of more hits, and then-

A raspy gasp escaped her lips as Conrad responded with a vicious one-handed swing, smashing into her right arm. Once again, the crunchy sound of wood cutting into flesh filled the air, and Lucia grimaced as her arm went numb. She took a weak, one-handed swing to push him away, and then hopped back to gain some distance.

Lucia grasped her arm and squeezed to give it some feeling again. She glanced down to see another welt, this one bleeding even worse than the one on her leg. In training battles, it was customary to hit with perhaps half of the usual force. The odd accident was prone to happen, but now she was certain that it wasn't a coincidence: Conrad was going all-out with his swings. Now, she was more certain than ever that the dark essence had changed him. Six-to-four, she thought, filling up with newfound determination.

Just as she was willing herself for another round, however, the strategist held his sword up, and she cocked her head. The baton had a crack in it from having struck her so hard. He dropped it, sadness overcoming his expression.

"I'm sorry... I surrender," he said.

CHAPTER 14
PLAN OF ATTACK

After surrendering, Conrad accompanied Lucia back to the house without saying a word to anyone else, despite their gazes. There was a feeling in the air that a conflict had been settled.

Alistair, Triston, Ebbie, Giles, Rolf, and Franco convened at the side of the house to discuss their battles as they drank fresh water from a well and rested.

"So then, should we have some more matches to see who the best is?" Giles asked.

"There ain't no need!" Triston said with pride on his tongue. "I'll tell ya who tha best fighters are, in order, based on what I've seen: Dalton, Kabel, me'self, and tha lass. With tha four of us fightin', we'll crush the forces o' evil fer sure!"

"Couldn't help but notice you put yourself ahead of Lucia… even though you lost to her," Franco said with a roll of his eyes.

"That's only 'cause I got tired!" Triston growled.

"So then, she has better endurance than you?"

"Yeh, but next time I won't let the fight go on fer so long."

Franco shrugged. "Still sounds like she's better, to me."

Triston pointed his baton at him with fire in his eyes. "Ya wanna test me fer yerself?"

Franco put his hands up in protest as Alistair held his brother back. After calming him down, the big man cleared his throat.

"I think yer forgettin' someone, brother! When it comes to battlin', we gots another top man who'll come through fer us against Drake's team!"

"Oh, yeh? Who?" Triston asked.

Alistair pointed to the house. Giles nodded along. Who would know Joel better than Alistair, after all? He had probably seen his skill up close more than anyone else, save Aldous.

"None other than tha great fairer of tha sea, CAP'N AUBER!"

Franco's cheeks flared out as he covered his mouth. Some chuckles managed to slip through.

"I thought you were gonna say, 'Joel,'" Giles said with a shrug. "I couldn't land a single hit on him. Conrad couldn't either, without cheatin'."

"Well, Joel don't count."

"Why not?"

"'Cause I said so!" Alistair shot back with venom on his tongue. "As my understudy, yer supposed ta listen to me!"

Giles fidgeted his mouth. "I'm willing to follow yer instruction, but… ye haven't *instructed me*, yet."

"Oh…" Alistair rubbed the back of his head and laughed. "A fair point, lad! I was so caught up in all tha goin's on 'round here that I forgot ta teach you! Hm… where ta begin?"

"The wee lad could use some strength trainin' fer sure, Ali." Triston nodded while prodding at one of his arms with an index finger. Giles groaned. "He's got noodles fer arms!"

"Good idea, brother! I suppose ta begin, we can have 'im play *the penalty game*."

"Oooo, that'll whip 'im into shape!"

"Dare I ask what this 'penalty game' is?" Giles asked, his stomach now in knots.

"It's real simple," Alistair said, holding up a finger and smiling. "If ya fail a task set by me, yer teacher, then ya have'ta make up for it by workin' off a penalty. Ya weren't able ta land any hits on Joel, right?"

"Right."

"Since you earned no points outta a possible 10 in yer practice duel, you must *run 10 laps* around tha house ta make up for it!" the big redhead said with a grin as wide as his broad shoulders.

"Oh…" Giles muttered, looking down. "Sh-should I start now?"

"Yer damn right, lad!" Triston said, slapping him so hard off the back that he stumbled forward. "And ya best believe we'll be holdin' ya to it! The penalty game is always in effect: When ya wake up, when ya eat… even when yer sleepin'! It's a time-honored MacRae tradition and not ta be taken lightly!"

With sheepish eyes, Giles looked at Alistair, who nudged his head toward the house. "Go on! Git goin'!"

Giles took a deep breath, put his head down, and began jogging around the house. 10 laps wasn't so bad, he thought with spirits uplifting. If he treated it like a game, maybe he could get results and have fun in the process.

~

"THE LAD'S in fer a helluva time, I'll tell ya that much!" Triston said while slapping his knee and laughing. "Remember when I was in charge of yer penalty game, Ali?"

"Oh, I remember," Alistair replied, eyes narrow. "I nearly reached me breakin' point when ya woke me up in tha middle of the night an' made me lift that big ol' anvil in the barn as many times as ya'd counted me snorin'!"

"Hundreds of times!" Triston's laughs grew louder.

"So, you just make up rules for de penalty as you go along, and yer student has to follow 'em?" Rolf asked.

"That's right," said Alistair.

"Doesn't seem fair to me, but it ain't my problem!" the lanky young man replied with a laugh.

"It'll toughen 'im up, is what it'll do! He'll be stronger than a block o' iron when I'm done with him!" Alistair said with a clenched fist and confident smile to match. "And in tha meantime, I can learn tha finer techniques from an esteemed swordsman, like Cap'n Auber!"

"I dunno why ye keep sayin' things like that," Ebbie said.

"Are ya tryin' ta say that he's *not* one of our fiercest warriors?" Alistair asked while cocking his head.

Ebbie scratched his chubby chin. "Well, I don' think-"

Franco nudged Ebbie and said, "It seems you've forgotten how *fierce* the captain can be. Remember that when he *cowers* or seems *weak*, it's because he is acting to catch enemies off-guard, or he's got 'land sickness'."

"The captain also mentioned cornerin' a man who wielded one of them blue swords!" Giles called out between breaths as he passed by them on his jog.

"Faster! Or I'll add another 10 laps to yer penalty!" Alistair shot back, to which Giles' shoulders shot up. He lengthened his strides while rounding the corner. The big man chuckled through his nose before glancing back at Ebbie. "He's got a good point, though. If Auber truly was able to fight off someone who wielded superior luxmortite as a weapon, then he is a lion of a man!"

Ebbie grimaced. "I can't believe it…"

Franco cast narrow eyes on him. "Now, Ebbie-"

"He had me fooled this whole time!" the first mate said with a laugh. Franco let out an amused breath. "I've gotta ask him to teach me a few moves!"

"Awright, den," Rolf interjected. "From what I saw and what I know, I dink it goes in dis order: Dalton, Joel, Kabel, Lucia, Triston, Conrad, Auber, me, Alistair, Franco, Giles, and Ebbie."

"What? I ain't the weakest!" Ebbie complained.

"An' I think yer underestimatin' the mighty Cap'n Auber! How rude!" Alistair added.

"Like I said before," Triston began with crossed arms. "I can beat the lass. She just has bettah endurance!"

"Endurance is a part of battle, too," Franco said.

"WHAT WAS THAT? I've had about enough of yer wise comments!" the elder MacRae bellowed.

"HOLD IT!" Alistair said, looking at Rolf with fire in his eyes. "Did I hear ya wrong, or did ya put the lass above *me*?"

"Err… yeh?"

"An' now that I think of it, ya put *yerself* ahead of me, too, didn't ya?" he continued while getting up in Rolf's face. "That's it! You an' me! Right now! Let's have a match!"

"Dat's fine with me," he replied with a confident smirk.

AT THE FRONT of the house, Joel, Aldous, and Dhogron observed the beginnings of a practice duel between Alistair and Rolf. Many of the others gathered and encircled the combatants, cheering them on as wood smacking wood filled the crisp air. Giles passed them by for a third time, and Joel smiled at the sight. He figured it had something to do with training under Alistair.

"They're still having matches?" Dhogron asked as he took in a puff of smoke from his pipe. "We should come up with a plan. Every moment we sit back puts Amis and the monolith in further danger."

"True enough," Aldous said, folding his hands. "The issue is that some of our group are known by Sampson, and thus pose a danger if they walk the streets in daylight."

Joel signed to the Wizards. The way he had it figured, Amis was likely being held captive in one of Sampson's buildings.

Aldous nodded along. "Sampson has enough control of this city that he can be discrete in taking prisoners. But I'm sure he owns many properties. Where do we even begin?"

"I may be able to help with that," Dhogron said as he let out some smoke from his mouth. "Well, not *me*, but a contact of mine. She always has inside information on Sampson."

"Oho! That is splendid to hear!" Aldous replied with an excited tap of his walking stick. "It is not safe for you in the city either, though. Some others will have to accompany you. Do you know where to find her?"

"Well, in the afternoon, she is usually performing out in the streets, so that shouldn't be a problem," Dhogron said. Joel and Aldous looked at each other in confusion. "She's what you'd call a 'belly dancer' by trade."

The mute made hand signals to his old friend.

"He wants to-" Aldous cut himself off. "Erm... *we* want to know how a belly dancer obtains such information. Are you certain of her credibility?"

Dhogron laughed. "Oh, I'm certain of that much. She has eyes and ears throughout his entire operation. If the lord of the land wasn't corrupt, then her shipload of evidence would see Sampson hanged publicly for his many wrongdoings!"

"Very well. Our first order of business will be to meet up with this contact, then. I also have an idea for how our compromised teammates can go out in public during the day: I can simply purchase some masky-do's and cloaka-majiggers," Aldous said.

"Alright, then. Shall we depart now?" Dhogron asked.

"First, let us gather everyone and make a plan."

Joel rounded up the group outside, prematurely halting Alistair and Rolf's duel and disappointing the crowd watching. Giles, on the other hand, showed appreciation for the early end to his running laps. Aldous, meanwhile, gathered everyone inside. The group convened in the dining area. Dalton, Kabel, and Mirabel sat at the table, sipping tea as everyone else filled in and sat or stood where they could. Mira waved Lucia over to sit with them, and she took the offer before

Conrad could finish patching up her minor wounds, much to his visible chagrin.

"I presume you have a plan?" Dalton asked as he took a sip of his drink and eyed the old Wizard.

"Time is short. With each passing moment, there is a chance that Drake's team has obtained the map to the monolith. We must rescue the Keeper of the Key within the next few days, I'd imagine," Aldous said.

"Well, ya told us that much already! But where do we begin searchin'?" Alistair asked.

"Our best lead is that Drake is allied with Sampson. I believe that if Amis were being held anywhere, it would be on one of his many properties. That is where our new friend Dhogron comes in," Aldous said, giving his fellow Wizard a confidence-filled nod.

"There is a woman who has eyes and ears within Sampson's operation. Her name is Satara. She operates as a belly dancer in the streets," the trickster Wizard explained.

"And why would a belly dancer know anything about a slaver?" Franco asked.

"Trust me. I know Satara well. Her information is reliable," Dhogron said.

"Methinks our Wizard friend has had a few *intimate dances* performed for him, eh?" Dalton asked, drawing some laughs in the room.

Dhogron darted his eyes away awkwardly before cracking a smirk. "If only…"

"Anyhow!" Aldous interrupted, striking his walking stick to the floor with enthusiasm. "Satara is our best lead at this time. Dhogron will be venturing into the city today, in the hopes of finding her and obtaining some information. With that said, he must be protected at all costs. If he is captured, we'll have no hope of protecting the Degenerate seal ourselves. Could I get some volunteers to accompany him?"

"I'm up ta tha task!" Alistair called out with enthusiasm.

Rolf snickered. "You couldn't even defeat *me*, out dere. We need our most skilled fighters to protect 'im."

"Oooo here we go!" the big man said, throwing his arms up. "You were only winnin' that duel by one point before Joel came in and interrupted! An' I was startin' to get tha upper hand out thar!"

"Is dat what you call it? Cause de enemy won't wait fer you to start improvin' mid-battle if we're attacked," Rolf retorted.

"We'll have'ta finish our battle when we get back! I'll put yer rude arse back in its place, lad!" Alistair said with a proud smile. "Besides, me preferred weapon is an axe! An' I'm sure we can have one of our best battlers come along if I won't be enough. I suggest the great Cap'n Auber! I've been wantin' ta see him in action!"

All in the room turned their attention to the gasping captain, whose eyes were as wide as cut cucumbers. Some, such as Dalton and Lucia, flashed amusement on their faces. While others, such as Alistair, Giles, and Ebbie showed the same enthusiasm that a child might show their hero.

"Erm… well, I-"

"I'm afraid he won't be able to go," Aldous said. Auber let out a nervous chuckle and relieved breath all in one. Joel was once again confused by his behavior. Had he still not gained his land legs? Or was his hesitation to battle similar to his own mental struggles? "We must refrain from drawing eyes to us. Sampson's men will know to look for the Auber pirates, Conrad, Lucia, and Dalton. If possible, we should avoid conflict before attempting to rescue Amis."

"I'll come along, then," Kabel chimed in.

"Count me in. Someone's gotta watch out fer me lil' brother!" Triston said before laughing and clapping a groaning Alistair hard on the shoulder.

"Is there anything that the rest of us can do to help?" Dalton asked.

Mirabel looked at him with a crooked smile. "Chores."

"You couldn't put 'em off forever," Kabel said with a chuckle, then sipped some tea.

"Don't think that *you're* off the hook, either. You've been avoiding any and all work these past few days," Mira added as the stocky man took a bitter gulp of his drink to the tune of chuckles throughout the dining room.

"What about you and Joel?" Lucia asked, nodding at the old Wizard. "The two of you should be more than enough to protect Dhogron. In the meantime, the rest of us could think up a plan of attack for when we figure out where our target is."

"Oho! A fine idea! However, the old boy and I will be headed into the city as well. We need to purchase some cloaka-majiggers and masky-do's so that the rest of you can travel the city by day if need be," Aldous said.

With that, the allies split up. Half of the group prepared for their journey into the city, and the other half got to work on chores. As Joel

rummaged through the horse carriage to tidy up, he came across something glowing beneath a pile of garments, and his eyes were alight. He
peeked back out of the carriage to see Alistair swinging his battle axe
wistfully through the air nearby. Smiling now, Joel retrieved the
glowing object, still wrapped up, and approached the big man.

As if sensing him, Alistair halted his swings and turned to the
mute, looking at his hands. "What's that ya got thar, lad?"

Joel's smile grew ever more as he unwrapped the garments. Alistair
gasped when the white glow bounced off of his brown eyes. In the
mute's grasp was the wind Rune that Zamarim had lent him back in
Thironas.

"That would be a mighty secret weapon, if only I could get it ta
work," Alistair said as his quiet friend handed the Rune to him. Wavy,
white symbols flared up on the flat stone, as if in reaction to his touch.
"I dun' understand… it worked that one time, ta send ol' meat-stain
flyin'! But I tried it a bunch o' times on our trip across tha Sigrian
Channel, an' nothin' happened!"

The mute looked upward in thought. He was far from an expert on
magic, but he had his hunches as to how Runes might work. He signed
his idea to Alistair.

"My feelings? What's that gotta do with it?"

Joel made hand signals, reminding him that he had made the wind
Rune work in a tense situation where all seemed lost. Had it not been
for his quick actions, Angus may have killed Aldous and Zamarim,
back then.

"Ah, I understand… but I don' remember how I felt at that time!"
Alistair replied with a laugh. "It happened in tha heat of tha moment."

A smile of encouragement spread across Joel's face, and he signed
those very feelings to the big redhead.

"Aw, thank ya, lad!" Alistair said, smacking him hard on the back.
"I'll think about it real hard. Maybe me brother will even give me some
respect if I can get this thing workin'!"

As Aldous descended the stairs of Kabel's tree-built home, his eyes
picked up on Conrad and Lucia waiting for him at the bottom.

"Have you come to see me off?" he asked with a knowing smile.

Conrad looked at Lucia, let out a sigh, and then turned back to
Aldous, who was now standing on the bottom step. "I apologize for

my rudeness the other day. You were right to worry about the dark essence. I think that it is building up my aggression."

"I'm glad that you've come to see reason," he replied before eyeing Lucia. She only nodded in return.

"You mentioned an Exorcist, before. Can you take me to see this person?" Conrad asked.

"Of course," Aldous said, placing a sure hand on his shoulder. "But I must ask that you wait a little longer."

"Why?" Lucia asked with a deadly concoction of despair and anger in her voice.

"When I first mentioned the Exorcist, time was on our side," the old Wizard said with a sigh. He relieved Conrad's tense shoulder of his hand. "The process can take up to a day. For reasons that I'm sure are not lost on you two, I cannot afford to be away for that long."

"I see..." Conrad said as he gazed at the floor for a moment, and then, as if catching a second wind, he looked back up with determination in his reddened eyes. "I can hold out until we rescue Amis."

"He needs that essence taken out of him *now*," Lucia interjected with a furrowed brow. "Could you not drop him off with this Exorcist, then come back to us for the day that it will take?"

Aldous shook his head. "They will need me there for the process."

"It's alright, really," Conrad said with an assuring smile in Lucia's direction. "Luckily, I have someone who will be there for me if need be."

The old Wizard flashed a grandfatherly smile and said, "I am happy for you both, as are the rest of us. Worry not, things will get back to normal, soon enough."

"Yeah..." Lucia muttered as Aldous walked past them, a slight pang of guilt striking him.

CHAPTER 15
THE STRANGERS

Dhogron, Alistair, Triston, Kabel, and Rolf separated from Aldous, Joel, and Giles when they arrived in the city center of Endoshire. True to its reputation, the city was packed with folk coming and going, hagglers on the streets, and performers such as Magicians, Gypsies, and snake charmers entertaining large groups.

The trickster Wizard led his protectors north up the main road; one that would take them to the wealthy district. Over time, the peasants, trolls, and centaurs became less abundant, and in their place appeared the rich men and women of the land, parading about with escorts. Knights walked around in half-armor, and prestigious steeds galloped, tugging expensive carriages along that tended to part crowds.

"She must be one hell of a dancer to work these streets. It ain't so easy, gettin' the wealthy to spend their notes and gold," Kabel said.

"I usually see 'em workin' closer to da slums," Rolf added.

"She's well-connected and well-regarded among rich men; especially the knights," Dhogron said with a smile. "Let's just say that she has ruined a few courtships in her day."

"I dun' understand what belly dancin' is. In Ghobmor, we dance with our arms an' legs, like normal folk. How tha hell're ya supposed ta dance with yer belly?" Triston asked, looking at his little brother. "Did ya see anythin' like that in Federland?"

"No, but me understandin' is that all settlements of that country are like their own lil' countries. They gots thar own customs n' such. That's what Joel told me, anyway," Alistair replied.

Kabel, Rolf, and Dhogron laughed in unison.

"What's so funny?" the big man asked with a huff.

"It's funny, seeing how disconnected you two are from the rest of the world," Kabel said with another chuckle.

Triston leaned in with deathly eyes. "Don't be *rude*, now."

The stocky man held a hand up and shook his head. "I don't mean it in that way. I was like you before movin' here. Since Endoshire is the trading hub of the world, a lot of different folk from a lotta different backgrounds tend to roam these streets, and they bring along with 'em many different customs and ideas. Livin' here is almost like gettin' a little piece of every country and what they have to offer."

"Well, ya don' gotta act so superior. It's rude, ya know!" Alistair argued back.

"It ain't *always* superior," Rolf added.

Alistair looked at Triston and shrugged. "I don' know what they're tryin' ta say!"

"It's simple. Endoshire's mixture of different peoples and cultures can be quite good. These streets will expose you to many new ideas, foods, and even forms of entertainment that you never would have known, otherwise. But some bad things come about from this way of living, too. Many of the cultures and ideas tend to clash, and as a result, there is little to unite the people living here," Dhogron explained.

"And that is precisely how someone like Sampson can operate in this city. No one resists, because no one cares." Kabel's normally calm eyes became fiery.

Dhogron smirked and whispered, "Belly dancing comes from my home country, southeast of here, and I think you'll soon find it to be a *good thing*."

After traveling north for some time, the group came upon a crowd that nearly blocked the entire road. In the gathering were many men, either noble or knight, watching and cheering as entrancing, foreign music played toward the center. The group pushed through the crowd as far as they could go, before it became too dense to get past without attacking those in the way. Even still, the taller group members such as Alistair, Triston, and Rolf could see what everyone was gazing upon.

"Is it the belly dancers? I can't see..." Dhogron muttered.

"I dunno..." Alistair said, his voice oddly quiet. He wore a slack-jawed smile, and his eyes were wide with delight. "If this is belly dancin', then I take back all tha bad thoughts I had about it earlier, eh brother?"

The big man nudged his brother, who himself had a dumb, crooked smile on his face.

"Yeh…" Triston replied, with no care or attention. His eyes were fixated on the show.

"Dey're dancin', alright," Rolf confirmed with a smirk. "But how do we know if dis is da right one?"

"We can either wait 'till the end of the show or…" Kabel trailed off, slapping Alistair on the back. "Why don't you put our Wizard friend up on your shoulders, big fella?"

Dhogron chuckled. "I'm sure we can wait until the end-"

"UP YA GO, LAD!" Triston interrupted, grabbing the trickster Wizard from behind, under his armpits, and hoisting him up onto Alistair's shoulders.

"I bet that's tha best view anyone has of these fine lasses!" the big redhead said with an obnoxious laugh.

After balancing himself, Dhogron looked to see five women dancing at the center of the crowd. Just behind them were a couple of seated men, playing a stringed instrument called the oud. It produced a different sound than many outside cultures were used to, and so it tended to draw a crowd in a place like Endoshire. They usually came for the music and stayed for the dancers.

The dancing women each wore a small vest in varying colors, with an exposed stomach and a long skirt at the bottom. Over the vest was a translucent cloth that flowed with their movements like paper dancing in the wind. Finally, all of the dancers wore a small mouth covering. The trickster Wizard knew this to be a tactic of secrecy on Satara's part, but thankfully, he'd seen enough of her performances to pick her out of a crowd.

The woman in the center of the dance, leading the others along, was his contact. She had long, black hair done up in a ponytail and striking brown eyes. A belly button piercing attached to a golden chain hung down past her swaying hips. Her dark olive skin gleamed in the sunlight, signaling to Dhogron that the dance was nearly over. For Satara to have worked up a sweat, she must have been dancing for some time, he thought.

"I think the dance is nearly over," he said. "Let's wait until the crowd dies down."

~

MEANWHILE, within the city center's shopping district, Aldous, Joel, and Giles strolled, looking for a place to buy cloaks or masks. After pushing through many herds of different folk, the group found a store that displayed a variety of masks outside of its doors.

Joel and Giles started for the store entrance, but then the mute caught Aldous retrieving something from a sack that he'd been carrying, and its dark glow caused both his legs and heart to freeze. Upon closer inspection, he was able to breathe a sigh of relief. It was not the black gold, but the summoning Rune that Zamarim had gifted the old Wizard. The swirling design on the smooth surface of stone emitted a dark, yet alluring hue. Joel cocked his head. Was he planning on leaving them?

"I'm sure you two can find some nice masks for our group. I need to pay someone a visit," Aldous said.

The mute signed, asking where he was going.

"To find help, I hope," Aldous replied with a half-hearted smile.

"Will you be away for long? Yer the one with the gold, after all," Giles said.

"Ah, a fine point, m'boy," he replied while reaching into a pocket. He retrieved some gold coins and handed them to Joel. "I shouldn't be long, but just in case, that oughta cover both the masks and the cloaks. I'll be sure to find you, so don't worry about waiting up for me."

The pair waved their Wizard friend goodbye as he exited into an alley with the glowing Rune in his hand. Not a single patron that he'd brushed by paid the magical stone any heed, living up to Endoshire's reputation: No one around these parts cared about goings-on that had nothing to do with them.

With that, the duo looked at each other, shrugged, and then entered the store to start browsing for masks. In such a crowded and tight space, the mute wouldn't be able to mouth any words, and prepared himself for the possibility that he'd have to mime any communication to Giles, should the need arise.

Many of the store's items were considered 'dancing masks' meant for a masquerade, but as Kabel had mentioned before their departure, they more often served as a way to hide one's identity during promiscuous activity. Most masks featured gems, feathers, or unique engravings upon them, while generally only covering from the eyebrows down to the nose. They came in a variety of colors, but the most common were black, white, and gold.

Joel smiled as he lifted a mask with bull horns protruding from the brow.

"For Alistair?" Giles asked with a smirk. The mute nodded. "It suits him well. If we fetch 'im a dashing mask, then mayhap he will take pity and not inflict a harsh penalty game on me, tonight."

Unlikely, Joel thought. Now that Alistair's mind was set on it, he was almost certainly going to carve Giles into a finely-tuned weapon; or powder, depending on how hard he pushed him.

Giles held up another mask that was shaped like a crescent moon. Unlike most of the others, half of it arced down to the chin, leaving the other half of the face exposed, except for a slight engraving around the eye. It was colored in a dark bronze.

"What do you think of this one for Lucia? With that tattoo around her eye, I thought it might be a good fit," he said.

Joel nodded once more, and then the pair went through several masks for each member of their group, until finally having enough for everyone. The mute was happy with their picks; for it felt as if each mask had been personally made for his friends, old and new.

After paying for the masks with Aldous' gold, Joel was surprised to receive Sigrian notes as his change. He flashed Giles a bewildered expression.

"You've never used notes before, eh?" he asked as they squeezed out of the bustling store exit with a sack of masks slung over their respective shoulders. Joel shook his head. "Think of 'em as a replacement for gold n' silver. Mithika once used precious metals fer money, but that was before I was born. These lil' pieces of paper are valuable, too."

The mute looked down at the notes with a raised eyebrow. They seemed like ordinary paper, aside from the crude portraits of Sigrian royalty that had been drawn onto them. As the pair walked the streets in search of a store to purchase cloaks, Aldous appeared out of one of the alleyways and began walking in step with them.

"That was fast," Giles said.

Joel signed to his friend, asking if he had managed to find help.

Aldous sighed. "I'm afraid not."

"Who were you lookin' for?" Giles asked.

"I paid a lil' visit to our friends in Thironas…"

With wide eyes, Joel made hand signals at a frantic pace.

"Yes, yes, I know. I had anticipated Zamarim's containment, given the circumstances. But even Pierce has been taken, it seems," the old Wizard said with despair on his tongue.

"They were imprisoned just for failing? What if it wasn't their fault?"

"It would be a lil' much to say they are 'imprisoned'. I'm sure that their accommodations are fine. But in situations like these, the Council will have many questions. They're likely trying to determine who was at fault for the Famine seal being broken," Aldous said.

A pang of nervousness came to Joel's stomach. If Zamarim had been taken in for questioning, he had to wonder if he'd be able to keep his vow to secrecy. The mute communicated his concerns via sign language to Aldous.

"Indeed, we will soon find out if Zamarim has given us away," the old Wizard said with a huff. "If so, they will come for me; and in that situation, you must continue to protect this seal at any cost."

Joel and Giles nodded at the same time, reflecting a bold, if nervous determination about them.

"And what of Thironas? Have there been any changes? Any improvements?" Giles asked.

"Unfortunately, I found it quite difficult to get around. The presence of the Wizard's Council was strong. We can only hope that means they are taking this attack on the seals seriously… but I wouldn't get my hopes up," Aldous said.

The trio continued along, hanging their heads under the weight upon their shoulders, ever-growing.

~

THE CROWD ROARED IN APPLAUSE, shaking the wealthy district to its core as the dancing show came to a close. Quickly, as if running back to their wives, the swaths of nobles, knights, and merchants began to disperse. Some stayed in an apparent attempt to get a better look at the dancers, but the men who'd been playing the instruments stood guard with hands at the ready to draw upon scimitars that rested at their respective hips. The dancers, meanwhile, convened and chatted while drinking water and eating fruits.

Dhogron and the others approached, but like the others before them, the musicians blocked their way. They wore cloth masks over their noses and mouths, along with white tunics and loose pants.

"The ladies will be taking no questions or requests as of now," one of them said.

"Please," Dhogron said with a smile. "I am a friend of Satara's. I only wish to say hello."

One of the musicians looked over his shoulder at the dancers, then fixed a cold glare back at him. "As he said, there will be no visitation. Come back later."

"OI! QUIT BEIN' RUDE!" Alistair bellowed, holding up a fist and shaking it. "He just wants ta see his friend! What's wrong with that?"

Kabel jabbed at the big man's ribs, to which he flinched. "Don't you have any control over that big mouth of yours? We don't wanna draw attention to ourselves."

"Sorry…" It was obvious from his tone that Alistair was attempting to whisper, but it came out at normal volume, instead.

"The answer is still no," one of the musicians said as a delicate hand grabbed his shoulder from behind. He glanced back with a raised eyebrow, and everyone looked past him to see one of the dancers. She had let down her long, dark hair and removed her cloth mask to reveal a striking, if cynical, expression.

"Who do we have here? More hagglers?" she asked.

Dhogron clapped his hands together. "Satara, it has been too long! Have you missed me?"

"Not even a little," she replied without flinching. Dhogron sulked as his cohorts chuckled from behind. "What do you want, this time? I trust you are not here to sell me any more junk? And I'm certain that you've run out of foolish schemes by now…"

"Could we speak in private?" Dhogron asked.

"Why should I give you any more of my time?" Satara asked while placing hands on her full hips.

"It is in regards to…" he trailed off, leaning in and lowering his voice to a whisper. "Sampson."

The dancer scoffed. "What could you possibly know about him that I do not?"

Dhogron rubbed the back of his turban, nervously. "Erm… I was hoping *you* could give *us* some information."

Satara laughed, then tapped her musician on the shoulder. "Good-bye, Dhogron."

"Hold on! We can make it worth your while!" Kabel called out as the musicians approached, their postures aggressive like bears defending their cubs.

"I have plenty of money," she replied without turning around.

"Awright, lads! Tha way I see it, we gots ta fight our way through!" Triston said as he drew his great sword: a weapon with immense reach, at the cost of less maneuverability. The musicians readied their scimitars and took crouched stances in response.

Alistair drew his battle axe, while Kabel and Rolf called upon their own blades.

"You're outnumbered," Kabel said with a cool smile. "There is no need for you to get hurt. We only wish to talk."

"You're the ones who are outnumbered." Satara's ice-cold voice drew everyone's attention. She wielded a hooked dagger and had it pressed up against the side of Rolf's neck. The other dancers circled the group with their weapons coiled.

Kabel sighed and lowered his sword. "I think most of us know that it is outlawed to brandish our weapons out in the streets like this. Instead of fighting out here, how about we go indoors and have a chat?"

"Fine," Satara said while lowering her weapon. Rolf let out a relieved breath. "Follow me."

The dancers and their musicians led the way through some alleys of the wealthy district, where many of the rooftop bridges cast their shadows. Eventually, they reached a set of stairs that hugged one of the tall, stone buildings.

"So, this is how people get up to them fancy bridges atop tha buildings?" Alistair asked as they ascended.

"Yes," Dhogron said with a timid nod. "But these 'rooftop deals' are often conducted by the wealthy and connected. Our presence up here may not be appreciated. I've seen commoners thrown from the rooftops, before..."

Satara scoffed and waved him off. "Don't forget who you're dealing with, Dhogron. Nearly every one of the scoundrels who dwell up here have made a pass at me or one of my dancers, and nearly all of them are married. They would not dare to cross me."

Nevertheless, as soon as they reached the top of the stairs, the group was greeted by a striking orange, sun-kissed coastline that was dirtied somewhat by the unsavory stares of well-dressed nobles who appeared to be exchanging papers. Satara paid them little mind while brushing past and crossing a bridge, where a man was sitting at the edge, letting his kicking legs dangle like an easily amused child.

The group crossed a few more rooftop bridges before coming to a new set of stairs that descended back into the alleys. However, to Dhogron's surprise, the passage below was completely boxed in by the surrounding stone buildings, and when they reached the bottom, they bathed in shadow; as if nighttime had already come upon them.

Within the walled-off space, Satara kicked some litter aside before leading them down yet another set of stairs that cut into the side of a building, like a wine cellar of sorts. At the bottom, she retrieved a key and unlocked the door. She gestured into the pitch-black abyss before them with a smile that looked sharp enough to cut steel, and Dhogron led his friends inside with careful steps.

Though it smelled of an intoxicating, feminine fragrance inside, the trickster Wizard couldn't settle his nerves. Satara had always been short with him, but today, she seemed especially aggressive. And on top of that, to lead him directly to her quarters was completely out of her character. For as long as he'd known her, she'd been sure to keep her distance and shroud herself in secrecy. What if she had been compromised by the enemy? What if they had just walked into a trap?

His dark thoughts were quickly dispelled with a soothing candle-light ahead and to the right, and then another to his immediate left. In short order, Satara and her dancers lit several scented candles to reveal a relaxing living area. There were padded seats, tables with playing cards laid out on them, and plentiful reserves of silk layered all about. With the soft confines of finely crafted and patterned carpet at their feet, Dhogron and his cohorts practically glided to their chairs with relaxation having taken over their previously wary minds. The dancers approached them and began massaging their shoulders, and all of them sunk into their chairs and let out sighs of happiness.

"Can we stay here for a while?" Alistair asked, dreamily.

"That depends," Satara said as she took a seat across from Dhogron at one of the tables. "Are you wealthy?"

"No," the big man replied. As soon as the word left his mouth, the dancers left each of the men and convened in a different corner of the room. "Aww!"

"Cut to the chase. What do you wish to know about Sampson, and what will you provide in return?" Satara asked.

"Amis has been kidnapped by a wealthy and powerful man with connections to Sampson. We believe that he is being held on one of his properties. Have you heard anything about that?" Dhogron asked.

"Maybe I have, maybe I haven't..." Satara said, smoothly crossing her legs. "You still haven't said what's in it for me."

Dhogron's brow furrowed. "You remember Amis, don't you? Would his rescue not be reward enough?"

"Yes, he was a nice, if smelly fellow from what I remember, but I am still not hearing anything that benefits *me*," she said. Now, her arms were crossed, and Dhogron felt a sweat come to his brow. She was running out of patience, fast. He would need to come up with something of value to her soon, or else-

Triston slammed his fist on the table, eliciting gasps from many in the room. "Now ain't tha time ta be cutthroat, lass! This man is bein' tortured ta death as we speak! Have ya no heart? Yer help could save someone's life!"

Satara let out a derisive laugh. "Don't lecture me on saving lives. I've saved more people in this city than your thick skull could count."

"Yer actin' so high an' mighty just 'cause yer dancin' is nice ta look at! Well, I hate ta break it to ya lass, but that don' save no lives!" Alistair shot back, pointing a righteous finger in her direction.

Dhogron turned back to the MacRae brothers and waved them off. "That's not what she meant. The reason she knows so much about Sampson is because, for years now, she has slowly but surely been rescuing his sex slaves."

Kabel's mouth fell agape as he looked around the room. "The dancers?"

"That's right," Satara said with a smile. "How did you know?"

"Most belly dancers in the slums and city center appear to be from the desert countries," the stocky man said, pointing to some of the women. "But I noticed different skin tones among your group and realized that your performances make for a great cover. After all, there are crowds blocking the view of them, and no one would think to look in the wealthy district for escaped slaves."

"And deir faces are partially covered," Rolf added.

"Very good. You are observant; I'll give you that much," she said.

Dhogron smiled and held up a finger. "And you even go so far as to change the color of their hair."

"Am I supposed to be impressed by you stating something that you've known for a while?" Satara asked with a snort.

"No, but it is dye purchased from me, is it not?"

"And?"

"You said that all of my products are junk," Dhogron said with crossed arms and a smile. "When in truth, they can be quite useful."

"Fine. They are *mostly* junk, then," Satara said to a few laughs.

"I feel that we are getting off-topic," Kabel interjected. The dancer cocked her head. "You wanna rescue more sex slaves. We wanna know where our ally is located. Let's help each other out."

"And how would *you* help me out?" she replied with contempt on her tongue.

"If you reveal our friend's location, we will go to free him. Such a task would be near impossible to pull off without at least a skirmish breaking out," he said.

"Ah, you mean to say that it would be a distraction?" Dhogron asked.

"Precisely," the stocky man said while nodding and smiling. "While we are rescuin' Amis, with all of the attention on us, y'all could probably rescue more girls than ever before. It's a win-win."

Satara sighed. "I suppose there's no harm in telling you this, but it doesn't matter whether you cause a distraction or not. Because tonight, Sampson is moving his prisoner, and he's bringing an unprecedented number of men with him. That's enough of a distraction on its own for me to save many women."

"Amis?" Dhogron asked, wide-eyed.

"I believe so. I don't know why, but he is considered an extremely valuable asset. From my understanding, they will be transporting him to a great, black ship on dock four," Satara said.

"That ship belongs to tha Dark Wizard. Cap'n Auber told me!" Alistair explained to the group.

"At least now we know where and when we can head them off and rescue Amis," Dhogron said with relief taking hold in his mind.

"Prisoners… Wizards… slave traders…" Satara trailed off with a shake of her head. "You seem like a troublesome lot. What kind of group involves themselves in affairs like this?"

"A group of strangers," Kabel said with a chuckle.

"You're *strange*, alright," she added with a laugh. Her expression then turned serious. "You realize that your chances of success are nearly zero, right? Sampson's influence cannot be overstated. You'll likely be captured and killed, and even that won't be the end. He'll find and enslave everyone you know and love. Why take such a brazen risk for one man?"

With a look of determination, Rolf said, "Da fate of da world is at stake."

"Well, I'll keep *the Strangers* in mind, next time the world needs saving," she said as her cohorts began laughing.

Dhogron and the others, however, did not join. They knew exactly what was at stake, even if some of them had not witnessed the horrors and atrocities of the Dark Savior up close.

As the group was leaving, Dhogron looked back to Satara. "Best of luck, tonight."

She huffed in return. "Save that luck for yourself."

While walking up the stone steps that led out of the cellar, Kabel said, "Y'know, I like that name: 'The Strangers'. That's what we should call our lil' group."

"But I'm gettin' ta know you all so well! Yer hardly strangers ta me, anymore!" Triston argued.

"Think of it as more of a symbol, big fella," the stocky man replied with a smirk. "Especially if we're gonna be wearin' masks and cloaks out on the streets."

"Well, all I'm sayin' is that we can come up with bettah! How about... tha Fearsome Goats!" Triston suggested.

"Dat's a terrible name," Rolf said.

"Oi! Quit bein' so rude, ya string bean!" Triston yelled as the group began walking up the shadowy steps, to the rooftops.

"Yeh! An' besides! Goats are mighty an' fierce! City-dwellers wouldn't know that!" Alistair added.

"We must return to the house as soon as possible," Dhogron said, breaking up the argument. "We need to gather everyone and get to the docks by nightfall. This is our one and only chance..."

All in the group quieted down. As they set foot on the roof, their strides lengthened. This was one task that they could not afford to fail. While crossing one of the bridges, Alistair came to a sudden stop, and all behind bounced off of him as if he were a stone wall.

"What's the hold-up?" Kabel asked.

Alistair was looking to his right and squinting. "Over thar, on that bridge..."

Dhogron fixed eyes on the rooftop bridge that Alistair was pointing to. No one was there.

"What about it?" Rolf asked.

"I coulda sworn I saw someone walking along it, starin' at us as he did," the big man replied. "Methinks we've got someone on our tails."

"Thar ain't no one thar, Ali!" Triston said with a shove. "Yer eyesight has always been below standard."

"If one of Sampson's men picked up on our trail, then we could lead them straight back to my house in the woods..." Kabel muttered, looking around with paranoia in his eyes. "I know that our mission tonight is important, but I could never live with myself if they got to Mira. I cannot leave her alone. Y'all will have to press on without me."

"Calm yourself, Kabel," Dhogron said with a confident smile. He gestured to the rooftops near the bridge. "There are no stairs near that bridge and no place to hide on those roofs. I think Alistair's imagination may be playing tricks on him."

"I s'pose…" the big man muttered while rubbing the back of his head.

As the Strangers continued along the rooftops, Dhogron kept his eyes peeled. Though his prior words had been rational and steady, Alistair's paranoia had also been contagious. For now, despite there not being a soul in sight, he could not shake the feeling that they were being watched.

CHAPTER 16
THE LEADERS

In the late afternoon, the two groups reconvened at Kabel's tree-built house in the wooded outskirts of Endoshire. Joel, Aldous, and Giles handed out masks and cloaks to their friends. All seemed happy to have their own personalized guise to wear out on the streets.

"Oi! This suits me well! Good pick, lads!" Alistair said as he fitted the bull-inspired mask tightly around his large head.

"Yes, these are quite nice to look at," Franco added, holding his tile-patterned guise up with a smile. "I imagine these fine designs must have set you back."

"Yeh, even I'm starting to run low on gold," Dalton said, frowning in his iron-inspired mask.

"You'd have more if you and my husband didn't spend every night at Cole's pub," Mirabel said with a snort. She had been given a fanciful mask with many colors and feathers, even though she was not to take part in the upcoming mission to save Amis.

"And I'd have more coin if Cole didn't make me pay for that broken window!" Kabel added with a laugh. He wore a dark blue mask with intricate, swirling designs on it.

"Let's worry about that after we've rescued Amis," Aldous chimed in, then *thunked* his walking stick off the floor. He wore a water-inspired guise with teardrop designs. "Dhogron and the others have obtained important information. Take it away, my friend."

Aldous nodded to the trickster Wizard, who wore a mask made of paper; one he had conjured for himself.

"Satara has informed me that Amis is to be taken from one of Sampson's buildings to a massive black ship on dock four. It's happening tonight."

"Aye, I'd wager it's the same vessel that Ebbie an' me encountered back in Bosfueras," Captain Auber said. He wore a black mask that happened to double as a proper pirate's hat. He swished his finger, back and forth, across the feather that stuck out from the hat.

"Why would they bring him out in public like that?" Lucia asked with arms crossed. Her crescent moon-inspired guise hung from a string at her hip.

"It's the Dark Wizard," Conrad said, gesturing with the mask that he held in hand. It was black with a swirling pattern that had been carved toward the middle of the brow. "He'll perform a ceremony on Amis with the dark essence, brainwashing him to their side. After that, he'll give away the map's location willingly."

"Well, what're we waitin' fer? Let's get down thar and set a trap fer them knobs!" Triston said with great excitement. He wore a bear-inspired mask.

"It's true that we don't have much time. Nightfall is already approaching," Dhogron said.

"We should at least make a plan. Sampson has hundreds of men at his disposal, including Sigrian knights. There are only a lil' over a dozen of us. We'll be slaughtered if we charge in unprepared," Kabel said, tracing the designs on his guise.

"My contact confirmed that a horde of Sampson's men will be guarding Amis along the way," Dhogron added.

"It'll be fine," Dalton said with a confident smile. Joel cocked his head. Had they ever faced such poor odds before? Had the warrior lost his mind? "Let's remember one important detail: They're takin' him to a ship at dock four."

All in the room remained contemplatively silent until Conrad's eyes widened and he looked to Aldous. "The water…"

"Exactly," Dalton said with a satisfied smirk directed at his Wizard friend. "All you've gotta do is wash them away like piss in the tide. Then, we'll perform the cleanup. They'll never know what hit 'em."

"Yes… that is a fine idea," Aldous said with a stroke of his beard. "I can hide among docks, in the water, and undetected. When they reach, say, dock seven or eight, I could hurl a great wave of water at them."

"Then, it's settled!" Ebbie cried with excitement. The tusks of a boar protruded out near the nose of his mask.

"But we can't just bunch up. Dat'll make us easy to find and catch," Rolf said. He held onto his black mask, which was complimented by a white feather sticking out of its edge.

Joel made hand signals to the group. His guise was black and simple, unlike most of the others.

"I agree," said Kabel. "We must split up into sub-groups. Each of these teams can hide in an alleyway before dock four."

"So, each group is a new line of defense?" Giles asked, twirling his blue, patterned mask around by the string.

"Yes, and each of these groups will need a leader," Aldous said. Joel pointed to the old Wizard, and many others looked at him as well. He then let out a laugh and held up his hands. "Oh, no, no! I couldn't!"

"There's no doubt about it; you brought us all together. And in many ways, you keep us focused. Hard to think of a better leader for this band of misfits," Dalton said with a smile. All others in the room appeared to share the sentiment.

The old Wizard sighed and then returned a warm smile of his own. "I shall accept the role with honor."

"Let's choose three more," Dhogron said with crossed arms. "The way I see it, we will need to split up into four sub-groups."

"I say Kabel is worthy," Dalton said. "Not only is he one hell of a drinker, but the best marksman around; one who knows this city all too well. And besides, we wouldn't have a place to stay without him, so we've gotta kiss his arse!"

The group laughed along for a bit, but as the chuckles tapered off, the suggestion became reality.

"All in favor?" Aldous asked.

All in the room shouted, "Aye!"

Dhogron cleared his throat. "We have chosen an expert marksman, sure, but what about ground combat? We need a leader with great skill in their swordplay. As far as I could tell, Dalton is our man."

"That might be Joel if he cared to try," Conrad said.

Lucia narrowed her eyes and nudged him with an elbow.

"I've never seen defense like Joel's," Giles said with wide eyes. "I'd hate to be on the other side of one of his offensives. He may be the best of us after all..."

"I suppose that is possible," Dalton said, looking to the mute with eyes alight. "Ever since you displayed your true abilities at Mt.

Couture, I've wondered how a duel would go between us. What do you say? You against me, winner gets to be a leader?"

Joel let out an inaudible chuckle, then shook his head. Until he resolved his struggles within, he could never hope to live up to such a responsibility. What he *did* hope was that tonight was the night where he could prevent needless death with swift action. It had proven difficult against the degenerates, who held no regard for their own lives, but perhaps Sampson's men would be different. He pointed to Dalton, granting his blessing.

"All in favor?" Dhogron asked while gesturing to the warrior.

"Aye!" the Strangers shouted, aside from Conrad and Giles.

"Dat makes dree leaders. Who should be da fourth?" Rolf asked.

"I say it should be Lucia," Conrad said while patting her on the back. She returned an odd if uneasy look, but he seemed to pay it little mind.

"She is certainly one of our best fighters," Dalton chimed in.

"Well, just a moment! Methinks I should be considered if she's gettin' votes ta be a leader!" Triston argued.

"She *did* defeat you, earlier..." Franco muttered.

"IT WAS ONLY 'CAUSE I GOT TIRED, YA HARD OF HEARIN' DOBBER!" he shouted, shaking his fist at the navigator. Chatter in the room began to pick up.

"I dink I'd be a good leader," Rolf added.

"We gots another Wizard! He should be a leader!" Ebbie shouted.

"HOLD UP!" Alistair called out. All in the room fell silent. "Yer forgettin' the most fearsome of us all!"

"Don' say it..." Captain Auber muttered, squirming in his seat.

"None other than tha fearsome king of tha sea, Cap'n Auber!" Alistair shouted. The captain's face went pale as fast as lightning could brighten the sky.

"Do you ever stop saying foolish things?" Lucia asked with hands to hips and narrowed eyes.

"What do *you* know, lass?" Alistair asked as he pointed to Auber, who Joel noticed was lowering his head into the collar of his shirt like a turtle into his shell. "This here fella has accomplished *way* more in battle than you!"

Lucia chuckled mockingly while waving him off. "You don't know what you're talking about, as usual."

"You and Joel are like brothers. You must know his capabilities,"

Giles added, nudging his new mentor. "Don't you think he should be leader?"

"Nah, half of our crew don't even know USL," Alistair said, rubbing his thick hands together and grinning. Giles cocked his head. "But I *do* think that a new penalty game is in order!"

"Oh, erm…"

"One pushup fer each mask n' each cloak that ya purchased today! By my count, that makes…" Alistair strained his eyes and began counting his fingers.

"28," Joel mouthed. 13 of the strangers had been given masks and cloaks, while Dhogron and Mira were gifted only a cloak and mask, respectively.

The big man cleared his throat. "R-right you are, lad! I was just about to say that!"

"No one believes that," Lucia said, to a few snorting chuckles around the room.

"Oh, shut it!" Alistair said before turning to Giles and jamming his finger onto the tip of his nose. "An' what are *you* waitin' for? Drop down and give me 28!"

"Y-yes, sir…" he muttered before lowering himself to the floor.

Lucia scoffed in Alistair's direction. "I have no idea why anyone is listening to your training advice, let alone your thoughts on who the final leader should be."

Alistair's face turned red, and he bared teeth like a ferocious beast. "WHY, YOU-"

"Wait!" Dalton called out before arguments could pick back up. "He's right."

The student looked at her mentor as if he had three heads, her mouth agape. A few others in the room gave Dalton their undivided attention.

"Let's not forget that Captain Auber is the man who gave Sampson a limp and lived to tell the tale!" Dalton said with so much enthusiasm that it almost felt fake, to Joel's ears. Franco's cheeks flared out and he covered his mouth, but a few chuckles escaped in the process. "I've also heard that he cornered a luxian in battle and nearly claimed his luxmortite sword as a prize."

Dhogron narrowed his eyes. "I don't know… his reaction was pathetically slow when I threw my paper arrow at him…"

"Well, I'm sure there's a perfectly good explanation," Dalton said.

"Erm…" Auber whimpered, then raised his hand, gaining the attention of the room. "I didn't have me land legs, yet…"

"THAT'S RIGHT!" Alistair bellowed, in triumph. "Yer all underestimatin' 'im just 'cause he don't gots his land legs, yet! But do ya see *him* judgin' any of *you* landlubbers fer gettin' seasick? I think not!"

"We can only hope the captain gets his land legs soon," Franco said before once again covering his mouth and failing to withhold laughter. "It'll be the key to our victory."

"Yeh! I've been told that the cap'n is secretly a cunning warrior!" Ebbie chimed in.

Dalton nodded with a knowing smile. "Good enough for me. All in favor?"

"Aye!" half the group called out.

"It is contested," Kabel said.

"We'll make it simple, then," said Aldous as he walked to the middle of the room. "If you oppose Captain Auber as a leader, raise your hand."

Lucia, Conrad, Dhogron, Rolf, Joel, and Aldous raised their hands.

"All for it?"

Dalton, Kabel, Franco, Ebbie, Alistair, and Triston put their hands up.

"Hm… that's still six-to-six…" Conrad muttered, stroking his chin.

"Oi! Lad!" Alistair said, prodding an exhausted Giles with the tip of his toe. He tumbled over in the midst of his most recent pushup, drenched in sweat. "I'll give ya a reprieve from tha pushups if ya vote fer *the right fella* as fourth an' final leader!"

"Auber… has… my vote…" he replied, breathlessly.

Lucia grimaced. "Well, hold on-"

"It's settled, then," Aldous said, making a grand gesture to the captain. "The fourth and final leader shall be none other than Captain Auber!"

Cheers and groans erupted all at once, as Auber heaved over, hands to knees. It looked like he was about to vomit. However, within moments, the captain stood, now grinning from ear to ear, and put hands to hips.

"I've been captain of the seas fer so long… I didn't think I was ready fer somethin' like this. But I'm gonna tell ye right now! The great Captain Auber won't let ye down! We're gonna take Amis back! An' maybe we'll loot some of their treasures along the way, while we're at it!"

"YEAH!" Alistair slammed his fist into the table, which seemed to rattle the entire house. The enthusiasm became contagious, though, and eventually, even the captain's detractors joined in the cheer.

After the cheers tapered off, Kabel cleared his throat. "While we're decidin' on things for our little group, I wanna put forth a name: The Strangers."

"Oooo, here we go!" Triston said, throwing up his hands. "I say 'The Fearsome Goats' is a bettah name!"

"Both seem like odd choices to me..." Lucia trailed off.

"'Strangers' makes perfect sense. We're all still gettin' to know each other, and to folk on the streets, the name will always match, 'cause we'll be in masks and cloaks," Kabel explained. Many in the room nodded along. "All in favor of 'The Strangers'?"

"Aye!" all in the room called out, aside from Triston and Alistair. The MacRaes were disappointed in the overall decision, but it didn't keep their spirits down for long.

Having sorted out the business of leadership and name, the Strangers began gathering supplies, to prepare themselves both physically and mentally for the rapidly approaching challenge: Rescue Amis, and survive the onslaught of the vile forces who sought to unleash Degenerate upon the world.

CHAPTER 17
MONSTER IN THE DEPTHS

Dressed in their cloaks and masks, the Strangers planned on splitting up into four separate groups to tackle their mission on different fronts. It was believed that Sampson's men would escort Amis from east to west along the docks until reaching the Dark Wizard's mighty black vessel at dock four. As such, the sub-groups were to hide in spots along the docks, awaiting Aldous' surprise tidal wave attack from somewhere near the sewer pipe. If all went well, they could swoop in and steal the dark force's prisoner before they even knew what hit them.

As the sun set, the Strangers traveled northwest, up through the slums and into the heart of the city. Though Endoshire's center remained crowded even as dusk blanketed the litter-filled streets, it was clear that people were making an effort to leave: Shops were closing up, the nobles were nowhere to be seen, and everyone was rushing. All seemed to know that nighttime was not a safe occasion in this part of the city. Soon, the degenerates would emerge from their wretched hive.

Upon reaching the near-abandoned wealthy district, they split up into the alleyways, ignoring the sidelong glances of performers who were packing up. The tall, stone buildings and their shadows brought with them newfound cover, and with that, faster strides. Amis and his captors could show up at any time after nightfall, after all.

Kabel, Rolf, and Dhogron reached a place that felt like a decent hiding spot: Behind a wide building across from dock ten. There, they could peek from the sides while remaining in the shadows and avoiding detection.

"Let's hope we made it in time..." Kabel muttered as he peered at the path along the docks. He could see no sign of the enemy, though, to the front-left, he did spy Aldous, Joel, and Giles heading for the coast-line between docks 9 and ten, where the sewer pipe lay below.

"'Nightfall' ain't da best description of when dey're comin'," Rolf said.

Dhogron smiled. "Just be glad Satara gave us any information at all. Usually, you've got to pay an unreasonable price for her services."

Kabel chuckled. "So, you *have* gotten some private dances from her, eh?"

The trickster Wizard let out a nervous laugh, then put his hands up in defense. "No, no... I couldn't possibly afford that."

"How much does it cost?" Rolf asked. Kabel snorted, then shoved him. "What? I'm only wonderin'..."

"If you have time to fantasize about things that'll never happen, you have time to scout on the other side of the building."

"Fine..." Rolf muttered. He skulked away until the shadows obscured him.

"Why are you so hard on him?" Dhogron whispered.

"To toughen him up, of course. The world is a harsh place," Kabel said, cracking a smooth smirk. "Besides that, it's fun to mess with him."

"I can appreciate messing with others."

"So I've heard. Maybe you can come up with some tricks to stop the enemy in their tracks," he replied.

"I've had a few ideas. Hopefully, I don't have to use 'em," Dhogron said while readjusting his turban, and then his paper mask. "Our enemy would have to be mighty strong to withstand a tidal wave."

DALTON, Lucia, and Conrad reached their hiding place in the shadows of an alley across from dock eight. The warrior raised an eyebrow when his student took off her lunar-inspired mask.

"The point of the masks was to hide your identity, y'know," he said with a snicker.

Lucia rubbed her chin. "It irritates my skin. I don't think it fits my face properly."

Conrad walked past the pair, then looked to his right out of the alleyway. He spotted Aldous, who appeared to be controlling a water geyser that held him, Joel, and Giles. He was steadily lowering to the sea. Aside from that spectacle, the road was empty as far as the eye could see under the light of the moon. He then peered to his left. Far off in the distance, he caught onto a green glow from the looming decks of the Dark Wizard's grand ship. There was complete silence about the air, however, which filled him with relief. If there truly were a great force transporting Amis, they would have made some noise.

He turned back to his teammates and smiled. "I think we made it in time."

"Now we only have to hope that Aldous can muster enough water to wash those knobs away," Dalton said as he leaned up against a building wall and sat.

"I think we all know what he's capable of," Lucia said.

He snorted. "Don't forget what monstrosities you witnessed in Bosfueras, foolish student. We should still plan for a battle, just in case."

"It's simple," Conrad added with crossed arms. "If Aldous' attack fails for some reason, we layer our attack on top of that. The others know that if *we* strike, it means that something went wrong, and they'll know it's time to ambush from all sides."

"There are also Sampson's slaves to consider. We need to use non-lethal force," Lucia said.

"Oh, *this* again…" Conrad muttered with a roll of his eyes. "We do what we must to recover Amis. They wouldn't hesitate to kill us themselves."

"You act as if they have a choice in the matter," Lucia said, shaking her head. "You heard the stories from Kabel and Mira. It is not only their lives, but their family's lives that are at stake. These are good people being forced into bad lives."

"And you act as if you know how they think," Conrad said, sharply stroking his chin. He pointed at her with righteous indignation. "It is obvious to me that some element of your past is influencing your hesitation, here. No wonder you sympathize with Joel. You have your soft spots, too."

"'Soft spots'?" She leaned in with a glare that normally would have left the strategist paralyzed, but for some reason, there was an unquenchable fire in his chest. Their dispute from earlier had not truly been settled, but perhaps her mentor could bring it to an end.

Conrad turned to Dalton. "I think that something happened in Luneria. Something she regrets. Something involving slaves. Does that sound about right?"

The warrior let out an uneasy chuckle and opened his mouth, but Lucia didn't give him a chance to speak.

"You haven't a clue what I witnessed in those lands, but if you are so eager for Dalton to settle this dispute..." she trailed off, looking at the warrior with sharp eyes. "What do you have to say? *You're* the leader. Make a call."

"Whoa, thar!" Dalton said while holding his hands up. "I don't wanna get between this lover's quarrel."

"It is not a lover's quarrel. This is a matter of the plan," she said.

Conrad let out a huff. "Dalton has killed slaves, too; because his life was in danger."

The warrior rubbed the back of his head. "Yeh, well, that was before I knew-"

"And our lives will be in danger this time, too."

Dalton groaned. "Give me a moment to think about it, would you?"

～

FURTHER DOWN THE ALLEYS, Captain Auber, Franco, Ebbie, Alistair, and Triston arrived in their hiding spot across from dock six. They were the closest to the Dark Wizard's grand ship and it filled Auber with so much dread that he could feel his knot-filled stomach collapsing into itself.

With their backs to each of the buildings, the MacRaes and the pirates all looked to the left and right of the path along the docks. There was no one to be seen, and only the green flames flickering aboard the Dark Wizard's ship provided any sign of activity.

"Looks like we made it in time, lads," Triston said in his probable best attempt at a whisper. It seemed normal volume to the Auber, however.

"Could ye keep it down? We don' wanna give our position away!" the captain said in a harsh whisper.

"We don't gots nothin' ta worry aboot, with you on our side!" Alistair said with an obnoxious laugh. He delivered a spine-shattering slap to the captain's back. Auber wanted to let out a wheeze from the impact, but he forced himself to take it in stride. Especially now that he was a leader of the group, he had no choice but to appear every bit as fearsome as he'd built himself up to be.

"Yeh! I can't wait ta see what the cap'n is made of! Hard ta believe that all this time, he was puttin' on an act ta lure our enemies into a false sense of security!" Ebbie said with child-like excitement.

"Yes," Franco said with a sly smile toward his captain. "But perhaps tonight, we'll see the captain go at it for real, eh?"

"Erm… right! I suppose tonight would be a good time ta give 'em a real beatin'!" Auber said with a cocky laugh and hands at his hips.

"Still, even if ya *are* that good, I wouldn't want this Sampson fella after me," Triston said. "If he catches ya alive, then yer probably gonna be enslaved 'n tortured fer the rest of yer days."

Somehow, the unbreakable knots in Auber's stomach tightened a little more. It seemed that every time he began to feel confident, a stark reminder that he had injured Sampson was brought up.

"Don' be ridiculous, brother!" Alistair said with a chuckle. "The great Cap'n Auber would nevah be taken alive!"

Auber laughed along while squealing internally. "Y-yeh!"

"Speakin' o' death…" Triston trailed off as he turned to his brother with grave eyes. "I want ya ta stay behind me at all times. We may be partnered up with death-defyin' pirates, but we both know that ya weren't meant fer the battlefield."

"No way! I can handle me'self out thar! Just watch!" the big man said as he drew his axe and pointed it to the docks ahead.

"Yer stayin' under me watch, and that's final!" Triston said with a vicious snarl. He then softened his expression, as if a parent trying to reach through to his child. "How many times do ya have'ta be shown that yer not a battler, Ali? Ya just don't gots tha instinct. I don' wanna see ya killed, or worse!"

"You'll see…" Alistair muttered, patting a bumpy spot beneath his cloak. Auber raised an eyebrow. He could swear that part of the cloak was emitting a weak, white glow.

His curiosity was interrupted, however, by a *whoosh* overhead. A hush fell upon the group and they all looked up to see nothing save the twinkling night sky.

"I take it we all heard that?" Franco whispered.

"But what was it? That big ol' buzzard?" Alistair asked.

"Naw, it must'a been the raven," Auber argued.

"You're both talking about the same creature…" the navigator trailed off with narrow eyes. "And I believe it was an avian."

"Who cares what it was? Let's shoot it down!" Ebbie said with a cheeky grin.

"I don' suppose any of ya gots a bow 'n arrow?" Triston asked. The group remained silent for a few moments. "Welp! There ain't much we can do, then! Gotta hope someone else picks 'em off."

~

ALDOUS, Joel, and Giles stood atop the water plume, directly across from the gag-inducing smells of the sewer pipe. An uninviting brown water drained from the inside, and the trio had simply been staring at it instead of entering.

"Come now, boys! This hiding spot is vital to the plan. We must enter eventually," said Aldous.

Giles shrugged and then hopped into the pipe. He immediately gagged upon entering. "How long're we gonna have to put up with this smell?"

Joel was next to enter. He pinched his nose in a vain attempt to block out the stench, but it didn't work. It was as if he could *taste* the smell, it was so strong.

"A small sacrifice to save this city, wouldn't you say?" Aldous asked while gently lowering himself in. With a single leap inside, the water plume became a mere wave and dropped to the sea below.

"How is the smell not driving you mad?" Giles asked between wheezes.

"Oho! When you've been around death as much as I have, you come to realize that there are worse smells than sewage."

As he was adjusting to the horrid stench, Joel looked behind and shuddered at a grizzly display. In the muddy water, he could see a variety of bones caught on clumps of waste. He tugged at Aldous' tunic with urgency, then pointed to the remains.

"Oh, dear…" Aldous muttered, wide-eyed. "Mayhap we should move elsewh-"

The old Wizard was cut off by a giant tentacle cracking out of the water like a whip, striking him with such force that he was flung out of the pipe and into the murky waters below with a great splash.

"Whoa!" Giles cried.

He and Joel drew their respective blades as the tentacle slithered back into the dark depths of the sewer drain. Joel looked back over his shoulder. There was no movement in the water where Aldous had fallen in, and his Wizard's artifact remained afloat, bobbing over the small waves.

The mute looked to Giles, then motioned toward the spot where Aldous had been knocked into the water. The pair ran for the sewer exit, but as Joel was about to jump out and into the sea, a great crash rocked the sewer pipe. The source of the collision came from his back left. He turned to find Giles pinned up against the wall by the big, dark tentacle that had attacked Aldous.

Giles gasped for air, but with each draw of his breath, less was exhaled, and his face began to turn purple. Try as he might to escape, the tentacle had him fully pinned. Joel readied his sword and rushed forward with it held over his shoulder and ready to chop down. However, when within range, he reconsidered. Even against a monster, his goal was not to kill, but merely to ward it off.

Joel lunged forward and stabbed the thick tentacle with his dark blue blade. A shriek echoed from further down the pipe as blood spurted from the feeler, and it retreated into the depths of the tunnel at top speed. Giles exhaled loudly as he fell to the muddy floor and then fell into a coughing fit.

"Like I said… Conrad was… too harsh on ye…"

Another shriek came from further down the sewer; its anger shaking both the pipe and the duo within. Without even a word or gesture, they turned tail and made a run for the exit. This time, they escaped into the water while evading capture.

As Giles emerged, however, Joel dove further into the depths to search for his Wizard friend. Almost immediately, he noticed a stream of white bubbles cutting upward through the muddy water. Along with them, a determined Aldous rose within his own protective air bubble. Just above the brow of his mask, the crimson red of a bloody gash painted intricate designs that leaked around the edges and down his jaw. If he weren't underwater, Joel would have gasped at the damage his Wizard cohort had taken from only one blow. Were they facing off against a Guardian of the monolith?

Joel surfaced, then soon after witnessed Aldous rise out of the water on a geyser. Giles tossed the Wizard his walking stick, to which he nodded as thanks. In Joel's time underwater, several tentacles had grasped onto the outside of the sewer tube. It groaned at the sheer stress of whatever was pulling at it. The mute watched on, eyes wide and wondering: What monster could possibly be lurking within the depths?

CHAPTER 18
ACT OF BRAVERY

Dhogron watched from the shadows as a crowd approached on the path along the docks. In his estimation, there were at least several dozen, but considering Satara's information, he had expected *hundreds*. The more he thought about it, the more he began to doubt that Amis was among the nearing group. After all, the Dark Wizard commanded a sizable portion of the Bosfueras townsfolk, and Sampson easily had hundreds that he could call upon, if need be. As his mind raced, other possibilities came up: Had the dark forces simply not considered the idea that they would be attacked while transporting Amis? Or were the Strangers walking straight into a trap?

"That group is smaller than expected," Kabel whispered.

"My thoughts exactly," Dhogron said. "I worry that this is a trap."

"Dere's not much we can do about dat, now. We either rescue Amis, or he gets on dat ship, and he never gets off," Rolf said.

The stocky man looked back and scowled at first, prompting his lanky friend to brace for a punch on the arm. Dhogron had already seen such a thing play out several times tonight. This time, however, Kabel let out a defeated sigh.

"You're right."

The trio watched on in silence as the ominous group marched ever closer. Dhogron hoped that Drake and the Dark Wizard had merely underestimated the Strangers and sent too few.

~

ANGUS GROUCHET LED a potent mix of Sampson's slaves, Sigrian knights, and his own team. The entourage was layered around the prisoner at its center. He limped forward in heavy chains that were wrapped around his wrists and ankles, guarded closely by Sir Job, Catalina, and Barret; the latter of whom wore a cloak to cover his hideous fly-face. All in the group were armed to the teeth with bows, arrows, pikes, swords, axes, and clubs.

Upon passing Sampson's shipyard at dock 15, Angus looked back to his underlings. "Be on high alert as we near the ship. Secure the prisoner at all costs."

The group let out a strangely enthusiastic cheer. It was all part of their strategy, Angus thought. He had retrieved the prisoner from one of Sampson's sex slave establishments and left with a team of his choosing along with some slaves and knights to aid him. Sampson had been confident that there was a mole within his establishment who was feeding information to the outside. He'd been sure to share tonight's plan with many of his slaves, hoping that it would lure out Aldous and his troublesome band of misfits.

Angus' team had brought along many torches, and he encouraged their chatter, to draw as much attention as possible. Even their route along the docks was planned out with a purpose: To travel near the sea for so long would almost certainly goad Aldous into a foolhardy attack.

Finally, the Dark Wizard ensured that his ship was alight in its usual green hue, to give the illusion that all of the Bosfueras townsfolk were still aboard. In reality, many were hidden in buildings across from the docks, ready to spring their trap at the signal: A tidal wave to be wielded by Aldous. Although there were many assumptions in this plan, they were safe ones; and even if no attack were launched against them, it would only mean their safe and simple passage to the ship.

~

DALTON PEERED out of the alleyway and then looked back to his teammates, who were still pouting at one another. "Save the dramatics for later. The dark forces draw near."

Conrad grasped the edge of the stone building and peeked out to see torchlights off in the distance. They appeared to have reached dock

13 or 14, in his estimation.Then, he felt Lucia's chin resting atop his head, and she pressed herself against him while wrapping an arm around his chest, presumably to get a good look at the street. He'd have thought it a romantic gesture, if not for her having been so frustrating to speak with, lately.

"We still haven't decided on the matter of fighting the slaves," Lucia said, releasing Conrad and then looking to her mentor. "Make a decision."

"I agree with that much," Conrad added with a nod. "Whatever your decision, we will follow your lead."

The warrior shrugged. "I don't think it will matter."

"And why not?" she asked with hands to hips.

"If Aldous washes all of them away, we probably won't have to fight," Dalton replied before smirking and letting out a snorting chuckle. "And if he *doesn't* succeed, then we are in deep shite, anyway."

Conrad shook his head. "You cannot call yourself a leader of this team without making some decisions…"

"Very well. In that case, let's not kill anyone, if possible. I'd wager they have Sigrian knights by their side, and if we spill any of their blood, it will anger the kingdom. We don't need that kind of attention."

Lucia smiled as if to rub the minor victory in Conrad's face, but before he could retort, his ears picked up on a couple of peculiar noises in quick succession: First had been a weak cry; perhaps one of surprise. Then had come a great *splash*. Both sounds had come from the sea, directly across from their hiding spot in the shadows.

"What was that?" As a natural reaction to his curiosity, Conrad took strides out of the alley, only to feel a firm grip on his wrist.

He looked back with a furrowed brow to see Lucia shaking her head and pulling him back. "What are you doing? You'll give away our position!"

"Are you telling me you didn't hear that? Someone has clearly fallen into the water, nearby. What if something is wrong on Aldous' end? We should investigate," Conrad said.

"He's a Wizard," Lucia replied as the strategist flicked his wrist to release her grip. "He'll be fine, whatever it is."

"What about that large snake you saw before? In the sewer pipe?"

Her eyes widened. "What about it?"

"We may have just sent Aldous, Joel, and Giles into a deadly trap without even knowing it. That could have been the Guardian Beast, for all we know," Conrad said.

"It is out of our hands, now," Dalton said with a sigh. "We have to stick to the plan."

With frustration mounting, Conrad gritted his teeth. "I'm telling you… something's not right. We have to adjust the plan."

The warrior's eyes sharpened, but he merely shook his head in reply. *Outnumbered again*, Conrad thought. It didn't exactly come as a surprise, seeing as they were student and mentor; but more importantly, he still couldn't shake the feeling that Joel, Aldous, and Giles were in grave danger.

ATOP A GREAT GEYSER of water that was nearly as loud as a waterfall, Joel could have sworn he'd heard some faint splashes come from further out at sea. Yet, neither he, Aldous, nor Giles could afford to pay such trifles any mind; for the source of the powerful, iron-bending tentacles was about to reveal itself from the depths of the sewers.

Joel wiped drops of water from his eyes to erase the sting of salt and get a better look at the monstrosity that finally appeared: Filling the inside of the pipe was a creature as dark as the muddy water pooling around it. With a long head that was both triangular and rounded at the end, it could best be described as a giant octopus and squid combined. Its eight massive tentacles granted the groaning metal sweat release, and began wriggling in apparent excitement; though its cold, wide eyes showed no such emotion.

"L-look at the s-size of that thing!" Giles cried between chattering teeth.

"Like a kraken from the legends…" Aldous muttered, his eyes as blank as his tone.

Against his better judgment, Joel switched his attention to behind the trio. All of the thrashing and splashing out at sea told him that he hadn't imagined the noises from earlier, and under the light of the moon, his eyes confirmed the same: He picked up on some men swimming toward them, but it begged several questions: Where in the world had they come from? Were they friend? Foe? Neither?

The mute's thoughts were interrupted by both Aldous and Giles' stuttered, panicked breaths. He returned his attention forward to see the kraken leaning back, revealing a gaping, uninviting mouth that was filled with rows of teeth. From there, it ejected a veritable fountain of dark liquid at the trio, to which Aldous gasped and swung his walking stick right; jerking their geyser in that same direction to avoid. Joel hung on for dear life as the geyser settled and the kraken's vile liquid steamed like acid upon striking the seawater. The group let out a collective gasp as it seeped into the water and emanated a horrid stench, managing to top the gag-inducing sewage nearby.

"Venom?" Aldous asked aloud.

No one bothered to answer, because a much greater problem now presented itself: The monster had disappeared. The tunnel before them was now empty, and as much as Joel hoped it had retreated, the water below was where his eyes wandered to, first.

The mute nudged his Wizard cohort and mouthed, "Cloak."

"Methinks you're right," he replied, darting his gaze back ahead. "Octopuses can change color. Perhaps a kraken can, too?"

Giles jerked his head back and forth, scanning the dark blue abyss below. "But it's so large. Surely, we'd be able to see-"

A harsh *whoosh* reached the trio's collective ears, just in time to still Giles' tongue and for Joel's eyes to catch the speeding tentacle of the kraken whipping their way. Aldous had caught on too, for he raised his walking stick with a grunt, and along with it came up a wall of water to soften the blow.

Joel shielded his face as water erupted all around him and he felt the odd sensation of soaring through the air. He opened his eyes to see that he was indeed flying, and Giles was along for the ride. Then, a sinking feeling came to his stomach, and now the mute understood that they'd been flung away like bothersome flies by the kraken's tentacle. With that realization came the sting of water striking his back, and a mouthful of said water rushing down his throat.

Regaining his bearings as he sunk, Joel kicked his legs with urgency to reverse course, until resurfacing. His head poked above water just in time for the final droplets of Aldous' broken geyser to rain down upon him. Yet, despite spinning in a full circle, he could find no sign of the old Wizard. Giles was next to surface, and after a great exhale, he locked frightful eyes with Joel.

"What do we do?"

At that moment, the mute realized just how much the prior attack had knocked him for a loop. He had completely forgotten about the kraken, who appeared to have blended back in with the water. As it stood, they were like helpless worms; powerless to stop the monster from having its way with them. Their only hope was-

Some splashes from behind caught Joel's attention, and he turned faster than the wheel of a runaway wagon, expecting to see Aldous. Instead, he was greeted with something else: Two men approaching, about 10 or so meters away. Their red eyes gleamed between strokes and the splashing water.

Bosfueran townsfolk, Joel thought with a silent gasp. Conrad had mentioned that their eyes turned red instead of yellow. The realization only brought more questions to mind, however: Why were they in the water alone? How had they gotten out to sea?

~

LIKE A RAGING BULL, Aldous burst from the sea and shot up a couple of stories high. Before he could start falling, a water jet exploded upward, catching him. With a simple, yet forceful gesture to his right, Giles and Joel were gently pushed aside, out of his path. Next, he punched the air forward, and in reaction, the water below turned into a giant fist, smashing into the kraken as it surfaced for another attack. The monster shrieked while being carried by the immense force of the water fist, headed straight for the sewer pipe behind.

The nearby docks rattled as seawater burst into the pipe and caused a massive eruption of a wave to rock the foundations of the city. As the tide calmed, however, Aldous gasped to see that the kraken's tentacles had latched onto the pipe's edges, to keep it braced. The monster leaned its long, rounded head back and let loose another stream of venom in his direction.

Thinking quickly, Aldous swung his walking stick ahead, and a great wave formed to catch and redirect the vile liquid at the kraken. The venom-filled tide smashed into the drain pipe at a furious speed, further rumbling the land and docks, and leaving a drizzle of black rain in its wake. Yet, the old Wizard knew that the fight was far from over. He was privy to the last-second escape that had just occurred: The kraken had contracted, as octopuses often did, to make itself smaller. With that decrease in size, it escaped through a narrow passage between the oncoming water and the pipe.

Searching frantically below, Aldous spotted a dark figure to his front-left and pointed his walking stick at it.

"Aha!" he cried as a giant plume of water shot up.

However, instead of revealing the kraken, nothing but ink-filled water surfaced. *Of course,* he thought with a groan. Squids could squirt blots of ink in the water to ward off attackers, so why not a kraken? Aldous scanned the depths once more, when, to his front-center, he spotted a tentacle shooting at him like a long, dark arrow aimed at his heart. The attack had some distance to travel, however, and he was able to ward the feeler off with his walking stick.

Mere moments later, it became apparent that the initial strike had only been a decoy, though; a separate tentacle coiled around his neck from behind and began choking the life out of him. Not only had the breath been sucked from his lungs, but the resulting pressure on his head was immense; it felt like his eyes were going to pop out, or his head was about to explode. Even worse, the tip of the tentacle housed suckers with such monstrous suction that Aldous could feel the skin of his neck stretching unbearably. In his estimation, he had only seconds to escape before his flesh was torn.

Out of desperation, Aldous used the static of his body to create a small shock, traveling along the kraken's tentacle until reaching its mantle and briefly lighting up the night. The weak bolt of lightning had succeeded in stunning the monster, as it released its grip from his neck and retreated underwater.

Aldous wheezed and coughed as he fell to his knees in relief and his water plume began to lower. The creature was powerful, but he was certain that it wasn't the Guardian Beast. It was too similar to beings of this realm, while Guardians tended to be otherworldly in appearance. Could the kraken have been one of the aforementioned 'pets' of the Wizard King Olius, instead?

The dark blue seawater bubbled below, as if some vile potion boiling over a cauldron, and Aldous refocused himself. The battle was far from over.

❧

Kabel sweated profusely as he gazed upon the malicious group passing dock 12.

"What's the status on Aldous?" he asked, motioning to Rolf on the other side of the building.

The lanky young man approached, shaking his head. "It looks like he's still fightin' some kinda monster."

Dhogron's eyes widened. "Why didn't I think of it before?"

"Think of what?" Kabel asked with a tilted head.

"The Wizard King who oversees the Degenerate seal keeps 'pets' to patrol the sewers. Usually, they stay deep within… unless they are hungry," he said with a frown.

"So, dat monster he's fightin' is lookin' fer food?" Rolf asked.

"Why don't we just feed it, then?" Kabel said.

"Dat's dumb. We don't got any food with us," Rolf replied with a playful jab.

"*You're* dumb," Kabel shot back before punching him in the arm.

Dhogron sighed. "The kraken will sometimes leave at night to hunt for fish if it is unable to find food in the sewers. I thought that Aldous and the others would be fine taking refuge in the northern sewer pipe, but I hadn't even thought about the creatures lurking within…"

"Well, why not?" Kabel asked, his nose crinkling. "The beasts of the sewers seem a bit important, wouldn't you say? Who among us would know them better than you?"

"A fair point, but you see, Amis provided this city with an unappreciated luxury: He took care of feeding these monsters every once in a while. He did so to keep them satisfied; to ensure that they wouldn't surface in the city. Without him around, it seems the kraken has grown hungry," Dhogron said before hanging his head. "But it is true that I should have thought of such a thing. I've let our team down."

"There is no use in dwelling on it. Now, we must think of an alternate plan," Kabel said.

"Didn't we agree to attack from all angles, anyway?" Rolf asked.

Dhogron shook his head. "Fewer men are guarding Amis than we thought, but their group is still much larger than ours. Attacking now would almost certainly invite death or capture."

Kabel drew an arming sword from his hip. "Well, I say we-"

Several commotions coming from the sea interrupted his words.

"What was dat?" Rolf asked.

"Sounded like people thrashing about in the water," said the stocky man.

"Could it be Joel and Giles? Escaping from the kraken?" Dhogron asked.

"Perhaps we can help them out of the water," Kabel said as he peeked out from behind the building. The torch lights were closer than ever, and so too were the loud noises made by the ominous group. He could feel the light rumbles of their march in the cobblestone at his feet. "Never mind. They have gotten too close. I say we wait to see what Dalton's and Auber's teams do. We're meant to attack from behind, anyhow."

∼

Sampson's slaves grumbled and chattered as they neared the titanic battle unfolding at the sea. Because of the crashing waves and flailing tentacles, it was difficult to tell who was winning or even who was fighting.

"What's this all aboot, then?" one asked.

"Is that a monster out thar at sea?" said another.

"Pay it no mind," Angus commanded, his husky voice dripping with authority. "Continue marching to the ship with the prisoner, and let no one stop you."

Peering past others in the group, Sir Job's eyes widened when getting a good look at the combatants. "Is that a kraken? I thought that they were merely legends told by sailors whose ships had sunk at sea… and who is that old man fighting against the monster?"

"I believe he is a Wizard; one of our enemies," Catalina chimed in.

"No one said *anything* about fighting a Wizard," the knight said, wide-eyed. "I've heard many-a-tale about the dreadful things they can do."

"Fear not," she replied with a smile. "He will be busy with the kraken for a while, I'd imagine. Besides, we don't expect you knights to do battle with a Wizard. Angus, Barret, and I will handle him if we must."

Sir Job scoffed before flashing a smug grin. "I could never let a precious flower like you take on such dangers. I don't know why you've accompanied us on this treacherous mission, m'lady, but I will ensure that no one harms a luscious hair on your head."

The knight then swept up her hand and kissed it, gently.

Catalina giggled and a light blush came to her cheeks. "Oh, my…"

His chivalry and charm had earned him many pleasurable nights and courtships in the past, and he did not plan for tonight to be any exception. Job smiled as he thought of ways to impress Catalina, should the need for battle arise. Perhaps he would behead one of the worms, or-

Job's dreamy thoughts were interrupted when he bumped into Amis, who'd slowed to a near crawl. The knight growled at his insolence and pushed him forward with the force of a bull. "Keep moving, whelp!"

The Gentish woman giggled once more. "Not as nice to the men as you are to the ladies, I see. Let's just say my gruesome nature may surprise you if we are forced into battle."

"Spirited, isn't she?" Job asked while nudging Barret.

The hooded man responded with a series of buzzes and hisses, to which the knight frowned. Between Wizards, a kraken, and the odd folk surrounding him, he began to wonder just what he was getting himself involved in.

~

As Angus' malicious group passed by dock 10, Kabel watched from the shadows, his calm eyes studying them for a potential crack in their proverbial armor.

"Interesting…" he muttered.

"What is it?" Dhogron asked.

"That formation… it has a weakness that we can exploit."

"How? It looks impossible to penetrate," Rolf whispered.

"They are lined up in a layered circle, likely to keep Amis surrounded at all times," Kabel said as his chubby cheeks flared out to form a mischievous smile. "If we attack 'em at an angle with our full group, in columns of three, we'll poke a hole in that circle, and disperse 'em from a weak point."

Dhogron's eyes lit up, and he rubbed his hands together. "They won't expect an attack from behind, either."

"We need de others dough, right?" Rolf asked. "How are dey supposed to know our change of plans?"

"Dalton is a military man, like me. I have no doubt that he'll pick up on the weakness of their formation. Once they pass our building, we'll travel between alleys to rendezvous with his team," said Kabel.

"And what of Captain Auber and his group?" Dhogron asked.

"Ehhh…" Kabel rubbed the back of his head. "No plan is perfect. We'll probably have to work around whatever they do."

~

Dalton peeked from out of the alleyway, then jerked his head back into the shadows.

"They've reached dock nine," he whispered. "From this point on, we need to stay hidden."

"Shouldn't we be attacking, anyhow?" Conrad murmured. "I thought the backup plan was to attack from all sides."

"That was before we knew their formation," Dalton replied.

"What about it?" Lucia asked.

"It is circular and layered; I assume to create a barrier around Amis. That said, such a formation has a weakness. If we make two or three lines of our own and attack from an angle, we can pop that circle like a bubble, and break them up," he said, poking his clenched fist and then opening that same hand up for emphasis.

"Sounds like a recipe for pure chaos," Conrad said while shaking his head. "Besides, how do we know that the others will join us in the plan? We have no way of communicating it to them."

"Kabel will know what to do; I'm sure of that much." He returned a confident nod.

Lucia narrowed her eyes. "And Auber?"

"Well…" the warrior trailed off with a chuckle. "No one said this backup plan would be perfect. We just gotta hope he plays to his timid nature and doesn't attack from the front."

"Have you *met* Alistair? There's no chance in hell that they'll wait," Lucia said, to which the trio chuckled in unison.

They abruptly fell silent, however, as the far louder cackles, chatter, cheers, and jeers of Angus' team approached. Dalton and his team raised their cloaks and bathed in the shadows to blend in as the rumbling of the dark forces' marching grew stronger.

Dalton kept eyes on the sea as Angus and his crew passed. Aldous continued his battle with the kraken, dodging tentacles and dark liquids alike while throwing around boatloads of water and the occasional, if small, bolt of lightning. Though waves erupted against the coastal path, they were a result of the ongoing struggle at sea; not the aimed tidal wave that had been integral to the Strangers' plans. Rather than a wall of water to wash the dark forces away, they were instead treated to refreshing showers of droplets and mist.

The warrior tightened his grip around the hilt of his sword. Soon, they would have no choice but to strike.

～

Across from dock six, Alistair peered around a nearby building before returning to the shadows with the others.

"They're gettin' close, lads. What do we do? Aldous hasn't done nothin', yet," he said.

"He's still fightin' that monster of the sea?" Ebbie asked.

"Yeh, seems they're havin' a real back 'n forth," Alistair said before widening his eyes and turning to Auber. "Oi! Cap'n!"

Auber, as if awakening from a dream, snapped his neck up. "What is it?"

"Ye've been a great fairer o' the sea fer some time, right?"

"What of it?"

"Surely ye've encountered a beast like tha one Aldous is fightin'. Is thar anythin' we can do?" Alistair asked.

"Erm…" the captain muttered, frantically searching for any excuse in his repertoire to avoid such a fight. "Naw, mate. The kraken be far too dangerous, even fer fearsome pirates. They can sink a ship with ease."

"I thought as much," Triston said, crossing his log-sized arms. "Even if ya are pirates, yer still human. Only a Wizard could battle such a creature an' live ta tell tha tale!"

"More importantly, Aldous has his hands tied at the moment. It doesn't seem he'll be able to provide us with that great wave for a distraction. What do we do?" Franco asked.

"Wasn't tha backup plan ta confront 'em head-on, so tha others could attack from tha sides and back?" Alistair asked.

"True, but…" Triston trailed off while peeking outside the alley. "That formation looks familiar. I seem ta recall it havin' a weakness."

"Nonsense, brother!" Alistair argued back. "Dalton came up with this plan. He's a military expert! Thar's no way we know betta than him."

Triston lifted his bear-inspired mask and scratched his nose. His brow twitched for a few moments before relaxing, and then he shrugged. "I suppose yer right."

"Tha only answer is fer Cap'n Auber ta lead us into battle!" Alistair cried with a raised fist.

Auber's stomach groaned and twisted to the tune of his increasing heartbeat. "Well, I-"

He was interrupted by the brief cries of men, followed by some loud splashes out at sea near dock six. A great fear burrowed into his mind. "Wh-what was that noise?"

Franco shrugged. "It's not important. What *is* important is saving Amis. One act of bravery to save this city, sir. I believe in you."

"Oh…" Auber muttered, a cold sweat beginning to gather on his brow. "That might be the nicest thing ye ever said to me, Franco."

"I believe in ye too, cap!" Ebbie added with balled fists and a child-like smile. "Can't wait to see what yer truly capable of in battle!"

Some anxious laughs escaped the captain's quivering lips. "Uhh, well, about that-"

"I think I speak fer us all when I say that I'm gonna feel invincible with tha great Cap'n Auber by me side! So what if they gots dozens o' bloodthirsty men? We'll crush 'em with our fightin' spirit!" Alistair said.

Auber narrowed his eyes and held up a hand as his stomach churned a little more. "Let's not get carried away, now-"

"I gotta admit that with a mighty pirate cap'n by me lil' brother's side, I feel he's safer," Triston said, giving the captain a hard slap on the shoulder. His jolly expression suddenly turned serious, however. "Don' go lettin' me down, mistah pirate."

"I-I… won't?" More nervous laughs gave way to the dripping sweat on his nose tip falling into his mouth. Auber fell into a coughing fit as the others looked at him in concern.

"Are you alright, sir?" Franco asked, patting him on the back.

"Y-yeh…" he said, wiping his mouth and clearing his throat.

Of course, he wasn't truly alright. That approaching group, armed to the teeth and ready to kill, would slaughter him, he thought. And all so he could impress a few landlubbers. It was such an unbearable situation: Either march out to his death or reveal that he was nowhere near the legend they all thought he was. Would his pride be able to handle the loss of so many wide-eyed followers who looked up to him? *No*, he thought. He had to lead by example, whether he liked it or not.

"Just one act of bravery…" the captain muttered before drawing in a final, fearful breath. With that, he erased his doubts and replaced them with double the prideful enthusiasm. For now, he would play the pirate he always wished to be, and prayed that it would be enough to survive the night. "Awright, lads! We go to battle! Let's show them landlubbers what the Strangers are capable of!"

Auber drew his saber and raised it in triumph. The excitement was contagious, and everyone else raised their weapons and tapped blades as a show of fellowship.

~

Angus smirked as much as his stone face would allow when he and his group reached dock seven. Although his enemies had been foiled by the kraken attacking Aldous, he was surprised that they hadn't attacked in some desperate attempt to retrieve the prisoner. Or perhaps, he thought, they had split up and were searching for him in different parts of the city.

His thoughts were interrupted when something caught his eye on the path ahead, however. The giant stopped and raised his bent arm as a signal. The group behind him halted, and chatter began to pick up.

Standing before Angus, just before dock six, was a man in a dark mask that was attached to a pirate hat atop his head. With a patchy beard, baggy clothes, and a saber that refused to settle in his rickety hand, the man before him hardly seemed like a pirate. In fact, the supposed pirate before him was quivering in his boots so much that his knees looked ready to buckle.

"And who do we have here?" Angus asked.

"Just a passerby," he squeaked out.

"A passerby who turns his weapon to us?" Angus asked as he made a fist, his knuckles cracking loud enough to echo over the crashing waves and whipping tentacles behind. "I'll splatter you in less than a second, you worm."

The pirate took a deep breath, and his shivering ceased. A cocky grin came to his face as he pointed his blade forward. Out from the alleyway to his right strode Alistair and a few others whom Angus did not recognize. Each of the men wore themed masks and had already drawn their weapons.

"Ye won't be passin' this here dock," the pirate said, his courage and ferocity shining through like a roaring lion.

Angus snickered. "Is that so? Says who?"

"So say the Strangers: You landlubbers have gone far enough! Release the prisoner and I *might* let ye escape with yer life!"

CHAPTER 19
HELPING HANDS

"*That idiot*," Dalton said in a harsh whisper as Auber and the others faced down Angus' team. Conrad and Lucia couldn't help but giggle in the background.

"He actually confronted them?" a calm voice asked from the shadows behind.

The trio turned with weapons drawn and ready to defend. Kabel, Dhogron, and Rolf revealed themselves and a collective sigh of relief was shared by all.

"I had hoped he would give in to that timid nature of his and stand down," the warrior said with a grimace.

Lucia shook her head while letting out a snorting chuckle. "As I said, the big-mouth would never allow that to happen."

"We cannot dwell on this for long," Conrad said, urgently. "What is our next course of action?"

"Indeed. It will only be a matter of time before bloodshed occurs," said Dhogron.

"We don't have enough manpower to break through that circle. The best we can do is two columns of three, or three columns of two," Kabel said, his posture slumping. "Even if we did break through, most of us would die in the process."

Dalton held up a finger. "That's *if* they are facing us and know we are coming."

"So, we use de others as a distraction?" Rolf asked.

"Given our situation, it's the best option."

"I see... we could wait until the first sign of battle, then strike," Kabel said with hope returning to his voice. "That would poke a hole at least halfway through their defenses before they even know what hit 'em."

"Try not to deal fatal blows when we penetrate the circle," Lucia said while donning her moon-inspired mask. "Many of these people are slaves being forced to carry out Sampson's will."

"Now is not the time to worry about such things," Conrad said with crossed arms. "We only get one chance at this. It's them, or us."

Rolf narrowed his eyes and started for the strategist, and Dalton knew why: He had once been a slave. Thankfully, he did not have to intervene. Instead, Kabel put a hand to Rolf's chest, halting him. The lanky young man seemed to immediately understand that now was not the time for quarrelling, and dropped his aggressive posture.

The group of six ran into the shadows, crossing into a new alleyway that was closer to Angus' squad. The plan was to attack from behind and at an angle, when Auber's group and the dark forces began fighting.

Just before dock six, there was a tense silence about the air. Auber had made some bold claims in his attempts to stop the malicious group, and Angus returned a murderous glare that sapped the strength out of him.

After what felt like an eternity, Angus finally ended the quiet with some low-pitched laughter. As his laughs began, the rest of his group joined along until it became a series of feverish cackles.

Alistair's skin audibly strained against the shaft of his battle axe, yet his flush, round face strained even more. "QUIET, YA BUNCHA KNOBS!"

To Auber's surprise, the rowdy crowd obeyed.

Angus scoffed. "Why even bother wearing a mask if you're gonna give yourself away so quickly, fat-head?"

"Listen here, meat-stain!" Alistair called out, pointing his axe at him. "Be rude ta me all ya want, but I won't let ya laugh at the mighty Cap'n Auber like that!"

Auber looked back to the big man with the fear of God in his eyes. *Why?* Why did he have to say his name aloud in front of their enemies?

"Oh?" Angus cocked his head. "Never heard of him."

"I don' expect a bog-barren oaf like yerself ta know much of anything," Alistair said with a potent mixture of pride and mockery on his tongue. Next, he made a grand gesture toward the captain, like a subject presenting his king. "This man here happens ta be tha one who struck down yer *precious* Sampson with an arrow! He is an expert marksman, but an even betta swordsman!"

Captain Auber let loose noises from his mouth that resembled desperate gurgles. He wanted to tell Alistair to shut up, but he was paralyzed by both fear and pride. Now, he was a dead man for sure.

"Well then, I suppose I'll take him in alive after we've slaughtered the rest of you cretins," Angus said. Auber took in a monstrous gulp of dread. "I'm sure Sampson would love to add a famous pirate to his collection of slaves."

"You'll never take 'im alive, swine!" Ebbie called out in a rage.

Auber felt his heart skip a beat. Death or enslavement? Neither prospect enticed him. Still, to go out with some pride was better than cowering. There was no escape now, he thought.

Angus reached into his cloak and retrieved a sword. Auber leaned in. Everything, from the blade to the hilt, was white.

"Why have I come across so many odd-colored swords, of late?"

"Careful, Cap'n! That thar sword is made of his bone, an' it's harder than steel!" Alistair said while planting his feet and taking a crouched stance. "Nothin' you can't handle, of course! If you can withstand luxmortite, then ol' meat-stain's sword should be no problem!"

Oh, come on, he thought with an internal groan. It was bad enough that the odds favored his death, but now it seemed that even if he survived the night, his prior *white lies* would be exposed. He regretted ever making up that story about besting a luxian in combat.

Angus pointed his bone blade at the Strangers. As he opened his mouth to give the probable command to attack, however, some screams echoed from out at sea, and they were followed closely by splashes. All darted their eyes out to the water in confusion, for the battle between Aldous and the Kraken should not have been so close to them. Auber gasped when he picked up on some unfamiliar men thrashing about in the water. He had expected it to be Joel and Giles, escaping from the intense battle back by dock nine, but these men were different; in fact, he could have sworn that there was a red glow to their eyes.

"What the hell?" Angus asked aloud.

As everyone else was looking out to sea, Auber caught a blur of red, white, and metallic gray rushing past him in his peripheral vision. He turned his attention forward to see Triston charging the unsuspecting dark forces with his great sword drawn back and ready for a devastating swing.

"Attack!" the elder MacRae shouted.

The Strangers took stuttered steps forward before turning them into full, confident strides. Angus and the others turned their attention back to them, their collective eyes wide and mouths agape at the brazen offensive. The giant pushed some of his men ahead while he sunk further into the formation.

"Hold the line!" he commanded.

EVEN WITH THE number advantage and his superior dark essence-fueled abilities, Angus' strategy was one of caution. He couldn't be sure how or why some of the Bosfueras townsfolk had been flung out to sea, and it filled him with worry. His first thought was that some other magical element aside from Aldous was at play. In that case, it was probably for the best to fall back and let the grunts take on the *mere humans* charging them, while he waited for the true threat to rear its ugly head. Anyone who wished to take the prisoner would have to go through him directly.

The giant's thoughts were interrupted by a *whoosh*, followed closely by a small wind brushing past his shoulder. His eyes picked up on an arrow flying through the thick of the group until it struck one of the men in his back. The man on the frontline gasped aloud in surprised pain before falling to his knees. Angus turned back with sharp eyes to see that it had been one of Sampson's slaves that let loose the arrow. With the aura of an enraged bear, he walked over to the marksman and stabbed him in the gut with his bone blade. Gasps sounded off in the crowd as the stabbed slave was lifted from his feet, legs twitching and sword still in his stomach, for all to see. He wheezed and coughed up blood before going limp, far above Angus' head.

"Only fire if you have a clean shot. *This* is what awaits overzealous fools," Angus said as he tossed the corpse away like a hunk of meat. The group did not complain or even mutter a word. Nods and loud gulps of nervousness were all that they could muster.

∼

AT THE FRONT of the formation, Alistair made the first move by swinging his battle axe into the crowd of opponents. Metal clashed with metal like an unbearably loud bell to signify the beginning of a chaotic skirmish.

The slaves at the front line swung sabers back at the big redhead, but Ebbie and Franco jumped in to defend their ally, blocking with their own blades. Ebbie in particular swung back with great vigor using several bends of his wrist. He seemed well-suited to battling crowds as opposed to dueling, which brought a battle-hungry smile to Alistair's round face as he, too, continued swinging wildly with his weapon.

Triston, with his great sword, swung into a group of slaves and knights. With his blade's long reach, they were all forced to defend. Before they could respond with anything, the elder MacRae angled his wrists the other way for a follow-up attack. This time, he struck a knight, but his sword merely *clanged* aloud as it grazed off of shoulder armor. Still, he continued his serpentine swings, allowing him to keep his distance from potential attackers.

The gargantuan swings of Triston's great sword had caused such a commotion that some of the men within the circle broke formation and approached to help their comrades. Alistair wanted to break free from the confines of his skirmish; to prove himself to his brother up close, but there were simply too many enemies. Stopping his attacks for even a moment almost guaranteed death. However, tucked underneath his cloak, bouncing against his leg in the heat of battle, lay his secret weapon: the wind Rune. Was it worth the risk to attempt using it now, though? There was no guarantee that it would work, and-

"Hold formation!" Angus' husky voice called out from the middle of the pack. Relief settled in Alistair's heart as the slaves stopped in their tracks and returned to their spots in the circle.

Captain Auber jumped into the fray, on Alistair's left, with several slashes of his saber. Now, the big man's relief turned to excitement. To fight alongside this man; this veritable legend, brought out an unquenchable fighting spirit within. He felt unbeatable.

"Take that, ye dirty dog!" the captain said with a stab attempt. He gasped as the blow landed in the lower-left midsection of a slave, who gasped out in pain and fell to the ground. "Oh… erm… s-sor-"

"That's Cap'n Auber for ya!" Alistair said with a stupid grin as he took another swing of his axe. "Already got tha first kill out of us all!"

"Aw! I almost had one of 'em!" Triston complained between breaths. His swings of the great sword had worked up a mighty sweat around and beneath the bear-inspired mask.

In the alleyway just before dock seven, Dalton and the others watched from the shadows. Each sub-team had lined up next to one another to make two groups of three. Dalton stood next to Kabel, Lucia rubbed shoulders with Rolf, and Conrad was alongside Dhogron.

"What are we waiting for?" Lucia asked, her tone sharp enough to cut stone.

"I didn't expect things to play out this way," Dalton replied without looking back.

"Why so cryptic?" Rolf asked.

Kabel looked back with a scowl. "Do you really wanna hear more about military formation and strategy? That information would be wasted on you anyway, dolt."

"Hey! Dat was uncalled for!" he shot back, shoving him. Kabel glared back and cocked his fist.

"Let's not fight amongst ourselves, now…" Dhogron said, holding up both hands and bobbing them.

"If not now, then when *do* we attack?" Conrad asked.

"That big fella is a better strategist than I thought," Dalton said with a chuckle. "I was certain that, given his opponents, he would unleash some waves of his men to try and kill 'em quickly. Instead, he is conserving them; letting each layer fight to wear Auber and the others down. It's almost as if…"

"He knows there are more of us to come," Conrad concluded.

"Yeh, it seems that way," Kabel said.

"There is no choice but to wait until Auber's group is worn down. That is when Angus will send more men in for the kill, I'd imagine," Dalton said.

"Why not call that what it is?" Lucia asked with crossed arms. "We are *sacrificing* them if we go through with this plan. They'll die while we attempt to break through the formation."

The warrior let out a sigh. "You're right, but what other option do we have? If we go out there and attack from the other side, their conservative defense will hold us at bay, just as it is doing against Auber's team."

"Or at least, they'll keep us back long enough to defeat the others, and then bring their focus solely on us," Kabel said.

"If only we had a distraction…" Rolf muttered.

A snorting chuckle came from Dhogron, and all in the group looked at him with interest. "I may have something…"

OUTSIDE THE SEWER pipe dumping into the sea, Aldous and the kraken continued their furious battle, kicking up so much destructive water that bits of the city's foundations were beginning to crack and fall into the raging tides. Joel and Giles watched on in awe as the monster swung its tentacle so hard and fast that it sounded like a cracking whip fighting against the wind. The duo gasped when it cut through Aldous' midsection like a hot knife through butter, but the mute knew better than to doubt his Wizard cohort; for it was not blood that spattered from the impact, but more water.

Giles had picked up on it, too, as he looked to Joel with confusion in his eyes. The mute could certainly sign how he'd pulled off such a feat if he weren't so busy waving his submerged arms to stay afloat. Even then, Giles did not know USL, and miming or mouthing to him the explanation of how Aldous had mastered the element of water and could thereby become one with it would be difficult.

Of course, even the most powerful of master Elementals could only become one with their element for a short time, and it was a great drain on their reserves of magic, too. Aldous likely had a plan to finish the battle soon, he thought as a small flash of lightning forced him to shield his eyes.

Upon lowering his arm and regaining focus, Joel noticed something missing: Giles. He looked around in a panic, but saw nothing save mist and waves; remnants of the battle before him. Had Giles been attacked by another monster of the sea? As if to answer his question, the mute felt something clamp down on his ankle, and he winced, anticipating it to be a bite. However, as he was dragged down, he realized it to not be the jaws of a monster, but the grip of a hand. *Of course,* he thought, stinging eyes wide as he descended into the depths of the sea, little by little. He looked down to see a pair of red, glowing eyes staring back up at him.

Just ahead, Joel could make out two dark figures struggling under the surface, and again, one of them seemed to have red eyes. How could he have forgotten? Their attackers were none other than the two Bosfueras townsfolk who'd been swimming toward them, earlier.

With the pressure of held breath welling up in his chest, the mute reached to his hip for the luxmortite blade, but the red-eyed man violently jerked him further down and grabbed his wrist in the process. He tried to free his hand, but it was no use; the red-eyed man refused to relinquish his grip. He next attempted to contort his body so that his other hand could reach the hilt of the blade, but once again, his bid was thwarted by the Bosfueran tugging him back and forth, disorienting him.

Throughout the struggle, Joel wondered how the red-eyed man hadn't needed any air. It felt like both his chest and throat were about to burst, but his attacker showed no such stresses; only the cold, dark abyss of his single-mindedness shined through in his actions. He glanced over to see Giles and the other crazed man becoming subdued in their motions, and that's when it hit him: They never planned to come up for air. It was a suicide mission. Fear washed over Joel as he wriggled; a desperate bid to free himself, but every time it seemed he would gain ground, his attacker adjusted his grip and dragged him further into the depths.

Joel was at the end of his rope. He let out a few more bubbles from his mouth; the last gasp before he would inevitably take in water. Was this how it would end? After all he had been through? Killed while no one was watching?

In those moments of despair, a torrent of bubbles smacked him in the face, causing him to swallow a bit of water. However, he resisted the temptation to take in any more of the disgustingly salty liquid, for in the commotion, he had somehow been freed from the grip of the red-eyed man. Though he could not see anything save the white of the bubbles that surrounded him, Joel clawed in a direction that he prayed was upward with what meager strength remained in his arms. Then, he burst out of the water's surface with an exhale so loud that he almost thought he'd recovered his voice. Alas, it was not so; he remained mute. On the bright side, at least he was still alive.

After regaining his bearings, Joel turned with an appreciative smile, expecting to see a triumphant Aldous hovering over him on a water plume. However, to his inaudible shock, the old Wizard was still in the midst of battle with the kraken. If it wasn't Aldous, then who had saved him?

Before he could ponder any further, Giles' body burst from the water, limp as a beached fish. Carrying him over his shoulder was a figure that did not look human. If it wasn't human, and it had the cunning and speed to comfortably rescue them while underwater, then it had to be a marinian, Joel reasoned.

The shining, crescent moon above helped illuminate the marinian for Joel to see when turning to him. He had no hair, but instead a rough, alligator-like skin. His eyes were dark at the center, but they appeared to have intricate designs around the pupil. The mute could make out webbed hands grasping Giles' shoulder, and the bottom half of his face was similar to a pushed-in snout.

Joel cocked his head as the marinian pushed Giles' body through the water and into his arms. He then spun his limp body in place, so that it faced him. The mute let out an inaudible gasp as the mysterious creature straightened out his webbed fingers and pulled his arm back, as if ready to stab.

He quickly dispelled the possibility that the marinian was trying to attack Giles, though. Otherwise, why would he have bothered to save them in the first place? Instead, he held his body steady, hoping that whatever was about to happen would revive his downed friend.

Swiftly, the marinian stabbed his hand forward and struck Giles where his chest and stomach met. In reaction, he heaved forward and vomited water. Joel patted him on the back as he hacked and yacked. When his coughing fit came to an end, Giles looked back to Joel, then forward to his rescuer.

"Y-you saved me... thank you..." he muttered, near-breathless. "But... who are you?"

The marinian cocked his head, then cracked a smile on his short snout and approached the shocked pair. Joel couldn't help but notice that the smile was comprised of rows of sharp teeth.

"Ah, so *that* is your language," he said in a low, gravelly voice. "I am Prince Xviktolo. It's nice to greet you."

"'Nice to greet' us?" Giles asked, looking at Joel with a knowing smile. "I think you meant, 'Nice to *meet* you.'"

The marinian pointed his webbed finger and smiled. "That's it; that is what I meant! It is a real hurt to memorize the human languages."

A snorting chuckle escaped Giles' nose. "'A real *pain*', you mean."

"Right, right."

Joel could understand how it might be tough. The beginning of his name sounded like the hiss of a snake, so it seemed that his language was far different than most human tongues.

"I am Giles, and this is Joel," he said, pointing to the mute.

"Jah… jaaah…" Xviktolo began, flaring his flat, wide lips out. "Ja-hiles… Jow-el…"

Joel and Giles looked at each other once more and smiled. There was an obvious language barrier, and it served as a much-needed moment of levity. However, such a moment brought with it a reminder of why some lightheartedness was needed: Joel turned his attention back to the battle ongoing between Aldous and the kraken. He then tapped Giles' shoulder and pointed to the conflict.

"Oh, right…" he said, turning to the marinian prince. "We are grateful for your help, but might we ask you for one more favor?"

"If it's about the other two humans, I tried to save them, but they attacked me. I had to let them go," Xviktolo replied.

Giles shook his head and smiled. "No, no, those fellers were bad. They were tryin' to kill us. I was gonna ask if you could help our friend."

He pointed to the clash between Aldous and the kraken.

"I see…" the marinian said as he pulled a weapon from underwater. It was a sword of crystalline nature, reflecting beautifully off the waves and the light of the moon. It reminded Joel of a gem, but how could a blade be made of something so brittle? "That man is bothering the kraken? I have little tolerance for those who harm innocent creatures."

Joel held his hands up in protest, and so too did Giles.

"No, it is the kraken who attacked us! That man over there is a Wizard. He would stop attacking if only the kraken would stand down."

"Don't you mean, 'stand up'?" Prince Xviktolo said while rubbing where his chin would have been, were he a man. Instead, it was more like the bottom of his snout. Giles only flashed a half-hearted smile and shrugged. "Anyhow, I think that I can calm her down."

Xviktolo dove underwater, and the remaining duo watched on as his powerful stream somewhat parted the water on his way to the battle.

Giles looked to Joel, and something about his expression told him he was about to ask something unanswerable.

"How does he know it's a 'her'?"

Like many other times that night, the mute could only shrug. The pair watched on as Xviktolo shot through the water like a speeding arrow, then got between Aldous and the kraken. The creature immediately stopped flailing her tentacles as the marinian held out his hand. Aldous had also ceased attacking.

Joel and Giles gasped when the kraken extended her tentacle out for Xviktolo to pet. She let out a low-pitched gurgle, then lowered the other tentacles. The marinian prince looked up at the sea creature, smiling. They remained silent for some time, with only the breaking waves of the tide and the *clings* and *clangs* of the battle above to serve as tension-breaking noise in the background. Joel couldn't put his finger on why, but he felt that they were communicating in some way. Nevertheless, the battle had ceased, and it seemed like peace had come upon the combatants, so Joel and Giles swam over to them.

～

Aldous lowered his water jet so that he was nearly at sea level. "Excuse me?"

The sea-dweller turned to face him, still petting the kraken's tentacle. "Yes?"

"Might you be marinian royalty?"

"You are correct," he said, turning back to the kraken. "I am Prince Xviktolo of the Coralstar Kingdom."

"I thank you, Prince," he said with a gracious bow. "I am Aldous, a Wizard of the Council. Might I ask what brings you here tonight?"

It was not lost on him that there was a battle going on further up the docks, but in this chance meeting, he saw opportunity. If what he suspected was true, Xviktolo could turn the tide of the battle and make Angus' number advantage meaningless.

"It may surprise you to learn that my kind have a distaste for the kraken, despite being fellow creatures of the sea. The reason that there are so few attacks on ships these days is that the marinians nearly wiped them out," Xviktolo said. "When I noticed this kraken venturing into Coralstar territory, I knew that she would be hunted down and killed. But I found that despite her intimidating appearance, she was peaceful… unless someone were to enter her domain."

"Oho! I found that out the hard way," Aldous attempted to clank his walking stick off the ground, but he had forgotten that he stood upon a geyser, and the result was a squirting of seawater that flew backward, showering an approaching Joel and Giles.

"Like any other creature, she needs to eat. So, once in a while, I visit the coast to bring her food, but only at night. That is the only time she ever seems to leave her dwelling," the marinian said.

"You know why she is so protective of her domain, don't you?"

He nodded. "I can communicate with her through the *sound of the sea.*"

"I knew it! So, you can understand her thoughts, can you not?" Aldous asked with excitement building up in his chest.

The prince rubbed his lower snout. "How can I say this in man-speak? It is more like I can understand her feelings, and through that, I can communicate with her."

"Well then, I'm sure you know that she is guarding something of the utmost importance. Something that could change the very fabric of this world in the wrong hands."

"Perhaps… that is not how she describes it. She guards this 'something' out of a sense of loyalty and duty; a love for her master," Xviktolo said while shaking his head. "I've never understood it. He doesn't even *feed* her."

"Nevertheless, it *is* important to her," Aldous said.

Xviktolo turned around and asked, "What's your tip?"

"Erm… I believe you mean, 'What's your point'…"

"Right, that is what I meant."

Aldous pointed to the ongoing battle down by dock six. "See that large group in the circular formation? They wish to infiltrate the sewers and destroy that which she guards. They have taken prisoner someone who holds a map that would allow them to reach what she protects. Help us by letting her know; and together, we can stop them!"

The marinian gazed upon him with uniquely patterned eyes that normally would have been a wonder to behold, but they were far too piercing at the moment to drink in their beauty. He swam up to him and held a hand out. Aldous cocked his head.

"You want my help, don't you? All you must do is sway my hand."

Despite Xviktolo's humorous butchering of human sayings, Aldous felt a wave of nervousness sweep over him. It was the fear of the unknown. Timidly, he accepted the invitation and felt the roughness of Xviktolo's skin as they shook hands.

"I see…" Xviktolo said with closed eyes before cracking a sharp-toothed smile. "Alright, I'll help you."

Aldous let out a sigh of relief, then widened his eyes. "Were you reading my emotions?"

"Indeed," the marinian said as he swam back over to the kraken. He grabbed the creature's tentacle and began using the sounds of the sea to communicate.

The old Wizard looked over to his cohorts, who shared a look of bewilderment that made him chuckle.

"I know that this is Joel's first time meeting a marinian," Aldous said, looking to the mute with a grandfatherly smile. He then turned his gaze to Giles. "How about you?"

"No, never. It's strange; like he's from another world."

"We live in strange times indeed, my friends. The marinians rarely involve themselves in human affairs, but if we are lucky…" Aldous trailed off as he looked to see the kraken shake her tentacles aggressively, as if angered or shocked. "That just may happen, tonight. I only hope that the others can hold on."

After some deliberation, Xviktolo approached the group, and behind him followed the kraken. "She has agreed to help. What would you like us to do?"

Aldous smiled and then leaned in. The tides were about to turn back in favor of the Strangers, he thought.

By dock six, Captain Auber's group continued their furious assault on Angus' team, but it proved to be a stalemate, and a stalemate was the same thing as a loss in their current situation. Worse yet, the Strangers were showing signs of fatigue, while the group of slaves and knights could simply cycle their formations to take the place of the wounded or tired.

Alistair, despite his earlier excitement, could feel the tides turning. He got the feeling that the enemy had gained control and were merely playing with their food. If they changed strategies and decided to go on the attack-

"Press forward! Flank from all sides!" Angus' husky voice echoed, as if reading his mind.

He gasped between tired breaths and swings of his battle axe. Earlier, they might have weathered such a storm, but now, they were sitting ducks; too tired to fight back with anything more than half-hearted defense.

"We must retreat!" Triston called out, his normally bombastic voice hoarse. He attempted to keep the rushing enemy at bay with a lengthy swing of his great sword, but it was in vain; slaves had already begun surrounding them.

"Retreat!" Auber's panicked voice cried over many loud *clangs*.

If even the mighty fairer of the sea was worried, then they were in trouble, Alistair thought. The Strangers began to fall back, but the slaves and knights had created a new circle around them before they could gain any true distance. Alistair, feeling the pressure, gripped the wind Rune under his cloak. Was now the time to use his secret weapon?

"Get behind me, Ali!" Triston called out, to which Alistair's stomach sank.

Now was the time to prove himself; that he *could* be useful in combat. Triston was being overprotective. His brother and many before had never given him the credit he deserved, but that was all about to change.

Gripping the wind Rune with a nervous ferocity, Alistair revealed the magical stone from under his cloak. "Brother! *You* get behind *me*! I'm about ta show ya how it's done!"

Triston cocked his head as a couple of slaves dashed forward and swung their sabers at him.

"Ali! No!"

Alistair pushed the wind Rune outward and closed his eyes. He concentrated on his emotions, as Joel had recommended. The big man used his sheer force of will to visualize the wind, and then let it out in a burst that erupted like a vicious clap of thunder.

Lightheaded and ears ringing, Alistair opened his eyes to find that he was soaring backward through the air. In that brief moment, he couldn't help but wonder what had happened. Dizziness overtook him until the sobering reality hit when he crashed into whoever was behind him.

After a few moments, the big man shook the cobwebs out and looked over his shoulder to see that not only had he taken down several of his own teammates, but some of the knights and slaves who'd been flanking them, too. His eyes then turned forward to find a couple of blades pointed at his face. It wasn't like before, he thought. Why had the wind Rune knocked *him* back? Alistair sulked. He hadn't saved the day; he hadn't helped. He had worsened their situation.

In the pile of bodies, Franco raised his saber and waved it around like a white flag. "We surrender!"

The men who had their blades pointed at Alistair looked back at their formation for instruction.

"Take the one in the pirate hat as a prisoner, alive. As for the rest..." Angus trailed off with a red glint in his eye and a wicked smile. "Kill them. Kill them now."

Cheers erupted from Angus' team as the men before Alistair raised their blades for the final blow.

"No! Get away from him, ya boggin filth!" Triston cried, trying to struggle free. It took six men to hold him back.

As the sabers chopped down, Alistair felt dread creep up his spine. He looked down and closed his eyes, unable to face the finishing blow. Perhaps his brother was right. No matter how hard he tried, he was substandard on the battlefield.

Alistair winced as he felt wind from the swing of the blades slap him in the face. Instead of chopped flesh, however, he heard a series of *dings*: metal striking metal. Next came the sound of steel *clanking* off the ground, bouncing like coins that had been dropped.

The big man opened his eyes and gasped to see his attackers still standing over him, both with broken blades in hand. Had that slap of wind actually been his savior? The Rune? *No*, he thought while looking down. It showed no signs of activation. Could an arrow have flown across and cracked the sabers? If that were the case, he thought, it would only crack one blade at most. To cut through both at once could only have meant one thing.

Finally, Alistair's eyes caught on to a glow between the slaves and himself: Protruding from the ground, like a majestic monument, was a dark blue dagger. It was longer than most such blades but shorter than a sword. The jewel just before the hand guard gleamed beneath an intoxicating blue aura that surrounded the blade and drew attention from all around. Based on the trajectory, Alistair looked up and to his right, and so too did the men who had attempted to kill him.

Standing atop the stone building's edge, cross-armed and bathing in crescent moonlight, was Pierce Thaeon. His inverted, two-faced mask held a pale frown with its vague features, striking a pang of fear into Alistair's chest. *The other*? *No*, he thought with a relieved breath and wide smile. While it may have been frowning, the right-side-up face of his Ometos mask held a sad, sorrowful expression. The malicious, grinning expression of the mask was upside-down. His left hand pooled blood into the sleeve of his cloak, and it had begun dripping onto the face of the building below. Yet, that bloody, helping hand had been sorely needed. Now, perhaps, the tides could turn back in the Strangers' favor.

CHAPTER 20
CHAOS

Angus glared up at Pierce with as much disdain as his stone face was able to show. That damned Ometos had been a thorn in his side for too long; another cockroach to be squashed, he thought.

The giant pointed up at the masked luxian and shouted, "Fire upon him!"

Marksmen of the group drew their arrows back and aimed at the rooftop where he stood, unflinching. Pierce tilted his head before revealing a Rune stone from under his cloak. A dark, glowing swirl was engraved upon its smooth surface.

Realizing what it was, Angus turned back to his men with urgency in his eyes. "Halt! Belay that order!"

It was too late: All of the arrows had been let loose and were already passing overhead. Angus turned his gaze back to the rooftop, the wind of the soaring projectiles fluttering his hair like sails on a ship. He could only watch on, helpless, as Pierce held the Rune out in response to the rapidly approaching volley. A rift in the air quickly shaped into a dark, swirling vortex, blotting out the masked luxian. Most of the arrows flew into the portal, and after taking notice of the starry night sky darkening, Angus looked up just in time to see that another vortex had appeared above a section of his team. A rain of arrows fell upon them, and soon after, the streets rumbled in the wake of bloody cries as limb, body, and armor alike were filled with arrow-heads, slices, and holes.

There was no time for Angus to assess the damage because Pierce wasn't done: He pointed at his dagger, and then at the giant. The blade pulsated a bright blue before dislodging itself from the ground, and then, like the fastest of arrows, it launched through the formation and parted the sea of men.

Angus turned to face the immense force and swung the bone blade with all of his might. The resulting clash reminded him much of the blast of wind that *ol' big-head* had hit him with back in Thironas, but this time, he'd been prepared: He stumbled back a few steps and his ears rung unbearably, but he had otherwise weathered the attack perfectly. He snorted as the luxmortite dagger floated back to its owner.

Pierce grasped the blade by its hand guard, then floated down from the building to the side of the Strangers, who, after all of that commotion, had regained their footing and begun to fend off the men surrounding them.

The giant grimaced. That Summoner Rune could have only meant one thing: The splashes and cries from out at sea had been Pierce's handiwork. His reserve of Bosfueras townsfolk, hidden within several of the stone buildings lining the road, was gone. Or at least, *some* of them were. The front line had been broken, and there were several injuries from the rain of arrows. He needed to regain control of the situation. Perhaps it was time for him to step in and kill one of the enemies himself, he thought.

However, a riling up of the men behind drew his attention. He turned to see members of his group shouting at someone.

"More rats in the streets..." Angus muttered. He gazed past the crowd to see a man in a turban standing still as the night. He had no idea who it was, but if there was even a possibility that this man was allied with the Strangers, then he couldn't chance letting him walk. "Kill him!"

Several men dashed ahead with sabers drawn, yet the man in the turban didn't move a muscle. The first of the slaves to reach him slashed down and diagonal at his torso, but to the gasps of all nearby, the man in the turban contorted and seemed to *float* while avoiding the attack. More men took swings to no avail. Like whimsical paper in the wind, he dodged each attempt.

After a barrage of attacks, one of the slaves finally connected with a stab to the gut.

"Got 'im!"

His elation was short-lived, however. Instead, he and the others grunted and cocked their heads as the man in the turban jutted backward and folded into the sword at its tip. Beneath the smacking tide of the sea, Angus could swear that he heard a crumpling noise, similar to paper. In fact, it did indeed appear that his men had been hacking away at mere paper, somehow; even though it had looked exactly like a man just moments ago.

The giant gripped the hilt of his bone blade until it burned his hand. "Just what in the world is going on-"

Then, out of nowhere, Angus caught wind of *yet another problem*: Dalton Rayleigh and a stocky man whom he did not recognize led a furious charge, at an angle, into the back of the circular formation. Each of them led two others in a line, and he quickly recognized Lucia and Conrad among them. That had not surprised him, but upon laying eyes on the man in the turban once more, he couldn't help but gasp and become even more confused. What sort of devilry was this?

No time to ponder, he thought as the two groups of three cut through the back lines of his circular formation. Of course, the men had been caught unprepared thanks to the many distractions going on around them, and the Strangers had breached them with ease. However, in the chaos of their offensive, Angus picked up on a potential weakness: The stocky man smashed his round shield into some unsuspecting slaves and knights, while Dalton attacked with the butt of his sword. They were avoiding fatal blows, and such a weak-minded strategy could surely be used against them, he thought. A smirk came to his stone face. He couldn't help but wonder where *Joel* was, in all of this.

His amusement soon turned to fury, as his enemies had cut deep into the formation, and were headed straight for the prisoner. So too had his pride been cut deep, for all that had transpired reflected on him poorly as leader. Things had gone far enough, he thought. Any more elements introduced would be pure chaos, and he needed to get the situation under control before that happened.

Angus mustered the strongest of his group: Barret, Catalina, and Job; and they surrounded Amis while awaiting the fast-approaching Strangers. They left many grounded men in their wake. The brazen group was near, now, and the giant had seen enough. Merely killing them would not do the job. He wanted to strike fear into their hearts before death.

He raised his bone blade with a ferocious battle cry as Dalton and his stocky ally skidded to a stop and looked up at him with terror in their eyes. However, in the split-second before deciding to bring his sword down, Angus noticed two things of great importance: One was that the men before him were not looking *at him* but *past him*. The other was a great shadow that loomed over them all, wrapping the battle-field in a blanket of black so tightly that it took his breath away.

Angus looked over his shoulder, mouth agape, to find a tidal wave that towered above all. It was already starting to break over the shore-line, giving him mere seconds to escape when he would need much more to avoid the great, unstoppable wall of water before him.

"Brace yourselves!" Dalton cried.

Those were the last words Angus heard before the harsh, salty water shot into his eyes and up his nose. His whole world became blue and began spinning, and he knew it was because he and the others had been washed away like helpless ants caught in a river.

Then, his flailing body struck something hard, stopping him cold as the heavy tide continued to pin him down. Though his head had taken some damage, he could feel it regenerating already, and now the water was receding. He opened his hazy eyes to find that he was sitting up against one of the many stone buildings lining the street. The tide was at his shoulders, but quickly lowered as it drained back out to sea.

With the sting of the salt leaving his eyes, his vision cleared and the carnage was revealed: None were left standing, not even his other dark essence-enhanced cohorts. Angus stood with wobbly knees and scanned the area for the prisoner. He spotted him lying on the ground, near an alley. Several limp bodies surrounded him, including Conrad, who sat up against a wall that his blood had been trickling down.

This was an opportunity, Angus thought, to kill one of his enemies and retrieve the prisoner. He would have to hurry, though: The tidal wave had certainly been Aldous' handiwork, and while that was meant to signal the Bosfueran reserves hidden in nearby buildings to attack, he couldn't be sure how many Pierce had disposed of. As he started for his target, however, something slimy struck him from behind; a blow that sent him flying through the air and into some of his men.

Despite the inhuman strength of the impact knocking a couple of men unconscious, Angus returned to his feet with little damage. He looked back to face his attacker, and yet another surprise awaited him. Sitting atop the ledge where land and sea met was what he believed to be a creature of legend: the kraken. It was far too large to be a mere octopus or squid, after all, and with the bad luck he'd encountered thus far, it almost made too much sense that a mythical ship-sinking monster would be attacking them.

The giant grimaced as the kraken's tentacles whipped around, striking any who dared to move or stand. Wanting to down his newest foe quickly, Angus made a cracking fist and pointed his arm at the sea monster. A sharp, white bone shot out of his forearm and flew toward it like an arrow.

The kraken let out a mighty squeal as the bone bolt pierced its mantle. Angus' arm dangled in a bloody mess while the bone and skin regenerated, as always. He then clenched his fist once more, preparing to fire another bolt, but something caught his eye, stilling the attack. Among the masses of struggling humanity on the streets, someone plowed through, charging straight for him. He was nearly as tall as Mur'del and wore a scaly tunic that glistened majestically in the moonlight with each lengthy stride. So too was his skin scaly, enough that it seemed more like the rough hide of some swamp creature. As this new foe drew closer, Angus came to realize that he was not human.

When within range, the marinian drew a crystalline sword. Angus smirked as he prepared his bone blade. His entire skeleton was capable of withstanding luxmortite. What could a brittle, if beautiful sword do against his own? The fool would never know what hit him. His eyes twitched as the marinian swung his weapon; for it was difficult to make out the exact trajectory of such a swing with all of the light refracting off of it.

Angus had judged that he would need to defend his upper right side, and he was correct: The blades clashed, and the big man scoffed in triumph, expecting the crystalline sword to break.

"What in the hell?" he muttered. The sword remained intact.

In the time that Angus had lowered his guard, the marinian brought his sword down and across for an unanswered slash to the midsection. The giant grunted and fell to a knee as his opponent pointed the crystal sword, dripping with blood, in his face.

"That sword… what is it made of?" Angus choked out as he held the gaping wound on his stomach. A waterfall of crimson spilled out.

"I was about to ask the very same of your white blade. I have never encountered a material that could withstand starlite," he replied.

"Star… light?" Angus asked, now feigning injury. He could feel the wound closing up.

"Ah, right. I suppose you wouldn't know what I'm talking about. It is a mineral that can only be found in my kingdom, after all," the marinian said.

"I see…" Angus trailed off while gripping his bone blade. "I'll be sure to make good use of it, then, after I kill you!"

The giant stood and simultaneously slashed with his bone, aiming for the marinian's upper body, but the surprise attack was blocked just in time. Despite his starlite sword being able to withstand the impact, the blow saw him stumbling back and onto his bottom. Angus took long, aggressive strides and stood over the fallen sea-dweller to finish him off.

He raised his sword for the final strike, but in doing so, felt something wrap around his right ankle. Had it been the kraken? No, its tentacles were larger, he thought. His eyes darted down to see the marinian's tail, pulling at his ankle and taking his feet out from under him. The sea-dweller then rolled to his left and let out a screech as Angus plopped to the ground.

As he rushed back to his feet, Angus noticed a change in the battle-field: The kraken had stopped flailing its tentacles around. He turned to the shoreline and found that the sea monster was now leaning back, its horrid mouth agape. Like a geyser of water, a black substance shot out, aimed at him. Angus, stumbling in his panic, scurried away on all fours. The black liquid flew past him and skidded across the road, splashing onto some of the slaves along the way.

Angus' eyes twitched as the men writhed in agony, steaming as the terrible toxins melted through their flesh all the way to the bone. *Poison*, he thought with a grimace. Such a dangerous foe needed to be dealt with immediately, and as such, he turned and pointed all ten of his fingers at the kraken. With so many bone bolts flying at once, he was certain that at least *some* would hit a fatal spot.

However, he did not get a chance to unleash the devastating attack, for the enemy had launched the latest of their surprise offensives: In his peripheral vision, Angus caught wind of a screaming-fast water geyser, a mere arm's length away from striking him. With that, his world turned blue and he spun helplessly once more; though this time, much more painfully.

∽

JOEL, Aldous, and Giles floated up to land on their water plume. The old Wizard looked to his former kraken foe and nodded, to which the sea creature acknowledged him with a soft squeal. Joel surveyed the carnage resulting from the tidal wave and kraken attack. The nearby roads and buildings alike were soaked, and many lay on the ground; groaning, unconscious, or dead.

Aldous' most recent attack, though, had done the most damage. It had knocked Angus across the road and through the wall of a stone building, creating a gaping hole that seemed to threaten its stability. On the other hand, the powerful stream had almost certainly granted sweet release to the slaves writhing in agony from the toxins melting their skin.

Next, Joel's eyes fell upon a man who was slumped over, shackled, and chained near the building that Angus had been blasted into. That had to be Amis, he thought. Dalton and Kabel were close to the prisoner, but they appeared to have their hands full against a couple of Sigrian knights. The mute tugged on Aldous' sleeve and emphatically pointed to his discovery.

"No time to waste, my friends!" the old Wizard said, dashing ahead. Joel and Giles quickly fell in step with him. "Be on your guards!"

The mute continued to take in his surroundings as he ran, and that was when he caught wind of Lucia, Rolf, and Dhogron. They stood in a triangle, fending off attacks from all sides by a mixture of slaves and red-eyed folk. Joel still wasn't sure where the Bosfueras townsfolk had come from, but it was safe to say that they had joined the battle after the tidal wave crashed down. Most of the slaves were soaking wet and stumbling in their movements, while the same could not be said for the others.

As the group neared the growing number of skirmishes to their center-left, Prince Xviktolo joined them, his tail wiggling with each long stride.

"That one in shackles... he is the one you need to rescue?" he asked.

Aldous nodded as they entered the battlefield. The marinian called upon his starlite sword and clashed with a Bosfueras townsman wielding a wood axe. The axe head cracked under the strain, and an unbearably loud ringing brought Joel's shoulders up to his ears.

With that, Joel brought out his luxmortite sword. He'd been preparing for this inevitable moment; the moment where he'd have to fight again. Tonight, he would have to find the correct balance between playing defense and attacking. Disarmament was his goal, but if his blade absolutely needed to meet flesh, he had to keep in mind the vital points; to avoid them.

Quickly, his new battle strategy was put to the test, as a slave wildly swung a short sword in his direction. Joel stood firm and met his swing with far more grace, an ear-shattering *crack* ringing out over all else on the battlefield. The slave let out a confused grunt as his swinging sword collapsed in half, the tip *clanging* off the ground. Joel and the slave stared at each other for what felt like an eternity, but it likely only lasted a couple of seconds. *Now what*?

The slave started forward as Joel's mind scrambled for a non-lethal method of incapacitating him, but before it came to blows, a loud *zap* sounded off behind his opponent. His shoulders sizzled and lightly smoked as he gasped and fell forward; crashing to the ground to reveal Aldous, whose crackling, outstretched hand bellied a grandfatherly smile. Joel looked down to see that the slave was still breathing; the shock had merely knocked him out. *This is the way forward*, he thought: He could disarm the enemy, and then Aldous could finish them off without dealing a death blow.

And so the next series of battle went: Joel fended off attackers with superior technique and weaponry, and then Aldous finished them off with non-lethal shocks. In addition, Giles' wild flailing of the sword often caused enough of a distraction for Aldous to down those enemies by knocking them off the head with his walking stick.

Eventually, the group of four reached the heart of the battle, where the remaining Bosfueras townsfolk gathered to surround and secure the prisoner. They wielded basic weapons such as pitchforks and wood axes, but those small details fell out of focus when a peculiar glint caught Joel's eye: Many of them carried black gold.

He nudged Aldous and pointed to the enchanting ore. The old Wizard gasped as he continued knocking their enemies away with fearsome swings of his walking stick.

"Whatever you do, avoid touching that black ore!" Aldous cried, in the heat of battle.

While their prior strategy had been effective in warding off the slaves, the red-eyed folk and their wills of iron proved much tougher to keep down. As Conrad, Lucia, and Dalton had once described, they seemed nearly immune to pain or fear.

As Joel continued warding off his foes, he noticed a figure out of the corner of his eye. Angus emerged from the hole in the building, with rips in his tunic and dry blood decorating his torso and limbs. In one hand was his bone sword, and the other arm sported a thick shield grown from wrist to elbow, in a long, rectangular shape that was rounded at the top.

The giant did not mince words, dashing for a groggy Conrad, who had his back pressed against the wall and was struggling to reach his feet. Blood trickled down the building where he sat, and it appeared to have come from the back of his head.

With an inaudible gasp, Joel nudged Aldous in the direction of their fallen friend. Angus pulled his bone blade back, ready to lop the strategist's head off, but Aldous had other plans. He hurled his walking stick like a javelin, and before the giant could start his swing, it struck him in the head.

Angus grunted and fell to a knee as the walking stick *clanked* off the ground. Without hesitation, Giles let out a battle cry and rushed in as the next attacker. He slashed down and to his left, attempting to cut where the big man's neck and shoulder met. Angus swatted his attack away with the bone shield, albeit with little precision or grace.

Joel was now within range of a dazed and wide-open Angus. The mute had been taking care to only disarm and avoid direct contact with flesh, but that wouldn't work on this opponent. Before him was a man who'd regenerated from a blade chopping halfway into his torso; a man capable of restarting his heart after a blanket of lightning had covered him. Like the degenerates, Angus did not fear the loss of his life, and that rendered Joel's disarmament strategy powerless.

His eyes fell on Angus' exposed neck. All around him became silent as his grip tightened around the sword's handle. What other choice was there? If he didn't strike now, he'd be putting himself and Giles in grave danger. Yet, the ghosts of the past continued to haunt him, and he couldn't bring himself to lop off Angus' head. The best he could offer was a compromise; a painful distraction to hold him off until Aldous arrived.

Joel chopped his dark blue blade into Angus' shoulder at about half-force. The awful, squishy sound made his stomach churn, but even worse was the spurting blood as he ripped the sword out of the wound. How many times had he seen that at the academy? Or even in the past year? However, unlike his prior victims, the giant hadn't even flinched. Instead, it was as if he had been awakened from his daze.

Angus, still on a knee, dropped the white blade and pointed his left hand, fingers first, at Giles, while pointing his right at Joel. The mute realized what was going on just as the bones shot out of his fingers.

Letting his reflexes take over, Joel brought his sword up to face-level and angled it just in time to feel one of the bolts bounce off. The rest whistled past him.

"It's nice that I can always count on your cowardice when we battle. I wonder how your teammate feels, though…" Angus nudged his head toward Giles.

Joel shuddered while looking Giles over. Three bone bolts had pierced him: One on the lower torso, another stuck out of his arm, and most alarmingly, one had gouged his right eye.

Giles lifted a jittery hand and felt around where his right eye socket was. He gasped when his fingertips made contact with the leaking blood, and then held his hand out to see it painted red.

"Oh… oh no…" he muttered before rushing his hand back to feel the bone bolt sticking into his eye socket.

His shock was quickly replaced with pain and fear, as Giles fell to his bottom and let out a primal cry that seemed to alert many on the battlefield. However, all other Strangers were embroiled in battles of their own, so only Joel was left to clean up the mess. He gripped his sword as Angus approached his fallen friend with the bone blade in hand.

The mute was stricken by guilt. If he had attacked with his best effort, then Angus wouldn't have had the opportunity to cause such harm. His previous battle strategy had shown promise against most opponents, but Angus was a living, breathing rejection of such solutions; a veritable wall in the face of his desire to help while not killing. Joel's mind went blank. He kept searching for answers, but there was nothing.

Angus stood over Giles, who had curled up into a ball on the ground, shivering. He pulled his sword back, ready for the final thrust, but he had not noticed Conrad's recovery. The strategist, fueled by desperation in his daze, plunged his saber into the giant's ribs with all of his might.

With a grunt, Angus stopped his attack, and Conrad twisted his blade in the flesh wound before ripping it from his ribs.

The giant calmly turned to face him. "I could have sworn that your skull was cracked…"

Conrad frowned as the gaping wound closed before his very eyes, leaving only a few trails of blood in its wake.

"I suppose it shouldn't surprise me that a bottom-feeder like you took in the dark essence."

Angus scoffed. "Your words sting more than your pathetically weak blade. You are hardly even worth my time, but I seem to recall that back at Mt. Couture, you stabbed me in the leg while I wasn't looking… perhaps it is time I return the favor."

Something caught Conrad's eye on the right, but the giant gave him no time to comprehend, lunging forward for a sword swing. Thinking quickly, the strategist threw his saber at a gasping Angus. The move had taken him by such surprise that he was unable to block; the blade pierced through his neck and stopped him in his tracks.

Angus gurgled and struggled while once again falling to a knee. He looked up with fiery eyes, and a pang of worry came to Conrad's stomach, but a great water geyser saved him from the consequences of his actions. The mighty torrent hurled Angus into the same building he'd emerged from, resulting in an explosion of water and stone that rained down on the battlefield.

Aldous approached with his walking stick in hand, and behind him was a marinian. The old Wizard placed a hand on his shoulder and smiled.

"Well done, but leave the rest to us. See to Giles, and then work on securing Amis!"

Conrad nodded and began making his way to where Joel stood, still as night and eyes an empty abyss. He was the only barrier between a prone Giles and a familiar, dark-haired woman who wielded two falcata swords. Each hand guard hooked around, protecting all of her fingers, and the blade was angled forward in such a way that looked meant for chopping. She appeared Gentish, to his eyes, but lacked the dull expression of the other townsfolk.

She cocked her head at Joel's lack of stance or care in her presence. "You have no intention of fighting?"

Joel offered no response.

"Ah, you must think I'm a typical farm girl," she continued while looking down at her bloodstained dress with a smile. "After all, that is what I used to be."

"I know better," Conrad said as he approached. He stood next to his friend, unarmed.

"Do I know you?"

"Maybe not, but *I* know *you*," he replied. "I was there that night; when you were sacrificed at the black mass. Catalina, wasn't it?"

She giggled. "'Sacrifice'? That was no sacrifice. It was a *rebirth*."

"Is that what they call slitting your throat in Bosfueras?" Conrad asked with barbs of sarcasm.

"A necessary step for the greater good. I was not cooperating, back then. I refused to see the will of the people. Now, I am part of something *much more*," Catalina said.

"Now, you are brainwashed; part of a collective that can't be reasoned with. I'm only sorry that I couldn't have saved you, that night," he replied before nudging Joel. The mute returned a gaze that simmered the flame in his gut. It reminded him of the Bosfueras townsfolk, somewhat. "You are in no state of mind to fight. Please, lend me your sword."

Joel looked down at his dark blue blade. Angus' blood still dripped down from the tip. Rather than wait, the strategist grasped the bottom of the hilt, and slowly removed it from Joel's hand. A look of concern swept over him, as the mute did not react. He remained slumped in posture, staring at him with that same blankness that could swallow up stars.

Conrad gripped the handle with both hands and a wave of murderous intent swept over him. Catalina closed in with both falcatas in position to strike. The strategist moved forward and took an elongated stance to keep distance. With his opponent dual-wielding, it was a requirement to pick his spots. That was, of course, if her blades were able to withstand the luxmortite. Conrad was confident that they could not, but it was unlikely that she would know such a thing.

Catalina lunged forward and attempted a succession of slashes with each falcata. Two *dings* rang out within a split-second of each other as Conrad blocked one attack to his left, then twisted his wrists to the right for his second successful block. He then gave a token swipe of the sword to ensure that the distance between them remained.

The strategist had surprised himself. Those two blocks and even the follow-up swing had been thoughtless; a sort of natural focus that had fallen over him. Catalina tilted her head as she stepped back.

"Your eyes..." she trailed off, a sly smile coming to her face. "You are one of us?"

Could it have been true? Had his eyes turned red? *No*, he thought. It had to be mind games.

"Perhaps you should pay attention to more important matters." With the dark blue blade, Conrad pointed at her falcatas.

Predictably, the Gentish woman looked down and gasped at the cracks in both blades. Conrad used that opportunity to lunge at her for a surprise attack. Catalina raised her specialized swords in vain for the block as the blue blur of his swing made contact. Just as planned, the falcatas shattered upon second contact with the luxmortite sword.

As she took a step back and the broken metal *clanged* off the ground, Conrad closed in some more and brought the blade high up and horizontally across for a blow that was impossible to avoid. Catalina gasped as the sword cut into her neck and chopped through with little effort. Her decapitated head flipped through the air and thudded off the ground at the same time as her limp body. Conrad turned to face Joel and held the sword out for him to take back.

"*That* is what must be done against these people. They are too dangerous to be left alive…"

Though Joel did not respond to his words or the offering back of the blade, something else was wrong. Conrad looked the weapon over, and after a few moments, he finally noticed: The blood on the sword had dried. It wasn't Catalina's blood, but Angus'.

He turned just in time to see a red streak flying toward him. It was too fast to avoid, and he could only watch, helpless, as the red blur pierced straight through his stomach like an arrow through straw.

With stuttered, painful breaths, Conrad looked to the ground to see Catalina's head sitting upright. It had little, dark red spider legs sprouting out from where the open neck wound should have been; but they almost seemed gelatinous, like blood clots. The culprit of his stabbing was her tongue, supernaturally extended and sharp as any dagger.

Just as abruptly as the tongue had pierced him, it retracted back into Catalina's mouth. Blood burst from Conrad's stomach as he dropped the luxmortite sword, grasped the wound with both hands, and then fell to his knees. The Gentish woman smiled with menace as she licked his blood from her lips. Her detached body then stood, bent over, and grabbed her head by the hair.

In short order, Catalina reattached her head, and clotted blood spurted out from her neck to form stitches, holding it all together. She rolled her neck and it cracked loudly as Conrad took notice of Joel leaning over to retrieve his dark blue blade.

"Finally ready to play?" Catalina asked. She then cocked her head as Conrad stood beside his friend with newfound energy. The wound at his stomach had been reduced to a series of large scabs, yet strangely, it pained him more than ever. "So, you *are* one of us."

"I'm… not like… you…" he replied between labored breaths.

"Red eyes, regenerating wounds, and…" Catalina trailed off as a Bosfueras native passed her. She opened her mouth and out shot her wretched tongue once more. It pierced through the man's head, and he fell to the ground, dropping a piece of black gold in the process. The Gentish woman grinned after her tongue returned to her mouth. "A raging desire for the black gold."

Conrad's eyes glazed over. His head pounded from cracking his skull off the building. His stomach ached from the hole that had been poked through it. He was almost certain that his old wounds from Bosfueras were returning, as well. He now began to fear that the essence forced into his body by Mr. Willoughby had run its course in healing his injuries. Despite the returns of these pains and aches, however, there was another sensation that overruled them all: an itch. One that was intangible and impossible to scratch, but very much real, and ever irritating. There was only one way to stop that itch, he thought. He *needed more* dark essence.

An entranced Conrad ran for the black gold and dove to the ground to obtain it. He let out a happy, relieved sigh as he sat up, smiling stupidly while stroking the black gold like a little pet.

Conrad's predicament had not escaped the notice of Lucia, despite having hands full with a variety of opponents attacking her in the triangle formation. Joel had gotten between him and the attacking Gentish woman, but after what had become of Giles, she did not want to leave anything to chance.

Steadily, Lucia had been leading Dhogron and Rolf, and by proxy their enemies, back toward Conrad and the others. Just as it seemed like the Gentish woman was about to launch her attack, the trio backpedaled rapidly, barging into her line of sight and dragging the Bosfueras townsfolk along with them.

As Lucia had planned, several battles broke out between where Joel and Catalina stood. The triangle of Strangers held firm amidst the chaos, warding off attacks from farming tools and basic weapons alike. Lucia looked over her shoulder while defending; she could see Conrad sitting just outside the wall of chaos, looking at the black gold and nothing else. His eyes had turned a glowing red. As concerned as she was, there was no way for her to come to his side without leaving the others. It was difficult enough to fend off the villagers with the three of them. Making it only two would be a death sentence, she thought.

As if reading her thoughts, Joel punched a hole through the surrounding townsfolk by striking them in the back of their heads with the butt of his sword. None had seen him coming, for a trait they all shared was a deep, intense focus on current tasks. It appeared that with all the fighting going on around them, Joel had also managed to drag Giles safely away. She hoped that it hadn't been his corpse.

With this opening, Lucia and Joel nodded to each other, knowing exactly what to do. The mute joined up with Rolf and Dhogron in the triangle, while Lucia used the opportunity to sneak past the attackers and come to Conrad's aid.

While the battles raged on behind her, Lucia's heart sank. A stupefied Conrad sat before her, paying no mind as she approached. His red eyes were locked on the black gold, like so many others had been before him.

CHAPTER 21
REINFORCEMENTS

Dalton's back pressed against Kabel's as the duo fended off oncoming slashes from the opposing knights. Sir Job Cardon, out for blood, took aim at Dalton, while another gallant made his attempts on Kabel.

Job swung for Dalton's head with fury, but the warrior parried and then followed up with a near-miss toward the midsection. Meanwhile, he could hear Kabel thwarting the other knight's attempts with hollow *thunks* of his shield. Next came the screeching sound of steel grinding on steel, telling him that his friend employed a peeking stab strategy, and had likely landed hits on armor; or perhaps their blades had simply clashed. Either way, it was time for a change of pace, he thought.

"Switch!" Dalton called out as his sword bounced off of Job's blade.

At a moment's notice, the duo each pivoted to their right in a half-circle while simultaneously swinging their blades across. Dalton's attack took his new opponent off-guard and tagged him in the ribs. However, thanks to his plated armor, it was not a crippling blow and only stunned him. It was enough of a distraction for the warrior to lay a boot square in the knight's chest, to which he let out a choking gasp and crashed to the ground.

Kabel's attempt had not been so successful. Dalton's ears twitched as he heard a grunt, and then the stocky man's back slipped against his. He looked over his shoulder to see him on a knee, holding his lower-right midsection. There was already blood seeping through his fingers.

In that moment, Dalton's eyes caught onto a reflection of moonlight, and knew what it was: Job's deathblow. Like lightning, he turned and swung his blade, meeting the Sigrian knight's sword just over Kabel's head. Next, he pushed forward with several quick flicks of his wrist, forcing Job to both backpedal and block.

As Dalton continued his offensive, he snuck glances back at his recovering friend. He was glad to see Kabel standing under his own power, but the knight that he'd felled earlier could smell blood in the water and approached while dragging his blade. The warrior wished to help, but he had his hands full with Sir Job, who was now beginning to push him back with a return volley of stabs and swings.

Another hollow *thunk* caught Dalton's attention as he backpedaled, and this time, he could see Kabel directing an upward, arced sword swing ever higher with his shield. He followed up with a quick stab of his arming sword, which plunged into the elbow joint of the knight's armor.

Blood spurted from the fresh wound as Kabel ripped his blade out, and he gave the knight no time to cry out in pain, for his shield had already smashed into his face. Although the knight wore a helmet, the impact was strong enough to send a tooth soaring through the air as he stumbled back. After a few uneasy steps, he finally collapsed to the ground.

"No killing!" Dalton called back while blocking Sir Job's most recent flurry of sword swings.

"He'll live," Kabel said, now side-by-side with his friend.

Job snorted while taking a few steps back and lowering his sword. "If you kill an honorable knight of Sigraveld, then you shall be marked men for life. Choose your next course wisely, peasants."

"A hollow threat from a desperate man," Kabel said with a smirk. The heel of Sir Job's boot pressed up against a building behind, stopping his retreat.

"Worry not. Our aim is not to kill, but to dishonor and defeat you. After tonight, you will never be hired for dirty work again," Dalton said, raising his sword.

He was distracted, however, by a buzzing in the air. The bothersome noises reminded him of a fly, but they weren't consistent; they happened in short bursts. Dalton looked to his right to find Barret charging at him, fluttering his giant fly wings. Because he had been drenched, the translucent wings were weighed down too much for him to fully take flight.

Dalton hadn't noticed the bug-man until it was too late. Barret tackled him with the force of a charging buffalo, but rather than take him to the ground, he attempted flight once more. This time, he was successful, but the trajectory was uneven due to the waterlogged wings and Dalton's struggles.

Kabel called out to him as he soared away, but the warrior couldn't make out the words due to the buzzing in his ears. In fact, his ears both rang and pounded like a tolling bell amongst all of the noise.

Panic set in as they climbed higher and higher. No matter how he struggled, he could not escape from Barret's iron grip. It was unsurprising, given the bug-man's enhancement by the dark essence, but it didn't stop him from flailing in desperation. He knew that it wouldn't be much higher before a drop became dangerous, even in the waters below. However, along with his flailing, came a realization: He had held onto his long sword throughout the ordeal. With no time to spare, he slashed away at Barret's arm.

A loud squeal, followed by a hiss, left Dalton in a daze, but he was relieved to feel the sensation of dropping as he plummeted from the sky. He looked up at Barret, who wildly veered off course and spiraled down toward the sea. The warrior was also headed for a watery destination and straightened himself out before impact to avoid injury.

Dalton remained underwater for some time, letting the calm tides settle him down. The nervous numbness of his body faded, and so too did the ringing ears. As peace came over him, he surfaced with a quiet exhale and then sheathed his blade underwater. The warrior let out a sigh of relief. Somehow, he had avoided injury.

With his senses having returned to normal, Dalton heard splashes from his back-right. He turned to see a horde of Bosfueras townsfolk swimming toward him. The warrior spun back around and began stroking for the shore.

～

A PANTING and pale Kabel fended off a flurry of slashes from Job with his shield. He no longer had the strength to respond with attacks of his own, as the wound in his lower-right torso continued to spill blood and sap the strength from that side of his body.

The stocky man looked over his shoulder to see what his options were. His eyes widened for a brief moment, a new strategy taking shape in his racing mind. Several battles raged on behind him, and, since he was weakening with each passing second, his best chance was to mix in with the crowd and hope it would distract his opponent. Kabel returned his concentration to a pressing Job with another shield block at his midsection. The knight grinned with killing intent; each successive attack had hit harder than the last.

At the next clash of sword and shield, Kabel pushed back with nearly all of his remaining might and staggered a gasping Sir Job. With that brief distraction, the stocky man turned and made a run for it, wheezing a little harder at each stride taken.

While running, he heard a callous cackle from behind. "How sad! You could at least die with some dignity!"

Sir Job's jeering voice sounded dangerously close, and dread began creeping up Kabel's spine as his run slowed to a hobbling jog. However, new hope and life came to him upon realizing that many of the Bosfueras villagers and slaves had been defeated. On the ground they lay, unconscious, with many splintered weapons littered about.

Kabel bashed one of the slaves in the back of the head with his shield, then broke through the unsuspecting crowd and collapsed in front of the trio of Strangers: Joel, Dhogron, and Rolf. His vision blurry, his breaths hoarse, and his mind in a panic, all he could do now was hope that his allies would protect him.

～

WITH THE COMBINATION of Dhogron's paper distractions, Joel's superior luxmortite blade, and Rolf's quick strikes, the trio of Strangers had held their own against the dark forces, despite a great numbers disadvantage.

Upon taking notice of a collapsed Kabel, Rolf broke the formation by jumping out to fend off attacks aimed at the stocky man. Joel and Dhogron shuffled over to reform the triangle while surrounding their leader like a protective cocoon.

Sir Job pushed past his allies and took aim at Rolf with his sword overhead and ready to chop down. Joel, as if activating a sixth sense, nudged Rolf and Dhogron. The trio, like one living being, all pivoted at once, so their triangle rotated.

As the knight brought his sword down, Joel held up his dark blue blade for the easy block. The shock of probable pain pulsed through

Job's hands as his sword *clanked* off of Joel's superior metal. An unbearable *crack* rang out as the knight's trembling hands dropped his sword, now shattered.

A surprised gasp was all he could manage before Joel laid a kick into him that simultaneously doubled over and pushed him back. Job then tripped over his own two feet and crashed to the ground.

The knight quickly sat up, grimacing, with disbelief in his eyes. "How? What kind of blade could do such a thing?"

Joel, of course, could not provide him an answer. Even if he *could* speak, the mute was too busy fending off more townsfolk and slaves. However, out of the corner of his eye, he caught wind of Sir Job drawing his sidearm, a dagger, and returning to his feet. He pushed his allies aside once more and held the dagger above head, facing downward.

"Answer me, waif!" Job cried as he brought the blade down with the ferocity of an eagle swooping on its prey.

With a snort, Joel whirled his blue blade up and across to meet the dagger. This time, the luxmortite cut clean through. Job halted his swing and watched on with wide eyes as the top half of his blade flew through the air, *clanging* off the ground many paces away.

The knight gasped, then held his hands up to signal surrender as Joel pointed the sword at his gut. Job gulped, and a nervous sweat came to his brow. The mute lowered his blade. With no more weapons in his arsenal, the knight was no longer a threat.

Their eyes met, and Job's expression turned to surprise. "Y-you are not going to kill me?"

A ghastly smile crept onto Job's face and Joel let out a silent sigh. This was the problem, he thought. Even after having successfully disarmed his opponent, he was still going to launch an attack. All of his opponents were prepared to die, but he was not ready to kill; not even against a monster like Angus, let alone some knight who was out of his depth.

"That's a nice sword you've got there..." Job trailed off with a chuckle. Joel cocked his head. "It seems a shame that a meek child like you should wield it!"

Job leaped out at a surprised Joel and tackled him to the ground, next to a recovering Kabel. The knight grasped his fingers around the hand guard of the blade with one hand, while wrapping the other around Joel's throat. The mute placed one hand around Job's wrist to help relieve the choking while fighting back for the sword with the other.

"Give me the sword! And I shall let you live!" Job cried with malice in his eyes. "It is the only wa-"

The knight's pleas were interrupted by a boot punting him in the head. Job's helmet flew off as he groaned and rolled over, and so too did his eyes roll back.

"Yer open…" Rolf muttered before spitting on the knight's armor.

Joel took a deep breath to recover, gave his lanky friend a nod of thanks, then rose to recreate the triangle and defend his leader. Within the formation, Joel could hear Kabel stirring. He snuck a look back to see that he was pushing himself up with his shield-wielding arm. With any luck, he'd catch a second wind, and he could leave the triangle to tend to Giles further. He was still alive, but barely. For now, he could only hope that Aldous, Lucia, or Conrad had come to his side. He could not afford to stand by while another ally was gravely injured.

FURTHER DOWN THE DOCKS, Captain Auber's group had defeated the last of their enemies, thanks in large part to Pierce. His charmed dagger had disarmed many opponents permanently, and the Summoner Rune was an efficient way to send difficult enemies away.

"Err… who is that feller?" Auber whispered to Alistair as the masked luxian kicked the last of his opponents, knocking the wind out of him.

"That thar is a friend of Joel's… well, in a way… sometimes he's Joel's worst enemy!" the big man said with a chuckle.

"And what is that supposed to mean?" Franco asked.

Alistair rubbed the back of his head and then snorted. "It'll take too long ta explain. Just know that when his mask looks like that, he's on our side."

"And if it's tha other way?" Triston joined in as Pierce approached the group.

"He'll become our enemy," Alistair replied. The others looked at him in disbelief, but there was no time to question it. Their new ally had reached them.

"Erm…" Auber trailed off, then outreached a hand. "Thank ye fer the assist! I'm Cap'n Auber."

The masked luxian clapped his hand and shook, firmly. "Nice to meet you. I'm Pierce."

"I prefer tha name, 'Ometos'!" Alistair said with a big smile and a hard slap off the shoulder. "Hell of a performance out thar, lad! But how did ya find us? Aldous said there was no sign of ya back in Thironas."

"It's a long story," Pierce said as he turned toward the battles up ahead. "For now, let's just say I had a 'guiding voice'. Can you fill me in on what's going on?"

"Hold on!" Triston interjected. Pierce turned his sharp gaze to him. "How do we know that we can trust ya?"

A muffled scoff came from beneath the Ometos mask. "Do you think I would fight off all of those people, only to backstab you?"

"Er… I may have mentioned yer *other side…*" Alistair muttered.

"I see. You can all be at ease, then. *The other* and I have come to an understanding. Drake and his team must be stopped. That will take precedence over any past grudges… for now," Pierce said.

"Awright, good 'nuff fer me!" Ebbie said with enthusiasm. The others seemed to share the sentiment, their faces brightening and their postures relaxing.

Triston scoffed. "Just like that? Yer all gonna believe that load of-"

"Are you a relative of Alistair's?" Pierce asked with a chuckle.

"Yeh, I'm his older brother! Why do ya ask?"

"No reason." His laughs tapered off into amused breaths before looking at all around the group. "So then, what is our objective?"

"There is a Keeper of tha Key bein' held prisoner! Tha dark forces aim ta transport him ta that ship down there," Alistair said, pointing to the Dark Wizard's great vessel. "We gotta rescue 'im, or tha enemy might figure out tha Degenerate monolith's location!"

"Understood." Pierce held his dagger out, and the others stepped back as he sliced his palm with the luxmortite blade.

"The hell're ye doin'? Have ye gone mad?" Auber shouted, his eyes bulging out.

The masked luxian remained silent as he let the blood drip onto his dagger. The blade pulsed light blue, and with that, he turned toward the fighting crowds further up the docks. He leaped ahead, and the dagger carried him forward like a speeding arrow, leaving a powerful wind in its wake that parted the dust into two parallel walls that nearly reached the rooftops. Auber and his group looked on with mouths agape as Pierce defied what they knew to be reality.

After a few moments of awkward silence, the captain said, "Erm… should we get movin'?"

"*You're* the leader, sir…" Franco muttered.

Auber cleared his throat and then pointed his saber ahead in triumph. "Onward to battle!"

As the series of skirmishes moved closer and closer to Amis' location, three combatants were left on their own: Catalina, Conrad, and Lucia; the latter of whom stood in a long guard position with her sword to keep distance between herself and the enemy.

Conrad, meanwhile, gazed at the sparkling dark ore with a thoughtless, blissful smile. Catalina also smiled but with a far viler intent behind it. Her lips were coated in dry blood, and that alone was enough for Lucia to surmise that she'd been enhanced in some way by the dark essence.

"Does it bother you?" the Gentish woman asked. Lucia remained silent and ever-watchful. "Your ally sits and does nothing, forcing you to defend him when you could be helping the others."

"That's not *him*. It is the black gold's doing."

"Well then, why not take it away?"

"That would be foolish. It would just infect me, too. Do *try* to keep up," Lucia said with narrow eyes.

Catalina scoffed. "Fine. As you can see, I am unarmed. Why not attack?"

"Too risky."

"I see…" she trailed off before turning devilish eyes to Conrad. "Could it be that he is more than just an ally to you?"

"Spare me your drivel, would you?" Lucia asked with an eye roll. "I'd rather we skip the pleasantries and get to the fight."

To Lucia's surprise, Catalina relaxed her posture, then motioned with a flick of her wrist, as if shooing a fly away. "I have no desire to fight right now. So, I will give you a chance to leave."

"What nonsense!"

"But it's true. I am giving you and that miserable heap over there your only chance to escape with your lives," she said.

"I would never abandon my allies. Besides, your word cannot be trusted. I'm sure you will attack at the very moment I lower my guard," Lucia replied, gripping her blade a little harder.

Catalina shook her head. "That blue sword is amazing. It shattered my falcatas like a brittle piece of glass. Our forces are already dwindling, and you've got a Wizard on your side… and even a kraken! I'd rather live to fight another day."

"Do you honestly expect me to believe what you say?"

With a chuckle, Catalina turned and began to walk away. "You can escape, or try to help your friends. It makes no difference to me. You will all perish soon, anyway."

Lucia propped Conrad up and over her shoulder as she watched Catalina walk up the docks, past the fighting crowds. Dark thoughts crept into her mind. If the Strangers truly did hold the advantage, then why was she so confident that they were all going to die?

Captain Auber's group ran past the chaos of the kraken's flailing tentacles, and then past the intense battle between Aldous, Prince Xviktolo, and Angus. Chunks of stone and water flew around like a wild storm of rain and hail, prompting them to cover their heads as they continued.

Further ahead, Alistair spotted Giles, laid out on the ground and motionless. In a panic, the big man diverted from the group and charged toward his fallen friend.

"Wait! Ali! Stay behind me!" Triston called out from behind.

"Balls ta that!" Alistair shouted back between breaths. "That's me understudy! I can't let 'im die!"

The big redhead's eyes widened as a red-eyed horde popped out of the alleyway with torches and pitchforks.

"Ya can't handle 'em! Wait fer me!" Triston pleaded, but Alistair only shook his head and charged forward with fiery eyes focused on his enemies. He drew upon his wind Rune once more, and its wavy symbols pulsed white.

"SAYS YOU!" he cried while pushing the Rune forward as if thrusting a blade.

A gargantuan gust of wind erupted from the stone, halting his hefty momentum and pushing him back enough that his resisting feet burned against his own boots. Alistair watched on in anticipation for what felt like hours to him, until the air burst collided with the townsfolk, and sent them flying back into the alleyways from whence they came.

All in Auber's group gasped at the spectacle of men and women, flying and flipping through the air helplessly. While some were lucky enough to land atop the nearby roof, others crashed into the building's wall or each other, quickly incapacitating them.

"Whoa! What did ya do, Ali?" Triston asked.

For once, Alistair was speechless. With wonder in his eyes, he looked down at the Rune to see that its white glow was fading. All of the doubt that had overtaken him earlier began to dwindle, and relief set in.

The big man's eyes widened, and then he said, "Oi! Giles!"

He and his brother ran to the downed Stranger. Auber and the others approached from the left. All hovered over Giles to see the heavy damage that he had taken: Angus' bone bolts stuck out of his arm, torso, and most notably, his right eye.

"Wh-what happened to him?" Auber asked.

Alistair clenched a shaking fist. "Angus…"

The big man grasped his wind Rune and turned to the raging battle in the rubble between his Wizard friend and the giant. He began to run toward the fight, but Triston stood in his path.

"Outta my way!" Alistair bellowed.

"I won't let ya run ta yer death," the elder MacRae said with crossed arms.

"I dun need yer protection!" Alistair said, holding the Rune up in his brother's face. "I've had about 'nuff of you underestimatin' me!"

"Ya got one lucky shot off, an' now ya think yer gonna help a Wizard in battle?" Triston said with a scoff. Alistair's eyes twitched in anger but then darted to the ground. Maybe he was right. "Besides, we still gots a mission ta complete. An' ya won't be honorin' Giles' memory by rushing into battle an' dyin'!"

"Erm…" Franco trailed off. He was on a knee and had placed a hand on Giles' chest. "He's still alive."

"Oh, thank tha mighty Gods o' Stone!" Alistair called out as he rushed to his downed friend's side.

"His injuries are severe. I can't be sure of how long he has. Do we know any doctors?" Franco asked.

"I know someone…" Ebbie trailed off. All in the group looked back at him with cocked heads.

"What're ye talkin' about? We don' know any doctors!" Auber said with hands to hips and a raised eyebrow.

"Well, y'see, he ain't a doctor… but he can heal Giles," the first mate said. "Thar's a priest who resides in a church on the east end of the city. His name is Father Vega. Back when we first had to escape from Sampson and them slaves, I took an arrow to the leg. He healed the wound so much that I nearly fergot about it!"

Auber scoffed. "Shouldn't ye have told us about 'im, earlier? He coulda helped us on this mission, ye fool!"

Ebbie sunk his head. "Sorry…"

Franco narrowed his eyes. "You're one to talk about withholding information, sir."

The captain let out a nervous laugh. "Yes… well, I suppose no one's perfect, eh?"

"There ain't no more time ta talk, lads!" Alistair said as he knelt, draped Giles' arm over his shoulder, and then lifted him with ease like a parent carrying their child. The big man turned his gaze to Ebbie. "Lead tha way!"

The first mate began walking toward a nearby alley.

"Hold up," Triston said. The group stopped and looked back. "We gotta help tha rest of tha team too, don' we? Tha fate of this city may well be at stake!"

"But we gotta get Giles ta tha priest, too! He could die!" Alistair argued.

All looked to Captain Auber for a final say.

"Oh… uhh…" he muttered, looking between the ongoing battles and the beckoning alleyway nearby. "We'll do both!"

"An excellent compromise, sir," Franco said with barbs of sarcasm.

"I mean it!" Auber said with newfound excitement. "Let's go over thar, crush the last of thar forces, and take the prisoner, all in one fell swoop!"

"YEAH!" Alistair cried with infectious energy. He led the charge of Auber's group, despite having to carry Giles over his shoulder.

The group began making their way toward the skirmishes ahead, where their remaining allies fought valiantly to break through the last barrier between them and Amis. On their way, however, they spotted Lucia sitting with her arms draped around Conrad.

Auber and the group stopped upon reaching the pair. The pirate captain cleared his throat. Lucia looked up with defensive eyes, but she relaxed her posture moments later.

"Auber's team, checking in," he said in his most proper voice. "Is everything alright, here?"

With a snicker, she said, "You don't have to act so officially just because you're a leader, now."

"Right..." Auber muttered with an unsure chuckle.

"We'll be fine. Go and help the others up ahead," Lucia said.

Alistair eyed the black gold in Conrad's hands and gasped. "I-is that what I think it is?"

"Ah, what's that he's holdin' thar?" Auber asked. The ore shined brilliantly in the night, despite its dark color, and it allured him so much that he reached out for it.

"NO! DON' TOUCH THAT!" Alistair shouted, to which Auber shot his shoulders up to his ears and whimpered. "That's tha black gold! It'll infect ya with Gold Fever!"

"So, *that's* the black gold we've heard so much about," Franco said while rubbing his chin. "I can see why it is sought after. Truly a sight to behold."

"I don't believe this to be the black gold that we encountered at Mt. Couture," Lucia said before looking up to Alistair. "Remember how we were able to break the Gold Fever's spell by reminding ourselves of the things that we care for? It's not working, this time. I've tried everything..."

"An' ta think that it got Conrad! He was tha most resistant to it of us all!" Alistair said, sighing. "What does this mean?"

"I believe this is the Dark Wizard's black gold, and that is why it's different," she replied with despair on her tongue. "If he had Gold Fever, there would have been a violent outburst by now. He's been little more than a motionless husk since laying his hands on it. There has to be some other way of breaking the spell... I just wish that I could get through to him, somehow..."

~

Lucia's words echoed in Conrad's dream-like state, but they had distorted so much that it may as well have been in another language. He was too busy enjoying himself, in blissful harmony with the black gold that he had been yearning for since *the itch* overtook him.

As he slipped further and further into a state of unconsciousness, Conrad began to understand the Dark Wizard's point of view. Back in Bosfueras, it had seemed outrageous to purport the black gold and dark magic as forces for good. However, he found the shadows surrounding him to be comforting, and after all, it was dark magic that allowed this special brand of black gold to exist. Without it, he wouldn't be experiencing this current euphoria. In fact, he would be dead. It wasn't that darkness was bad, it was simply that Conrad had *feared the unknown*.

With that realization, he came to sympathize with the Dark Wizard's plans. What was wrong with everyone being in such a peaceful state as he was? If all were given *this* black gold, then the entire world would be at rest, and there would be no worries. Everyone would be happy.

Still, it seemed to Conrad that there was no need to lament. It was all out of his control, after all. He instead decided to focus on the relaxation of his muscles and the easing of his mind. Nothing could separate him from this happiness, he thought.

That was when he heard it: *the breathing*. They were the pained, excited, and shrill breaths all in one, but most importantly, they were familiar. Could it be? *Mr. Willoughby*? No, Conrad thought. The foul beast had exploded before his very eyes in Bosfueras. Then, what? What else could make that infernal noise?

Conrad shivered as the calming shadows gave way to pure darkness, and then a pair of glowing, red-ringed eyes appeared in the distance. Slowly, they approached.

"No..." he murmured.

Memories came flooding back: The desperate chase, the terrifying deformities, and the breathing; that *horrid* breathing. In the distance, another pair of red eyes appeared, and then another. Before he knew it, Conrad was staring down many red eyes, and now some of them had shrunken down into concentrated dots. *They had taken notice*, he thought with a shudder.

Before they could reach him, however, the red eyes faded away. Conrad let out a sigh of relief, but it was short-lived. Mr. Willoughby's deformed face shot out of the darkness and roared a demonic combination of man and beast, mere inches from him. The monster was as gruesome as ever: It had a drippy, tar-like hide, with traces of its previous humanity such as the odd skin patch or hair clump serving as decorations on its body. Its nose was pushed upward and crunched in, and its lips were receded to the top its wretched gums and uncannily long teeth; quivering, as if begging to open wide for its first meal in a long while.

With that, Conrad snapped out of his stupor and dropped the black gold. He breathed heavily for a few moments, then turned to see everyone else in his group standing. They weren't facing him, however. The strategist climbed to his feet and rubbed his eyes, as if having woken up from a daylong slumber, and then peeked over Lucia's shoulder to see what had drawn their attention.

"What the hell am I lookin' at?" Auber asked with the fear of God in his voice.

Ten monsters, all tall, lumpy, and with inhumanly stretched limbs, lumbered toward them with irregular steps. Each took a similar appearance to Mr. Willoughby and let out high-pitched breaths or moans periodically. It sounded like they were trying to suppress maniacal laughs.

"They are reinforcements," Conrad said as a familiar, nervous pit took hold of his stomach.

CHAPTER 22
ESCAPE ROUTES

Angus Grouchet emerged from the rubble of a decimated building, surprised to find his opponents no longer paying him any mind. Though he had successfully prevented Aldous and Xviktolo from reaching a downed Giles or any of the other Strangers, the rest of his team had failed in claiming any of their lives, as far as he could tell. The duo had overwhelmed him with a simple strategy: Angus had no choice but to respect the threat of the starlite sword, and while distracted, the old Wizard only needed to wash him away with a torrent of water. There was little he could do while they were working so well together. And now, it appeared that the Strangers were closer than ever to retrieving the prisoner.

Even if he and his team had a fool-proof contingency, the giant had at least hoped to claim a few of the rodents' lives in battle. The duo had foolishly turned their backs to him, and he crept forward with his bone blade, ready to backstab. However, as he neared his targets, Angus looked over their shoulders, to the west, and understood what had distracted them.

Plodding up the road were Willoughby-like monsters, their shrill breaths echoing in the night, and their pale imitation of human strides chilling even Angus' fiery bones. Behind them were chanting hordes of Bosfueras townsfolk, carrying torches, pitchforks, and wood axes. There were well over 100 on their way to intercept and take back the prisoner. Meanwhile, the enhanced avian Mur'del buzzed around the agitated kraken like an annoying fly. The sea monster swung its tentacles violently, as if cracking a whip, but the speedy avian casually flipped, dove, and barrel-rolled to avoid.

The biggest surprise came when he locked eyes on the Dark Wizard, walking among his acolytes like a shepherd amongst sheep. His great, dark robe fluttered in the gentle wind, signaling the storm soon to come. One of Drake's bodyguards walked alongside him in his tall, cloaked form.

"About time..." Angus muttered with a chuckle. Aldous and Xviktolo peered back over their respective shoulders. "The reinforcements have arrived. You never should have challenged us out in the open like this. You will all be slaughtered, or perhaps experimented on."

Aldous snorted at him before softening his expression and looking at Prince Xviktolo with a half-hearted smile. "You have done more than enough to help us. I can't thank you enough. But there is no need to further endanger yourself."

"No sense," the marinian replied with a toothy grin.

"Err... I think you mean, 'nonsense'."

"Right, right," Xviktolo said, his tail wriggling with apparent excitement. "These fights have been great fun. I did not know you land-dwellers had such a thirst for battle!"

"Not normally, no... but I daresay you showed up for quite the occasion," Aldous said before turning back to the approaching Dark Wizard and his horde. "Still, you should leave, while you have the chance."

"What about you?" Xviktolo asked.

"I must stay and confront this Dark Wizard menace," Aldous said.

Angus scoffed. "If you had any sense at all, you would run for your lives."

In a flash, Aldous turned and whirled his walking stick around to strike Angus in his jaw. He soared through the air; a familiar feeling, though not a pleasant one anymore. Next, his back and flesh crunched against the rubble of the building, and then all turned gray. As that gray slowly faded to black, the giant smirked amidst the rubble. Drake's prediction had come true: He was no match for Aldous near the water; though he wished he could have proven him wrong.

～

"THAT'S ENOUGH OUT OF YOU…" Aldous muttered, eyeing the rubble to ensure that Angus stayed down, this time.

"I admire your bravery, but you seem tired. Could it be that this Dark Wizard has sent his soldiers to wear you down so he could easily slay you?" Xviktolo asked.

"Oho! A fine observation indeed, Prince!" Aldous said as he clanked his walking stick off the ground. "It is almost certainly a trap. That is the only conceivable reason to show himself before me… but y'see, this Dark Wizard's identity is of the utmost importance. I must confirm it."

"Very well," Xviktolo said with his starlite sword at the ready. "Then, I shall fight by your side."

"Direct those helping hands *their way*," Aldous said, nudging his head toward the Strangers. Their struggle against the final barrier of villagers and slaves between them and Amis continued at a furious pace.

"What fun!" Xviktolo cried as he began long strides toward his new allies, the crystalline sword glistening under the stars themselves to reflect his excitement.

Aldous grunted and held his walking stick out toward sea. Three great streams of water shot up into the sky like a vicious hydra emerging from its slumber, and then they arced down toward him as a crashing wave would on the shore. Before striking him, though, the old Wizard cradled the three masses of liquid and combined them to create a stationary jet stream. He stepped on the watery platform, and by raising a free hand, it propelled him high into the air, well above the nearby stone buildings. Aldous then pushed his walking stick forward, and so too did the geyser push ahead, allowing him to travel high above all commotions on the ground.

The old Wizard passed the kraken and enhanced avian, and then the ten hobbling monstrosities who led the hordes. Since the great stream of water traveled along the ground, it cut into the thick lines of the Bosfueras townsfolk, forcing them to break their rows.

Finally, Aldous halted his water plume just before the Dark Wizard, who stared up at him, a grin slicing through the guise of his hood. Another cloaked man leaned forward, but the Dark Wizard held his arm out, and he immediately stood down. Aldous lowered the water enough to speak with his adversary, but out of reach from the villagers, who had all turned their red, glowing eyes to him.

Yet, those droning eyes shifted to the Dark Wizard when his deep, powerful voice filled the air and he pointed ahead. "Proceed."

Without a second thought, all of the townsfolk returned their attention to marching ahead, where the Strangers battled their allies.

"That's a nice lil' army you've got there," Aldous said with a huff.

"An 'army', you say? No, they are merely a collective who have come to see things as they truly are. What you see before you are future visions of a better world, where all are focused on the greater good," the Dark Wizard said.

"And who decides what 'the greater good' is? Might that be you, perchance?"

"Naturally."

"You simply cannot leave well enough alone, can you? Always meddling; poking and prodding at people until they are your puppets! Your title amongst the Council is indeed a fitting one!" Aldous said.

The Dark Wizard cocked his head. "Oh? And what might that title be?"

"The Oppressor," Aldous said. The Dark Wizard remained silent. "Not to your liking? That's alright, you've had *many names* over the millennia for which you have plagued the world! The Harvester! The Tyrant! The Deceiver! The Demon!"

A low-pitched laugh from the Dark Wizard sent chills through Aldous' body. "You are mistaken."

"Is that so? Because you act much in the same way as he would. It is always the same pattern: Enslave a group of humans and force them to do your bidding. And then you try to morph them into your twisted vision of what they should be. Worse yet, this time, you dare to risk our entire world by involving the Dark Savior in your selfish causes!" Aldous said.

"Again, you are wrong," the Dark Wizard said as he brought his hood down to reveal a demonic face with malice-filled eyes. He had long, dark hair and pale skin, as if he had bathed in darkness his whole life.

The old Wizard narrowed his eyes. He could never forget what Wilhelm the Oppressor had looked like all of those years ago. Despite his wicked demeanor, he had resembled a prince or nobleman, emitting a natural charisma that could sway anyone. The only thing that *this* Dark Wizard had in common with him was the long, dark hair.

"Don't take me for a fool! I know that you can change your appearance. Conrad revealed much to me," Aldous said.

The robed man cackled and placed a palm over his face. He then dragged his hand down, and as if cleansing the surface of a table, his face transformed. Aldous gasped at the sight of an old, frail face, lined by a trim goatee. It was his friend from the Council, Utrix.

"Do you miss talking to him?" the Dark Wizard asked with a smirk. His voice perfectly mimicked Utrix's, adding to Aldous' despair. "I wonder what happened to that old man... Summoner magic can be *quite dangerous*, after all..."

"So, back then, in the Dead Woods, I was not talking to my friend... it was you..." he trailed off, still in disbelief.

"On the contrary..." the Dark Wizard said before wiping over Utrix's face and returning to his prior appearance. "The last time you spoke with Utrix, it truly *was* him. Of course, I expect that you would be able to tell the difference between my presence and his, but Conrad certainly couldn't..."

"What is your interest in him? Why did you lead him to Bosfueras?" Aldous asked.

"I am always on the lookout for the next generation of Dark Wizard, and the boy reminds me much of myself when I was young and full of curiosity. He wondered what was being done with the black gold, so I showed him," the Dark Wizard said, then let loose a venomous grin. "I showed him how much better life would be with my brand of the black gold, and then, I took it away to show him the harsh realities of life without it."

"Your twisted game ends here. I won't allow you to poison him any further!" the old Wizard said as the water around him began to bubble, matching his ferocity.

"Too late. He will come crawling back to beg me for more. It is only a matter of time."

"The dark essence will be removed from him, and so too will your malicious grip over the boy," Aldous replied.

"I was unaware that he had taken in more dark essence... interesting..." the Dark Wizard trailed off. His smile grew ever wider. "If that's true, then he has had it within him for weeks, which means that my grip over him has only *strengthened*."

"For someone who claims not to be the Oppressor, you have much in common with him."

The Dark Wizard scoffed. "Yes, well... let's just say that *the old man* is not relevant at this time."

"Fine. If you truly aren't the Oppressor, then who am I dealing with?" he asked, the frustration mounting. The Dark Wizard remained silent. "I already know your plan, your allies, and your connections... a name wouldn't hurt, would it?"

"You presume to know much, my foolhardy friend, when you in fact know very little. Still, you are correct about one thing: It doesn't matter if you know my name. It wouldn't even matter if I was who you claim me to be. The Council has lost faith in you. They won't believe a word you say," he replied. Aldous grimaced, because he may well have been correct. "I am Oneth. Remember that name if you survive this night, for it will be I who ignites the flame that shall burn this world's limiting institutions to the ground. And in their place, the ultimate solution to man's woes will arise! *My* solution."

The water around Aldous flared up once more, like a viper coiled to strike. "Just know that whatever it is you have planned, I will oppose you to the end. I'll never stop-"

"I know you won't!" Oneth interrupted with a potent mix of venom and excitement on his tongue. "That's what I'm counting on! The more you interfere, the more you help me! *You* have been my greatest asset, Aldous! Who else could cause such chaos and discord inside the Council, but *you*?"

"You lie!"

"Do I? The Mt. Couture plan truly was a long shot, but you made it happen. After all, it was you and that quiet boy who sought to save those miserable miners. Without your help, they all would have perished in the mines, and the Greed seal never would have been destroyed," the Dark Wizard said as Aldous darted his eyes away in shame. "Even better, the key is no longer in your possession, and having to guard that portal stretches the Council's resources. A few more seals broken, and..."

"I won't let that happen! It ends tonight!" Aldous cried as he raised his walking stick, ready to strike with the full force of a tidal wave. Before swinging his Wizard's artifact, however, a green glint off in the distance caught his eye, stilling him.

From Oneth's great ship, a large pair of bone arms faced one another, palms first. Between the hands was a ball of bright, green light. *Dark Hands*, Aldous thought, his stomach sinking like a rowboat filled with holes. With that realization came another discovery: The Dark Wizard was now whispering an incantation for the wretched spell.

"Without making a sacrifice? But how?" he asked.

"Plenty of sacrifices have been made ahead of time," Oneth said with a smirk. At that moment, Aldous spotted another green light out of the corner of his eye; this time to the left. There was another pair of Dark Hands atop a nearby building. "Of course, talking to an idealistic old fool like you is sacrifice enough, and *time* enough…"

Aldous' eyes widened as he saw more Dark Hands all around, with orbs of light ready to fire at any moment. Soon, the night sky was filled with green, and so too was Aldous' heart filled with dread. He was surrounded by over a dozen Dark Hands, by his count.

"As much of a useful tool as you have been, I fear that your well of worth has begun to run dry. Perhaps it would be easier if you die, and *I* impersonate *you*," Oneth said as a high-pitched, sizzling noise caught Aldous' ear. He focused his eyes just in time to see that the Dark Hands on the great, black ship had fired a brilliant beam of green light, headed straight for him.

With a gasp, Aldous swung his walking stick to the right, and his water plume jerked in that direction as he felt the immense heat of the blast pass him by. The liquid at his feet began to bend and wobble, like a snake dancing for a charmer, to make his movements unpredictable. The strategy worked for the next couple of light beams, which were off their mark by a considerable margin.

"Scure Namille Greles!" Oneth's thunderous command rattled Aldous to his core as all remaining Dark Hands fired their wayward soul energy all at once.

In desperation, Aldous dove off of his watery platform for the sea, but in mid-air, his breath was taken away to find that the beams of light had not been aimed at him, but *at each other*.

～

ALL ON THE battlefield froze as a blinding green light and ear-ripping *sizzles* overtook the streets. Alistair put a forearm to his brow and watched in awe as the many beams of energy combined into a great ball no smaller than the nearby buildings. In a near-instant, the mighty orb struck a falling Aldous and carried him out over the sea like a comet across the sky. In mere seconds, Aldous and the green energy disappeared into the horizon, bringing the night sky and its stars back to prominence.

What remained of Aldous' water plume collapsed without its master, splattering on the road like blood against a wall. Next to fall were the tatters of Aldous' tunic, followed closely by green puffs of smoke that the nefarious attack had left in its wake.

"Aldous!" Alistair cried, running for the sea before Lucia got in his way. "Move! I ain't gonna say it more than once!"

"We've got other things to worry about," she said while nudging her head toward the approaching monsters and villagers. "Aldous is a Wizard. He may have survived."

"I don' know how anyone coulda survived somethin' like that!" Auber said, to which Lucia narrowed her eyes.

"Even if he didn't survive, Aldous would want us to complete the mission. It was more important to him than anything," Conrad said.

"What's goin' on with you, anyway? First, yer sittin' there droolin' like a simpleton, and now yer alright?" Alistair asked.

"I'm fine," he replied while turning to face his battling comrades up ahead. "Let's go. We have a mission to finish."

With that, Conrad ran off, and Lucia and the others followed, albeit with more hesitation in their strides. Alistair looked out to sea one more time before sighing and then dashing ahead, after his teammates.

~

IN THE THICK OF BATTLE, a hunched-over Kabel took a half-hearted swing with his arming sword, which was easily blocked by one of the red-eyed villagers of Bosfueras. The townsfolk had created a thick line in front of the alley where Amis sat, dazed, and in chains.

Joel had been able to break a few more of the villagers' weapons with his luxmortite sword, but he had also found that they were quick to adapt. Rather than directly clash weapons, the crazed mob had made efforts to dodge and swing at awkward areas where the mute would struggle to generate power behind his swings. Dhogron's paper trickery had also lost its effectiveness over time. His substitutes were simple to identify when letting wind do the work; it would smack against and cause them to flutter or crumple. Rolf, too, had fought valiantly, but he found it impossible to break through the barrier of people without causing them great harm.

There was reason to have hope, however. Prince Xviktolo arrived on the scene with a bang, taking out several townsfolk with one swing of his starlite sword to disarm them, and then a harsh swipe of his tail to knock them back. Although Kabel, Rolf, and Dhogron had never met the marinian, Joel gave them a nod to assure his allies that he was on their side.

Soon after Xviktolo's arrival, Joel looked over his shoulder to see the remainder of his allies charging in his direction. A quiet sigh of relief escaped his lips to see Alistair carrying Giles. However, a cursory glance past them revealed that saving Amis wasn't the only reason for their rush: A small battalion of townsfolk and monsters loomed behind them.

Letting panic set in, the mute charged into the crowd, hoping to miraculously break the line, but it was in vain. They merely pushed him back with their strength of numbers. Dhogron and the others looked back to see what Joel had seen, and they too began to attack with greater ferocity.

The trickster Wizard stepped back from the fighting and then held his hands overhead. In short order, a large, triangle-shaped paper formed in his grasp. Dhogron hopped in the air a few times, but there was no effect.

"The hell're you doin'?" Kabel asked as he blocked a token strike from one of the villagers with his shield.

"Trying… to… glide over them…" he said between each hop.

Finally, as he was starting to pant, an updraft of wind caught hold of Dhogron's makeshift glider and carried him up into the air. There was a glaring problem, however: The direction of the wind was taking him backward, to the Dark Wizard and approaching monsters, instead of ahead, toward Amis.

In a panic, Dhogron let go of the glider and crashed to the ground as Captain Auber's group approached.

"Oi! Are ya alright, mistah Wizard?" Triston asked, outstretching a hand.

Dhogron rubbed his back as the Elder MacRae hoisted him up. "I've gotta master that thing, someday."

"Looks to me like you need to learn the *basics* of it, whatever it is," Lucia said with a snicker.

The trickster Wizard chuckled. "Well, you see, it's a simple piece of p-"

"NO TIME FER TALK, LADS! WE GOTTA GO!" Alistair shouted, charging past his teammates and straight at the skirmish in the alleyway.

"Wait, Ali! It's dangerous ta go alone!" Triston called out, running after him.

The rest of the Strangers followed close behind the MacRaes. Alistair wasted no time upon arriving at the battle; even with Giles draped over his shoulder, he swung his battle axe at the line of townsfolk between him and the Endoshire Key Keeper. Soon after, the other Strangers joined him in battle.

Lucia stabbed into the crowd with her long sword, throwing all caution for her opponent's lives to the wind out of apparent desperation. Conrad only wielded a dagger and appeared sluggish. He took sparing swings into the crowd, and all were easily blocked. With the reach and power of his great sword, Triston had to be mindful of his teammates in the confines of the alleyway, and the slower speed of his swings made for easy reads by his red-eyed opponents.

Captain Auber cut into the wooden shaft of a townsman's pitchfork with his saber and said, "Hah! Take that, ye dirty landlubber!"

Ebbie and Franco followed along with their leader, slashing into the crowd with vigor, though the attacks had little effect.

Joel looked back once more to see that the large, dark, and lumpy monsters had passed the kraken, who was still preoccupied with the enhanced avian in the sky. The horde of townsfolk weren't far behind them.

Alistair, seeming to notice his worry, flashed a confident smile. "Don' worry, lads! I gots a secret weapon that'll blow these tosspots away!"

The big man unveiled the wind Rune from beneath his cloak. Its glowing, wavy lines lit up his round face.

"Now ain't tha time, Ali! We don't know if it'll work!" Triston chimed in.

"That's right! Keep tellin' me I can't do it! That's how I got it ta work, last time!" Alistair said with a wide grin, then held the Rune outward at his enemies.

His smile was short-lived, however, as just before the explosion of wind erupted in the collective faces of the Strangers, Joel picked up on his lemon-sucking frown. *Fitting,* he thought while flying away in a swirling cloud of dust; for they were about to experience the bitterness of defeat.

After skidding harshly across the road, Joel shook the cobwebs out and surveyed the damage: Some of the Bosfueras townsfolk had been downed, but most of the wind had been directed at the Strangers. Dhogron, Conrad, Lucia, and Triston had all flown away with him and were in the process of struggling to their collective feet. Meanwhile,

Alistair was carefully maneuvering Giles' limp body, which was draped over him, on the ground. Triston extended a burly hand and hoisted his brother up.

"Idiot…" Lucia muttered while dusting herself off.

"W-was that *magic* you just performed?" Conrad asked, eyes wide.

"That ain't important right now!" Alistair said as he hoisted Giles over his shoulder once again. "We gotta get back ta tha battle! We're almost outta time!"

"You *could* do that…" a familiar voice said from behind. Joel and the Strangers turned to see Pierce with his glowing Summoner Rune in hand. "Or, you could take the path of least resistance."

All in the group gasped as the stone's dark glow flared out, opening a vortex of darkness before them, howling like the heaviest of storm winds.

"How can we be sure that you are trustworthy?" Conrad asked, staring blankly at the portal.

"We can trust 'im," Alistair said in an unusually calm tone. "This here is Ometos. We met 'im back in Thironas. He's on our side!"

"How can we be sure that Alistair knows what he's talking about?" Lucia asked with a roll of her eyes.

"Shaddup!" the big man said as light chuckles broke out within the group. Joel began making hand signals to confirm what his friend was saying, but Alistair interrupted. "See? Joel's gonna vouch for 'im, too, but we don't gots time fer that!"

"Very well…" the strategist said with unease in his eyes. "I just want to be sure that we'll be sent to a safe location."

Pierce pointed past the crowd in the alley. Upon squinting, Joel spied an exit portal swirling behind, where the crazed villagers weren't looking. "That is your destination. As soon as you're through, retrieve the prisoner and make a run for it, and you *might* survive."

Without as much as a word, Alistair barreled through the swirling darkness. Triston, chasing after his brother, went next. Dhogron followed close behind, and Conrad and Lucia entered at the same time while holding hands. Joel, however, gasped to be stopped by a luxmortite dagger held up to his neck.

He turned his head slowly to see that Pierce's Ometos mask had shifted to its more sinister expression. How could he not have realized? He hadn't even thought to look, assuming that *the other* would never help him or his friends.

"It happened on your watch, didn't it?" he asked. Joel cocked his head. "That fellow with the bolt in his eye... I'd bet anything that you allowed it to happen. I told you that your allies were better off without you, didn't I?"

The mute grimaced. It was true that it had happened after his blow failed to fell Angus. He'd been trying to push it out of mind; to focus on the task at hand, but along came Pierce, reopening that wound.

"After all of this is settled, and we've dealt with the threat to the seal... you and I have unfinished business. Next time we fight, one of us will die," Pierce said, withdrawing his blade. "You will either live on as a killer or die as one."

Joel, ever defiant, huffed and walked past him and into the void without flinching. After exiting, the mute was shocked to find his friends running past him. Triston carried Amis over his shoulder. Alistair, still carrying Giles, followed close behind, while Conrad, Lucia, and Dhogron brought up the rear.

"What're ya doin', lad? Run!" Alistair called back.

He looked ahead to find a horde of townsfolk charging at him like angry mother bears in defense of their cubs. Good thing his shin had healed, he thought. Joel turned and ran at top speed, his hair fluttering in the wind and his burning scrapes cooling. In little time, he caught up with the others.

"You're... quite nimble... eh?" Dhogron asked between breaths. Joel nodded with a smile.

The quartet charged ahead until reaching the two slowing MacRae brothers. They now panted heavily, and their legs began to drag. Not only were their bodies larger than the others, but they were carrying Giles and Amis, respectively.

Lucia looked to Conrad with concern in her eyes. To Joel, there was good reason to worry: The strategist's strides were becoming sloppier and his face was going pale. Whatever was going on with Conrad and the dark essence seemed to be slowing him down at the worst possible time.

"We have to split up," she said.

"But... why?" Dhogron asked.

"Some of us are beginning to slow down. They are carrying an extra *weight*," she replied, eyeing Conrad. He huffed in response but didn't argue.

"Are ya... callin' me fat?" Alistair asked, his voice dripping in as much exhaustion as he was sweating. He began to lag behind. "Cuz I'll have ya know that I'm mostly... muscle..."

"Yeh…" Triston chimed in. His normally hardy voice had turned breathless. "Us MacRaes… are built like iron… an' iron just happens… ta be heavy!"

Dhogron looked over his shoulder as the shadow of a rooftop bridge blotted out the fleeing Strangers. By the time they returned to the comforting confines of moonlight, he was smiling.

"I've got… an idea."

"We're open… ta suggestions…" Alistair said. His tongue was out and he panted like a dog while falling further behind by the stride.

Still running, Dhogron twisted his upper body back toward the approaching Bosfueras townsfolk and held a hand out, palm forward. His whole face, from his thin brow to chubby cheeks, twitched with such ferocity that his beads of glistening sweat appeared to triple in number. Then, with a forceful thrust of his palm and an equally forceful breath through his nose, he unleashed his greatest trick yet.

Just behind the lagging MacRae brothers appeared a gigantic boulder, filling the alleyway from building to building, and reaching the bottom of a rooftop bridge overhead. The other Strangers looked back and gasped in collective shock.

"Whoa!" Alistair said with an excited breath. "So, you can create… more than just paper! That's handy-"

Rip

The harsh sounds of shredding paper behind drew all of the Strangers' attention once more. Their eyes were greeted with the peculiar sight of the boulder ripping to shreds, along with several of the Bosfueras townsfolk barreling through and tumbling to the ground, poking holes in it. It took a moment to register, but now Joel understood: Dhogron hadn't truly conjured a boulder, but a great blanket of paper that mimicked one.

More of the crazed mob crashed through the paper distraction until the bottom of it was in tatters, on the ground. Only its upper half fluttered in the gentle breeze from the roof bridge.

All of the Strangers looked at Dhogron with narrowed eyes. He let out a dry chuckle. "Guess they didn't fall for it…"

Despite the failed attempt at trickery, the distraction had succeeded in allowing the group to gain some extra distance. That gap was rapidly closing, however, as all besides Joel and Lucia began to slow down.

"We have no choice but to split up," Lucia said. Joel nodded. If they separated into two groups and made for the branching alleyways, it might confuse the dark forces, hot on their tail. With Alistair and Triston in particular slowing, it was their best chance at escape.

"Where… do we meet up… then?" Dhogron asked.

"We all know… where to inevitably meet up…" Conrad said. Now, Joel was certain that something was wrong. Before, on the Mt. Couture expedition, it had taken considerably longer than this brief run for his stamina to wear. "Do what you… have to do… to evade them. We can always… meet back up… at Kabel's place… when things blow over."

"I gots ta… take Giles to tha church…" Alistair said between breaths.

"Conrad and I know the way," Lucia said with a smile. "We'll lead you there… let's just hope the little fella can hold on, until then."

"I'm comin', too! I can't… leave ya alone, Ali!" Triston said with what seemed to be his last burst of energy. Joel shook his head emphatically. "Well… why not?"

"He's right…" Conrad's voice was now hoarse, like a man who'd been stranded in the desert for days. "That crazed mob… can't be sure… which of you is carrying… their prisoner from afar… but if you both… go the same way… they will only chase the one group."

"But I can't leave Ali-"

"NO TIME TA ARGUE!" Alistair shouted as he, Conrad, and Lucia darted down an alleyway to their left without warning.

"But-but-" was all Triston could get out before acceptance seemed to overtake him.

Joel looked over his shoulder to see that the group of glowing, red eyes had shrunk down. He was thankful that there were fewer enemies on his tail, but there were still more than enough of them to over-whelm the trio. With that in mind, he led Dhogron and Triston down an alley to their right, in search of a place to hide.

BACK BY THE DOCKS, the remainder of the Strangers stood outside the alleyway, where mere moments ago, they had been engaged in an intense battle with the crazed villagers. Amis had disappeared, and so too had half of their group.

"So… erm… what happened?" Auber asked, his shoulders and face alike slumping.

"We were all here with you. Why would we know da answer to

dat?" Rolf replied. He winced while rubbing his shoulder, and it looked like a bruise was taking shape on his sharp cheekbone.

"They must have secured the prisoner, somehow," the marinian chimed in.

"And who are ye, anyway? I don' remember any fish-guy bein' a part of this team!" Auber said with crossed arms. The marinian returned an amused smile, flashing some sharp teeth that turned his indignation into caution.

"That's not important," Pierce said, approaching the group.

"And this guy! Who the hell *is he*?" Auber asked while bombastically gesturing with both hands. "It seems like half our allies are strangers fallin' from the sky!"

"I don't know who all these new fellas are helpin' us out… but I sure do appreciate it," Kabel said, cracking a smile. The exhaustion in his voice was apparent.

"Alistair mentioned that the man in the mask could be trusted," Ebbie said. "Good 'nuff fer me."

"We are *all* wearing masks, aren't we?" Franco rolled his eyes.

"But I dunno who the fish-guy is," the first mate continued.

"'Fish-guy'," the marinian said to himself, shaking his head and hissing some inhuman form of laughter. "You land-dwellers are funny. Call me Xviktolo."

"Enough of this small talk," Pierce demanded, getting the attention of all in the group. "We have to escape. Right now."

Kabel took a deep breath, then felt the fresh wound on his lower torso. His fingertips found themselves covered in a fresh coat of crimson. "I dunno how much farther I can make it."

Pierce unveiled the Summoner Rune from beneath his cloak. "With this, you won't need to go far."

No sooner had the Strangers laid eyes on the stone's peculiar glow, than a white streak shot into the small crowd and struck it. The Rune flew from Pierce's hand and skidded across the ground for several paces before settling. The dark glow of the engraved swirls on the stone faded.

All turned with a collective gasp to see Angus approaching, his muscled, bloody arm limp at his side. Behind him were a few dark, uncanny monsters that hobbled in lumpy forms, their red rings for eyes glowing. The brainwashed townsfolk of Bosfueras brought up the rear, though much of their reinforcements had disappeared. The kraken had retreated into the water, and so the enhanced avian landed next to the giant.

Pierce let out a hollow huff from beneath the mask and drew his dark blue dagger. "You lot make a run for it. I'll hold him off for a bit."

"That man survived battles with both the kraken and Aldous," Kabel said, shaking his head gingerly. "What makes you think *you* stand a chance in hell?"

"I'll be fine. I have fought him before."

"And what of the avian?" Xviktolo asked, drawing his crystalline sword. "You'll need help in fending off multiple opponents."

"And what good will a fragile diamond sword do?" Pierce asked with a scoff.

The marinian snickered. "You humans amuse me."

"I'm as much 'human' as you are 'fish-guy'… but if you wish to throw your life away so badly, then feel free," Pierce said before looking back to the rest of the Strangers. "The rest of you should make a run for it."

"Don' gotta tell me twice!" Auber said as he pushed his pirate cohorts along the dock path. Ebbie in particular showed signs of resistance, but he eventually gave in. Rolf and Kabel followed, albeit slowly.

"What about Aldous and Dalton?" Franco asked as they jogged up the path, past dock seven.

"They are… leadersss for a reasssson…" Kabel trailed off, his words starting to slur. He tumbled over in a daze, but before hitting the ground, Rolf caught him.

"We gotta find someplace safe to rest," he said.

"What about that church you mentioned before?" Franco asked, looking at Ebbie.

"Ah! Right! Thar lives a priest who may be able to heal ye!" he said.

"Lead… the way…" Kabel choked out as he draped an arm over Rolf's shoulder.

~

Further down the docks, Oneth the Dark Wizard and Hector stood in silence, observing the wreckage of the battlefield, now calm.

"Mm, even Endoshire's residents, used to nighttime destruction as they have become, will find it hard to believe that the degenerates caused all of this damage. Perhaps Sampson can pull a few strings to quell their eventual concerns..." Oneth said before turning to Drake's bodyguard with a vile smile. "You have been patient all of this time. Would you like to have some fun?"

He returned a single nod, and nothing more.

"Very well," Oneth said with a deep chuckle. "You may hunt down a few, and *only* a few. Avoid the Mercer boy and his group."

Hector bowed before his master, then strode up the dock path with startling speed and stealth, like a tiger in search of his prey.

CHAPTER 23
TRAPS IN THE ALLEY

Their eyes alight with bloodlust, Angus and Mur'del approached Pierce and Xviktolo with smooth, careful strides, as if stalking prey. The giant drew his bone blade and then bent his left elbow toward the enhanced avian. Out from his arm popped a sharp bone, which she caught.

"Normal weapons will be useless against these two," Angus said.

She tweeted at him derisively. "As if I *need* a weapon to crush my prey…"

"*You're welcome,*" he replied while rolling his eyes, which then fell on Pierce. "You should have stayed in Thironas. At least then, you could have enjoyed a few more years of peace and freedom."

"Did you think that you could march up to my seal, break it, and then get away? I will only return home after claiming your head as my prize," Pierce said while emphatically slicing his palm open with the dark blue dagger. Blood dripped onto the luxmortite, and sure enough, to go along with Xviktolo's gasp, it pulsed a light blue.

"Obviously, you didn't learn your lesson last time," Angus said as he flexed his free arm. The cracks in the bone of his forearm shield closed up, and a new sheen coated it. "Between you, Endoshire's Key Keeper, and the quiet one, I am beginning to think stubbornness is a trait of all luxians."

"Perhaps…" Pierce trailed off.

All four combatants remained silent for a few moments, with only gentle gusts and the weak tide below to entertain their ears. Then, a piece of cracked city foundation fell to the sea with a great *splash*, and Pierce took that as the signal to begin. He pulled his arm back and across his body, and then flung the dagger forward with all of his might.

The streaking blue blade flew toward the giant at the speed of an arrow. Angus swatted it away with his shield, but harming him had not been the goal of the attack: Pierce ran in the other direction until he neared the Summoner Rune on the ground, and then dove out for it as he heard a whistling of the wind to his right.

Bone bolts, he thought while cradling the Rune and rolling. With no time to spare, Pierce turned his upper body while on a knee and held the magic stone out. His eyes caught a mere glimpse of five small streaks of white before he was blotted out by the portal before him. He next focused on the exit vortex's location: Above Angus' head.

Pierce heard a couple of *thunks* in rapid succession as he willed the portals shut, but Angus' pained grunting revealed that at least some of his counter-offensive had landed. After the last remnants of darkness disappeared before him, he could see that three of the bone bolts had pierced the giant's chest, and he was stumbling back. Sensing blood in the water, the masked luxian gestured two authoritative fingers toward himself, and like a dog obeying commands, the charmed dagger flew into Angus' upper back.

Taken aback once more, Angus gasped up clots of blood and fell to a knee while grasping the tip of the blade protruding from his chest in vain. Pierce responded to his pain by inflicting more: He crunched his fingers, as if grasping a knob, and then began to twist, and so too did the dark blue blade twist. The giant winced and let out a weak, raspy cry before crashing to the ground like a great tree that had been tugged down by rope. A darker-than-human blood pooled around his upper body, but Pierce knew he would simply regenerate if left alone.

While gesturing to the ground with his hand, hoping to pin the giant down, he looked at a stunned Xviktolo and shouted, "The head! Go for his head!"

The marinian nodded and made a run for Angus' limp body, his tail wiggling in the wake of his speedy strides. Without wasting a single movement, he brought his starlite blade down in one smooth motion, aiming for the neck. However, at the last moment, Mur'del jumped in and blocked with the bone blade that Angus had provided her. Xviktolo took a few steps back and flashed discomfort on his face while shaking a free hand. Pierce snorted as he commanded the luxmortite dagger to return to him, and so it did. Angus was already stirring.

Mur'del chirped as she looked down at her weapon. "I suppose it came in handy, after all."

"You seem quite large for a sky-dweller," the marinian said while switching his sword to the right hand and using that opportunity to begin shaking the left. "And strong, too. It is not often I lose feeling in my hands while wielding this blade."

"'Sky-dweller', you say? Would that make you a bottom-feeder?" Mur'del asked with an obnoxious tweet.

"She is not naturally powerful, of course," Pierce said while approaching them. Within moments, he stood next to his newfound ally with his dagger at the ready. "This pathetic lot did not *earn* their abilities. They were *granted* by devilry; a dark essence."

"Tough talk coming from a lesser being," Angus said while pushing himself to his feet. The hole in his chest had healed, and there was no hint that it had ever existed save for blood blotches and rips in his tunic.

"Not a scratch on him…" Xviktolo muttered, wide-eyed. "How do we slay one with such strong regenerative abilities?"

"I fear we may have missed our best opportunity," Pierce said, a hollow snort bouncing beneath the Ometos mask. "If you wish to run, I can send you elsewhere with the Rune-"

"No opportunity," he replied while shaking his head.

"You mean 'no chance'?"

"Indeed," said Xviktolo while grasping his starlite blade with both hands and then crouching into a sideways stance. "I am rarely given a chance to do battle, but a battle to the death against such abnormal opponents? Unheard of. I would be a fool to miss out on this opportunity!"

Mur'del chirped and then smirked at Angus. "I say we feed these maggots to the kraken after we've had our way with them."

"A fine idea," said the giant while raising both his sword and shield.

Try as he might, Pierce could not think of a way to kill Angus or Mur'del save decapitation, and that would be near-impossible to pull off against one of them; let alone two. Yet, he somehow felt at ease with a smiling Xviktolo by his side. Did his new ally have an ace up his sleeve? Or was he simply crazy?

~

Joel led Dhogron, Triston, and Amis through the alleys of the wealthy district in a series of zigzags meant to throw their pursuers off. Although the group was exhausted from all of the running, it was beginning to pay off; the sounds of the Bosfueras townsfolk faded more and more with each new alley passed through.

"Can we... take... a rest?" Triston asked, panting like a water-deprived dog.

Joel nodded, and at the next edge of a building, darted behind, into the shadows. Dhogron and Triston followed, and upon finally stopping, the elder MacRae plopped to the ground and rested up against a wall.

"Don' think... I ever ran so much... in me life..." he choked out while letting Amis sag from his shoulder. "Oi! Are ya awake?"

Dhogron wiped the sweat from his brow before kneeling, so that he was face-to-face with Amis. The Keeper of the Key's eyes widened.

"Y-you came for me..."

"Of course, my friend. I'm only sorry that we couldn't reach you sooner," the trickster Wizard said while placing a hand on Amis' shoulder. His long hair was ragged, and so too was his getup; yet curiously, Joel did not spot any obvious wounds. Perhaps Drake and the Dark Wizard had wished to forgo any sort of interrogation and planned on skipping straight to black gold indoctrination to get what they wanted.

"How're ya feelin', lad?" Triston asked.

"I've felt better, but when you spend as much time in a sewer as I have, it tends to harden your resolve," he replied with a weak chuckle.

"Is the map's location secure?" Dhogron asked.

"I didn't tell 'em anything." Amis smiled while shaking his head. "That is one thing I'd take with me to the grave."

Now, Joel was certain that Amis' transfer to the Dark Wizard's ship was precisely to combat his stubbornness. If he had refused to give them the map's location willingly, then a dose of the altered black gold may have changed his mind. After having borne witness to the droning Bosfueras collective up close, he had no doubt that it would have worked in extracting the map's location from Amis.

The mute began making hand signals to convey his thoughts to the group, but he stopped amid picking up on their puzzled expressions. In their rush to get away from the pursuers, Joel hadn't realized that he'd chosen to escape with people who couldn't understand his sign language.

Joel smiled and let out an inaudible chuckle. His thoughts would have to wait until later. Sitting around and talking for long was ill-advised, anyway. Though the footsteps and voices of their pursuers had initially seemed far away, both their noise level and numbers seemed to have grown over time. He worried that they might have discovered their location and been making preparations to flank them in the alleys.

"Oi! I still don't understand what yer sayin', lad!" Triston said with a loud laugh. The mute held a finger up to his mouth to shush him. "Right… my mistake…"

He peeked around the corner of their hidden alleyway to see a few of the crazed mob looking around and approaching. Joel looked back to his allies with a frown.

"They draw near," he mouthed.

Dhogron held a hand out for his friend. Amis took it and was boosted up. He looked around at the others with gratefulness in his eyes.

"I owe you all many thanks… and my life," he whispered while shaking his head. Joel then approached and drew his sword. Amis held his hands up and his mouth fell agape. "Whoa, whoa! What are ye doin'?"

The mute lowered his blade at a snail's pace until it tapped one of his shackles. Amis squinted at the luxmortite sword and then gasped. "You are… luxian?"

Joel nodded while smiling.

"I have many questions," Amis said while holding his chains out. "But we shall save that for after we've escaped from these fiends."

In a sideways stance, Joel chopped, one-handed, and sliced through the chains, which crumbled like rock turning to dust. Then came an additional swing, to break the chains binding his ankles. The shackles themselves would have to wait, he thought. Not only had the voices of the mob gotten even closer, but he couldn't help but notice the rickety state of his hand while taking the swings. The last thing he wanted was to feel responsible for another maiming of an ally. A pang of guilt struck through Joel as the realization hit: *He had let Giles down.* Not only had he failed to prevent Angus' devastating attack, but he hadn't even accompanied him after the fact. Wasn't that the least he could do?

"Judging by the buildings, I'd say we are still in the wealthy district," Dhogron whispered, looking further down the alley. Joel shook the cobwebs out. Now was not the time to lose focus. He could make it up to Giles later. "The further south we go, the safer we'll be…"

That wasn't entirely true, Joel thought. It was getting late enough in the night that the degenerates would be out and causing trouble. He couldn't sign it to his friends, so instead, he grabbed his eyelids and widened them to bring attention to his eyes; a way to remind them of the yellow eyes, he hoped.

Instead, Triston belly laughed while pointing at him. "Ya look like a bug, lad!"

All others in the alley pressed fingers up to their lips with narrow eyes.

"Right, right… sorry…"

Joel eyed Dhogron, then jerked his head toward the other end of the alley, signaling that it was time to go. The voices nearby had gone silent, but they could still hear footsteps.

"Follow me," the trickster Wizard said, then began walking down to the other end of the alley.

Dread set in, however, when the darkness of the alley receded to reveal a dead-end. They looked back to see shadows of their pursuers stretching past the only remaining exit under the glow of the moon.

"We have no choice but to stand and fight," Amis said, grasping the broken chains attached to his shackles.

Triston drew his great sword. "YE-"

Dhogron slapped a hand over his mouth, muffling whatever remained of his bombastic words. Joel and Amis let out snorting chuckles as the trickster Wizard pointed to the building ahead.

"Everyone, please sit up against that wall," he said.

With grumblings and skidding steps hurrying their pace, the group did as Dhogron said, and then, with his arms spread in a grand gesture, a long piece of paper appeared in both hands. The trickster Wizard swiftly sat down next to them and nudged his head to the upper edges of the paper. Joel grabbed onto the top-left, while Alistair and Amis took hold of the top-right.

"Let us pray that the wind doesn't find us…" Dhogron muttered as five shadowy figures approached from the other side of the paper.

Through their outlines, Joel could see that the Bosfueras townsfolk carried pitchforks, wood axes, and torches; but most noticeable were the glowing, red eyes. They seemed to look through both the paper and his soul. He did everything in his power to resist shivering in the wake of chills running up his spine, but because of their body language, or lack thereof, he was unable to tell if they had taken notice of them. They merely stood there, staring. Then, without uttering a single noise, the men and women turned to leave, as if one body sharing limbs. There had been no verbal or physical communication.

After waiting some time, Dhogron spun the paper around to reveal a highly detailed picture of the very spot where they sat.

"Impressive!" Triston said.

"I always knew your tricks would come in handy," Amis said while clapping his friend off the back.

Joel merely gave him a nod of encouragement.

With that narrow escape, Dhogron led the group out of the alleyway and to their left, toward the west. As they walked, something new caught Joel's ear: Creeping up behind them was an odd, uneasy, breathing. It was both shrill and excited; like some monstrosity sneaking up on them for the kill. The others had to have heard it, too, because their pace had doubled in the past few seconds. No one wanted to find out what it was.

～

MEANWHILE, Lucia, Conrad, and Alistair traversed the east end of the wealthy district with Giles in tow. Their pace had slowed considerably, despite the shouts and noises coming from behind them. Conrad was well aware that he was partially responsible, but it made him feel better that Alistair was right there with him, albeit for different reasons.

Lucia stopped the group upon reaching the end of an alley. Instead of leading to more alleyways, it emptied into a main street. Conrad peeked beneath a gap between her arm and torso to see that the coast was not clear. A large cluster of Bosfueras townsfolk were on patrol, sometimes turning over crates or searching underneath vacant food stands. On the bright side, he recognized this spot as the same road where Sir Job had confronted them the other day. The church was not far off.

"Let's take a moment to rest," she said.

"Not too long, though..." Alistair muttered with uncharacteristic softness. He looked back to an unconscious Giles, still draped over his shoulder. "Me understudy needs tha help as soon as possible..."

Despite the nearby dangers and Giles' poor condition, Conrad was eager to sit and press his back up against the building wall. He let out a deep breath as his head became light as a feather and his thoughts fluttered away. Of course, he suspected that his prior fiddling with the black gold was responsible for his current state, but something was different this time. There was no comfort or relaxation; nor were there any sensations of anger or resentment. Instead, he felt nervous; as was evident by his churning stomach, the cold sweat at his brow, and his limbs feeling heavy as lead. The itch, pains, and aches of before had given way to a natural dread; one that reminded him of his time in Bosfueras. It seemed as if the shadows of the walls were closing in on him.

Attempting to get himself together, Conrad decided to focus on something else: Lucia. He looked at her with a tired smile as she peeked around the corner of the building once more. She then gazed back at him, and oddly enough, the moon-shaped mask on her face had gone from crescent to full. The eye slits slanted downward and the mouth opening smiled with menace.

"Do you truly believe you can escape my grasp, boy?" a deep, dark, and distorted voice echoed. Conrad tried to shake the cobwebs out. Lucia's lips were moving, but it wasn't her voice. Her eyes began to glow red through the slits of her mask. "I am all-encompassing; inescapable; irrevocable… just like your pain and suffering…"

Conrad shuddered and pushed himself further back up against the wall while choking out stuttered breaths. There was nowhere for him to go. The walls closed in, and so too did Lucia. Her lips moved, but her words were as mute as Joel.

"Wh-what?"

"I said, 'How are you feeling?'" she asked, tilting her head.

The strategist let out a relieved breath, then pushed himself back to his feet. He could practically feel the color returning to his face.

"I'm alright…" he said before letting a long breath out through his nose. The shadows of the walls retreated and the mask upon Lucia's face twisted and turned back to its normal state. "What is the plan from here?"

"We are not far from where we were a few days ago, when the knight confronted us," Lucia said. "The church is near."

"What're we waitin' fer, then?" Alistair asked as he rose.

Lucia held a hand up. "They are patrolling the main streets, from the look of things."

"We'll have to cross a road, eventually," Conrad said.

"I agree," Lucia said as she turned and peered around the building corner once more. After a few moments, she looked back at her allies. "As for how we cross the road, I have an idea. But we will need to head south."

"So, we gotta cut through some more alleys?" Alistair asked.

Lucia nodded. "Indeed. How is Giles faring? Do you think he can hold on a little longer?"

Alistair shook the little man on his shoulder. "He's still breathin'."

"Excellent. Let's go," Lucia said before striding past her cohorts.

The Strangers glided through the alleys and in the shadows. In addition to walking the streets, there were several villagers on patrol in the alleyways with farming tools and primitive weapons at the ready.

While traveling southward, Lucia suddenly darted into a new alley on her left. With stuttered steps and confusion filling his head, Conrad followed, and then Alistair brought up the rear. The group hid in the shadows until they heard footsteps and vague chanting. Lucia looked to Conrad with a furrowed brow, and he immediately knew why. She had probably expected Alistair not to pick up on the enemies, but he hadn't realized how close they were, either. She may have thought that his senses were dulling.

In truth, his senses were *heightening*. The steps and grunts of the Bosfueras townsfolk sounded thunderous as they trotted by. Then, in less than a moment's notice, everything save his tired breaths muted. The shadows of the alley cradled him, but they did not bring comfort or feel gentle; they felt malicious and invasive. For a moment, he heard his own breath strain and become high-pitched, just as Mr. Willoughby's breaths had been. Before jumping to any conclusions, though, the noise around him unmuted.

It was then that Conrad realized he had slumped against the wall. He looked up to see a concerned Lucia leaning over. She placed her hands on his shoulders, and he closed his eyes in relief at her warm touch.

"Hey…" she trailed off.

Conrad smiled and opened his eyes, and then his mouth fell agape. Staring at him were a pair of glowing, red-ringed eyes. Lucia's face began to deform: Her lips receded upward and into her gums. Her skin darkened and melted into a tar-like form. Her teeth grew unnaturally long and clumps of hair began to fall from her head. The tip of her nose fell off entirely and she let out an otherworldly hiss that paralyzed him, save for his shivers.

Then, with a single blink of his eyes, Lucia's face returned to normal.

"You hear me? You're going to be alright," she said before planting a kiss on his forehead.

"Y-yeah..." he muttered, looking down. What was happening to him?

"Awright, awright! Cut tha lovey shite out, an' let's get movin'!" Alistair said. Lucia darted her eyes at the big man and frowned.

"*Fool.* Keep your voice down," she hissed.

"Well, I-" Alistair held his tongue and then sighed. "Fine. I'll keep quiet. I'm just anxious about Giles. Can we go, now?"

Lucia nodded before turning to Conrad and holding a hand out. He meekly grasped her offering and was hoisted up.

"Just a little further," she said with a reassuring smile.

"Right..." Conrad was anything but sure.

The group turned left out of the alley and traveled further south. Eventually, they reached a set of stairs that hugged the edge of one of the buildings. Lucia stopped on the first step and then looked back at them.

"Stay low."

Conrad and Alistair only nodded as they crept up the stairs. The strategist was kicking himself for not having realized her plan earlier. One of the rooftop bridges crossed above the main road, and the likelihood that anyone was patrolling up there was low. Otherwise, they'd have probably been spotted by now, and likewise, they'd have spotted the enemy above when surveying the street, earlier.

Sure enough, upon reaching the rooftop, the Strangers encountered no enemies. However, there was an obvious problem with their current trajectory: The railings of the bridge were low, and if even one of the Bosfueras townsfolk decided to look up for any reason, they would be spotted.

While taking crouched, careful steps, Lucia looked back. "Not much cover here. I say we crawl. Will that be a problem?"

To Conrad's surprise, she looked at him, not Alistair.

"N-no problem."

"I'll stay behind you, just in case."

And so, Alistair led the way, crawling across the rooftop bridge with Giles draped over his back like a fancy fur coat. Conrad lagged behind him somewhat, the aches and pains of his previous wounds flaring up with each movement of a limb.

"I'm right here if you need me," Lucia whispered from behind.

Conrad groaned internally. He tried to shake the sluggishness out of his arms and legs occasionally, but it was no use. To make matters worse, when he looked back ahead, the bridge seemed to stretch out, and Alistair now felt impossibly far away. He sighed and let his body sink while closing his eyes. One deep breath gave way to several that were calm, and the strategist found new determination to continue upon opening his eyes back up. However, there was one problem: He was now across the bridge, draped over Lucia's back.

She looked over her shoulder with a huff. "You're heavier than you look."

"Sorry to have been dead weight," he replied, rolling off of her and then propping himself up on one knee. Alistair was already by the stairs, across the rooftop. "But I feel much better, now."

"Good. We'll have plenty of time to rest at the church. For now, let us be quick, for Giles' sake."

Though he was conscious throughout the process, time passed for Conrad in a blur as he followed Lucia and Alistair down the stairs, and then through a dark alleyway that felt familiar. As his eyes wandered to the ground, he caught streaks of red; the same blood he'd spilled at the expense of the slave just days ago. It was dry, of course, but the strange flow of time around him made it feel fluid and alive; like a moving painting. A thoughtless smile came to his face as the blood curled into a crescent moon, just like the tattoo around Lucia's eye. Such beauty reminded him of just how much she'd helped him tonight. Ideas of how he could thank her ran across his mind: A piece of jewelry? A fancy dinner? Or perhaps-

Conrad's happy thoughts were interrupted when a cold, hard reality hit: *the breathing.* Shrill, stuttered, and excited all at once, the strategist looked up to see that his Stranger cohorts had stopped. The alley walls shrunk inward and darkness swallowed up the path, and then he saw the red-ringed eyes of the lumpy beast plodding toward them. *It's not real,* he thought. Just another vision.

"That thing, again! It be a strange beast!" Alistair bellowed, snapping Conrad out of his stupor. It *was* real.

"H-how? How could it be alive?"

Lucia looked back at him with wide eyes. "If Willoughby was a result of the Dark Wizard's tampering with the dark essence, who's to say he couldn't make more monsters just like that?"

"More importantly," Conrad said, gazing over his shoulder. "We have to get out of here."

"An' lose all tha progress we just made? Giles is barely hangin' on as it is, lad!" Alistair argued while drawing upon his battle axe. "I say we stand and fight!"

Conrad turned to Lucia. Surely, she would disagree with the big man on principle, he thought. She had witnessed the terrifying might of Willoughby and had to know that there was no chance of victory in direct combat.

"I hate to say it," she said as Conrad's heart sank. "But he's right. We don't know how long Giles has."

The strategist snarled. "You know what it's capable of! The only reason I ever survived against such a monster is that I was able to hide and use elements of surprise! We don't have that here. It will slaughter us all."

"Don't forget that we are a team. For Giles' sake…" Lucia trailed off while drawing her long sword. "We have to try."

Alistair placed Giles up against the wall of a building, then walked side-by-side with Lucia; both had weapons at the ready. Conrad remained frozen. What could he do? The situation was hopeless.

"There is a way…" a deep voice echoed in his mind as darkness began clamping down on the alleyway around him.

"Get… out of my head…" Conrad muttered, grasping his skull and twisting it, in the same way that his mind was twisting.

The darkness receded momentarily, but his efforts were in vain. A sinister cackle reverberated about the increasingly narrow and darkening path and it resumed its closing. Lucia and Alistair, who were just ahead of him, began to fade away. The alley became a tunnel of wind, and the gusts sounded like blood-curdling screams of desperate men.

"Such a shame that you turned down my offer back in Bosfueras. I could have helped you conquer the dark," the voice said. Aside from the howling wind ripping at his ears, it was all that Conrad could hear.

"Is that right?" Conrad asked with doubt on his tongue. "With your black gold? I don't wish to be your slave."

"I gave you the black gold to demonstrate how I would heal what ails mankind, and that is all."

"You forgot to mention how you took it away, and let me rot in a dungeon."

"A valuable lesson. All that awaits man is death and misery without it; that is how it has been for thousands of years. They cannot handle the stresses and pains of the world on their own. They are not like us, Conrad," the Dark Wizard said.

The strategist scoffed. "I'm afraid we don't have much in common, fiend. Or should I call you by your true name? Wilhelm the Oppressor..."

"I see Aldous has shared his misguided theory with you. I am not quite this 'Oppressor' that you refer to. I can be quite merciful, in fact," he replied with a bass-filled chuckle. "For instance, the monster that stares you down in the alley… it is one of my *creepers*. A fitting name, wouldn't you agree?"

"Get to the point," Conrad said with vitriol.

The Dark Wizard snorted. "I will get straight to it, then: I control the creepers myself, meaning I can call them off at any time. Kill one of your friends, and I shall spare the rest of you."

"Wh-what?"

"Make your decision, quickly…" the deep voice said, fading away with each word.

"No! Wait!" Conrad called out, but his vision had returned to normal. So too had the noises and surroundings of the real world. His two allies had barely moved since the conversation in his mind took place.

"Sorry, lad. We gotta try!" Alistair said without looking back.

Conrad looked over the shoulders of his friends to see the grotesque creeper looming. *No way*, he thought. There was no conceivable way to win in a direct confrontation with the monster. His eyes darted to the right and settled on an unconscious Giles.

There *was* a way, but it would require a sacrifice, he thought. He drew his dagger, then turned toward Giles. His stomach churned with each step taken toward his prone ally; he held his blade downward, ready to stab.

"Conrad! No!" Lucia's voice called.

No time to explain, he thought as the thudding steps of his comrades neared to stop him. With his heart racing, Conrad brought the dagger down and closed his eyes. Only the miserable sounds of the hissing creeper, peeling flesh, and spurting blood remained to comfort him.

～

Captain Auber's group continued to walk up the coastal path. They had reached dock 14 upon hearing curious noises coming from behind. However, when they stopped and looked back, there was nary a foe to be found. All they could really see were Pierce and Xviktolo as specs, battling Angus and the enhanced avian off in the distance.

"Why do I keep hearin' things?" Auber asked aloud with a shiver.

"I dunno. Maybe yer right crazy in da head?" Rolf replied.

"No…" Kabel said, eyeing the alleys to his right. "There is someone, or *something*, out there."

"Perhaps it is one of those unsightly monsters from before?" Franco asked.

"I don't think so," the stocky man said before letting out a breath of exhaustion. It was becoming difficult to keep his eyes open. "Those beasts were slow-moving. Whoever this is, they are fast. *Inhumanly fast.*"

"Oh, come on!" Auber whined while rubbing his grumbling stomach. "This is the kinda situation that makes me imagination run wild! Now, I'm nervous."

"I didn't know that the *mighty* Captain Auber got nervous?" Kabel said, eyeing him with a cheeky smile.

"R-right… well, ye shoulda let me finish!" the captain said, putting hands to hips and snorting with pride. "I'm nervous 'cause I don' wanna get tied up battlin' a monster when we've gotta focus on getting' ye to safety!"

"How kind of you," he replied with barbs of sarcasm before turning his attention to the road ahead. "We aren't far from where we need to be. There is a road near dock 19 that will take us straight to the church."

With that in mind, Auber and Kabel's combined team continued along the coastal road with no resistance or presence from their enemies. That was, until reaching dock 18. Across from the docks was a road that led southwest, where dozens of brainwashed Bosfuerans patrolled. Auber and company froze in place as a small horde stared straight ahead with glowing, red eyes and walked toward them. They drew weapons and prepared for battle, but let out collective gasps to find that they turned around after reaching a certain point on the street.

"I dun' get it… why're they leavin' us alone?" Ebbie asked.

"They are a single-minded lot," a woman called from the roof of a building at the end of the southwest road. "Their orders were to attack anyone on that road, and nothing more."

The Strangers looked up to find a dark-haired woman sitting on the roof's edge with a carefree smile and a dainty hand cradling her cheek. Her floral dress, further decorated in blood splotches, fluttered in the gentle breeze.

"So then, *you* are the one who's been following us," Kabel said.

She shrugged. "I'm afraid not. I have no interest in dead men walking."

"Is that right?" he asked before pointing up at her with his rickety arming sword. "Then, why don't you come down here and prove it!"

The woman chuckled. "I have nothing to prove."

"You can't fight her, she's just a helpless woman stuck on a roof!" Auber said.

Her chuckles turned to hysterical laughter as she closed her eyes and tilted her head up to the sky. After settling down, she opened her eyes, which now glowed a piercing red in the dark of night. She opened her mouth and out slithered a tongue that was as long as a snake, and it danced like one, too.

"Another freak," Kabel said with a groan.

She retracted the tongue back into her mouth, but her smile remained. "That is unkind of you to say; especially since I planned to impart some friendly advice to you."

"And what advice might dat be?" Rolf asked.

"I suppose it doesn't matter much, since you won't live to see another dawn, but... if you wish to live a little longer, you may want to take your chances down *this* path," she said, pointing down the southwest road, where the drones patrolled.

Auber scoffed. "What nonsense!"

"That is my advice. Take it or leave it," the woman said while hopping to her feet. "You lot are boring me. But at least Hector will see to it that I am treated to a chorus of your screams..."

Just as mysteriously as she had appeared, the woman vanished into the shroud of night. The Strangers looked at each other in bewilderment.

"Stay the course?" Kabel asked.

"It's obvious that we should!" Captain Auber said. "Why would we listen ta her? She's *the enemy*."

"True, but something about her tone bothered me," Kabel said while stroking his chin. "Usually, such confidence is reserved for those telling the truth."

"Perhaps her confidence is linked with those noises from before," Franco said.

"She mentioned somethin' about a fella named Hector. Maybe one of dem dark beasts is followin' us after all?" Rolf suggested.

"But wait, them noises went away. They must'a been her!" Ebbie said.

"Yeh, she's just tryin' ta lure us into one of the alleys where she can trap us; or worse, pit us against them crazy villagers!" Auber said.

After a few more moments of thought, Kabel nodded. The captain's logic was sound. She likely wanted to trap them between the villagers or in an alley to pick them off easily, he thought. Still, something ate away at the back of his mind, but he couldn't figure out what it was. He was too exhausted and sore to think clearly.

With the road they wished to travel nearby, the Strangers made their way past dock 18 and up to 19. Across from that dock was the path to the church. The eastern side of Endoshire had far more open space than the city center, slums, or wealthy district. Grassy hills dominated the landscape, with modest houses and cottages scattered about.

As soon as the group turned right down the path, they began to hear noises again. To Kabel's ears, it reminded him of an animal scurrying along a stone path. Neither he nor the rest of the group would be kept in suspense for long, however: Dashing out from behind one of the houses ahead and onto the road was the tall, cloaked man who'd been standing by the Dark Wizard's side, earlier.

The Strangers stopped to observe him. The bottom of his cloak tented outward as if it were hiding something large at his feet. Beneath the hood were glowing, red eyes; though they were hardly a surprise.

"This must be that Hector fellow the woman mentioned. Be on your guards," Kabel said.

"I'll handle him," Auber said to his teammates, stepping forward. He looked out to the cloaked figure with a toothy grin. "Ye best be turnin' back, landlubber! The Strangers don't have much tolerance fer needless obstacles such as yerself!"

He remained silent and motionless. The captain looked back to his team with a notable drop in his confidence before returning to them. Without a spoken word, all in the group drew their weapons. Hector only cocked his head in response.

After a few more moments of dead silence, the skirmish began:

Hector kicked up a cloud of dust while charging ahead and that familiar noise returned. It truly was the sound of scurrying, Kabel thought. Not only that, but he was fast; too fast for them to escape.

That was when it hit him: The woman from earlier wasn't trying to lure them into the alleys, or even into a trap. This mysterious, cloaked figure had been trying to lead them out into the open. That way, there would be no hiding, and his superior speed would give him the edge.

"Prepare yourselves!" Kabel cried with renewed energy as he held his shield up in position and pointed his sword outward.

A jolt of pain shot up the stocky man's arm, however, and his shaking blade lowered. That brief moment of weakness was all that Hector needed: He swatted at Kabel's arming sword, to which it spun and flew away like a pinwheel taken by the wind. He then laid a shoulder into his shield, knocking him back and into the trio of pirates nearby.

Rolf, the last one standing, had already begun retaliating: He swung a blade horizontally with all his might, but to the gasps of all, Hector blocked it by merely holding his arm out.

"I-impossible!" Rolf shouted as the bottom of the cloak lifted.

A giant scorpion tail emerged, then coiled back. Before Rolf could express his shock any further, the tail's stinger struck like a cobra and pierced deep into the stomach of its prey.

Breathless and dry heaving all at once, Rolf fell to his knees as the black-tipped tail ripped from out of his midsection. Kabel's vision blurred with horror and rage alike as his friend reached out for him, pale and struggling to breathe. The hole in his stomach quickly turned an ugly combination of red and black.

The cloaked man loomed over them all with his scorpion tail wiggling in delight. Kabel gritted his teeth and balled his fists. Angry as he was, despair still managed to overpower that feeling. What could he do against such a monster?

CHAPTER 24
BATTLE IN THE STREETS

Prince Xviktolo thwarted a downward and diagonal swing from Mur'del's bone blade with a hollow *thud* off of his starlite sword. He swiftly responded with a slice that traveled in the same direction as her attack's follow-through. The enhanced avian cawed in surprise as he landed a heavy blow on her wing.

Not wanting to let up, the marinian whirled his sword as the smatterings of her dark blood misted the air, and he lunged out for an unopposed stab. The starlite blade plunged straight through her midsection, and after a gurgling, crimson-soaked cough, she slumped over. Though still standing, it felt to Xviktolo like the sword was all that held her up.

"Perhaps you should have spent more time attacking from the sky, where you belong. In close combat, you're no match for me!" he said while tugging at his crystalline blade.

His blade halted, however, when Mur'del grabbed the sword with both of her wings. Beneath the dark feathers, he spied two talon-like hands, each large enough to claw apart flesh with ease. It made him wonder why she bothered engaging in a swordsman's duel, to begin with. Struggle as he might, Xviktolo was unable to pull the blade away.

Mur'del straightened and let out a chirp. The wound on her wing had healed. "Funny. Soon, your corpse will be fish food on the seabed. That is where *you* belong, bottom-dweller."

Before he could react to her taunt, she plunged the bone blade into Xviktolo's shoulder. The searing hot sensation in combination with spurting blood granted the prince a jolt of energy, allowing him to rip the starlite sword from her grip and put some distance between them.

After taking a few backward strides, Xviktolo switched to a one-handed grip and felt the wound with his other hand. It was deep, but in a non-fatal area, he thought. Still, he could feel the energy being sucked from that arm, meaning he would have to continue the battle one-handed.

"What was that you were saying about 'close combat'?" the enhanced avian mused.

"Yes, well, I didn't know that you could regurgitate."

Mur'del narrowed her eyes. "That's *regenerate*."

"Yes, of course… that is what I meant…" Xviktolo trailed off, searching his mind for ways to defeat her. The burning of his shoulder blocked all rational thought. "There has to be *something* that you cannot recover from."

At that moment, Pierce hopped back from his most recent clash with Angus and stood side-by-side with Xviktolo. He wiped the blood from his chin, breathing heavily.

"It is impossible to defeat us. You are *lower beings*, after all," Angus said with a smirk.

"But we both know that you can be beaten. Zamarim was about to rip you to shreds back in Thironas. You only got lucky," Pierce said.

"Mayhap, but last I checked, neither of you could ever begin to compare with a Wizard King."

"He's right…" Pierce whispered to his ally. "My only idea is to cut off their heads, and I'm not even sure if *that* would work. We need something more powerful."

Xviktolo's eyes widened at a revelation. With a slick smile, he turned to Pierce and whispered back, "I have an idea, but it is dangerous. We'll have to make a run for it, on my signal."

"I can fly us away with the dagger, or transport us to safety with the Rune," Pierce replied. "What are you planning?"

"Just get ready for my signal. If we don't escape in time, it will kill us, too."

Pierce nodded as the marinian prince closed his eyes and lowered his head. He pushed through the burning pain in his shoulder and concentrated on the sounds of the sea.

"Are you giving up?" Mur'del asked with an amused chirp.

"Don't be ridiculous. This stubborn group never gives up," Angus said as he held a hand out, fingers facing forward. "I'm not waiting around to find out, either way. Farewell, Ometos."

Xviktolo could practically feel Pierce looking at him with urgency, but his eyes were still closed and his head adrift; as if he were praying. He heard the great *crack* of Angus' bones, signaling the attack soon to come. Next, he felt Pierce grasp his webbed hand. Through him, he could feel the pulsating power of the dark blue dagger.

"Good choice..." Xviktolo muttered with a toothy grin. For what he had planned, they might still get caught up in the attack if they tried escaping through a portal. With that thought, the offensive was ready, and his eyes burst open. "Now!"

At the same moment that the pair took off, Xviktolo's senses were assaulted by the five streaking bolts of white whistling through the air, and a great splash erupting from the sea. In less than a second, the marinian pushed his burning shoulder and arm out of mind to admire the enormous amount of ground they had covered: He estimated their enemies to be at least 20 meters away, now. However, even at their eye-watering speeds, the extra weight of Xviktolo coming along for the ride had a price. The marinian watched on, helpless, as one bolt passed by him and lodged into the back of Pierce's leg. There was no time to admire such a spectacle, though, as he felt two burning blows to his back, sending shockwaves through his whole body.

The allies crashed to the ground and tumbled for a short distance, but upon stopping, they did not immediately tend to their newfound wounds. Instead, their attention was to their enemies, now shadowy figures, to their eyes. The kraken had shot up out of the water and tilted her head back. Mur'del began to lift off and Angus pointed his other arm at the creature of the sea, but it was too late. A mass of poison blotted the sky above them, and it came down in a torrential downpour.

Angus and Mur'del writhed in agony on the ground as their cries and screeches filled the air, complimented by a high-pitched *sizzle*. Even from afar, Xviktolo could see that the poison was not only melting away at their skin, but their bones, too. Soon, their panicked screams of agony turned to weak moans, and then, the smells of the sea became overpowered by burning flesh and putrid poison.

When the effects of the poison finally wore off, Angus and Mur'del had been reduced to unrecognizable creatures: Each had become so, so, small, and only retained the thinnest layers of muscle to hold what remained of their bones together. Bodily juices leaked from places where appendages should have been, and there was not a hair or feather to be found on either of them. The little, red creatures squirmed like demonic newborns, occasionally flailing and making vague gurgling noises from mouths that looked painful to open. No immediate regeneration was apparent. The kraken hopped down from the coastal ledge and returned to the sea.

"It worked!" Xviktolo said, now on a knee. He ripped the bone bolts out of his back, and it was quite painful, but he was too elated with their victory to care.

"I didn't realize that the kraken was on our side..." Pierce said while stumbling to his feet. He grunted while ripping the bolt out of the meat of his leg.

"Let's finish them off," Xviktolo said as he drew his starlite sword.

"Wait!" he said, stilling the marinian. Pierce pointed ahead. Past Angus and Mur'del's rotting forms, a few green lights twinkled off in the distance. "It's that wretched attack again! The one that felled Aldous! We have to go!"

Pierce held his Summoner Rune outward as the green lights intensified. Though Xviktolo knew the wicked intent behind the glow, he couldn't help but look on in awe as they overtook the dark blue of the night sky. Then, he heard a howling wind and turned back to see a dark, swirling portal.

"Where does it lead?" Prince Xviktolo asked as the environment grew greener and a new sizzling sound tickled his ears.

"Somewhere better than here," Pierce replied as he nudged his head toward the gateway.

Without a second thought, the pair jumped into the portal, sure to avoid a fate similar to Angus and Mur'del.

～

"WHAT THA HELL... IS THAT THING?" Triston asked, eyes bulging at the sight of a lumpy monster plodding down the path behind them.

Joel's group had traveled southwest through a series of alleys, and as they did, the breaths of the inhuman monster had grown louder. Eventually, the beast revealed itself, but to their puzzlement, it had not charged at them. Instead, its pace was deliberate.

"When those fiends interrogated me..." Amis said between breaths while hobbling along to the tune of his jingling chains. "They threatened to 'let the creeper have its way with me'. I wonder if they were referring to this monster?"

"Hold on…" Dhogron huffed. "What about your sword? Surely… it could slay the beast…"

The group stopped beneath the shadow of a rooftop bridge to catch their collective breaths. There was no sign of the red-eyed lump of darkness down the stretch of alley, but Joel suspected the calm wouldn't last long. Though it moved slowly whenever appearing before them, it seemed to always catch up with them quickly when out of sight.

"They took it from me," Amis said, sulking. "That weapon is one of a kind in this day and age."

That was an understatement, Joel thought. With luxmortite in the hands of the enemy, he shuddered at what they may be able to accomplish. Then again, Angus' bones seemed about as strong as the rare metal.

"Where are we, anyway? We've been wanderin' these alleys forever!" Triston said.

"I'm trying to take us to the western coast. The degenerates usually don't stray that far. Seems like the safest route," Dhogron said.

The mute felt relief set in. Even if he hadn't been able to relay his thoughts about the crazed mobs that roamed the city at night, he was glad someone else kept them in mind.

"Ain't nothin' safe as long as that monstah's followin' us!" the elder MacRae said before nudging Joel. "What about you, lad? You got one of them fancy blue blades, too! Slay that beast!"

Before he could reply, the red eyes of the creeper beamed into view from down the path, and a realization dawned on Joel: No matter how sharp his blade was, it could not compete with the regeneration of his dark essence-enhanced enemies. Especially in this confined area, striking anything but a killing blow would see a repeat of what had happened to Giles, or worse.

Joel turned to his allies, shook his head, and then motioned for them to continue running.

"Aldous told me about your apprehension to harming men or women, but why not a monster?" Dhogron asked.

The mute gritted his teeth. This was all a misunderstanding. Regardless of whether he fought or not, they didn't have a hope of winning at this time. He wasn't sure what he could mime or mouth to get the point across.

Triston groaned, and then Amis stepped forth while holding out his hand. The creeper continued at its lumbering pace, letting out shrill breaths along the way. "Allow me to borrow the sword, and I will vanquish the beast."

Joel shook his head once more, and the others frowned. He wished that someone were there to translate for him.

"Please... I ask you as one of your fellow countrymen; nay, as one of your *brothers*. We share blood that has nearly gone extinct. Surely, that must count for *something*. Entrust me with your blade, and I will rid us of this nuisance!" Amis said. After a few moments without response, he turned to Dhogron and shrugged. "He doesn't trust me."

"Mayhap you'll trust me, then!" Triston said, holding out a hand. Joel once again motioned for the group to run. The creeper was close, now, and each of its ringed eyes had focused down into solid dots.

"There is no time to argue!" Amis cried as he swiped the sword from Joel's hip. The mute was too shocked to react.

"L-let's remain calm!" Dhogron said, holding out a hand.

"Too late fer that!" Triston shouted, then drew his great sword and charged the monster alongside Amis.

The pair launched a dual attack that the creeper didn't even try to avoid: Triston slashed into the lumpy gut of the creature, while Amis cut into its neck. All at once, the creeper's upper body flipped through the air, and so too did its head; both landed as the remaining lower half of the body fell to its knees and collapsed in a heap of rotting flesh and tar-like substance.

"See that?" Triston asked, looking back to Joel and Dhogron. "It was no mat-"

A harsh squeal came from the disembodied head at the elder MacRae's feet, stilling his tongue. All in the alley covered their ears as the head of the creeper sprouted red, spider-like legs at its bottom stump. Pieces of the creeper's body began to mold, like clay, into red spider creatures, each about the size of a dog. Their fangs, covered in black, twitched with excitement.

Amis shuddered and began running back to his allies. Triston didn't realize he was retreating until one of his jingling chains bounced off of his leg. The brief distraction was enough for the monster to unleash a ball of clotted red from its mouth, which then netted out into a flying web.

"Gah!" Triston cried as the web caught onto his arms and flung them into the side of a building, where the stickiness kept him trapped. Struggle as he might, he was unable to free himself without the use of a sword.

As Amis ran past, Joel swiped the luxmortite blade back from him and made a run toward the creeper and a struggling Triston. No more allies would be harmed on his watch.

Four spider-like creatures approached the elder MacRae with careful steps, each like a fox about to pounce on a rodent. Joel rushed in and sliced through the red webbing with his dark blue blade. However, in doing so, he left himself open.

The creeper's head leaped out with its massive jaw agape and ready to snap down. Joel let his reflexes take over: He dropped his sword and then caught the head by two of its spider legs. The head thrashed about in his struggling arms, chomping down with bone-crunching power mere inches before his face.

As Joel felt his grip weakening, however, a sword plunged through the face of the monster and then cut down to slice it in half. Dark red blood erupted as the head deflated and collapsed to reveal a panting Triston.

"Let's get the hell outta he-"

He was interrupted by a spider creature jumping on his back. Joel let out an inaudible gasp, thinking that it would tumble Triston over, but he remained on his feet, grabbed the spider by one of its legs, and threw it off. It splattered into a dry, blood clot-like substance upon striking the nearby building wall.

Triston opened his mouth once more, but Joel retrieved his sword and tapped him off the shoulder as he ran past, deterring him from speaking further. Instead, he dashed alongside the mute.

Screeches from the regenerating creeper head reverberated about the alleys as the four Strangers converged and ran further west, down the path.

"EXPLAIN YERSELF!" Triston said, shoving Amis as they escaped. "YA LEFT ME BACK THAR TA GET EATEN BY THOSE THINGS!"

The Key Keeper stumbled but regained his footing quickly. He looked back at the big man with fire in his eyes, but only for a moment. He quickly shifted to a remorseful expression.

"I'm sorry..." Amis muttered between breaths. "I didn't want... them to capture... me again..."

"You are not one... to shy away from battle... either..." Dhogron choked out while panting. "What did they do… to make you… so afraid?"

Amis opened his mouth to answer, but all in the group were distracted by another creeper, hobbling toward them from the other end of the alley. They looked back to see the red spiders crawling along the walls of the buildings, not far enough behind for comfort. In a panic, Dhogron turned left down the next alleyway.

"Damn!" said the trickster Wizard. The end of the path appeared to branch into a main road. "I wanted to… avoid the city center… but we have… no choice…"

After a mad dash down the passage, the Strangers burst out of the shadows and found themselves bathing in the moonlight for the first time in what felt like an eternity.

There was no time to stop or rejoice, however. In mere moments of being out in the open, the Strangers found themselves under attack. Not from the creepers, but the degenerates that they had so badly wished to avoid. A horde of yellow-eyed men and women swarmed the group, swiping at them with knives, fingernails, punches, and kicks; cackling and screaming as they did so.

A crazed woman with blood streaming down her nose jumped out from behind a market stand and tackled Amis to the ground as he ran. Triston drew his great sword, and without hesitation, swung horizontally to push back the group of attackers looking to dog-pile his downed comrade.

"Get off me, ye crazy wench!" Amis cried as he pushed a hand up into her bloodied face. She swiped away while straddling him like a rabid animal lusting for the kill.

Dhogron grabbed the collar of the bloody woman's dress and jerked back. She let out a surprised gasp as the trickster Wizard sent her flying into the crowd of pursuers, knocking several of them over in the process.

"Stronger than he looks!" Triston called out, still on crowd control.

Amis smiled as his friend held a hand out for him. He took it to be hoisted up. Afterward, the group resumed their attempts to escape westward. However, like flies drawn to rotting meat, more and more degenerates appeared out of the woodwork and gave chase.

While running, Joel felt something lasso around his leg. He looked down, in the process of tripping, to see a tongue that stretched from out of his view. It had to be the handiwork of the disembodied monster head, he thought.

As he was falling from the sudden constriction, Joel turned, and in one sweeping motion, drew upon his luxmortite sword and slashed the tongue clean off. When his bottom hit the ground, the mute used a backward somersault to propel himself back up, then pivoted and ran forward once more. When it was all said and done, Joel looked up and to the right to find a creeper head perched atop a nearby building, retracting its cut tongue while letting out an otherworldly howl. Meanwhile, the sliced piece of tongue flopped on the ground like a fish out of water.

The Strangers pressed onward and didn't dare look back at the chanting hordes behind them. However, just as it seemed they were leaving the angry voices behind, they ran into another obstacle: More creepers entered the main street via an alley up ahead. They strode along at a slow pace, hissing and taunting them with their shrill breaths. As much as their red-ringed eyes frightened Joel, the mob of yellow-eyed degenerates to their rear made him equally nervous. They had slowed their pace, much like the monsters ahead, and all wore smiles that perfectly reflected their ill intent.

"Let's put 'em to sleep!" one of the men called out. Several in the crowd laughed.

"Break them!"

"Beat them!"

"Carve them!"

"Hang them!"

"What do we do?" Triston asked aloud.

"We've got no choice but to fight," Dhogron said.

Joel shook his head in defiance.

"Enough of this peaceful nonsense. They are trying to kill us!" Amis said.

While what he'd said was true, the mute had another plan. He turned, walked up to one of the approaching creepers, and drew his sword. The monster cackled at him while pulling its unnaturally long arm back, ready to take a full-strength swing.

"What're ya doin', lad? Get outta thar!" Triston cried as the creeper swung its arm.

Joel was surprised by the quickness of the swing, but his reflexes prevailed; he hopped back and avoided it, only feeling the light sting of wind slapping his face as a consequence. The creeper hissed, then lunged forward with another swing. Joel dodged once more by jumping backward.

The process continued until he passed by the stationary Strangers, all watching on in silent confusion.

"But wait! Yer gonna run into them degenerates, soon!" Triston called out.

"Hold on. I think he's got a plan," Dhogron said with a confident smile.

"I see, now…" Amis said, then walked up to another approaching creeper.

"Now, where's *he* goin'?" Triston asked.

With his most recent dodge of the monster, Joel looked over his shoulder to see a degenerate approaching him. The man had long, black hair, and decrepit skin that reflected the poor state of his mind. Some of his teeth were missing, and he excitedly clenched a small war hammer that was drenched in blood.

"What's the matter, lil' boy?" the crazed man asked with a vile giggle. "Are ye cold? I can warm ye up! Drippin' blood keeps ye warm!"

The vile man howled with laughter as he swung the hammer for Joel's head. With ease, the mute ducked, and the war hammer smashed into the creeper standing behind him. A combination of rotten meat and dark red blood flew through the air as the monster let out an unbearably loud bellow, forcing all in the vicinity to cover their ears.

Such a cry caught the attention of the other degenerates. Their yellow eyes met the red-ringed gaze of the creeper, and many of them wore excited grins filled with malice and hate.

"Such an unsightly beast!" one woman called out.

"Such a pathetic creature!"

"Another tool of the Imperialists!"

"Let's skin 'em alive!"

"Make 'em cry out in pain again!"

Joel dove out of the way as several degenerates and the creeper went to battle. Men and women flew over him as he crawled back up the street, unnoticed, to safety. The creeper let out a monstrous howl as the degenerates tried to hack away at the regenerating creature.

No matter how many times it got damaged, the creeper regenerated, and no matter how often the beast swatted them away, the degenerates continued coming back for more. The immovable object had truly met the irresistible force, Joel thought.

Meanwhile, another section of the degenerates closed in on Amis, who had led the monster past Triston and Dhogron, on the other side of the road from Joel. The same bloody-nosed woman who had attacked the Key Keeper earlier hopped onto his back and bit him on the shoulder.

Amis cried out in pain, then grabbed her by the hair and flipped the woman over his back. She landed with a *thud* on her bottom, at the feet of the creeper. She looked up in wonder at the dark creature, who lowered itself so that they were face-to-face.

After a bizarre moment of tranquility, the monster pulled its head back while stretching its mouth inhumanly wide. Before the crazed woman could so much as speak, the creeper sprang its head forward so that her head was inside of the mouth. It then clamped down using its grotesque, long teeth, and a loud *crunch* echoed between the buildings in the streets.

The decapitated body of the woman spurted blood from the stump at her shoulders before going limp and plopping to the ground.

"HOLY HELL!" Triston shouted.

"That could have been us…" Dhogron muttered, wide-eyed.

Amis wiped the blood that had splattered onto his cheek and stood as the separate group of degenerates ran past him and began attacking the creeper.

"This is our chance!" he said as Joel joined the Strangers.

Without another word, the group ran down the street, leaving the battle that they had started behind. Shrill cries and careless cackles filled the air. Joel took one last look back to see mobs throwing their torches at the large, red spider creatures. The creepers themselves swung with their long arms, knocking the degenerates away in clumps. However, they continued coming back for more and the fight raged on as the Strangers turned onto an alleyway on the left, to enter the slums.

Lucia heard the wet, fleshy sounds of blood spatter as she tackled Conrad in the midst of his stab. The pair crashed to the ground and up against the building wall. She could feel the warmth of fresh crimson dripping down her shoulder as she sat up.

Conrad hunched over against the wall; tensed and shaking. Alistair marched over, his wide, fiery eyes on Giles' limp body, before turning to the strategist. He grabbed him by the collar, lifted him with the ease that a parent would their toddler, and then slammed him against the wall like a rag doll.

"How could you? *Why* did you?" the big redhead asked with betrayal on his tongue. Conrad looked away. "Don' got much ta say fer what ya did, eh? Maybe I should bash yer head in ta get ya talkin'!"

"Wait!" Lucia said, standing with an outstretched hand. Alistair looked at her with more demand than she'd ever seen in his eyes. She could hardly blame him, but…

"He is not himself…"

"I don' care! He just killed our ally! Our friend! Me understudy! It was *my job* ta protect 'im!" a teary-eyed Alistair said before grabbing Conrad's scalp. With a twisting of the wrist, he turned his head to Giles' motionless body, slumped up against the wall next to him. "Look what you did!"

"Worth it…" Conrad muttered.

"What was that?" Alistair asked, incredulous. His face was reddening by the second.

Lucia gripped her long sword with a grimace. If it came to blows, she would need to step in. Understandable as Alistair's rage was, he simply did not grasp the dark essence and its effects on the mind.

"I said…" Conrad trailed off as he raised his left, bloody hand. It pointed at the dark monstrosity, which had turned around and was making its way down the alley. "It was worth it."

Both Alistair and Lucia gasped. Conrad's hand was shaking, but not due to nervousness or emotional shock. There was a gaping, bleeding hole in his palm. The big man pushed him back into the wall and ran to Giles. He placed his hand on his chest, and sure enough, it began bobbing with each tiny breath that he took.

"H-he's…"

Conrad held up a finger to silence his friend and then motioned to the monster exiting the alleyway off in the distance.

"It left because you stabbed yourself?" Lucia asked, finally loosening her grip on the long sword and relaxing her posture. "I don't understand."

"Back in Bosfueras, when some of the dark essence was injected into me, I would sometimes hear a voice chanting wicked spells or some such thing. I came to find out that it was the Dark Wizard contacting me. The connection between us was much weaker, back then, so it usually happened in my dreams…" Conrad said, looking at his twitching, bloody hand.

"Did he contact you just now?" Lucia asked.

"Yes, and he has been trying ever since we escaped into the alleys, I think. Whenever our connection is established, it seems to distort the very world around me. It's as if the shadows on the walls are closing in on me," he said while cleaning off his dagger with a rag. "Those monstrous creatures are called 'creepers', apparently, and they are under his control. He offered to call it off if I killed one of you."

"Thar's somethin' wrong with that fella!" Alistair said.

"Understatement of the millennium," Lucia replied with a roll of her eyes.

"Oh, shut it!" the big man bellowed before turning to Conrad and slapping him on the shoulder. "Sorry I ever doubted ya, lad! When it all came down to it, ya even sacrificed a hand fer us!"

"Not exactly," Conrad replied with a sly smile. He held up his hand, and under the dried blood was no longer a wound, but a large scab down the middle of his palm. "The dark essence heals me, to a certain extent. On this night alone, I cracked my skull, got pierced through my stomach, and gouged my hand... but you'd never know it."

"Don't ignore the downside. You're not *you* when under the influence of that *toxin*," Lucia said with crossed arms.

Conrad frowned, but his combativeness faded quickly. "Right... well, it is up to Aldous to remove the essence from me. Until then, I may as well enjoy the benefits."

"We don't even know if Aldous is alive after that green ball of light hit him," she said with worry in her heart.

"That's true! I've nevah seen nothin' like that in me whole life! I hope he's alright..." Alistair said in lowered spirits.

"There is nothing we can do but move on, either way," Conrad said as his two cohorts looked to him with tilted heads. "If the Dark Wizard killed him, then I'm certain that Aldous' wishes would be for us to see this through and defend the Degenerate Seal."

Lucia searched his face for any sign of worry or sadness, but couldn't find it. All she saw was cold, hard, calculation. No one save for Joel identified better with Aldous than Conrad. Just over a year ago, he would have been torn up at the idea of any of his allies dying, she thought. Now, she couldn't even find a spec of despair in his voice or mannerisms. It had to be the dark essence within him. Worries were creeping into the back of her mind that without Aldous, there would truly be no way for him to be rid of it.

"An' what about Dalton? I didn't see him around when we made our escape," Alistair said. Lucia's eyes widened. How could she not have noticed?

"If he perished in battle, we'll have to determine a new leader for the group," Conrad said, rubbing his chin. "Come to think of it, the same goes for Aldous."

"We don't know what became of either of them," Lucia replied with an icy glare. "Your callous thoughts are beginning to get on my nerves… remember when the death of a friend used to bother you?"

Alistair gasped, then looked away, red-cheeked, like a child whose parents were arguing.

Conrad frowned in return. "Who says it *doesn't* bother me?"

"Everything about the way you've been acting tells me otherwise. I try to tell myself that it is just the dark essence controlling you, but-"

"Incorrect," he interrupted. "It *doesn't* control me."

"I have to believe that it does."

"And why is that? Because you have grown wary of me?" Conrad asked. His aggressive demeanor became more obvious with each word.

"You know that's not true," Lucia said.

"I'm not so sure-"

"OI! ARE YA DONE WITH THA POINTLESS ARGUIN', YET?" Alistair shouted, drawing their attention. After a few puffs of his chest, his voice lowered. "In case ya fergot, we gots a friend ta save."

The big man pointed to Giles, still sound asleep up against the wall. The pair let out a collective sigh, then nodded in unison. Any further arguing would have to wait.

Alistair scooped Giles up and draped him over his shoulder. The trio continued down the alleyway without a monster or enemy in sight. Despite the clear path, uneasiness and uncertainty loomed over Lucia. Between the crazed mobs, monsters, and Conrad's instability, something had to give.

~

ON THE EAST side of Endoshire, Rolf's head smacked off the cobblestone terrain after falling. A pool of blood soon became apparent underneath his twitching body, and Hector's scorpion tail wriggled with excitement at what it had done. The hole in his midsection oozed a nasty combination of black and red.

Kabel, who'd previously been dazed from blood loss, let out a desperate battle cry and grabbed his arming sword while aligning his shield for optimal protection.

Auber and his crew watched on from the ground, mouths agape, as Kabel charged Hector, full speed ahead. From the perspective of the captain, it was inspiring. *There goes a true leader*, he thought.

"Fellas…" Auber said as he stood with his saber drawn.

"Yes, sir?" Ebbie asked, also reaching his feet. Franco rose and dusted himself off.

"Are we just gonna sit here an' let our comrades die?" Auber asked, gripping the hilt of his blade so tight that his hand burned. His crew looked at each other with raised eyebrows. "Or are we gonna go out thar and slay that beast?"

"Slay the beast! Slay the beast!" Ebbie shouted, raising his blade to the sky.

"You tell us, sir," Franco said with an eye roll.

Captain Auber frowned back at him. "'Course we're gonna fight! Let's bring that scum ta his knees fer what he's done!"

"Yeah!" Ebbie cried.

Franco shook his head and smiled. "When did you become such a brave heart?"

The captain's cheeks turned red, but instead of flashing embarrassment, he put forth an assured smile. His crewmates nodded, and with that, the trio charged forward with sabers held high.

❧

Kabel approached his target at top running speed. Hector swung his tail to intercept him, but rather than dodge left or right, the stocky man slid under the attack, bringing him into close-quarters combat. Next, he hopped up and swung his sword with an angry grunt, connecting with the chest.

Hector let out an inhuman screech that rang Kabel's ears, but his hands rang even more. It felt as if he had struck a rock. Under the tears in his enemy's robe, he could see traces of a purple ooze leaking from a light underbelly that was quickly regenerating. Kabel had correctly guessed that his scorpion-like opponent would have a rough outer shell and weaker underbelly. However, much to his horror, his blade had barely harmed him, even in his supposed weak spot.

There was little time to think about strength and weakness,

however. Hector swung his right arm for Kabel's head. He held his shield up and intercepted the blow perfectly, but both confusion and the sensation of flight overtook him as the enemy's robed form grew further away and the wind roared in his ears. It was only after passing the charging pirates that Kabel understood how hard he'd been hit; and with that reality sinking in, he crashed to the ground and uncontrollably rolled backward before skidding to a stop.

At first, his blurry eyes struggled to focus in on Auber and his crew swarming the scorpion-man ahead, but then, a dull pain sharpened his senses. Kabel looked down at his heavily dented shield, and then that dull pain turned abominable and made him wince.

"I don't believe it…" he muttered with a chuckle, dropping the shield and letting his inflamed arm dangle. "That knob broke my arm."

As the pirates attempted chopping him down at all angles to little effect, Hector removed the glove on his right hand to reveal that it was not skin covering his body, but a brown exoskeleton. On the edges of each finger were several small spikes, effectively making two adjacent fingers their own pincher claw. He held his index and middle finger out, like a pair of scissors ready to snip.

Ebbie gasped and ceased clubbing away when Hector spun without warning to face him. In one swift motion, he snipped his ring and pinky fingers off with the pinchers.

"Gah!" Ebbie cried, wide-eyed, as blood squirted from the stumps of where his two fingers used to be. The scorpion-man finished him off with a shot to the ribs, courtesy of his tail. He hadn't even bothered using the poison tip.

"Hang in thar, Ebbie!" Captain Auber said as he jumped back to avoid the very snips that had maimed his first mate. Hector hissed as the remaining pirates backpedaled to gain distance between themselves and him.

"Distract 'im for a moment, will ye? I gots an idea!" Auber said as he began searching his pockets.

"Are you trying to get me killed?" Franco asked with a raised eyebrow. "We stand no chance against this monster. Our only hope is to recover the others, and then make a run for it."

The captain firmly shook his head. "That's a direct order!"

"Yes, sir…"

As Franco did his best to distract the enemy without dying, Auber pulled a small, brown sack out of his pants pocket, and grinned like a child making mischief. Kabel's fading eyes widened in realization. Those must have been the beige berries, he thought. Both Auber and Dhogron had spoken at length about how they might be used against their enemies. For they were not truly berries, but cleverly disguised pellets of poison that, when ingested in small doses, caused a volatile stomach. Though he did not anticipate such a cheap trick felling their monstrous opponent, Kabel did see it as a very probable distraction and readied himself for one final, desperate attack.

"Oi! Landlubber!" The captain's tone was drenched in bravado. Franco gained some distance as Hector turned his attention to Auber. "Ye look like ye've worked up a mighty hunger!"

He cocked his head as Auber grabbed a fistful of beige berries and threw them at his face. Franco let out a groan as the pellets bounced off the unflinching scorpion-man.

"Perhaps he is not hungry, sir..." the navigator muttered. Kabel began creeping into position with his sword at the ready.

"Nonsense!" Captain Auber said. He grabbed another handful of the berries, then looked to Hector, who cocked his head once more. "Weren't ye listenin'? *I said* it'll satisfy yer hunger. Next time, eat 'em when I toss 'em to ye!"

Auber wound up and threw another batch of beige berries. This time, Hector lunged out, and they flew into the void of his hood.

"Ye idiot! I got ye!" Auber said, pointing and laughing.

Hector let out a hiss, and from under his hood spewed the chewed-up beige berries at the captain. Auber could only frown helplessly as the chunky liquid splattered on his face. The scorpion-man let out a low-pitched chuckle, but in that moment, Kabel saw an opportunity to strike. With one arm dangling, he gathered all of his anger and worry for Rolf into one powerful lunge, stabbing his blade into Hector's hood until he felt it lodge into something. The stocky man smiled, but his face soon turned sour upon hearing the *crunch* and shattering of his blade.

"No way..." he muttered while pulling his sword back, to find half of it missing.

In jerking his weapon back, Kabel had inadvertently pulled down Hector's hood, revealing his face. It only turned his frown into a wide-eyed expression of horror. Like other parts of his body, Hector's face was not coated in skin, but a brown exoskeleton. His jaw was exaggerated and square, and sprouting from his mouth were two sharp mandibles. He did not possess a nose or any traces of hair, and much like his enhanced allies, his eyes reflected glimmers of red when viewed under the moonlight.

Kabel stumbled back and fell to his bottom, defenseless. He looked at Rolf's limp body one more time and felt regret seep into his soul. He had failed to both protect and avenge him: the ultimate dishonor that a leader could incur. He wanted more than anything to lash out; to use his despair and anger and summon the strength needed to win, but he'd already tried that. There was no winning this fight.

His weary eyes wandered up to Hector's coiled scorpion tail. He hoped that Mira would be alright without him. *Mira*, he thought, a newfound fire lighting in his gut. He couldn't leave her behind, and with that thought, he noticed a different fire: Torchlights approaching from behind the looming Hector.

Before the scorpion tail could strike, a torch was thrown onto Hector. He let out the squeal of a thousand desperate bugs as the flames quickly spread down his robe, and he fell to the ground in a fiery heap.

"Looks like we gotta few stragglers, tonight!" a grinning, yellow-eyed man called out with a toxic mixture of insanity and joy on his tongue. He led an entire horde of degenerates, armed to the teeth with weapons and torches.

"Not the saviors I was hoping for…" Kabel choked out as he struggled to his feet. He turned his attention to Auber, who appeared about ready to puke from the spewed-up beige berries coating his face. "We need to make a run for it."

"In your condition? How are we supposed to outrun *that*?" Franco said, pointing to the approaching mob.

"There ain't no time ta argue! We gotta get Ebbie an' Rolf outta here!" Auber said.

"We can help with that," a muffled voice said. Kabel looked back to see Pierce approaching with one hand dripping blood, and the other gripping his Summoner Rune. He was accompanied by Xviktolo.

The marinian walked up to Rolf and scooped him up with one arm. "This one still draws breath, but barely. What should we do?"

"We… gotta take 'im… to the church…" a pale-faced Ebbie said, staggering away from the approaching crowd. He grasped the bloody stumps where his two fingers used to be.

"Very well…" Pierce said as he held out his Summoner Rune. A dark portal materialized before the Strangers. "You can lead the way after we've escaped."

With that, the group jumped into the gateway, one by one, until only Kabel and Pierce remained.

Pierce tilted his head. "You wish to stay?"

Kabel nodded toward Hector, who was struggling to his feet. His cloak had burned off, revealing a charred, insect-like body that appeared to be regenerating as the flames around him simmered.

"Let's finish this bastard off."

"You are in no condition to fight him, and thanks to his regeneration, I doubt that I could beat him, either," Pierce replied before gesturing toward the degenerates, who had gathered into a semi-circle around the scorpion-man. They began chanting, jeering, and grinding their weapons off the cobblestone in anticipation. He looked to the crowd and said, "Burn him alive."

All in the crowd let out a malice-filled cheer as Kabel followed Pierce into the portal, hearing the remnants of Hector's screeches over the roaring wind as he did.

CHAPTER 25
RESTORATION

Alistair burst through the church doors with an unconscious Giles draped over his shoulder, and Conrad and Lucia flanking him. The benches were splinter-filled and rotting, and the carpet going down the empty aisle seemed old and dirty. Some candles lit up the area, but only enough to reflect off a few murals.

"Oi! Mistah priest!" the big man called out. His voice echoed in the emptiness. "We gots a man down! We need yer help!"

After a few moments of silence, Lucia heard some rustling come from behind the stage. Then, the glow of a candlestick appeared, and it traveled down the aisle.

A frizzy-haired Father Vega stopped before the Strangers and raised his candle toward their faces. His emerald green eyes reflected a cautious curiosity.

"How can I help you?" he asked, his mouth fidgeting; as if holding back a yawn.

Conrad and Lucia looked at each other with raised eyebrows. Had he forgotten them already? They then chuckled in unison. Their masks were still on.

After removing the guises, Vega smiled. "Ah, I remember you two. Lucia and Conrad, right?"

The pair nodded as Alistair removed his mask.

"An' I'm Alistair, a friend o' theirs! I'd love ta chat, but we gots an emergency, here!"

Vega's eyes locked onto the limp body over the big redhead's shoulder. "I understand. Bring him up to the stage, please."

Alistair ran down the aisle while the others followed at a hurried pace. Father Vega lit candles all around the altar, then knelt to examine Giles: He gasped at the finger bone sticking out of his right eye socket. Though the bleeding had stopped, it was obvious that the wound was already festering. The bolts lodged in his arm and torso continued to cause bleeding, but they appeared to have struck non-vital areas.

"He must be low on blood, by now," the priest said while feeling Giles' pale forehead. "I will get to work on healing him, but first, I must remove these... arrows..."

"You may find this hard to believe, but they are actually finger bones," Conrad said with a half-hearted smile.

"Strange as it may be, we must dislodge them before I can heal him. There is a bowl in the back. Would you fetch it for me?" Vega asked, looking to the strategist.

Conrad nodded and then ran to the back. The priest straightened Giles' body out as Lucia and Alistair watched on.

"I am relieved to see that he is asleep. The removal of the bones would otherwise be quite painful for him," Vega said, looking back to the others. "Just in case, I'll ask that the two of you hold him straight. I require a great degree of focus for his eye wound."

"Do ya think he can be healed?" Alistair asked, in high spirits.

"He has lost very much blood, but I believe he will make a recovery, yes. Unfortunately, I am unable to recreate a functional eye, so he shall live on with only one for the rest of his days," the priest said. The big man sulked.

"Could be worse," Lucia said with crossed arms.

"*Much* worse," Father Vega added. "The eye wound is already infected. If it had an opportunity to spread, he would not have lasted long."

Before anyone could contemplate further, Conrad returned from the back with a bowl in hand. He laid it next to Giles' body. Then, as per Vega's request, Alistair held his understudy's shoulders down, while Lucia pressed down on his boots.

"Let's start with the hard part..." Father Vega trailed off, holding his hand out over Giles' eye.

A golden glow enveloped his fingers, and slowly, the bone bolt dislodged from the socket. Vega raised his hand along with the bone, like it was held on a string. After fully removing the projectile, blood spurted up from the open wound, and Giles squirmed around. Alistair and Lucia held firm as the intensity of the golden glow increased around the priest's open hand.

While putting her full weight atop Giles' kicking legs, Lucia distracted herself by taking in the miracle playing out before her: From the open eye wound ascended a smattering of floating blood. It must have been the infection, she thought. Father Vega directed his hand over the bowl, and the bone bolt followed, along with the infected blood.

"Jus' hold on, lad! We're helpin' ya!" Alistair said.

Giles began to cry out in pain, thrashing his knees, midsection, and elbows, the only parts of him that weren't restrained.

"Keep him steady..." Vega muttered as he held his golden hand over the open wound once more.

Second after a painstaking second, the skin around Giles' eye began to grow and stretch across the open wound. After much thrashing and screaming, the one-eyed man finally settled down and fell back asleep. The priest let out a sigh of relief.

"The worst of it is over," he said, wiping a profuse sweat from his brow.

"He's gonna make it?" Alistair asked.

Vega nodded, and all Strangers let out a collective breath. The remaining two bone bolts were much easier and less dangerous to remove by comparison. Giles stayed asleep for the duration, and when all was said and done, Father Vega fetched a wet cloth to place on his forehead as he rested.

"That was incredible!" Alistair shouted while clapping the priest hard off of his shoulder. He looked to his hand with a raised eyebrow and then shook it. "Yer a sturdy fella, too! I s'pose that'd make ya a Wizard!"

Vega held his hands up and chuckled. "Oh, no, no! I am no longer a member of that Council and therefore am not a Wizard. I suppose they would classify me as a Warlock."

"What? But ain't Warlocks supposed ta be evil?" the big redhead asked with crossed arms.

"Yes, I'm sure helping and healing people truly suits his *evil agenda*," Lucia said with an eye roll.

"Who asked you, anyway?" Alistair shot back.

"I've been told that it was a term created by the Wizard's Council. A Warlock can be good or evil... or perhaps neutral. They are simply mages who are not Wizards or Dark Wizards, right?" Conrad asked, looking at the priest.

"There are more classifications, like Witches, but you have the right idea."

"Be careful what ya say…" Alistair said with uncharacteristic quietness. His cheeks flared out, trying to withhold laughter. "I think tha lass is a Witch in disguise. It's tha only reason anyone would have such a *stupid* tattoo on their face."

Lucia scoffed. "If I were a Witch, you'd have been turned into a toad long ago. Though you wouldn't look much different, it would surely solve the problem of having to listen to you speak."

"Yer really askin' for it, today!" the big man bellowed while drawing his battle axe. "You an' me, right now! Let's settle this once and for all!"

She laughed and shook her head. "I'd hate to spill blood on hallowed ground."

"Yes, if you could limit the fighting to outside, I'd appreciate that…" Father Vega added, holding his hands up.

"But ain't them degenerates outside?" Alistair asked, lowering his weapon. "We can't go out there 'till it's light out."

"They wouldn't bother you as long as you stayed on the lawn," he replied.

Conrad's eyes widened. "Now that you mention it, the streets were flooded with those crazed mobs… except around the church."

"Oooo, it must be a spell ta ward off evil!" Alistair said with a clenched fist to go along with a face-widening grin.

"It's far simpler than that," Father Vega said with a chuckle. "This is a house of worship, but just as much, a temple of reflection. In here, they must face their worst enemy: themselves. No matter how hateful their rhetoric or wicked their deeds, they will never hate someone more than they hate themselves."

"But is it truly their fault? What if there is an external force that causes them to act out?" Lucia asked, looking at Conrad out of the corner of her eye.

The priest flashed surprise on his face before settling into a smile. "I get the feeling that you are not mere passersby. The lot of you know far too much."

"Ya don' know tha half of it!" Alistair said with an obnoxious laugh.

"But to answer your question…" Vega said, looking back to Lucia.

"Everyone is different. There is more hope for some than others. I have come to find that for every poisoning of the mind, there is an antidote… to a point. To find that cure, you must understand the meaning of their behavior. Almost all of the degenerates in this city come from the slums. *If* they can find work, it is backbreaking labor, and the pay is low. They are reminded every day, by the wealthy district, how badly they live."

"So, what is the 'antidote'?" Conrad asked.

"To put it simply? Compassion."

"Hah! Yer jokin', right?" Alistair asked.

"Laugh if you wish, but it's true. When someone feels oppressed, and that there is no escape, they will eventually lash out. There is only so much that one can take. Sometimes, all it requires is a little *push*. The only answer, even when it is obscenely difficult, is to show them compassion," Father Vega said as he pointed around the chapel. "You see, it wasn't so long ago that these hallowed grounds were pristine. The degenerates, however, decided to come in and wreck the place."

"Then, how'd ya ward 'em off?" Alistair asked, making a fist. "Did ya pound 'em into submission?"

"No, no, not at all," the priest said with a laugh. "I did something that many in this city are unwilling to do: I showed them mercy. And *it worked* on most of them. They began attending services and cleaning their lives up."

"If you were able to do that, maybe we should get more of them in here," Conrad said.

"Well, you see, the rest of the degenerates took notice of the people I was reforming. As I mentioned before, some had been poisoned too much by their hate. Those who were able to resist simply use fear to keep the rest of the degenerates away from this church. As I said before, it is a fear and hatred of themselves."

"I noticed that you were able to draw the infection out of Giles, back there… would you be able to take other substances from a body?" Lucia asked. Conrad darted his eyes to her, but she pretended not to notice.

Father Vega, too, understood. He looked to the strategist and said, "You need not be cross with her, for her concerns are not unfounded. I feel a dark substance within you. I felt it the last time you were here, too. But I'm afraid that such a thing could only be removed by an Exorcist. Otherwise, the process of removal would kill you."

"It's fine, really," Conrad said with a huff, then looked at Lucia with cold eyes. "She is just overprotective. I can manage-"

Conrad was interrupted by the church doors slamming open. The Strangers stirred and readied their weapons as the dark figures rushed into the hallowed halls.

"Degenerates?" Lucia asked aloud.

"It can't be..." Vega muttered.

"We need some help, here!" Kabel cried as he hobbled up to the stage. His arm dangled and his midsection was soaked in red.

Arriving behind him was their new marinian ally with Rolf over his shoulder. Next to come in were Auber and his pirates, and then finally, Pierce. Lucia's eyes widened: All had sustained various degrees of injury since they'd separated.

"It's going to be a long night, isn't it?" Father Vega asked with an amused snort. "Now, then... who needs treatment first?"

As the night began to wind down, Dalton Rayleigh emerged from his hiding place on a ship at dock seven. He had found that it was empty, and after realizing that his allies had escaped, decided that hiding was his best option until the Dark Wizard and his forces left.

Upon setting foot on the road along the docks, Dalton was shocked to find that not only had everyone left, but all of the unconscious and dead bodies had disappeared, too. The only evidence that anything violent had happened on the dock path were the bloodstains, broken weapons, and a decimated building.

Dalton felt a great exhaustion sweep over him. He hadn't had a good night's sleep in days, and the intense battle to rescue Amis hadn't helped. Most tiring of all, however, was the stress. Had his team survived? Had they retrieved the prisoner? He had no way of knowing.

To decompress, the warrior reasoned that he could use a few drinks before heading back to Kabel's house in the outskirts. He made his way eastward along the docks until taking a right onto the main street of the wealthy district.

Most of the buildings and property remained intact around this area, to Dalton's surprise. The streets were quiet as could be: Only the sound of his footsteps and breathing convinced him that he hadn't gone deaf. He looked for any sign of life or evidence that his friends had been down the road, but there was a complete absence of any prior activity. It was as if the streets had been built anew.

After a long walk through the wealthy district, Dalton found himself in the city center, which showed all the signs of life that he had been looking for: Fruit stands had been split in half, cinders remained from fires started in the middle of the road, litter whirled and twirled in the wind, and dry blood painted the walls of buildings. It almost looked as if the city had seen war, he thought. However, he couldn't find a single person out on the streets.

The warrior continued southward, toward Cole's pub, practically frothing at the mouth for a drink. The destruction all around filled him with anxiousness. It felt as if the enemy could pop out at any moment and spring a trap on him. However, that moment never came. Instead, he happened upon a man who was sweeping in front of a tailor shop. His tunic, though ragged and torn, looked fit for a businessman of lesser wealth. Likely the owner of the shop, he thought. Certainly not an enemy.

Although Dalton saw the pub at the end of the road, and he badly desired an ale, his curiosity overtook him. They were the only two men outside, after all. He had to know *why*.

"Excuse me, sir," he said, approaching from behind.

The tailor turned with a frightful look in his eyes. His graying mustache crinkled, and his peasant's hat fell off as he flinched at his presence.

"Oi, I dun' want no trouble, now…" he said, holding his broom up in a defensive position.

"Nor do I, good sir," Dalton said, waving him off. The tailor cocked his head, but he also relaxed his posture and then lowered himself to retrieve the downed hat. "I am a foreigner, y'see. I was just wonderin' about these empty streets."

"Well, if ye've been walkin' these streets at night, then surely ye know about them degenerates runnin' amok!" he replied while dusting off his hat. "An' then, every mornin', we all gotta come out an' clean up their messes! I could tell they were really lightin' it up tonight, so I decided to get an early start!"

"Right, right… but I don't understand. Why do you all put up with it? Surely, the lord of the land would put a stop to this," the warrior said.

"Hah! We put up with it because in this city, if ye don' have money, then yer opinions ain't worth a damn! Do ye know what happens when commoners like me'self complain to the lord?" the tailor asked, leaning in. "We get sent back to the slums! Or worse! I've worked hard to get this close to the city center. Ain't no way I'm gonna risk that."

"I see… but what does the lord gain by letting these mobs incite chaos?"

"Hell if I know…" he muttered, then got back to sweeping.

Dalton narrowed his eyes and gave a sarcastic wave as he continued down the street. "Nice talkin' to you too, fella."

Upon finally reaching the pub at the end of the road, Dalton gasped to see Cole locking up. He made a run for it, to catch up with him.

The barkeep turned and let out a groan as he approached. He held up a hand, to which Dalton halted and tilted his head.

"Pub's closed," he said, slicking back his dirty blond hair.

"Aw, c'mon… I've had a rough night."

"Every night's a rough night fer me, ye right ape," he shot back, crossing his arms. The bags under his eyes appeared even heavier than usual. "But do ye see me drinkin' me'self to death all the time? No. Go home."

Dalton let out a sigh and shrugged. "I've never met a man so eager to turn down easy money."

"There ain't nothin' easy 'bout servin' a langer like you, that's fer sure."

"Come on…" Dalton trailed off, wrapping an arm around Cole's shoulder. "I just want a drink… or two…"

Brushing his arm off, the barkeep began walking away. Even though he was often cold, Dalton found something endearing about him.

"See you tomorrow, then, when the sun goes down!"

Cole returned a sarcastic wave without looking back. Dalton shrugged as the barkeep disappeared into the night. If he couldn't get drunk, then his only option was to go home and get some rest. It was a distant second place to his first preference, but still not bad.

Dalton began walking down the southeast street, which remained barren and empty. The glow of the crescent moon in the clear night sky bounced off the streets, showing him the path ahead.

However, the warrior didn't get much further than past the edges of the pub before something else caught his eye: A woman stood in the alley between Cole's pub and another building. She was tall, with dark brown hair flowing out of the hood of her purple cloak. He couldn't make out her face, aside from striking green eyes that seemed to beckon him. He had always been drawn to emerald eyes. Even more appealing to him, the cloak had a slit down the side, revealing a bare, toned leg that went on for days.

He turned to face the mysterious woman. "What are you doing out so late, m'lady?"

"Looking for a good time," a smooth, soothing voice replied. Something about it made him feel at home.

"I'd offer you a drink, but Cole truly is a grump. I think he closed up early, tonight."

"We can have fun without drinks…" she said while beckoning him with a bent index finger while disappearing into the shadows.

"Mayhap the night can be salvaged, after all…" the warrior muttered as he followed into the alleyway.

Dalton stopped to marvel at the cloaked woman, who had pressed herself up against the sidewall of the pub and arched her back to accentuate a beautiful figure. He couldn't wait to get under those clothes, but a thought popped into his head before proceeding any further.

"Before we do this, I wanna make sure… you are not expecting payment, are you? Just looking for a good time?"

The woman giggled. "Don't be silly. I wouldn't do that to an *old friend…*"

Dalton cocked his head, then let out a confused laugh. "Do I know you?"

"You don't recognize my voice after all of these years? Perhaps you will remember my face," she said while bringing her hood down.

With a gasp, Dalton's tired eyes widened. She had a cute little nose and delicate cheeks to round out a feminine jawline. Her lips pouted, but naturally, and her eyelids came down just enough to obscure the tops of her loving, emerald eyes. In some ways, she bore a resemblance to Lucia, and for good reason: She was her mother.

"Anora…" Dalton choked out. His legs numbed, then buckled, and he fell to his knees. Tears began to stream down his cheeks.

"You poor thing," Anora said while wiping the tears with her delicate hand.

"H-how are you alive? I… watched you die… back then…"

"Seeing is believing, is it not?"

"I just-" Dalton got out before exhaling in disbelief. "You died in my arms. How am I supposed to believe that you're… you?"

The emerald-eyed woman put hands to hips and flashed a puzzling mix of stern and playful on her face. "Edvard… you know better than to doubt me."

Dalton let loose another laugh out of pure shock. Aside from his parents, only Anora and his mentor, Adrian, had ever known his middle name. She had used it, back then, whenever scolding him.

"There is so much to catch up on. How did you get here? Why haven't I heard from you in all of these years?" Dalton asked, rapid-fire. His heart and mind alike raced until he came to a realization. He grabbed Anora's hand. "And Lucia! She is all grown up, now! I have to take you to her! Do you want to see your daughter?"

Anora let out a pleasant chuckle. "All in due time. But first, I have a favor to ask."

Dalton smiled. "Yes, of course. Anything, anything!"

"Would you help me break into the bar, so we can drink the night away?"

He raised an eyebrow. "But… Lucia. Don't you wanna see her?"

"Of course," Anora said with a smile. "But first, I'd really like to have a few drinks with you…"

Conflicting thoughts clouded Dalton's mind. Anora had never been much of a drinker, he thought. Then again, much could change in 13 years.

"I dunno… I like Cole, even though he's a real knobber sometimes. I don't think it would be right to break in. Weren't you always tellin' me about 'doing the right thing'?"

Anora tilted her head and the friendly gaze upon her face turned stone cold. "Weren't *you* the reason that I died, back then?"

Dalton shuddered. All of the energy and enthusiasm drained from the depths of his soul. He looked to her, sweating bullets. "W-well, I-"

"It's the least you can do, isn't it?"

"Right…" Dalton said as his head and heart sunk further.

He walked around to the front of the bar, then smashed a window with the butt of his sword. Dalton would do anything to set things right, even if none of it made any sense.

CHAPTER 26
RISING SUSPICIONS

Captain Auber and Kabel led their fellow Strangers through the wooded outskirts of Endoshire under the clear night sky. Father Vega had healed them all to the best of his abilities: Giles had lost his right eye, but kept his life. Rolf had the scorpion venom drained from his stomach, bringing him back from the verge of death's door, but kept a scar as a reminder of the attack. Ebbie's fingers could not be grown back, but they had been sealed tight, preventing further pain or infection. Kabel's broken arm and stab wound had left some soreness, but otherwise, he was as good as new.

The remainder of the Strangers had also found their minor ailments mended before the night was through. After departing the church, Pierce had separated from the group, stating that he would need to pick someone up before meeting with them at Kabel's house in the outskirts.

Upon reaching the tree-built home in the woods, everyone breathed a sigh of relief.

"I can't believe we made it outta that alive!" Auber said.

"But at what cost?" Alistair asked, looking at Giles. He hadn't been the same since losing his right eye; all of his energy and enthusiasm seemed a distant memory. There was a white cloth tied around the side of his head, to cover up the eye socket.

"Yeh, I'm gonna miss me fingers..." Ebbie said, holding up his three-pronged hand.

"Cheer up, lads! We're still alive, ain't we? And we completed the mission!" Auber said with pride.

"That remains to be seen," Kabel said as he approached his door and attempted to open it. It rattled but held firm. The stocky man shook his head and chuckled. "Locked outta my own home."

"You don't have the keys?" Franco asked with narrowed eyes.

Instead of responding, Kabel turned back and pounded on the door. "Oi! It's me! Let us in!"

The metal latch in the door opened and a pair of demanding eyes looked through. "Don' be rude! What's tha password?"

Kabel cocked his head, then shot him an icy glare. "It's *my house*, Triston. Let me in…"

"Sure… if ya give me tha password! Or are ya a filthy, double-crossin', Dark Wizard dobber?"

The stocky man huffed, then stepped aside. "As you can see, all of your teammates are waitin' outside for you to get your arse goin' and open that door!"

"Not gonna happen without a password!"

"Oh, oh!" Alistair called out. "Tell 'im tha password is 'fearsome goats'!"

"This is ridiculous…" Kabel muttered before sighing and turning back to the door latch. "The password is… fearsome… goats?"

Triston shut the metal latch, then burst open the door and surprised Kabel with a bone-crunching bear hug.

"Ya made it! Ya really made it!" the elder MacRae cried as Kabel gasped for air.

"When… the hell… did you two… come up with that idiotic password?" Kabel asked between wheezes, looking back at Alistair. Finally, Triston set him down. Even after all of the dangerous encounters he'd survived tonight, that hug had frightened him the most.

"It's always been our password, what're ya on aboot?" the big redhead said with a snort.

Lucia snickered. "You wanted to make our group name the same as your password? Why am I not surprised?"

The group laughed while entering the tree-built home to a round of cheers. The Strangers wasted no time in gathering and beginning to converse, though the chatter didn't last long. Kabel and Auber stood in the midst of a circle and cleared their throats in unison, silencing all.

"Awright, everyone, listen up!" Auber called out.

"Look at our captain, acting like a *real leader*," Franco said to Ebbie. Both of them chuckled.

"Everyone, get comfortable and find your sleepin' place for the night. Then, come back here. We have much to discuss, obviously," Kabel said.

THOUGH EVERYONE DISPERSED AT THE LEADERS' command, the sleeping arrangements remained largely the same as previous nights: Kabel and Mirabel naturally had claims to their own bedroom, while Rolf shared his room with the pirates and their ill-made cots, and Lucia and Conrad remained in the downstairs living room.

Accommodations had to be made for the newest additions to the Strangers, however: Dhogron led Amis to the room that he and Aldous had been sharing, while Joel, Giles, Alistair, and Triston showed Prince Xviktolo to their crowded bedroom.

"Erm… we should'a asked this earlier… do ya sleep in tha water, or do ya need us ta set up bedding?" Alistair asked the marinian.

"I can sleep in the sea, or on land," he replied with a toothy grin. "I am one of the Elite, which means I can breathe air, *or* take in water, as I wish."

Alistair tapped his foot. "Bedding, then?"

Xviktolo nodded. "I shall not trouble you for long, but if you could provide bedding for the night, I would appreciate it."

With that, Alistair got to setting up his sleeping arrangement. It involved the folding of many blankets, as both cushions to the floor and a pillow.

"Well, if ya don' mind me askin', what *are* ya here for?" Triston asked. Joel narrowed eyes at him for the rudeness.

The marinian let out a hiss-like chuckle. "Tonight's battle was the most fun I've had in years. I'd like to stay a while longer, to see if anything else of interest happens. Life is short, my friends. I would hate to miss out on anything."

"*That's* what ya call 'fun'?" Alistair asked, wide-eyed, while folding a blanket. "Don' get the wrong idea; I like stickin' it ta tha enemy, too, but we barely scraped by, out there! I don' know how so many of us survived!"

"I suppose land-dwellers wouldn't know much about life under the sea. In my kingdom, Coralstar, we like to 'butt heads'. Tests of strength, speed, and combat ability are how we entertain ourselves."

"What's tha problem, then? Sounds like a good time ta me! Ghobmor has games like that, too! We throw big rocks around ta see who's strongest!" Triston said.

"The problem is that no one is willing to challenge me. It's because I am one of the Elite."

"Ya keep callin' yerself elite… but it's rude ta brag so much, ya know!" Alistair said.

Xviktolo laughed and shook his head. "No, no. There are different kinds of marinians. Elite can breathe air or take in water. Then there are the Arxen, who must come up for air once in a while, and the Aqven, who cannot breathe air at all. An Arxen or Aqven attacking me would be much like if one of you picked a fight with a prince up here."

"Fine, then just fight with another Elite!" Triston said.

"They don't want to. The Elite are almost always royalty, and so they would rather watch someone else fight for their own entertainment," Xviktolo said, his spirits lowering. "And as I said, life is short. Most Elites are happy to waste away and accomplish nothing while being served by their subjects. Is it wrong of me to want something more?"

"Oooo, so everyone wants ta worship an' serve you, eh? I'm weepin' for ya, I really am!" the elder MacRae said in mockery, then let out an obnoxious laugh. Alistair joined in.

"That was a long-winded way of tellin' us that yer bored, lad! But I tell ya what! Tomorrow mornin', I'll be happy ta spar with you! I need tha practice!" Alistair said before looking back to Giles, who'd been silently standing in the corner. "And you! You've been through hell tonight, but don' think yer off the hook! Rest up, 'cause tomorrow, there will be no more mopin' around! The penalty game is still on! And believe it or not, I've been goin' easy on ya, up 'till now."

Giles nodded and then seemed to force a smile, at least to Joel's eyes. The mute was not sure how to approach him. He could not deny his inner guilt for the gouging of his eye. Had he struck a fatal blow to Angus, it wouldn't have happened. On the other hand, he wasn't so sure that a death blow had been possible in that situation. After all, decapitation had not slowed down the dark, lumpy monsters chasing them in the alleys.

"A 'spar', you say? That sounds interesting! Is it like butting heads?" Prince Xviktolo asked.

"Erm… somethin' like that…" Alistair muttered before casting eyes back on the doorway. "Anyway, whaddya say we get back downstairs, lads? We gots much ta discuss!"

All in the room nodded and began making their way into the hallway. However, Giles stopped just short of exiting, so that only he and Joel remained. The mute looked into his eye, to search for some hint of his demeanor, but it was impossible to read.

Giles sighed. "Joel, I want ye to know that I don't blame ye for what happened to my eye…"

A mixture of relief and awkwardness seeped into the mute's mind. Happy as he was that there was no grudge, he still didn't know what to say. Not that Giles would understand his hand gestures, anyway.

"Alistair's penalty game is a might bit insane if I do say so myself… but it has also helped to expose my vulnerabilities. *I* couldn't dodge or block those projectiles… and *you* could," Giles said as he held a finger up to the cloth covering his eye socket. "This is my own fault."

Joel smiled while placing a hand on his shoulder, hoping it would convey not to be hard on himself. He hoped that Giles was choosing to use the lost eye as motivation; to better himself. With that, he took a step forward to leave, but Giles pressed his hand against the door frame, blocking him. The mute raised an eyebrow.

"But there is somethin' else I want to say: Conrad was right about you," Giles said, to which Joel cocked his head. "Ye hesitate with every swing of that sword, and ye might be skilled, but there will always be some opponents who can take advantage of that. I saw it up close, twice: Once against the degenerates, and a second time against Angus. Don't misunderstand. My weakness is what put me in danger, as it has many times before. For as long as I can remember, I have been a weak link who needed others to bail me out of trouble. Oftentimes, folks like you or Aldous saved me. This time, I wasn't so lucky."

The mute opened his mouth, but as usual, no words came out. He found the sudden urge, more so than he'd felt in years, to speak. Try as he might, however, it was a one-way conversation.

"But the day will come when someone is carryin' their own weight, while also countin' on you… and yer hesitation gets them killed. I don't know how yer vow of peace came about or why ye cling so strongly to it, but I do know this: I will push myself to the absolute limit until I am no longer a burden on this team. And when that day comes, I will *not* be the victim of yer inner struggle," Giles said, pounding his fist against the doorframe as Joel's heart sank. "Since we are a team, I will always have yer back, but I will *never* count on you to have mine again."

Even if Joel could speak, he was certain that he'd be speechless. Never before had he been cut so deep by mere words. His mind began spinning. It had become a ritual for him to run through all of the justifications of his peaceful ways, but this time, he came up blank. All he could do was nod in return, to show that he understood what the one-eyed man was telling him.

After an awkward silence, Giles bowed out of the room and made his way downstairs. Joel stayed behind and stared into space.

DOWNSTAIRS, Conrad and Lucia sat side-by-side in their makeshift bedding as people came and went from the living room. Much to her puzzlement, the strategist had concern written all over his face. It almost filled her with relief, as she hadn't seen anything save coldness or anger in his eyes for days.

"Something bothering you?" Lucia asked. He jerked his head back as if breaking out of a trance. "Are you finally starting to worry about Aldous? Or Dalton, perhaps?"

"I think they'll be alright…"

"How can you be sure?"

"Haven't you noticed? Against all odds… over a hundred enemies, some of them strong enough to kill us in a single blow… *none of us died*," Conrad said.

"We've survived worse, haven't we?"

Doubt crossed his face. "Yes, well, most of the miners died at Mt. Couture, if you remember. It was fortunate that most of our inner circle survived; that's all."

"I think you are giving our group too little credit," Lucia said with a playful shove, longing to see his smile in return.

Instead, he frowned. "Something is not right."

"Yeah, *you're* not right," she replied, rolling her eyes.

"I mean it," Conrad said with tension on his tongue. "Think about what transpired tonight. The Dark Wizard shows himself, blasts Aldous away, and then just *stands there* for the rest of the battle. Why?"

Lucia cocked her head. "Alright, I'll give you that one. That spell looked powerful, though. Perhaps it drained him of his magic?"

"Then, why did he call off the creeper back in the alleyway?"

"Simple. He has taken an interest in you and wished to test the lengths you were willing to go for him. Don't forget that he wanted you to kill one of us," Lucia said, wrapping an arm around his shoulder. "Any other foolish questions I can answer?"

Conrad let out an amused snort, then darted his eyes away. "I suppose not..."

~

AFTER SOME LEISURE TIME, Kabel and Auber stood in front of the crackling fireplace and called everyone back. The Strangers made a circle around their remaining leaders and listened in.

"Good work out there tonight, everyone," Kabel said to a few cheers from the crowd. "Next time we head down to Cole's pub, drinks are on Auber!"

"Yeh!" the captain cheered along with the others, then gasped. "Wait, what?"

Some laughs filled the room as the stocky man cleared his throat. "But truly, tonight could have ended much worse. We are fortunate to have so many cunning warriors fighting side-by-side!"

Joel sunk his head as most others in the room let out another cheer. Giles wasn't cheering, either. He was staring at him with one judgmental eye.

"Our next order of business should be to find Aldous and Dalton," Kabel said.

"Yeh! Let's go out thar an' find 'em, fellas!" Auber added.

"Not tonight." Kabel shook his head. "The enemy may still be out on patrol. We wait until morning."

Prince Xviktolo stepped forward. "If they are not back by morning, I will search for them by sea."

To escape Giles' gaze, Joel focused elsewhere and found himself watching Conrad, of all people. He was tucked tightly between Lucia and Alistair's towering forms, across the circle. Had the mute's eyes not been wandering, he never would have noticed him staring at Xviktolo with such fiery apprehension.

As far as Joel knew, the pair had never even spoken before. Why the death stare?

"We'll need to take shifts standing guard outside." Dhogron's voice ended Joel's train of thought. "It is unlikely, but the enemy could have followed us, or discovered our location. I'd be happy to take the first shift. Any other volunteers to watch alongside me?"

Now, Joel caught visible shock on Conrad's face. Something about what Dhogron said had almost certainly helped him to realize something. But what was it? Something about the enemy? What would that have to do with the marinian prince?

Alistair raised his hand. "I wanna sleep easy tonight, knowin' that tha best of us are out there protectin' tha coop!"

"Then, why are you volunteering?" Lucia asked, drawing a few laughs.

"If you'd quit flappin' yer gums, you'd know that I wasn't volunteerin'!" the big man shot back. "Tha fella I wanna nominate is tha fiercest an' most cunning of us all!"

"Oh, no…" Auber muttered.

"CAP'N AUBER!" Alistair shouted, pointing to the sulking pirate.

"Well… erm… I'm a lil' tired…" Auber said, rubbing the back of his head. His heavy eyes told Joel that he was at least telling the truth about that much.

"I'd rather have a tired Auber, than no Auber at all!" Kabel said with a little too much cheer and then slapped him off the back. The entire group roared in approval.

The captain narrowed his eyes at Kabel. "Throwin' me overboard to the sharks so ye can get some rest, eh?"

Kabel only afforded him a wink and smile as his response.

With that, the Strangers began to chat amongst themselves in the circle. It didn't last long, however. Amis stepped forth and all around looked to him in curious silence. He had cleaned himself up to such a degree that he almost looked like a different person: His previously messy brown hair was now up in a ponytail. All of the grime on his body had washed away, and though he could have dressed nicely, he instead wore a baggy tunic with rolled-up sleeves that he'd borrowed from Dhogron. His ankles were exposed by stockings that also had to be rolled, for they were too long. It was a reminder to Joel that he needed to get to know his fellow luxian. Since they were about the same size, he'd have been better suited to some of his garments.

"I just wanted to thank you all. If you hadn't come to save me, I would almost certainly be dead," he said, letting out a breath of relief. "And the Degenerate seal would be in grave danger."

Again, Joel caught onto Conrad's inquisitive, yet apprehensive gaze. *First Xviktolo, now Amis*, he thought. Given his reaction to what

Dhogron had said about the enemy possibly finding them here, did the strategist suspect a traitor in their midst? Perhaps he was suspicious of *those two* for being relative outsiders. That would have been out-of-character for Conrad one year ago, but with the dark essence coursing through him, he'd been acting different, of late.

Soon, the strategist's stare became less aggressive and more studious. As others in the circle talked, it became mere background noise to Joel. He instead put his mind to figuring out what was going on with Conrad. He worried that, given his recent tendency toward rash, aggressive behavior, he might stir up a problem with either Xviktolo or Amis. Needless panic and discord were the last things the Strangers needed, tonight-

A silent gasp turned into a heavy gulp as Joel realized that Conrad was now staring back at him with crossed arms. His cheeks reddened and he darted his eyes away. He'd been caught, but perhaps it wasn't such a bad thing. In fact, he was almost certain that Conrad would explain himself. He just wasn't sure if it would be tonight.

As chatter between the Strangers began to die down, the circle dispersed. Most went to bed, while Dhogron and Auber went outside to start their shift on the watch. Before Joel could make his way upstairs, however, Conrad grabbed him by the shoulder.

"Could I have a word?" he whispered before nudging his head toward the dining table, drenched in shadow.

The mute feigned confusion by cocking his head. Before even sitting to talk, he wanted *confirmation.*

"Please, this is of the utmost importance. I wouldn't disturb your sleep if it wasn't something time-sensitive. The safety of the group is at stake..."

So, he *was* suspicious of someone, Joel thought. Once again playing dumb, he let out an inaudible sigh while nodding.

As the pair walked past the makeshift bedding where Lucia lay, she sat up and tugged at Conrad's sleeve.

"Aren't you coming to bed?"

"Soon enough. Joel and I have a few things to discuss," Conrad said with a pleasant smile that Joel felt certain was fake.

"Don't tell me this is about your ridiculous suspicions..." Lucia said with narrowed eyes.

"No, no," he replied with a chuckle, holding his hands up. "It's a little something that only we men can talk about. It is a little embarrassing if I'm honest. You understand..."

"Oh..." Lucia replied, wide-eyed. "Erm, sure, I will try not to eavesdrop..."

Conrad let out an amused huff while nudging his head toward Joel. "There won't be anything to listen to."

"Right..." she trailed off while rolling over.

Upon sitting across the table from one another, Conrad lit a lantern, and in its dim flicker, Joel noted that his cheerful expression had turned to stone.

The mute raised an eyebrow as Conrad signed to him instead of speaking aloud. He asked how he had met Prince Xviktolo. Joel responded with hand signals of his own, explaining that the marinian saved him and Giles from drowning at the hands of crazed Bosfueras townsfolk. He had originally come to feed the kraken and happened upon the battle between her and Aldous. After stopping the fight with his 'sounds of the sea', he had convinced the sea monster to aid them in battle.

Conrad nodded along before sending more hand gestures back to Joel, asking why he thought that Xviktolo would stick around with the Strangers, despite having no stake in what they were doing.

Joel signed back that the marinian had taken a liking to Aldous, and wished to ensure his safe return. He also explained Xviktolo's desire to fight, due in large part to circumstances surrounding the culture of his kingdom, Coralstar.

With a stroke of his chin, the strategist shifted topics: He next made hand signals to ask about Amis, and if Joel had noticed anything odd about him while escaping from the dark forces. Before answering, however, Joel asked what his questions were truly about. What was the potential threat that he had mentioned?

Unwavering, Conrad repeated his question in USL form. Joel let out a quiet huff and signed back that he did not know Amis well enough to comment.

With narrowed eyes, Conrad asked if Amis had done anything that bothered him, or seemed out of place.

Now that he'd mentioned it, Joel did have some reservations about the Key Keeper's behavior. He made hand signals in return, saying that Amis had swiped his luxmortite sword from him without permission, to use against the creeper in the alley.

Conrad smiled and asked how he knew that they were called creepers. Joel told him that Amis knew their namesake and that they'd been used as a threat by the enemy to make him talk. The strategist only nodded along, and Joel looked past his shoulder to see Lucia watching them with one eye open. He still wasn't sure where Conrad was going with all of this, but her apparent worries made *him* worry.

However, the strategist's demeanor had significantly calmed. It was almost as if Joel had eased his worries, and now their conversation felt more casual. He next asked if Amis did anything else out of the ordinary. After some thought, Joel signed back that despite his aggressive behavior toward enemies, the Key Keeper had paradoxically run away and abandoned Triston when one of the creepers had him dead to rights.

With an easy-going shrug, Conrad made hand signals saying that he couldn't expect a shackled man to fight against a monster like the creeper, and that, given the vile nature of his prior captors, fear and even cowardice were understandable reactions. After finishing his hand signals, though, something changed: His eyes widened, and his mouth fell agape.

Joel shook his head and signed that he had cut the chains with his luxmortite blade, to make running and fighting easier for him while they escaped. A cold sweat broke out on Conrad's brow, and his eyes looked back and forth as if searching his mind for something.

What was it about the chains and shackles that had riled him up? The mute made hand signals to ask, but Conrad denied there being any further problems. The goosebumps lining his arms betrayed such an obvious lie, but Joel had hit a stone wall. Conrad stood while thanking him for his help in USL.

As Joel ascended the stairs, to head up to bed, he peered down at Conrad. He had nestled into the bedding with Lucia and already looked to be fast asleep. No matter how calm he appeared now, however, the mute couldn't get that terrified image of Conrad out of his head. Something was still bothering him, and he couldn't even begin to imagine what it was.

CHAPTER 27
KILLING INTENT

While lying in bed with eyes wide open, Conrad began to hear the light snores of Lucia, to his left. It was time, he thought, to confront the threat head-on. If the conclusion he had come to about Amis was true, then *everyone* was in danger, and *no one* would believe him. The final piece of the puzzle was something that only Conrad had witnessed; something that he had neglected to mention to anyone. He had almost forgotten about it entirely. To make matters even more difficult, Lucia and many of the others believed that the dark essence was altering his mind, so any claim made about someone whom they'd worked so hard to save would be met with skepticism at best and condemnation at worst.

Conrad reached under his pant leg to retrieve a stashed dagger; the same weapon that had saved him from certain death a startling number of times. He crept up from his bedding with pinpoint precision, so as not to awaken Lucia, and tip-toed his way up the stairs.

At the top of the staircase, the strategist hesitated. If what he believed was true, a dagger wouldn't be enough to stop the threat. Joel's luxmortite blade, perhaps? *No*, he thought. Cutting him would do nothing. The only other weapon he could think of was Alistair's wind Rune, but he didn't dare risk awakening the second loudest member of the Strangers, and even if his theft ended up successful, he was unsure of his ability to wield it.

It seemed the only option was to confront the threat himself and expose it to the others. That plan presented great risk; not only to his life, but to the relationship with his friends. If, when trying to expose the threat, he was caught and thwarted, then he would almost certainly be seen as the murderous villain, when the true fiend had hidden in plain sight.

Flipping his dagger downward into a stabbing position, Conrad crept past the doorway of the room where Joel and the others were sleeping.

"Oi… what're ya doin'?" Triston asked in a sleepy state. Somehow, the words had still managed to come out at normal volume.

Conrad widened his eyes and darted to the corner of the doorframe, out of sight.

"It's chilly, I need another blanket," Alistair said from within the room.

"Ya already got one. Quit tryin' ta steal mine, ya weasel!" the elder MacRae shot back. Conrad let out a sigh of relief.

Continuing down the hallway, the strategist snuck past Kabel and Rolf's rooms, which were parallel to one another. The final room, at the end of the hallway, was where Amis slept. Thanks to Aldous' absence and Dhogron keeping watch outside, there would be no one to stop Conrad from confirming his suspicions.

Entering the room at a crawl's pace, Conrad set eyes on Amis, who rocked his hammock ever so slightly with each breath taken in and snore let out. Conveniently, he lay on his side, facing a window that bathed him in pale moonlight.

As he crept toward the hammock with dagger at the ready, he recounted his justification for the coming attack. In a battle where less than a couple of dozen had accomplished their mission against over a hundred enemies, two casualties at most didn't feel right. In addition, the Strangers had all gathered in one spot; a prime opportunity for the dark forces to take them all out in one fell swoop. The final piece of the puzzle came when Joel reminded Conrad that Amis had worn shackles throughout his torture and rescue.

Conrad approached the hammock with his dagger raised overhead. He had originally thought not to use lethal force, but the more he considered it, the more he realized that it didn't matter.

As he stood over the hammock, about to strike, Conrad's eyes widened to see Amis turn over. He looked up at him in a groggy state, then, as the glint in the dagger reflected in his eyes, he put his hands up and began to breathe heavier.

"Wh-what're you doing?"

"Don't move a muscle," Conrad said in a harsh whisper. "And no loud noises."

"What is this? Some kind of joke? *We are on the same side...*"

The strategist scoffed. "You've done well to fool everyone, and you almost had me fooled, too; but it's like I told you back then... spending enough time with someone tends to reveal their *true nature.*"

"Wh-what are you on about?" Amis asked, squirming in his hammock. "Could you put the dagger down, at least? We can talk about this..."

"Yes, let's talk about those wrists of yours."

"My wrists?"

"Your ankles, too," Conrad said, pointing to the lower part of his legs, where the stockings were rolled up. "Am I supposed to believe that you wore shackles for days, and walked across an entire city in them, only to receive no lesions on your wrists or ankles?"

"I-I don't know what to tell you... perhaps I was lucky," Amis said with a nervous shrug.

"I imagine it is quite difficult to play the part of a battered prisoner when your wounds keep on regenerating. There is no need for you to continue this facade. It's only you and I, after all. Show me your true form, *Brice.*"

"You're not making any sense," Amis said, slowly reaching outward with a rickety hand. "Why don't we put down the dagger, and-"

"Stay back!" Conrad said in a harsh whisper. Amis backed off and put his hands up once more. "If you won't willingly show yourself, then I will force it out of you!"

Conrad brought his dagger down, aiming for the chest. Amis intercepted and grasped Conrad's arm with both hands, however, before the blade could reach him.

"Help!" he called out.

"*Damn it...*" the strategist muttered as he wriggled himself free and then hopped back.

"Help meeee!" Amis cried as he fell out of his hammock in a panic.

Conrad's heart sank as he heard the frantic shuffling of feet coming from behind. One of his worst-case scenarios was about to play out. He would have to convince his friends, who had already come to distrust his word, that the man whom they had just saved was not who he claimed to be. Worst of all, he would have to convince them in short order.

"So, what's your plan?" Conrad asked, holding his dagger up in defense. "How are you planning to summon your allies here? There must be a way for your master to reach you…"

"Yer crazy!" he shouted back as the first of the responders, Alistair, Triston, Xviktolo, Joel, and Giles entered the room.

"Oi! What's goin' on, here?" Triston asked, shining a candle ahead and squinting.

"Ah! Is this 'sparring'?" Xviktolo asked, looking to Alistair with enthusiasm. The redhead could only shake his head with narrow eyes.

"This loon attacked me!" Amis cried, pointing at the strategist as Kabel and Mirabel entered from behind.

"He's not who he says he is!" Conrad said, pointing to the suspected fake with his dagger.

"Huh? What's that supposed ta mean?" Alistair asked.

"This is *not* Amis. He is an impostor; a part of Drake and the Dark Wizard's team!"

"He's been talkin' this nonsense ever since he got up here! I don't know what he's on about!" Amis retorted.

"Alright, why don't we just put the dagger down?" Kabel said, slowly approaching with an arm outreached.

Conrad held the weapon out in front of him and the stocky man stopped in his tracks. "Keep your distance! I know that you don't believe me, but it's true!"

"Alright, if dis isn't Amis, den who is he?" Rolf asked, rubbing his eyes. Ebbie and Franco filled the doorway behind him.

"This is Brice Garin. I don't know how, but he's gonna lead Angus and the rest of them here to kill us all."

"A bold claim," Franco said.

"Ain't that what we've got a watch outside fer?" Ebbie asked.

"A watch don't matter if dere are hundreds attackin' us…" Rolf said with a roll of his eyes.

"I say bring them on, then." Xviktolo chimed in with a hand on the hilt of his sword.

"But hold on, isn't Dhogron his friend? Surely, he would have noticed if it wasn't Amis," Mirabel said.

"He can take the form of his victims," Conrad said, eyeing Amis. "After eating their brains, he's able to copy that person in any way. Appearance, voice, even memories…"

"What a load of nonsense!" Amis shot back, as the group began to grumble and argue amongst themselves.

"Brice… where have I heard that name before?" Alistair asked aloud.

"He is one of the hooligans…" Lucia said, pushing through the crowd. "Or what is left of them, anyhow. Dalton fought him back in Bosfueras."

"Is what he says true?" Kabel asked, gesturing to Conrad. "Could Brice have perhaps transformed into Amis?"

"I never saw him do anything like that. In fact, I saw very little of him at all. Based on what Dalton told me, he had speedy regeneration and could morph his arms into deadly tendrils," Lucia said as her eyes fell on the strategist. "Still, I see no reason for Conrad to lie-"

"But what about that dark essence?" Giles asked aloud. All in the room looked at the one-eyed man. "Wasn't it affecting his mind? I saw him make plenty of questionable decisions while under its influence."

Conrad snarled at his detractor. He was tempted to bring up how he had stabbed his own hand just to save him earlier in the night, but that was a whole other argument, and he was certain that time was short.

"We can still settle this peacefully," Kabel said, holding his hands out between Conrad and Amis. "All we gotta do is find Dalton, and he can confirm-"

"He can't," Conrad interrupted through gritting teeth. "I'm the only one of us who has seen this ability. He has used it to trick me once before. We don't have time to discuss this. He's going to lead the enemy here, to kill us all. So, you have to decide… do you believe me? Or do you believe him?"

"This fella is crazy! I think I saw a red glow in his eyes when he attacked me! Just like the people who kidnapped and tortured me!" Amis cried, practically delirious.

"Red eyes… like tha people attackin' us tonight?" Alistair asked.

Joel began making hand signals, but they all went ignored. Conrad thought to ask the mute to vouch for him, but half of the people in the room wouldn't understand his USL, anyhow.

"Yeh, now that ya mention it, most of them enemies had red eyes," Triston said, then pointed to the strategist. "What if *he's* tha real traitor?"

"No! He's trying to turn you all against me!" Conrad shouted as

Amis started walking toward the crowd. "And you! Don't take another step!"

Amis froze in place and then pointed a shaking, judgmental finger at him. "You see? Red eyes!"

Conrad turned to see most in the group eyeing him with suspicion.

"Wh-what are you all looking at?" he asked.

"Oh… lad…" Alistair muttered with uncharacteristic sadness.

Kabel shimmied his way over to Lucia and stood on his tip-toes to whisper in her ear. She leaned back and flashed surprise on her face. After seeming to gather herself, she returned a nod.

Lucia pushed through the tense crowd and began a slow walk toward Conrad.

"You really should have told me what was on your mind," she said as he held the dagger out toward her. She stopped in her tracks and raised an eyebrow.

"I knew that you wouldn't believe me," said the strategist.

"Pointing a weapon at me won't change that," she said in a stern tone, then continued her approach.

"Don't come any closer."

"You have given me no choice," Lucia said as she took another step forward. "Put the dagger down, before you make a regrettable decision."

"*You're* the one who will regret it," Conrad shot back.

Lucia took a deep breath, and then another step. She was only a few paces away, now. "I don't believe that you'll attack me, even with that vile substance controlling you."

Conrad shook his head and lowered his weapon. "That's not what I meant. We need to get out of here. The enemy is-"

Out of the corner of his left eye, Conrad caught wind of Kabel charging at him. The split-second he had before impact was filled almost entirely with shock: Lucia had used herself as a distraction.

While the stocky man wrapped arms around his waist, Conrad pulled his dagger back, and as he was dragged to the floor, he threw the weapon at a wide-eyed Amis. The sound of peeling flesh and splattering blood was nearly drowned out by the two men hitting the floor with a *thud*.

And then came *the gurgling*. Conrad looked up to see all in the room staring past him, mouths agape. The strategist looked over his shoulder to find a staggering Amis. The dagger had found its way into his neck. He swiped around at the air in desperation, spitting out a storm of red from his mouth as he did. After a short struggle, the Key Keeper's eyes rolled, and he fell back into the hammock. Only the sounds of tensing rope filled the room as the hammock rocked back and forth at the command of Amis' limp body.

Conrad looked back up at Lucia. He had never seen such a look on her face. It could best be described as *condemnation*.

"You idiot!" Kabel's angry, panicked voice snapped Conrad out of his stupor. He found the stocky man standing over him, face-to-face, his fist cocked.

"Wait-"

A thunderous right hook cracked into Conrad's jaw, to which he recoiled, but Kabel caught him by the collar. A second and third blow to chin and cheek respectively numbed his face and rang his ears. Yet, instead of responding or trying to escape, he turned his eyes to Amis' rocking body.

Why? Why hadn't he regenerated and revealed himself? Back in Bosfueras, he had found that stabbing Brice was the only way to make him involuntarily reveal his true form. Or at least, it was the only way that he knew of. Yet, there Amis' body lay, without a single sign of life or change. Dread seeped into his heart. Had he been wrong? Even with so much evidence of his suspicions?

The crowd surrounded Conrad and Kabel, taking the strategist's eyes off the body in the rocking hammock. Alistair pulled Kabel back and restrained him.

"Steady, lad! Steady!"

"Yeh, methinks he's had enough!" Triston added.

"That's where you're wrong! Let me go!" Kabel cried as he struggled and wriggled, but it was no use. The big man had an unbreakable hold around his arms and shoulders. "I'll decide when he's had enough!"

"Now what?" Franco asked, his back turned to Conrad. He was staring at the body rocking in the hammock.

"We went drough all of dat effort of savin' Amis, just fer one of our own to kill him… and y'know, now dat I dink of it, he seemed overly eager ta kill slaves out on da battlefield," Rolf said with disappointment on his tongue. "I say we give him a taste of his own blade. An eye for an eye!"

The lanky young man drew a dagger of his own and began pushing through the crowd.

"You'll do no such thing!" Lucia said, stepping between them. Joel stood next to her with crossed arms.

"Stand aside," Rolf said. Giles came to his side.

Joel and Lucia shook their heads and stood firm. Grumbling, and then a series of arguments began to break out amongst the entire team, but it didn't last long. Dhogron and Auber burst into the room, near-breathless and with eyes wider than gold coins.

"The enemy is coming!" the trickster Wizard said in a panic. All in the room fell silent.

"What do you mean?" Mira asked, leaning in.

"Hundreds of 'em! Carryin' torches just up the path!" Auber clarified. A thick tension filled the air. Suddenly, there were new priorities.

"I knew it…" Conrad grumbled through his bloodied teeth.

"That doesn't mean you get to kill a member of the team!" Kabel shouted, then tried to escape Alistair's grasp once more. He almost slipped through, but the big redhead retightened his grip and held firm.

"I don't know what's going on here, but we need to leave…" Dhogron said with the fear of God in his eyes. The group remained motionless and silent out of an apparent shock. "Now!"

"What're ye all frozen solid for? Let's get movin'! That's an order!" Auber said with demand on his tongue.

The silence was broken up by a series of chuckles. All in the room looked around in confusion, as those chuckles turned to howls of vile, callous laughter. Finally, Conrad and the rest of the Strangers looked to the body in the hammock, which sat up. The bloody dagger *dinged* off the floor like a bell tolling at a funeral.

Staring back at the group with a poisonous grin was Brice. No evidence of a prior wound existed on his neck, save for dry blood, and his arms had transformed into tentacles, wriggling with a ferocious, wicked joy.

"None of ye are goin' *anywhere.*"

Dhogron looked at the big-nosed man wearing his tunic with mouth agape. "A-Amis? What happened to Amis?"

Brice cackled with delight. "We tortured him fer days, and then he squealed like a pig before I ripped him to bloody pieces and ate his brains!"

All of the Strangers gasped before a terrified silence overtook the room. Yet, no one was more horrified than Conrad to find out that he'd been right all along. It was just crazy enough to be real, and now the enemy was in their midst. Even worse, Brice had found a way to summon his comrades, making escape nearly impossible. The entire mission to rescue Amis had been a multi-layered trap.

With a breath of desperation, Dhogron ran forward and punched a gasping Brice in the cheek, which sent him flying into the wall, splintering it in the process.

"You all need to run!" the trickster Wizard cried, looking back to his allies.

"B-but where can we go?" Auber asked. "The enemy is just down the road!"

"I have a place we can go to!" Kabel said, then wriggled free from the weakening grasp of Alistair. "Everyone, grab your essential items, and meet me downstairs!"

"But... our home..." Mirabel muttered, her tone drenched in despair.

"Sorry, dear," Kabel said as he took his wife's hand and led her out of the room.

The rest of the Strangers began piling out, but in the meantime, Brice snuck a tentacle up behind Dhogron and wrapped it around his neck.

"Like I said, yer not goin' anywhere!" A villainous grin warped Brice's jaw as he tightened his chokehold. Dhogron's face began turning purple.

Conrad pushed his swelling face out of mind, ran up to the struggling pair, swiped his dagger off the floor, and then jumped up for extra power while stabbing down. However, Brice caught him in midair with another tentacle and began to constrict the life out of him, too. The strategist opened his mouth to breathe, but nothing came in; only weak, desperate exhales were allowed.

The dagger slipped from Conrad's hand, but as it bounced off the floor, it found a new owner: Joel swooped in, and with the same motion that he had grabbed it, swung the weapon upward, into the tentacle holding the strategist. Less than a moment later, Lucia plunged her dagger into the feeler that restricted Dhogron.

Neither attack had been enough to cut all the way through, but they had weakened Brice's grip enough that Dhogron escaped. Conrad, only having a human's strength, remained breathless and in the big-nosed man's grasp.

Adding to the combination of attacks, however, was Prince Xviktolo, who plunged his starlite blade between the eyes of a gasping

Brice. Dark red blood erupted from the big-nosed man's face as he finally released Conrad, who fell to the floor in a wheezing heap.

Not letting up, Dhogron marched forward and laid a vicious elbow into Brice, which sent him soaring through the window and crashing to the ground outside.

"There is no time to waste! Grab what you can!" Dhogron said to the remaining Strangers.

Lucia held her hand out to a struggling Conrad, but he turned it away. Very much had changed between them after what had just transpired, but the strategist tucked it all away, for now. In silence, they were the last to leave the room. It wouldn't be long before the enemy was upon them.

~

DOWN THE ROAD from Kabel's tree-built home, Drake Danvers and Sampson led over a hundred of the Bosfueras townsfolk, slaves, and shrill-breathed creepers up the path, anticipating the surprise of their enemies. Ned the bodyguard walked beside his master, striding smoothly, as if gliding through air; he hissed with excitement.

"Ye really outdid yerself, this time!" Sampson said with a heinous laugh. "When some of my girls went missin', I thought I'd never see 'em again. I never woulda dreamed that they'd dare to infiltrate one of my buildings! Those fools never knew what hit 'em! And this? This plan o' yers is even better!"

Drake flashed a smooth smile. "Yes, well, I tend to see these things like a game of chess. Those street performers thought they had you all figured out and were emboldened to strike tonight, only because we *wanted* them to think that way. They had our king in check with a bishop, without realizing that our queen was pointed right at their only weapon."

"Err… yeh, well, I ain't much of a chess enthusiast, but ye weeded out the moles in my organization; all while allowin' me to recapture some of my lost girls. Brilliant! I think we're gonna have a long, prosperous partnership!" the slaver said with a slimy grin.

A chuckle escaped Drake's lips. "And what could be a more fitting way to end the night than burning our enemies and their quaint little home to the ground?"

"They'll never see it comin'!" Sampson held up a fist that shook with obvious excitement. "I only wish I could get my hands on the wretched pleb who dared strike me with an arrow!"

"Come, now..." Drake trailed off as he held a hand back. Ned retrieved two wine glasses from within his cloak and handed them to his master. "I brought you here tonight to enjoy the show. The Dark Wizard isn't the only one who can put on a light display. *Mine* will be filled with the music of blood-curdling screams, courtesy of our enemies. Perhaps you can take solace in the fact that burning to death is one of the worst ways to go."

"I suppose..." Sampson said as the Village Elder handed him a glass. While Ned poured wine for them, Sampson let loose a cheeky grin. "If I didn't know any better... I'd say ye were tryin' to outdo the Dark Wizard. Do I detect trouble in this partnership?"

"Not at all," he replied with a nonchalant sip of his drink. The group had reached the house. "Tonight, I simply wished to show you my role in this alliance. With my strategic dominance, the Dark Wizard's vast powers, and your influence, we'll be unstoppable."

"I'll drink to that!" Sampson said and then began to gulp down his wine.

The slaver spit out his drink as Brice flew from the window of the tree-built home and crashed to the ground, a bloody mess.

"*What?*" Drake asked aloud, his voice cracking.

"Say, ain't that the fella we were relyin' on?" Sampson asked.

Instead of answering, the Village Elder walked up to a groggy Brice. The big-nosed man looked up, slowly regenerating from a series of sustained wounds.

"What happened?" Drake asked with demanding eyes.

"They're tryin' to escape..." Brice replied, in a daze. The gash in between his eyes was closing up.

Drake shook his head. "I assumed as much. The Dark Wizard will be displeased. This is twice now, you've failed us."

"It wasn't my fault!" Brice shot back as he stood. "I don' know how, but Conrad figured it out just before ye got here."

"That *damned Mercer boy... again...*" Drake muttered with a snarl. "Our Wizard friend's fascination with him has gone on for long enough. Find him, and kill him. Do *not* fail me, this time."

Brice's eyes twitched. "Don' get all high an' mighty, orderin' me around! I only take orders from the Lord of Darkness! I bet he wouldn't care much if I crushed that dainty lil' neck of yers..."

A tentacle formed in place of his arm and wriggled toward an unflinching Drake. It stopped short, however, and the Village Elder knew why. He could practically feel Ned hovering behind, in a battle-ready position. Then, there were the creepers, whose shrill, excited breaths could still just about anyone. They were begging for an excuse to kill. With a scoff, Brice retracted the tentacle.

"A wise decision," Drake said with a sip of wine. "You'd do well to remember that it was *I* who convinced the Dark Wizard to take in your crew, and to make you into something more than hapless miners."

"Thanks a bunch," Brice said with an eye roll. "All of my friends have either died or been transformed into freaks. Ye did us a *real favor*, back then!"

"Don't blame me for your shortcomings. I've given you nothing but opportunity. Tonight, I served up for you the easiest possible win to get back in the Dark Wizard's good graces, and you *still* wasted it. I'd recommend taking at least *some* casualties if you wish to show yourself before him again. I can tolerate mistakes; *he* rarely does."

"Yes, sir..." the big-nosed man replied through gritted teeth. He, Ned, and a couple of the creepers approached the tree-built home.

With one of his dark tentacles, Brice splintered the front door in half and entered into the darkness. After some time searching within, it became apparent that their enemies had gotten away. Drake groaned as he heard Brice cry out in frustration from within the house.

"I suggest you get out there and find some of them, Brice! Ned, you shall be his backup! Utilize the creepers, if you must!" Drake called out.

After a brief crashing noise on the other side of the house, the Village Elder and his hordes of torch-bearers stood in silence.

"Now, what?" Sampson asked.

Drake threw his glass down, shattering it with angry conviction. "Let us burn this ugly house to the ground."

The red-eyed collectives and slaves approached from behind with torches in hand. The short-lived home of the Strangers was to be eradicated without a second thought.

CHAPTER 28
DECLARATION

Dalton Rayleigh opened his heavy eyes to a squint as the sunlight of the early morning struck his face. His back groaned as he sat up over the bar counter, where several empty mugs and bottles lay. With a gasp of realization, the warrior looked to his left to see an empty chair: Anora was gone.

Had he imagined it all? He could hardly remember the prior night, and his pounding head didn't help matters. It had to be real, he thought. She sounded like Anora, looked like her, and she even knew his middle name. The warrior had felt her warm touch for the first time in 13 long years, yet he could never forget the feeling; it felt like home.

With a disappointed snort, Dalton stood and turned to see the window he had smashed in last night. It was all a haze, but he chose to focus on the positives, rather than the negatives nagging at his mind.

"Sorry 'bout the mess, Cole… but it was worth it…" Dalton reached into his pocket and left some gold coins on the counter. It wasn't enough to cover the broken window, but at least it would take care of the drinks.

As he approached the window, Dalton spotted some commoners in ragged clothing coming and going from the slums, but the streets were otherwise uncrowded. When the coast was clear, he slipped out of the window and began walking to the southeast, in the direction of the outskirts.

Ominous, dark clouds formed seemingly out of nowhere as the warrior traveled, though his mind was anywhere but on rain. How could he get back in contact with Anora? He strained his brain, trying to remember details of their late night, but there was nothing save empty space; a blank memory.

Raindrops began striking Dalton's dark hair as he lengthened his strides and the streets emptied. Thunder echoed off in the distance of the fields ahead, and a familiar metallic smell filled the air. It wasn't much longer before the downpour began. While everyone else was frantically running for cover, the warrior couldn't be bothered to care when he had so much on his hazy mind. He was nearing the woods, anyway; a good cover from the rain.

After walking down the wooded path of the outskirts for a time, Dalton stopped. He could smell smoke, and it hadn't been from a single campfire, either; it was all-encompassing, like a thick fog. His mind jumped to the idea of a wildfire, or perhaps the worst possible scenario: The enemy had struck Kabel's home. With that possibility taken to heart, he continued down the muddying path with his sword drawn.

Further and further Dalton traveled into the haze, his lungs filling up with burnt wood. He badly wanted to cough, but he stopped himself with each temptation. The enemy could have been around any corner, or in any crevice, ready to strike. The path became more confined to the smoke with each pace forward until it seemed like he was unable to see his hands in front of him.

Then, as if awakening from a dream, the warrior stepped out of the smoke and his view became clear as day: Before him, where Kabel's tree-built home once stood, were a pile of logs, ashes, and dying cinders. Dalton's stomach sank as he tightened the grip of his sword and proceeded to investigate up close.

Upon inspection, he was unable to find burnt bodies or any sign of prior life. After all, there would still be remains of a charred body. The horses were missing from their small stable, which gave the warrior hope that perhaps his friends had fled on the swift steeds. But Aldous' carriage had also been reduced to burnt wood, which could have meant that the enemy had stolen, released, or killed the horses. Had his friends escaped? Or had they been captured? For once, Dalton was at a loss for what to do.

His thoughts were interrupted by a twig's *crunch* off in the distance, behind him. Dalton ran back to the wooded path and looked into the thick trees across from it. All he could hear now were raindrops bouncing off leaves, muddy puddles, and the grassy ground.

"You may as well show yourself! I'm in no mood for hide n' seek!"

After a few moments of silence, a man in a peculiar mask stepped out from behind a tree. It bore two faces: One was sad, frowning, and right side up; the other was menacing and upside down. He adjusted a dark blue dagger to Dalton's direction with each deliberate step taken to reveal himself.

"Who caused this?" Dalton asked, motioning back to the burnt-down house with his head. "You?"

"Would I be sitting around here if I did?"

"Seems like it'd be a good idea if you wished to pick off any stragglers who avoided the fire."

"Or perhaps *you've* come back, looking to kill stragglers?" he asked.

Dalton chuckled while lowering his blade. "That's a fine luxmortite dagger you've got, there. Are you a friend of Joel's, perchance?"

"Depends on my mood," the masked man said as he, too, lowered his weapon. "I cannot recall seeing you in battle with the others last night."

"Funny, I don't recall seeing you, either. But that blue blade tells me you're on *our side*," the warrior said.

"'Our side'? You refer to the Fearsome Goats?"

"Erm… no… the Strangers," Dalton said with narrow eyes. "Alistair and Triston kept tryin' to push that lousy name on us, but it got overruled."

A hollow chuckle came from beneath the mask. "I overheard Alistair talking about it, yesterday. I suppose the name wasn't final, back then."

"It ain't hard to overhear Alistair! Unfortunately, half of what comes from his big mouth is nonsense!"

"That 'big mouth' is the only reason I found you lot, to begin with. His shouting in the alleys and on the rooftops led me straight to him and the others."

"What brings you to Endoshire? I don't believe Joel has mentioned you," Dalton said, then slicked back his mid-length hair, drenched by rain. "That dagger leads me to believe you are a Key Keeper, like Joel was. Is that right?"

"I was Keeper of the Key in Thironas, for a time. But much like Joel, I have been placed on probation by the Council, for failure to protect the Famine seal," he replied.

"Ah, so you must be this 'Ometos' fella that they mentioned."

He removed his mask to reveal two brown, dagger-like eyes and an iron expression. "That's right. Or you can call me Pierce if you prefer."

"The name's Dalton," the warrior said as he approached. With a thunderous slap that echoed off the trees, the pair shook hands, instantly forming a trustful bond. "I suppose we should retrace our steps to figure out what happened."

"Yes… I'm sure you noticed, but there are no bodies in the debris of the house. They either escaped or were captured by Angus and his goons," Pierce replied.

"When was the last time you saw them?" Dalton asked.

"To escape with the prisoner and avoid the horde of those red-eyed folk, we split up. Most of us reconvened at a church to the north of here. But the prisoner was not among them. Joel was missing, too. We assumed that they had made it back to this house, so that was the next destination after leaving," the dagger-eyed man said.

"Good! So, they succeeded!" Dalton said with clenched fists and a big smile.

"Perhaps… I cannot be certain. I had to split up from the group to pick up… well…" Pierce trailed off, then turned back to the trees. "You can come out now if you wish."

Out from behind the trees stepped a small woman with olive skin, long, dark hair, and a slight bump protruding from the midsection of her muddy dress. She waved to Dalton with a pleasant smile.

"'Ello there! My name's Greta. Ye got any food?"

Pierce looked back to her with even sharper eyes than usual, while Dalton shrugged, and pointed back to the cinders that remained of Kabel's home.

"The name's Dalton, and sorry to say, but all of my stuff was in that house," he replied and then leaned in for a whisper to Pierce. "That your wife? She's adorable."

"Well… she is the mother of my unborn child, but after Thironas fell on hard times, it became nearly impossible to marry. Perhaps, after all of this is over, we could use that church in the city. The priest seems a nice enough fellow."

"Methinks we are a long way from settling this conflict," Dalton said with disappointment on his tongue. "Did you notice anything else after picking her up? Perhaps you saw the enemy marching to or from here?"

"When we first arrived in Endoshire, my top priority was secrecy.

The slums in the west, by the shoreline, seemed best to remain hidden from the eyes of our enemy," Pierce said as he looked back to Greta with a smile. She was stomping in the mud to entertain herself. "Unfortunately, that meant crossing the entire city amid the chaos happening in the streets. It was fine by myself, but on the way back…"

"Tell 'im about that big ol' group we almost ran into!" Greta blurted out.

"I was getting to that…" Pierce muttered before snorting. "Anyhow, on the way back, we were nearly discovered by a huge group leaving the outskirts. They were led by two people that I did not recognize: A well-dressed man with slicked back, blond hair; and a portly fellow in a fur coat."

"That'd be Drake and Sampson, probably," Dalton said.

"Ah, so *that's* Drake. I've only ever dealt with his right hand, Angus, but it was clear from the outset that he was leader of their operation."

"And that operation just got a whole lot bigger with Sampson on his side. From what I am told, he carries with him more influence in this city than anyone else."

"Tell him about them creepy monstahs, too," Greta said, peeking over his shoulder, as a child might do.

"Yes, in addition to the battalion of men they commanded, there were these odd, shrill-breathed monsters. I believe they were unleashed toward the end of the battle at the docks. They were oozing that same dark essence that Angus used to enhance his abilities," Pierce said.

"It was frightenin'! I could feel my heart poundin' when they trotted on past us. Or mayhap that was the child kicking," she said, rubbing her pregnant belly.

"It is far too soon for there to be kicking," Pierce said with a chuckle. He then turned back to the warrior. "Anyhow, we came back here to find the house in ruins, and have been waiting for some sign of life ever since. What happened on your end?"

"My story's a lil' simpler," Dalton said while smirking. "A bug-man lifted me into the sky, I cut him in mid-air, and then we both crashed to the sea."

"A bug-man? I wonder what he would look like…" Greta said.

Dalton snickered. "Uglier than you can imagine. By the time I recovered and climbed aboard an empty ship, the battle seemed to have ended, but some enemies lingered nearby. So, I hid on board until the streets were cleared."

"And you didn't encounter anyone or anything on your way back?" Pierce asked.

"Well… I, uhh… may have stopped for a drink on the way back…" Dalton trailed off, red-cheeked.

"I hope it was worth it," the dagger-eyed man said, nudging his head toward the smoking debris.

"Let me put it to you this way: Greta is carrying your child, so you must care for her deeply, right?" the warrior asked, to which Pierce nodded. "Let's say you go 13 years without seein' her even once. She invites you out for a drink. Do you go out for that drink?"

Pierce rubbed his chin and remained silent for long enough that it became awkward.

Greta shoved him, albeit playfully. "Why're ye takin' so long to answer?"

"Well, I-"

Cracking branches from behind the wreckage of the house quieted the trio. Dalton and Pierce drew their weapons and prepared for battle, as Greta ran back into the thick of the woods to hide.

～

DRAKE DANVERS BOARDED Oneth's great ship, covered by a cloak that protected him well from the heavy rain. Flanking him were his two bodyguards, Hector and Ned. However, the scorpion-man hobbled along rather than glide in his normal, elegant way.

Catalina approached the trio as they arrived on the main deck, much to Drake's surprise. Normally, it had been Angus who led visitors to and from the Dark Wizard. Mur'del had usually tagged along for her own amusement, but she was also missing.

"Greetings, Sir Drake," Catalina said with a polite bow.

"You are to address me as "My Lord', from here on. Understood?" he replied with a scowl.

A warm smile crossed Catalina's beaming face. "As you command, My Lord. Shall I bring you to the master?"

Drake's nose scrunched up. *He* was the brains of the operation, and the Dark Wizard was the brawn. They were meant to be equals in the partnership, but it was becoming clear that some of the underlings saw it differently. Catalina viewed Drake as a visiting lord and Oneth as her *true master*. Brice had also come to see it that way; though he'd shown even less respect for him last night. Had it not been for Ned and the creepers, Drake may well have even been killed by the big-nosed man.

"Yes, and let us be quick. I have urgent matters to attend to."

Catalina bowed and then led the trio up to the third deck. She knocked on Oneth's cabin door, and after a brief delay, he opened up. Drake often forgot about his imposing stature. He not only dwarfed the Gentish woman before him, but he even reached the door frame in height.

"I have been expecting you," Oneth said while gesturing inside. "Come in."

The entourage entered, while Catalina waited outside for orders. Oneth silently pointed back down to the bottom deck, and with a bow, she left them.

Drake sat at an old wooden table, flanked by Ned and Hector. The Dark Wizard sat across from him with hands folded.

"Brice informed me of his failure last night," Oneth said. "It would be wise to develop a new strategy for dealing with these pests."

"Did he tell you *why* the mission was a failure?" Drake asked.

"Perhaps your plan wasn't so foolproof, after all."

"The Mercer boy… Conrad found Brice out and exposed him. You can't pin this one on me. How many opportunities have you had to kill him?" Drake asked as the Dark Wizard raised an eyebrow beneath his hood. "Enough playing with your food. We *must* slay him before he truly becomes a problem."

"The same could be said for that entire group," Oneth replied. Drake was surprised at his sense of calm. Normally, tempers would have flared by now.

"Now, we haven't a clue where they are, so I'm not sure what you wish for me to do about it," the Village Elder said. He leaned in, expecting an enraged response, but again, there was nothing but his cold, calculating eyes staring back.

"I don't expect you to do anything about it. In fact, I think it is time you focus more on our business dealings. Leave the upcoming battles to me," Oneth said.

Drake let out a haughty laugh. "You *must* be joking."

"You had your chance to finish off our enemies. Now, we do things my way."

"How quickly you forget that we'd be nowhere without my plans!" Drake shot back. "Mt. Couture? That was all me. The deal with Ometos in Thironas? Me. Hiring the Montgomery bandits? Me. The partnership with Sampson? You look upon the one responsible!"

With a deep, dark chuckle, Oneth said, "I think you've forgotten that none of this would be possible without *my* black gold. *My* dark essence. *My* information."

"And that is precisely why this is a partnership, not a pecking order. You don't order me around," Drake said.

"Be that as it may, it has become clear that battle is far from your specialty. Your plan relied too much on allowing the Strangers to live through our initial confrontation-"

"Not true," Drake interrupted while wagging his finger. "I specifically said that half of the Strangers needed to live and that Brice was not to harm anyone while taking the Key Keeper's form. That way, their remaining forces, including any stragglers, would gather in one spot for us to wipe them out. All plans have restrictions. It is unfair to punish me for our underlings' shortcomings on the battlefield."

"Don't act as if you've lost your place in this cooperative. It's best not to think of it as punishment, but more as the two of us focusing on our strengths," Oneth said.

The Village Elder let out a long breath through his nose. "The battle plans should still be run through me. It is important that we both have a say in how our team handles its enemies."

"Do you see me interfering in your business decisions?" Oneth asked, to which Drake cocked his head. "No. And that is because I know you'll make good choices for us. Working with Sampson will pay off in many ways, for instance. It is the same for me when it comes to our battle strategies... I have shed more blood than you ever will in your lifetime, Drake. You could never hope to reach my level of expertise on the battlefield."

"Tough talk, and yet our enemies still elude us..." Drake trailed off. The Dark Wizard opened his mouth to retort, but screams of agony rumbled the floor, stilling his tongue. The Village Elder leaned in. "Brice's punishment?"

"Angus and Mur'del, actually," said Oneth. "Last night's battle dealt them quite a bit of damage; more than their doses of dark essence were ever meant to handle."

"Will they be alright? We need them in top shape for the sewer infiltration, tonight."

"Yes, they should be fine. Unfortunately for them..." Oneth trailed off as more flesh-peeling screams vibrated from the ship innards "It is a very painful process, to heal these ailments."

"Speaking of which, Hector looks to be in poor condition," Drake said, nudging his head back at his hunched-over bodyguard. "Could you heal him before the afternoon? I have a business trip to make, and I'd like both he and Ned to accompany me."

"I will take him to the bowels of the ship to be replenished," Oneth said, looking Hector over. "I don't detect too much damage, so it won't take long. If you wish to return to your quarters, I can send him back to you when I'm finished."

"Excellent," Drake said, then stood. "And to be clear, I expect to be included in tonight's plan."

"Of course, you'll be given a layout of the plan…" said the Dark Wizard, who also rose until towering over him. "But *I* will be taking command of this one."

"Unacceptable."

Oneth snarled, but he quickly regained composure. "I know that you're keen on making deals, so here is my proposition: Let me take care of the sewer infiltration, and when we succeed in releasing Degenerate, I will bestow his powers upon you."

Drake's eyes widened. "You're serious?"

"Of course," he replied with a sly smile. "I know that much of your concern has to do with the power balance in our working relationship. If it would keep you aboard with our plans, then I am more than happy to fuse you with Degenerate himself, making you the first to receive the Dark Savior's inordinate power. You would become the most powerful man in the world."

"Consider it a deal: I will not interfere in your plans to infiltrate the sewers; and in return, I shall be the one to assimilate Degenerate," Drake said, each word more satisfying than the last. As he turned to leave, the Village Elder looked over his shoulder. "Oh, and by the way, I'd like to have Rose's ceremony performed as soon as possible. Perhaps tomorrow… have you made all necessary preparations?"

Oneth nodded. "Indeed-"

A splintering noise interrupted him, and it was followed soon after by groaning wood. Then came a great crash, rocking the vessel so much that Drake stumbled and had to catch himself against the cabin wall.

He and the Dark Wizard rushed to the door and opened it to find one of the great masts toward the middle of the ship, collapsed and ablaze. Though the downpour may have been all that was needed, several of the Bosfueras townsfolk had already gathered buckets of water to put out the fire. A horde of lightning bolts split and lit up the sky at once, striking water around the ship as the storm raged on.

"What are the odds that we'd be hit?" Drake asked aloud with a groan.

"Quite good, considering that they were directed at us…" Oneth said, staring off into the distance.

"Aldous?"

"Yes… it seems he survived my specially prepared Dark Hands," the Dark Wizard replied with a scowl. He looked over the docks, and then out to the horizon, but there was not a soul to be found. "It is as I feared. Right now, I do not possess the means to kill him; especially not during a storm like this. If the rain persists through the night, we will need to delay our attack."

"Ridiculous! We can work around him!" Drake argued.

Oneth glared back with eyes that could freeze even the hottest of coals. "Have you already forgotten our deal? Leave the planning to me. A storm like this presents Aldous with unlimited ammunition against us. He could wash our forces away in one fell swoop, or shock them all to death."

Drake frowned but held his tongue. The idea of obtaining Degenerate's power had interested him so much that he was willing to keep his hands out of the upcoming battle strategies.

"It begs the question: Why would he attack us now? All he has done is alert us to his presence," the Village Elder said.

"This was no mere attack," Oneth said as he turned back to his cabin. "It was a declaration of war."

CHAPTER 29
THE ITCH

Tension released from Joel's chest in the form of a long, silent breath to find Dalton and Pierce wandering the wreckage of the burnt-down house. Kabel and Rolf joined him in a joy-filled jog over to their comrades, who had drawn weapons at first, but showed similar signs of relief as they approached. Then, out from behind a tree appeared a pregnant Greta, who meekly hovered behind the dagger-eyed man as everyone greeted each other.

Kabel and Dalton shook forearms, as was their custom, while the others aside from Greta gave each other pats on the back for a job well done the prior night. Joel's nerves ramped back up upon realizing that Pierce's Ometos mask was off. Now, there was no way to tell if it was his friend or *the other* standing before him.

"I told you we'd meet again, brother, didn't I?" he said, placing a hand on his shoulder and nodding assuredly. Finally, Joel could relax. He smiled back and returned a nod.

"What happened here?" Dalton asked, seeming to search Kabel's calm eyes for answers.

"We did not bear witness to the deed, but Drake and his men probably burned it down. We escaped just in time," the stocky man replied, solemnly, and then looked to his empty stable. "It appears they stole the horses, too…"

"Worry not, soldier," Dalton said, nudging him. For some reason, that had raised Kabel's spirits. "We'll make 'em pay, soon enough."

"And what of the prisoner? Is he safe?" Pierce asked. Joel began signing, but the dagger-eyed man held up a hand. "Sorry, but I still haven't learned USL. I've been meaning to, but there is no one to teach me."

"Kabel could teach you," Dalton said.

The stocky man raised an eyebrow. "You say that as if *you* don't know sign language…"

"Well, you know me. I ain't much of a teacher," he replied with a shrug.

"Then, why do you have a student?" Kabel asked with a tilted head.

Dalton's eyes widened. "That reminds me-"

A howling wind from behind silenced Dalton, and it shot the collective shoulders of the Strangers up to their ears. Joel and the others spun around to find a dark portal opening up behind them. All who were able drew their weapons and awaited the worst. However, their postures softened when Aldous the Wizard walked out with a noticeable limp; his Summoner Rune was glowing a dark hue in his hand.

The old Wizard's blue tunic was ragged and wet from the abuses of dark magic and the waves of the sea. Some of his skin showed signs of burning, and he used his walking stick to brace himself while hunched over.

Joel ran up to him and held hands out, as if to catch the wheezing, weakened Wizard, but he steadied himself, then held a hand up to show that he was alright.

"You look like you've been to hell 'n back," Rolf said.

"Haven't we all…" Aldous trailed off, looking at the burnt-down house. His frown then turned to a grimace when locking eyes with what remained of his horse carriage. "I'll be fine, so long as Amis and the map are safe…"

"He's dead," Rolf said, to the gasps of Dalton, Pierce, and Aldous.

"But, how?" the dagger-eyed man asked, looking to Joel. "It seemed to me that you all made it back here without getting caught by the enemy."

"We did all make it back here…" Kabel began, his eyes falling to the muddy ground. "But it turns out, all of last night's battles were meant to distract us from a trap laid out by our enemies."

"I was aware of a trap set," Pierce said, holding up his Summoner Rune. "Those red-eyed men and women were hiding in the buildings along the docks, waiting to ambush you all; but they never got the chance. I sent them out to sea."

"So, dat time we heard screams n' splashes out in da water…" Rolf trailed off.

"It was you?" Kabel asked, pointing to the Summoner Rune. Pierce nodded.

"Then, there was some other trap we were unaware of?" Dalton asked.

"Yeh… Amis *was* the trap," Kabel said.

"He was compromised by the enemy? With the dark essence? But I thought that was the whole reason for bringing him to the ship," Aldous replied.

"We believe it was meant to look that way."

"But da truth is dat Amis was dead all along. He was bein' imitated by someone else, usin' some kinda devilry," Rolf said.

"Only the Dark Wizard could do such a thing," Aldous said, his brow raised. "And he is the one who attacked me. There is no conceivable way that he could be in two places at once…"

"It wasn't the Dark Wizard, but one of his minions: a fella named Brice. His imitation was so convincing that none of us believed Conrad when he tried to warn us," Kabel said.

"Brice…" Aldous trailed off while splashing his walking stick off the muddy ground. "Ah, yes! He was one of the hooligans, back in Faiwell. Conrad did mention that he had taken in the dark essence. So, it gave him the ability to transform into whomever he wishes?"

"Odd, I don't remember him having that skill," Dalton said with a furrowed brow. "Back in Bosfueras, he had these odd tentacles that could branch out into tendrils, each as sharp as a sword."

"After Conrad exposed him, Brice did let loose those vile tentacles. It seems he gained more than one ability thanks to the dark essence," Kabel said.

"We know dat Amis is dead because of how Brice copies people. He can't just do it to whoever he wants. He has to eat deir brains, first," Rolf explained while hanging his head.

"Poor Amis…" Aldous said, in lowered spirits. "Dhogron must be crushed. But at least, mayhap, he took the location of the sewer map to his grave…"

Kabel shook his head and let out a frustrated sigh. "It gets worse. When Brice copies someone, it is not only their appearance and voice, but their mannerisms and memories, too."

The old Wizard's face went pale. "Then, last night was all for naught…"

Dalton cleared his throat. "There is little time for regret. We have to regroup and make a plan. If they have obtained the map as we fear, then the enemy could attack those sewers as soon as tonight."

"I think that I may have bought us some time, in that regard," Aldous said with a half-hearted smile. "They would be brave to oppose me in the sewers where there is so much liquid for me to use, but just plain foolish to make an attempt during this downpour. I directed a lightning bolt at the mast of the Dark Wizard's ship to send a message."

"You shoulda burned the whole thing down, to show 'em how it feels," Kabel said with a scoff.

"In my current condition, I didn't want to get into a fight. But it is surely what they deserve," Aldous replied, then bowed in the stocky man's direction. "I'm sorry about your house, m'boy. I fear that I may have brought upon you all a great burden."

Kabel shook his head and a fire came to his normally calm eyes. "It is clear to me that all of this is far bigger than me or my house. These knobs are messin' with forces beyond all of our understandings. They must be stopped at all costs."

"Well said," Dalton chimed in with crossed arms. "But we still need to regroup. Where are we gonna stay, in the meantime?"

"I've got that covered." Kabel's fury faded, and a sly smile spread across his face. "Don't forget that I've had backup plans in case Sampson ever caught wind that I was housing Rolf, one of his escaped slaves. Burning down homes is one of his favorite things to do. As far as living arrangements go, it's a lil' rough around the edges, but far more interesting than a regular house, anyhow."

"Does this place have food? I'm hungry…" Greta said, stepping out from behind Pierce. All of the group looked at her with wide eyes. Joel waved at her and smiled. "Ah! Joel! It's nice to see a familiar face!"

As she crunched him with a big squeeze of a hug, Pierce shrugged, looked at the others, and said, "She is the mother of my unborn child, Greta."

"Are you from Mithika, by chance?" Kabel asked her, amusement written all over his face.

"That's right. Why do you ask?"

"You remind me a bit of my wife," he replied with a laugh. "I'm sure y'all will get along well."

"I look forward to meeting her, but... food?" Greta asked, drawing a few chuckles.

"Some of the others were out on a hunt when we departed... I worry that all of this rain will see them coming up empty, but I'm sure they'll at least pick some berries."

With that, Joel jumped to the front of the pack and motioned for the others to follow him. The Strangers traveled with haste toward their new hideout.

∼

AT THE WESTERN coast of the Endoshire outskirts, Prince Xviktolo exited the woods to be greeted by torrential downpour. Earlier this morning, he'd searched for Aldous by the docks but found no sign of him. The kraken had also chosen not to show herself near the sewer pipe, but since she usually only emerged at night, her absence hadn't been a surprise.

Though he suspected that some in the Coralstar Kingdom were wondering where he was by now, he couldn't help but stay with the Strangers for just a little longer, to see if another battle would break out. Then, he hoped, he might carve his name out in legend; at least among land-dwellers.

The marinian hissed some laughter as he approached the sheer cliffs of the coast. His recent patrol of the woods had hardly been legendary. He hadn't come across a single soul, in fact. Yet, Xviktolo could feel it in his bones: Battle was on the horizon, and if he waited just a bit longer, his appetite would be satisfied.

Now at the coastal edge, Xviktolo walked along a cliff that protruded out a few steps further than the others. Far below lay rocky waters and rough tides, but more immediately downward were an easy-to-miss set of stairs carved out of the bedrock, spiraling down. Minding his balance on the mossy, slippery steps, the marinian found himself turning and descending into the gaping hole of the rock wall. Echoes of crashing water and chatter from his allies passed through his body as the cove on his right came into view, where stormy waters thrashed and splashed up onto a rocky land. The cave ahead went deep into the foundation of the cliffs, where several rooms had been dug out.

According to Kabel, the Strangers' new hideout once housed pirates who had left many of their belongings; including old chests, tables, chairs, bedding, clothes from a bygone era, and even a couple of small rowboats that had been left tied to a post. The cove was big enough, however, to host a mid-sized ship.

In the back corner of the cave, Auber, Ebbie, and Franco sat at a table, playing cards. The captain slammed his fists onto the old, rickety surface after losing another game, and Xviktolo let out a bubbly snort. Auber had been losing since all the way back when he first went out on patrol.

"Glad that you remembered to grab the cards before we escaped last night, sir?" Franco asked with a chuckle.

"Not even a lil' bit!" Auber shot back.

"At least it gives us somethin' ta do…" Ebbie muttered.

"You could have gone for a swim with Xviktolo." The navigator's words were drenched in sarcasm.

"He's a real nutter, that one," Auber said, looking over his shoulder at the marinian.

Prince Xviktolo waved back at them as he dipped into the rough tides of the cove and lay up against the rocks while half-submerged. Turbulence from the waves rocked him, and sometimes they even broke over his head, but to him, it was relaxing. The others had flashed bewildered or horrified expressions when he'd asked if they wanted to join, earlier.

"It is his element, after all," Franco said while slapping down a card.

"Bah!" Ebbie shouted, throwing his hand down. "I'm gettin' a lil' tired of cards, and gettin' very much hungry!"

"Quit yer whinin'! The others'll be back soon," Auber said as a stomach groan echoed off the cave walls, wriggling Xviktolo's ears.

"Your body says the opposite of what your mouth does, sir," the navigator replied with a snort.

Though he seemed a silly man, Xviktolo couldn't wait to fight alongside Auber. He'd been assured by Alistair that his usual demeanor belied a fierce disposition when on the battlefield.

FURTHER IN THE CAVE, in a room filled with candles, Giles stood on his aching hands, upside-down and up against the rocky wall. His whole body shook with exhaustion, and it was made even worse by the fact that Dhogron sat across from him, relaxing on his bed.

"Why do you feel the need to tire yourself out like this?" Dhogron asked while conjuring a small, paper lion in his hands.

"Alistair's orders," he replied with a heavy breath. "Gotta stay like this until he returns."

"Yes, but why listen to him? It is a strange request."

"It ain't a request," he growled back. Sweat had rolled down from his chin and seeped into the bandaging around his right eye socket. No sting came to his non-existent eye, of course, but the pooling perspiration was still irritating. "It is the penalty game."

"Would you like me to remove the wrapping?" Dhogron asked, leaning forward. Giles nodded, and with that, the trickster Wizard leaned over to slide the bandaging off. "Better?"

"Yeh, thank ye."

Dhogron sat back down and stared at the empty eyelid. "Does it ever hurt?"

"Not at all," he replied. "It's just odd. Like one of my eyes is permanently trapped in darkness."

"It must be difficult, what you're going through," the trickster Wizard said as he crunched his hands together. Upon opening them back up, a little paper bird began flying about the dim-lit room.

"I'm just happy to have a second chance at life," Giles said, looking at the paper distraction. "This time, I won't waste it. This time, I will not be the weak link."

"We were all helpless and unprepared last night; not just you. Otherwise, Kabel's house would still be standing. Otherwise, Amis would be..." Dhogron shuddered, then lowered his head. "Well, there was no saving Amis last night, but the responsibility still lies on me. If I had been by his side when those fiends kidnapped him, he may have stood a chance."

"That may well be true, 'cause unlike me, ye add somethin' to this team. As a Wizard, yer a force to be reckoned with. Me? I've always been weak," Giles said, grunting in the hopes that it would somehow cool his burning shoulders. "I could only cower under my sheets when my family was killed, back in Thironas. Worse still, I was defeated in seconds by the filth who wished to break the Famine seal. And last night, my greatest failure yet reared its ugly head. I slowed everyone else down, endangering them; and all because I couldn't defend myself."

"You are being a bit hard on yourself," Dhogron said.

Giles shook his head. "For too long, I have latched onto others, hoping they would bring me strength and security. Where has that gotten me? Nowhere. Last night, it became clear to me that out on the battlefield, all that matters is the *iron law of the strongest*. A team is only as strong as their weakest member, and I'll tell ye now: I ain't satisfied with the strength of our team. Especially against Drake an' the rest of them bottom-feeders, I need to be stronger; smarter; more skilled. Otherwise, I'm draggin' the team down."

"Perhaps you should consult Joel," Dhogron said. Suddenly, all pain and exhaustion left Giles' body. Now, there was only rage. "You remind me a bit of him, and I've been told he is quite the swordsman. Perhaps he could show you some moves."

"I wish that everyone would stop comparing us," Giles said with a snarl. "We couldn't be more opposite. While I am physically weak, he is *mentally weak*. I'll always give it everything I've got on the battlefield, and he will forever hesitate. Eventually, I will overcome my barriers. But will Joel do the same? I doubt it."

Dhogron put his hands up and let out nervous chuckles. "I only meant that you look alike, somewhat..."

"Right..." the one-eyed man trailed off, and then let out all tension with a single breath. The aches and pains of his penalty game returned. He hoped Alistair would also return, soon.

~

FURTHER INTO THE caves of the hideout, Conrad and Lucia sat in silence. They had a room all to themselves, but they may as well have been in different countries.

Conrad had closed his bruised and battered eyes from the moment they arrived. Though he could hear her speaking once in a while, the words were unintelligible; muted to his ears. In fact, all of his senses had dulled in favor of one, single feeling: *the itch*. If he could just have some black gold, he thought, he'd be able to keep his problems at bay. His injuries would heal, he'd be relaxed, and that *damned itch* would go away.

It was as if his insides needed to be scratched, but it was simply impossible. The strategist tried to push it out of his mind, but it only intensified his need for the black gold. He could feel the dark walls of the cave closing in on him, so much that it reminded him of the corridors at Mt. Couture. In a strange way, it was nostalgic. It had been a brutally difficult time, filled with strife and chaos, but at least back then, he and his friends were on the same page. It was a simpler time, in his darkened eyes.

"How long do you plan to just sit there?" Lucia's voice echoed.

Conrad opened a single eye, to see her deformed, Willoughby-like face; she let loose shrill breaths and had that awful tar-like skin, dripping and running like blood. He knew that it wasn't real; a hallucination induced by his growing desire for the black gold, but he couldn't bear to see her that way.

"As long as it takes."

Lucia scoffed and then crossed her now-monstrous arms. "How many times must I apologize?"

"I don't need your apologies..." he trailed off, closing his eye again. "I need a return to normalcy."

"On that much, we agree."

Conrad didn't respond, because he was certain that she had misunderstood. For him, normal had become the calming sensation of the black gold; or at least, it had become his ideal state of mind. While holding that precious ore, he was at peace. The anger in his heart would fade, and he would be able to think clearly once again.

Her idea of normal was a waste of time, he thought. The dark essence hadn't done anything to alter his mind as far as he was concerned. His current way of thinking had been molded by experiences at Mt. Couture, and especially Bosfueras.

"That's right..." a deep voice echoed from afar. Conrad opened his eyes, but he was no longer in the room with Lucia. Instead, he found himself within an empty, dark void. "I have shown you that my way would be best for all, and now you finally understand..."

"You can't... fool me... you wish to... rule over everyone..." he squeaked out. His entire body ached, and worse yet, he could feel the itch again; it was *everywhere*, even under his very skin.

"And what's wrong with that, if everyone is happy?" the Dark Wizard asked. His bass-filled voice grew louder with each word. "Having experienced it for yourself, you cannot deny the truth any longer."

"No, I-" Involuntary shivers ended any semblance of speech he could produce. He hunched over and started scratching his arms, to no avail: The itch remained, and then it intensified.

"Your body knows what your mind is not yet willing to accept," the Dark Wizard said, appearing out of the dark void before Conrad in his great, cloaked form. "Do you understand why you feel it? *The itch*?

Your heart knows that the black gold is what is best for you, but your mind still resists."

"I need it to stop…" Conrad muttered. His mind had nearly gone blank from discomfort. He wanted to rip his skin off.

"You know the way," he said, holding his hand out. "I can provide you with what you need, and so much more."

With gritting teeth and his entire body shaking, the strategist muttered, "I-I can't… I won't…"

"You must!" the Dark Wizard shouted. His voice had grown unbearably loud and it intensified the itch, the shivers, and his all-around discomfort. "Take my hand, Conrad! It is the only way!"

Conrad felt his hand slowly extend, but it was not his conscious decision. His bodily instincts had taken over. There had to be something; someone, he thought, to stop him. Conrad looked around the void. Lucia was nowhere to be seen. Where had she gone? Where had all of his friends gone? He needed them now, more than ever, to step in.

Mere inches from grasping the Dark Wizard's hand, a walking stick cut through his body. He faded away like smoke in the wind, and with him went the dark void. Conrad's bruised eyes opened wide as he let out a violent exhale. He had returned to the normal world, and Aldous the Wizard stood before him, leaning over with a warm smile.

"Oho! Sorry for the wait, m'boy! Are you ready for this dark substance to be removed from your body?" he asked. "I shall take you to the Exorcist right away."

Looking around the room to see Joel, Dalton, and Lucia, Conrad opened his mouth to speak, but nothing came out. What had just happened? It was such a surreal experience, and it filled him with dread, thinking of how close he had come to taking the Dark Wizard's hand.

After sitting back for a moment to take everything in, Conrad began scratching his arm. He would do anything to make that damned itch go away.

"More than ready."

"Very good!" the old Wizard said as he extended his hand.

Conrad took the boost, and then Aldous unveiled his Summoner Rune. The engraved swirls upon the stone emitted a dark glow, and within the room appeared a swirling vortex that howled like a hungry wolf and blew out the nearby candles.

The strategist hesitated, but then felt both Joel and Dalton pat him on the shoulder. He looked to his friends, who flashed him encouraging smiles, then let out a deep breath. Aldous stood before the portal, gesturing toward it as Conrad walked.

However, before reaching his destination, Lucia blocked the path. Conrad looked up at her with a half-hearted smile. They shared no words before his departure; only a long, tight embrace. Afterward, she kissed him on the forehead and stepped aside.

Like many times before, Conrad could feel himself stepping into uncertainty as he entered the portal. His hard feelings in regards to his friends' distrust remained, but he chose to push it aside, to relieve *the itch*.

CHAPTER 30
TRANSACTION

Conrad Mercer stumbled and fell over a clump of sand as he exited the howling portal. The sand practically seared his skin, but before he could even think to wince, he felt Aldous' leg crash into his downed body.

"Oof!" The old Wizard tripped over him and ate a face-full of sand.

After sitting up and pushing through the sting of the boiling sun on his face, Conrad scanned the area. He gasped, and his throat became a little dryer. All around, there were nothing but hills and dunes of sand.

Aldous chuckled while propping himself up with his walking stick. He brushed the sand from his ruffled tunic, and then from his beard. "I had hoped to forget the taste of sand… but alas, it is the only thing to eat around here."

"Are you sure this is the right place?" Conrad asked. Again, he looked over the desert landscape, straining his eyes to find signs of life. There was nothing.

"Well, of course!" the old Wizard said, smacking the ground with his walking stick. "Welcome to the Endless Desert!"

With wide eyes, the strategist stood. "You mean to tell me that not only does this Exorcist live in a desert, but *the largest one in the world*?"

Aldous held up an index finger, his demeanor never dimming. "On the bright side, he *does* live in an oasis."

"That is comforting, but…" he trailed off, looking around one more time. "I'm not seeing an oasis."

"Ah, I'm afraid we'll have to do a bit of traveling to reach it. You see, there is a powerful barrier-majigger that surrounds this particular oasis; one that prevents me from summoning us there directly."

"Blocked off from the world and in the middle of a gigantic desert? I can take a hint when it's given to me," Conrad said with a chuckle. Aldous smiled back at him. "I only hope you took us to the right place. What do you have as a reference? What direction do we need to go?"

The old Wizard flashed confidence in his eyes. "It may not seem it, but I know this spot *very well*. In fact, I could never forget it!"

Conrad struggled to find anything special about the area: Everything looked the same to him. Even still, he found hope in Aldous' smile. It was tired but assured. He was a Wizard, after all, and would certainly find a way to reach their destination.

"We are in for a bit of a trip, but nothing too bad. Trust me when I say that many before us have had it much worse in this desert," Aldous said as he began hiking up a large dune. "Follow me!"

With that, the pair set off on their journey to the oasis.

∼

Alistair, Triston, and Mirabel descended the slippery stairs of the Strangers' new hideout, to the fanfare of the pirates. The elder MacRae carried a bloody sack over his shoulder, while Alistair held all of the weapons, and Mira carried a basket filled with berries.

"Finally! I'm starvin'!" Auber said, standing while wringing his hands.

"We still gotta cook tha meat, Cap'n!" Alistair said as he tossed the weapons into a corner of the cave.

"Oh…" Auber muttered, then lifted his spirits once more. "Well, how about them berries?"

"You will still have to wait," Mirabel said, eyeing him with suspicion. "The hunters get to eat first."

"Oh, come on! We're starvin' over here!" Auber argued. Ebbie nodded along, while Franco seemed to shrink in his chair.

"What were *you* doing while we went out to gather the food, besides sitting on yer arse, playing cards?" Mirabel asked while wringing out her drenched, dark hair.

"Well… uhh…"

"She has a point, *sir*," Franco chimed in.

"Yer just as guilty as I am!" the captain shot back.

"Why don't you all just eat some fish?" Prince Xviktolo asked as he stepped up from the harsh waters of the cove with a salmon wriggling in his webbed fingers. Some of the Strangers let out a gasp when he bit the fish's head off. "We are near a plentiful supply, and I would be happy to catch some for you."

"Yer supposed ta cook it, lad! Or it'll make ya sick!" Triston said.

The marinian gazed down at the half-eaten fish, then looked back up with a toothy smile. "Oh yes, I forgot that land-dwellers sometimes need to… eh, light it on fire, right?"

"Ye mean *ye* don't?" Auber asked with a cocked head.

"He *does* live in the water, sir," Franco said.

"I know that! I was just sayin' that he could come to the surface and cook it, is all!"

"Ah, you're back!" Kabel called out as he exited a dark hallway in the depths of the cave. Behind him were Joel, Dalton, Pierce, Greta, and Rolf. "How did the hunt go?"

"Not a large haul, but in a storm like this, tha animals ain't gonna be out an' aboot, methinks!" Triston said, holding up the bloody sack.

"Without me watching over them, we'd be eating nothing but berries," Greta said with crossed arms.

"Well, if ya didn't keep yellin' at me while I was tryin' ta aim, I woulda gotten us food fer the whole week!" Alistair argued.

"Most of yer arrows fluttered harmlessly through the air, Ali…" Triston whispered with uncharacteristic care.

"I was distracted!"

"Is there anything I can eat, *now*?" Greta asked aloud. All in the cave fell silent.

Mirabel smiled. "And who might you be?"

"This here is Greta," Kabel said, gesturing to her. "She is from Mithika. I thought you two might get along well."

"This is no place for a pregnant woman," Mira said with concern in her eyes. "We need to buy her some proper bedding."

"We're a little short on coin, methinks," Dalton said while patting his empty pockets.

"Has the great Dalton Rayleigh finally run out of gold from his war spoils?" Kabel asked with hands to hips.

"Well… the rest of it is hidden away back in Faiwell. Everything I brought with me is gone," the warrior said, his spirits sinking to the depths of the sea. Suddenly, his ears perked up, and he looked at Captain Auber. "Unless…"

All others in the room turned their collective gaze on the pirates.

"What?" the captain asked with a shrug.

"Remember how I gave you some gold back in Bosfueras?"

"Oh… oh no… yer gonna ask me fer it, ain't ye?"

A snorting chuckle escaped Dalton's nose. "I'll pay it back, someday."

"Oh, come on!" Auber whined. "We were gonna use that to buy a new ship!"

"You are part of something much bigger than a pirate crew, now," Dhogron said as he entered from the hallway behind. "We are all small parts of a whole. That is the only way to combat Drake, Sampson, and the Dark Wizard: to function as one."

"So, we pool our money together for now?" Kabel asked, then looked to his wife. "I like the idea. What say you?"

"Better than you spending it all at Cole's pub," she replied with a shrug.

"What about you?" Rolf asked, pointing to Xviktolo. "Ain't you a prince? You should have piles of coin layin' about."

The marinian let out a hissing chuckle. "I am not so sure that our currencies would match up. I've noticed that land-dwellers use some sort of paper."

"Around here that is common, but we also take gold and silver," Mirabel said.

"Wait! I gots an idea!" Ebbie said, slamming a fist into the table and drawing everyone's attention. He then pointed to Dhogron. "Yer able to make anything outta paper, right?"

"Indeed. What of it?" the trickster Wizard asked.

"Why don't ye just make some Sigrian notes fer us to use?" the first mate asked. Nearly all in the room groaned and shook their heads.

"Counterfeiting is a grave offense around these parts; enough that I would be hanged for the crime if caught. Besides, it is bad for my Anima," Dhogron said.

"The hell's Anima?" Ebbie asked.

"Methinks we should be quiet, now," Franco said with rosy cheeks.

"I thought it was a good idea…" Auber muttered.

"Anyhow, gold and silver are quite uncommon below the surface," said Xviktolo.

"They aren't common up here, either," Pierce said.

"I mean that there isn't enough to use as money. They are thought of as collector's items. I'll see if I can dig anything up, though," he said before turning back to the rough waters of the cove. "Now, I shall take my abandon."

"Ya mean 'take my leave'?" Alistair asked.

"Right, right," he said while shaking his head and laughing. "With Aldous' safe return, I now only need to check on the kraken. Afterward, I shall venture back to my kingdom, and see if I can bring back anything of value."

"Could you catch some fish along the way? We will certainly eat it when cooked," Dalton said.

The marinian nodded, then dove into the harsh waters. Dhogron walked past the group, to the opening in the cave where the rain raged on.

"When the storm calms, I will be taking a trip into the city. If any of you would like to come along; to stock up on weapons or supplies, your company would be welcome."

"It will be dangerous to leave after what happened last night," Dalton said with crossed arms. "We must always stay in groups, from here on. Going out alone could lead to the enemy capturing or killing one of us. I hope whatever you need in the city is worth the risk."

"There are some items back at my shop that may help us, but I also wish to check on Satara. She and her dancers put themselves at great risk last night, thinking that Sampson would be undermanned and unprepared… but it seems to have been a ruse," Dhogron said.

"Very well. I'm happy to accompany you," Dalton said before pointing to Kabel. "You can come along, too."

"I can?"

"I think that he should stay and help out around here," Mirabel said, eyeing her husband.

"Sorry Mira, but he and I have somethin' *real important* to talk about," Dalton said with an assured smile.

"It better not involve another trip to the pub," Mira said, putting hands to hips.

"Not this time, I promise!"

"I'm glad we're makin' plans… but what about the food?" Greta asked, rubbing her pregnant belly.

"We still need to cook," Mira said, then held up her basket. "But in the meantime, I have some berries that you could eat."

"I'll take anything, at this point!"

"But what about the rest of us?" Auber asked, eyeing the basket.

Mirabel huffed. "You can wait."

The captain sulked as everyone else laughed.

In the wealthy district of Endoshire, Drake sat in his quarters, waiting for Hector to return from the Dark Wizard's ship. Rose sat across from him at the luxurious dining table, picking at some fruits in a bowl. Standing on each side of her were two other women adorned in long, dragging gowns and white bonnets.

With each fruit eaten, one of the servant women wiped her mouth with a handkerchief, much to her visible discomfort.

"Please… there is no need to trouble yourself," Rose said with a half-hearted smile as the servant blotted her cheeks.

"We are happy to serve you, m'lady," she said.

Drake cocked his head. "What's wrong? Are they not to your liking?"

"It's not that…" she muttered while looking down at her fidgeting hands.

"Speak up. My future wife will need to have some backbone," Drake said, a smirk coming to his sharp face.

With a deep breath, he could feel Rose summoning all of her courage, amusing him even further. She looked him square in the eyes. "I used to be a slave, too, and would never want anyone else to experience that life. Could we not release them?"

The Village Elder leaned in with hands folded. "These two… they were once sex slaves like you, but they managed to escape. Recently, Sampson caught them. Do you know what kind of punishment he doles out to escapees that he catches? Torture to the point of disfigurement. I've actually done them a service by making them your servants. Isn't that right?"

Drake looked at the servants, and they nodded with smiles that he knew to be forced. His words hadn't only been for Rose's education, but to serve as a reminder that they should be thankful and obedient to him.

"I thought they would make good company for you, if anything," he continued with a nonchalant shrug. "But if you'd prefer I send them back…"

"No, no! I'm happy to have them," Rose said. Now she was forcing a smile, and Drake couldn't help but find it adorable.

"Very good. Then, they shall stay your servants. Make good use of them, or they will be replaced."

"R-right..."

"Is something else the matter? You have been so quiet today," Drake said.

"It's just..." Rose's eyes wandered back down to her hands, and a stuttered laugh escaped her lips. "I am anxious about this 'ceremony' you've been talking about."

"Ah, yes. I had thought to schedule it for tomorrow, but as it turns out, our Wizard friend has some freed-up time. It shall be performed tonight," he replied with a warm smile.

"And this will allow us to have a child?"

"Indeed. It seems that you are not as fertile as I'd hoped," Drake said as Rose lowered her head. "But fear not. After the ceremony, you will be more than ready. After all, it tends to fix that which ails us."

"Will this ceremony be painful?"

Immensely, Drake thought; but that word never left his mouth. Instead, he chuckled and grabbed hold of her hand to caress it. "Not at all, my dear."

Drake could still detect her nervousness, but it couldn't be helped. The best he could do was comfort her, for now. Painful and scary as it was to be, it was a necessary sacrifice.

After some time lounging at the table, Hector strode into Drake's quarters, heavily cloaked and brimming with newfound energy.

"Feeling better?" Drake asked as he stood. The scorpion-man returned a single nod. "Very well. I suppose it's about time we make our transaction. Hector, fetch the horse and carriage, would you?"

Hector bowed and then glided out of the room as if sliding over ice.

"Shall I come along?" Rose asked, leaning forward in her chair.

"That won't be necessary," he replied while fitting himself into a fancy coat.

"I would like to learn more about these business deals," she said, tightening her grip on the table's edge. "If I am to be queen, then I will require a strong understanding of what we do."

Drake walked up behind Rose and put his hands on her shoulders, to which they tensed. He then leaned in and kissed her on the cheek. "In time, my dear. For now, I need you rested up for the ceremony tonight. You must focus on the objective at hand. Soon, we will have our heir."

"R-right..."

"Let us depart, Ned," the Village Elder said while heading for the door. The cloaked bodyguard strode out of the shadowy corner of the room to follow his master. Before exiting, Drake stopped and looked back at the two servant women. "See to it that she is taken care of while I am gone."

"Yes, Master," they replied in unison.

Outside of the building, Drake grunted in annoyance as the rain pounded down on him. He retreated to the archway, in wait of his horse and carriage. After a short while, Hector finally arrived with a couple of dark steeds pulling a finely-crafted coach.

With half of his body hanging out of the coach, Drake looked at his bodyguard with narrow eyes. "What took you so long?"

Hector only hissed in response. Drake sighed as he entered the comforts of his carriage. Sometimes, he truly missed being able to speak with his bodyguards.

To Drake's surprise, though, Hector hopped down from the front position and accompanied Drake inside the coach.

"When was the last time you let Ned take the reins?" he asked with a raised eyebrow. "I'm starting to think you don't enjoy rainy days."

With that, Ned steered the horses out of the wealthy district and took a right onto the coastal line where the docks lay. The waves thrashed and rocked all docked boats, and a thick fog could be seen off on the horizon, drifting inland.

Drake grimaced as rain continued to pummel the carriage. It didn't seem like the storm would let up by nightfall, which meant the attack on the sewers would indeed be delayed. Although it also meant he could get Rose's ceremony over with, the Village Elder found his mind to be on those pesky Strangers.

Had the Dark Wizard not toyed with Conrad in Bosfueras and simply killed him, Brice would have succeeded in leading them to the enemy hideout, undetected. The plan was foolproof, he thought. Why, then, did it feel like he had taken the blame? Even if he had promised to stay out of future attack plans, Drake couldn't help but want a chance at redemption; to be responsible for the trampling of their ant-like enemies.

Perhaps there was more to it than mere redemption or satisfaction, though. Drake could feel his grip on the partnership weakening. Oneth's promise to fuse him with Degenerate could have been a lie to quell concerns regarding his dwindling role. On the other hand, he still had *some* advantages. As long as he continued to make the ever-important deals for his team, there would always be a role for him. Still, there was a sense of foreboding in Drake's mind. Provisions were needed to combat a possible betrayal.

One such provision was precisely the business transaction that he was traveling to; something that would add to his value in the partnership. The other provision was explicitly for after a betrayal, in the case of his death. He would take care of that after returning to his quarters, he thought.

Ned steered the horse and carriage onto a road that cut through the fields of east Endoshire, where workers labored tirelessly in the misery of the mud. For most of them, missing one day of pittance meant a day without food, and so a storm was something they simply had to work through.

Near the end of the fields, Drake and his bodyguards crossed into an enclave of huts, where loud *clangs* and *clanks* echoed over the smacking rain, and the smell of melted metal overpowered all else. The steeds skidded to a halt in the muddy road, next to a hut that was under construction. The small accommodation looked to be assimilating the hut next to it, to form one building.

Drake exited his carriage and entered the hut with Hector and Ned in tow. Waiting for them at the front counter inside was a man with a scruffy beard who wore old armor over his tunic.

"Greetings, Sir Drake!" he said with folded hands. "So glad ye could make it in this harsh weather."

"I would never miss a business transaction, much less with Reginald, the greatest goldsmith in Endoshire," Drake said with a cool smile.

"I thank ye kindly, sir," Reginald replied with a bow. "Hold tight. I shall return with the product."

The scruffy man exited through a back door that led out into the pouring rain. Soon after, he returned with a tall, thin man. Both lugged a chest through the door, then plopped it onto the counter. It was so heavy that the surface buckled.

"Quite a hall today," Drake said while opening the chest. His green eyes lit up when the sparkles of black gold presented itself to him. He grinned, then shut the box. "Excellent work, as always."

"I'm able to make more, and at a higher quality, thanks ta all the work ye've given me. Recently, I hired a young man ta help with the workload," Reginald said while gesturing to the thin man. "This here is Clarin."

"A pleasure ta meet ye, sir," Clarin said. His voice was squeaky like a mouse.

"The pleasure is all mine, young man," he replied before turning back to Reginald. "And I notice that you have been expanding."

"Well, it's all thanks to yer business, sir."

"Your quality of work is high, and so long as it stays that way, we shall always do business," Drake replied.

"An' speaking of which, it's time for ye ta get back ta work, lad," Reginald said while patting Clarin on the back.

"You should listen to everything this fellow teaches you. He is truly among the greatest," the Village Elder added.

With a smile, Clarin nodded, then exited the hut.

"He's a nice boy, but has a ways to go, in this craft," Reginald said.

"I'm sure you will be able to hire many more like him in the future."

"Ah, an' that reminds me…" the scruffy man said, digging beneath his counter. He retrieved a piece of paper that was filled with barely legible writing and a custom seal at the bottom. "Here's yer bill… I still don' understand why ye asked me ta charge more per coin on this job, but I do appreciate the extra money."

"Think of it as a little bonus, so you can more easily pay for the extension of your building," Drake said while inspecting the bill. After a few moments, he pulled some Sigrian notes out of his coat pocket to pay. "Of course, it won't stay this way forever. But for now, enjoy that extra money, my friend."

"I certainly will, Sir Drake," Reginald said as Ned approached. He grabbed the chest handle with one hand, then lifted it as if it were weightless. The scrappy man gasped. "What strength! It's almost… inhuman!"

"How right you are," Drake replied with a smirk, then turned to leave. "I look forward to our next meeting."

"F-farewell…" Reginald muttered before the pounding rain overtook all other sounds once more.

As he sat in the carriage with Hector by his side, Drake smirked at his handiwork. A price increase would be just one of many business nuances that only *he* could handle. After all, a businessman like him was expected to be an expert in negotiation, and he could have Reginald lower the prices on a whim. If the Dark Wizard ever questioned the value of his partnership, then he would simply *invent* problems that no one but him could solve.

CHAPTER 31
GAZE OF THE EXORCIST

Conrad let out a dry, raspy cheer. Between the ripples of intense heat off in the distance, he had spotted the oasis. Sweat crept down from his brow to his eyes, but even such an unbearable sting could not break his focus. What Aldous had called 'a bit of a trip' ended up feeling more like a cross-country trek, to him.

There was little sense of time in the Endless Desert; only sand and the sun, and neither were kind to him. He could feel his skin turning red from the blistering rays of light, and his head pounded with each plopping step through the sand. Yet, there was only one thing on his mind: water.

"We are almost there, m'boy," Aldous said with cheer while hobbling through the sand.

"I noticed," Conrad replied. He meant for his tone to be curt, but it had instead been dry and breathless. "I don't suppose you have any water?"

"Not to worry! There is plenty of it where we are going!"

"Right..."

After continuing through the harsh sands and sun for a while longer, the heat ripples dissipated and the oasis came into full view ahead. Among the yellow landscape, it stuck out like a sore thumb. Several palm trees sprouted up from rich, green grass. They were mixed in with shacks and huts, but Conrad's eyes were drawn to something else: At the center of the oasis was a small pond that reflected the sun's fury beautifully, bringing forth a smile that stung the blisters on his lips. How could such a thing exist in the middle of a desert?

"I don't believe it…" he muttered.

"Oho! After all you've seen, nothing should surprise you, anymore!" Aldous said.

As the pair drew near, Aldous' cheerful demeanor seemed to vaporize beneath the sun's oppressive heat. His smile had turned to a frown, and his pace became frantically fast.

"Is something wrong?" Conrad asked.

"There…" He pointed to a palm tree, just ahead.

Conrad placed a flat hand perpendicular to his brow, and when his eyes adjusted, he spotted a man sitting underneath the tree. His tattered, dark blue Wizard's robe hung off of his sitting, slouching form like a bad curtain. Belying his ragged clothes was a well-trimmed, white beard, and dark skin that gleamed so perfectly under the sun that it almost looked as if he was encased in light.

"Is he the Exorcist?" Conrad asked.

"No. He is the leader of the Wizard's Council, Zequim," Aldous said with a certain chilliness that made Conrad forget about both his thirst and the pounding sun.

"I see… and why would he be here?"

"I am unsure, but if he asks you, you are *not* from Faiwell, and you have *never* heard anything about the seven seals. Understood?"

If Conrad had enough moisture in his mouth, he'd have taken in a heavy gulp. Instead, he merely nodded. The duo altered course and headed for the Wizard under the palm tree, yet even in the face of what was sure to be a fascinating meeting, Conrad's mind was still on *water*. He prayed for the conversation to be swift. The oasis was but a short walk away.

When the pair arrived under the shade of the tree, they found Zequim to be sleeping: His head was down, and he let out an occasional, heavy snore. Aldous cleared his throat with obvious impatience.

"Oh-wha-wha!" Zequim cried before starting forward and looking around, frantically. Soon after, a new calm washed over his face while looking up at the duo. He stood and dusted the sand off of his robe. "Ah, Aldous… it's only you."

"What are you doing here, Zequim?"

"Perhaps I was looking for you."

Aldous crossed his arms. "Unlikely. I have not set foot on these grounds in years."

"Yet, here you stand," Zequim replied with unwavering eyes.

"Not here to lecture, I hope?" Aldous asked.

"Guess again." Now, he was smiling.

"Am I reinstated to the Council?" The leader shook his head. "Excommunicated?"

"No. The Council hasn't deliberated, yet." Zequim chuckled, but it quickly turned into a series of coughs.

Aldous huffed at him. "I must insist that you not play games. We are in a bit of a hurry, y'see…"

"Have patience. I've been waiting under this very tree for, oh…" Zequim trailed off while looking up. "A week? Give or take a day or two."

Conrad's eyes widened. "Excuse me, sir."

"Yes, what is it, young man?" he replied. Aldous shot a distraught glare at Conrad.

"Why suffer out here, when there is an oasis just ahead?" he asked, to which Aldous' expression softened.

"Unfortunately, I am not welcome around these parts. I can't imagine why…" Zequim flashed a knowing smile at Aldous.

"You are lucky they haven't attacked you, up to this point," the old Wizard said, looking over his superior with a critical eye. "Especially in your current state. Why are you so depleted of magic? What happened to you?"

"I paid a little visit to our friend, Olivier. We had a few disagreements," Zequim said with a pained laugh.

"Could it be that the esteemed leader of our Council has finally decided to listen to a lowly Scout?" Aldous asked, relaxing his posture and laughing along.

"We are truly living in strange times," Zequim said with a nod. "I admit that your pleas felt more like rambling, at first. But now, the evidence feels undeniable. The final straw for me was when the Famine seal broke."

"Oho?" Aldous tilted his head. "So, the attack on the seals continues…"

Conrad did everything he could to keep a straight face. Aldous wasn't much of a liar.

"I'm afraid so. For that reason, I was authorized by the Council to accompany some up-and-coming Wizards in their most recent attempt to remove the Mountain King from his post," Zequim said, his expression darkening. "I asked him if he'd felt a Dark Wizard's presence on the day of that disaster. Unfortunately, he was not so cooperative in telling me what I needed to know, and when persuasion fails..."

"I could tell that dark magic had made him more powerful, but to have brought so much harm to even you..." Aldous muttered.

"Mmm," Zequim hummed while nodding along. "I certainly underestimated him, in the beginning. After throwing a castle at me for the first time, I took the fight more seriously."

"He threw *what*?" Conrad asked, his dry voice cracking.

Aldous chuckled. "That's our esteemed leader, for you! I was fortunate one year ago, when Olivier went easy on me. Otherwise, he'd have killed me in short order. It sounds like he went all-out against you, though."

"Yes, well, I was not permitted by the Council to bring my artifact along. That made for a more challenging fight. Still, after a few days of battle, I got him on the defensive, and he finally let slip some details on the dark presence that you no doubt felt on the day that Greed was released," Zequim said.

The hairs on Aldous' arms stood on end. "And? What did he tell you?"

"He did not give a name, but he did describe him to me..." Zequim said with dire eyes. Conrad leaned in with anticipation, but he was surprised to see the Council leader smile. "Would either of you care to guess who it was?"

The old Wizard sighed. "More games?"

"My apologies. I could not help but try to clear the tension from your faces," Zequim said while holding up his hands and smirking. However, his smile quickly faded. "Olivier described a 'dark presence' just outside the mountain, you see..."

Conrad stopped a gasp from escaping his mouth. Back then, the old man Cyriack had been right. He, too, had sensed a dark presence, and that had been the beginning of their troubles. It had to have been one of the 14 men he was leading. Who had been deceiving him that entire time?

"One of Olivier's roaming eyes got a good look at him. He was a tall, gangly man-" Zequim's calm voice faded away as Conrad's mind lurched. That description alone was a dead giveaway. "-ginger hair, and a playful, affable expression."

With eyes wide and his mind cycling through all the events up to now, Conrad stood in astonished silence. All of that time, he had been fooled. He knew that a dark presence had been under his nose back then, outside of Mt. Couture; but even afterward, he hadn't noticed it while in plain sight.

"Does that sound familiar?" Zequim asked.

Aldous stroked his sandy beard while looking up in apparent thought. "Mayhap… but a name doesn't come to mind…"

The strategist looked to his Wizard friend, asking only with his eyes if he was permitted to speak. He knew who it was, and the revelation shocked him to his core. As if reading his mind, Aldous returned a nod.

"There was a miner on the expedition who fit that description: His name is William."

"Oh? And how might you know that?" Zequim asked.

"I was among the survivors of the Mt. Couture disaster," Conrad said, looking down. "Now that I think of it, all of the signs were there. I had found black gold in his tent, back then. He must have used some devilry to trick me because when I confronted him about it, they turned out to be mere rocks…"

"Sounds like Dark Shapeshifting magic, wouldn't you say?" Aldous asked, looking at his leader.

"Or Dark Mind Augmentation," Zequim said.

Conrad looked at Aldous and snorted in disbelief. "William also led me straight to the Dead Woods on that day you were speaking with Utrix. Could it mean that *he* is the same Dark Wizard that we encountered last night?"

"Oh, you've confronted another Dark Wizard, recently?" Zequim asked with judgment on his tongue.

Aldous showed apprehension at first, but some quality about Zequim's eyes seemed to drive confession. The old Wizard let out a breath and said, "Have you ever heard of a Dark Wizard called Oneth?"

The strategist cocked his head. Was that the true name of the one who'd been haunting his mind? The one who had teamed up with Drake? Had William simply been a disguise all along? Or worse, some poor, innocent man that he had murdered and then imitated?

"I'm afraid not, sorry," Zequim said with a shrug. "I must confess that I did not travel here to meet up with you."

"Shocking," Aldous replied with a chuckle.

"I had hoped that our *mutual friend* could help me identify the Dark

Wizard by description," he continued, gesturing to the oasis. "But alas! He has not answered my call."

"That is to be expected. You could wait out here for a full year, and he still would not have come out to greet you, methinks."

"It matters little. Now that I have a name, the Council can investigate further. For that, I thank you both."

"You could take us back to Faiwell with you," Conrad said with brimming enthusiasm. "I can take you straight to William. I know where he lives."

Zequim shook his head. "I sense a dark presence within you... I would assume that Aldous has brought you here for an *exorcism*. That should be your top priority, for now."

"Why don't you state the truth? You can't be seen with us, can you?" Aldous asked.

"I wish you had listened to me back in Port City." Zequim sighed. "Now, the Council suspects that *you* were behind the Famine seal's destruction. They wish to bring you in for more questioning."

"I'm sure they do," Aldous said with a snort. "But I have more important matters to attend to."

"Protecting another seal? I can help you with that," Zequim said.

"I said nothing of the sort."

"Are you sure that you don't want my help?"

"Not if it involves the Council," Aldous said.

"Well, you know that I have no choice, in that regard. I'm taking a large risk, just speaking with you," Zequim said.

"I'm surprised you were able to shake *that vulture* off of your tail," the old Wizard said.

"Ah, right... I snuck away from Axar back in Arkhuthal. I'm sure he's worried sick, by now," Zequim replied with a strained chuckle. "I should be going, then."

"Farewell," Aldous said with a bow. Conrad mimicked his motions, hoping to show respect.

"Oh, and by the way, that pesky Mountain King had *soul slaves*," Zequim said while wiping some more sand off of his tattered robe.

"Yes, he used them against me, as well. It is truly startling how far the black gold has twisted his mind," Aldous said with a grimace. "I would assume that you being here means he was defeated, and in that case, it would be wise to ensure defenses against the black gold's effects for the next Wizard King."

"Olivier fled to avoid capture, but he had taken heavy damage. It is only a matter of time before his capture, I'm sure. The Council is working on a solution to the black gold as we speak. It has taken the breaking of two seals, but it seems that we are finally addressing the threat."

"That remains to be seen," Aldous replied.

Zequim let out a light snort. "*Anyway*, the reason I bring up soul slaves is that one of them recognized you when I took your form to deceive Olivier."

"Henic..." he muttered with despair on his tongue. Conrad darted his eyes at him.

"So, you *did* know him," the leader said.

"Yes..." Aldous trailed off.

"Just know that once Olivier is captured, I will ensure that he releases the soul-enslaved so they can finally rest in peace," Zequim said with a reassuring smile.

The old Wizard remained silent, so Conrad bowed and said, "Thank you, sir."

"You are most welcome, young man," he replied, bowing in return. "I hope that the exorcism will cure your ailment."

"Well, it's not-" Aldous placed a firm hand on his chest, silencing him.

Zequim began walking off into the gaping desert landscape. Without looking back, he said, "I trust you two will stay out of trouble?"

"If only..." Aldous muttered as his leader transformed into a falcon, let out a ground-quaking screech, and then flew with great haste to the east.

"Shapeshifting magic?" Conrad asked, eyes wide.

"Quite right. Think of the most powerful, wondrous creatures in the world. He can change into most of them," the old WIzard said, now headed for the oasis.

"Why didn't you tell me about Henic?"

Aldous sighed. "I think you already know why."

"Enlighten me."

"If you knew that the Mountain King had kept Henic as a soul slave, you'd have tried to return to Mt. Couture. And I'm sure the others would have accompanied you," he said.

"And what's wrong with that?" Conrad asked.

"Joel and I didn't go through all of that trouble, only for you lot to return to that cursed mountain and throw your lives away," Aldous said in a stern tone. "I don't think you fully grasp just how lucky you are to be alive. That mountain has swallowed up more lives than you could possibly imagine."

"That would be my choice, *not* yours," Conrad replied with ice-cold eyes.

Aldous frowned in return, but he softened his expression after letting out an exhale. "I understand. You felt responsible for him, back then. But he is not your responsibility anymore. Leave it to Zequim."

Conrad remained silent for a few moments, but he was not done talking. "I will simply go back after our business in Endoshire is settled."

"You wouldn't even make it to the mountain before the Council caught you," Aldous said while shaking his head. "Leave it in Zequim's capable hands. There is nothing else we can do."

"If he is so capable, then why did he need to come all the way here for help? I'm sure there are plenty of men in Faiwell who fit William's description, but how many of them are survivors of the Mt. Couture disaster? Is the Council incapable of conducting a simple investigation? That's all it would have taken."

"Oho! I had the same thought, but I don't think that it is so simple…" Aldous trailed off. The strategist raised an eyebrow. "Zequim is finally beginning to realize that the Council is compromised. It is the only explanation for their behavior, of late."

"Compromised?"

"I don't wish to imply anything that I cannot confirm myself, but there was a time when the Council was efficient; so much that they would have figured out a solution to this problem by now and taken action. Yet, here we are," Aldous said.

"You mean to say that dark influences are coming from within?" Conrad asked.

"I cannot confirm, but let me put it this way…" the old Wizard said with a half-hearted smile. "Something is *not right* within the Council."

The pair continued to walk in silence until the grassy patches of the oasis first touched their feet. They stopped before a yellow-tinted barrier that encased the entirety of the small community. It hummed like insects in an open field and vibrated the ground enough that Conrad could feel it in his feet.

"They like their privacy…" Aldous muttered before cupping his hands. "I seek council with the Exorcist!"

After a few moments, a door-shaped opening carved itself out of the barrier. The process was so loud and unnatural that Conrad's shoulders shot up to his ears. It best reminded him of someone banging a hammer off of steel, except a thousand-fold faster.

"Come along, then." The old Wizard walked through, and Conrad followed. Then, he heard a hollow, windy noise and turned to see that the doorway had closed. He flashed Aldous a concerned expression. "Worry not, my friend. You are in good hands."

"Well, at least I can finally drink some water," he replied, looking to the pond at the center of the community. Many huts, tents, and shacks surrounded it, but they were of no concern in the face of his thirst.

Conrad lunged forward, to make a dash for the water he desperately needed, but a firm tug of his shirt stilled him. He looked back, incensed, to see Aldous' iron grip on his sleeve.

"Not yet," he said, wagging his finger.

"Why not?" Conrad replied in a near-growl.

"Think of it as part of the exorcism process."

"What? That doesn't make any sense!" Conrad cried, his tone shifting to dry desperation.

"It will, soon enough," Aldous said as he guided him toward a tent off to the right. "But for now, just trust me."

The strategist groaned as he was pushed toward the beige tent. It had several gold, wavy designs on its side, and was flanked by a couple of palm trees that bore fruits unfamiliar to Conrad's eyes.

"Should I knock?" Aldous asked before smirking. Conrad narrowed his eyes. "Not in a joking mood, eh? I understand. It must be the dark essence."

"That is one possibility… or it could be that I'm desperate for water and you won't let me have any," he replied with crossed arms.

Aldous chuckled as he held the tent flap open and gestured a hand inward. Conrad entered to see a surprisingly spacious area: Multiple rooms were separated by flaps, and the central area was large enough to house several people, in his estimation. Ahead, he spotted a bubbling pot that sat over a fire. Skulls of many different creatures hung from the ceiling by strings, and several weathered tomes decorated the floor.

The flap to the left brushed open, and out stepped a man who wore a black, open vest, exposing a muscular torso and set of arms that looked fit to wrestle a python. His necklace, made of small bones, bounced perfectly to the smooth rhythm of his strides, and so too did the ribbon-like bottom hems of his white pants. Although he was no taller than Conrad himself, his presence filled the room, as if he were the size of a dragon. The fire flared out as he neared it, reflecting an intense terracotta off his bald, ebony head. Yet, nothing had quite prepared Conrad for his piercing gaze. It felt like an arrow had struck and gone through his whole body. Somehow, he knew that those wide, dark eyes held more power and knowledge than he could ever conceive of.

"Now, what do we have here?" Though not as deep or dark as Oneth's voice had been, it carried even more intensity; enough that Conrad was too nervous to open his mouth.

"Hello, there!" Aldous said with cheer. He placed a hand on Conrad's shoulder, somewhat easing his worries.

The bald man gazed upon them with a ferocity that had made Conrad feel like a mouse cornered by a snake. After a few intense moments, however, he smiled, and the flames underneath the bubbling pot simmered.

"I thought I recognized that voice," the bald man said as his smile grew into a mischievous grin. "It has been a while, Aldous. I would have known it was you sooner, if not for that Anima of yours… yes… swinging in the other direction, is it? Taking a turn toward *the dark*? What's an upstanding Wizard to do?"

Conrad looked at Aldous to see an unamused frown on his face. As he recalled, Anima was vital to a Wizard's survival in their advanced years. Had the events of the past year brought him to the brink of death?

"I am not here for myself," Aldous said while patting Conrad on the shoulder. "This old boy is in need of an exorcism."

"And who says I'm willing to do the favor?"

Aldous put hands to hips. "Such a cold reception. Is that any way to treat an old friend? Is your sour mood because of *Zequim's* presence?"

"*Don't say that name,*" the bald man shot back as the room dimmed and the flames beneath the pot tucked themselves away as if hiding. The skulls in the tent *clanked* off one another in taunting applause, while Aldous and Conrad each took a step back.

"I'd say you were correct…" Conrad muttered as the flames flared back up, and the room's lighting returned to normal.

"My apologies…" the old Wizard said while holding his hands up and letting loose nervous chuckles. "But I must say that I'm surprised you let him stay so close to the oasis. Surely, you could feel that he was weakened."

"Are you implying that I *need* to face him while weakened? That I could not crush him into dust for my potions while he is at top strength?"

"Ehrm, no, no! Not at all!" Aldous said between more anxious laughs.

The bald man sighed. "I feel that you are one of the few good Wizards left, Aldous. But *don't* test me. I have my limits."

"Right… I'll cut straight to the chase, then. This here is Conrad. There exists within him a vile substance, which only someone of your talents could possibly remove," Aldous said, then gestured to the bald man. "Conrad, this is Hexzar, an Exorcist and master of dark magic."

"D-dark magic?" the strategist stammered, then took another step back. "I've experienced *enough of that* for my lifetime."

"You see that?" Hexzar asked with a crinkled brow. Aldous began to sweat. "That term… means *everything*."

Aldous cleared his throat. "R-right, sorry, I meant to say-"

"No!" he interrupted, pointing to him with conviction. "You keep on using that term, just like a *good little Council member*."

"What is he talking about?" Conrad asked, looking to his friend.

With a sigh, Aldous said, "The truth is that 'dark magic' wasn't always named as such. It used to be called 'occult magic'."

"That change was the Council's doing," Hexzar said with crossed arms.

"I don't care what it's called; all I know is that it isn't *good*," Conrad said.

Hexzar held a finger up, and the strategist fell silent. "Just because you have the capability of flapping your lips, doesn't mean you should."

"Please, don't be too harsh on the old boy. He has had many bad experiences with… erm… occult magic," Aldous said.

"Be that as it may, he must learn that his way of thinking is *flawed*."

"How so?" Conrad asked. His tone had gone from apprehensive to inquisitive.

"You seek an exorcism, do you not?" Hexzar asked. Conrad nodded. "And what kind of magic do you think that is?"

Conrad rubbed his chin. "Dark magi-"

"Occult magic," he interrupted. "Perception is *everything* in this world. You have been told over and over that this so-called *dark magic* is bad; you even had bad experiences with it, and for that reason, you know it to be true. Yet it is not the truth. It is nothing but a fabrication created by the most powerful and influential group in the world."

"You say that the Wizard's Council created this lie? For what purpose?" Conrad asked.

Aldous snorted. "It is best not to get him going…"

"No. He deserves to know the truth."

"We don't have time for this…"

"You lied to the boy, so now, you will *make time*," Hexzar shot back, then looked to Conrad with a fiery gaze. "Think of every powerful institution. What do they all have in common? They wish to *keep that power*, by any means necessary. Think of the Wizard's Council as the ultimate power in this world. They wield strength beyond measure; an influence that is ever-present, yet goes unseen by the masses. Even mages who do not call themselves 'Wizard' must operate beneath their oppressive thumb. Now then, if another group were to rise up in competition with the Council, how do you think they would react?"

"Poorly," Conrad replied, without hesitation.

"How right you are. Occult magic can be used for evil, but so can any tool or weapon. There were far more Witch Covens a couple thousand years ago than there are now… some used their magic for good, and others evil, but the Council did not discriminate. They attacked them all, friendly or not," Hexzar said.

"I must say that I've only ever heard bad things about Witchcraft," Conrad said.

"And that is by design. They'll find their justification, whether it is true or not," the bald man said with a solemn shake of his head. "And so, when I gathered fellow Occultists and formed the *League of Wizards*, they treated us as a threat, rather than co-existing."

"Hold on," Conrad said, looking at Aldous. "Didn't you tell me that Anima swings in the direction of good and bad deeds? And that Dark Wizards come to be from the latter?"

"Well, generally-"

"I'm disappointed in you, Aldous. You've fed this young man many lies," Hexzar said before snorting in his direction. "As I said, *anything* can be used as a tool for good and evil, including the occult. Exorcising demons and vile substances from others is a good thing, is it not?"

"You have a good Anima, then?" the strategist asked. Hexzar nodded in return.

"You're not telling the whole story, old friend," Aldous replied with a frown. "Occultists are different from Dark Wizards, in my mind; far rarer, too. Dark- or, erm, occult magic requires *sacrifice*. There are only two ways that can go: Self-inflicted sacrifice, or the sacrifice of others. The former is the only path to a good Anima between the two, yet it is far more difficult to achieve. It is basic instinct, after all, to choose yourself over others."

"And yet here I stand, with a good Anima, thrice your age!" Hexzar said as an angry wind swirled around the tent, shaking the animal skulls on the ceiling. "You say that Occultists are rare, but you know not how many are in hiding, for fear that the Council will hunt them down!"

Aldous stood firm in the face of his anger. "You may recall that I made this argument to the Council, but they refused my changes to the classifications."

"As I said, you are one of the good ones, but you've omitted some important details. If you are thinking of taking the boy as your protégé, he must learn all aspects of magic."

Conrad smiled at the old Wizard.

"Erm, yes, well…" Aldous muttered, then cleared his throat. "I never said any such thing. We are only here for the exorcism-majigger."

"As interesting as this conversation has been, I must excuse myself," Conrad said as Aldous and Hexzar cocked their heads in unison. He didn't care how disrespectful it was. He needed water, *now*, and started for the tent flap.

"You'll leave when I've excused you," Hexzar said as Conrad's legs froze. His mind was telling them to move, but they refused.

"Oho! He must be quite thirsty, by now," Aldous said.

The strategist twisted his upper body to see Hexzar grinning, holding a small straw doll by its legs.

"I'm afraid you won't be drinking any water for the next day or so. Your body belongs to me, now," Hexzar said while twisting the doll in his hand. Involuntarily, Conrad's legs faced forward.

"Wha-why not? What have you done to me?" he asked, his heart and breaths alike racing.

Hexzar chuckled as he waggled a strand of blond hair that was wrapped around the doll. "People are always shedding their pesky hair… of course, even hair can be a useful tool in the right hands."

"Worry not, m'boy! This is all part of the process," Aldous said.

"Yes… the exorcism begins *now*," Hexzar said, then moved the doll's legs with his fingers. Conrad began walking to the tent flap on his right. "See yourself into the room."

Conrad's mind went blank with fear as he passed through the flap, into a room drenched in darkness. He tried to resist as his legs turned, then crouched to sit in a padded chair. He attempted to stand, but his legs didn't even offer a struggle. What he had been told would be an exorcism, was beginning to feel like imprisonment.

CHAPTER 32
PAIN

Joel, Dalton, Kabel, and Dhogron walked through the rainy slums of West Endoshire with hoods up and masks on. The mute had joined up with the trio to get some distance between himself and Giles, for the time being. Even though he had claimed not to hold a grudge for the loss of his eye, Joel could feel resentment irradiating from Giles every time they were in the same room.

Even worse, Giles' harsh words from the prior night stuck with him like a stubborn tree sap. Did the rest of his allies see him in such a poor light? As someone who's refusal to kill would eventually get them killed? The only other Stranger to make his opinion known on the matter, Conrad, had not quelled his concerns in the slightest. He hoped that had been the dark essence talking.

The group slipped in and out of alleyways to avoid contact with even a single person, until reaching Dhogron's shop. They entered through a smashed-in door to find the store in disarray.

"So, the place was ransacked by the enemy," Kabel said.

"It was like this a few days ago, too. I don't think they've been here, recently," Dhogron replied as he weaved between some junk on the floor.

"What did you need here, anyway?" Dalton asked. He retrieved a door handle from the floor, narrowed his eyes, and then flung it over his shoulder.

"Just a few odds n' ends. I think they will help us against the enemy," he said from the backroom.

Joel held up a small, brown sack and looked inside to see a dark powder. Worried that it could be something akin to the beige berries that Auber had bought from this very store, he quickly closed the bag without inhaling its contents.

"What was so important that you had to drag me out here for?" Kabel asked, directing a critical eye in Dalton's direction. "Mira will be displeased that I didn't help with chores today..."

"She'll get over it," he replied with a crass chuckle. "Besides, this is a big deal."

The stocky man leaned in. "Well? Don't keep me in suspense..."

"Last night, near Cole's pub, I came across a woman," he said, smiling from ear to ear.

Kabel scoffed. "Yer a real knob, y'know that?"

Dalton tilted his head and pointed at himself, in obvious confusion. Joel let out an inaudible chuckle.

"You dragged me out here to talk about another one of yer damn conquests?"

"No, no, it's much more than that!" Dalton said between laughs. "The woman was none other than *Anora*."

Kabel shook his head and shrugged. "Am I supposed to know who that is?"

"You know... Anora... Adrian's wife? Lucia's mother?"

Joel and Kabel's eyes widened in unison. Weren't both of Lucia's parents supposed to be long since dead?

"Right... right, I never met Anora, but Adrian could never shaddup about her," Kabel said.

"Turns out, she is somewhere in the city. We had drinks last night, but like an idiot, I got drunk and fell asleep... she was gone when I awoke, but at least now I know she is out there. We must find a way to get in contact with her," Dalton said, his fists clenched and his eyes alight.

Kabel sighed. "Sorry to tell you, but no, she is *not* in the city."

"What do you mean? I saw her with my own two eyes! Spoke to her! Felt her touch! You don't forget somethin' like that, even after 13 years!"

"I've been meaning to tell you about this, but every time we go out, it keeps slipping my mind..." Kabel trailed off with nervous laughter.

"Tell me what?"

"Before y'all came here, about two or three weeks ago, methinks, I got a knock at the door," Kabel said. Joel shuddered. He had told this story before. "When I opened the latch to see who it was, Adrian was standin' there, smilin' at me."

"That's not possible..." Dalton said, wide-eyed. "I saw him die. He fell into that deep ravine. No one coulda survived that..."

"Exactly. And weren't you with Anora while she was on her deathbed?"

"I-I was..." he muttered, now exasperated. "What are you tryin' to say?"

"Aldous told me that a Dark Wizard can read our minds, and then take the form of those we know and love. But y'see, they often aren't able to imitate perfectly as a Shapeshifter Wizard can; they usually don't study their subjects to the same degree," Kabel said, raising an index finger. "I could tell somethin' wasn't right with Adrian when he spoke to me. He looked like him, spoke like him, and even had his mannerisms, but there was somethin'... somethin' 'off', that I cannot quite describe. He felt like an *imitation*."

"So, it was all a lie..." Dalton muttered, his eyes and posture alike drooping.

"I'm sorry to say, but yes."

Dalton scoffed and shook his head. "Glad I didn't tell Lucia, then."

Joel cocked his head, then signed to him, asking why he hadn't told her about the encounter.

"I wanted to arrange a meeting between the two, to surprise her," Dalton said between dejected chuckles. "I shoulda been smarter than that. After all, life is a bloody struggle, and then you die."

Kabel frowned and opened his mouth to say something, but Dhogron exited the backroom with several sacks draped over his shoulder and drew his attention. "Ready to go?"

"What's all of that you've got, there?" the stocky man asked with a smirk.

"As you all should have gathered by now, I enjoy a good prank. You could say it's one of the few ways we find entertainment in the slums. I never thought I'd be using these things to save the city, but when we get back to the hideout, I will show you their uses," Dhogron replied with an assured nod.

With that, the group left Dhogron's shop and began making their way north, toward the tailor and weapon shops. With the remaining gold pooled by the Strangers, they purchased various garments and arms for the team. However, they only bought whatever could be carried by hand. Their horses had either escaped or been captured during the fire last night, and a wheelbarrow or cart was likely to draw unwanted eyes to them.

Tension ramped up as the group passed into the wealthy district, and all four of them kept hands free, so they could draw weapons as needed. After all, running into Drake, Sampson, or the Dark Wizard in the pouring rain meant that there would be no place to hide. The streets were nearly empty.

Luckily, by the time they reached a set of stairs that led to the rooftops, not a single enemy had approached them. Even the rooftop deals that Endoshire was famous for seemed to be paused until the storm subsided. After crossing a few bridges, the group descended into the boxed-in alley where Satara resided. Joel took in a nervous gulp as they were swallowed by shadow. It was possible, after all, that she had been captured by Sampson. Her living quarters may have been occupied by the enemy.

Dhogron turned back and pressed a finger to his lips before walking down the stairs and entering the building cellar. Inside was well-lit by over a dozen candles, adding to Joel's anxiety. It meant that *someone* was here.

As the group walked further inside, they found a dazed Satara lying out on a sofa. Her face was covered with cuts and bruises, and the translucent silk that draped over her vest had been ripped. Sitting next to her was a man holding a scimitar, but its tip rested on the floor; as if he were too weak to even lift his weapon. His clothes were painted in dry blood, and his face was swollen and bumpy.

"What do *you* want?" Satara asked with sharp eyes.

"We came to ensure that you were alright," Dhogron said, looking around the room. "There weren't nearly as many of Sampson's men as we had anticipated, last night. I knew that could only mean one thing: There was a trap set for you. Sampson *wanted* you to try and rescue the sex slaves."

She snickered. "You have a talent for pointing out the obvious."

"If it makes you feel any better, they set a trap for us, too," Kabel said with a half-hearted smile.

"Ah, so 'The Strangers' are no more, eh?" her musician said with a chuckle that turned into a coughing fit.

Satara glared at him and then chopped him in the ribs. He doubled over and began dry-heaving. "We *don't* laugh at other people's misery just because we ourselves are in pain, Najih."

"S-sorry…" Najih muttered while hunched over.

"We were fortunate, actually," Dhogron said. "We're all still alive, with relatively few losses, all things considered."

"Speak for yerself! They burned my house to the ground, and nearly everything I owned!" Kabel shot back.

Ebbie had lost some of his fingers, and Giles had lost his eye, too, Joel thought. In addition, the Strangers' morale seemed to have been crushed. He looked at Dalton, who simply stared ahead with little care or apparent thought. He hadn't been the same since Kabel revealed to him that his reunion with Anora had not at all been what he thought it was. In fact, he hadn't spoken a word since leaving Dhogron's shop.

"Try having nearly all of your friends either killed before your eyes, or worse: Forced back into their bondage by the very man you were supposed to protect them from," Satara said while clawing at the fabric of her sofa until it ripped. Then, she let out a long breath through her nose. "As you can see, we'll survive. You can go, now."

"I came for more than simply checking up on you," the trickster Wizard said.

"You cannot possibly want more favors…"

Dhogron shook his head. "Not a favor, but an *offer*."

"What can you conceivably offer me? In case you hadn't noticed, everything I've been working for went up in a cloud of smoke, last night. There is nothing you can sell that would satisfy me," Satara said.

"That's precisely my point: After last night, Sampson knows your face. I'm sure your inside contact is dead, too. You must start anew," Dhogron said. Satara crossed her arms and turned her nose up. "Join us. Sampson is our enemy, too. What more do you have to lose?"

"My dignity? My life?"

"Neither of you looks dignified to me," Kabel said with a smirk. "But Dhogron is right. The Strangers could always use more members, and Sampson is one of our worst enemies. Who would know him better than you?"

Satara looked at Najih, wide-eyed. He stood with his chest puffed out, breathing heavily. "After last night, I have nothing left. We cannot perform on the streets anymore; I know that much. There is nothing left to do but *fight*."

The dancer frowned at Najih, then softened her expression and let out a sigh. "I suppose you're right."

"So, you'll join?" Dhogron asked, in high spirits.

"We're in," Satara said. Najih nodded in unison with her.

"Hold up," Dalton said in a stern tone. All in the room turned their gazes to him. "How do we know it's *really her*?"

Joel's eyes widened. It seemed so unlike him to suggest such a thing. It was cold, calculated, and straight to the point.

"What are you on about?" Dhogron asked with a raised eyebrow.

"The Dark Wizard can take whatever form he wishes, can he not?" Dalton asked.

Kabel held a hand up. "Well, hold on, now. There are two of 'em. I don't think-"

"And didn't we just get through with Brice, another man who could imitate his victims?" the warrior added.

Joel made hand signals, indicating that Brice would reveal his true form if harm came to him, according to Conrad's findings.

"So be it, then," Kabel said with crossed arms. "If the two of you wanna join, you'll need to slice your palms open."

"What an outrageous request," Satara said with a scowl. "Can't you see we're already in enough pain?"

"Sorry, but they're right," Dhogron said. "Two of our enemies can mimic others perfectly. The only weakness that we can find is that if they are cut or stabbed, it reveals their true form."

"Very well," Najih said, then sliced the scimitar across his palm without a second thought. He winced, and blood spurted from the fresh wound. After a few moments, all in the room let out sighs of relief.

"I don't like your idea of 'initiation'," Satara said with sharp eyes. She held her hand out and cut into it with a hooked dagger. "But since I have no choice…"

Once again, the group waited with bated breath, and after some time, Dhogron stepped forward with a cloth in hand.

"I think it has been long enough."

"Wait," Dalton said. All in the room looked at him once more.

"What, now? They proved themselves, didn't they?" Kabel asked.

"One of 'em could still be the Dark Wizard. He probably doesn't have the same weakness as Brice," Dalton said before casting eyes on Satara. "You, there. You're a belly dancer, right?"

"What of it?"

"Come and give me a personal dance, to prove you're the real deal," he said with a stone face.

The other Strangers narrowed their eyes at him and groaned. Perhaps Dalton wasn't acting so different after all, Joel thought.

"Have you no shame?" Dhogron asked with a frown.

"He doesn't..." Kabel muttered.

"What's the problem? If she is the Dark Wizard in disguise, then I'm takin' one for the team! And if not, well..." Dalton trailed off with a wink and a smile.

"This is ridiculous! I thought you all said the city was at stake? We have no time for nonsense," Najih protested.

"I have no problems giving a personal dance," Satara said as she approached Dalton and tickled his chin with her index finger. His face lit up with glee. "For a price."

"Name it!"

"3,000 notes," she said.

Dalton frowned. "I was hoping it would be more like 300..."

"You get what you pay for," Satara said in a mocking tone.

The warrior looked back to his friends. "Could any of you spare some coin?"

"Absolutely not!" Dhogron shot back.

"It shouldn't be a problem. We all pool our money together, right? So, paying her is like paying the Strangers, isn't it?"

"Not happenin', fella," Kabel said with crossed arms. The rest of the Strangers stood firm as Dalton hung his head.

"I should have known that friends of Dhogron would be cheap," Satara said with an eye roll, then nudged Najih. "Pack your things, and *pack light*. We don't want to be spotted."

With that, the dancer and her musician began to gather their belongings.

∽

CONRAD SAT IN THE DARK, bound by rope and thrashing around in the padded chair. His mouth was agape, gurgling the essence that consumed him. In the midst of his desperate movements, he leaned over to vomit some of the vile substance.

However, before the dark essence could hit the floor, it froze in mid-air. Hexzar held a hand out, then gestured toward a nearby jar. The liquid obeyed his command and floated into the container. He tightened a cap over the jar, then picked it up and inspected its contents. He had dawned a glowing, white face paint, drawn in the shape of a skull.

"Do you recognize it?" Aldous asked.

"This is surely the work of the occult, but..." Hexzar trailed off, squinting at the dark essence. "There is something else within. It feels dark, but in a different way from what I normally see... almost as if it were *blank*."

"It was drawn from Greed's imprint: the black gold."

"And how would someone have gotten their hands on that?"

"There is much you need to be caught up on, old friend," Aldous said with a half-hearted chuckle. "The black gold has spread further than we ever could have imagined, in recent years. Humans came into contact with it, and a Dark Wizard was able to obtain some as a result."

"I see... and this dark mage sought to combine their magic with the black gold, to achieve some sort of submissive effect in men?"

"Yes. He managed to take over an entire town with it. There are probably thousands under his command, thus far," Aldous said while stroking his beard. "Worse yet, he created a concentrated dose, giving magic-like abilities to humans."

Hexzar's eyes widened and his expression became deathly serious. "This mage's actions... they remind me of-"

"I know what you're thinking," Aldous interrupted, shaking his head. "But he did not lay claim to the title of 'Oppressor' when I confronted him."

"It sounds like something he would do," Hexzar said, letting out a breath of relief. "Then again, he *was* cast into the Great Chasm. He shall never walk among us again."

"Are you certain of that?" Aldous asked as Conrad thrashed in his seat some more. "I've often wondered: If we know that the Great Chasm nullifies magic and keeps the body alive, then surely someone must have escaped to tell the tale, right?"

"Do you really think Zequim and I would have thought up such a plan without being sure?" Hexzar asked with a derisive laugh. "There are small patches of land around the Chasm that hold those effects. Believe me, we did *many* experiments. There is no way to escape, save clawing his way up hundreds of meters of sheer rock wall with a broken body."

"Fair enough. I have my suspicions, is all I'm saying."

"You continue to butt heads with this dark mage, correct? Why not allow the Council to take care of him?" Hexzar asked.

"Oho! I often forget how long it has been since you last worked with them. The Council has changed much since the previous Wizard War. This Dark Wizard has been in the process of attacking the seven seals for over a year, and the Council has done little in response," Aldous said.

"It doesn't surprise me that the Council would be more hesitant to act, these days. After all, their incessant persecution of others and provocative actions helped Wilhelm rise to power, last time," he replied while shaking his head. "Still, to think that they wouldn't take a threat to the seven seals seriously..."

"Sad, but true. They have completely lost their way. It would seem that these days, I am in danger of being excommunicated."

"Yes, well, if that were to happen, you could always stay here with us Occultists. You're one of the few Wizards of substance left, after all, and we could use an Elemental with control over water in this little community," Hexzar said.

"Oho! I'm afraid not. Even if they were to excommunicate me, my place will forever be defending the seals, as I swore to!" Aldous replied with a prideful smile.

"Stubborn as ever, I see." Hexzar chuckled. "I do wonder, though... if this dark mage has access to black gold, then why bother with the other seals? What benefit is there to unleashing the Dark Savior's split identities? They would pose a great danger to everyone, including *himself*."

"I am unsure what his true intentions are, but he did mention 'stretching the Council's resources'," Aldous replied.

"I can understand why you thought he was Wilhelm, at first," Hexzar said as Conrad vomited more dark essence. He stuck his hand out, and it froze in the air once again. "The first thing he would want to do is dismantle and destroy the Council."

"If you say so. No one alive today would know him better than you," Aldous said with a smirk. For a brief moment, Hexzar's hand wavered, and so too did the dark essence. However, he quickly regained control and placed it in another jar.

"Did this Dark Wizard give you a name?"

"He called himself Oneth."

Hexzar looked up and rubbed his chin. "I've never heard the name, but one of the Occultists in our community may have. I will ask around after the exorcism is complete."

"Thank you for helping us," Aldous said with a bow.

"No need to thank me. This substance is highly volatile, so you'll be feeling great pain as sacrifice for its removal... I'm sure you are well aware of that, though. You must be fond of the boy."

"Yes... I think he has the potential to become a Wizard, should he apply himself to the craft."

"There is potential, true. I can sense a great curiosity within him. Perhaps that would lend well to becoming an Elemental, like you. Then again..." the bald man trailed off with a devious smile. "There is a certain darkness within him. I can't help but wonder if he would make for a great Occultist..."

Aldous let out a huff, then held out his hand. "Let's get this over with."

"Very well," he replied, grasping his hand.

Hexzar shot his free hand out toward Conrad, who began to convulse. Aldous winced at the shock to his system that one might feel when being stuck by a knife, but in his case, the feeling was all-encompassing and everlasting. Regardless, he held on tight to Hexzar's hand and ground his teeth. *It's going to be a long day*, he thought.

CHAPTER 33
CEREMONY

Night came upon Endoshire, but the storm did not let up. Drake and Rose sat in their comfy carriage, pulled slowly by dark steeds that had to trudge through mud and puddles. The sluggish pace was excruciating to Rose, for their destination was the Dark Wizard's ship, where *the ceremony* was to take place. Having had so much time to think about it, she was now a bundle of nerves.

Why did she have to undergo the ceremony? After all, it was *Drake* who likely needed help with conceiving a child, at his age. What would happen if it was a failure, and a pregnancy still couldn't be reached? Would he toss her aside like common trash? It felt as if his attachment to her had weakened with each failed attempt at conceiving.

"You look nervous. Don't be," Drake said.

Rose looked out the window on her side of the carriage, and then down upon her new personal servant. She panted like a dog while trying to keep pace with the carriage, and her dress had become muddy all over. The bonnet atop her head sagged under the weight of the rain, exposing wet, wild hair that likely hadn't been washed since beginning her servitude. Such a lowly position to be in, Rose thought.

"Did you hear me?" Drake asked, in a sterner tone.

"Yes…" Rose trailed off. She continued looking outside as a flash of lightning illuminated her servant's face. Even that brief flash told all: Her desperation, her fear, her misery.

"Well, then…" he trailed off before grabbing and jerking her arm, nearly pulling it out of its socket. The bride-to-be winced before turning to him with a fiery grimace. She quickly returned to her down-trodden demeanor upon seeing those devilish, green eyes staring back. "Look at me while I'm talking to you."

"I'm sorry," she squeaked out.

"This is not how a queen acts," Drake said.

"How does a queen act, then?" Rose asked.

He cocked his head and crinkled his nose. Rose was already at her breaking point. Nothing he did or said could scare her more than she already had been.

To her surprise, Drake relaxed his posture, then let out a long breath through his nose. "A queen does what she must for the sake of her kingdom. We *have* no kingdom without an heir."

Rose looked down, straining her palms against her knees. It was time, she thought, to say what was truly on her mind. "If I undergo this ceremony, and it still doesn't bear a child, will you cast me out as a commoner? Or will you take responsibility and undergo such a proce-dure for yourself?"

Now, Drake's eyes were intense, but not angry. They were *focused*. Once again, to her surprise, he relaxed his posture and then cracked a cool smile. "Have I ever told you about how I came to power back in my home village?"

"No…"

"It is not a story that I often tell. You see, I wasn't born into wealth, like most nobles. I was instead raised by a family of miners. We were all crammed into one tiny home, and would work all day, every day, for a pittance," Drake said, looking up and smiling. "They were all so happy, despite their poor living conditions. *I hated every moment of it.*"

"How did you gain wealth, then?" Rose asked.

"Back then, I was under the illusion that I could work hard to reach the top," he replied with a scoff. "But my family and many other miners worked themselves to near-death every day, and they remained peasants, for all intents and purposes. They all died young, except for me. I lived long enough to find myself leading expeditions into the mountains."

"You must have found your fortunes while mining, then, right?"

"In a way? Yes…" Drake trailed off with a chuckle. "Except some-times, our biggest achievements come disguised as trying times. One day, at the end of one of our most successful expeditions, a tunnel collapsed, trapping us. Luckily, everyone survived, and our spoils remained intact."

"You got everyone out safely, I trust?" she asked.

"Listen closely, my dear, for this is the most important part of my story," Drake said, holding up an index finger. "After a counting of our supplies, it was clear that we only had enough remaining water to last us half a day. I was certain that it would take us at least two days to break through the collapse. The space to chip away at the rock was narrow, and so only half of us could work on it at once. So, that night, when everyone was asleep, *I did what I had to do.*"

"Y-you killed them?" A hush came over Rose's voice.

"Half of the crew had to be sacrificed for *the greater good*. With their supplies carefully rationed off, we survived for two, long days; tirelessly chipping through the collapse," Drake said with pride. "When all was said and done, we returned home with half the men and all of the spoils. Not one of the surviving crew members ever reported me or complained about what I had done. Instead, the Miner's Guild hailed me as a hero; for making a decision that none of them wanted to make, and saving us all. They made me president of the Guild for my efforts, and with that, I created new policies that brought about a golden age for the entire village. One dirty deed; one difficult sacrifice… and at the end of it all, there was *a greater good*."

"The sacrifice wasn't yours to make! How could you do such an awful thing and be rewarded for it?" Rose asked, her skin crawling.

"To make such decisions takes conviction… strength… knowledge… things that filthy commoners don't have. *We* must make these decisions *for* them," Drake said while playfully twirling a few strands of her hair. She closed her eyes while shuddering, praying that he wouldn't rip out any more of her locks. "For you see, I am not a businessman, a Guild president, or even a Village Elder. I am a *king*, and that is what kings and queens do. They rule over their lowly subjects and make decisions that the weak are incapable of making. And rest assured, the commoners *are* weak. They would be living in ditches, eating and drinking their own waste without people like *us* to rule over them."

Rose took a few heavy breaths to compose herself, then opened her eyes to see Drake's usual, cool smile. "I don't understand… how could it not bother you? How could you toy with people's lives like that, and still wear that handsome smile?"

"Because, to answer your earlier question, I am strong enough to make whatever sacrifice necessary so that my kingdom comes to fruition. The reason I am here today, wealthy and connected, is because I am strong," Drake said, then pointed to one of the servant women outside the window. "That could easily be *you*, out there. Do you understand that? Much like the mining cave-in for me, this is your opportunity, your defining moment. The question is, will you seize power and claim your rightful place? Or will you squander this once-in-a-lifetime opportunity? Strong or weak? Make your decision."

Rose's mind swirled like leaves in the wind. Her breathing became heavy and slow as she looked outside to see her downtrodden servants, trekking through the mud in a heap of misery. She'd have guessed they were each crying beneath the guise of rain pounding their faces. Deep down, in her heart of hearts, she was certain that they would never speak out of turn or defy her orders. They were completely subservient, just as she had been under Sampson's oppressive boot.

In a sad way, her servants were helpless pets who would die without her helping hand; even if it wasn't their fault. They hadn't been given a choice, like her. Rose took in her own surroundings. She sat in a luxurious coach with the finest fabrics inside, adding to her comfort. She had grown accustomed to her many sets of jewelry and dresses, each of which cost more than a group of shacks in the slums. There was plentiful food and drink in her vicinity at all times, and now she even had servants to wait on her every whim.

There was no question that her life had drastically improved since Drake took her in. The true conundrum was whether she was making the morally correct choice in ruling beside a man who had no problems with hurting or killing others. She had tried to do the right thing all of her life, but it never got her anywhere. Everyone she ever knew or loved had died or been sold into slavery.

With that, the thought crept into her mind: What if there was something to what Drake had been saying? What if there *was* a greater good beyond her ineffective and small deeds? Did she have the strength, the willpower, to crush her opposition in her ascent to the top?

Rose took one last look outside to see her servants hobbling along in the mud, coughing and struggling beneath the cold rain. She let out a sigh, then looked at Drake with as much determination as she could muster. "I'll do it."

"A wise decision," Drake said with a sly smile, then kissed her on the cheek. "I knew that you would make for my perfect queen... a few moments of sacrifice and pain, all for the greater good; the beginnings of our kingdom!"

The bride-to-be remained quiet. Drake had finally let slip that the ceremony would bring her pain. Even so, Rose wouldn't allow herself to become like the miserable servants outside. Never again would she settle for less.

With that conviction seeping into her mind, time seemed to fly by. Soon, the horses and carriage arrived at dock four of the harbor, where Oneth's ship loomed over all.

"Best of luck, m'lady!" one of the servants said with an overly enthusiastic smile. There was mud all over her face and dress.

Rose mustered a half-hearted smile and nod while looking back. Only she, Drake, and the bodyguards were permitted onboard. The servants would have to wait out in the rain.

The group was greeted on the main deck by a young woman with a beaming smile. "Lord Drake, it is my pleasure to see you again."

Drake smiled and nodded back. "The pleasure is all mine, Catalina."

Her eyes then fell onto Rose. "And this must be Lady Rose. It will be an honor to serve you, m'lady."

Catalina curtsied, and Rose responded in kind with what she hoped resembled gracefulness. The smile on Catalina's face felt forced; cold, even.

"Shall I take you to the Master?" she asked Drake.

"Yes, we have a meeting with him that is of great importance."

"Right..." Catalina trailed off. She returned her gaze to Rose, and her smile grew inhumanly large; into a malice-filled grin that sent chills down her spine. *"The ceremony."*

"Ah, so he has made you aware," Drake said, clearing his throat. "Very good. Take us to him, on the double!"

"Right away, My Lord," Catalina said with a bow, then turned to the stairs behind.

Drake and his entourage followed Catalina up to the third deck, where she knocked on the grand door of Oneth's quarters. After a few moments, the door opened to reveal a large man in a hooded robe. Rose shuddered at his mighty presence; the wind and rain seemed to shift direction, so that the drops ran away from such a fiend and struck her in the face, instead.

"Ah, good... I was just finishing up preparation for the ceremony,"

Oneth said, smiling down upon the crowd with what looked to be devious intentions. "Won't you come in?"

"Wait out here for a moment," Drake said, looking back at Rose, Ned, and Hector. "I'd like to have a word in private."

The Dark Wizard bowed to those outside on the rainy deck, then closed the door behind him and Drake. Rose looked at the two bodyguards with fear in her eyes. Just moments from the ceremony, she was getting cold feet, and needed some reassurance.

"You've both undergone a ceremony. Please… just tell me the truth. What will it do to me? Will I become like you?" she asked, her voice reflecting a primal desperation.

Hector and Ned only hissed in response, to which Catalina let out some playful giggles. The bride-to-be's heart sank.

"You should know by now that they are never in the mood for talking," she said. Rose looked over her shoulder to see Catalina's eyes glowing somewhat red between the drops of rainfall. "But that's alright, I don't mind telling you about the Master's ceremonies…"

Rose turned around and gasped. "He performed one on you?"

"Indeed. Twice, now. Once to become part of the collective, and a second time to bestow me with *inhuman power*."

"Did it hurt?"

"The first time? Fear and desperation clouded any feelings of pain. The second time, I felt no pain *or* fear. Both times, it was the most alive I've ever been," Catalina said, then narrowed her eyes and smirked. "I won't lie to you, though. What the Master has planned for you, will be far more taxing than what I went through. It will be the most painful experience of your life. Most would pass out, then die from what he is going to do, but you will be wide awake for it all."

Rose's heart began pounding. It was as she had feared. Even still, there was *some* comfort in the back of her mind. "I must say that I'm relieved… I was worried that the process would turn me into a monster, but you seem to have come out of it without transforming."

Catalina's smirk grew uncannily wide as some giggles escaped through the sides of her expanding lips. "Well… for the most part…"

The blood clot stitches around her neck began to unravel as she placed a hand atop her head and grabbed her soaked, jet-black hair. Rose gasped with both hands held up to her mouth as Catalina decapitated herself. She held her disembodied head outward, and let loose her tongue, which twisted and turned inhumanly long; like a snake coiled to strike.

"You can hold my head if you want," Catalina said.

Rose, breathless and wide-eyed, found herself unable to respond and looked back at Hector and Ned for support. Thunder erupted and the sky lit up to reveal a small notion of their deformed faces under the hoods. Rose jumped back and let out a frightened cry as Catalina cackled and the two bodyguards hissed in jovial unison. All around her had become monsters; what would the ceremony do to *her*?

With that thought, the cabin door opened, and the Dark Wizard filled the doorway with a hand outstretched.

"It's time..." he said with such power and bass that Rose's entire body shivered.

"I-I've changed my mind... I-I don't wanna go through with this..." she muttered, taking a step back.

Oneth let out a deep chuckle. "It is natural to fear the dark, but I can assure you that this is for the best."

"N-no! I won't do it! I won't!" Rose shouted as she took another step backward.

Just as the idea entered her mind to flee, Oneth pointed a finger, and the world around her distorted. Thunder clapped overhead, but deeper and slower than normal. Rain striking the deck echoed in her ears as the environment darkened. After a few moments, all she could see was the Dark Wizard standing before her with a hand held out.

"This is the only way..." the deep voice echoed.

"No! I must leave!" Rose cried. Panic struck her even harder upon realizing that her mouth hadn't moved, but the words had come out all the same.

"I'm afraid you have no choice in the matter," Oneth replied, his powerful voice consuming her like a ravenous piranha. "But fear not. You do not yet realize your vital role to play. It will come to you during the ceremony, and then all will be right within your heart."

Rose closed her eyes and strained them, wishing for it all to go away. Upon reopening her eyes, she gasped to find herself inside the cabin. Drake and the Dark Wizard were in the process of strapping her to a swiveled table. The bride-to-be's breathing grew heavier and more erratic as she took in her surroundings. Time had somehow skipped. What had he done to her?

"Please..." Rose muttered, looking at Drake with teary eyes. "Let me go... I don't wanna become a monster..."

Drake cocked his head and then laughed. "Where do you get these silly ideas?"

"I-I saw! I saw the faces of Hector and Ned! And that woman! She ripped her own head off and lived! They are all monsters! Abominations! I don't wanna be like them!"

Drake scowled in the direction of the Dark Wizard, who shrugged. "You'll have to forgive Catalina. She has a flare for the dramatic."

"She'll *pay* for her insolence," Drake said before looking back at his bride-to-be with a cool smile. "Worry not, my dear. I wouldn't want a monster as my queen, would I? This ceremony will make you fertile, and nothing else."

Rose shook her head in desperation. "Please, let me go... we can figure something else out."

"Calm yourself. This attitude is not befitting of a queen," Drake said, his tone harshening. He then looked at Oneth like a clueless king might look upon his advisor. "She has nothing to fear, right?"

"Of course not," the Dark Wizard said, waving him off. "Soon, all she'll have to worry about is giving birth... and might I add, this process will prepare and strengthen her body for the birthing to come. So many die during labor, but after this ceremony, she will be ready to have many more children without risk, if you wish."

"Yes... I think there will be many territories to rule in the future. Multiple heirs would be ideal," the Village Elder said with a smirk. "And just to be sure, you *are* giving her the basic blend of the essence, correct?"

"Indeed," Oneth said as he bit his thumb with such force that it began to bleed. "Let us begin. Unhein cluis diabonis!"

Rose's eyes became large and frightful as the nail of the Dark Wizard's index finger grew long, red, and razor-sharp. She began to sob as Oneth pointed his claw at a spot on her dress, underneath her belly button. He dragged the red nail across, easily ripping the fabric. He then pinpointed a spot just below and repeated the process.

With his unmodified hand, Oneth pulled the rectangular piece of cloth off, to expose Rose's lower belly. It pulsed up and down in rapid succession, mimicking her strained, horrified breaths.

"It's alright, my dear," Drake said, patting her on the shoulder. Rose held her breath. For a fleeting moment, she felt a bittersweet happiness. He was finally showing her some compassion. It wasn't much, but desperation had fully taken hold. "I will buy you a new dress, after this."

With that, Rose's eyes, heart, and stomach sank all at once. As had always been the case, Drake couldn't offer her *true comfort*. Everything had been *material* with him, and now was no exception.

Tears filled her eyes as Drake retrieved a small, rectangular, and wooden block from his pocket. Several tooth-shaped indents marked its top and bottom.

"Bite down on this," Drake said as he shoved the block into her mouth. Rose grunted in confusion between her muffled sobs. "This will be quite painful. I don't want you biting off your tongue."

Before Rose could react, she felt a burning sensation across her lower belly; it had been like a glowing poker dragged across her stomach. She looked down in horror to see that the incision had begun. Blood spilled over the flaps of her fresh, open wound as she let out muffled screams while biting down on the block so hard that it stung her nose and gave her a headache.

Her spine flexed upward as Oneth made the next cut, vertically down and to her left. She could feel the warm, thick liquid rushing down her hip and leg, through the dress. However, that awful sensation paled in comparison to the next incision; this time, downward and on her right side.

Rose began convulsing and thrashing as the Dark Wizard peeled her lower stomach flesh back. Her mind went blank. There was no more fear; no more dread; only *pain*. Raw, strenuous pain.

"Hold her still!" Oneth's voice thundered. "I am cutting into her womb, now. If I hit the wrong organ, we may not get the desired results."

Among the dreadful sensation of air touching her innards for the first time, Rose felt a pair of hands grab her at the shoulders and push down on them. There was little time to comprehend that, however, as the worst pain yet ripped through her midsection. An unsavory squishy noise accompanied by squirting blood sent Rose into a feverish frenzy. She shook her head back and forth, squirming under the pressure of Drake's hands, and letting out muffled screams.

And then, just as suddenly as the procedure had begun, Rose felt an oddly cooling relief, and her posture slouched. Now, there was only tingling lightheadedness. Her eyelids wavered, her ears rang, and the wooden block fell from her slacked jaw.

"She's dying! Hurry!" Amongst the ringing and her fading consciousness, Rose could almost make out the worry in Drake's voice.

"Relax." The Dark Wizard scoffed. "Everything is going according to plan."

Rose tilted her head, and let it fall so that she was looking at Oneth through her hazy eyes. He had gestured his hand toward one of his cauldrons; the one on the right. From it emerged a dark, wobbly liquid that slithered toward her like a snake in the air.

Then, her world went dark, and just before losing consciousness, even over her ringing ears, she heard the powerful voice of Oneth:

Slara teat feinum
Pleite an chroide
Resnu domin altigh
Etus perios doam laitem
Teig dorchae accadh tu
Etus imverte isteam doam nearem
An duino as exuan

CHAPTER 34
PREPARATION TIME

Conrad awoke from his dark essence-infused stupor with a start. He shot to his feet, ready to fight, but the sight of an unconscious Aldous on the floor settled his fiery intentions. He looked down at his steady hands, in awe. How long had it been since he'd felt such calm? Such clarity?

"It appears the exorcism was a success. Good." Hexzar's appearance elicited a gasp from the strategist. His white, skull-like face paint stood out in the darkness like a sore thumb, yet, somehow, only his voice had alerted him. The bald man knelt and then lifted Aldous over his shoulder like a sack of meat. "Come with me."

They passed through the tent flap, crossed the main section of the tent, and then entered through the leftward flap. Inside the room was a bed that was surrounded by various plants in pots. Weathered papers and folded clothes littered the floor.

Hexzar laid Aldous on the bed, then let out a sigh of relief. He looked back at Conrad as if sensing his concern. "He'll be alright, after some rest."

"I'm glad to hear it. I did not know that the exorcism would bring harm to him..."

"Given your obvious disposition for stubbornness, I can see why he may have withheld such information from you," Hexzar replied with a chuckle. "But that is the nature of the occult. A sacrifice must be made.

In this case, neither of us could be sure how strong of a hold the dark essence had on you. So, we offered our own magic as sacrifice."

Conrad raised an eyebrow. "How is it that you are unaffected, then?"

"Aldous took the worst of it, so I could focus on the exorcism. Of course, it wouldn't have been enough to knock me off my feet, but when dealing with the Dark Savior's inordinate power, one can never be too careful."

"Yes, well-" An impossible dryness overwhelmed Conrad's throat. "Water… I need… water."

Hexzar laughed with hints of menace as the strategist let out dry coughs. "You *were* out for a little under a day. It is no surprise that your throat would be dry. I will take you to the pond. You could use some fresh air."

Conrad shielded his eyes from the intense sunlight as he exited the tent. Hexzar led him through the community of tents and shacks until they reached the small pond at the oasis' center. Conrad wasted no time in cupping the water and throwing it into his mouth.

After several scoops and gulps, he let out a satisfied exhale.

"Feeling better?" Hexzar asked with a wide smile.

"In many ways," he replied before wiping his mouth with a fore-arm. "I don't understand why you and Aldous wouldn't let me take a drink before. I could have died of thirst."

"Don't be dramatic, boy," the bald man said with crossed arms. "It was all a part of the process."

"I'll need more of an explanation as to how water deprivation was supposed to help," Conrad said with narrowed eyes.

"It's simple, really. All possessions and addictions are the same by nature. The subject and the possessor become codependent on one another. That manifests itself in certain sensations that make you crave more of whatever the possessor desires; whatever keeps it thriving within you," Hexzar explained.

"The itch…"

"Yes… and did you feel this 'itch' when you became thirsty?"

"Not at all," Conrad said, wide-eyed. "Now, I see. Aldous had me walk through the desert on purpose. He could have taken us straight here, but that long walk was *aiming* to make me thirsty."

Hexzar nodded. "It saved precious time. The exorcisms tend to go easier when something else is on the subject's mind. Thirst and hunger are our usual strategies, and if that doesn't work, *pain* is a good motivator."

Conrad bowed before him and said, "Thank you for curing me."

"It is Aldous you should be thanking. He did the heavy lifting," Hexzar said before looking up and scratching at his face paint. "Though I must say, it fascinated me; that dark essence within you. I shall keep it here to study."

"Just be careful."

"And who do you think you're talking to?" Hexzar said with gaping, frightening eyes.

"R-right… my mistake…" Conrad muttered.

"Your mistake, indeed," he said with a snort. His angry demeanor quickly shifted to inquisition, however. "Aldous clearly sees something in you. I can sense your desire to learn. Yet, during the exorcism, I also felt your ambition to inflict punishment on your enemies. Tell me, which do you desire *more*?"

The question was some sort of test, Conrad thought. Admitting that he wanted to harm others was obviously going to be the wrong choice. Yet, for some reason, he could not bring himself to lie.

"I'm not sure, to be honest," he replied with a sigh. "Before the exorcism, my head felt hazy, but my judgment was absolute. Without question, I was more interested in hurting those who had hurt me, back then. Now… I am unsure."

"I want you to understand something," Hexzar said in a grave tone. "The exorcism won't magically change the way you think or act. What you thought and felt back then was all you, except amplified."

Conrad snorted. "That fact is going to disappoint some people."

The bald man held up a finger and his nostrils flared out. "Only if you choose to disappoint them! That is what I'm trying to tell you. You cannot use the dark essence as an excuse anymore. It's up to *you* to be at your best. Take control of your life back."

"If you demand that I be at my best, then why not teach me to control myself? Show me the ways of the occult," Conrad said.

Hexzar let out a derisive laugh. "I only teach *the best*. You are hundreds of years too early to be requesting my tutelage!"

"What must I do to prove myself?"

The bald man smiled. "If you happen to survive whatever Aldous has gotten you wrapped up in… all you must do is cross the Endless Desert, and find this oasis all on your own; no help from a Wizard allowed. And don't try to cheat your way through: I will know if you do, and you will pay *dearly* for it."

"Sounds like a deal-" Conrad interrupted himself with a gasp. "It has been a day… the enemy will attack the Degenerate seal today. I'm certain of it…"

The strategist began walking away at a hurried pace. Hexzar followed close behind. "And where do you think you're going? I'm not finished talking to you."

"Sorry, but Aldous and I have to leave. Now."

"You will *stay*, as long as required," Hexzar said while placing a firm hand on his shoulder.

Conrad's legs turned to mush, and he collapsed, eating a face full of sand in the process.

"But… we have to… get back…" he muttered, spitting out sand between his words.

"Have patience. Aldous shouldn't need much more than a few hours to recover."

"I'm not sure if we have that long," Conrad said as he got to a knee. "Say, why don't you come along with us? We could use a powerful mage like you. I'm certain you could overwhelm the dark forces."

"I set aside any notion of involving myself with human affairs long ago," Hexzar said while shaking his head.

"But this is the *Dark Savior*, we're talking about. The world could be at stake!"

"If that is how it was meant to play out, then so it shall be," he replied. "I have my role to play in all of this. Perhaps, if you can muster the will to trek through the Endless Desert on your own, you will come to understand."

Conrad smiled as he stood. "Just be ready with some lessons to teach."

~

IN THE COVE hideout obscured by the waves, rocks, and cliffs, the Strangers had gathered around a table, planning out their defense of the Degenerate monolith.

"There are too many things we don't know," Lucia said with crossed arms. "Where will the enemy strike? And when?"

"Since it has finally stopped raining, it would be fair to say that they consider Aldous less of a threat. My wager would be on *today*," Pierce said.

"Awright, then *where* will they attack from?" Alistair asked between bites of his cooked fish on a stick.

"They would be foolish to attack from the north sewer entrance. In such a narrow area, the kraken would slaughter them all," Prince Xviktolo said. The lower half of his body was submerged in the water, while he leaned and rested his arms on rocks protruding around the cove's perimeter.

"That leaves the east and west entrances," said Kabel, who himself was eating some berries.

"Well, don't them degenerates loiter 'round tha eastern pipe? They wouldn't try ta get past them, would they?" Triston chimed in.

"Then, it's settled, lads!" Auber said as he smashed a fist onto the table. "We defend the west pipe!"

"YEH!" Alistair cried, spewing pieces of chewed fish all over the place.

Dhogron shook his head. "I'm not so sure they'll take that route."

"What makes you say that?" Dalton asked.

"We know that the enemy has Brice on their side, and he assimilated Amis…" the trickster Wizard trailed off with a frown. "Amis would know the west pipe better than anyone, and therefore, so would Brice."

"Oh, that's right," Franco said, raising a finger. "We first met him by happenstance, when he exited that drain."

"What's in tha west entrance, then? Can't be worse than a kraken!" Alistair said.

"Olius, the Wizard King of the Endoshire monolith, likes to keep 'pets'. The kraken is one such pet, but another, which he once kept for his amusement, has grown into a problem of sorts…" Dhogron said. "You see, Olius kept a pet swine down in the sewers. Because it consumed so much sewage, this swine changed into a grotesque monster before reproducing. Now, there are many of these black hogs running around, spewing toxins and goring those who dare to enter their domain. Each is roughly the size of a horse."

"I've heard about the swine of Endoshire before, but they always seemed like fool's tales to me," Satara said, sitting at the table across from Auber and Ebbie, who were ogling her.

"I can assure you; they are quite real," Dhogron said as a dark portal opened up in the depths of the cave. All of the Strangers looked back with hands at the ready to draw weapons, but they collectively sighed in relief to find Conrad and an exhausted Aldous emerging from the vortex.

"Just in time, lads!" Alistair said with a cheeky grin.

"There is no time to waste..." Aldous muttered with heavy breaths, approaching the group at an unbalanced, yet hurried pace. "The rain has stopped; we must hurry to intercept them!"

"I don't think they will make a move until tonight," Dhogron said.

"And why is that?" Aldous asked with a cocked head.

"It's because Brice has Amis' memories, isn't it?" Conrad asked to some nods in the room. "Amis must have known something about the sewers that we don't."

"That is correct. We all know about the kraken at the north drain, but there are also the mutated swine roaming the western pipes. Amis used to go down there and feed them once in a while, so they wouldn't surface in the streets," Dhogron said.

"Oh, right! Them boggin degenerates will leave their spot in tha east sewer drain at night! That's when it'll be easiest fer them ta strike!" Triston said.

"And what of the Guardian? Does it not guard the eastern entrance?" Aldous asked, now leaning up against a wall.

Dhogron shook his head. "The beast stays close to its master and the seal unless otherwise ordered."

"Hold on," Rolf said, drawing the eyes of all around. "If da enemy's ship is right near da northern entrance, and dey have dese all-powerful soldiers at deir disposal, wouldn't dey still try and press drough da kraken?"

"In such a tight space as the pipes, I don't see how they could break through. She could unleash her poison on them, like before. Except this time, there would be nowhere to escape to," Xviktolo chimed in while stepping out of the water. "But I can patrol the docks if it would make you all feel better. Perhaps Aldous could accompany me. His command over the water would come in handy."

"I believe we'll need Aldous wherever the enemy decides to strike the hardest," Kabel said, looking around the room. "Are we in agreement that they will send most of their forces to the east sewer entrance?"

"It makes the most sense," Conrad said while nodding. "Not only because of the degenerates but the inconvenience of traveling through a packed city with hundreds at their command in the daytime. It would cause a huge commotion, and hardly be worth the effort. If they are going to strike at night, why not the entrance that will have been abandoned by the degenerates, by then?"

"The degenerates will not come out all at once," Lucia added. "Drake's team may lie in wait somewhere near the sewer drain."

"There are fields to the north of the river, but if there are so many of them as you say, I don't think they could hide," Najih said while sharpening his scimitar with a rock.

"That leaves the beginnings of the woods, to the south, then," Aldous said, looking at Dhogron, Joel, Auber, and Franco. "We used those same woods as cover, a few days ago."

"They'd have to cross the bridge over the river to reach the woods," Satara said while putting her feet up on the table. Franco narrowed his eyes. "Perhaps we should intercept the enemy there."

Joel tugged at Alistair with urgency. An idea had come to him; one that had been creeping up in his mind since a couple of nights back.

"What is it, lad?"

The mute made hand signals in response.

"Oi! Everyone listen up! Joel gots a plan!" the big redhead shouted.

With a deep breath, Joel laid out his idea for Alistair to translate. One that he hoped would land their enemy a massive defeat.

When the planning was all said and done, the Strangers agreed to split up, with the leaders taking command of their own groups as they had two nights before. This time, however, they were split into three.

Captain Auber and his crew were set to team up with Prince Xviktolo at the northern sewer entrance, to ensure that the dark forces didn't attempt a surprise attack in the kraken's domain.

Kabel was to lead Pierce, Rolf, Dhogron, Satara, and Najih to the west drain of the sewers. Their focus would be to lay traps and strike with range, should the enemy attempt to infiltrate from there. Upon finding out that he would be in the same group as Joel, Giles asked to accompany Kabel's team instead; and the stocky man reluctantly agreed.

Dalton and Aldous would combine their forces, leading Joel, Conrad, Lucia, Alistair, and Triston in their attempts to defend the eastern sewer entrance.

Finally, Mirabel would stay behind and tend to a pregnant Greta.

"Hold up!" Alistair said, halting any conclusion to the plans. "What about *inside* the sewers? Methinks tha enemy is gonna have a map, so they'll know where they are goin'! What about us?"

"Ideally, they will never make it to the innards of the sewers, but…" Dhogron trailed off as he removed his turban to reveal a shiny, bald head. He then retrieved a folded piece of paper. As he unfolded it, a picture magically appeared to reveal a map. "You have a point. I don't like the idea of more sewer maps existing, but for tonight, I make an exception. Give me some time to study this, and I shall make a copy for each team."

Joel was tempted to ask if he could redraw the maps himself, but there was no time for that. After agreeing on their plans, the Strangers disbanded to prepare for the battles ahead.

～

As the crowd in the cave cleared, Conrad noticed Kabel approaching. He hadn't forgotten about his attack two nights prior and remained on guard.

Kabel put his hands up and smiled. "Easy, now. I come in peace."

"My swollen face begs to differ."

The stocky man let out a chuckle and rubbed the back of his head. He looked back to his wife, Mira. She returned him a nod. "I feel real bad about bashing yer face in, that night. So, I got you a lil' something. Come with me."

Conrad followed him into the bowels of the cave, where he took a left into one of the rooms. Various sheathed weapons, clothing, and armor lay on the floor and stacked against the walls. Kabel leaned over and grabbed a thin, sheathed blade, and then tossed it to Conrad. The strategist unsheathed it and gazed upon its beauty.

"Dalton tells me yer fond of the rapier. Thankfully, you can find just about any kind of weapon in the shops, 'round here. I hope that it is to your liking," Kabel said as Conrad whisked the blade through the air, gently. It was certainly nicer than his previous blade. The hand guard provided all-encompassing protection with wiring in a beautiful, if chaotic, pattern.

"This will do nicely. Thank you."

"So, we are all even? No grudges?"

Conrad smiled. "As long as you don't give me a reason to hold one…"

"Right… well, I'll leave you to play with yer new toy. Best to stay focused for tonight," Kabel said, then turned and waved as he walked out the door.

The strategist was ready to follow, but Dalton walked into the room before he could leave. He eyed Conrad's new sword.

"You like it? We figured it'd be a little more useful than a dagger."

Conrad snorted. "If only you knew how many times that dagger has saved me. But yes, this will serve me well, tonight. Thank you."

"And how are you feeling? Is your head all clear?" Dalton asked.

"Clearer than it has been in some time," he replied with a smile.

"Good… we'll need you in top form tonight." Dalton said no more, but he continued to stare at his blade. Conrad could tell that there was more on his mind.

"Is there something else?"

"You came into direct contact with the Dark Wizard, right?"

"More times than I'd like, in fact," Conrad said.

"Mayhap this is a question for Aldous, but I thought I'd ask you, too," Dalton said, then looked down. He'd never seen the warrior in such an odd demeanor. It was almost meek, but there was anger mixed in, too. "Have you seen him shapeshift, in the past?"

"Yes, that was how he tricked me into leaving for Bosfueras, back then. He disguised himself as a member of the Wizard's Council," Conrad replied, leaning in. "Why do you ask?"

Dalton's expression turned grave. "Do you think that… he'd be able to change himself into someone he couldn't have ever possibly known or seen? Someone dead?"

"I don't know that he could pull off such a feat…" Conrad trailed off, looking up in thought. "It sounds something more along the lines of Brice's ability."

Dalton smirked and then shook his head. "Not possible, in this case. She has been dead since long before Brice took in the dark essence."

Conrad raised an eyebrow. "And who is the 'she' you are referring to?"

The warrior's eyes widened and his mouth fell agape, but he quickly shifted to his usual, confident smile. "Nobody that you know, don't worry."

"Fair enough. The truth is that we don't know the full capabilities of this Dark Wizard. You may be better off asking Aldous. He may have a few ideas."

"Yeh, you're probably right…" Dalton said as he turned to leave. However, before exiting the room, he stopped and looked over his shoulder. "By the way, now that you got that vile substance out of your system, I hope that you will make amends with Lucia. I can tell when somethin's bothering her, whether she wants to admit it or not."

"And who says the dark essence had anything to do with our issues?"

"It sure sounded like it," he said, turning to face him. "I was always pushing for the two of you to become entangled because it seemed you were both happiest when with one another. That was *before* Bosfueras, though. Things feel different, now."

Conrad narrowed his eyes. "Are *you* trying to give me courtship advice, Dalton?"

Both chuckled for a moment before Dalton cleared his throat. "Ridiculous, I know. But once upon a time, I was quite close to settling down. I have always regretted not being able to."

"We will work things out after tonight," Conrad said with a nod.

"See to it that you do. She and I have had quite a string of bad luck and disappointments over the years. *Don't* be the next disappointment."

With that, Dalton left the room for Conrad to contemplate.

FURTHER INTO THE HIDEOUT, Joel and Aldous sat next to one another on some bedding. The old Wizard leaned his back against the wall to rest. However, the mute insisted on signing to him.

"Oh, I'll be alright, m'boy. Just need to rest up a bit for the battle to come."

Joel made more hand signals, asking about Conrad and the exorcism.

"Thankfully, it was a success. That dark essence-majigger took a lot out of me, though," he said before choking out a laugh.

With more sign language, Joel conveyed his guilt for Giles' eye injury. He told Aldous of his worries, namely that he might accidentally kill someone tonight in an overzealous attempt to prove his worth to the team.

"Yes, well, against our dark essence-dependent opponents, you can cut into them with confidence that it will not be a killing blow," Aldous said as Pierce walked into the room. Greta followed close behind.

"What's this about 'killing'?" Pierce asked, looking to Joel. "Have you finally called an end to your self-destructive vow of peace?"

The mute shook his head, much to Pierce's visible chagrin. It was difficult to explain. Despite the wretched actions of Drake and his team, he held no desire to kill them. However, he did wish to *hurt them*, and Aldous had made a good point. With the regenerative capabilities of Angus and the others, Joel could go all-out without fear of killing them.

"Leave 'im alone! There's nothin' wrong with peace!" Greta said, smacking the dagger-eyed man in the arm, then putting hands to hips. "I think what he's doin' is honorable."

"It isn't realistic, especially not against the fiends who we are opposing," Pierce argued.

Joel made hand signals in response.

"Well, he is adamant about 'hurting' our enemies..." Aldous trailed off with a raised eyebrow. "That would be a first."

"Ye mean he hasn't even been tryin' to *hurt* anyone, so far?" Greta asked.

"That was certainly the case when we fought back in Thironas," Pierce said with a smirk. "It was frustrating... for *the other*, anyway."

"You *fought* him? What kinda friend are you?" Greta asked with a frown. "Joel has been nothin' but kind to us! I think ye owe him an apology!"

"It's not that simple..." the dagger-eyed man trailed off with a defeated chuckle.

"Regardless, I do hope that someday we can live in a world where Joel's attitude is the norm. It is quite admirable," Aldous said, smiling at his friend.

⁓

Out by the cove, before most of the Strangers, Dhogron showed off some of his items. They were normally meant to be distractions, but due to how outnumbered they were, the trickster Wizard was confident they would come in handy.

"This here is itching powder," Dhogron said, holding up one of the smaller sacks. "I think that the name speaks for itself."

"I say we try it out on Auber, just to be sure," Dalton said to some laughs.

"Oh, come on! Why do ye always gotta single me out?" the captain whined.

"Don' get down, Cap'n! They're just jealous of ya!" Alistair said with a raised fist.

"Anyway…" Dhogron said, clearing his throat. He retrieved another bag and pulled out a little white pellet.

"Smoke pellets? I've used 'em before. They can certainly come in handy," Dalton said.

"Not quite, my friend," he replied with a devious smile. "I call these *haze pellets*. They do provide a smokescreen, but more importantly, they will leave the enemy preoccupied."

"So… just like a smokescreen, then," Lucia said with an eye roll.

"Well, I crushed up some feather mushrooms and added them to the mix, you see… so, it makes the target hallucinate," Dhogron said with a chuckle. "It is quite nice, actually. But most importantly, it will pacify whoever breathes it in. Be careful while using this one."

"Yes, do be careful, sir," Franco said, eyeing his captain.

"Why're ye givin' *me* that look? I'm always careful!" Auber shot back.

"Now, these here are my own invention," Dhogron said as he reached into a different bag and retrieved a piece of paper that had been crumpled up into a ball.

"So what? It's just paper!" Triston said with crossed arms.

"It's *never* just paper, with him," Rolf added.

"How right you are! I call this my Supreme Paper Surprise! Just throw one in the direction of your enemies…" Dhogron trailed off before tossing the paper ball onto the table where Satara and the pirates sat. "And you get a spectacular surprise!"

The ball exploded into a small pack of paper spiders. Everyone at the table got up to avoid them, except Auber, who fell over in his chair as one scurried up his arm. Most of the group laughed at the display, and after a few moments, the spiders ripped themselves up into little shreds.

"*This* is your idea of useful?" Satara grimaced at him while gripping the back of her chair.

Dhogron held a finger up and let loose a nervous smile. "To be fair, there are several things that it can do. That's why it is *a surprise*. Be glad it wasn't the most annoying of all. I call it *Death by a Thousand Paper Cuts*! Truly, the least comfortable of all my pranks."

"Hold on, are ya sayin' we can use these Supreme Paper Surprises, even though we ain't mages?" Alistair asked with a wide, giddy smile.

"That's right. I infused my magic into them, so they will work in anyone's hands," the trickster Wizard said.

"Anything else?" Satara asked, her face resembling stone.

"Well…" Dhogron muttered, searching through his things. He then retrieved a net and held it up before the group.

"Is there anything special about it?" Franco asked while dusting himself off.

"Erm… no, it's a regular net," he replied, red-cheeked. The group erupted into an odd combination of groans and jeers.

"Well, a net can be useful, too! For fishin'…" Ebbie trailed off, then looked to Prince Xviktolo. "No offense intended."

The marinian shrugged. "I eat fish, too."

"An' let's not ferget the genius of the beige berries!" Captain Auber said with muffled laughs. "Our enemies won't know what hit 'em! They'll be messin' thar pants in no time!"

"How charming," Satara said, eyeing Dhogron with obvious judgment.

"I'm sure we'll find uses for the items," Kabel said with a smile. "For now, everyone should gather their weapons and armor, if they have it. Tonight's battle might make the skirmish at the docks look like child's play."

With that, the Strangers dispersed and began gathering their items while mentally preparing themselves for the hardships ahead.

CHAPTER 35
IN THE EVENT OF MY DEATH

Drake Danvers exited his bedroom with a satisfied smile and strolled into the dining area. Awaiting him at the table, picking at food, was Angus.

The giant stood and bowed before his superior. Normally, Drake would have maintained a commanding presence, but he was in too good a mood to hide his grin, and instead, he beckoned Angus to sit with him.

"I trust the ceremony went well?" Angus asked.

"Yes, I think it went about as well as it could have. Somehow, I can tell that she has finally become fertile. This time, I shall have my heir," Drake said with a grand, spread-out gesture of the arms.

"Congratulations, sir," Angus said, uncomfortably shifting in his chair. "But if I may ask, is Edith not your rightful heir?"

"You needn't worry about your future, my friend," Drake said with a crass chuckle. "You and my daughter will be given a territory to rule over when all is said and done."

"And I appreciate that. But that leaves the obvious question: When and how will Edith assimilate Greed? It is the only way to cure what ails her, is it not?"

"Have patience. Right now, the Wizard's Council has their eyes fixed upon Greed and Mt. Couture. Once we begin to stretch their resources thin, however..."

"With all of the monsters we must face tonight, I worry that I might die before then. Do I have your promise that you will take care of her, in the event of my death?" Angus asked.

Drake cocked his head. What a silly question, he thought. Couldn't Angus tell that he had practically discarded Edith? Why else would he have sacrificed her to Greed back at the mountain? Why else would he be seeking a new heir? She had long since become damaged goods.

"Of course." It took enormous restraint for him to stifle a laugh.

"I thank you for respecting my last wishes," Angus said.

In that moment, Drake was reminded of something important that he needed to do, and it involved the possible event of *his* death. He had manipulated the purchase of black gold coins to look like there was a price increase; something the Dark Wizard would need a businessman like him to handle. But what if his partner didn't understand that value?

The idea of a betrayal hadn't been lost on Drake. Oneth had been secretive about many of his dealings, happenings, and ideas, of late. It felt as though he had gained the majority of control in their partnership. In the event of such a betrayal, he wanted to ensure that it would be something the Dark Wizard regretted dearly.

Drake had always been skilled at thinking ahead. So much that he had gathered something in Bosfueras one day, on a visit. Something that the Dark Wizard did *not* want in enemy hands. He had originally thought to keep it for himself, just in case he ever wanted to be the betrayer in their collaboration. However, recently, Drake had committed himself fully to the plan: He would either succeed and assimilate the *inordinate power* of Degenerate, or fail and die trying. There was no turning back, now.

"Ah, that reminds me. I have an important matter to attend to. Excuse me for a moment. I'll be right back," Drake said while pushing in his chair. Angus merely nodded in reply.

The Village Elder entered his room. Rose lay in bed with the covers up; turned over and facing away from him.

"Are you awake, my dear?" he whispered.

"Yes."

"How are you feeling?" Drake asked. Rose let out an exhausted breath as if to answer the question. "I know it has been a tiring day for you, with the ceremony, and our conception. Get some rest…"

"I think it worked…"

"You mean the ceremony?" Drake asked in a jovial tone. "Was there ever any doubt?"

"Yes… I suppose you were correct all along… I feel… different… I think there is a bump in my belly, already… should that be happening?" she asked.

"I wonder if your pregnancy will be quicker than normal due to the ceremony…" Drake said as he began rummaging through one of his drawers in the corner of the room. "I will ask Oneth about it when he arrives."

Drake retrieved an envelope that made light clicking noises as he lifted it; like marbles banging together. He walked over to his desk, picked up a quill, and began writing on a fresh piece of paper. After some time, he stopped writing, folded up the piece of paper, and placed it into the envelope.

Upon the envelope, and in large print, he wrote:

CONRAD MERCER
FAIWELL SETTLEMENT, FEDERLAND

After sealing the letter with his personal insignia, Drake walked up to his bed and kissed Rose on the top of her head. He had grown accustomed to her flinching whenever he got close, but much to his shock and delight, there was no such recoil from her this time.

"Rest easy, my dear. Soon, we shall rule the masses," he said while exiting the bedroom.

Back in the dining room, Drake walked over to one of Rose's servants, who straightened out both her posture and face, like a soldier would near their captain. Then, she bowed before him.

"How can I help you, Master?"

Drake handed her the sealed envelope. "Do you know where the city mail carrier is?"

"Yes, sir."

"See to it that this piece of mail reaches them, on the double," he said, then handed her some Sigrian notes. "This should more than cover the charge."

"Right away, m'lord!" she replied with a timid nod and then exited his quarters with a hop in her step.

A smug smile grew on Drake's face; one that he didn't often let slip. If the Dark Wizard had the gall to betray him, then he would pay dearly for it. If, on the other hand, he had been truthful and planned to bestow him with the incomprehensible power of Degenerate, then he would retrieve the letter upon returning safely to Faiwell. It was a simple, yet effective strategy to ensure that his presence would be felt, dead or alive.

"I wonder who that was for..." Angus muttered while chewing loudly on some grapes.

The arrogant smirk on Drake changed, as it so often had, to a finessed smile. He let out a small breath, then said, "Oh, just an update for the Village Elders, back home. I am here under the guise of a diplomatic mission, after all. The poor fools think that Endoshire's businessmen or even the lord care about trading with them. Only men who have never ventured far outside of their quaint little village could believe such a thing."

"Yes... it seems to me like the idea of Endoshire as a whole is that *they* come *here* to bring their services, and not the other way around," Angus replied with a scoff. "Though I doubt the lord of this city has much use for mining."

"How right you are," Drake said as he took a seat across the table. "But they needn't worry. I shall bring them a new enterprise, soon enough."

"Aren't you worried about how they will react to indentured servitude? Could Federland not amend their laws to forbid it, just like slavery?" Angus asked.

"By the end of tonight, my friend, that will be of no concern to me. I will have assimilated Degenerate, gaining his inordinate power, and Federland will be mine to take. Should they have a problem with indentured servitude, *I will make it legal.*"

"Ah, I was unaware that you had Federland in your sights to rule over. Pardon my ignorance, but I had thought you despised the country," the giant said.

"Oh, but I do," Drake said with a menacing grin that was offset by properly folded hands. "That is precisely why I wish to mold it to my vision. I will transform it to my liking, erasing or enslaving the worms beneath who try to resist. For it is my will, and I don't just hate them; I *resent* them. I won't allow them to slip quietly into the black gold's trance, no! They will fight, and not me, but each other! They will become degenerates, and when all are begging for an answer to the senseless violence; the horrid living conditions; the sheer terror and helplessness of it all... I will give it to them: my answer. And in the end, they will thank me! Bow before me! Sing my praises in poems and heroic stories, which shall become anthems for my new kingdom-neigh! *My empire.*"

A loud creak drew Drake and Angus' attention. They looked to the main door to find Sampson and a couple of his slaves approaching. He carried a sheathed sword in both hands as if it were some sort of holy relic.

"You sounded awfully excited as I was walkin' in!" the slaver said as he placed the blade on the table. "What did I miss?"

"Oh, not much..." Drake said. He pulled at the sheath, gently; unveiling a dark blue blade. He let loose a smirk in the direction of Angus, whose stone face did its best to smile back. "Just thinking about my vision for the new world."

"Yeh, well, I've been thinkin' about somethin' else: food! I'm starved! Ye got anythin' besides grapes lyin' 'round here?" Sampson asked.

Drake glanced back at Rose's other servant, who stood in the corner of the room with hands behind her back. "Fetch him something to eat, would you?"

"Right away, m'lord!" she replied with a bow, then exited at a hurried pace.

Sampson grinned. "I trust *the help* has been good? I must say that I hope one of 'em messes up, so they gotta come back to work fer me. There is a certain pleasure to inflicting punishment on the runners, y'know what I mean?"

"That will be up to Rose," Drake said, trying to hold back a frown. Sampson had a habit of spewing bile for words, he thought. Punishment for failure was understandable, but *hoping* for failure was foolish, in his mind. "As long as she is happy with their services, I am happy to have them around."

"Good, good..." he muttered, wringing his hands. "Now, how about this sword? I assume ye asked me to bring it because there is somethin' special about it?"

"In a word? Yes. That sword is made of a special metal called luxmortite. It is far stronger than iron or steel, and is therefore excellent in battle," Drake said, looking over the blade with curious eyes. "Ages ago, blades like this one were wielded by an ancient civilization. It holds many secrets that have been lost to us for thousands of years."

"I see... and are you looking to study it? So that you can make more?" Sampson asked.

"Not quite. It was the Dark Wizard who requested you bring it," Drake said, nodding toward the giant across from him. "Angus' bone can rival the luxmortite, so I have no use for it."

The servant woman entered the room with an entire platter of food. Roasted chicken was surrounded by various fruits and vegetables. Sampson eyed the servant with cruelty in his smile as she placed the tray on the table, bowed, and then returned to the corner of the room.

For a little while, Drake, Angus, and Sampson enjoyed the food on offer. Then, they spoke on a few other topics concerning the city, until the Dark Wizard arrived with Barret, Catalina, and Brice in tow. Soon after, Mur'del entered from the grand window that overlooked the streets. Hector and Ned appeared out of the shadows of the room to complete the menacing group. All major players in the fellowship to destroy Degenerate's seal had gathered at one table.

"Here's the sword ye wanted," Sampson said, handing the sheathed blade to Oneth.

"Excellent…" he said, a grand smile brimming from beneath his hood. Catalina pulled up a chair for him to sit in.

"I must ask, why do you need such a blade when Angus can make something just as strong?" Drake said.

Oneth remained quiet for a moment, looking over the sword with intense focus. Without looking up, he replied, "I don't need it for anything. There is someone that I would like to give it to."

Drake sighed. "You cannot possibly be talking about *him*, can you?"

A tense silence filled the room until Sampson cleared his throat. "Awright, I'll ask, then. Who are we talkin' about, here?"

"You need not worry yourself," the Dark Wizard said with a low-pitched chuckle. "We should instead focus on tonight's plan."

"I think they deserve to know. After all, it's why we're all here," Drake said with crossed arms. He searched Oneth's posture for any trace of anger or bother, but couldn't find it. Lately, it had seemed like he was an impenetrable wall. By comparison, they were getting into heated debates as recently as a few days ago. What had changed?

"Know what, exactly?" Angus asked.

"The reason you have all been assembled here, as a team," he replied while eyeing Oneth, who remained emotionless. "You see, we were not the first ones seeking to break the seven seals. Our Wizard friend once allied himself with another group who called themselves *the Masons*."

"What went wrong, then?" Brice asked.

"I have never been told, exactly, but after having met their leader, I can take a good guess," Drake said, now smiling at Oneth. "Considering what an *unstable man* he was, I can only assume that his group was much the same."

"You forgot to mention that I had to save you from him," the Dark Wizard said with an amused chuckle. "I suppose he simply wasn't lulled into a false sense of security by your charm, as so many others have been in the past."

Drake scoffed. "The point is, these Masons are a group of unreliable radicals. That is why we, the better and more focused team, are here; on the cusp of victory."

"Don't get ahead of yourself," Oneth shot back, pointing at him with a weighty finger. "There is still a monumental task at hand. It is very much a possibility that we fail, and in that event, I feel that we should work with the Masons. Handing the sword over will be a good first step in reestablishing a partnership."

"What nonsense." Drake shook his head. "They may wish to break the seals, too, but their end goal is far different from ours. Eventually, we will find ourselves in conflict with them."

"Let us focus on the here and now," Angus chimed in, looking to the Dark Wizard. "It is as you say: We have a monumental task at hand. How might we best accomplish our mission?"

"Very well," Oneth replied while putting the luxmortite sword down. "Tonight, our plans are quite simple. Sampson, you and your men are to infiltrate from the north sewer entrance. The kraken will surely attack in response, and from there you must lure it out to sea. There, Barret will assist in distracting the beast. It seems to have trouble with aerial opponents. After that, some of your men will be able to infiltrate the sewer."

"I never woulda guessed that there was a monster livin' in the sewers. I suppose there were always rumors, but I thought it was just peasants makin' conversation," Sampson said with a laugh. "But rest assured, we will make it in. Tonight, there are even more Sigrian knights at my disposal."

"Excellent," Oneth said before turning his gaze to Mur'del. "You shall accompany Hector and I to the western sewer entrance. We will be sailing to and anchoring near there for ease of access."

Mur'del nodded. "Am I to patrol the skies upon our arrival?"

"Correct," he replied and then cast eyes on Angus. "And I believe you know your role by now. Lead Brice, Catalina, Ned, and our largest group to the woods at the southeast end of the city. After the degenerates leave the east sewer entrance, lead the charge. If you time it right, your group should be unopposed until nearing the monolith."

"Hold on," Drake said, raising an index finger. "You are using both Ned *and* Hector? I'll be left defenseless!"

"Against Aldous and his little team?" Oneth asked with a deep, dark scoff. "They will be too busy scrambling to the defense of the sewers. Their numbers are far too low for *you* to be worrying about them."

"Point taken, yet still, your plan lacks subtlety," he said, to which the Dark Wizard cocked his head. "This is far too simple, especially for a group who managed to figure out our complex scheme a couple of nights ago. They will anticipate your strategy and put a stop to it."

"On the contrary, simplicity is exactly what our plans have been lacking, of late," Oneth said. Drake's brow twitched. "Your plans *sounded* great, but they failed to take into account unideal conditions in execution. That is why our enemies escaped with their lives. Instead, we can brute force our way through, expecting maximum resistance."

Drake was disheartened to see all around the table nodding along. He cleared his throat in a fruitless attempt to stifle the frustration. "Very well… but I still feel that I should accompany one of the groups. Perhaps I could come up with a backup plan, in case things go wrong."

Oneth shook his head. "That would be ill-advised with degenerates, monsters, and the enemies opposing us. You're our *invaluable businessman*, after all, and we cannot afford to lose you."

The Village Elder opened his mouth to speak, but he stopped himself as the creak of the front door caught his ear. Rose's servant had returned from delivering his piece of mail. He smiled as she crept into the corner of the room.

"I have always been hands-on with my business ventures. You must forgive me for my intrusions…" Drake said.

"I can understand that much. But we are trying something different tonight. All you have to do is stay here and take care of your future queen. By now, I'm sure that you both have a child on the way…"

"About that. Would the ceremony cause her pregnancy to progress quicker? She can already feel a lump in her belly."

"I cannot say for certain, but it wouldn't surprise me. After all, the dark essence tends to heal what ails us. It may see the long length of pregnancy as an ailment," said Oneth.

"Alright, I will keep an eye on her…" Drake muttered, sinking into both his chair and his thoughts.

"As for the rest of you…" Oneth trailed off while taking a couple of maps out from under his robe. "I have forged two copies of the sewer map. I shall hold onto the original for my group."

The Dark Wizard passed the copies out to Angus and Sampson, then said, "Use them well. And should you run into the monolith, *destroy it with extreme prejudice.*"

All within the conspiring group let out a cheer, save for Drake.

He had every reason to be satisfied, but something about his lack of inclusion in the plans filled him with worry. It felt as if he was being phased out. Still, if the team were to succeed, and he was to assimilate Degenerate, then all would be well. However, there remained a possibility in his mind that it all might fall through. That was why, in the case of his death, Drake had delivered mail that would drive a spike into the Dark Wizard and his plans. If he couldn't bring success to the team, then *no one would.*

CHAPTER 36
UNEXPECTED ENEMY

Joel watched the streets from behind a deteriorating shack of the slums as dusk set in. Tonight, he wore a dark, protective coating of gambeson over his usual tunic. Kabel had initially purchased it for himself, but he found that it was a little tight around his barreled chest. Even though there was no need to hide their identities, he and all of the Strangers had elected to wear their decorative masks for the battle yet to unfold.

As the sun set, field peasants were rushing home, in a hurry to avoid the impending threat of the degenerates. The mute had paired up with Aldous, Alistair, and Triston. To his chagrin, they couldn't seem to keep their voices down. Even though Aldous had been worn out from Conrad's exorcism, he had gotten to chatting with Triston, and the elder MacRae's bombastic nature had become contagious.

Alistair, meanwhile, kept making small talk, and Joel could tell there was something more on his mind. After a while, he gave up on keeping quiet and signed to ask if something was troubling him.

"Well, it's funny you should ask..." Alistair said, twiddling his thumbs. Joel would have let out a scoff if he could have. "Y'see, I just don' get it..."

He retrieved his wind Rune, its wavy, engraved lines emitting a white glow that was similar to moonlight. Joel let out a silent gasp and then held his hands out. The intense knockback from a few nights ago was still fresh in his mind.

"Oh, don' worry, lad. It won't be lettin' out any bursts of air unless I tell it to!" Alistair said with a loud laugh, followed quickly by a thunderous slap to the mute's shoulder. "But y'see, tha real problem is that I can't seem ta control *which way* tha wind goes!"

Joel narrowed his eyes. He was well aware of Alistair's lack of control. Yet still, he couldn't help but indulge. He signed back to him, asking if he had used his emotions as he'd recommended a few days back.

"Yeh, that's tha confusin' part!" Alistair said while looking at the glowing stone. "That one time I got it ta work, I was arguin' with Triston 'bout comin' ta Giles' aid. So, I've had me big brother's doubts in mind ever since then… but it keeps blowin' up in me face!"

Giles, Joel thought with a silent groan. Even just hearing his name brought a pit to his stomach. Already, he could tell that the one-eyed man was trying to convince others that he could not be relied upon in combat. He only needed to point at his missing right eye as an example.

Yet, those bitter thoughts brought with them a realization about the Rune: It hadn't been Alistair's desire to prove Triston wrong that got it working, but his will to save Giles. The mute quickly signed his revelation to the big man.

Alistair's eyes widened. "I think ya done gone an' solved tha mystery, lad! Those damned dirty dogs will never know what hit 'em!"

With a half-hearted smile, Joel shrugged. Aldous or Pierce probably could have told him the same thing, having quickly mastered their respective Runes, but he was happy just to help. At least Alistair still valued him as a teammate. He was not so sure about the others, but one thing he was sure of was that tonight, he would prove the doubters wrong with a display so dazzling that its mere description would shut Giles up about his supposed shortcomings. Tonight, he would prove his worth to the Strangers.

～

FURTHER DOWN THE line of shacks, Dalton sat in the shadows while Conrad waved his new rapier around with exaggerated wrist motions, and Lucia adjusted her shoulder pads while keeping her eyes peeled on the streets.

Dalton cleared his throat. "I'm gonna go scout further down the street. I'll be back."

With swift strides, the warrior left the pair alone. After a few moments, Lucia let out a long exhale through her nose.

"I suppose we should talk," she said, looking over her shoulder.

"What about?" Conrad asked in a jovial tone. He wore a thick, leather vest over a white long-sleeved shirt.

Lucia narrowed her eyes under the lunar-inspired mask. "If you'd rather not speak, you need only say so…"

"We can talk after defending the monolith. Our entanglement seems a bit trivial compared to the fate of this city, and perhaps the world. Wouldn't you agree?" Conrad replied while continuing to whisk his rapier through the air.

"Tell me this much," she said, now fully turned around. "Do you feel better after the exorcism?"

"Yes. My head has not been this clear in some time," he replied with a playful snort. "Although, I may end up missing the regeneration factor."

"You'll just have to stop being reckless, then," Lucia said with an eye roll.

"Simply being here tonight is reckless."

"All I'm saying is that it was worth the pain of having you exorcised. I can already tell you are… *yourself* once more."

"Ah, but you weren't there to hear the Exorcist's full assessment," Conrad said, wagging a finger. "According to him, the dark essence only heightened what was already within. Like I've said many times before, it didn't change me. I have *been* myself this entire time. The only difference now is that I find it easier to restrain myself."

"That is still a part of who you are. We all have urges, and they might be bad, but it is our conscience that guides us in the end. You did not have it back when the dark essence was controlling you," Lucia argued.

Conrad shook his head and laughed. "I think you've created this idealized version of me in your head. My *experiences* have shaped me, not the dark essence. Even now, if I had Brice, Drake, or any of those people's necks under a guillotine, I'd pull the lever without hesitation… in fact, that is too easy of a death for the likes of them. I would want them to feel a bit of the pain that their selfish actions have inflicted on others."

"So, maybe you're a little self-righteous," she said with a warm smile. "Deep down, maybe we all are. That doesn't mean I'm ready to abandon you."

"That's not the issue. The problem is that back when Brice was impersonating Amis, you assumed the worst of me. You even used yourself as a decoy so I could be taken down. Yet, if I had not acted, many of us would be dead right now."

"Are you looking for an apology?" Lucia asked with impatience growing in her voice.

"No. Let's just see how things go, tonight. I will trust you on the battlefield, as I always have. The question is: Will you trust me?"

Lucia turned back around to watch over the streets. She then let out a gasp, prompting Conrad to peer over her shoulder.

Angus, Brice, Catalina, and Ned led hundreds of Bosfueras townsfolk, slaves, and knights over the river bridge. As predicted, it seemed the enemy was focusing most of its forces on the eastern sewer pipe. Half of the conditions for Joel's plan had come true: The dark forces had arrived before the degenerates could emerge from the sewer depths. The next crucial step of his strategy would depend on their positioning and a little bit of luck in the timing.

Kabel led Rolf, Pierce, Dhogron, Satara, Najih, and Giles through the western slums of the city. Many peasants ran past them, often pushing, shoving, or stumbling as they did. It was hard to blame them, for soon, the degenerates would roam the streets.

"Nightfall approaches," Dhogron said while putting his paper mask on. "Let us hope we were correct in predicting their strategies."

"Your guess cannot be any more costly than mine was," Satara said, then raised an eyebrow. "By the way, I meant to ask earlier… why are you all wearing masks?"

"We *are* the Strangers, after all," Kabel said with a laugh. He wore a dark brigandine over his tunic, with a shield strapped to his back, a bow tied to one hip, and an arming sword sheathed at the other.

"Oh, right. You ended up taking that name. You *do* know I said that to mock you, right?" she asked while wrapping her silk mouth covering around the bottom half of her face.

"What can I say? We liked it," he replied.

"Well, besides Alistair and Triston," Giles chimed in. A cloth was wrapped around his right eye socket, and he was fitted in chainmail over a tunic that was a couple of sizes too large. Out of all the Strangers, he had been gifted with the most new armor and weapons; a side effect of having taken so much damage in the previous battle. "They wanted 'The Fearsome Goats'."

"What a silly name," Najih said with a scoff. "Everyone knows that camels are the mightiest of all."

"Right…" Kabel muttered with narrow eyes.

"Why does everyone keep namin' docile creatures like dey're mighty? Why not 'Mighty Lions' or somethin'?" Rolf asked with a shrug. Kabel ensured that he, too, had been gifted with plentiful armor, thanks to his near-death experience a few nights prior. The chainmail was rounded out with shoulder pads and a thick, leathery tunic.

"'Cause the lion is Sigraveld's symbol, idiot," Kabel said before punching him in the arm. He cracked a smirk at the sting in his knuckles. The money had been well worth it.

"Hey! Dat was unnecessary!"

"You are quite tough, hurting a kid like that," Satara said with an eye roll.

Kabel shrugged. "It's all in good fun."

"Fer *you*, maybe," Rolf said.

"Quit yer whinin', soldier! With all of that armor on, nothin' should be able to hurt you!" Kabel said while smacking his shoulder padding.

"Speaking of 'good fun', would any of you like some of the traps I've devised before we reach the coast?" Dhogron asked, holding up his bags and shaking them.

Kabel, Pierce, Satara, and Najih shook their heads in unison, while Rolf and Giles showed interest.

"Against these bastards, I'll take whatever I can get." Giles grabbed a few of the traps and stuffed them in his pockets.

"Yeh, we gotta take every advantage dat we can against dese monsters, or dey'll kill us," Rolf said as he, too, accepted Dhogron's inventions.

"On second thought…" Pierce trailed off, holding out a hand. He donned his Ometos mask in the sad, frowning orientation, and wore a dark tunic with a red sash around the waist. "I'll take one of each."

Dhogron supplied him with the items. "But as I said before, be careful with those haze pellets. You'll hallucinate so much that it will seem like you're in another world. We cannot afford such distractions against *this enemy*."

"Worry not," Pierce said with a nod. "I prefer to fight at a range."

"Good man!" Kabel said, tapping the swaying bow at his hip.

"That reminds me..." Satara trailed off, drawing her curved dagger. "I feel ill-prepared for battle. This is my only weapon."

"Your dance could be used as a weapon," the stocky man said with a big smile.

"Not everyone's gonna be distracted by that," Giles said while shaking his head. "In fact, them red-eyed folk don't seem to get distracted by *anything*."

"Let's not forget that the enemy should know their best chances lie at the east sewer entrance. We are only here in case they make attempts to infiltrate the west," Dhogron said, raising a finger. "And even if they do, their hands will be more than full with the swine of Endoshire. They are large beasts with a nasty temperament."

The Strangers continued at their quick pace until reaching the west coast. The sun had set, and the streets were nearly empty. As they began heading north, a massive black ship came into view, hugging the coastline and approaching rapidly. A spec could be seen flying around the sails of the vessel.

"Erm... I-isn't that the Dark Wizard's ship?" Giles asked.

"Damn... so they *are* attacking this one at full force..." Kabel said, grasping at his bow.

"Not necessarily," Pierce said while drawing his luxmortite dagger. "They are not so different from us, in regards to their strategy. They seem to like splitting up into sub-groups. All we know for sure is that the enhanced avian has accompanied this group."

"Well, it's da Dark Wizard's ship, ain't it? Surely, he'd be ridin' it. An' most of us saw what he did to Aldous a few nights ago. We don' got a chance in hell of beatin' a fella like dat," Rolf said.

"Strike with precision, and anyone can be brought down," Najih said with a confident nod.

"I agree. Even if he *is* a Wizard, his mortality remains," Satara added before eyeing Dhogron. "Besides, we have a Wizard of our own."

Dhogron wiped sweat from where his turban and brow met. "I'm afraid the element of surprise is all we have if the Dark Wizard is on that ship. Only Aldous could stand up to him. I am no match."

"Let's not get ahead of ourselves. Maybe the Dark Wizard is on that ship, or maybe he isn't. All we can do is wait and see," Kabel said.

"And make a plan," Pierce added, holding up one of the bags that Dhogron had gifted him. "If we play our cards correctly, we could stop most of them from even making it into the sewers."

~

AT THE NORTHERN docks of Endoshire, Captain Auber and his crew approached the ledge between docks nine and 10. They looked down to find nothing but wavy reflections of themselves staring back at them.

"Ugh, it smells! Why do we gotta get stuck doin' the dirty jobs?" Auber complained.

"Everyone was given a sewer drain to protect, sir," Franco replied.

"Err… right… but ours was the farthest away! It ain't fair!"

"I just wanna get some battlin' in! Wish we weren't saddled with the boring part of the mission," Ebbie said with clenched fists.

"Don't be so quick to wish for excitement. Remember what happened last time," Franco said, eyeing the two stubs that remained of his pinky and ring fingers.

"Right…" Ebbie trailed off with a nervous chuckle. "I just meant that it woulda been nice to face regular, human opponents, is all! They didn't stand a chance against me furious sword swings the other night!"

"Quit yer braggin'! We're here on serious business," Auber said in a grumpy tone. "Where is that fish-guy? He shoulda beaten us here if he was such a fast swimmer!"

Auber yelped as the water below shot up into his face. Flying up from the explosion in the sea was Xviktolo, who landed next to the pirates. The captain fell over and grasped his chest, letting out pained, weak breaths.

"Are ye alright, Cap'n?" Ebbie asked while kneeling next to him and placing a sure hand on his shoulder.

He let out a great sigh of relief while getting to his feet, and then cleared his throat. "I'm fine, of course! Just a lil' scare, is all!"

"What took you three so long?" Prince Xviktolo asked with hands to hips.

"Pardon me, but it sure seemed like *we* got here before *you*," Franco said.

The marinian let out a raspy chuckle. "Oh no, I've been waiting here for a whale."

"What? Why were ye waitin' fer a whale?" Auber asked with raised eyebrows.

"I think he meant, 'for a while', sir," the navigator whispered.

Xviktolo shrugged. "Yes, that is what I meant."

"What were ye doin', sneakin' around in the water like that, anyway?" Auber asked.

"Ah, right… I became bored while waiting for you three, and so I decided to scout the area for any signs of the enemy."

"Did you find anything?" Franco asked.

"Down at dock 15, there are many men gathered, boarding ships within some kind of building. There are at least dozens of them, if not over a hundred. I figure it must be our enemy," Xviktolo said.

"Oh yeh, I noticed that building the other night! Looked like a ship-yard of sorts," Ebbie said.

"And I think we know which influential figure of Endoshire likes to say he's a shipwright as a front for his slave trade," Franco said, looking to his captain.

"Aw, come on! Ye mean to say we're goin' up against Sampson?" Auber asked, slumping his shoulders.

Xviktolo cocked his head. "Will that be a problem?"

"Well… y'see…" the captain muttered, rubbing the back of his head.

"Our captain got a bit overzealous with his *superb marksmanship*, and struck Sampson in the leg with an arrow," Franco said, a smirk cracking on his slender face.

"Why is that a problem? He is our enemy, is he not?" Xviktolo replied.

"Yeh… well… you try havin' a target on yer back, with the most powerful man in the city takin' aim at ye!" Auber said.

"Our poor captain will almost certainly become a slave if Sampson ever gets his hands on him," Franco said, twisting Auber's stomach into knots.

"Well, better to attack than *be attacked*, right?" the marinian asked.

"Are you suggesting that we go on the offensive before they set sail?" Franco replied.

"Exactly! That building is built *on a dock*."

"So what?" Auber asked.

"So, that means we can sink the building and all of their ships in one fell swoop," he replied with a toothy grin.

"Oh… I don' like the sound of this…" Auber trailed off while clutching his groaning stomach.

"I love the idea! Let's go thar an' crush 'em!" Ebbie said with a loud cheer.

"And how might we sink this dock? Unless marinians have

monstrous strength, I don't see how we could do it," Franco said.

"Aren't you lot pirates?" Xviktolo asked as the trio looked at each other, each reflecting bewilderment. "Why don't you steal a ship, and then crash it into the dock?"

"Are ye mad? That's dangerous!" Captain Auber complained.

"Any more dangerous than Sampson on the prowl for your hide, *sir*?" Franco asked with barbs of sarcasm.

Auber gritted his teeth. He then leaned in next to his crewmates and whispered, "But we've never *stolen* anything so big before..."

"Well, don' that ship in Bosfueras count?" Ebbie asked.

"Hardly..." Franco muttered.

"But wait, ain't everyone gonna be inside, 'cause of them degener-ates comin' out at night? It should be *easy* to steal a ship," Captain Auber said, his spirits picking up.

"Yeh, we can do this!" Ebbie said with unfettered excitement.

"Why are you lot whispering? We're on the same team, after all. Shouldn't you include me in the plan?" Xviktolo asked.

Auber cleared his throat. Then, in an official tone, he said, "Yeh, we're gonna steal a ship an' ram it into the dock. We *are* pirates, after all. Them landlubbers will never know what hit 'em!"

Truthfully, the captain wasn't sure what had hit *him*, to agree to such a suicidal plan. Was it the impending doom of Sampson? Or did he simply wish to make a good impression in front of Xviktolo?

SOUTHEAST, near the outskirts of Endoshire, Angus and his forces had gathered in the woods across from the river. As Joel had predicted, they appeared to be lying in wait for the degenerates to emerge from the sewers before making a move.

The mute gave the signal to his fellow Strangers, and they exited the shadows of the shacks, letting the light of the crescent moon shine down upon them for the first time that night. The group of seven marched up the street and took a right onto a path parallel to the river. After a short walk, they took a left down a small, inclined path that led straight to the sewer entrance.

Joel and the others stopped short, however. Many yellow eyes stared back at them from the great drain that the river flowed into. Rows and rows of men and women resided within, extending into the infinite black of the sewers.

"By tha Stone Gods… there's so many of 'em…" Triston muttered. He seemed well aware of his vocal volume, for once.

"We have come this far. And they have their beady, yellow eyes locked on us. No turning back, now," Dalton said.

"The question is…" Aldous said with a tired breath that was as deep as the depths of the sewers appeared to be. "What is our next move?"

With a sly smile, Joel made hand signals to the group, detailing the rest of his plan.

"Right…" Conrad said, wide-eyed. "We poke the hornet's nest."

All in the group looked at Aldous. The old Wizard cocked his head at first, but quickly seemed to understand, and nodded his approval.

"Very well," he said while pointing his walking stick in the direction of the river. "I assume we will be running to the woods after I've stirred them?"

Joel nodded emphatically. The only way they could combat the horde at Angus' command was to distract them with *other enemies*. It was something that he had realized a few days back; when he, Dhogron, Triston, and a disguised Brice had escaped from the degenerates and creepers. It had only been possible because they began fighting *each other*.

Aldous closed his eyes, then strained them. Joel quickly realized that something was wrong. To his Wizard friend, controlling water was as natural as breathing.

With a weak exhale, Aldous fell to a knee. The Strangers rushed to his side to find him pale and hard of breath.

"You don' look so good!" Alistair said while holding out a hand.

The old Wizard took the boost and stood, but needed to hold himself up with his walking stick. "It seems I am still a bit winded…"

"This is my fault," Conrad said. He drew his rapier and began walking toward the yellow-dotted abyss. "The least I can do is lead them out."

"Wait," Lucia said, grabbing him by the shoulder. He stopped and looked back with a raised eyebrow. "I don't think you could create a big enough distraction. For Joel's plan to work, all of them must come out. We have to make a *big splash*."

"If not Aldous, then who could do such a thing?" Dalton asked.

Joel rubbed his chin. Then, his excited eyes darted to Alistair. He gave the big man a hard slap on the shoulder.

"Wha? Me? But what am I supposed ta do?"

"I'm all for using Alistair as bait, but it presents the same problem as Conrad trying to lure them out," Lucia said with crossed arms.

"Oh, here we go again! Ya can't go more than a few days without sayin' somethin' nasty about me, can ya, lass?" the big man shot back with a clenched fist. "Well, fer yer information, I gots a wind Rune, which is *way* more powerful than anythin' you can do!"

All in the group looked at him with critical eyes.

"Oh…" he muttered while retrieving his Rune, glowing as white as ever in the dark of night. "Right… how could I ferget?"

"Hold up!" Triston said, standing in front of his brother. "I don' think it's fair ta put this one on Ali! We never know if that thing is just gonna blow up in his face! It rarely works! I say it's too dangerous!"

Alistair looked back at Joel, who gave him a nod of approval. The big man walked up to his brother and clapped his shoulder.

"Brother, I know ya mean well, but I think I gots this Rune thing figured out."

Triston snorted. "Well, I say-"

"JUST SHADDUP AN' WATCH!"

Alistair walked past his stunned brother and trudged down the slight decline along the river with the Rune pulsing in his hand.

"I hope he knows what he's doing," Aldous said.

"Hopeless…" Lucia said with a frown.

"One can never be sure, with Alistair at the helm. He might steer us in the right direction, or crash us into the rocks," Conrad added with a chuckle.

Triston watched on, in silence. Joel couldn't tell if he was horrified or impressed at his brother's bravado.

Alistair walked along the riverbank at a crawl's pace while dozens, and then hundreds of yellow eyes began following his every move. He stopped just short of the sewer entrance, and even from afar, Joel could hear his nervous *gulp*. He prayed that he hadn't just sent him to his death.

"Oi! Who let the cow go astray?" one woman called out from the great drain.

"We should cut 'im up! Cows make fer a good meal!" another shouted, to a chorus of hollow, echoing laughs.

"Methinks he would be bad meat!"

"Let's skin 'im, anyway!"

"The only good Imperialist is a dead one!"

As suspected, however, none of the degenerates made a move. The most they could offer were nonsensical jeers. Joel was surprised that Alistair hadn't fired back with insults of his own, yet it also filled him with confidence in the big man. *He was focused.*

That was when the mute noticed it: A gentle wind parting at his cheeks, and if his fluttering, red hair and the bending blades of grass at his feet were any indication, then the source was Alistair.

"Oi! Are you smelly, boggin knobs talkin' ta me?" Alistair called out with bravado that shined greater than the sun.

Howls of laughter emerged from the great drain, and following that were so many taunts and jeers that Joel couldn't even tell what they were saying in return.

"I think you lot need a bath! But don' worry! Ya won't even have'ta go to a bathhouse! You can stay right there!" Alistair shouted.

"What's he doin'?" Triston said, taking a step forward. "They're gonna kill 'im!"

IN THE BEGINNINGS of the outskirts to the south, Angus peeked around one of many trees that provided him and his team with valuable cover.

"I'd know that obnoxious voice anywhere..." he muttered while squinting. He could make out some shadowy figures off in the distance.

"Have the degenerates come out, yet?" Catalina asked, peering around the same tree as him, but on the other side.

"No... I cannot tell who else is with him, but Alistair is causing a ruckus near the sewer entrance, from the sound of things," Angus said.

"Those damned Strangers... they just can't help themselves," Brice said while shaking his head. The giant looked back with an eyebrow raised. "That's what Aldous an' his lil' group have been callin' themselves."

"So, they came up with a name. Adorable. We should have a name for our team," Catalina chimed in.

"Their names won't matter after tonight. This time, we don't hold back. Crush them into nothing, should they dare show themselves before you," Angus said.

"Ye don' gotta tell me that much. Still... what could they be doin' by the sewers?" Brice asked.

"Perhaps they anticipated our arrival?" Catalina asked.

"That is certainly possible, given the lack of subtlety to our strategy.

Still, there is little they can do against our full might. We will trample them like horses over a rodent," Angus said, then squinted some more at the dark figures by the riverbank. "But be on your guards, regardless."

~

BACK BY THE SEWER ENTRANCE, Alistair smiled with confidence as the degenerates stirred in their angry hive. They were about to get *much angrier*, he thought. The big man took aim with his Rune, pointing it to a position in the water just before the giant drain.

He focused his thoughts. This was not just for himself, or to prove Triston wrong. The fate of his team and the entire city hung in the balance. Though, it would have been easier to call on his protective nature if he wasn't surrounded by so many capable warriors, tonight; and it would have been exceptionally easy if Giles hadn't *rudely* switched teams at the last second. His smile grew larger as he thought of some penalty games to inflict upon him. First, there was the matter of defeating *ol' meat-stain* and his team. With those thoughts, a burst of wind shot from the stone, the intense recoil shocking Alistair as he flew back and landed on his bottom. It had happened as if it were second nature, like walking or sleeping.

When he looked up, Alistair saw a large wave breaking in mid-air, sending shiploads of water bursting through the pipe and onto the bridge above. The big redhead looked down at the Rune in wonder as he heard the awe-struck gasps of his allies behind.

As the water receded and the river returned to its normal state of flow, Alistair could see that most of the degenerates had been bowled over by the sheer impact of the wave. Some laughed hysterically, while others coughed and grumbled. The noises gave way to angry chanting as more and more of them stood.

Just as Joel had predicted, the angry hornet's nest had been success-fully swatted at, and the first degenerates to stand began a charge outside.

Alistair looked on, in trance, as hundreds of degenerates flooded out of the tunnel ahead, each armed, and each with murderous intent in their yellow eyes. He felt two tugs: One on each shoulder, and looked back to see Joel and Triston hoisting him up.

"Come on, Ali! We gots ta go!" Triston said as the rumbles of the charging crowd reached their feet.

Falling out of his daze, the big redhead let loose a huge grin. "I DID IT, LADS!"

"Well done! Now, let's get the hell outta here!" Dalton called back. He and the others had already started making a run southward, to the trees.

The trio began their mad dash for the woods as the degenerates closed in. Hundreds of the crazed mob had flooded out to attack, and they hurled weapons and insults alike while giving chase.

∼

ANGUS' eyes widened as he watched the Strangers run toward him and his team, with hordes of the degenerates chasing after them.

"Those cheeky bastards," Brice said with a venomous grin. "They don't have the manpower to face us, so they enlisted the next best thing!"

"It matters not to the likes of us," Catalina said, licking her lips with a tongue far too long to be human. "Just more fodder to play with."

Sir Job Cardon approached Angus with a few other Sigrian knights in tow.

"What's this commotion all abou-" A gasp stifled his words. "Are those the degenerates of the sewers? Why are they charging at us? I thought the whole point of us hiding here was to wait until they left so we might avoid them."

"The plan has changed," Angus said without looking back. He clenched a fist, cracking his deadly bones in the process. "Prepare your men for battle."

"Very well..." said Job. They retreated into the thick of the woods, where fellow gallants of the Sigrian crown awaited them.

"If they are going to bring the degenerates to us, then we may as well attack first, wouldn't you agree?" Angus asked, looking back at his subordinates. Brice cackled as his arms transformed into dark tentacles, while Catalina giggled with glee, and Ned let out a low-pitched hiss.

The Strangers had introduced an unexpected enemy into Angus' plans, but he planned to meet them head-on and demoralize them in the process. Soon, they would understand the true gap in their abilities.

CHAPTER 37
THE HERD

Dalton led a charge toward the woods, where the dark forces lay. Conrad and Lucia followed close behind, while a panting Aldous lagged back to where Joel, Alistair, and Triston were making a mad dash for their lives. The ground at their feet trembled more and more from the horde of angry degenerates gaining on them.

"Damn…" Dalton muttered between breaths.

"What is it?" Lucia asked, lengthening her strides to catch up.

"They know… we are coming…" he replied, pointing ahead.

Out from the woods stepped Angus, Brice, Catalina, and Ned. Behind them, rows upon rows of men and women appeared, some with red eyes glowing, and others making themselves known with the glints of their weapons under the moonlight.

"This isn't good…" Conrad muttered between breaths. "They aim to sandwich us… between themselves and the degenerates… we'll be crushed!"

"Keep… movin'! Full… speed ahead!" Aldous cried. He held out his Summoner Rune as he ran. "I'll… get us… outta trouble…"

The Strangers collectively put their heads down and pressed forward. The degenerates were now no less than five meters behind, in Joel's estimation. He glanced over his shoulder to see that many had drawn weapons such as swords, daggers, axes, and clubs, while some carried lit torches in a position that looked ready to be thrown.

As they neared the trees, it became apparent that not all of their enemies wielded conventional iron or steel arms. Some carried white weapons.

"They must be… using Angus' bone…" Conrad said.

"Damn that… meat-stain!" Alistair choked out.

Angus cracked a smile on his stone face. He then pointed his bone blade forward and called out, "Charge!"

With that command, the knights, Bosfueras townsfolk, and slaves dashed out of the woods. Soon to follow were some creepers, plodding along unsteadily with glowing red dots-for-eyes fixed on new targets.

"What… do we do?" Dalton asked, looking back at Aldous. Now, the old Wizard was drenched in sweat, and his breaths were hoarse.

"Keep… going!" he insisted, gesturing his Rune forward once more.

A collective nervousness gave way to visible fear as the dark forces charged at the Strangers, and the rumblings of the chanting horde behind grew stronger.

"Almost…" Aldous muttered. About 20 paces away from Angus' team, the old Wizard pushed the Summoner Rune forward with a desperate grunt. "Now!"

A dark, swirling portal opened before Dalton; so close that he had no time to react, and fell through. Lucia and Conrad were next to jump in, followed closely by Triston and Alistair. Joel and Aldous brought up the rear, with one degenerate getting so close that the mute felt the wind of a sword swing strike him in the neck as he hopped through the vortex.

Just as quickly as they had been sucked up, the Strangers crashed on a road along the shacks where they had first hidden. Joel hopped to his feet and looked to the southeast. Off in the distance, the degenerates and dark forces had already gone to battle. *Clangs* of steel, cries of pain, and shouts of joy echoed from afar.

Joel stumbled forward after a hard slap struck his back. He turned to see a grinning Alistair, still huffing and puffing from their mad dash. "Good plan… lad! This'll hold 'em off… fer sure!"

"For now, perhaps…" Aldous said, standing markedly slower than the others and dusting himself off. "The degenerates are dangerous, but they are no match for the dark essence-infused or the knights."

"In other words, all we've done is buy ourselves some time," Dalton said with crossed arms.

"Time, and mayhap a thinning out of the herds," the old Wizard said before smiling at Joel and lightly patting him on the shoulder. "Still, good work, m'boy! Your plan has helped us, greatly."

The mute nodded and returned a smile, but there was still more to be done. He made hand signals, suggesting that they venture to the great sewer drain, as a last line of defense for the inevitable arrival of Angus' forces. All agreed, and so the Strangers took no time to rest. They headed east, where the unknown of the sewer's depths awaited them.

~

KABEL and the others got into position as the Dark Wizard's massive ship arrived at the western coastline of Endoshire, just before the sewer drain poking from the rock foundations below. Upon dropping anchor, a wooden plank plopped onto the metal where the sewage-filled waters flowed out.

Several of the Bosfueras townsfolk showed themselves on the main deck. Their red, glowing eyes became fixated on the sewer entrance. They began walking toward the plank, but they came to a stop when noticing Satara, who stood atop the ledge overhanging the pipe. She shook her hips and swayed around naturally, like leaves in the wind, but her audience did anything besides look on in desire. Instead, they looked to their master, Oneth, who let out a low-pitched chuckle at the display.

"Fire upon her."

From the crow's nests, archers appeared, and within seconds, arrows streaked through the night sky. The projectiles found their target, striking Satara in the chest and midsection. She shot back from the sheer impact and flopped to the ground as if not a single muscle in her legs worked. Of course, it was because there *were* no muscles in her legs.

Behind one of the slum shops off the coast, Satara peered around the corner to find Dhogron's paper replica of her riddled with holes.

She frowned. "I must be losing my touch."

"Don't take it *too* personally," Kabel said with a cheeky smile as he pushed an arrowhead into the flames of a torch. The oil-soaked metal was lit ablaze. "These folk have no desires, except to serve their master. It's a lil' sad if I'm honest…"

The stocky man rounded the building's edge with a flaming arrow at the ready in his bow. He looked across the road to see that Rolf, who was also equipped with a bow and fire arrow, had drawn back on his string and took aim at the ship.

With a nod to his friend, Kabel pulled back on the string of his bow and aimed for the sails of the ship.

"Three... two... one..." he muttered, then let go. Rolf fired his arrow in unison, and the two flaming arrows carved the air like shooting stars in the night sky. Kabel smiled. *Right on target*, he thought.

However, a dark streak caught his eye, ending all excitement and bringing a lump to his throat. It was Mur'del descending from above with dragon-like speed; even faster than the fiery projectiles flew. Yet, Kabel did not fret, for there remained a contingency; and that contingency revealed itself when she was a mere arm's length away from intercepting the arrows.

A blue streak of light shot past the arrows and angled upward at Mur'del. The enhanced avian maneuvered while still diving to face Pierce's charmed dagger, and she swiped at it with her great, black wing. In response, the dagger darted downward so that only her feathers harmlessly brushed through its tip, and then it aimed up once more, to continue its original trajectory.

In a split-second, the streaking dagger poked a hole through her neck, like an arrow through wet paper. Gagging noises echoed from above as Mur'del grabbed her throat and began to spiral. Blood rained from the sky while she plummeted like a swatted fly, until crashing into the sea with a great splash.

Meanwhile, the flaming arrows had found their targets: Two of the monster ship's sails had caught on fire, prompting the Bosfueras townsfolk to begin gathering buckets of water. Hector parted their efficient ranks on the deck and approached his master, Oneth.

The Dark Wizard muttered something to the scorpion-man, and with only a nod of acknowledgment, he glided across the deck. With inhuman strength, he leaped like a grasshopper onto the ledge above the sewer entrance.

Rolf shuddered and took a rickety step back as the cloaked figure approached, but Kabel shook his head and gestured with a hand for him to calm down.

"We'll get 'im, don't worry," he whispered. The lanky young man nodded, but even from afar, he could hear his frightened *gulp*. It was hard to blame him, considering just how close Hector had brought him to death's door just a few nights ago.

Hector strode forth along the slums' edge without fear. Kabel smiled as some crumpled-up paper balls rolled out at his feet, stopping him. The scorpion-man cocked his head and leaned over to grab one of the balls, but all at once, they exploded: One ball into a pack of little paper spiders, which scurried up onto his cloak. The other shot out many small pieces of sharp paper, which, while cutting through his garb, did not even produce the tiniest of nicks on his armor-like exoskeleton.

Giles, Najih, and Satara hopped out from their hiding places behind the buildings for a surprise attack. The dancer brought her curved dagger down vertically, while her musician swung his scimitar horizontally, aiming for the midsection. Giles followed up with an attack from behind, aiming for the back.

Gasps echoed in the streets as Hector caught Satara and Najih's blades between his pinchers-for-fingers, all while swatting Giles' sword away with a scorpion tail that darted out from the bottom of his billowed robe. With desperate battle cries, the one-eyed man continued his assault from behind, but the flailing tail managed to keep him at bay. Meanwhile, the dagger and scimitar each groaned under the clamping force of the pinchers. Sweat dribbled down Kabel's twitching brow as he watched on with an arrow pulled back in the drawstring of his bow. They didn't have long, he thought. Across the street, his eyes caught onto Rolf, about to bathe a new arrow in flame. He shook his head, stilling him.

"Not yet," he mouthed.

Then, he picked up on a blue blur parting dust and litter in the street. Pierce's charmed dagger streaked past both Giles and the scorpion tail before plunging into Hector's back with a fleshy *splat*. Kabel remembered the hollow *thunks* of his ineffectual blade against the scorpion-man's exoskeleton a few nights back. Pierce's attack had done true damage, and it was their best chance to strike a finishing blow.

Kabel doused the arrowhead in flame and took aim at a shrieking Hector. Out of the corner of his eye, he saw that Rolf had done the same. Pierce strolled ahead, casually, as the scorpion-man dropped Satara and Najih's blades and turned to face his attacker. The dagger-eyed man gestured two fingers toward him, driving the blade into his spine all the more. Hector fell to a knee, and Kabel nodded at Rolf while smiling.

"Time for a little payback!"

The flaming arrows flew fantastically through the night, but there was little time to admire their beauty; for in mere moments, they pierced Hector's right torso and left leg, respectively. And then, his robe was alight with swiftly spreading flame. Kabel and Rolf jumped out into the street and tossed their remaining oil onto the flames, which erupted into an explosion. All in the area shielded their eyes as Hector's hissing and clicking rang out over the crackles of the fire.

Upon lowering his arms and opening his eyes, Kabel gasped. Hector had dropped out of his fiery garb, but the flames continued to rage upon his molting, oil-soaked exoskeleton. He turned and ran for the coast with horse-like speed, but a groggy Pierce remained in his path.

"Pierce! Get down!" Kabel cried. The dagger-eyed man dove out of the way just in time to avoid the man-sized fireball. "He's headed to sea! After him!"

Kabel started forward, but he stopped himself when Pierce, while down on a knee, held a hand up. In that hand was his Summoner Rune, pulsing a dark, mysterious hue.

"He's not going anywhere…"

Hector hopped over the ledge of the coastline, but, in mid-air, an unavoidable portal appeared before him. The scorpion-man fell through, and Pierce turned eastward while crossing his arms. The rest of the Strangers looked down the road to see a ball of fire growing in size, parting dust, dirt, and litter alike as it did. All aside from a scoffing Pierce readied themselves for another round of battle, until an ear-piercing squeal rang out, and Hector collapsed, still several buildings away. Now, only the weak crackles of fire could be heard. It grew outward and high, feeding off the fuel of the burning carcass below.

"That's one down," Pierce said as the luxmortite dagger floated to his bloody, outstretched hand. It fell into his palm as the bright blue glow faded.

"Excellent work, everyone," Kabel said with a grin. "Now, we just gotta take out that damned Dark Wizard. The rest of 'em will be helpless without their master."

"The avian will resurface, soon. A dagger to the throat is not enough to bring her down," Pierce said, looking out to sea.

"Dey seem to really hate fire," Rolf said, looking over his shoulder at Hector's deteriorating corpse. "It's a shame we wasted all of our oil on *him*."

"They are not Gods. There must be other weaknesses," Najih said.

"The kraken's poison took care of the avian a few nights ago, but we don't have anything *that* potent," Pierce replied.

"In that case, we pound that monster into the ground 'till she stops movin'," Giles said, crunching a fist in his open palm.

"I agree. There is no choice but to keep hurting her until she submits," Satara said, swinging her curved dagger through the air with a smile pointed at Giles. "I like a brutal man."

The one-eyed man blushed but did not have time to respond, as Mur'del burst from the sea with a great screech that took the Strangers' collective attention.

However, instead of charging for them, she hovered over the great, black ship of her master.

"Mur'del!" Oneth's thunderous, growling voice seemed to shake the foundations of the coastline itself. "We are entering the sewers. See to it that *they* don't follow. Do not fail me, as Hector did, or I'll see to it that you are begging to be burned to death, as he was!"

"I think that we can handle the avian," Dhogron said, stepping out of the shadows of a nearby alley while looking up at Mur'del, who circled the monstrous ship, picking up such speed that gusts of wind fluttered the collective hairs and garments of the Strangers. "But I do not know what we can do against the Dark Wizard."

"Ah, the hero shows himself," Satara said with a snort. "How is it that a Wizard is the only one of us to shy away from battle?"

Dhogron shrugged. "I specialize in tricks, not fighting. My Supreme Paper Surprises helped, did they not?"

"No time to bicker. The Dark Wizard is getting away as we speak," Kabel said while aiming at the enhanced avian with his bow and arrow. "We have to hope those fabled swine of Endoshire can hold him off for a while."

"Hold your fire," Pierce commanded, holding a hand out.

The stocky man eased up and raised an eyebrow. "I thought that *I* was the leader, here."

"I have an idea." A hollow, if amused, snort whistled beneath Pierce's Ometos mask. "Shall I tell you? Or would you prefer I hold my tongue for the sake of your title?"

"Let's hear it."

"I'll take the avian," he said, then pulled out his Rune. "While she is distracted, I'll send you lot to the ship, down below. You should be able to enter the sewers from there."

"But how will we stop the Dark Wizard?" Dhogron asked.

"I leave that to *you*."

∼

MUR'DEL EXITED her holding pattern and darted down, faster than any arrow, in the direction of the Strangers. The wind howled and grumbled under the stress of her magnificent speed. With great haste, Pierce pulled the luxmortite dagger across his palm. Blood spilled onto his blade, and it became encased in a light blue aura.

Pierce pointed up at her, and then the glowing dagger shot into the air with a similar burst of speed to her own. Mur'del narrowed her dark eyes. This time, he would not catch her by surprise. In mere moments, the dagger was upon her, and she took evasive maneuvers with a twirl. A surge of pleasure coursed through her veins as the *whir* of the blade passed her ears. Now diving at top speed, there was no way it could catch back up to her, she thought.

However, while continuing her descent, the enhanced avian caught wind of a peculiar, dark glow. Pierce was holding out his Summoner Rune. Yet, it was just another possibility that Mur'del had prepared for. With the ground rapidly nearing, she spun and let loose one of Angus' bone blades. Upon straightening herself out, she could already tell that it was far too quick for Pierce to react to.

The bone shot into where his left arm and shoulder met, with such force that it plowed straight through without getting stuck. Pierce groaned as his legs buckled and he fell to a knee. The bloody bone blade bounced behind him, and Mur'del let out a mocking tweet. The dagger-eyed man seemed to keep his composure, however, and gestured his right hand back toward himself.

Mur'del looked over her shoulder to see the dagger streaking back toward her. She had wanted to get a second strike in, but knowing that her target was now injured, there was no longer a need to rush into attacking. She instead somersaulted to avoid the glowing blade and then returned to a holding pattern, high in the sky.

While lurking above, Mur'del caught onto two things: Pierce was flipping his mask around, for some reason; and the other, more alarming observation was that the rest of Strangers had disappeared. She had been so focused on dodging the dagger and counterattacking that she hadn't noticed them sneaking off.

The enhanced avian turned her gaze toward the west coast to find the remainder of the Strangers on her master's ship. They were dashing for the plank that led into the sewers. Her eyes widened. The Summoner Rune! It hadn't been meant for her but for those damned rats!

"Little pests!" she shrieked, then darted for the great vessel at top speed.

Before getting far, Mur'del was caught up in a portal that she was going too fast to maneuver around. Upon exiting the gateway, she found herself just a meter off the ground and flying toward Pierce.

The dagger-eyed man gestured down with his right hand, and before Mur'del could react, the luxmortite blade descended from the sky like a blue ray of light through parting clouds. It plunged into her back with such force that she was pushed to the ground, and skidded and rolled uncontrollably for several paces before finally coming to a stop.

Her limp body tingled as it regenerated, though the sting of Pierce's dagger ripping out of her feathery back ruined any good feelings that it might have brought. She struggled while looking up and over her shoulder to see the charmed blade floating gently into his grasp. He stalked toward her with his left arm bloodied and dangling, yet he was still able to grasp the Summoner Rune in that hand.

Mur'del let out a frustrated squawk. "I grow tired of your portals and trickery, luxian scum!"

She gasped as her eyes tracked a blue light, the glowing dagger, headed straight for her. Then, Mur'del's world turned black. The confusion did not last long, for the searing pain in her face reminded her that the blade had been approaching just a moment ago. She brought a trembling hand up to her face, or what remained of it, to find a gaping, bloody hole.

"Get used to it, fell beast," Pierce's harsh voice echoed in the dark.

Mur'del cocked her head as her beak-like nose began reshaping itself. The switching of the Ometos mask's orientation and the coldness in his tone were dead giveaways. It was no longer Pierce who stood before her. *The other* had entered the battlefield.

~

KABEL and his team shielded their faces from sewer's stink as they jogged down the pathway of stone to the right of the muddy river. The green gasses made it difficult to see and inflicted a lightheadedness upon the Strangers. There was a stone-laden path running parallel to them, across the stream, but Dhogron, squinting at the map before him, was certain that the Dark Wizard would have studied the correct way to the monolith's location, and taken the path that they were currently on.

From the western sewer entrance, the quickest way to reach the monolith was via a passageway on the right, which led to one of the swine nests. They had been placed there by design, to stave off any intruders who dared to try their hand at finding the Degenerate seal. From there, they would have to make their way through a series of maze-like tunnels to reach their destination.

Most curious to the trickster Wizard, however, was that he couldn't see the Dark Wizard and his group up ahead. The correct path to take was the second possible right within the main sewer line, but that turn was still far off; at least a few blocks into the slums, he thought. Surely, they couldn't have gotten that much of a head start-

A series of high-pitched squeals broke Dhogron's train of thought.

"The swine?" Kabel asked as the group skidded to a stop.

"Yes..." Dhogron muttered, darting his eyes to the left, across the river. Further ahead, there was a tunnel that could be taken into a different swine nest. "I did not anticipate this, but I think the Dark Wizard went the wrong way..."

"So, maybe those swine will do the job for us," Giles said.

"Dat would be *too easy*," Rolf replied while shaking his head. "Nothin's ever easy, with dese guys."

Kabel nodded. "True. Everyone, be on your guard."

As the group continued onward at a markedly slower pace, the squeals became louder and more frequent. They echoed throughout the vastness of the sewer passage, in one ear and out the other, striking fear and nervousness into the heart of Dhogron.

Soon, they reached a point where the first passage to the swine nest was directly across the river from them. More squeals erupted from the tunnels, and with squinted eyes, Dhogron stopped to see an entire herd of the mutated boars marching, with men riding on their backs.

"It can't be..."

The Strangers watched on as the swine, who filled up the tunnel before them in rows, emerged from the green haze. The leader of the pack, who had the Dark Wizard riding upon it, came to a stop, and so too did the others behind.

Standing before them, snorting heavily, were the mutated beasts of the Endoshire sewers. Thought to be old wives' tales or myth by most,

the swine were dark and slimy, like the filth they lived in. They were each roughly the size of a horse, but twice as stout, and tenfold as restless; huffing and puffing, just itching for the opportunity to charge and gore the stunned group before them with their thick tusks. Several mutations grew from each of the swine, from generations of feasting upon sewage and garbage: Some featured extra eyes, or spare nostrils on their snout. Others had formed additional tusks underneath their chin, or growths on their body that had not fully developed into legs.

Oneth cackled with menace. "I must say that you are a tenacious group. By all accounts, Mur'del and Hector should have been able to slay you... but I had a feeling you might continue your needless pursuit, somehow, and here we are. *This time*, you won't be escaping. This sewer shall be a fitting tomb for a pack of rats like you."

"How did you gain control of the swine?" Kabel asked, his tone apprehensive.

"Nature..." Dhogron muttered with a defeated sigh. The other Strangers looked at him with demanding eyes. "He must know Nature magic... I hadn't anticipated this..."

"You are only half-right," Oneth said with a deep, dark chuckle. "Nature magic allows the user to communicate with animals, the plants, the trees, and even the weather... but there must be an agreement; cooperation. *Dark Nature*, on the other hand..."

"You filth!" Dhogron shouted before turning fiery eyes to his teammates. "He has the swine under his complete control. They are *forced into subservience*."

"That's not a charitable way to put it," the Dark Wizard said with a venomous grin. "Think of it more like I'm borrowing their minds, for the time being. If you are so against hurting these smelly, ugly creatures, then perhaps you should stay still while they gore you and feast upon your flesh!"

Howls of laughter echoed from beneath Oneth's hood, and the Bosfueras townsfolk laughed along from atop the swine behind him.

"Listen to these sub-humans, laughing at the plight of animals; of us. We can't let 'em win," Giles whispered, looking to Rolf with a nervous smile. He raised an eyebrow at first, but when the one-eyed man reached into his pocket and retrieved one of the haze pellets, his confusion turned into a smile. "It's time for desperate measures."

The swine across the river began kicking up dust, ready to charge. The other Strangers, meanwhile, drew their weapons in anticipation of the herd attacking them. Dhogron took in a nervous gulp while eyeing the pellets in Giles' and Rolf's respective hands. They were on the verge of pure chaos, but in their present predicament, what other choice was there?

~

DRAKE SAT at his dining table with arms crossed. Rose remained in her room, quiet as the night, while the servants stood by her door, awaiting orders.

In such solitude, he couldn't get it out of his head that he was being phased out of the very team he'd helped to build. While true that they would need his business sense, Drake felt that he was being unfairly blamed for the failure a few nights prior. After all, Brice had only been caught due to the Dark Wizard's foolish fascination with *that damned Mercer boy*.

To make matters worse, the sewer infiltration plan was brutally nearsighted and easily anticipated by the enemy. It was almost as if the Dark Wizard *wanted to fail*, Drake thought. While true that he'd agreed to stay out of tonight's proceedings, he found it impossible to sit back and relax, knowing that the chance at *inordinate power* was within his grasp. There was no good reason for him to stay behind, aside from Oneth attempting to push him away from the group and its dealings.

That couldn't happen. After all, they would be nowhere without the genius of his planning. Tonight, he would prove himself the most valuable member of the team. Drake stood with sudden vigor and intensity. Rose's servants looked to their master like lambs to a shepherd.

"I've become bored," he said with a cool smile. "How about you, my fair ladies?"

"It is not important, my Master," one of them replied with a bow. "We live to serve, regardless of our feelings."

"Good answer," Drake said with a chuckle. "Your reward shall be an introduction to untold excitement, and the birth of Federland's true king, tonight."

The Village Elder stood, then grabbed his fancy fur coat off of a rack. He then retrieved a belt that was decorated with several holsters; each sheathing expensively decorated daggers.

"But what of Lady Rose, my Lord?" one of the servants asked.

"She'll be fine," Drake replied with a dismissive wave. He then took hold of a few swords, each with a beautifully crafted, gold-crested scabbard protecting it. He kept one for himself while gifting the others to the servants. "I hope you each know your way around a blade."

"We have wielded similar weapons before, Master," one of them said.

"Good. You may need it, tonight."

"M'lord, if I may…" the other trailed off.

"Speak," Drake said with authority.

"Should we really leave? It's just… I fear for my Master's safety," she said.

"Is that right?" he asked, walking up to the pair, who squirmed more and more with each step he took.

"S-sorry, sir. She was out of line," the other woman said. They bowed before him in unison.

Drake drew his sword and put it up to the servant's neck. She let out a squeak but spoke no further as the cold of the blade put a cap on any noise she would dare to make.

"There is no place for cowardice within my ranks, no matter how lowly you may be," Drake said, pushing his sword further up against her neck. "You have three choices: You can be sent back to Sampson, I can cut your heads off right now, or you can come along with me tonight for the experience of a lifetime. What is your decision?"

"W-we'll go," the free woman said, putting her hands up in protest. "We shall fight by your side if it is required."

"Very good," Drake said as he withdrew his sword and turned. "Come! Survive this night, and you might find yourselves in a higher position than mere servants."

He smiled at the tepid steps behind him. They were simply not prepared for the glory to come, he thought. Soon, he would become a God, to them.

CHAPTER 38
MOTHER

Captain Auber let out a nervous sigh as he crept up dock 12 with his crew and Prince Xviktolo in tow. He had set his sights on a mid-sized vessel, ahead and on the left. The marinian looked back at the pirates with a furrowed brow as they continued to sneak.

"Why the secrecy? You *are* pirates, aren't you?"

"Yeh, an' what's yer point?" Auber asked.

"If you are pirates, then you should steal the ship by force," Xviktolo said.

"That would require us to be intimidating," Franco said with an eye roll.

"I can be intimidatin'!" Ebbie shouted with clenched fists.

Auber turned back and slapped his first mate off the back of his head. "Ye idjit! Keep yer voice down!"

"Aren't you a leader of the Strangers? If you are fierce enough to contend with the likes of Aldous, then surely commandeering a ship will be of no consequence," Xviktolo continued with a critical eye pointed at Auber.

"Erm… well… ye see…" he stammered, searching his mind for excuses.

"You'll have to excuse the captain. He hasn't gotten his land legs, yet," Franco chimed in.

"'Land legs', you say?"

"That's right!" Auber said with an unassured chuckle. "I haven't gotten me land legs, yet. Only brave travelers of the sea would understand, of course, but I need time to adjust to the land. The sea is my natural home, after all!"

"The sea is *my home*, too..." Xviktolo trailed off.

"Er... right... but it's different fer me, 'cause I travel on a ship," the captain said with desperation on his tongue. "But after I recover, I'll become a force to be reckoned with!"

Prince Xviktolo paused, leaving Auber on edge. It was difficult to read his facial expressions.

"I see... in that case, I will be happy to fight for you until you've gotten your land legs. You don't *look* tough, but then again, Aldous appears to be a chubby old man. I look forward to seeing your true skill shine in battle, Captain!"

"Aren't we all?" Franco muttered with a knowing smile. Auber scowled at his navigator.

After a short walk, the group reached their intended target, which did not have a plank stretching out to the dock.

"The crew must be staying on the ship," Franco whispered.

"Aye, best to turn back and find another ship, then," Auber replied.

"Aww, c'mon, Cap'n! We can take 'em!" Ebbie whined.

"I must agree," Xviktolo said, drawing his starlite blade. IT gleamed majestically under the light of the moon. "Time is of the essence. We cannot waste the night away looking for an empty ship. The enemy could be departing at any moment."

Captain Auber narrowed his eyes. "Yer really just lookin' to brawl tonight, ain't ye?"

"Perhaps..."

"Fine," the captain said with a dramatic sigh. "But we do it carefully! We still gots the element of surprise. As an esteemed leader of the Strangers, it is my duty to keep me crewmates safe."

"How selfish," the marinian said.

"Oh, come on! I'm just tryin' to keep us alive, is all!" Auber shot back.

"Methinks he meant 'selfless', sir," Ebbie said.

Xviktolo hissed a chuckle between sharp teeth. "Right, right, that is what I meant."

"But more importantly, what is our plan?" Franco asked.

"We could just throw the landlubbers overboard," Auber said.

"They'll make a ruckus, that way," Ebbie argued, smashing his fists together. "The only way ta deal with this is to beat 'em into submission!"

"Or we can just tie 'em up," the captain said with a shrug.

"But they may call for help," Prince Xviktolo said, raising his crystalline sword in a triumphant pose. "I must agree; we need to beat them into submission, then tie the land-dwellers up."

"Yer a violent lot, y'know that?" Auber asked with narrowed eyes.

"Please don't lump me in with the brutes, sir," Franco said.

With that, the group hopped over the railings to infiltrate the ship. They immediately located some rope that was coiled up near the bow of the deck. It was overly long; not meant to tie anyone up, but it could certainly be cut, especially with the superb sharpness of the starlite sword in Xviktolo's grasp.

Afterward, they crept around the ship, looking for containers and chests. One such chest contained rags, which they intended to gag the crew with after they were tied up. With the needed supplies, the Strangers made their way toward the cabins. Inside the main hall that led to the rooms, a candle was alight. Auber and the others pressed their backs up against the wall outside.

"Someone must be on guard duty," the captain whispered.

"We can take 'em, Cap. Let's all charge in thar!" Ebbie said in a low, but harsh voice.

"No. I gots a better idea," Auber said, trying to withhold laughter. He retrieved a small sack from his pocket. Franco and Xviktolo groaned.

～

WITHIN THE CABIN HALLWAY, a young sailor sat at a chair with only a candle and his solemn thoughts to keep him company. Discomfort, hunger, and tiredness crept up on him; for it was his third night in a row on guard duty, and he had only been given bread and water to eat over that period. The captain had punished him for missing roll call one day, out at sea.

The punishment had begun to affect his work. Without enough sleep, he had not the proper energy to complete his daily tasks efficiently. The young sailor prayed that this would be his last night on watch as his stomach grumbled in protest.

As if to answer his prayers, the sailor noticed a blueberry rolling down the hallway. At first, he jumped out of his seat in a sudden rush of panic, but then, he felt great relief. It was his first time so much as sniffing something other than meager bread in days. With a big smile, he knelt over and grabbed the berry. Without a second thought, he plopped it into his mouth.

It was flavorful, but it didn't taste like blueberry. Perhaps it was an odd side effect of not having other foods for so long. Even so, it was nice to have some variety, the sailor thought as he sat back down. It seemed odd, though, that a berry would just roll down the hallway like that. After all, everyone else was asleep in their rooms. Had a container toppled over, spilling the food?

With that thought, the young sailor stood up to leave, but then he felt it: A rumbling in his stomach, and *not* the kind that signified hunger. Instead of heading to the containers of the ship, he made a dash for the bow, where slits for relieving oneself resided. As he turned around and lowered his trousers, he gasped to see a scruffy, giggling man standing before him.

"Erm… who goes thar?" the sailor asked, red in the face while relieving himself

"I can't believe ye fell fer it!" the scruffy said, bursting aloud with laughter. He held a rope in one hand, with a saber pointed at him in the other.

~

THE STRANGERS TIED up the hapless sailor and gagged him after he finished his business at the bow. Then, they snuck back into the cabin area. Most of the crew slept on cots in one room, while the captain of the ship had his own quarters. Auber and the pirates handled the crew members discretely by using Dhogron's itching powder to lure them out of bed, only to tie them up when they were isolated. Meanwhile, Xviktolo disposed of the captain himself, with little effort or aid.

After leading all of the tied-up crew out to the deck and gagging them, Captain Auber looked over his team with a big grin.

"Raise the anchor, fellas! We're goin' on an adventure!"

"We are only traveling a few docks over, sir," Franco replied with a sigh.

"But it's still excitin'!" Ebbie shouted with a raised fist. "Down with Sampson!"

"This Sampson fellow is sure to hate you after this," Xviktolo said, looking at the captain with a toothy grin.

"Oh… erm… right…" Auber muttered, a bundle of nerves. After recomposing himself, he let out a confident chuckle. "Well, that's what he gets for opposin' the great Cap'n Auber!"

"Still," Franco said, crossing his arms. "Between the arrow to his leg and what we're about to do, I'd *just hate* to be captured by Sampson. He would probably torture me until the end of my days."

Auber eyed his navigator with a combination of contempt and fright.

"A man of Captain Auber's skill and cunning has nothing to fear, I'm sure," the marinian said with a nod.

"We can only hope the captain gets his land legs in time to defend himself," Franco added with barbs of sarcasm.

"When *will* you get your land legs, exactly?" Xviktolo asked.

Auber frowned and then let out a defeated sigh. "A long time, lad… a long time…"

Preparations began for departure of the ship, while the sailors huddled up in the corner, gagged and tied up. Auber couldn't help but chuckle at their ignorance. If only they knew what kind of trouble they were all about to find themselves in.

DALTON AND ALDOUS' group watched the unfolding battle between the degenerates and the dark forces from the bridge above the river. They had originally planned to head straight for the sewer drain, but their current vantage point was best for scouting out the enemy. Many shouts of agony and pleasure erupted as men and women fell into bloody heaps from the battle.

Most of the Bosfueras townsfolk and slaves struggled to fend off the ravenous degenerates; they simply could not match their aggression, intensity, or ruthlessness. However, evening the odds were the Sigrian knights and the creepers. Led by Sir Job, the knights easily defeated most enemies using their superior armor and skill. However, every once in a while, a knight was taken by surprise and fell to the mobs of angry, yellow-eyed folk.

Strength in numbers was how the degenerates began attacking the creepers, who, despite their sluggish movements, proved incredibly dangerous in close quarters: A single swipe from their long, deformed arms could maim or even kill. In response to the dark beasts, the yellow-eyed folk lit torches and threw them around recklessly. Fires littered the field between the river and woods, but they never grew large enough to spread. Most flames reached a body and stayed there, regardless of whether it was living or dead.

As the conflict's intensity ramped up, the dark forces began pushing back the degenerates. The unnatural strength, speed, and abilities of Angus, Brice, Catalina, and a mysterious cloaked figure gave their group a decisive edge.

Brice unleashed dark, serpent-like tendrils from his body in many different directions, skewering enemies and even his allies like common finger foods. He threw their limp bodies at the other degenerates, but the crazed mob was not demoralized, and only attacked with more ferocity. In addition to fighting, the big-nosed man got in a few good meals, tearing open the heads of some enemies and eating their brains to acquire new identities for the future.

Catalina's tongue stretched through the chests of three degenerates running toward her, killing them instantly. Her hands had each been cut off at the wrists, but moved independently of her body; crawling up the legs and torsos of her unsuspecting victims and crushing their throats with the iron-bending strength of her fingers. As the battle raged on, her tactics became more and more brutal. Joel shuddered at what seemed to be her favorite move: Severing the spine of her enemies with a strong jab to their back, then, as they lay paralyzed on the ground, stomping on non-vital parts of their bodies to completely crunch their bones.

Angus and the hooded figure, meanwhile, took no-nonsense approaches. The giant, wielding a long sword made of his own sharpened bone, broke the weapons of his enemies and finished them off in no fewer than three strokes. The cloaked figure left his weapons sheathed. He elected to use his own gloved hands, which contained such strength that he could dismember opponents with simple tugs or pushes. Most commonly, however, he tore the heads off of the degenerates who opposed him.

"What a brutal battle…" Alistair muttered.

"*This* is what I've been tryin' ta keep ya from," Triston said with a shake of his head. "This is what *war* is like, Ali."

"Well, besides the monsters and dark essence-infused people, anyhow," Dalton said.

"As I thought, the degenerates cannot hope to stand up to Drake and the Dark Wizard's forces," Aldous said, leaning up against the railing of the bridge. "Still, the herd will be thinned by this battle. It will make our job easier."

Joel made hand signals, asking if the time was right to head into the sewers and stand guard. He could see that the battle was creeping north, toward them, as it raged on.

"You seem more eager than usual to do battle." Dalton pointed his intrigued gaze at the mute.

"There is little to look forward to against these monsters," Conrad said, wide-eyed at the carnage unfolding across the field. "We must make a plan. Fighting them head-on would be foolish."

"How are you feeling?" Lucia asked, leaning next to the old Wizard on the railing. "Could you muster up the water of the river to wash them away?"

Aldous pointed a rickety finger at the river below. Ripples formed in the water and it started to rise, but after a few moments, his grasp of it weakened, and it came crashing down as he hunched over in exhaustion.

"No good…" Aldous muttered between tired breaths.

Conrad shook his head. "If I had known that the exorcism would take this much out of you, I never would have gone along with it."

"Precisely why I didn't tell you as much, m'boy," he replied with a weak chuckle.

"There is no use in regret," Dalton said with crossed arms. His eyes reflected an uncommon intensity. "Life is a bloody struggle, after all. We must instead focus on what we've got *now*."

Joel fidgeted his mouth. Ever since Kabel had revealed to Dalton that the Dark Wizard was imitating their departed friends, he hadn't been the same. He worried that the warrior's head was in the wrong place, but didn't dare speak out about it. After all, he'd spent the past few weeks dealing with a mental struggle of his own, and it was starting to get his allies hurt. *Not tonight*, he thought.

"I've got me wind Rune!" Alistair said with a big, confident smile. "Just get them knobs in front o' me, an' I'll blow 'em away!"

"The odds are just as high that it will blow up in your face," Lucia said, stoically.

"Did ya *not* just see me make it work, back there? I can do this!" the big man argued.

She scoffed. "All you've proven is that it works for you *half the time*."

"But I figured it out! Now, I got the wind under me command!"

Alistair shot back, pointing the Rune at her. "But if ya don' believe me, I can always show ya!"

"You already did, when it blew up in our faces the other night," Lucia said.

"She's right, Ali," Triston interjected.

"You still doubt me?" Alistair asked, wide-eyed.

"We can use the wind Rune as backup," Dalton said, dismissively. He then turned his hard gaze to Aldous. "Even if you are tired, the Summoner Rune can still be used, can it not?"

Aldous nodded. "Indeed. The Rune works independent of my magic… though it has limits of its own."

Joel signed to the group that getting the strongest of Angus' team into a portal would be difficult. They would have to be knocked in.

"Right you are, m'boy. But I may have a few more trickly-dos up my sleeve that don't involve magic," Aldous said with a wink.

As the battle in the field raged on, it continued pressing northward, passing the halfway mark between the woods and the river.

"I think Joel is right," Conrad said. "We should head into those sewers and prepare ourselves for battle. The degenerates' numbers are dwindling. It won't be long before they are soundly defeated."

"Very well," Dalton said as he began walking down the pathway of the bridge. The other Strangers followed close behind.

At the end of the bridge, they took a left down a steep path, which brought them by the river. After another left, they walked along narrow patches of dirt that led to a platform by the entrance of the sewer.

Upon reaching the sewer entrance, the Strangers came to an abrupt stop. Inside, the river raged straight through a spacious tunnel, echoing from as far as the ear could hear. A noticeable stink permeated throughout, and a green haze obscured their view, deeper inside.

On each side of the river were long stretches of stone platform, where passageways could be entered or exited every so often, leading into a network of paths to form the maze. Most notable to the Strangers, however, were the hundreds of yellow eyes staring back at them from deep within.

"Well…" Aldous trailed off with a nervous chuckle. "I suppose poking the hornet's nest doesn't send *all* of the lil' buggers out to sting you, eh?"

Joel felt a pit in his stomach. He and his team found themselves between a rock and a hard place. They could return to the bridge and hope that the degenerates would hold Angus and his team off, but everything he had witnessed told him that it would only delay the inevitable. The dark forces were going to infiltrate the sewers unless the Strangers could find a way to stop them.

~

On the west side of the sewers, Kabel and his group stood in both anticipation and dread. The herd of mutated swine kicked up dust as a prelude to the charge. The Dark Wizard and his brainwashed masses grinned from atop their backs.

Satara's sharp eyes fell on Giles and Rolf, however. They nodded at each other, and each was holding something small in their hands.

"They're up to something…" she muttered while nudging Najih.

Oneth kicked his swine at its swelling sides, and it let out an unbearable squeal before charging ahead. The others followed, perfectly in step with the head of the pack.

"Prepare yourselves!" Kabel called out, drawing his sword and shield.

In unison, Rolf and Giles threw the haze pellets at the swine as they were dashing across the muddied river. Gasps echoed in the tunnel as the little balls exploded into a shroud of smoke, halting the swine and blurring everyone's vision. Satara pressed a hand to her mouth covering while stifling coughs, and to her left, she could just barely make out Najih in his tall, muscular form. He, too, was pressing a hand to his silk mouth cover.

At first, the struggles of the enemy and their swine were apparent thanks to their squeals, coughs, and splashes in the water. However, after a few seconds, all fell eerily quiet. She did not dare make a move, for fear of the swine attacking. Now, all she could do was wait.

As the haze cleared, Satara found that all allies aside from Najih were either lying on the stone path or leaning up against the tunnel wall. Each of them wore dazed, loopy expressions. Satara herself was somewhat off-balance and lightheaded, but she otherwise kept her wits about her.

"Load me up with another drink, Cole!" Kabel said with a stupid grin. He cupped his hands in the river water and leaned in to drink it.

Satara ran over and slapped the water out of his hands. "Are you *trying* to poison yourself?"

Meanwhile, Dhogron, with eyes nearly shut and giggling, looked at

Najih. "Pssst… hey… I've got a plan that will end this whole conflict. It's a prank… they'll never see it coming."

"Well? What is it?" he asked.

The trickster Wizard's giggles tapered off into a contemplative silence. "I… I can't remember."

Najih looked at Satara with a twitching brow. "Something is wrong with the others…"

"This sword… is *so heavy*!" Giles said, nudging Rolf with one hand and dragging his blade with the other, limp-wristed. The pair started laughing uncontrollably.

"You think?" Satara asked with an eye roll. "I feel a little strange, too. It must be the haze pellets…"

"Could it be that our mouth coverings spared us these odd effects?" Najih replied.

"For now…" she muttered, trying to conserve her breaths. It felt like each inhale took in a little more of the haze that had incapacitated the others.

The pair looked across the river to see several Bosfueras villagers sprawled out on the unforgiving stone tiles, having toppled over from their rides. The swine, meanwhile, either laid down or walked around in circles, dazed and confused. The Dark Wizard sat atop his boar in the middle of the muddy stream while looking at the palm of his hand.

"What… what am I doing here?" Oneth muttered, his breaths growing heavy. He then buried his face in a palm. "This… this isn't right! I should *not* be here!"

Satara and Najih looked at each other with a mixture of fright and confusion in their eyes, and then back to the Dark Wizard, who seemed to be having a mental breakdown. All of the others had devolved into children. Even the mutated swine had pacified, but there was a clear element of danger, or instability, in Oneth.

"It's all wrong," he said, shaking his head. "Mother, what do I do?"

"'Mother?'" Najih asked, turning to Satara.

"Don't look to me for answers…" she replied.

"Why won't you answer me, mother?" Oneth asked in an accusatory tone. He was looking at Satara, now, and she was taken aback. In all of her years in this strange city, she had never found herself in such a bizarre situation.

"These haze pellets… didn't Dhogron say that they make you hallucinate?" Najih asked.

"He did. So what?"

"Can't you see? He is hallucinating so much that you look like his mother; at least in his warped mind."

Satara turned her gaze back to Oneth with a furrowed brow, filled with sweat. He'd been staring at her for long enough that nerves had come into play. It felt like her life depended on telling him what he wanted to hear. *Time to improvise*, she thought.

"I… err…" she trailed off, searching for direction in her voice. "My apologies, dear. Mother is here to help."

"Where are we?" Oneth asked. Satara was taken aback by the change of tone in his voice. She could have sworn that there was a certain innocence or naiveté to it.

"We are in the sewers of Endoshire," Satara replied. All good lies were woven between truths, she thought. And something told her that she could not afford to be caught in a lie. So, her strategy was to tell as much of the truth as she could afford while playing the part of his mother.

"Endoshire? We are so far from home!" Oneth said, frowning. "Mother… have you been practicing *Witchcraft*, again?"

"Of course not, dear."

"Don't lie to me. I can smell the stink of your sacrifices," Oneth said in a stern tone. Satara did her best not to scoff at the assertion. "You know what will happen if they find out you have been partaking in more devilry, mother. They will come for you, and then they will burn you alive…"

Satara did her best impression of a motherly chuckle. "Worry not, my son. What you smell is merely the sewage that runs through this river. Would I lie to you?"

He sighed. "I suppose not."

"You, on the other hand, have been bad, haven't you?" Satara asked. Najih cocked his head, to which she shrugged.

"Yes…"

"Tell mother what you have done."

"O' mother…" Oneth trailed off, each passing syllable growing darker and more treacherous. "Where ever shall I begin in confessing my sins to you? There does not exist a sum of money in this world that could pay off the debts I have accrued in my acts against God. But alas, it is for *the greater good*, and it must be done for a better world. So, you see, when I crushed little Gwendolyn's skull and sacrificed her, it was not done in malice. It was done to help others. You understand, don't you?"

"R-right…"

"And then, of course, there was Mr. Bertrand. You remember him, I'm sure. He was such a nice old man, but when he discovered my experiments… I had no choice… he threatened me, and that meant he threatened my better world. The poor old boy had to be chopped up. I fed his toes to the dogs, his fingers to the squirrels, his head to the fishes-"

Satara regretted her prior question. Each grizzly detail felt like a hair being yanked from her head. On, and on he went, describing his atrocities in increasingly feverish detail. It got so bad that shivers shot down her spine, forcing her shoulders to shift up and her neck to crick down.

"Is something wrong?" The Dark Wizard's face remained eerily calm.

"I… I think that it is time for you to leave, dear. Go home, and take your group with you," said the dancer. It was a risky play, making any demands, but she had grown immensely uncomfortable and feared the turn that their conversation was taking.

Oneth looked over his shoulder at the Bosfueras townsfolk, floundering on the ground or lying atop their respective swine, dazed.

"You bewitched them, didn't you?" he asked with contempt on his tongue.

"Would you be a dear and take them back onto the ship?" Satara asked in a pleasant tone. Oneth glared daggers at her; ones that pierced her heart and took her breath away. "A-after all, y-you wouldn't want *them* to catch me, and to burn your mother alive, would you? You love mother, don't you?"

There was a long, breathless pause that overtook the sewer. Oneth's face became unreadable. All Satara could be sure of was that she was either his next victim, or would be one of the lucky few to escape his grasp. There would be nothing in between.

"Yes… I suppose I could take them," he said to collective sighs of relief from Satara and Najih. "However, you must come with me. It is clear that you cannot withhold your cravings for Witchcraft. It is for your own safety that I must watch over you."

The dancer shuddered. "Wha-"

Oneth strode across the river, as if gliding atop the water's surface, and grabbed Satara's wrist, freezing her in place. She would have fallen, if not for the strength of the Dark Wizard holding her up.

He looked back at the folk from Bosfueras. "Back to the ship. Now."

Without question, the sluggish men and women stood or dismounted their swine, and began walking down the stone path, toward the sewer exit. Oneth followed close behind with a breathless and helpless Satara in tow.

She looked back to Najih, also paralyzed with fear, in sheer desperation. The dancer could not speak, for she knew it meant death, or worse; but her eyes said it all. Satara was pleading for help with her gaze.

As the Dark Wizard and his group marched down the tunnel, approaching the light of the moon outside and the ship, Satara felt dread set in. While on the vessel, there would be no escaping from an all-powerful Wizard. When he inevitably awoke from the spell of the haze pellets and realized that she was *not* his mother, there would be hell to pay. Despite fully realizing that she was walking to her death, the dancer continued in her approach. Her legs betrayed her thoughts and followed the orders of the large, robed man with a tight grasp on her wrist.

There had to be some way out, she thought; a path of escape that eluded her thoughts, which both fear and the haze pellets had successfully clouded. No matter how her mind raced, it reached no tangible conclusion. It simply droned on without much in the way of helpfulness, much like her legs.

A sense of irony and despair struck Satara through her heart. For years, she had spent her efforts on rescuing slaves. Now, she was getting a small taste of what it felt like to be one.

CHAPTER 39
STANDOFF

"Careful with them crates!" Sampson bellowed as a couple of his slaves lost their grips and dropped a container. "Ye want yer families to stay safe, right? Do the job, and do it well! Don't give me a reason to harm 'em!"

"Yes, Master," they said in unison while readjusting the crate.

Sampson and his men stood on one of the larger ships in the docking area of his grand wooden building, stacking crates to be used in their planned attack against the kraken. The slaver had loaded the containers with many hazardous materials such as mercury and lead. The idea was to poison the sea monster before it could release its own deathly toxins upon them.

Barret lurked by Sampson, buzzing and watching the slaves in their preparation. Sampson couldn't help but stare at the grotesque bug-man every once in a while. He'd experienced his share of oddities over the years, but Barret was unlike anything he had ever seen. It didn't happen often, but Sampson found himself struggling for words when attempting to speak with him.

"So… erm… yer aware of the plan, are you not?" he asked.

With several hisses and buzzes, Barret responded, gesturing with his arms as if he were talking like any other man would.

Sampson snorted. "Just so we're clear, I'll tell ye the plan again: We are takin' two ships out to sea. One is the decoy, which will drift near the sewer entrance first. It's gonna have loads 'n loads of toxic material on board, so we need that vessel to be destroyed and sunk. That way, the beast will take in the poison through the water. Ye follow so far?"

The bug-man buzzed, to which Sampson narrowed his eyes.

"Nod fer 'yes', shake yer head fer 'no'."

Barret nodded his grotesque fly-head.

"Good. Now, this is where *you* come in. I have been told that the kraken has trouble handling targets who can fly. The big ol' beast will swing its tentacles 'round wildly, and so we need ye to get it to strike the decoy ship. Make sure it really destroys it, too. The crates o' poison will do the rest of the work," Sampson said with a filthy grin. Barret nodded once more. "Afterward, you'll join up with the rest of us on a second ship, an' we can infiltrate the sewer together. I gots a map that will take us straight to the target."

Reaching into his fur coat's pocket, the slaver retrieved his copy of the Endoshire sewer map and waved it around, proudly. "The ships are almost all prepped an' ready to go. Stand by for departure."

Sampson walked down the plank, back onto one of many platforms where ships had been docked for repair. He studied the map, filled with maze paths and confusing landmarks alike. From his perspective, it seemed that the north drain was the worst of the possible entrances to take.

"Ah, well…" he muttered, rolling up the map and stuffing it back into his pocket. "After we down that kraken, nothin' will stand in our way. We'll have plenty o' time."

～

THE PIRATES, Prince Xviktolo, and the tied-up sailors departed from dock 12 with a strong breeze pushing them out to sea. Auber took hold of the steering, while Ebbie manned the crow's nest in watch for anything out in the dark waters worth pointing out. Franco and Xviktolo, meanwhile, watched over the captive sailors with weapons drawn.

"Is this necessary?" the navigator asked, whisking his saber about in the wind.

"Do you *want* them to escape?" Prince Xviktolo asked, shaking his head.

"It is only fair that we cut them loose before crashing the ship," Franco said as muffled cries of plight came from the sailors sitting before him.

"See that? Now, you've got them riled up," Xviktolo said, tapping his starlite sword off the deck.

"We can hardly blame them for being nervous. I'm sure we can quell those fears by assuring them that they may jump ship before the crash."

"What say you, Captain?" Xviktolo asked, looking to Auber.

"O' course we gotta let 'em go before crashin'! They never did nothin' bad to me, so I gots no reason to kill 'em!" Auber said with false bravado as his queasy stomach gurgled. Just speaking of the upcoming crash filled him with dread.

"Very well," Xviktolo said while pointing his sword at the sailors. "We will allow you to jump overboard, but only *just before* we crash."

"I dunno why yer bein' so strict about it," the captain said with a shrug.

"Because they could stop us if we're not careful. They outnumber us," the marinian replied.

"That's awright!" Ebbie called down from the crow's nest, holding up the folded net that he'd obtained from Dhogron. "If they try anythin' funny, I'll just drop this useful net down on 'em!"

"I fail to see the practicality of a net in this situation," Franco said with an eye roll.

"As a sea-dweller, I have to say… I've seen better," Xviktolo added.

"Ye lot just can't appreciate the beautiful simplicity of the net! But watch n' see! I bet it'll come in handy, tonight! If not against the enemy, then maybe we can catch some fish… or somethin'…" Captain Auber said.

The ship picked up speed as it swooped past dock 13. Sampson's wooden shipyard building loomed in the distance, at dock 15. Ebbie reported dark figures marching in and out of the building, but no boats had set sail, filling the captain with some relief.

"Shall I start releasing them, sir?" Franco asked, pointing to the sailors, who were now struggling to free themselves from the bindings and gags.

"Let's play it safe. Wait 'till dock 14 to set 'em free," Auber said.

Soon enough, the ship came upon the dock before Sampson's shipyard. Franco began to untie the sailors and push them overboard, one at a time. Xviktolo, meanwhile, kept his sword pointed at each prisoner being expelled from the vessel.

One by one, the crew of sailors were thrown out to sea; all were untied, but they remained gagged to keep them quiet in the dead of night. As the ship neared dock 15, Franco knelt over to start untying the captain of the sailors. He was an older, burly man, with salt and pepper hair and a scraggly beard.

However, as he attempted to undo the knots, the captain revealed a hand that had already slipped free, and landed a stiff jab to his nose. Franco stumbled back as the sailor captain hopped up, stole his saber, and held it up to his neck. The navigator's nose bled as he held up his hands in defeat.

"Awright, lads. Drop all weapons if ye want yer friend to see another dawn," he demanded.

Xviktolo placed his starlite blade on the deck, while Auber did the same with his saber. The burly man inched his way up to the steering wheel of the ship, using Franco as his hostage.

"I'll be turnin' this ship 'round, now, if ye please."

"Erm…" Auber let out a nervous chuckle. "Ye look hungry! Could I interest ye in some berries?"

Auber gasped as the burly man laid into him with a backhanded slap. The captain stumbled back and fell to his bottom, his face numb and his mind blank.

"What a brute…" Franco muttered. The lower half of his face was dripping crimson red.

With one hand on the saber pointed at Franco, the sailor captain used the other to spin the ship wheel. The vessel made a sharp turn to the left so that it faced north, toward the open sea.

Captain Auber looked up to the crow's nest as the vessel traveled further and further out and away from their intended destination. He nodded up at Ebbie, who looked down upon him with the net in his grasp.

With little warning, Franco dove to the deck, out of the burly man's reach. "What the hell're ye-"

"Go, o' mighty net! Go!" Ebbie shouted as he let loose the mesh from above.

The sailor captain looked up to see the net descending upon him, and there was no way to dodge in time. It ensnared him, and in his desperate struggle, he tumbled over. It only made his entanglement worse, and eventually, he began wriggling around like a worm.

"What's with these parlor tricks? What kinda pirates are ye?" he complained as Auber, Xviktolo, and Franco loomed over him.

"We're the Auber Pirates! An' don't ye ferget it, landlubber!" the captain said, following up with a triumphant right hook to his jaw.

"I'll keep that in mind..." the burly man said, now sitting up straight. A small welt took shape, just underneath his lip.

"Oh... err... I thought that was gonna knock ye fer a loop, at least. Or maybe even knock ye-" Auber yelped as Franco nailed the sailor captain in the back of his head with the butt of his reacquired saber. "-out..."

"Pardon me, sir," the navigator said as the burly man collapsed to the deck.

Auber returned to the steering wheel as Xviktolo tossed the dazed man overboard in unceremonious fashion. The captain spun the wheel hard to the right, jerking the ship so that it was facing the shipyard and shoreline ahead.

"Ebbie! Get down from thar!" the captain called out, looking up at the crow's nest. He then pointed his gaze at Xviktolo while smiling nervously. "Erm... by the way... I gots a favor to ask ye..."

"What is it?"

"Well, y'see... even though I'm a brave fairer of the seas, I spend most of me time on a ship, and not so much in the water," Auber said. He eyed the rapidly approaching shipyard ahead with a strange mixture of excitement and dread. "What I'm tryin' to say is... could ye guide me through the water after we jump overboard?"

Prince Xviktolo returned a wide-eyed stare. "I'm surprised, Captain! I'd have thought such a fearsome pirate would be one of the best human swimmers if nothing else!"

"Sadly, even the *fiercest of warriors* have their weaknesses, and the captain is no exception," Franco said in a facetious tone.

"Very well. I shall take you in my arms as we jump overboard," Xviktolo replied, much to Franco and Ebbie's visible amusement, and Auber's chagrin.

～

INSIDE THE DOCKING YARD, one of the slaves ran up to Sampson with urgency in his eyes.

"Master! There is a ship headed straight for us, outside!" he cried. All of the workers stopped what they were doing.

"*What?*" Sampson asked with a snarl. "Show me."

The pair ran to the back of the building, up to a window that overlooked the sea. The slaver gasped to see a vessel fast approaching from the north. So close was the ship that he could see the crew steering it in his direction.

Sampson gritted his teeth to see the raggedy pirate who had dared to shoot him in the leg a week prior. His lips quivered with rage.

"*Auber*," Sampson growled as he punched the wooden wall, splintering it and slicing up his knuckles in the process. A vein popped in his forehead as he watched the pirates and marinian jump overboard. "I curse you! You damned pirate! You'll know nothing but endless days on the fields when I'm through with you!"

"Master? What shall we do?" the slave asked.

"Isn't it obvious?" Sampson said, shaking his hand. The boat was but a few meters away, now, coming at full speed. "Brace fer impact!"

The splintering of wood and the sensation of falling dominated Sampson's senses as the room gave way and collapsed in on him and his slave. Then, all around him became a salty, black abyss.

IN THE EASTERN entrance of Endoshire's sewers, Joel drew his luxmortite blade as a horde of yellow-eyed degenerates approached from the depths of the tunnel.

"Hold on, m'boy," Aldous said, clasping a hand on his shoulder. It almost felt to Joel like he was using his shoulder to keep himself propped up. "We don't need to fight them. Not yet."

"What other choice do we have?" Alistair asked, looking over his shoulder. "We're sandwiched in, here! We either fight 'em in tha stink of these sewers, or we face both the degenerates *and* Angus' team outside."

The old Wizard nodded at his Summoner Rune with a knowing smile. "Anywhere I have been, or can see, is within my reach."

Joel sheathed his blade and smiled. Aldous had wisely reasoned that he could make a portal behind the degenerates, off in the distance of the gassy, green tunnel. Pierce had done the same thing for them back at the battle by the docks, and it had completely fooled the enemy. However, the degenerates were not single-minded in the same way as the Bosfueras townsfolk; they were *always* looking for someone or something to harm.

With various hand signals, Joel communicated that the group should wait to use the Rune until Angus' team reached the insides of the sewer. That way, the lurking degenerates could find new targets.

"Makes sense to me," Dalton said, dreary-eyed. "On another note… do any of you feel lightheaded?"

"Mayhap yer just tired," Alistair said.

"No, that's not it," the warrior replied, shaking his head. "I have felt this way before. It's like when your body takes over, without a thought. Sometimes, I get that feeling in battle, especially if I'm angry; it is an instinct to strike."

"Acting on impulse," Conrad said with a nod. "I know it well."

"I am beginning to suspect that the foul stench of the sewers is not merely human waste…" Aldous trailed off in an ominous tone.

"Well, of course! There's all kinds o' waste in here! Tha centaur, avian, and trolls gotta relieve themselves, too, ya know!" Triston said with an obnoxious laugh. Alistair joined in.

"I believe he refers to the effects of Degenerate…" Lucia looked at her mentor with a crass smile. "It makes sense that *you'd* be the first of us to fall victim."

"What does it say about *you*, dear student, to call such a degenerate your teacher?" Dalton asked, unwavering. Her smile turned to a frown.

"So then, Greed makes the black gold, Famine makes the violet fruits, and Degenerate makes… the green gas?" Conrad asked aloud.

"It would explain why the degenerates have made this their home base, at least," Aldous said, looking to the approaching horde with a tired smirk. "But that presents a problem: It is not certain how long we can withstand the gasses before succumbing to degeneracy ourselves. Perhaps an impulse to attack is the beginning of the symptoms."

The comment gave Joel pause. *He* had been itching for battle before any of the others. In most situations, it was the other way around.

Still, the jeers of the approaching degenerates did not see him dwelling on it for long. They marched down the stone pathways at each side of the tunnel, not rushing, but rather, savoring their next targets.

"Looks like we got a few wanderers from the surface, lads!" one called out.

"I can't wait to carve 'em up!" said another.

"Or drown 'em in the sewage!"

"Kill!"

"Kill!"

"Down with the Imperials!"

"Make 'em pretty!"

"Make 'em squeal!"

Chatter descended into laughs of complete and utter madness as the yellow-eyed horde drew weapons. Some began running at them while growling and howling like feral beasts.

"Erm… mista Wizard…" Triston muttered, taking a step back.

"Not yet…" Aldous replied, standing sideways. He looked to his right, where the sewer entrance was, then back toward the tunnel depths.

The degenerates, foaming at the mouth with vitriol, were closer than ever.

"Aldous!" Dalton called out with uncharacteristic urgency.

"A lil' longer…" the old Wizard said, then looked back once more. Shadows of the enemies yet to come poked into the sewer entrance. "Now!"

Aldous held out his Summoner Rune, and a dark, howling portal took shape. Time was short, and so all of the Strangers jumped in, showing no hesitation or resistance to the idea.

Upon exiting the vortex, Joel wasn't sure whether to be frightened by the darkness blanketing him or disgusted by the all-encompassing gas that he was breathing in. His eyes picked up on a source of light behind, and his ears wriggled at the echoes of pitter-patter coming from the same direction. The mute turned to see the crowd of degenerates nearly blotting out the dim light of the entrance off in the distance. In some strange way, it reminded him of Mt. Couture's tunnel collapses.

Still, Aldous' plan proved to be a success. *Clangs* of metal striking metal and cries of agony and glory echoed from down the tunnel. Angus' team had infiltrated the sewer, but now, they were embroiled in a second skirmish that was sure to wilt away their forces a little more.

"Now what?" Alistair asked with hands to hips.

"We must prepare ourselves for battle," Conrad said. "The enemy will almost certainly break through."

Aldous brought out the sewer map and squinted at it for a few moments.

"This is no place for us to fight," he said while hobbling deeper into the green haze of the tunnel. "Come! There is an open area up ahead; one that I think we'll find fitting for our final confrontation with Drake's team."

~

Sɪʀ Jᴏʙ Cᴀʀᴅᴏɴ dove for cover on the grimy stone platform as several degenerates soared: Two of them struck the ceiling and fell into the muddy river, motionless. Another flew over Job's head and rolled further up the platform until crashing into a crowd and knocking them all down. The last of the bunch mashed into the rocky wall on the knight's left, the crunch of his bones and the raining of his blood eliciting a shudder.

Yet, it was not just the brutality of battle that had struck him. It was the godly strength and blatant disregard for their enemies, Job thought while reaching a knee and looking over his shoulder. Angus loomed over both he and a couple of his fellow knights, who had also wisely dove for cover. The giant had been treating the degenerates like bothersome flies to be swatted away.

It made sense that he would afford little time for those beneath him, though. Most of the combatants had gathered on the left path of the tunnel, causing a blockage at the entrance. Swaths of the slaves and Bosfueras townsfolk were relegated to the outside, unable to pass through the mass of degenerates and even their own allies. Flaming torches kept the creepers at bay, and their large, lumpy bodies made it all the more difficult to get by. For that reason, the knights and dark essence-enhanced had been the only ones truly pressing forward.

Job's eyes wandered over to Brice, who howled aloud in laughter as his tendrils pierced through four yellow-eyed men at once. To his visible chagrin, the crazed folk laughed along with him before falling limp. He tossed the corpses into the river, like trash that he couldn't be bothered with.

Ned, meanwhile, continued to break limb and body alike with the sheer strength of his grip. All who stood before him fell, except when one of the degenerates threatened him with a flaming torch. He took a step back as the yellow-eyed woman swung the flame around with little in the way of strategy.

"Burn! Imperialist scum!"

However, a twisting and turning red streak interrupted the attack by piercing her temple like the sharpest of daggers. More devilry from Brice? *No,* Job thought with a gasp. The unnaturally long tongue slithered back into Catalina's mouth, and she licked her bloody lips with glee as the woman fell into the river, motionless. He stifled a disgusted groan and instead settled for a frown that she could not see beneath his helm. To think, just a few nights ago, he had been *lusting for her*.

"On your feet, Sir Job!" one of the knights called out, refocussing him on the task at hand. It had been the sturdy voice of Sir Gareth, who, along with Sir Elric, was in the process of crossing the river. "The path of least resistance lies across!"

Indeed, he thought with a nod. Nearly all of the degenerates had migrated to the left walkway, and it would be a risky, lengthy process to plow through them all.

Although the gap of the river was wide, Angus found it a trivial matter to clear. To call his attempt a 'leap' would be a dramatic overstatement. Instead, it looked more like he'd taken a casual *skip* onto the right pathway. The same could be said for Ned's jump, while Brice pulled himself to the platform with his dark tentacles-for-arms. Catalina, meanwhile, plopped down on all fours, and like some sort of feral cat, she leaped across the gap. *Truly a vile woman,* Job reassured himself as he jumped into the river and began swimming after his fellow knights.

Heavy armor meant slower swimming, however, and to make matters worse, Job heard splashes behind them. He was sure that the degenerates had jumped in to intercept them. And so, he and his fellow Sigrian gallants desperately paddled across as the stream pushed them further into the rotten depths of the sewer. After putting his head down and stroking his arms through the water as fast as he could, Job felt the slippery surface of the right pathway slide across his palm. At his feet, ever kicking, he felt what seemed to be hands grasping at him. With one more burst of energy, the knight pushed himself up while kicking as hard and fast as he could. He let out a breath of relief when the heel of his boot struck something, and he heard the surprised groan of his pursuer. To his left, Job caught the glint of armor. Sir Gareth stood over him, outstretching a hand.

Job took the boost, and looked behind to see the degenerate floating downstream, unconscious. However, his relief was short-lived. One of his allies was missing.

"They got Sir Elric..." Gareth said, pointing further up the stream to a lifeless, floating body. "He deserves a proper burial."

"Those damned degenerates..." Job trailed off, looking ahead. Angus had just finished slaying his latest foe, whose head rolled and plopped into the river below. The dark essence-enhanced monsters marched up the path, unhindered, until fading into the green haze. A muffled snort bounced beneath Job's helm. "Believe me, I'd much rather honor Sir Elric than see what further devilry or atrocities our new allies have in store. But we cannot let his sacrifice be in vain. There is a job to be finished. We shall retrieve his body after the completion of our mission."

Sir Gareth returned a slow nod, and with that, the pair dashed ahead, unsure of what the nauseous confines of the green gas had in store.

~

Angus led his teammates further into the sewers while looking down at the map. He could feel Brice hovering behind him, trying to read it for himself, but he constantly shifted his shoulders to make it difficult for him.

"Where are we headed, anyway?" Brice finally asked with a huff.

"Straight," Angus replied, without looking back.

"Alright, and *then what*?" Brice pressed, his tone growing more combative by the word.

Contempt began to erode at the stone foundations of Angus' expression. "Know your place, little one. It is *I* who will make demands of *you*, not the other way around."

"I've had about enough of yer self-righteous shite, Angus," Brice said with a clenched fist. "Yer not a noble, and ye ain't much of a leader… yer clearly just a brainless oaf, which is why soon enough, *I'll* be the leader of this group."

"Is that a threat?" the giant asked, coming to an abrupt stop. He turned and readied his bone blade. If need be, he would beat the insubordination out of him. Brice, meanwhile, had changed his arms into the dark tentacles, coiling and ready to strike.

"Now is not the time to be fighting, boys. We have a seal to break. Let us not forget how many threats we face, deeper in these sewers," Catalina said with hands at her hips. She then smiled and looked over her shoulder. "Besides, all of this infighting will dishearten our brave, handsome knights."

Clanking armor rang through the tunnel walls, until out of the darkness, Sir Job and Sir Gareth arrived, both panting.

"Did… we miss… anything?" Job asked.

"Nothing, yet," Angus said as he turned and looked back down at the map. "We are to continue straight until reaching a chamber of sorts. There, we will need to take a path to the left, I believe."

"'You believe'? Yer not even sure where to go?" Brice asked with a scoff.

Angus glared back, but then he relaxed his posture. "You and I obviously have a score to settle… but it can wait until after we have completed our mission. For now, try not to let your childish desires dictate any decisions you make."

"Why you-" Brice took a step forward, but Catalina caught his shoulder. She whispered something to him, and it brought mischievous smiles to both of their faces.

Angus was smirking, too. Did they truly believe that they could match him if it ever came to blows? He had already devised a strategy to handle both of them, just in case they ever decided to go rogue. Neither had particularly quick deaths in store if they ever dared raise a finger against him.

With that thought, Angus led his team down the tunnel. The further into the bowels they walked, the darker and greener their surroundings became. After walking for some time, he could see that the tunnel opened up into a chamber, off in the distance.

Echoes of the river intensely pushing and shoving against stone filled their collective ears, and as they grew closer, it became clear why: Ahead, at the beginning of the chamber, were three paths that the river split into. One curved to the right, another to the left, and then straight ahead there was a slit in a massive, stone platform that peeked out of the water and spread to the end of the chamber.

They traversed a small arch over the right river path, leading to the platform above water. The ceiling featured some barred slits where the light of the moon poked through; meant to relieve any potential flooding in the slums on rainy days, no doubt. Most notable about the chamber, however, was an abrupt end to the semi-circular platform, cut off by a wall where a great statue loomed.

The sculpture depicted a dragon that was unfamiliar to Angus. It was long and coiling; serpent-like in appearance, as opposed to the large, beast-like bodies they were known to have. The statue also lacked their great wings that allowed them to travel faster than any other known creature. Otherwise, it depicted some familiar, dragon-like features: An angular head with a long snout baring sharp teeth, mighty horns sprouting from its scalp, and four three-pronged claws stretching across its coiled body. Below the statue stood a small stone monument that had long since seen its inscribed text obscured by an outgrowth of moss.

Angus did not remain focused on the chamber-filling statue for long, however. Standing on the left side of the platform were the Strangers. They blocked the arched path over the leftmost stream, which led to the tunnel that Angus and his team needed access to. The two groups each formed a line, standing across from one another in anticipation of the coming battle.

"I suppose this confrontation was inevitable," Angus said, drawing his bone sword, and growing a thick, white shield on his forearm. This time, however, several more sharp bones sprouted from his arms and up to the shoulder, making close combat with the giant even more dangerous.

"Turn back while we're still affording you the opportunity," Dalton said before drawing his long sword and taking a bent stance.

Brice cackled. "Ye have no authority here! Yer skills with the sword won't mean a thing when I'm tearin' ye to bloody pieces!"

"And what do you know of authority?" the warrior shot back. A cheeky smile spread across his face. "I seem to recall your leadership *folding*, back in Bosfueras. Is that why the big fella is callin' all of the shots?"

The big-nosed man growled like an angry attack dog, but Angus cleared his throat, and it stilled him.

"Do not listen to the ramblings of a drunk who cannot handle reality. After all, who else would follow the empty words of a dead woman?"

"*What was that?*" Dalton asked with fire in his eyes. That fire quickly faded, though, and he looked down, as if coming to terms with the truth. "I thought that maybe… that night… it had been real, somehow. But in the presence of such treacherous dogs, I should have known better. You lot have been playin' around with other people's lives for too long. Tonight, it ends!"

Lucia looked at her mentor with a furrowed brow, but she did not speak.

"You too, Brice," Conrad said, his tone colder than a mountain's peak. Lucia looked to him, next, and Angus did his best to stifle a laugh. *The poor woman is surrounding herself with unstable men*, he thought. "You are little more than an abomination. Tonight, I will put you down, just like Daniel… just like Willoughby… and even Wolfgang. Rogues like you have no place in this world."

The strategist drew his rapier and took a staggered, sideways stance. He held the blade outward with one hand while placing the other on his hip.

"We'll just see about that!" Brice said as his voice grew monstrous and his arms formed into several wriggling, dark tentacles. "Ye were lucky to escape Bosfueras! I'll make up fer my mistakes! Yer death will be slow and plagued with suffering, as it will be for the rest of yer pitiful friends!"

Aldous let out a deep breath as he *clanked* his walking stick off the ground. His tired expression shifted to one of vigor and determination. "You shall go no further, servants of Drake and Oneth!"

Joel drew his luxmortite sword and bent his stance with the front foot facing forward and the back perpendicular. He held the blade diagonal and upward, but pulled the hilt in, toward the bottom corner of his stomach. Angus recognized it as a position meant for quick strikes, but now it was harder than ever not to laugh.

"How amusing," Catalina said while drawing upon a small bone blade that Angus had gifted her. "The quiet boy is acting tough. We all know that you are incapable of harming others. Why don't you just go home?"

"True though it may be…" Lucia trailed off, calling upon her sword and adjusting her stance to the long guard, with lengthy, powerful legs staggered and the blade outreached. A smile filled her face as she looked down at Joel, who remained still and calm, unlike all of the others. "But the night is young, and full of surprises yet to come."

Catalina let out a vain chuckle. "You were frightened of me a few nights ago, too. It seems that between you and the quiet boy, the Strangers are filled with cowards."

"HAH!" Alistair shouted, to the annoyance of Angus' ears. "No team with Cap'n Auber an' Alistair MacRae leadin' tha charge can ever be considered cowardly! Before tonight is over, it'll be *yer* sorry arses runnin' away! An' *maybe* if I'm feelin' nice, I'll let ya go! BUT PROBABLY NOT!"

Ned started for Alistair, but Angus held up a hand, stilling him.

"Settle down, Ned." Angus cracked a smirk in Alistair's direction. "This fat-head is all bluster. Let us savor his final, pitiful moments."

Alistair scoffed while bringing out his battle axe. He held it across his body with a grip so firm that the handle groaned. "I'll show ya who's really been tha boisterous one!"

"Ali…" Triston muttered while bringing out his great sword. "That fella's dangerous. You'll die if ya face 'im one-on-one."

"Nonsense!" Alistair called out with a mighty laugh, followed by a hard slap to Triston's back. "Tonight's the night I'll prove me'self to ya, brother!"

The elder MacRae only returned a half-hearted smile.

"Sir Dalton…" Job said while lowering to a knee and holding his sword up as if praying. "I have waited painstaking days for our rematch. Tonight, I shall prove that Sigrian knights are superior to Federland's warriors."

Both gallants took a ready stance, but Dalton didn't reply. There was a careful, methodical intensity to his movements as he inched forward.

"That's an interestin' stance!" Alistair said, taking a knee himself and holding his axe upward. "I'll try it out, too!"

"Brother, I think it's meant ta be ceremonial…" Triston whispered, to the best of his ability.

"Surely, you both understand the evil that your allies are committing," Aldous said, looking to the knights. "I'd advise you to turn around and leave, and to return to your duty as honorable gallants of the Sigrian Kingdom."

"Stupid old man," Sir Gareth said with a chuckle. "I could kill you with but a simple stroke of my blade. Why should we listen to you?"

"No…" Job muttered with a marked nervousness. "That there is a Wizard. He is the one who fought against the kraken, a few nights back."

"Indeed, and if you wish to remain unharmed, I would advise leaving immediately," Aldous said.

"I know not if it was from the kraken or my Master, but you look pale and weak, old man," Catalina said with crossed arms. "We have nothing to fear from you."

"What you fools don't understand is that we went easy on you a few nights ago. Brice's infiltration of your team and the surprise attack at the outskirts required that *at least* half of you live. Tonight, we have no such restriction placed on us." Angus clenched a fist, and his bones responded in kind with chilling *cracks* that echoed off the chamber walls. "You dare to present a pathetically weakened Wizard, some humans, and a luxian who is too scared to fight, against us, who have transcended mankind? How shortsighted! How naïve! Understand this: Your legs are too short to lock eyes with veritable titans. None of you are leaving these sewers alive."

"Are you ready to fight? I don't think I can take any more of this idiotic chatter," Dalton said. All semblance of patience had left both his voice and posture.

The Strangers and the dark forces inched closer to one another in their lines, all with weapons at the ready. The dragon statue, bathing in moonlight from slits of the surface world, watched them in anticipation. Tonight, it was sure to witness a decisive battle.

CHAPTER 40
WHAT LURKS IN THE SHADOWS

Joel leaped forward to the tune of gasps from all within the chamber. He pulled back his luxmortite blade for a stab attempt on Angus. The giant smirked and brought his bone blade down to meet the stab. When the swords met, however, Joel tilted his angle upward while continuing the momentum of his thrust.

A shocked silence overcame the chamber as the dark blue blade pierced Angus' throat. The giant gurgled on an uncontrollable stream of blood and the superb metal that blocked its flow to his head. Joel then ripped the sword out, and a very pale Angus toppled over like a tree.

As if a signal for the battle to begin, Brice let out an excited hiss and pulled his tentacles back to strike, with Joel as their target. Before he could launch the attack, however, Conrad jumped in with a lunging stab to his temple.

Brice remained motionless as the strategist ripped the rapier from his head, but he was disheartened to see that the tentacles still wriggled with killing intent, independent of their master. Conrad hopped back as one of the tentacles curled, then flung forward with startling speed like a cracking whip. He quickly deduced that dodging would not be enough, and curved his blade while swinging it across his body; deflecting the attack leftward.

Joel, meanwhile, casually sidestepped and swatted at the tentacle streaking toward him, cutting it horizontally in half. The appendage landed on the stone floor and wriggled around before slithering back to its master. Conrad flashed him a quick smile in the heat of battle. Just like back at Mt. Couture, he was letting his true skill shine in the face of monsters. There were no hesitations in his attacks.

Catalina let out a gleeful shriek, drawing Conrad's attention as the mutated tongue burst from her mouth. In response to the streak of red heading straight for him, the strategist held his rapier up to block. However, the tongue wrapped around his blade instead of deflecting, and she began retracting it. Conrad dug his heels in and grasped the hilt of his blade with a second hand as the Gentish woman slowly pulled him into her reach, against his will.

To make matters worse, out of the corner of his eye, Conrad caught wind of one of Brice's tentacles streaking for his head. He ducked just in time to feel the howling wind of the attack flutter his blond hair. Catalina's confused cry next caught Conrad's attention. He smiled to see Lucia finishing up a decisive chop of her sword, which had cut Catalina's tense tongue in half. An initial spurt of blood from the cut appendage gave way to clots, which stopped the bleeding, and the stump retracted back into the Gentish woman's mouth.

It quickly became apparent that the severed tongue had a mind of its own, as it slithered up to Lucia and coiled around her leg like a constricting snake. She winced as the snake-like appendage became so tight around her boot that she stumbled. Still, Conrad could see in her expression that she had remained calm. Lucia reached under her skirt, drawing the dagger that was strapped to her thigh, and began cutting the tongue as if it were rope.

While Lucia was distracted, Brice took the opportunity to extend one of his tentacles in her direction. Conrad jumped in and deflected the dark feeler with his rapier, then lowered to a knee and retrieved the trusty dagger from his boot. In one swift motion, he threw his blade, which the big-nosed man attempted to swat away with both appendages. However, Conrad's aim had been true, and the dagger pierced Brice's head as the tentacles swung, striking nothing but the air.

Brice toppled over in a bloody heap as Lucia finished cutting the binding around her leg. She turned to see Catalina lunging at her with a white dagger in hand, pointed downward. Lucia wisely sidestepped instead of blocking the steel-cracking bone with her sword, and she followed up with a heavy swing to Catalina's right midsection.

The Gentish woman grunted as the blade cut into her side and the mushy sound of chopped flesh and gushing blood filled the rotten air. Catalina ceased her reckless attack and slumped over, held up only by the strength of Lucia's sword.

"Can't you cut all the way through?" Catalina asked in a jovial whisper. Lucia's eyes widened. Red, web-like clots grew from the wound and ensnared her sword, and then muscle, fat, and skin began to take shape around it. *"How sad."*

Lucia ripped her sword out of the regenerating wound and took a step back. Unbeknownst to her, the tongue remnants that she'd sliced up were wriggling along the ground behind her.

"Behind you!" Conrad cried. He knew that it was too late.

Before she could even turn to see what he meant, the tongue ribbons coiled, and then shot into the back of Lucia's left calf, through her boot.

She fell to a knee and let out a stuttered cry as blood erupted from the fresh hole in both her boot and leg.

"Hang on!" said the strategist as he started for Lucia, but he ground to a halt when she held up a finger.

"Keep your focus on Brice," she said through gritting teeth.

He turned to see Brice stirring on the grimy stone floor, but couldn't help keeping focus on Lucia's battle. The tongue remnants squirmed out of her bloody boot and inched their way back to Catalina, who waited for them with a smile. With fire in her eyes, Lucia leaped forward, stomping on the appendages with a loud *splat*. She then hobbled backward with her sword outreached defensively as the tongue pieces writhed in agony on the floor.

"I hope you enjoy the taste of my boot," she said with a defiant smile.

"Not as much as the taste of your *blood*," Catalina retorted as she knelt, picked up the tongue remnants, and swallowed them. The Gentish woman's prior wound had completely closed, with the only signs of it ever having existed being the red, clotted stitches exposed by the ripped fabric of her bloody dress.

Brice, meanwhile, began to cackle while lying out on the ground. Conrad watched on as one of the dark tentacles pulled the dagger out of his head, constricted, and then threw it back at him.

The strategist directed the projectile to his right with a single swing of the rapier and quickly refocused his eyes upon the abomination before him. Brice used the tentacles to push himself up, and his cackles turned to howls of laughter that filled the entire chamber with menace.

The wound on his forehead finished regenerating as the laughs tapered off.

"Yer truly a hopeless cause, y'know that?" he said, shaking his head. "How many times are ye gonna try to harm me before understanding? Yer only human, and yer attacks are *weak*."

"I worried that might be the case," Conrad replied without wavering. Brice's eyes grew wide, and he started scratching at his head. His breathing grew heavy, and his eyes nearly crossed upward from trying to look at what bothered him. "And so, I coated my dagger in *itching powder*. A mere prank on the outside, but on the inside, I can tell you that *itch* is *unbearable*."

"Y-you!" Brice cried, frothing at the mouth and scratching at the top of his head, ripping at his skin, which regenerated with each swipe. He let out a howl of despair and fell to both knees, smashing his head against the stone floor; desperate for relief. "I'll have yer head for this!"

"Perhaps the itching will fade, as it does when exposed to skin. Or perhaps not," Conrad said without a modicum of sympathy. He turned and picked up his trusty dagger. Afterward, he began walking to Lucia and Catalina's ongoing battle. "In the meantime, suffer on the floor where you belong, *filth*."

~

As Joel had anticipated, Angus sat up, awakening from his brief slumber, and showed no signs of the prior damage he'd taken. The mute attempted a second stab while he was getting to his feet, but this time, Angus blocked with his mighty bone shield.

In return, the giant swatted with his white shield to push Joel's sword back and then swung downward and diagonal at him with the bone blade. A lightning-fast flick of his wrist saw Joel's blade meeting the attack; and then he fired back with a down and diagonal slash of his own, aimed at the knees. The giant hopped backward, but his eyes widened at the sight of the mute pressing forward like a hungry animal in pursuit of his prey.

With a pained grunt, Angus pulled both arms back and flexed his mighty chest. Two sharp pieces of rib shot out at high speed and close range. Joel had less than a second to react, yet his newfound focus made it an easy decision: He swung at and knocked away the bone spear to his right while falling in that same direction to avoid the other one. The hollow *thunks* of bone bouncing off in the distance slowed his heart a fraction, but it started thumping again when Angus' oppressive boots stopped before his face.

He looked up to see that the giant had pulled his bone blade back, ready to take a swing that he was not in a good position to avoid. The nauseous green gas around them parted out of respect for the immense force of Angus' slash, and now all Joel could do was close his eyes and prepare himself for the burning pain and wretched sound of his own flesh being chopped.

Instead, the mute only heard a hollow *thunk*. Overhead, he caught wind of a brown blur pushing Angus' sword back. Aldous' walking stick had made the block, and that wasn't all he had in store: He next took a furious, two-handed swing with his Wizard's artifact, and Angus snarled as he raised his shield to block while taking a few tepid steps back. Joel, sensing blood in the water, sprang to his feet with a new surge of energy and leaped out for a stab. Angus was too slow to respond, and simply allowed the dark blue blade to pierce his arm. He groaned as the mute ripped his sword from the wound while twisting it.

Not a word needed to be spoken between the Wizard Scout and Key Keeper. Though they had not often fought together in the past, tonight was an exception. Tonight, they would team up and end this menace before he could break another seal.

"Your pitiful attacks are of no use here, old man," Angus said with poise. "It is telling that you have not used the sewer water to your advantage, yet."

Aldous looked over his shoulder at the river flowing along the carved path next to their grand stone platform. He hunched over, drawing heavy breaths. Joel prepared himself for a swift response from Angus while he concentrated. However, the attack never came. Instead, Angus only smirked. He had reason to be confident, too. In Aldous' current condition, there was no way he could control a mean- ingful amount of water.

"You're right..." the old Wizard said with a smile of his own. Joel and Angus both raised their eyebrows. Given the situation, his demeanor was all wrong. "Yet, there is still much that I can do to stop you."

The giant cocked his head as Aldous brought out his Summoner Rune, its dark hue clashing with the slivers of moonlight from above beautifully.

"You mean to send me away, just as Zamarim did in Thironas?" Angus asked with a scoff. "This time, I won't make it easy."

With the Rune outstretched, Aldous let loose the dark, swirling, portal before Angus. "Oho! Sometimes, it matters not what goes in, but *what comes out!*"

Angus gasped as a massive stream of water shot out from the gateway, crashing into him like a waterfall at full force. He dug his bone blade into the stone floor and held on tight as the stream pressed him back more and more.

Then, the portal closed, and the final splashes of water settled. Angus, who had been sprawled out, hanging onto his sword for dear life, got to a knee and looked up with bloodlust. The strong smell of waste permeated from him.

Brilliant move, Joel thought. He had created a portal to the sewer river so that it would temporarily flow out onto the platform, in the giant's direction. Outside of sending their opponents away, this was almost certainly how a Summoner Wizard would fight.

There was little time for pats on the back, however. Aldous had provided Joel with another opening, and he planned on taking it. He would not be the weak link in this battle. Angus gasped as the mute rushed in and swung at his sword-wielding wrist with ruthless aggression. The giant could only watch on, helpless, as the dark blue blade cut halfway into his wrist. Joel gritted his teeth at the painful vibrations in his hands; punishment for striking the immovable object with the unstoppable force. Yet, the resounding *crack* of Angus' wrist bone brought a triumphant smile to his face. It was comparatively thin next to his blade, after all, and now, he was disarmed.

Grunting in pain, Angus swung at the mute with his great white shield, forcing him to jump back. Aldous returned to the fray, swinging his walking stick for the big man's head, which was subsequently blocked by the shield.

Joel attacked in tandem with his Wizard cohort, resulting in a flurry of swings from both battlers that forced Angus to stay on a knee. His defense began to falter under the barrage, and as the speed of their attacks picked up, he lost track of where to block. Aldous nailed the giant in the head with his walking stick, knocking him for a loop and forcing his shield-wielding hand to the floor. Joel followed up with an unanswered stab to the gut.

Angus fully toppled over and fell into a bloody coughing fit, but the mute did not let up. He crunched his boot onto his chest and then ripped his sword out from the wound, again while twisting it for extra damage. The giant dropped his bone blade and staggered to his feet in a panic, backtracking with a certain clumsiness that revealed just how much he'd been weakened. Aldous took that weakness as his next opportunity to strike. He gestured the Summoner Rune at the giant's feet, and suddenly, he was gasping and falling into a dark abyss. The portal had taken shape on the ground, this time.

However, Angus reached his arm over the hole in the floor and dug his shield into the stone, hanging on by a thread over the darkness below. Like ravenous attack dogs, Joel and Aldous swarmed and prepared their next attacks.

"Enough of this!" Angus cried, flinging himself up from the bowels of the portal with the strength of just one arm.

Upon touching down on solid ground, Joel and Aldous fell still and readied their defenses. Angus pushed off with such force that chunks of the floor flew as he lunged forward and laid a shoulder tackle into the mute, with the spikes on his arms leading. Joel blocked a few of the sharp bones with his sword, but there were simply too many to avoid, and one pierced his shoulder while another dug into his top-right chest plate. He let out a silent gasp of pain as the impact sent him crashing to the ground and rolling along the grime for a distance.

He looked up with dreary eyes to see the hazy form of Aldous closing in on the giant with his walking stick overhead and ready to strike. In response, Angus turned and pointed the fingers of his right hand at him. Out from his fingers shot the dreaded bone bolts, traveling fast as an arrow and headed for several points on Aldous' body at once.

With great urgency, the old Wizard swung his walking stick in a circular motion, striking each of the bone bolts along the way and deflecting them. However, the projectiles had merely been a distraction. By the time Aldous finished the follow-through of his swing, the giant had closed the distance between them. He clubbed him in the chest with his white shield, eliciting a pained, surprised gasp as he flew through the air and crashed to the floor in a miserable heap.

Angus retrieved his bone blade. "Your parlor tricks won't save you. My entire body is a weapon. The two failures of Mt. Couture shall die by my hand, tonight."

"The only way… you'll be leaving… here tonight… is unceremoniously, by a portal…" Aldous squeaked out between wheezing breaths.

The giant only snorted as he began inching forward with his shield up and bone blade at eye level, pulled back and ready to strike.

Aldous pushed himself up with his walking stick, but he stumbled several times along the way. Joel began clawing in their direction, slowly. His body had still not recovered from the shock of Angus' prior attack, but he was determined to aid his Wizard cohort, even if it meant serving as a mere distraction.

~

DALTON BACKPEDALED as the two knights swung their blades simultaneously at him. Since the beginning of the battle, most of his time had been spent dodging, with the occasional block.

"What's wrong, Sir Dalton? No jovial platitudes or snappy comebacks for us tonight?" Sir Job asked with a boastful chuckle.

It was true that the warrior had little to say. He felt not the natural reflexes or calm of his previous battles; only a primal urge to lash out that he had not felt in years. Experience told him that such impulses were good on lucky days, but bad on most others. Yet, he could not regain his focus. The gases of Degenerate clouded his mind and made him all the more prone to losing control.

Any time he tried to focus on the battle, his frustrations and impatience had weighed him back down into dark thoughts; thoughts about Anora; thoughts about that damned Dark Wizard. It made him want to lash out and kill his opponents brutally all the more. He simply hadn't found the opportunity. It was hardly a surprise that Sigrian knights had been nearly flawless in their attack formations thus far. However, even the most skilled swordsmen would slip up, eventually.

For the time being, Dalton kept his anger in check and awaited his opportunity, like an ember about to burst into flames.

After a few more sequences where the knights pressed on, that opportunity finally came when Sir Gareth slid his boot across a damp portion of the stone platform. The knight caught his balance almost immediately, but it was enough of a distraction for Dalton to make him pay. The warrior ducked a slash attempt by Sir Job, then tagged Gareth in the hand with his long sword.

Sir Gareth cried out in pain and fell to a knee. His hand was gloved and covered by thin metal plating, but the impact of the blow had still certainly shattered it. Before Dalton could deal further damage, Job jumped in and began a flurry of downward, diagonal cuts.

The warrior blocked each swing and halted his movement backward. He only had one opponent to worry about, now. Dalton opened his next attack pattern with a feigned swing to his left, prompting Job to switch stances to his right. However, Dalton curved his blade as he brought it down so that it struck the plated left arm of the gallant.

Job backed off while huffing in apparent surprise. It hadn't drawn blood, but it had dented the armor enough for it to bruise his arm. Dalton used that break in the action to focus on Sir Gareth, who clenched his broken hand in pain.

Gareth gasped as he caught notice of the warrior's attack: He plunged the long sword into the gap between his arm and shoulder plates. Sir Gareth fell to his knees in agony as Dalton ripped the blade from the wound, leaving a geyser of blood in its wake. He pulled his sword back, dripping in crimson, for a final blow. He couldn't help but smile. For some reason, he couldn't wait to see Job's reaction to the beheading of his fellow knight.

With malice growing in his heart by the second, Dalton cackled while swinging his sword as hard as he could, aimed at a small gap between plate and helm where the neck lay. However, Sir Job intercepted the blow before it could come across at its fullest force. With an angry grunt, he pushed Dalton back with his blade.

"What bad form! To attack a defenseless man on his knees! Despicable! I shall carve you up until no one can recognize you, and then your burial will be in this stinking hellhole," Sir Job declared with a hint of delirium inserting itself into his tone. "For that is what you deserve, Sir Dalton!"

Dalton knew that both he and the knight were succumbing to Degenerate's gases; that they were overreacting to things they normally would have shrugged off mere days ago. Kabel had told him all about how degenerates would become violently angry whenever someone did something that they themselves tended to do. There was nothing rational about these people, and he was becoming one of them. Yet, this fact, which should have startled him, did not. He simply did not care. All he wanted to do now was inflict pain and death.

"I've had about enough of you knobs. You are fighting side-by-side with a bunch of freaks who seek to do ill upon this world. And for what? A nice payday? Favors from Sampson? How idiotic can you be?" Dalton said, gritting his teeth. He felt his head lighten a little more, yet it was belied by a strange heat that passed through his whole body. It was a thoughtless, burning desire to attack at full force. His sword shook from how tightly he gripped it.

"And I've had about enough of your meddling! We settle the score here! I have decided that even these sewers are too good a burial ground for you. So instead, I shall burn your wretched corpse, and then piss on the ashes when it is all said and done!" Job shouted as he ran forward with his sword at the ready. Dalton bared his teeth and did the same. The battle resumed, but with tenfold the intensity of before.

～

AT THE BATTLEFIELD'S EDGE, near the river, the MacRae brothers inched back as Ned glided toward them in his cloaked form. So far, neither party had even attempted a blow; both had taken their time, but for vastly different reasons. The cloaked man seemed to be in no rush against two mere humans, while the MacRaes could not agree on how best to launch an attack.

"Awright brother, we're runnin' outta room," Alistair said, looking over his shoulder to see the running river. "Let's go with *my plan*."

"No way, Ali! That'll get ya killed!" Triston said while shaking his head. "We gots ta go with *my plan*.

The brothers' argument was interrupted by battle cries coming from down the tunnel. Along with them came many *clangs* of metal striking metal. They looked at each other, slack-jawed.

"We're 'bout ta have company…" Triston muttered, returning focus to Ned, who continued his stroll at the pair without an apparent worry in the world.

"There ain't no time ta waste, then!" Alistair said with a grin as he brought out his wind Rune.

Triston held a hand out, in protest. "No! It's too danger-"

An explosion of air burst from the stone, and Triston flinched. Yet, his fear did not last long, for it became obvious that the wind pointed at Ned, who was knocked back so hard that his robe ripped and tore off while skidding across the floor. The battles all around the chamber and in the tunnel halted, albeit briefly. Alistair's ears rang unbearably, but he couldn't help but feel that the pain was triumphant, in a way.

"I-it worked?" Triston asked, eyes wide.

"Was there ever any doubt?" the big redhead replied, his grin even wider. After a few awkward moments of silence, Alistair raised an eyebrow. "What's wrong?"

Pointing ahead with a markedly shaking finger, Triston said, "What tha hell *is* that thing?"

Alistair squinted at an uncloaked Ned as he stood. He, too, was taken aback by his appearance: The creature standing before them could hardly be called 'human', anymore. His face had turned dark and insect-like, with antennae on his forehead, twitching every so often. Ned's eyes had become glowing, red dots, and mandibles sprouted from his mouth, which now sported wide and tall slits, so it could open both horizontally and vertically.

Ned's arms had become thin and jet-black, with long, sharp hairs poking out. His fingers, too, were long and sharp, but retained their human shape. Most noticeable, however, was the extended abdomen, which, like an ant's, was bulbous and nearly reached his feet. It curved slightly past the front of his legs, and at its end was a stinger, dripping with poison. Though he wore a tunic, there seemed to be little point to it, aside from tradition. The brown garb was ripped and stretched around what little of his humanity remained.

"Hideous!" Alistair said in disgust. "I don' know why anyone would wanna take in tha dark essence when they turn into somethin' like that!"

"But more importantly…" Triston trailed off as Ned began walking toward them, a translucent, green liquid dripping from his mandibles as he did. "Even that great blast o' wind did nothin' to 'im! What else can we do?"

"We stand and fight!" Alistair said, gathering his battle axe and standing firm.

"There ain't no way in hell! You'll be killed!"

There was little else to say, however. The brothers had already backed up to the edge of the platform, with the muddy river running behind as their only possible refuge.

Ned stopped a few paces from the pair and let out a squeal that brought the brothers' collective hands to their ears. Alistair's eyes twitched as a couple of more arms sprouted from his ragged, brown shirt. He then reached down to the sheaths that hung from his hips and drew four short swords. Alistair had seen those blades before: They were thick and specialized for chopping; often referred to as falchion.

"What're we supposed ta do against *that*?" Alistair asked.

Triston held his great sword outward and stomped his feet like a territorial animal. "Now, Ali, there is no choice. As you said, we've gotta stand an' fight!"

"Yes! That's tha spirit, brother!" Alistair said, clenching the axe handle so tightly that it burned his hand. "As true warriors, we must slay such a monstah!"

～

As the battles raged on in both the chamber and nearby tunnel, Sir Gareth walked over to the edge of the grand stone platform, where the muddy river split three ways. The pain in his broken hand and gouged shoulder had numbed, but so too had his mind. Dark thoughts had crept up on him, and rather than focus on the fights, he found an odd desire to leave the sewers and roam the streets, naked and free; taking and destroying whatever he wanted. All inhibitions had crumbled before his feet.

However, before reaching the arch that led to the exit tunnel, he felt something bounce off his helmet. It was not heavy or impactful, but the gallant had still felt the light tap. Gareth scanned the stone floor and locked eyes on a clump of black hair.

"How odd..." he muttered while kneeling to pick it up with his uninjured hand.

What reason would someone have to throw hair into the sewers? Furthermore, how could such a thing have landed on his head? There were barred-off drains designated to the slums above, but he was not standing beneath one. It mattered little in the grand scheme of his degenerating mind, but his curiosity had been piqued.

Sir Gareth's brow furrowed as he grasped the hair. Contrary to what he'd anticipated, it did not feel wet or have any weight to it. With that realization came one far more startling: *The hair was moving*. His breathing grew heavy and newfound awareness swept over him in the form of pain. He began to feel little pricks, like pins and needles, on the top of his hand. *It wasn't hair at all*. Swarming the gallant's gloved hand were little spider-like creatures, each with rows and rows of red dots for eyes. These little monsters, easily numbering a hundred or more, were the darkest of black. Their scurrying and digging legs, each sharper than a nail, had burrowed through much of his glove in mere seconds.

A horrified, undignified cry escaped from Sir Gareth's trembling lips as the spider creatures broke through the glove's final defenses. He could feel them ripping, tearing, and biting at the flesh of his hand. They were so ravenous that he couldn't bear to look at the damage, for fear of finding nothing left but bone and blood. Worse still, the pins and needles began to feel more like hot nails rapidly driving into him. Now, they were traveling up and underneath the armor on his arm, wreaking unseen, but very much felt destruction along the way.

In a panic, the gallant ran forward, flailing uselessly as the proverbial fire in his arm seemed to spread to his upper chest. They were spreading so fast that his mind immediately jumped to desperate measures: the river. He had to hope that it would drown the little beasts. Gareth altered course and took a couple of long strides before jumping into the muddy water. He smiled in anticipation of the relief to come as the stink and splashes enveloped him. It never came.

Not only did the searing pain remain, but it continued to spread, too. Now, he could feel them clawing and gnawing away at his neck, and his chest sagged as if a great hole had been poked in it, letting all of the air out. More horrifying still were the screeches of the little monsters, right in his ear. They began ripping at his lobes, and he could feel them crawling onto his face; up his nose and even forcing their way into his mouth. Sir Gareth tried to brush them off, but his arms had long since lost feeling and ceased to work. He next thought to cry out for help, but it was far too late for that. His throat became clogged with the little spiders, and to his horror, all he could do was gag on them. As the pins and needles traveled down to the innards of his chest and his lungs began to burn, the realization hit that he was doomed.

Gareth drifted down the south river path and allowed the darkness to swallow him up. He prayed that his death would come before finding out what else lay in the shadows of this wretched place.

DRAKE DANVERS STRODE along the northern coast of Endoshire with Rose's servants in tow. He wore a fancy, red tunic, and at his hip were the scabbards of some blades that he had never used before. Still, they struck him as a nice fashion statement, and they didn't hurt to have, just in case.

More concerning to him, however, was the sight of a sagging dock 15. The back half of the shipyard building was collapsed and submerged, and poking out of it were the remnants of a sunken vessel. Even the dock itself did not appear stable, swaying and groaning against the wind. About half of it had been brought down, with only the seasoning of its floating, splintered wood remaining of it. In the distance, his keen eye caught onto several men coming and going from the building; a rarity for this time of night.

"As I had feared..." Drake muttered. "That bumbling Dark Wizard's plans were too simple."

"What shall we do, Master?" one of the servants asked.

"You wish to go home?" he asked, looking back with a critical eye. "It won't be that easy, I'm afraid. In fact, this means we may have to get our hands dirty."

"But Master, I don't think we are equipped to-"

"Calm yourself," he said, holding up a hand and flashing his signature smile. "I won't let anything happen to you."

The trio continued their walk along the docks until reaching the collapsed building on dock 15. Several slaves came and went, lugging supplies, most of which were chests. Some men had already gotten to work in attempting to patch up the building.

Drake stopped one of the slaves as he walked onto the dock. "What happened here?"

"Oi! A ship gone an' crashed right into us!" he replied, shaking his head. "A right idjit, they must'a been!"

"Where is Sampson? Is he alright?"

"He's up in his room. The Master's a tenacious one, ta be sure! He was at the back o' the buildin', where the ship crashed! You should'a seen the other fella that was with 'im..." the slave trailed off with blank eyes. "I never seen a man in such a mangled state... but Sampson is awright, save fer a few bumps and scratches..."

"I see. I will be visiting him, then," Drake said as he started for the shipyard building. The slave stopped him, however, by grabbing his shoulder.

"Oi! The Master's restin' fer the night! He explicitly told me '*no visitors*' unless it was a large fella in a dark robe. You ain't no large fella wearin' a robe, so I'm gonna have'ta ask you to turn back, kind sir."

"I am Lord Drake, one of Sampson's invaluable business partners. I'm sure he will make an exception," Drake said, brushing the hand off his shoulder. This time, he didn't even take a step forward before pausing. The unsheathing of a blade kept him still.

"I really must insist that you turn back," the slave said, pressing a dagger up to the side of Drake's neck.

Rose's servants began to quiver as Drake let out an annoyed sigh. This was normally where he would sick Hector or Ned on the brute. Of course, the servants he had dragged out were only good for Rose, not himself. At best, they were fodder, and at worst, they were useless, he thought.

"You serve your master with such loyalty and bravery," Drake said while slowly reaching into his pocket and retrieving a gold coin. "I suppose it's a good thing that I snuck past you, unnoticed, isn't it?"

With wide eyes, the slave took the gold, and then he let loose a big smile. "Yeh, an' it must be me lucky day! To find a gold coin on the ground like that!"

Drake strode forward once more, nodding at the slave as he walked by. Rose's servants followed like chicks behind a mother hen. Most other workers and slaves were too busy rushing around and recovering sunken goods to notice the trio as they walked into the building.

Inside, even Drake was shocked to see just how much damage had been done by the crash. The area to the right, normally filled with ships being fixed by the workers in an intricate system of smaller docks and pulleys, was almost entirely waterlogged. Some ships remained afloat, but most were in the process of sinking or already had. The men scurried about, diving into the water to salvage as much as they could.

After looking over the damage for a short while, the trio walked left until they reached some stairs. While ascending, the Village Elder couldn't help but let those same dark thoughts from earlier cloud his mind. Even Sampson's slaves didn't show him the respect that he deserved. They were told only to take Oneth's company. Yet, it was Drake who had introduced the two in the first place. It was even more evidence that he was being phased out, and now he was beginning to suspect that Sampson was in on it.

At the end of the stairs, the trio entered a hallway with a grand door at its end. Drake walked up to the door and knocked.

"I said no visitors!" a grumpy voice called back.

"It's Drake. I'm coming in," he said before opening the door.

He entered with the servants in tow to see Sampson lying in bed. Although there were small bumps and scratches on his face, Drake's eyes immediately focused on the dry blood around his mouth. It spread all the way from the bottom of the slaver's nose to the ends of his chubby cheeks.

"What happened to you?"

"That damned pirate! He's attacked me once more! Only this time, the bastard went an' brought down half of my shipyard! When I get my hands on him…" Sampson said with a growl, then clenched his hands so hard together that they cracked.

"It would seem that our adversaries decided to attack us before we could attack the sewers," Drake said, letting out a breath of feigned concern. "You are lucky to be alive."

"You ain't kiddin'! I was right thar, where the ship crashed. By all accounts, I should be dead, but…" Sampson trailed off, looking down at his hands.

"Did something happen? Something that helped you survive?" the Village Elder asked, prying deeper.

"I dunno… when the impact happened, I blacked out," he replied, looking up and rubbing one of multiple chins. "When I came to, the slaves were pullin' me off the corpse of that other fella that was with me when the crash happened… you shoulda seen his body… contorted in ways I ain't never seen before, with holes in 'im and everything… I must'a been on top of him in some vain attempt to save the poor bastard, but then… how am I not hurt? How am I not *dead*?"

Drake used all of his willpower to stop his eyes from rolling. Such a selfish man would never try to save anyone other than himself. No, he thought; it had to be the dark essence. Could the Dark Wizard have given him a concentrated dose? One that had turned him into a powerful monster without his knowledge? The Village Elder made a mental note to be careful around him until he got a straight answer from Oneth.

"It may be the dark essence. As you've experienced before, it can heal minor injuries. Of course, there may have also been dumb luck involved," Drake said, flashing him a cool smile. "But regardless, I am happy to see you alive and well, my friend."

"Yeh… thanks…" Sampson muttered, in a daze. He looked down at his hands once more, then shook his head. "But now, the plan is ruined. Both of the ships I planned on takin' to confront the kraken sank. I got a whole mess to clean up 'round here, too."

"Worry not." Drake nodded at him with confidence. "I am happy to take the reins on this one."

"Are ye sure? We've got some other boats that can be used, but they ain't much bigger than rowboats. You can maybe hold a dozen men at most, and very few supplies. All the other ships that remain afloat belong to my clients," the slaver said.

"That should be fine. As long as Barret comes along, we can still distract the kraken, and then poison the beast," Drake replied with crossed arms. "I trust you still have the tools to chip away at stone? We will need them, should we reach the monolith."

"Yes, but all of the poison sank along with the ship. So far, we haven't been able to recover it," Sampson said, shaking his head. "Yer absolutely certain ye wanna go?"

Drake noted the doubt in his eyes. Even *he* was beginning to question him, now. "Tonight, you will see that I *always* get the job done."

Sampson shrugged. "Well, if yer so insistent, I'll be happy to show ye where the boat and supplies are. I'll gather some of my men to go along for the trip."

"Excellent," Drake said as Sampson stood from his bed. "After all, my prize is in those sewers. Why shouldn't I be the one to pursue it?"

"Point taken..." Sampson trailed off as he opened the door. He stopped and then flashed a greasy grin at Rose's servants. "By the way... will ye be leavin' the ladies here when you depart?"

Drake looked back to see the pair trembling at the thought, then let out an amused breath. "No. I promised them an adventure, and tonight, that is what they shall get."

"Are ye sure? You really should take as many of my men as you can. They know how to fight, 'n such," Sampson said.

The thought of such a vile man having his way with Rose's servants sickened Drake to his very core. Even if he had hated them, he *still* wouldn't have subjected them to such punishment.

"I'm sure."

"Very well. Follow me," Sampson said while stepping out of the room.

As Drake and his servants followed along, he couldn't help but feel excitement building in his chest. After tonight, no one would be able to deny his place in the partnership or his cunning. More importantly, tonight would be the beginning of a new era; one that promised to see his influence spreading across the entire world.

CHAPTER 41
OLIUS THE TRAVELER

Pierce Thaeon grunted in frustration as the glow of his luxmortite dagger faded and *clanked* off the ground, across the street. In most situations, it would have been a simple matter to retrieve it, but in this case, there was a giant, enhanced avian blocking his path.

Since the other Strangers had followed Oneth into the sewers, it had been a war of attrition in the streets. Pierce had kept his distance while Mur'del dedicated most of her focus to dodging the charmed weapon. The problem, however, was that the long game favored his opponent. With each passing second, his shoulder wound leaked more blood, and on top of that came each slice of his palm to power the dagger. Pierce was becoming lightheaded, which made him prone to bad decisions; one such decision was going for an extra slash with his dagger, rather than bringing it back in to feed it more blood.

"You are out of options, luxian," Mur'del said with a haughty tweet. She spread her great wingspan to reveal talon-like hands.

"In that case, end your tiresome chirping and attack me," he replied with a scoff. "That is, of course, if you can find the bravery in your black heart to do so."

"That is what *your kind* and the humans don't understand," she said, stalking toward him and shaking her head. "You never savor, nor do you stop and think things through. You are happy to mindlessly consume, and faster than anyone else. What a hasty bunch, you are. No wonder you're extinct…"

"Don't talk to me of haste, fool," Pierce snapped back. "There can be nothing hastier than what *your group* is attempting. You mess about with powers far beyond your or anyone else's control. All in the name of conquest. But rest assured, it will lead you to ruin, soon enough."

"Those are some fine last words, luxian scum," Mur'del said as she stopped in front of him. Up close, the dagger-eyed man was struck by just how large she was. He didn't even come up to chest level. Now sweating, he slipped a hand into his pocket. "I suppose as Key Keeper, you must have been alive for when the avian were enslaved by your greedy, grubby kind, right?"

"No. The avian were free, even back then."

"As if I'd believe your lies!" Mur'del said with a loud chirp of amusement. "We never forgot; not what the luxians did, and not what the humans did, either. The stories have been passed down for ages. I know how poorly we were treated, and believe me when I say that retribution is coming."

"I never said anything about being treated *well*. Only that the avian were not enslaved when I was around. To us, you were moderately more intelligent carrier pigeons," Pierce said with a shrug. "But if you are so bitter, then come and take your revenge."

"And what is that you've got in your pocket?" Mur'del asked, cocking her head. "Do you really believe I'd charge in and fall into your trap?"

"Relax. They are only seeds. I thought you would enjoy picking at them off the ground." A derisive laugh bounced beneath his Ometos mask.

"You won't be laughing when I'm ripping you to pieces!" she cried while lunging forward with a hand outstretched.

From out of his pocket, the dagger-eyed man threw Dhogron's itching powder, striking an enraged Mur'del in the face as she was dashing toward him. From both the force of the throw and the speed she was dashing for him, the powder buried into the deepest crevices of her dark eyes while simultaneously getting up under her beak-like nose.

Mur'del squawked as she fell to her knees, desperately scratching at her face with those talon-like fingers and turning it an odd combination of black, gray, and red.

While she was distracted, Pierce ran across the street to fetch his luxmortite dagger. After picking it up, he turned back to see the enhanced avian flying toward the sea.

"I doubt salt water will be of much use… for her eyes, anyway," he muttered to himself.

He held his palm out, ready to cut it once more and feed his charmed dagger, but a voice from behind stilled him:

"Hey!"

Pierce looked down a nearby alley to see Najih running toward him.

"Ah, you're back," he said, relaxing his posture. "Where are the others?"

"It's… a long story…" the musician said as he arrived, panting. "We used the haze pellets… it worked… that large man in the robe left… but he took Satara… got to get her back…"

"Sounds like *her* problem, not mine," Pierce said with crossed arms.

"What?" Najih asked, both his nose and mouth covering crinkling. "She is our ally! We *have* to help her!"

"If the Dark Wizard has departed, then that is a win for us. Sometimes, there are casualties in the process of a win."

"Please… you have to help her… he will kill her once he snaps out of his stupor! I cannot do this alone!" Najih pleaded, looking over his shoulder, out to sea. "They will depart soon. If we don't hurry, there is no hope of rescuing Satara!"

"That avian will be back at any moment to attack us. The Dark Wizard has a small army at his command and wields an unholy dark magic. There is already no hope," Pierce said, shaking his head.

"We must try!"

"And why would I do that?"

"Because she is one of the few good people left in this rotten city! She has taken in many rescued slaves as her own, myself included, and given us new purpose. I owe her my life! Can you understand that?" Najih asked.

Pierce looked down and felt *the other* departing from his body. He placed a hand on his mask and then rotated it so that it was in the sorrowful orientation.

"Indeed, I can understand that," he said, then pointed out to sea with his dagger. "Let us be quick!"

~

INSIDE THE CHAMBER of the dragon statue, Conrad and Lucia battled Catalina together as Brice continued to twist and turn in agony on the cold, stone floor. Despite the Gentish woman's numerous advantages, she had not landed a single blow on the duo. Both knew to avoid clashing with the bone blade; and likewise, they had avoided severing any more of her appendages, giving her little opportunity to land surprise attacks.

Instead, Lucia and Conrad had been slowly poking holes in her with carefully placed stabs. Over time, Catalina's attacks had become more erratic; she was whipping her tongue around and flailing in all directions. However, Lucia's calf was burning more and more with each dodge or attack. Conrad's strategy to irritate the Gentish woman had worked well so far, but she hoped he had something in mind to finish her off, too. Her leg could not take much more strain.

"Fight me directly! Enough of your poking and prodding!" Catalina howled.

"I don't know…" Lucia trailed off, looking at Conrad with a smirk. "It seems to me that a skillful opponent would have hit us by now. What do you think?"

"I must agree," he replied with a knowing smile. "She is much like Brice: Powerful and brash, flailing away at us until she falls into our trap…"

"What trap?" Catalina asked, clenching the bone dagger and baring her teeth. "What have you done to him? You rats!"

"You'll find out, soon enough…" Lucia said, playing along.

"I've had enough of these games!" Catalina cried as she bent her neck downward and raised the dagger to its back.

The duo gasped as she chopped through her neck in a single swing. Catalina's body collapsed while her head rolled on the floor.

Lucia snorted as she started for her decapitated head. "Poor fool couldn't control her emotions. Let's destroy the head, just in case-"

"Don't fall for it!" Conrad said, stilling her. She looked back at him with questioning eyes. "This is how she got me a few nights ago. Much like her other body parts, she can independently control her head, even when decapitated."

"You hear that?" Lucia asked while taking a step back and raising her guard once more. "We haven't fallen for your silly trick."

Out from the stump below her chin sprouted red webbing that formed into little crab-like legs. Catalina's head propped itself up, and she smiled back at them.

"Who said anything about 'tricks'?" she asked as her body reached its feet, walked forward, and then stopped next to her head. "There are two of you, so I am evening the odds."

Catalina opened her mouth, giving way to her streaking tongue, sharp as an arrow and aimed Conrad. The strategist managed a deflection by swinging to the right with the rapier, but the disembodied head had already begun scurrying toward him in that time.

Like a spider pouncing on its prey, the Gentish woman's head leaped out, aiming for Conrad's face. He sidestepped and then flinched as the streak of dark hair flew by.

Lucia had started forward to help him, but she found herself having to dodge the wild swings of Catalina's body. It quickly became apparent that without the use of her eyes, the Gentish woman's body was truly lost. It posed little to no danger, despite its many abilities. However, she also realized that attacking in response and landing a hit would give away her location. If she was going to attack, it would have to be meaningful.

A perfect opportunity presented itself just moments later, as Catalina lunged out for a stab. Lucia sidestepped and brought her blade down upon the wrist. Like a knife through warm butter, the sword cut through, and the Gentish woman's hand fluttered through the air, dropping the bone dagger when it hit the ground.

Immediately, Lucia kicked the bone blade away and then stabbed the body's midsection. For most opponents, she knew such an attack would be more than enough, but not Catalina. She finished the sequence with a kick to the gut that ripped the blade from her body and sent it toppling to the floor. She followed up by crunching her boot onto her back and littering it with holes and gashes by way of stabbing and chopping. When all was said and done, the twitching body had upwards of a dozen wounds, and they were slow to regenerate this time.

Lucia licked her lips. *Time to finish it,* she thought, calling upon her dagger once more. She twirled it until the tip was oriented downward, and then, with a surprising amount of glee, she brought it down for the stab. Both the squishing and ringing noises brought a satisfied smile to her face. She had pinned the body through the thinnest point of its midsection and into a crease of the stone below. But that wasn't enough. Now, she twisted her blade, and both the writhing body and stone underneath resisted, but she didn't care. It only added to her enjoyment.

"Don't let the gases cloud your judgment!" Conrad's voice tolled in her ears like a morning bell, awakening her from a bizarre slumber that she both enjoyed and despised. She turned to see him nodding at the disembodied head of Catalina. "Eyes on the prize."

Catalina's head scurried toward Conrad for a second attack, but this time, he retrieved a paper ball from his pocket and threw it in front of her. Before she could react, Dhogron's Supreme Paper Surprise exploded into hundreds of little shards. The Gentish woman closed her eyes and grimaced while her face filled up with paper cuts.

As the cuts rapidly healed and Catalina opened her eyes, she gasped to see Conrad right in front of her, pulling his rapier back for the stab. He jabbed it into a crevice of the stone as she leaped back with her little crab legs, and then she opened her mouth to sick that dreaded tongue on him again. Lucia had other ideas. She sprinted forward and then punted her head with as much force as her tiring body could muster. It flew far into the depths of the chamber before landing and rolling by the monument of the looming dragon statue.

Brice snarled in desperation as the dark tendrils carved into his forehead, then ripped his head entirely in half. Blood, bone, and flesh alike erupted as the little black strands clawed away at the innards of his head, in search of relief. His body fell limp, and then, after a few moments of rapid healing, he came back to his senses.

With a maniacal laugh, Brice stood and pointed at Conrad. "Ye see that? I did it! The itch is gone! Yer a dead man! And yer death won't be quick!"

Catalina's head scurried to his side, while Conrad and Lucia stood shoulder-to-shoulder and resumed their stances.

"I know you are trying to rile them up, but what's our end game?" Lucia whispered to him.

"At first, I'd been hoping to distract them for long enough that Aldous could send them away with his portal Rune," he replied, nodding his head forward. Well past Brice and Catalina, who were also chatting amongst themselves, Lucia could make out three figures struggling in the green haze. "But it looks like his hands are full. Luckily, you've given me a new idea."

"Do tell."

"Have you noticed that when we stab or cut into their bodies, the wounds heal *around* our blades?"

Lucia nodded. "That happened earlier. I had to rip my sword out of Catalina's stomach, or I might have lost it."

"When our blades are lodged in there, the regeneration doesn't push them out. If anything, it holds them in there," Conrad said. He smiled while tapping his head. "Now, let us apply that elsewhere."

Her eyes widened. "Oh…"

Conrad's gaze wandered over to Catalina's body, which was beginning to stir, but remained pinned by the dagger. "You had the right idea, earlier, but aimed for the wrong target. Her body may act independently from the severed head, but I am confident that her brain still controls it. If we stab into her skull; or better yet, pin it to the floor, then part of her mind will not regenerate, and it may very well incapacitate her."

"I see…" Lucia muttered, nodding along. "And I assume the same goes for Brice."

"Yes," he said, smirking. "Outside of making him suffer a bit, my use of the itching powder had purpose: Brice just showed us that damage to his head will not kill him, but it *will* keep him on the ground."

"Very good. I say we go for Catalina, first. She is already decapitated. It is but a matter of plunging one of our blades into her skull."

"Let it be mine," Conrad said, whisking his rapier and parting the green gas around them. "She will undoubtedly attack you with her tongue again, and when she does, be sure to block it with your sword."

Lucia shook her head. "Bad idea. She'll just-"

The strategist wagged his finger and let loose a sly smile. *"Trust me."*

"Will you trust me, in return?"

"Certainly-"

Conrad was interrupted by *clinks* and *clangs* of metal ringing behind. They turned and gasped in unison at the sight of a crumpled-up piece of iron bouncing toward them.

The metal ball stopped skidding near Lucia's feet. It was about the size of a coconut, and it looked familiar, somehow. She picked it up but flinched as blood began to drip out and stain her hand in red.

"A helmet… from one of the knights?" she muttered.

"So it would seem…" Conrad looked over his shoulder and into the shadows behind them. "Something lurks in the depths; something deadly."

Catalina and Brice approached the duo with smiles from ear to ear.

"I believe this is yours," Lucia said with a snort, tossing the bloody, metal ball.

Brice caught the helmet and scoffed after examining it. He threw it over his shoulder, then wiped the blood off of his hands.

"What was it?" Catalina asked.

"One of them knights. No big loss."

"That attitude is precisely why we will win this fight," Conrad said with barbs of judgment. "Who would want to be allied with someone that doesn't have their back?"

"I suppose camaraderie is important..." Brice trailed off. His dark tentacles began wriggling. "But ye know what else is key to keepin' a team together? *Power*. Neither of ye have it. So, maybe ye do work well together, but here's a fact: Tonight, ye'll *die together*, too."

As Lucia took her stance next to Conrad, she couldn't help but grimace. The gash in her leg was paining her more and more, and the gas was getting to her, too. She hoped that whatever the strategist had thought up would end the battle quickly.

~

NEAR THE CENTER of the great stone platform, a weary Aldous fended off brutal strikes from Angus' bone blade. One such swing knocked the Summoner Rune away, but the old Wizard continued to defend admirably without missing a beat. However, a surprise swipe of the giant's white shield knocked his walking stick away, and in that distraction, the bone sword was plunged into his breast.

Aldous let out a bloody gasp as Angus smiled in triumph. In response, the old Wizard gripped his stabbing arm and closed his eyes. With all of his remaining might, he called upon what little lightning he could find in the chamber and unleashed a shock that lit up the dark confines of his shut eyes for but a moment. He soon opened them to find both he and Angus encased in a steaming aftermath.

As the vapor cleared, however, Aldous' eyes widened to see Angus still smiling down upon him. With a swipe of his shield, the world began spinning, and then he found the grimy ground.

"It almost feels too easy when facing you at your weakest." The giant's husky voice echoed in his reeling mind. "But then, my mission is not to get a good fight out of you. I shall finish you off here. Mayhap I can find some use for that Summoner Rune..."

Letting out a breath that sounded more like a whimper, Aldous turned himself over to face the final blow. Angus loomed over him, his bone blade pulled back.

"Even if you defeat us... there is still the Guardian... and the Wizard King..." he said with a weak laugh. "And you don't stand a chance against them..."

"That is no longer your concern, old m-" Angus stumbled forward and winced. The tip of a dark blue blade poked through his leg and spurted red.

Aldous leaned past the giant and smiled at Joel. Splotches of blood and grime stained his tunic and he was propped up by an elbow and knee on the floor.

The problem was that Angus, too, was smiling. With his wound healing around the sword, he turned back to the mute.

"Now, this is familiar..." he trailed off, his voice darkening with each word. "Ah, yes. Just like a few nights ago. You landed an ineffectual blow on me back then, too. And just like that night, you will only be able to sit there and watch as I finish off your friend. But this time, it will be bloodier."

Angus turned back to the old Wizard, whose legs had ceased to work out of exhaustion and the stab wound to his chest. He shared Joel's visible despair and reached out in desperation for something; anything that could stop Angus. However, he had run dry on magic, and his Summoner Rune had been knocked too far out of reach. The realization hit as the giant began his stabbing motion: He was powerless, much as he had been every time he had tried to defend the monoliths.

All of his efforts thus far had been in vain. Could it have been that assembling this team of misfits and strangers had needlessly endangered them all? Would Endoshire continue its descent into degeneracy? Or would Drake have his way and claim the monster's power for himself?

All thoughts of despair popped like a bubble as Aldous' dreary eyes caught onto *gold*, of all things, whisking through the air, beautiful and swift. The gilded object nailed Angus as he was in the process of his attack, and sent him flying, leaving a trail of blood and teeth behind as he bounced off the unforgiving floor.

Aldous looked up in his exhausted stupor to see a man with dark gray hair standing over him. He wore an intense, striking expression, as well as a long, black coat with high collars, and pants of the same color. He wielded a golden staff with a small replica of a gryphon spreading its wings on top. For some reason, though, Aldous couldn't stop staring at his odd haircut: His hair pointed like an arrow down to his brow. It made him chuckle, albeit in a dazed, stupid way.

The man shook his head, yet his odd arrow for a hairline remained still as if it were painted on. "Bloody tosspots think they can just walk in here like they own the place…"

With each passing word, Aldous' mind began to clear. It hadn't occurred to him until just now that the man, who had turned to face Joel, was a Wizard, staff and all.

"I don't suppose you're with the likes of him?" he asked, pointing to Angus, who was beginning to stir. Joel shook his head. "Yeh, I thought so… still, you shouldn't be down here. This is no place for commoners to be. You couldn't possibly imagine what lies in a place like this."

"We are no mere 'commoners'," Aldous interjected with newfound energy. After all they'd been through, nothing could have been more insulting to his ears. He pushed himself back to his feet but remained hunched over and exhausted. "You speak to the Keeper of the Key for Greed. And I am the Wizard Scout for that seal."

"I think you mean, 'Former Key Keeper and Wizard Scout,' don't you?" he asked with a scoff. Aldous tilted his head in surprise. "I am well aware of who you are, Aldous. And I'm sure *you* are well aware that as a Council member on probation, you are not to be anywhere within the vicinity of another monolith!"

"But… we are here to help…" Aldous muttered, the despair pouring out of his voice.

"I *need* no help," the Wizard replied while surveying the area. Several fights unfolded across the stone platform, and a series of skirmishes approached from the east tunnel. "It seems you have a lil' group here, helping you. Admirable of you to put forth such an effort, but doubly foolish. That is another violation of the Council. It is time for you to step aside. The Guardian and I are more than enough to handle this *trash*."

"Trash?" Angus asked as he began walking toward the trio. The bleeding gash on his cheek was already in the process of healing. "Who are you to say such a thing to me? I have progressed beyond humanity and become something superior. Before you stands the next step for mankind. I shall succeed in my tasks, and you shall fail like the others before you, little man."

The Wizard struck the ground with the bottom of his staff, stilling Angus before he reached them. Aldous felt the power of the strike in his feet, and nearly toppled over. Joel, too, looked to be off-balance. He had still not managed to stand and was now trying to prop himself up with his luxmortite blade.

"I am Olius the Traveler, Wizard King of the Degenerate monolith. Do you truly believe yourself to be better than a man? Because I can guarantee that before this night is through, your limitations will become apparent, and you will beg for death."

Angus let out a husky chuckle and raised his shield while holding his bone blade outward. "Like so many before, you are overconfident."

Aldous smirked. It was Angus who had let overconfidence cloud his mind. While it was true that he had snuck past Olivier and felled Zamarim with the aid of some devilry, he had no such advantages this time. Unaided against a Wizard King, he had a near-zero chance of winning. Yet, that small chance nagged at the back of his mind. He hoped Olius would take him seriously and finish the fight swiftly.

"Do you know why they call me 'the Traveler'?" Olius asked. His gaze almost seemed to look through Angus, as if he were insignificant; a fly hardly worth swatting at.

"I care not for your stories or tall tales."

With a toothy grin, Olius waved his hand, and underneath Angus appeared a portal. Unlike Aldous or Pierce's gateways, however, this one had a green tint to its swirling darkness. The giant grunted as he fell through, but he wasn't gone for long. A new portal appeared just above the old one, and Angus fell from it and back into the vortex from before. The process repeated itself over and over, and eventually, cries of anger from the giant were heard. However, each shout was cut off by the sudden silence of him falling into the abyss once more.

"It's because I have been to many places," the Wizard King said with a chuckle. "You, on the other hand, will be staying here for a while!"

ON THE NORTHERN coast of Endoshire, the Auber pirates and Prince Xviktolo sat with their legs overhanging dock 10, looking out to sea as they dried off.

"That was exhilarating," the marinian prince said, looking over the pirates with a toothy smile. "I have never commandeered a ship, much less caused so much destruction to a shipyard before. And to think it was to thwart a scoundrel like Sampson! I could not have been paired up with a better group, tonight."

"I'm just glad it all worked out," Auber said, breathing a sigh of relief. His expression grew livelier by the second. "The rest o' the team will surely be impressed by how easily we took Sampson down!"

"And to think, you were almost taken captive by one of *our hostages*, tonight," Franco chimed in.

Auber narrowed his eyes at him. "Now, don't ye go spoilin' me fun! We got outta that mess, didn't we?"

"Only 'cause of the mighty net!" Ebbie said, grasping the mesh in his hands with a grin. "Otherwise, we'd have been in real trouble."

"You realize that in any other situation, that net is useless, don't you?" Franco asked.

"Not for a marinian," Xviktolo said. "You might say that nets are our natural enemy while submerged."

"I still think the beige berries were the best of Dhogron's items," Auber said, trying and failing to withhold his muffled laughter.

"Yeh, those are funny! We gotta try 'em on more enemies!" Ebbie said.

"Once again, in most situations, those berries are useless," Franco said with a shrug.

"Why can't ye just admit that them items saved our arses many times tonight?" the captain asked with a scoff.

"Well, I-"

"I don't mean to interrupt the conversation, but..." Xviktolo trailed off, then pointed to the east, along the docks. "That boat is headed toward us."

With squinting eyes, Auber spotted a small boat, with men rowing on each side. At its back were some passengers sitting, but they were partially obscured by supplies and crates. He did, however, recognize Barret. His hideous form and fluttering wings were hard to miss.

"Oh, *come on!*" Auber whined, throwing his hands up. "Ye mean to tell me after all of that, they're *still* sendin' their men over here?"

"Perhaps Sampson has sent some men to capture and enslave you, sir?" Franco said. The captain's stomach groaned.

"More importantly, what else can we do to stop 'em?" Ebbie asked.

Auber looked at the first mate with fear in his eyes. However, after a few moments, a devious smile came to his ragged face.

"I gots an idea."

~

D‍RAKE SAT at the rear of the boat with arms crossed. The slaves around him rowed in unison while Barret stood, buzzing and jerking his head in seemingly random directions, as insects liked to do. Rose's servants sat nearby, watching the fly-man with fearful eyes.

"Don't worry about him," Drake said, putting a hand on one of the women's shoulders. "You may not see it now, but we need him in order to survive. Isn't that right, Barret?"

The fly-man looked back at him and let out a low-pitched hiss. He then gazed down upon the quivering servants and nodded at them.

"Just assume he said 'yes'," Drake said with a crass chuckle. "But more importantly, prepare yourselves. Tonight, you will see creatures you thought to be mere legend! And what's more, you shall bear witness to an *inordinate power* beyond your wildest imaginations!"

Half-hearted nods from the servants nearly made Drake scoff, but, as had been the case so many times over the years, he put a cool smile on display. There was plenty for him to be happy about, anyway. His enemies likely thought that bringing down Sampson's building would stop them all in their tracks. He almost certainly had the element of surprise on his side.

From there, it would just be a matter of Barret distracting the kraken, and then they could infiltrate the sewers. Drake pulled the map out to mentally plan out his route through the tunnels once more. He would need to travel far to the south until reaching a central area, where he could traverse a network of tunnels that would lead into the maze. With his sharp mind, he had already pinpointed where the monolith was and how to get there.

It was obvious from first blush that the path from the north would take longer in terms of sheer distance, but if the kraken was the only safeguard of that spot, he might still be the first to make it, if not the only.

As the boat got closer to the sewer pipe, the rowers steered it so that they would arc around dock 10, then straighten out in the direction of the entrance. While they were passing the final dock before their destination, however, a great splash erupted ahead of them.

Out from the waves appeared the mighty kraken, cracking her tentacles like giant whips and squealing at the sight of intruders. The slaves on board stopped rowing and simply stared in awe at the approaching sea monster.

"What do we do? *What do we do?*" one of the women asked in such a panic that her voice was squeaking.

Drake, too, felt his heart pounding. He'd thought the size of the monster to be exaggerated in the stories, but the kraken proved to be every bit as large as foretold, up close; something big enough to crush their boat like an annoying insect.

"That's right..." he muttered before eyeing Barret. "It's up to you! Take flight and distract the kraken while we enter the tunnel!"

Barret nodded at him while buzzing loudly. His translucent wings began fluttering and the whole boat hummed and shook at the force of such a takeoff.

Beyond the sounds of buzzing, however, Drake heard something else. Something that sounded quite odd to him. It was faint under the great ear-straining sounds nearby, but unmistakable:

"Go! O' mighty net!"

The Village Elder looked up to see a great net descending upon his boat. Before he could so much as make a noise, the mesh fell upon them, halting Barret's flight and crashing him back into the boat, which rocked so much that it nearly tipped over. Even after the boat settled, there was no calm. Everyone was struggling to remove the net, and it only entangled them all the more.

"Remain calm!" Drake called out as the slaves and servants thrashed about, ripping and gnawing at their entrapment. The net was large enough that it covered the boat and hung overboard, into the water.

Barret hissed and buzzed as his wings tried fluttering, but the net blocked them. Drake began gathering the bits of mesh around them, hoping to free himself, but deep down, he knew that it would take too long. The fly-man, on the other hand, used his enhanced strength and pulled at the threads, freeing himself.

Drake felt relief set in as Barret's wings began to flutter once more. However, something else gave him pause: Drops of water raining down on him and the boat crew. He looked up once more to see the kraken's massive, dark tentacle whipping down with such force that the very air around it wailed out in pain.

Was this it? Was he to be struck down before attaining the power he rightfully deserved? It was unfair, he thought. He had gotten them all so far, only to be crushed like a fly; and for what reason? Because that *damned Dark Wizard* refused to hear out his plans. Yes, he thought, that was the cause for all of this. If their plans had not been so easily predicted, he never would have found himself in this frustrating predicament.

For all of his dissatisfaction and anger, Drake, in that brief moment, could only whimper as the tentacle came crashing down. All went numb and black.

CHAPTER 42
A TERRIBLE FATE

Satara sat alone on a crate, staring at a shoreline that shrunk with each passing moment. The Dark Wizard, still under the effects of the haze pellet, had ordered a swift departure. All of the Bosfueras crew seemed off-kilter, as if simple commands were confusing. As she understood it, the red-eyed folk were all brainwashed. It seemed to her like something about the haze pellet's effects and the mind control hadn't mixed well.

If it weren't for the imminent threat of Oneth, Satara would have jumped overboard. He sat atop his throne on the third deck, and as far as she could tell, he hadn't taken his eyes off her even once. As if it weren't strange enough that he had mistaken her for his mother, it was even more bizarre how he was treating her. More than anything, she felt like his prized possession.

More troubling still, the ship was traveling south rather than north, where the docks lay. Satara hadn't a clue where he was taking her, but depending on how long the haze pellet's effects lasted, it may not have even mattered. Whenever the Dark Wizard's state of mind returned to normal, it would spell her doom.

~

AT THE WEST SHORELINE, Pierce and Najih came to a stop and watched as the ship sailed southward. The dagger-eyed man searched for

Mur'del in the waters below, but to his surprise, found no signs of her.

"Give me more details. Why did the Dark Wizard take her?" he asked.

"He seemed to think that she was his mother. The effects of the haze pellets must have been quite strong," Najih said.

"How odd," Pierce said, now looking out to sea. The decks of the great ship were surprisingly still. "Anything else?"

"He started acting differently than before. How can I say this? He seemed more vulnerable, yet, more dangerous all at once," he replied and then widened his eyes. "Oh, and he became quite protective of her; talking about how she had been 'practicing Witchcraft', and that people would 'burn her alive for it'."

After a few moments of contemplation, Pierce retrieved his Summoner Rune. "I have an idea, but whether it will work… I make no promises."

"Alright, what's the plan?" Najih asked while drawing his scimitar. "I am a bit lightheaded, but can still fight."

"I will be going alone."

"Unacceptable! You need backup!"

"If I went in with the mindset of fighting them? Yes. But my plan requires no violence. I'm taking a gamble, but from what you have told me, it just might pay off," Pierce said with an assured nod. "In the meantime, you may want to help the others out of those sewers. They, too, could be in danger, depending on when the swine snap out of their daze."

"Right," Najih said with a nod of his own. "Good luck out there."

Pierce concentrated on the ship sailing away from them. In front of him opened a portal, and its swirling darkness invited even darker thoughts. He was about to step into a den of sleeping lions. One false move would see him ripped to shreds.

With that chilling thought came a well-rehearsed calm; one that he would need to survive. Pierce stepped through the portal and onto the wooden deck of the monster ship. His breaths and strides stuttered alike. He had summoned himself mere steps from where Oneth sat on his throne. The Dark Wizard turned his vile gaze to him, sending deathly shivers down his spine. It wasn't often that his composure was shaken, yet, much as Najih had described, the man before him felt dangerous and vulnerable all at once.

"And who might you be?" The Dark Wizard's tone was accusatory.

Pierce, feeling a tightness in his chest, cleared his throat. It was now or never.

"I come to you with tidings from the Wizard's Council, good sir."

"Oh? And what news do you bring?" Oneth asked.

"Difficult news, I'm afraid. You see… it concerns *your mother*," Pierce said. He awaited a response with bated breath.

The Dark Wizard looked past him and down to the main deck with concern in his eyes. Satara was down there, sitting on a crate. She returned an expression that Pierce could only imagine was pure bewilderment beneath that mouth covering.

"What of her?"

"You needn't play the fool," Pierce said, to which Oneth looked back, reflecting deathly intent. The dagger-eyed man clenched his fists, feeling the pressure; knowing that just one wrong word could spell his demise. "We are… aware of her practicing Witchcraft."

Oneth relaxed his posture, then let out a sigh. "It is as I had feared, then…"

"Indeed. There are people after her now, it seems," he continued, looking around with feigned concern. "They mean to burn her alive."

"You hear that, mother?" The Dark Wizard's voice boomed so that it encompassed the entire ship, but it was obviously aimed at Satara. "Look at what you have brought upon us! Think of how many I will have to slaughter just to protect you!"

"That won't be necessary," Pierce said, holding up a hand. "We at the Council are willing to take her in."

"And why would you do that?" Oneth asked with a snarl. "What business is it of yours?"

"Well, you see…" he trailed off, searching his mind for lies. "The Council has seen a great potential in you."

"Really?" His deep, dark voice lightened.

Pierce nodded. "And for that reason, we are willing to take your mother and put her in hiding."

"Very good… I wish that it hadn't come to this, but sacrifices must be made," Oneth said, then looked down to Satara once more. "You hear that, mother? We are going into hiding! I hope you have finally learned your lesson!"

"'We'?" Pierce muttered, in shock. This couldn't possibly work, he thought. "Sorry to say, sir, but I must take her alone, for now."

The Dark Wizard tilted his head and raised an eyebrow. "What for? She is my mother. I should be there with her. I am a *good son*, after all."

"I'm sure you are, but... erm..." Pierce searched his racing mind for a new excuse. As if to answer his woes, he spotted Mur'del's great shadow swooping over the ship. He pointed to her with as much panic as he could muster. "There! An angry villager! She means to bring your mother back to the others! It would be a terrible fate, to let her burn alive!"

Oneth glared up at the sky and stood from his throne. "An avian? I don't remember living among any avian... yet, somehow... she seems familiar..."

A new knot twisted in Pierce's stomach. Was he unintentionally jogging the Dark Wizard's memory?

"There could be any number of spies among us. I must take your mother with haste!" he said.

"*Not* without me," Oneth shot back with a chill-inducing leer. He then looked back up to the sky. "I will handle this."

The Dark Wizard clenched his mighty fist until blood seeped out between his fingers. He then pointed three of those bloody fingers at Mur'del. "Laqibe diabonis, tris dighear!"

Dripping blood on his hand began reversing course, and flowed upward into the three pointing fingers until they became rose-red. However, they did not remain fingers for long. Swiftly, they extended into three stems with small spikes lining their shafts, and by the time Pierce's mortal eyes could track them, they had already reached Mur'del's soaring heights and wrapped around her midsection.

She let out a surprised squawk as Oneth clenched those three fingers back into a fist, and then yanked on the spiked stems as if they were a lasso. Pierce gasped at the grizzly sight of Mur'del's body splitting in two. Dark blood and avian innards rained down on them as each part of her separated body spiraled down, crashing onto the ship's second deck with a splintering *thud*.

"Let us gather some information from this treacherous spy," Oneth said.

"Right..." Pierce replied, nearly breathless. The display of power had far surpassed his expectations. As he had worried, the Dark Wizard was more than capable of killing him at a whim.

The pair descended the stairs to find Mur'del's top half painting the floor red. She slowly crawled on the deck toward her lower half, which was twitching.

"Master... why?" she whimpered.

"'Master'?" Oneth asked while cocking his head. He turned a critical eye at Pierce. "Is she talking to you?"

"She will say anything to trick you. Don't take your eyes off of her," the dagger-eyed man said.

"He… is… the enemy…" Mur'del's normally chirpy voice was hoarse, as if she'd been stranded in a desert for days.

"There is some trickery going on here," Oneth said with crossed arms. "I feel… there is something that I'm not remembering…"

"O-Ometos…" she squeaked out.

"'Ometos'?" Oneth asked aloud. "Yes… that name sounds familiar…"

Pierce, growing desperate, reached into his pocket.

"Him… in the mask… enemy…" Mur'del hissed.

"Ometos… yes…" the Dark Wizard said with growing vigor. "Now, I remember. We were supposed to make a deal with that fellow back in Thironas, and he went back on it! He is the enemy. So then, *you* are Ometos?"

As Oneth turned around, he was met with a haze pellet exploding in his face. The second deck quickly erupted into a series of coughs and hacks. Pierce dashed for the stairs, knowing that time was short.

He came to a sudden stop when a few Bosfueras townsfolk appeared between him and Satara. However, they seemed docile; content to stand there as dressings of the ship, rather than attack or obey their master. The dagger-eyed man looked back up to the second deck, where the haze began to settle. The coughing had long since stopped.

If he was going to have to deal with Oneth, then he at least wanted to know instead of being hit by one of his devastating attacks from behind. Upon a complete clearing of the deck, Pierce felt a great relief to see the Dark Wizard slumped up against the back wall, sleeping. Mur'del remained on the floor, with each half of her severed body motionless.

Pierce pushed through the bumbling townsfolk to find Satara sitting on the same crate, sweating bullets.

"Ready to leave?" he asked in a jovial tone.

"Damn right," she said, then jumped up and embraced him with teary eyes. "I thought this was the end for me. You've saved me from a terrible fate. Thank you!"

With a smile, Pierce retrieved his Summoner Rune and brought forth a portal. The pair walked through, leaving their dazed enemies to drift through the dark seas.

~

INSIDE THE DRAGON STATUE CHAMBER, Dalton swung for Sir Job's head, prompting a duck to narrowly avoid the blow. The knight responded with a horizontal strike toward the midsection, but Dalton parried, and the pair backed off to catch their breaths.

As a matter of pride in their swordsmanship, both had been attacking and parrying non-stop since Sir Gareth's retreat, but neither could gain the upper hand. It was clear that Dalton had the speed advantage thanks to his lighter wear, but the armor of Job had come in handy, as rather than fully dodging or parrying, he could take glancing blows and respond with dangerous attacks faster than normal.

Dalton grimaced between his labored breaths, then took a lowered stance. Job, on the other hand, relaxed his posture.

"I must say, Sir Dalton, that it is odd to see you like this." Job shook his head. "It won't be as satisfying to strike you down while you're so glum."

The warrior let out a breath, then lowered his guard. "I don't think you grasp the magnitude of what occurs here tonight, do you?"

"As I understand it, there lies a treasure deep within these tunnels, and I intend to find it," he replied.

"I'll let you in on a little secret," Dalton said, looking over his shoulder, to the tunnel behind. "That path is where you wanna go. But there ain't a 'treasure' at the end… all that awaits within is a terrible fate."

Job scoffed. "You cannot deter me. Not in battle, and not with your words!"

Dalton frowned. "Does none of this seem odd to you? Your allies are monsters come to life, mind-controlled servants, and a slaver. Do you understand who you serve?"

"I serve no one save the king, fool," the gallant said with a crass chuckle. "Sampson pays me large sums just to be here. He has no true sway over me."

"I do not refer to him, but the *Dark Wizard*. One of the true master-minds behind all of this."

"That large fellow in the robe? And what of him?" Sir Job asked.

"He is a tormentor and manipulator by trade. Those red-eyed village folk… he brainwashes and confuses them so they will obey his every command," Dalton said, shaking his head. "What's worse is that he can take the form of your loved ones with his black magic, and peel away layers of your sanity for his own amusement."

"So, he tormented you in the image of your beloved, I take it? My heart weeps for you, truly," the knight replied with barbs of sarcasm. "Being the miserable creature you are, I suppose it would only be polite for me to put you down."

Dalton sighed. He felt those same thoughtless, violent tendencies flare up once more. "Y'know, I had every intention of lettin' you go, but men like you just can't help themselves..."

"Are you about done, then?" Sir Job asked, taking a stance. "Because I say it's about time we settle the score. Sigraveld vs. Federland: Whose warriors are superior?"

"Very well," Dalton said as he staggered his stance and held his sword straight up, in front of his chest.

Job cocked his head. "What kind of stance is that?"

"Crown form. A risky play, but in skilled hands, unbeatable."

"Let us put it to the test!" the knight cried, charging forward for a big swing.

～

ALISTAIR AND TRISTON fended off the ruthless attacks of Ned, sweating bullets with each successive swing from the ant-man's falchions. It felt as if one slip-up would seal their fates.

Ned swung two blades at once toward Alistair's head, but the range of Triston's great sword allowed for a block. He then brought his blade back around in a quarter circle to block the next strike from the other side of the ant-man's body. This time, however, the heights of the falchions were staggered; one was low, and the other high.

The elder MacRae blocked low while simultaneously bending back to avoid the upper falchion of Ned. A sharp edge whisked the edges of his beard, and then he took a few steps back to gain distance. Alistair followed suit.

"We can't... keep... doin' this, Ali..." Triston said, nearly breathless. "I can't... keep... coverin' fer us both!"

"Then, I'll... take 'im... alone!" Alistair said.

"Don ya get it? Yer slowin'... me down! Yer place... just ain't on... tha battlefield, Ali!"

Alistair shook his head. "After all I've done... how can ya still doubt me?"

"Ya gots the heart of a lion… but the claws of a housecat! Please… fer both our safety… jus' stay outta this one, brother!"

Before the big redhead could respond to the discouraging words, some Bosfueras townsfolk appeared out of the shadows, having crossed the small arch and onto the chamber's center platform. Just as suddenly as he'd appeared, one of the red-eyed men stabbed Triston in his thigh with a pitchfork, and he stumbled forward while grunting.

Another townsman came at the elder MacRae, now helpless, with a wood axe, but Alistair intervened by smashing him off the bridge of his nose with the butt of his battle axe. Blood sprayed as the brainwashed man toppled back and fell to the harsh stone floor like a sack of potatoes. The man with the pitchfork took aim at Triston next, but he managed a desperate block by wedging his great sword in between the prongs of the farming tool.

Alistair charged in with his battle axe at the ready, to help his brother. However, as he got within range, he caught onto something in his peripheral vision: *yellow eyes*. Still running, he turned his head just in time to see a group of degenerates tackling him from the left.

The big redhead was bowled over by their combined might; he crashed into the struggling Bosfueras townsman and Triston. A strange mixture of limbs and metal obscured his vision, and his head felt light as a feather. By the time Alistair got his bearings, he was greeted by a flurry of punches and kicks, courtesy of the deranged degenerates on top of him.

"Oi! Looks like we gots a couple a' piggies in our midst!" shouted one as he laid a devastating kick into Alistair's ribs.

"We should dice 'em up an' make some pork!" cried another, while pounding the side of Triston's head with his fist.

One of the degenerates stood and held a dagger over his head, ready to thrust it down upon an unfortunate soul within the tussle on the floor. However, before he could make a move, a giant stinger pierced through his back and out of his abdomen. The yellow-eyed man gasped, but let loose a deranged smile before the potent poison took its effect and he fell to the ground, foaming at the mouth; pale and motionless.

Alistair shuddered to find Ned looming over him and his brother. The attacking degenerates and Bosfueras townsman seemed insignificant in the face of certain death. He had been attempting to reach for his Rune, but the punches, kicks, pushes, and shoves prevented him from getting ahold of what seemed to be their only lifeline.

It was in that moment of panic that Alistair noticed something odd: A clump of hair had fallen, seemingly out of nowhere, onto the back of the Bosfueras townsman. Amid the flurry of attacks, the big man gasped when the hair began to move. It wasn't hair; not at all. Hundreds of little spider-like creatures, each with many glowing, red eyes, scurried about on the spine of the brainwashed man, piercing skin with each of their pin-like legs.

The creatures made their way down to the legs, where they began dragging the townsman, who scratched and clawed at the floor in vain while falling into the shadows. The MacRaes, degenerates, and Ned all stopped to look into the darkness as the sounds of carving flesh and breaking bones assaulted their ears. Next came the blood spatter, which poured down like a heavy rain onto the crowd.

Semi-clothed bones bounced out of the shadows and landed before the stunned group. Alistair felt the ground shake with each step of the monster lurking in the dark, until finally, it revealed itself, and he immediately understood what it was. The beast was dark, as all Guardians were, with an enormous spider-like body, nearly the size of a whale. It had eight monstrous legs extending to the floor, where its spiked feet poked holes in the stone. There were also eight additional legs mirrored upward, with sharpened feet digging into the ceiling. Lining the top of the Guardian's face were rows and rows of red eyes, and the bottom half featured a long snout, similar to a crocodile's. Inside the mouth were many fangs the length of human hands, bathing in a vile poison. At the back of its fat abdomen were two stingers, pointed in opposite diagonals and dripping that same nauseating poison.

"The Host!" one degenerate cried while running away.

"Run! Run fer yer lives!" another of the yellow-eyed men shouted, also making a mad dash from the beast before them.

Alistair watched in horror as the massive creature opened its mouth, then hacked out another group of spider-like creatures, taking the appearance of hair clumps. They flew at the fleeing degenerates and struck them in the back. The struggle was fierce, but it did not last long. The terrible little creatures dug into their flesh with their tiny, pin-like legs, and the degenerates were dragged back to where the behemoth awaited, salivating poison from its gaping snout. The MacRaes and Ned only stared, in awe, as the giggling degenerates were brought upon the Guardian, who wasted no time in skewering them like common finger foods with its spiked feet.

The Host lifted their corpses and tossed them into its mouth, not even bothering to chew; it swallowed them in a single gulp, then turned its attention to the remaining three. It let out a low-pitched hiss; one that triggered an unfamiliar urge in Alistair to flee. However, running was not an option for an injured Triston, and therefore the same applied to him.

Ned, too, had decided to stay. Yet, for reasons beyond Alistair's comprehension, he seemed to ignore the Host and crept up on him, instead. The big man pretended not to notice, and feigned fear at the Guardian Beast as Ned pulled back his falchion to strike him.

Then, the big man swiftly twisted his body, and in one smooth motion, swung his mighty battle axe, striking a stunned Ned across the chest before he could chop down with his blade. However, the reactions reversed as soon as Alistair heard the bone-chilling noise of shattering metal. The axe had exploded into many pieces upon impact, and with it came a secondary surprise: Alistair looked down to see the stinger of Ned's abdomen pointed at him, poised to strike.

Contorting his body to the best of his ability, Alistair felt relief set in as the stinger shot forward and upward, only stabbing the empty air next to him. Ned followed the attack up with a casual side swipe from his bottom arm. The big man caught his dark, insect-like hand, but for the second time in succession, heard a loud *crack*. This time, it was the sound of bones shattering in his hand, and with that realization came a searing pain that buckled his knees. He collapsed to the grimy floor next to Triston, who, struggle as he might, could not seem to gain footing after the leg wound.

Alistair grasped his wrist and gritted his teeth while staring a hole through his red, swollen hand. He then looked up at Ned, who loomed over them with all four of his falchions raised and ready to strike.

"Damn it!" cried the big redhead. His frustration was not focused on the fear or pain, so much as on his failure in combat. Now, he was out of chances to prove himself.

Yet, some strange mixture of hope and dread crept into his heart when a shadow blotted out what little light poked into the chamber. Ned halted his attack and looked up with blank, red eyes. The ground rumbled slightly behind, and Alistair swore he could hear the sound of pickaxes chipping away at ore. Except, he realized, that wasn't what it was. It was the sound of the Host's foot spikes plunging in and out of the stone platform and ceiling above.

In a rush of excitement and desperation, Alistair retrieved his wind

Rune and activated it. This time, however, he thought not of saving anyone, but instead of proving his brother wrong. The stone activated, and as the two dangerous opponents descended upon them, an explosion of air fluttered his cheeks and hair alike; his world spun into a bizarre mixture of black and green, and his ears rang, but Alistair couldn't help but smile. *Just as planned,* he thought while skidding along the platform and away from the inevitable clash.

Alistair quickly shook the cobwebs out. He looked up from his sprawled-out position to see that Ned had inadvertently struck the Guardian's leg with two falchions, breaking them in the process. Much like the Nightcrawler and Lake Watcher before it, the Host's hide was too durable for *mere steel.*

The Guardian let out a shrill cry as Ned backed up, on the defensive. The Host hacked out more of the spider-like creatures from its gaping snout, but the ant-man swatted them away with his two remaining blades. In that time, however, the beast had already initiated its second attack: It stomped a massive leg down, attempting to skewer him with its spiked foot.

Ned hopped back to avoid, and the chamber shook at the striking impact of the spiked foot. He followed up by plunging the stinger from his abdomen into its leg. The Guardian shrieked as if it had truly been hurt, much to Alistair's surprise. The Host scurried back with flailing legs above and below, clawing out sections of rock and stone foundation alike in the process.

It was not a sign of retreat, however, but a counterattack. The Guardian lifted its bottom legs off the floor so that it hung entirely from the ceiling. Then, its massive abdomen coiled back and struck with a sting attempt of its own. The sheer mass of the abdomen swinging forward brought about a wind that reached Alistair and Triston, but while his brother shielded his face, the big redhead could not deny his watering eyes the unbelievable spectacle playing out before him. The ant-man jumped far-right to avoid the stingers, then attempted a stab with one of his falchions upon the exposed abdomen. Much like before, the sword shattered on contact with the beast's rough hide.

What Ned hadn't noticed was that the stingers were not limited to sticking out the bottom of the Host's abdomen. After missing with the first attempt, both stingers had shot out like spears on a rope, attached to a dark, organic, web. They curved back around and plunged into an unsuspecting Ned's back as he sought to retreat.

The ant-man shriveled and let out a distorted shriek as so much poison was injected into him that it began leaking out of his fresh back wound in buckets. He struggled against its debilitating effects, but it was already too late. His legs gave way as the Host pulled its stingers from his back and retracted them into its abdomen. As Ned fell to the ground, the Guardian brought one of its spiked feet down, crushing him against the unforgiving stone like a common bug.

Squirm as he might, the ant-man was unable to free himself from his pinned predicament, and his movements faded fast. His tense posture seemed to relax as the monster lifted its foot, but it was only to stomp back down on him even harder than before; as evidenced by the growing faults in the stone floor. The Guardian continued to trample Ned, and with each successive step, he squirmed and resisted less and less. Soon, a pool of dark red blood gathered around his near-motionless body. Only his antennae twitched.

From there, the host lowered and opened its snout, lifting Ned like a small piece of meat and tilting its head back. As it began chomping, the ant-man folded and severed, until disappearing between the Host's many poison-filled fangs. The MacRaes watched on, horrified and entranced all at once, as the sound of bones crunching and guts splattering filled the foul air.

More degenerates, Bosfueras townsfolk, knights, creepers, and slaves alike began pouring into the chamber, but all seemed irrelevant in the presence of such a monster. All that remained of Ned was a single, dark arm, hanging out the host's mouth. It quickly corrected the error by sucking it up and swallowing whole as if it were the remnant of a noodle.

Triston looked at his brother with wide eyes. "Ya saved us, Ali…"

"Eh?" he replied, tilting his head.

"That coulda been us, back there! But thanks to yer quick thinkin', we were saved from a terrible fate!" the elder MacRae said, giving him a congratulatory slap on the shoulder. "Maybe I was wrong. If it were all on me own shoulders, we'd be dead right now! Mayhap you'll become a fierce warrior, yet!"

Alistair opened his mouth, but then he stopped short and smiled. It was a rare case where he had nothing to say. Instead, he focused on enjoying the moment, however short it may be. Finally, his brother had accepted him as a worthy ally in battle.

CHAPTER 43
DESTINATION

Sir Job Cardon fell to his knees, breathless and helpless. He had lost his sword and helmet, and a shot to the ribs had felled him. Dalton held his blade over the knight's neck, like an executioner.

"What are you waiting for?" Job asked, looking up with conviction in his yellow-tinted eyes. "Finish the damned job!"

Dalton pulled the sword back, his brow tightened and his teeth clenched. Despite his hardened expression, he could not deny looking forward to Job's head rolling. With all of his might, he began his swing, but then, a piercing shriek struck him like a blow to the gut, and he held up.

"The Nightcrawler?" Dalton asked aloud with wide eyes.

Both he and Job turned and looked upon what could only possibly be this monolith's Guardian. Hanging from its long snout were a variety of limbs and corpses that had been crunched by its great fangs. Further back, a stampede of intruders entered the chamber.

The warrior let out a loud exhale through his nose, and his calm returned. He couldn't help but smirk while lowering his blade. Ironically, what he thought to be the Nightcrawler's dreaded cry had snapped him out of the spell of degeneracy.

"You see?" Dalton asked as the monster began attacking the chamber's new arrivals. "There is nothing here for you or your knights save a slew of painful deaths."

Job watched with twitching eyes as his backup forces and the degenerates flooded the stone platform. All of them seemed insignificant compared to the Guardian, who vomited out clumps of what seemed to be moving, sentient hair. It mowed down and ripped to shreds all who were unfortunate enough to be in its path.

"What a horrid creature..." Job muttered as he stood, slowly.

One of the creepers hissed, opening its mouth and letting loose a streak of red that bounced off of the Guardian's tough hide. The attack hadn't succeeded in hurting the beast, but it did get its attention. The Guardian swung at the lumpy creature with its spiked leg and tore off the upper part of its body; only the lower half of the stomach and legs remained standing for a brief few moments before toppling over.

The creeper's upper body, meanwhile, had splattered against the chamber wall into a dark pile of liquid and blood. It quickly began to swirl around, reforming the monster's upper body. It then divided both the lower and upper bodies into several red, spider-like creatures.

Another creeper joined in on the battle, and it, too, extended its tongue supernaturally long. This time, it wrapped around the Guardian's leg. In response, it hocked out more clumps of its own spider-monsters. Some landed inside the creeper's open mouth and crawled down its throat to wreak havoc on the monster's insides. It groaned and squirmed, letting out erratic breaths and squeals until the spider creatures burst from its chest in a shower of dark red blood.

From the side came the dark red spider-monsters to aid their ally, shooting webbing onto the little hair-like creatures to trap them. The Guardian stomped one of its spiked feet, shaking the stone floor, but it only managed to squash one of the blood-red spiders in the process. The others shot webbing at their target, and a couple of the creatures reached its legs and began sinking their fangs in.

The Guardian hissed so loud that all nearby covered their ears, and it flung the creatures off of its legs before lifting them so it was hanging from the ceiling. It pulled its bulbous abdomen back, aiming its stingers at the regenerating creeper standing before it.

In a flash, the stingers jutted forward, and the creeper did nothing to avoid it. One of them plunged into the lumpy monster's midsection with such force that it fell back and skidded along the floor until falling into the river. The Guardian, meanwhile, had pulled its stingers back, and, attached to an odd, dark webbing, flung them about the chamber by whirling its fat abdomen around in a circular motion. The spinning stingers left over a dozen downed opponents in their wake, and they did not discriminate between friend, foe, or neutral. Degenerates, slaves, townsfolk, and knights alike lay on the floor, twitching and foaming at the mouth in response to the potent poison they'd taken in.

Sir Job watched on, mouth agape, at the carnage unfolding before him.

"Don't think this is over..." he muttered. There was no threat in his tone, though. All fighting spirit had been sucked from his body.

Dalton snorted. "Only the weak-minded would see what you've seen tonight, and continue to ally themselves with a buncha knobs like this."

"What makes you think that you can speak to me in such a way?" the knight asked, picking up his sword. "Y-you got lucky, and that is all! I am an honorable knight of Sigraveld! And you? You are but a peasant! I ought to speak with the lord and have you hanged for your insolence. Or perhaps I should gather a battalion and hunt you down like the animal you are!"

"You will do no such thing."

Job snarled. "And why not?"

"Because your honor has been called into question. Remember this, Sir Job: Life is a bloody struggle... and then you die." Dalton prodded the gallant's chest plate with the tip of his blade, eliciting a stuttered breath from him. "But tonight, I saw to it that you did not, in fact, die. You owe me your life, and as an honorable knight of the crown, you would do well to repay your debts."

The knight's eyes were twitching, now. "Y-you cannot be serious..."

"Oh, but I am. Your repayment will start with this: Call your men off. Leave these sewers, *immediately*!" Dalton growled.

The fire left Sir Job's eyes, and he sighed. "Very well. This hardly seems a cause worthy of my men's lives, anyhow."

He turned and began running for his scrambling men, near the tunnel to the east.

"Fall back!" Job called out to his comrades as he dashed for the arch over the river. "That is an order! Retreat!"

The other gallants lowered their weapons and looked at each other in apparent confusion as the head of their operation made a run for it. The inhuman shrieks of the Guardian and creepers seemed like they helped convince them to follow.

Dalton smiled. Job was far from repaying his life debt, and he was sure to be a useful mole to the Strangers, moving forward.

~

OLIUS LAUGHED AS ANGUS' cries turned angry and bitter. He had been falling through the loop of portals for some time, shouting obscenities that Joel often struggled to understand; they were usually cut off each time he fell through the bottom gateway.

"Let me-" Angus fell through, then appeared in mid-air. "-out!"

"Worry not, big fella. You will be sent *far away* from here, soon enough. But not before I have a bit of fun," Olius said with an overly amused laugh.

Instead of shouting his next time through the portal, the giant pointed in the Wizard King's direction as he fell. Joel's eyes widened. *Bone bolts*, he thought. The mute reached out to Olius, but his silent pleas fell on uncaring ears, and there was no time to shove him out of the way.

Angus shot his bone bolts as he fell through the green-tinted swirls once more. Olius snorted and then twirled his golden staff in a circle, deflecting each bolt as if they were boring little distractions.

"Curse you!" Angus cried while falling through yet another portal. "Face me... up close... coward!"

Olius cocked his head. Aldous reached a rickety hand out. "Don't listen to him! Please, finish him, Olius! He is too dangerous to be toyed with!"

The Wizard King looked back at him and scoffed. "To *you*, perhaps."

"I beg you! This is our best chance to defeat him..." Aldous said, but each passing word sounded less and less convinced of itself; as if he knew that Olius wasn't going to listen.

Joel's stomach sank. Each opponent in Angus' path had underestimated him in some way, and they had paid dearly for it. The unfolding situation was beginning to look familiar; like the fall of yet another mighty Wizard King to come.

"Mm... he is beginning to bore me... perhaps it *is* time to end our little game," Olius said while smirking at the falling giant. He pointed a finger at the portal on the ground, and it vanished. Angus crashed into the stone with a loud *thud*, denting the tough foundation with the sheer speed of his fall. "It is time you learned your place: *At my feet.*"

The Wizard King walked up to Angus' motionless body with a smirk. That was when Joel caught wind of another sneak attack to come: A sharp bone quietly slid out of his wrist and into his hand. The mute crawled forward, reaching out, trying to say or do something to alert Olius, but nothing worked.

In one swift motion, Angus swiped at Olius' leg with his sharp bone. However, instead of a fleshy, splatting noise, the hollow *thunk* of bone bouncing off metal sounded off. The Wizard King had anticipated his attack once more, blocking casually with his golden staff. Now, the bottom of that same staff was headed for Angus' face.

Teeth and blood alike flew as Olius' strike connected and sent the giant skipping across the floor like a rock over a pond. As he skidded to a stop, the Wizard King waved a hand and then stepped through a portal. By the time Angus sat up, face bloodied, Olius had already covered their distance and struck him down with the golden staff once more. Over and over he smacked him, and each time, Joel found himself wincing a little more. Whatever fire had come over him earlier, had certainly faded. Angus' normally stone face was beginning to seem more like a bloody stump.

Between blood-spewing coughs, Angus squeaked out, "If I could only retrieve my sword… you would be dealt with… in an instant…"

Olius smirked, then looked back to where the bone blade lay. Aldous shook his head, mouthing the word 'no', along with Joel.

Despite their silent pleas, a portal appeared underneath the bone sword, and then one opened over Olius' hand. The blade fell through, and then he caught it. After examining the white blade for a few moments, he dropped it before a fast-regenerating Angus and nodded at him.

"Go on, then."

With a rush of energy, Angus hopped up while grabbing his sword, then unleashed a monstrous swing in the direction of Olius' head. Yet, with only one hand, the Wizard King swatted the blade away with his staff. He then cupped the other hand over his mouth, and Joel's wiggling ears picked up on what he thought to be a yawn.

The giant let out a desperate growl and next swiped with his shield, knocking the staff back enough to leave him wide open. Joel and Aldous gasped as Angus followed up by plunging the sword into Olius' midsection.

However, Angus was also gasping, and the reason soon became apparent: His white sword had not stabbed into Olius, but a portal about the size of a grapefruit. Its tip stuck out from an exit portal and into his own chest. He gently pulled his bone blade back, so that it slipped out of his fresh wound and back through both gateways.

Olius laughed derisively and swung his golden staff at the giant, skidding him across the floor like he was some tiny object to be thrown.

"Had enough?" he asked.

"Never..." Angus said. The Wizard King tilted his head. "You will never be able to stop me. I shall simply continue regenerating until you've finally worn out... your defeat is inevitable."

"Ah, yes. That regeneration of yours is an issue, methinks," Olius said, rubbing his chin. "But then again, I was just having a bit of fun while deciding."

"'Deciding'? On what?" Angus asked with a scoff.

"On your destination, of course!" he replied. "You look like a fella who enjoys *warm places*. How about I send you to one?

"Wha-" was all Angus could let loose from his stone lips before falling through a portal at his feet. This time, he did not return.

Aldous and Joel hobbled over to the Wizard King.

"Where did you send him?" asked Aldous.

"As I said... somewhere *warm*." Olius tapped his golden staff off the floor. "I wonder if he can still regenerate after bathing in lava..."

"I have so many questions..." Aldous muttered, nearly breathless.

"Sorry, ole' boy, but I've got more trash to take care of. That big fella seemed to me like the leader of his group, so I'm sure the others won't be as interesting or strong. I shall dispose of them in short order," Olius said.

AFTER ROUNDS OF BATTLE, the moment of truth finally arrived: Lucia held her long sword up to block Catalina's snaking tongue, and it wrapped around the blade. As she reeled herself in to close distance, Conrad jumped in and plunged his rapier into her skull, halting her momentum and pinning her head to the stone floor. Lucia then ripped her sword from the tongue's grasp and flipped it so that she was holding it by the blade itself. The strategist released his grip from the rapier, and she chopped down with the sword, striking the handle with her cross guard like a hammer to a nail.

Catalina's little red legs squirmed for a few moments, but soon they went limp. Her eyes became droopy and a trickle of blood ran down her nose.

"Curse you..." she moaned. "What... have you done... to me?"

Conrad and Lucia looked back to her main body, which had made considerable headway in removing the dagger pinning it down thanks to Catalina's disembodied hand pulling at it. Yet, all struggles ceased, and the duo smiled at each other.

"That's one down," Conrad said.

"But you've lost your weapon," Lucia replied, eyeing Brice. He hadn't just been standing there while Catalina was soundly beaten. Conrad had been keeping him busy with several of Dhogron's Supreme Paper Surprises.

"I've lost *a* weapon." He wagged his dagger at her mockingly, but his smile fell while staring down Brice. "I'm the one he wants. This time, *I* will be *your* bait."

"That may not be necessary. We could overwhelm him together."

"I think you know that's not true. Brice specializes in crowd control. We would both be skewered in seconds," Conrad said while shrugging and taking a step forward. "If I keep the focus on me, then I'm confident you'll be able to sneak in and chop his wretched little head off. We just have to hope that he cannot survive a severed head, like Catalina."

Lucia sighed. "There must be a better way-"

"Ye dirty rats ganged up on her!" Brice cried, pointing at Catalina's head. His face was covered in drops of blood; artifacts from the many paper cuts that had regenerated.

"Don't speak as if you wouldn't gladly do the same," Conrad replied while holding his dagger up. "Even with all of your advantages, you still struggle this much against *mere humans*? You deserve to lose."

Brice's face turned beet-red. "I've had enough of yer bottom-feedin' talk! I'm gonna kill ye! But before that, I'll peel the flesh from yer gal's bones, nice and slow! And I'll make ye wat-"

Before Brice could finish his threat, he fell through a portal at his feet, which then disappeared just as mysteriously as it had shown up. Lucia and Conrad turned to find an older man with a silly, pointed haircut. He nudged Catalina's twitching body with his boot.

"Curious..." he muttered, next eyeing her disembodied head, which, despite her dazed state, continued trying to wriggle out of the rapier's pinning. "Her head and body can move independently of each other?"

"Correct," Lucia said, tilting her head. "Are you the Wizard King of this seal?"

"Indeed. I am Olius the Traveler. I had wanted to play around with these scoundrels a bit before sending them to their doom, but it seems they brought a small army into my sewers," he replied, looking over his shoulder at the beginnings of the chamber.

"Damn you…" Catalina's head croaked. Lucia and Conrad took steps back and readied themselves. Even with a part of her brain not regenerating, it seemed she was still a possible threat.

"Oh?" Olius' eyes widened and his jaw became slack, but something about his expression reminded Lucia of a parent humoring their child's silly accomplishment. "You can still speak?"

"Where…" she moaned. "Where did… you send… him?"

"Ah, the small fellow? Would you like to pay him a visit?" With a wave of his hand, a portal appeared, and it swallowed up Catalina's head, rapier and all. He then returned his striking gaze to her squirming body. "Let's give her a parting gift, then."

Olius made a circular gesture just above the Gentish woman's body, and another portal appeared. This one dropped a collection of spears and swords, each piercing into her flesh and making her writhe and squirm like a worm that had been hooked.

"Well, there goes another rapier…" Conrad muttered.

"Better than your plan to let Brice skewer you," Lucia said with a playful shove.

To finish her off, Olius pointed with his golden staff at the body, and it disappeared into the swirling abyss below.

"If she *does* survive where I have sent her, finding her body will certainly be a difficult task," the Wizard King said with a satisfied smile.

Olius disappeared just as quickly as he'd shown up to help the duo, but in his place, Dalton appeared. Lucia looked past him, though. She could see several gateways off in the distance, with men and women alike flying through them. The portals then disappeared, and the people shooting through them splatted on the floor like squashed bugs. The creepers attacked next, but they were dealt with swiftly when Olius sent them away with his portals. The dark forces began retreating as the Wizard King, Guardian, and degenerates continued to wreak havoc near the exit tunnel.

"I can't believe this…" Lucia muttered, hobbling toward her mentor. "After all we've gone through, Olius and that monster are handling Drake's group like they're *nothing*."

"Yes, well, a giant monster and a Wizard King are better equipped than we are," Dalton said, looking back to the Guardian. "That thing must be this seal's version of the Nightcrawler. If we could have harnessed such a power, I'm sure they would have been defeated back at Mt. Couture, too."

"It's more than that," Conrad said, approaching the pair. "It looks like Olius defeated Angus, as well. There is no sign of him. Between Angus, Brice, and Catalina… even Aldous at top strength could not have taken care of them so easily."

Lucia snickered. "Well, it's nice to see a Wizard King doing their job efficiently for once."

"I've been thinking about that," Conrad said, rubbing his chin. "The Mountain King was corrupted by the black gold. From what Aldous and Joel have said, it sounds like the Psychic Zamarim was caught off-guard and low on Anima thanks to many years in isolation. Olius is a Summoner Wizard. He would not be affected by problems like the green gases of Degenerate or the isolation these sewers bring. He is always one portal away from going somewhere else."

"Whatever the case, I can see why Dhogron said that Olius preferred to work alone. Between his abilities, the Guardian Beast, the degenerates, the kraken, and the swine… this place ain't a sewer. It's a fortress," Dalton said.

"And then there's the maze-like layout," Lucia added. "We haven't even traveled *that far* into the sewers."

"Maybe we won't need to. It seems to me like Olius doesn't need the help of the Strangers," Conrad said.

"In any case, I say we meet up with Aldous and the others." Dalton pointed to the center of the chamber, where a small group, including the old Wizard, had gathered. The trio nodded in unison and began walking to their allies.

JOEL SMILED and pointed behind a limp-wristed Alistair. Lucia, Dalton, and Conrad were halfway to them, but in the time they'd taken to travel that far, Olius and his Guardian had soundly defeated the dark forces. Some were slaughtered, but most were either sent away by portal or forced into a retreat. The last of them were being chased out by the degenerates, who howled with laughter like a pack of hyenas and tossed obscenities and weapons alike as they did.

It was not a moment before the seven Strangers reunited that Olius stepped out of a portal to address them.

"Y'know, I tend to make examples out of intruders…" he said in an ominous tone. The group looked on, helpless, as the Guardian charged in their direction with long strides that tore up both the ceiling and the floor. Its shriek and multi-eyed gaze struck fear in a way that only a Guardian could. Some prepared their weapons, yet others, like Aldous, did not move a muscle. "But I suppose tonight can be an exception."

With a snap of Olius' fingers, a giant vortex opened up before the charging Guardian. It ran through before having a chance to stop, and the portal immediately closed behind it. The Strangers let out a collective sigh of relief.

"Your hearts were in the right place, I suppose," he continued while turning and gesturing a hand. A new, smaller portal swirled before them. "This will take you to the streets above. From here on, you are *never* to return. If the sewers are ever under siege again, the Scout can send me a message with his paper magic. Next time, I will not show you such kindness."

One by one, the Strangers walked through, most at a markedly slow pace thanks to their injuries. Each gave the Wizard King a nod or wave of thanks, but he seemed to take little pleasure in their gratitude. Before Aldous stepped through, Olius held a hand out and stopped him by his pudgy midsection. Only Joel had stayed behind with him.

"A word of advice…" he trailed off. Aldous raised an eyebrow. "Flee far from this city. Your little group may have been trying to help, but *you* also know the rules. You have trespassed on forbidden ground while on probation, and as far as I can tell, you have been bringing direct harm to humans without special permission, too. I will be reporting to the Council as soon as you leave. You've all but assured your excommunication if it was ever truly in question."

Aldous let out a strained breath. "I have witnessed two Wizard Kings crumble before their duties in protecting the seals… I am only glad that you have remained sharp in this difficult time. I apologize for the intrusion."

He bowed before his superior, then began hobbling toward the gateway before him.

"Be swift, if you don't want them catching you," Olius said, undeterred.

Before leaving, however, Aldous paused and looked over his shoulder. "You should be careful, though. The Key Keeper is dead, which means they have a map and the key…"

Olius scoffed and then rummaged through some pockets on the inside of his coat. He revealed a dark blue, hexagonal medallion with luxian symbols inscribed on it. "As I have said… I *need* no help."

With a chuckle, Aldous turned and exited the sewers through the portal. Joel gave the Wizard King a nod as he walked through, the last to leave.

Now, many questions remained, but only one was in immediate need of answers: What was next for the Strangers?

CHAPTER 44
THE UNCERTAIN FUTURE

Oneth the Dark Wizard awoke to the sun coloring his pale face out at sea. He was slumped up against the back wall of his ship's second deck, and upon taking in his surroundings, found Mur'del laid out before him, cut in half from the waist.

"Why…" she rasped. "Why did you attack me? Why can't I regenerate?"

The Dark Wizard scoffed as he stood. "Those meddlesome fools hit me with something that affected my mind… they probably think they have found a weakness, but soon enough, even my mind will be guarded to the utmost degree."

Mur'del only groaned as he loomed over her.

"Then again, *I did* tell you not to let them in the sewers, didn't I?" Oneth asked, shaking his head. "My Demon's Snare was a fitting punishment for your ineptitude, even if I was not myself when catching you with it. For you see, it is a curse; and curses are particularly effective against the impure. Even now, it continues to eat away at your flesh like an unstoppable disease."

"P-please… undo the curse…" she begged.

"You're under the impression that your punishment is through? My dear Mur'del, it has only *just begun*," Oneth said as a couple of Bosfueras townsfolk approached. "Take her to the bowels of the ship."

"N-no…" she whimpered as the brainwashed folk carried both halves of her body away.

Looking to the horizons at each side of the ship, the Dark Wizard was unable to spot land. He held a hand out, palm up, and above each finger appeared the apparition of a small skull. Some of the skulls faded away, while others remained.

"I see... so, they were sent away," Oneth said before clenching his fist, erasing the skulls from the air. "I may have no choice but to realign with *the Masons*..."

Oneth returned to his throne on the third deck, where he sat and contemplated his next move. He gave no orders to his brainwashed servants, feeling content to drift away into the clutches of the ocean while thinking. The battle had been lost, but *the war* was far from over.

~

AT COLE'S PUB, the Strangers celebrated their victories, much to the exhausted barkeep's chagrin. Just before leaving and closing up for the night, the group had stopped him and demanded entry into the pub. The rowdy festivities had gone on into the early hours of the morning.

"Load me brother up with another one, Cole!" Triston said, pounding a fist on the countertop. His leg was tightly wrapped with a blood-soaked cloth. "He's a hero, after all!"

"Can't ye give me a moment's rest, ye big ol' buffoon?" Cole asked with sagging eyes.

The entirety of the bar let out laughs, to which Cole sighed, and filled the drink up. He slid the foaming mug over to Alistair, who, sure to grab it with his uninjured hand, wasted no time in guzzling it down.

Some of the Strangers had sustained painful injuries, but all had survived their confrontations with the enemy. As they had it figured, Father Vega could heal them later in the day, just as he'd done a few nights before.

Giles let out a satisfied exhale as he placed his mug back down on the countertop. Alistair leaned in and inspected the mug, then pointed at a few drops of drink that remained.

"Oi! That's wasteful!"

"Huh?"

"Ya didn't finish it all, lad!" he said, smacking him off the back and laughing along with Triston. "Ya know what that means?"

The one-eyed man sighed. "Penalty game?"

"Yer damn right!" said the big man, before turning to Cole. "Two-No, *three* more drinks for me wasteful friend, here!"

Giles groaned and rested his head on folded arms atop the bar counter. "C'mon… can't ye take it easy on me? I still got a headache from those damned haze pellets…"

Alistair cocked his head, then rubbed his chin, in thought. Of course, he was only thinking of ways to make the punishment worse. By the mighty Gods of Stone, he *loved* the penalty game. "Oi! Cole! Make it four- no, five!"

A weak groan escaped Giles' trembling lips as the MacRae brothers howled with laughter.

"You'll be immune to tha alcohol before this night is through, lad!" Triston smashed his fist onto the counter in his hysterical fit, startling Giles so that he sat straight up, and shaking the foundations of the pub in the process.

Aldous and Joel sat at a table in the back corner of the pub as everyone celebrated. Rather than join in on the excitement, they'd elected to nurse their injuries and rest. Aldous rocked in his chair, eyes half-open, as one usually did mere moments before falling asleep. Joel, on the other hand, was too preoccupied by soreness to nod off. He couldn't wait to visit Father Vega and have his wounds healed. Angus' bones had left stubborn holes in his body that refused to stop bleeding, and it distracted him. He worried about infection, or that they might be more than temporary ailments.

"How are you feeling?" Conrad's voice echoed, snapping him back to reality. He was looking at Aldous.

"Oh, I'll survive…" The old Wizard's weak laugh hardly inspired confidence.

Joel made hand signals, albeit with a furrowed brow. Even benign movements sent waves of pain through his chest and shoulder. He pushed through the surges and communicated what Olius had said to Aldous before exiting through the portal.

Conrad frowned. "That is troubling news."

"It's no trouble at all, actually," Aldous said, grasping his Summoner Rune. "After I've rested up a bit, I'll take a lil' trip away from here. The way I see it, I can come and go whenever I please."

The mute signed some more while wincing. The threats of a Wizard King were not to be taken lightly.

"I agree with Joel. We must get you out of the city, immediately," Conrad said.

"You say that as if you know what the Council is capable of. Hexzar got into your ear, didn't he?" Aldous asked.

"He did more than that..." Conrad trailed off, then let out a long breath through his nose. "That is actually why I've approached you: to say goodbye."

Suddenly, Joel's wounds didn't hurt anymore. Now, he was stricken with guilt. Had the Strangers' prior distrust in Conrad pushed him away? He made hand signals in rapid succession, hoping to convince him to stay.

Conrad chuckled and held up a hand. "I hold no ill feelings toward our group."

"Did Hexzar offer you his tutelage?" Aldous asked, raising an eyebrow.

"He said that if I could find his oasis in the Endless Desert, he would teach me the ways of the occult."

Aldous sighed. "I could have taught you a thing or two, y'know."

"You would have been my first choice," Conrad said with a smile. "But to teach is not your calling, my friend. It is your destiny to defend these seals, and I firmly believe that if not for your interference, there would be three seals broken; not two. With that said, it has become apparent that as your student, I would bring with me many distractions. If it hadn't been for me, you would have been at top strength last night, and you would have made quick work of Angus. For your sake, and this city's sake, I needed to choose a mentor who is not embroiled in this conflict."

"I hope you know what you're getting into! Hexzar will work you to near death, and then, within an inch of yer life, work you some more! He is quite strict; dangerously so. Understand, m'boy, if you are even able to reach him, that the confines of the Endless Desert are a gently rocking cradle compared to the trying nature of his community," Aldous said.

"I admit that he scares me, somewhat. He has untold power, and looks willing to use it, should I step out of line. But for some reason, that makes me *want* to learn under him."

"And you will learn much," Aldous said with a gracious smile and nod.

Conrad turned to Joel. "Your determination tonight did not go unnoticed. You were the quickest of us all to jump into the fray. I hope you can forgive me for ever doubting you."

The mute nodded, then made hand signals.

"I'll be sure to visit, so long as I'm allowed," said Conrad.

"I would be more than happy to bring you back n' forth once in a while, m'boy!" the old Wizard added, flashing his Summoner Rune once more. "Though, methinks our group will miss your cunning."

"I have full confidence that the Strangers will keep this city in order while I'm gone…" he trailed off with chuckles. "And if all else fails, Olius and the Guardian make for excellent backup."

Aldous' tired eyes widened for a moment, and then he stood. "That reminds me… is Prince Xviktolo still here?"

Joel and Conrad looked at each other with raised eyebrows.

"He's hard to miss," the strategist said, pointing to the other corner of the pub. Xviktolo loomed over all, chatting with Greta and Mirabel.

"So, how many eggs do humans typically lay?" Xviktolo asked.

Greta and Mirabel stared at him for a while, before the latter finally cleared her throat. "Erm… none…"

"You mean to say that the child is produced outside of a shell?" he pressed, tilting his head.

"How did you *not* know that?" Greta asked.

"Well, some marinians give birth outside of an egg, but that happens in the sea. It is easy to hide the children from creatures looking to steal or eat them. But how will you defend your child?"

"With weapons, of course," Mira said, then put hands to hips and frowned. "And that is only if my husband fails to defend us. I'm sure he'd be here, downing a few while some bandit attacked us…"

Xviktolo put his webbed hands up and chuckled. "Relax! It was only a speculative question. You're not pregnant, are you?"

"Hold up," Greta said, eyes twitching. "Pierce ain't human… he's luxian… they're a lil' different… what if I *do* lay an egg?"

The trio looked at Pierce, who sat at the counter nearby. He let out a light groan and turned his back to them while sliding his drink over.

"Ah, Xviktolo!" Aldous said, slipping in between various members of the group before reaching him. "Could I have a word in private? I have an idea; one that may quell the degeneracy of this city. I wouldn't be able to do it without you, and perhaps some other marinian, if you can muster them."

Prince Xviktolo let loose a mischievous smile. "You never disappoint when it comes to holding my interest, do you?"

~

GILES SNUCK between many Strangers like a mouse, searching for a new place to blend in. While he had committed himself to Alistair's training, his pounding head and stumbling footsteps demanded that he no longer play *this particular* penalty game. He'd managed to convince the MacRae brothers that he was headed to the privy and hoped the plentiful drinks would erase their memory of him, for now. Eventually, he came upon a table where Rolf, Dhogron, Satara, and Najih sat.

"So, whadda we do now? Da enemy is beaten, but dey may come back. Hell, dey could come back at any time, really," Rolf said.

"From what Aldous told me, we may not have to worry so much about the sewers. I knew Olius was strong, but to hear that he disposed of those dark essence-enhanced folk like they were nothing... I now understand why he didn't find it necessary to include Amis or myself in his plans," Dhogron said with a smile and shake of his head.

"In that case, I say we move on to other things," Satara said, slapping the table with authority. Giles' shoulders shot up to his ears and then he looked back. Alistair hadn't turned around from the countertop, to which he breathed a sigh of relief. "Outside of that evil Wizard and his cult, *Sampson* is the chief problem of Endoshire."

"But what can we do against him?" Najih asked with crossed arms. "There is no one save the lord of this land who even approaches his level of influence. I hate to say it, but we are fortunate to be alive and free after Sampson sprung that trap on us the other night."

"Yes, yes, you need not remind me of the captured dancers... they are still fresh in my mind..." she muttered, looking down. "I will do what I must to free them if they are still alive. I owe them that much."

"Yer a part of this team, now. So, *we* owe them," Giles said with a nod of approval. Satara returned a half-hearted smile.

"Funny ye bring dat up. Me an' Kabel were tryin' to free slaves here 'n dere before all of dis 'monolith' business popped up an' took over our lives," Rolf said, then gulped down the rest of his drink. "I used to be a slave, so ye don't gotta convince me. I'm in!"

"If we are to remain a team, then I agree we must set a new objective. It'll have to clear with the leaders, though," Dhogron said.

"I can be very persuasive," Satara said with a knowing smile. "Who would be the easiest to convince?"

Giles let out a snorting chuckle. He looked to where the pirates had just taken seats: next to Alistair and Triston. *A perfect distraction*, he thought.

"Auber. Definitely Captain Auber."

CAPTAIN AUBER BELCHED after finally finishing a single mug of his drink. All of the others were well into their fourths or fifths, and in the MacRae brothers' cases, uncountable amounts.

"Would you like another, sir?" Franco asked with a smirk.

"Nah, I think I'll-"

"Load up another fer tha mighty Cap'n Auber!" Alistair shouted, smashing his fractured fist into the counter with excitement. Auber somehow found himself wincing at a pain that was not his own.

"Oh, that's nice of ye, but I think I'm content, fer now..." he muttered.

"Nonsense! Tha great fairer of tha sea, Cap'n Auber, can't possibly be slain by just one drink!" the big redhead insisted while sliding a new drink over to him.

"Enjoy it!" Triston added with a toothy grin. "From what I heard, ya single-handedly stopped them knobbers up by tha north!"

"Well... it didn't exactly happen that way..." Auber rubbed the back of his head while eyeing his crew, nervously.

"Don't be so humble!" Alistair said, then looked to his brother. "This mad lad went an' crashed a ship into Sampson's shipyard! He brought half tha building down!"

Franco and Ebbie looked at their captain with narrowed eyes.

"Uh... erm... well y'know, I had a lotta help..."

"An' ain't it true that ya stopped Drake Danvers himself with a *mere net*?" Alistair asked with clenched fists. Again, he did not seem to pay any heed at all to his swollen hand. "Yer so damned skilled that ya never even needed ta raise yer weapon!"

Auber let loose a nervous chuckle. "It didn't quite go that way..."

"Yeh! I deserve credit, too!" Ebbie said with a potent mixture of excitement and frustration in his tone. "I'm the only one who seems to appreciate the almighty net!"

"I appreciate it, too! Just not as much as…" Auber choked back a few laughs. "The beige berries…"

"Hold up," Triston said, looking at the pirates with suspicious, if drunken, eyes. "So, who threw tha net that defeated our enemy?"

Ebbie and Auber tried talking over one another and then began arguing.

"Allow me to explain," Franco said, silencing them. "Ebbie was using the net before, but when we spotted Drake and crew approaching the sewer, the Captain tried taking it to use for himself. They struggled for a bit, then accidentally dropped it out to sea. It just happened to land on Drake's boat. The kraken took care of the rest. Xviktolo only found a few bodies. The rest went missing, so I'd presume she ate them…"

Alistair's rosy cheeks cooled, just a bit. "Well, that was lucky!"

"Let me tell ya what *wasn't* a matter o' luck, though! That wind Rune really saved me hide! It also helped us throughout tha battle!" Triston shouted with glee. "I'm happy ta see ya comin' into yer own, lil' brother!"

"That's right! With the wind at me side, I'm a force ta be reckoned with! But still, I can only hope ta reach tha same level as Cap'n Auber someday!" Alistair said, then guzzled his drink.

Auber leaned in and whispered to Franco, "How am I gonna keep this act up? What if they find out I'm a big ol' wimp?"

The navigator shrugged. "More importantly, what is our next course of action? We are still without a ship, and I don't get the feeling that the Strangers are swimming in piles of gold at the moment."

"I say we stick around!" Ebbie replied with cheer and excitement. "We'll make money, somehow!"

"Didn't I tell y'all that I had somethin' in mind for you?" Kabel called from further down the counter. "Stick around, and you will see that I'm a man of my word."

The stocky man raised his mug and nodded at them with a smooth smile. The pirates shrugged in response and raised their drinks in unison before taking a swig.

"Hogwash!" Mirabell called from the other end of the pub to a chorus of laughter. Kabel ducked his head and hunched over in his seat.

~

Joel hobbled through the pub, catching the one-eyed glare of Giles as he passed a filled table. That was one of many issues unresolved, he thought. The mute then passed the rowdy pirates and MacRaes to find Pierce near the counter's end. The dagger-eyed man smiled and they clanked mugs as a toast to one another.

"It appears we have survived yet another one of these attempted seal destructions, eh?" Pierce asked. His left arm was in a sling, and his palm had been wrapped with bandages. Joel only smiled. "I'm glad that it was prevented, this time."

Joel began to make hand signals, but then he stopped himself.

"Right… I suppose it's about time we were able to communicate. It looks like Greta and I will be here for a while. May as well start teaching me now."

"Oooo! I can help!" Alistair called out, nearly bowling over Auber and the pirates to reach their spot at the counter. "I can translate for ya!"

Pierce and Joel flashed each other looks of concern, but once the big redhead had his mind made up, there was no convincing him otherwise. At the very least, a very drunk Alistair trying to teach the complexities of USL would be entertaining.

~

"You're really leaving? Just like that?" Lucia's grip trembled around her mug, and Conrad worried that she might break it. His gaze wandered down to her bootless leg, which was wrapped in a bloody cloth. She didn't need any more injuries. "Is it because of me?"

"It has nothing to do with our struggles, really," Conrad said, holding a hand up and bobbing it.

"I don't think you've truly thought this through. What if the Dark Wizard returns with an even larger army of Gold Fever-infected?" Lucia asked.

"You saw what Olius and the Guardian could do. From what Aldous tells me, the Dark Wizard cannot compare with this Wizard King's might. I tend to agree, based on what I saw. Angus and the others seem to have been dealt with, and Drake is probably kraken-food, by now," he replied, then took a sip of his drink. "That leaves

Sampson as the remaining plague of this city, and I know you are capable of handling him."

"And you choose to learn magic from a man in a desert while abandoning the next righteous cause? While abandoning *me*?" Lucia asked.

"You are welcome to join me if you wish," Conrad suggested with a knowing smile.

"Not a chance. I'm staying here." Lucia crossed her arms and her brow crinkled, giving the illusion that the crescent moon tattoo was pinching her eye.

"I thought as much."

"You can claim that it is your interest in magic all you like, but I will always suspect that it was my fault..." Lucia trailed off, darting her eyes away. "And that... that makes me..."

"Angry?" he asked with a chuckle.

"Bothered," she clarified. "Was it not apparent tonight that we still hold an unbreakable bond? That we still trust each other? Our teamwork was flawless; so much so that we defeated a dark essence-enhanced human, and we were well on our way to defeating another before Olius showed up. That is more than anyone in this entire pub could say."

"I cannot deny that brute force and strategy make for a great combination," Conrad said with a warm smile. It soon faded into a contemplative frown. "Still, my experience with the dark essence and its exorcism helped me to realize some of my flaws; flaws that can only be corrected by exploring them."

"We can do that together," Lucia said.

"Remember the tension between us these past couple of weeks. Now, imagine that same tension, but instead for *years*. It would destroy our bond," Conrad replied, shaking his head. "I don't want that to happen. The man whose tutelage I seek... there is no one better, I think, to help me harness my demons toward good causes."

Lucia sighed. "When do you leave?"

"I hope to catch a ship this morning."

"I hate that this is how it ends."

"Oh? Are you calling off our entanglement?" he asked, now smirking.

"Well, no, but-"

"Aldous has agreed to take me back and forth between here and the desert. So, consider this my vow to return; if not for the Strangers, then most certainly for you."

"I'll hold you to it," Lucia said as she held out her mug. The pair toasted and finished their drinks in unison.

~

DALTON LAID his head out on the bar counter and shielded the light from his eyes with his arms. He'd hardly been drinking since the celebration started, yet still, his body groaned and his stomach churned. Something else wasn't sitting well with him.

A hand grasped his shoulder.

"Conrad is departing soon." Lucia's muffled voice barely reached his ears. "I thought it would be nice if our original group saw him off."

The warrior looked up at her and belched. "Nah."

Lucia shook her head and then shrugged. "You need to cut back on the ales."

After she left, Kabel slid his stool over and leaned in.

"You sure you don't wanna see him off?" he whispered. "If he truly intends to trek the Endless Desert, then he may never return."

"Whether he returns or not, Conrad has proven to be yet another fella who is predisposed to disappointment. Take it from someone who knows all too well," Dalton replied.

"Hold up. Yer not drunk… why the act? You've been layin' here for a while, now…" Kabel said.

"Maybe I wanted to be left alone."

"Is this about Anora?"

"Do you know how long it took me to come to terms with her death?" Dalton asked, not looking up.

"A long time, apparently," Kabel said.

"*Years*," the warrior said, shaking his head. "I put off taking care of Lucia, as I had promised, during that time. Instead, she bounced around between relatives who didn't want her. By the time I took her in, it was obvious from her expression alone: she was demoralized; dead inside. And today, for the first time since she came back to me, that same dead look in her eyes returned…"

"I'd tell ye to slug Conrad for it, but I already did that a few nights ago," Kabel said with a laugh.

"Don't get the wrong idea," Dalton said with a clenched fist. "I can forgive Conrad for making the same mistakes as me. But the Dark Wizard… he will pay."

Kabel put a hand on his friend's shoulder. In silence, the two of them guzzled their drinks.

∽

Conrad said his goodbyes to the Strangers as Lucia gathered survivors of the Mt. Couture disaster to see him off. Joel, Aldous, and a very drunk Alistair accompanied them.

After the small group left, Cole cleared his throat, getting the attention of the remaining Strangers. "So, who here is gonna pay the tab?"

The room fell so silent that every breath and creak in the floor could be heard.

"I propose a new rule!" Kabel called out, turning in his stool to face the others. "Newest members gotta pay!"

Satara and Najih's collective jaws nearly hit the floor. The dancer shook her head, emphatically.

"No way are we-"

"All in favor?" Dalton asked over her.

"Aye!" the entire pub replied.

"How could I forget that these are friends of Dhogron? *Of course* they're all cheap!" Satara said with crossed arms, to a roomful of laughs.

The festivities continued with much singing, dancing, drinking, and cheering. It was a happy day for the Strangers despite the great uncertainty looming over them. They could not be sure of what exactly had become of their enemies or what their next plans were. Despite this, they found strength and courage in their newfound numbers. The Strangers had gathered, and there was a certain feeling about the air: Changes were coming to Endoshire, and nothing, whether it be the dark forces, Sampson, or the degenerates, would get in their way.

EPILOGUE

Drake Danvers awoke from his slumber with a start. His quick, straining breaths echoed along with the running water in the dark. There was a splitting pain on his forehead, and the foul odor emanating about the area only increased his discomfort. While the stench of human waste made it apparent that he had somehow been taken into the sewers, there was another odor mixed in that truly filled him with worry: rotting flesh.

It was a smell he had become more and more familiar with over the years. Whether they were threats to his good name or people simply in his way, Drake's ascent to the top had come at the expense of many victims.

The Village Elder winced as he felt his forehead; there was a size-able gash, but nothing that had crippled him. He reached all around his body, searching for more wounds or pains. To his relief, he could find no more injuries. His eyes were beginning to adjust to the dark, and the early onsets of panic were fading, steadily turning to confidence. After all, he'd survived an attack from the kraken that had probably killed most of the others. Perhaps it was fate. Now, he was closer than ever to the *inordinate power*.

With that thought, Drake reached into his pocket and retrieved a soggy, torn map. Disappointment and frustration overwhelmed him. So close to his goal, and he would have to leave rather than pursue it. His entire body had been drenched from the capsized boat, and with his eyes having adjusted to the dark, he could see that water wasn't the only thing covering him.

"Ugh…" he muttered. There was excrement all over him, so much that it now overwhelmed all of his senses.

Drake scanned what little of the environment was not blanketed in darkness to see that he was in a rounded chamber of sorts; one with a sloping walkway that circled a great pool at the center. To his right, he noticed a stream flowing out of a slit in the wall. It traveled down a carved-out irrigation system and into the pool. Almost directly across from him, he could make out vague notions of light; likely a tunnel leading to the exit, he thought.

"Master Drake…" a weak voice whispered.

Nearly gasping, Drake looked to his left to see one of Rose's servants, shivering, festering, and ragged. She was not well: Half of her clothing had melted away, and whatever had done the deed reached her skin, burning it several layers down. The servant's face was covered in boils, and much of her hair had fallen out.

"P-please… help me…" she wheezed, reaching out with a rickety hand.

Drake jerked his body backward to avoid. "Don't touch me. I don't want whatever got on you touching *my skin.*"

"S-sorry…" the servant said, slumping her posture.

"What happened? Have you seen any of the others?"

"The monster… it… spit on me… some kind of poison… it burns… it hurts… it hurts!" she cried aloud. Drake held an index finger up to his mouth to silence her. "Sorry, Master…"

"And what of the others? Have you seen anyone else?"

"Isabel… the monster… spit all over her… she melted away… then it… ate her…" she said between sobs.

"Who is Isabel?" Drake asked.

The servant stopped her sobbing and looked at him with wide eyes and a slacked jaw. "The… the other servant…"

"Ah, right. I had forgotten for a moment, there."

"What is *my name*, Master?" she asked with suspicion on her tongue. He remained silent. "You don't know it, do you?"

"Do I *need* to?" Drake snapped back, to which she began sobbing again. He let out a long breath to recompose himself. "I apologize, m'lady. What is your name?"

Between sniffles, she squeaked out, "Maria."

"Well then, Maria..." the Village Elder said while standing. "What do you say we leave this foul place?"

The servant attempted to stand, but she fell back onto her bottom. "It's no use... I am too weak... this place is my tomb..."

"That is your choice, and yours alone," Drake said with crossed arms.

"I have... nothing left to live for, anyway..."

"And what if I told you that escaping these tunnels with me would end your servitude?" Drake asked, flashing a cool smile. Maria looked up with newfound hope in her eyes.

"Truly?"

"You have my word. What benefit would there be in lying to you now?" Drake asked.

Maria nodded, then began to stand. Her knees wobbled and her pained groans were louder than Drake would have liked, but after a few moments, she finally reached her feet.

"We must be quiet... Master Drake..." she trailed off, pointing to the pool of dirty water. "It's in there..."

Drake nodded, and the pair began their trek around the circular chamber, using the dim light of the tunnel across from them as their guide. As they walked, the Village Elder noticed several bones with rotting flesh on them, along with various other odds and ends that he wouldn't expect a sea monster to collect.

Halfway around the circular path, a great splash erupted from the pool, stopping the pair in their tracks. The monstrous tentacles of the kraken sprouted from the muddy water like giant, dancing snakes. One such tentacle was wrapped around a struggling Barret, who hissed and buzzed, but try as he might, could not find the strength to break free.

Maria began to breathe heavily as the dark kraken rose, pinning the fly-man against the ground. Its mantle was turned to them.

"Keep moving," Drake whispered.

The servant obeyed, and they continued, tepidly, on the circular path. Their eyes were no longer upon the tunnel, however. Instead, their heads were turned toward Barret's struggle. The kraken slid its tentacle down so that his wings were freed.

With a sudden burst of energy, the fly-man fluttered his translucent wings, attempting to take flight. He managed to lift off into the air, but the kraken's tentacle was still wrapped tight around his waist, and like a dog at the end of his leash, he was only able to get so far before snapping back. The kraken ended his attempts by slamming him down onto the circular path several times until he began to deform. Dark bloodstains drenched the stone floor where he was laid; broken, buzzing lightly, and occasionally twitching.

Out of the pool appeared another tentacle, which grasped onto Barret's left wing, while the other grabbed the right wing. The kraken lifted him by both wings, then began to stretch them outward. Barret hissed and flailed with his broken arms and legs as the appendages ripped, thread by thread. Even Drake found himself wincing at the unsavory noises.

Finally, the wings came completely unattached, giving way to an eruption of dark blood from Barret's shoulder blades. The fly-man fell to the nasty stone floor once again, where he squirmed in agony. Just as it seemed like his situation couldn't get any worse, the kraken tilted back and unleashed the vile poison from its mouth, drenching Barret completely.

Sounds of searing flesh crackled off the walls as the fly-man squealed and squirmed. The toxin easily melted through his insect-like hide and leaked down to his innards. His regenerative abilities were not fast enough to keep up with the corrosive substance. Soon, his struggles ceased, and the kraken picked his decaying body up, tilted back again, and dropped him into its gaping mouth.

The crunches and splatter of Barret's body echoed off the chamber walls and seemed to strike Maria. She yelped like a frightened pup as they neared the exit tunnel.

Drake looked back at her with fiery eyes. "What the hell are you doing?"

Maria covered her mouth, then turned away. "I-I'm sorr-"

She was interrupted by the squeals of the kraken, prompting the pair to stop and turn around. The sea monster had already finished its meal and cast sight upon them as the next target. It pulled itself out of the pool with the flesh-tearing strength of its tentacles and had already gained considerable ground on them.

Maria clenched her fists and nodded. "We must hurry, Master Dra-"

As she was turning and beginning to run, Drake pushed her with all of his might, sending the servant crashing to the floor. The Village Elder fired one last look of discontent at her, then turned and made a dash for the exit tunnel ahead.

"Bastard!" she called out from behind, but he dared not look back. "I curse you! I curse you and that whore you call a queen!"

Drake entered the tunnel and felt exhaustion set in, but now was the time to dig deep and continue the mad dash for his life. Maria's final, bitter words would serve well as a distraction for the monster nearby.

"No! No! I don't wanna die! I don't wanna d-"

The splatter of the kraken's poison stamped out any sign of Maria's weak voice. As he ran, all Drake could hear was the sound of searing flesh, and the moans of a woman soon to be dead.

Now, it seemed obvious that Maria would have slowed him down, he assured himself. She had to die. Tough decisions like that would be commonplace once he came to power. Her sacrifice was key to his survival, and that's all there was to it. She had revealed her true nature with those vile last words, anyhow. Everyone revealed their true nature before death, he reasoned.

At the end of the tunnel, Drake found paths going both right and left. The stream running alongside him combined into a river that flowed to his right. At the end of that path was a natural light that called to him. The hisses and squeals of the kraken behind convinced him to make a quick decision, and before he knew it, the Village Elder found himself running along the right side of the flowing river.

Shielding his eyes as the light at the end of the tunnel grew stronger, Drake felt relief set in; the horrid smell began to dissipate, and so too did the shrieks of the kraken. Upon reaching the end of the tunnel, Drake celebrated his freedom by diving into the ocean with glee. It was still muddy, disgusting water, but compared to where he was, it was practically bathwater.

Searching around, Drake spotted a ladder going up the side of the sewer pipe. He could hear the hustle and bustle of the crowds above, and it filled him with excitement. Against all odds, he had made it out of the deadly kraken's lair. He had not achieved his goal, but at least he was still alive, and that was more than any of the others who had accompanied him could say.

Upon reaching the top of the ladder, however, Drake was greeted with a surprise: Down near dock 10, Joel, Aldous, Conrad, Alistair, and Lucia stood, conversing with one another. He could see baggage over the strategist's shoulder, but all of the others were empty-handed.

"Returning to Faiwell, eh?" Drake muttered to himself. "I'll have to ensure that I get back there before him, for that letter… I am still alive, after all…"

Drake smirked as Lucia hugged Conrad, and the others gave handshakes to bid farewell. They would all be dismayed to hear the news of his tragic death, he thought with a malicious smile. The Dark Wizard's interest in the Mercer boy had cost them too much. He'd carry the hit out himself if he had to.

The Village Elder's thoughts were interrupted by a group of nobles staring at him. He looked down at his excrement-stained clothing, then took one sniff to understand why; he was presenting quite an unkempt appearance in a section of the city where high-class folk roamed.

Looking around, however, Drake came to realize that it wasn't just the nobles; a few avian tweeted while looking at him out of the corner of their eyes. Children giggled and pointed as they walked by, and even the servants of the wealthy folk glanced his way.

With a scoff, Drake began walking toward his quarters, where he could wash up and make himself presentable. The looks and stares he was drawing were unbefitting for a king. In fact, he thought, it should have been *him* looking down at *them*.

After a brisk walk, Drake reached his building to find it empty. It was exactly as he had left it before departing for Sampson's shipyard the prior night. If none of his allies had returned, did that mean they had been defeated? Or were they still battling for the monolith in the sewers? He had no way of knowing, and it was yet another frustration stemming from his lack of inclusion in the plans.

Drake began to wash up on one of the bottom floors as he looked to the future. Next time he saw Oneth, he would need to be summoned to Faiwell, but it was a delicate subject; he couldn't let him know that he was going back to obtain his letter before Conrad could open it.

He would also demand to be let back into the group's plans if they had failed. It seemed clear as day to him that the Dark Wizard's strategies were far too simple. They needed more nuance, which was something that he could provide.

After washing up, Drake ascended to the top floor, then entered the bedroom to find Rose lying on her side, with her back to him. It seemed like she hadn't moved an inch since yesterday.

"Are you awake, my dear?" he asked while beginning to change clothes.

"Yes… where have you been?" she replied.

Drake looked over his shoulder and smiled. It seemed like she was in better spirits, today. "I had a meeting with Sampson. How are you feeling?"

"Well… it's hard to say…" Rose trailed off, then grunted and rustled the bed sheets.

"How so?"

She grunted once more, and the bed groaned. "I'm not sure how, but… it feels like I've come along faster than normal, in my pregnancy."

"Ah, well, that's to be expected, isn't it?" Drake asked as he pulled up a new pair of pants and began buttoning them. "After all, the dark essence is designed to eliminate weakness. It must have seen the long pregnancy as one such vulnerability."

"Right…" Rose said, her voice as calm as a gentle breeze.

Drake turned and let out a gasp. Sitting before him on the bed was a very pregnant Rose. Her belly had grown so large and round that it seemed to take up half of her body. He hadn't anticipated it to be *that quick*.

"My goodness!" he said with an exasperated chuckle. "I may need to fetch the doctor. It looks like you could give birth at any moment!"

"Could my servants not fetch him?" Rose asked with a warm smile. Drake searched her eyes for any suspicion, but she wore a cool smile that seemed impossible to read, yet felt genuine all the same. "I believe their names were Marley and Bella, or some such thing? They have been missing all morning. At this rate, I will have to reprimand them."

He was taken aback once more. Now, she was beginning to sound like a proper queen: demanding, yet fair.

"They… were sent out on some errands," Drake said. Of course, he never planned on telling her that they had become kraken-food. Finding replacements would only be a matter of speaking with Sampson. "And their names are Maria and Isabel, by the way. It will be useful to know your servant's names."

"Their level of service has been quite poor, of late. I may just send them back to Sampson before bothering to learn their names," Rose said with a shrug. Drake searched her face for deception once more, but she remained unwavering in her cool, calm smile.

"You must be hungry with a child growing inside of you so fast," Drake said with a smile of his own.

"Oh darling, *I'm famished*," Rose said, licking her lips.

"Very well. I shall fetch you some food, then," he replied, turning to leave.

"Wait," she said. Drake stopped, then looked over his shoulder to see her rubbing her pregnant belly. "The baby has been kicking, lately. Come over and feel."

Drake cocked his head as Rose beckoned him with a gesture of her index finger and lifted her dress. He returned a warm smile while approaching, and then knelt while pressing a hand up to her belly. He was surprised to find that it was tight as a drum; triggering the long-forgotten memories of Edith's conception.

"You were right, back then," Rose said.

"About what?" He smiled up at her while waiting patiently for the kick to come.

"The *greater good*, of course," the bride-to-be replied, now stroking his hair. "I think that this child, your heir, will prove to be a wonderful addition to our cause."

Drake raised an eyebrow but kept his smile. "Yes, well, I'm glad you finally see things my way. Since the ceremony, I have noticed a change in you, and it has been for the better. You will make a fine queen for our new empire."

"I cannot explain it, but now I am refreshed. I have never felt such clarity of mind and purity of soul. Perhaps it is the newfound responsibility of our child that has given me vision," Rose said, her smile growing wider. Drake continued to feel the pregnant belly. He was beginning to wonder if the so-called 'kicks' had simply been her imagination. "To have such a clear mind… it got me thinking about what you said on the night of my ceremony; about making one difficult sacrifice for the greater good…"

"It is something that important people like us must do on a daily basis. By undergoing the ceremony, you have proven your worth and earned your place at my side, my queen," Drake said with a smirk. "And there shall come times where we will have to make more of those difficult sacrifices and decisions. The masses are foolish and weak, and so we must guide them with our strength and wisdom."

"I agree that sacrifices must be made, but I have a question for you," Rose said.

"What is it, my dear?" Drake asked as he felt a rumble in her belly. Finally, he thought, the baby was going to kick.

"If it is for the greater good, *are you ready to sacrifice yourself?*"

Drake raised an eyebrow. "Wha-"

He gasped as a fissure opened vertically down Rose's belly, and then it spread into a gaping hole with hard, jagged edges. Drake fell forward as his arm was swallowed by the now-open midsection, and he felt the gooey, sticky insides of her womb for a brief moment. Then, like the mighty jaws of a dragon, the jagged edges of Rose's belly snapped shut on his arm.

He whimpered in confusion as the *crunch* of his bone shattering and the taut skin of his forearm *ripping* polluted his mind. Drake's eyes widened with an unspeakable dread as he pulled his arm, bitten off just below the elbow, from the jaws of Rose's belly. Those jagged edges were just like teeth, he realized, and they chewed on his flesh like a ravenous monster with a mind of its own.

"Gah!" Drake cried as blood squirted from the stump of where his forearm once was. He fell back, bottom first, to the floor, and looked up at his bride-to-be, whose warm smile had turned to a menacing grin.

His mind told him to keep calm; to escape while he still could, but his body had different ideas. Drake screamed in agony and grasped his stump of an arm while slipping and sliding with his backpedaling feet off the floor. His breaths grew faster and faster until he began to hyperventilate, and his movements became subdued. He could feel the color leaving his face.

Rose, meanwhile, remained still as the night on her bed, looming over and striking fear into him with her gaze alone. She licked her lips once more and then giggled at the struggling, sweaty mess of a man before her.

"No!" Drake shouted, beginning to understand his situation. Oneth had given Rose the concentrated blend of dark essence, despite explicit directions not to. His fear turned more and more to anger as he grasped the profusely bleeding stump of his arm. "That damned Dark Wizard! He lied to me! Double-crossed me! He will pay! You will both pay!"

"And what can the likes of *you* possibly do to *me*?" Rose asked with narrowed eyes and the grin of a demon stalking her prey.

For once, Drake was at a complete loss of words. There was no rebuttal, recourse, or defense for him. He began whimpering again. Now, all he could do was grovel.

"P-please… spare me…"

Rose let out a crass chuckle, then stood over him with judgment in her eyes. "This is not behavior fitting of a king…"

Drake's eyes widened, reflecting a brief rage at her mockery, but then they returned to their sorrowful, desperate state. "I-I'm sorry… I-I only wanted… what was best for you… my dear…"

"Tell me, then," she said, tilting her head so far sideways that it was unnatural. "What is best for me, your queen?"

With hoarse breaths and eyes darting back and forth, Drake ran through his mind, searching for an answer that would allow him to live.

"A-anything, my queen! I… I'll do anything you ask…"

"You will call me 'Master', from now on," Rose commanded, to which Drake returned a dumbfounded expression.

Yet still, he put his head down. "Yes, Master…"

"Very good, my loyal subject," Rose said, putting hands to hips. "But you see, I don't think such a pathetic little man should be king…"

"Huh?" Drake asked aloud, snapping out of his desperate act. A rage built up in him, but there was nothing he could do besides cower at her feet, for now.

"Yes… I think you shall be my servant from now on…" she said, her grin growing so wide that it reminded him of Catalina's inhumanly wide smile. "My *indentured servant.*"

"Why, you-"

"Is that a problem?" Rose snarled back, to which Drake flinched and lowered his head once more.

"No, Master. I-I'm sorry… please… let me live… I live… to serve you… from here on…" Drake said between whimpers.

"That is a very wise position for you to take. You must make sacrifices for the greater good, after all," Rose said as Drake let out nervous chuckles. He could no longer bear to look her in the eye, and the blood loss from his arm brought with it lightheadedness. "There is just one problem, though…"

"What is it… my Master? I will do anything… anything! Just say the word!"

"You see, I think that you would make for a fine servant, but that is not to be your sacrifice," Rose said as the jagged jaws of her pregnant belly opened up once more, this time so wide that the entirety of her womb could be seen. Drake flinched and cried out in fear at the horrid sight. "No… your sacrifice will be for *our child!*"

Out from the open womb shot a red, fleshy, umbilical cord. It wrapped around Drake's neck like a snake would its prey. Gurgles escaped from his mouth as the cord tightened and slowly began dragging him in toward the open mouth of the belly. He grabbed at it with his remaining hand, but it only tightened in response to his resistance. He had become too weak from blood loss; though he suspected that even at top strength, it would not have made a difference.

Drake ceased his struggles as he neared the great jaws of her belly. He saw movement inside of the womb, and then a protective layer being ripped apart. Emerging halfway from the tissue was a little blond boy with gleaming green eyes.

"M-my son…" he choked out, a smirk cracking on his now-purple face.

The pride in his child was short-lived, however, as the baby's hands grew larger than his head, and his nails turned into long, red claws. He then opened his mouth so wide that it was comparable to the opening of a barrel, and filling out the inside were several rows of monstrous teeth.

"N-no…" Drake rasped as he drew nearer to his doom. "Y-you've made… a monster… burn in hell… both of you…"

Rose laughed as the umbilical cord pulled him to his feet and brought them face-to-face. The jaw of the belly closed around Drake, each tooth gouging deep into his torso and arms like arrowheads. He began convulsing at the searing pain until his legs gave out, but a second clamping and *crunch* of his ribs held him up. With his light-headedness reaching its apex, Drake coughed up some blood onto her cheek. She licked it up with pleasure.

"P-please…" he mumbled. The emotion emptied from his words faster than the leaking blood of his wounds. "We can still… be king and queen… of this world… just… let me go…"

"Your role has already been determined," Rose said as a sharp pain in his stomach sent waves throughout his body. It was being ripped and torn apart, he realized, on both the outside and inside. "You are to be baby food."

"Gah! No!" Drake cried with his last reserves of energy. He could feel his intestines snaking out of him; slurped up, little by little, like spaghetti. "Someone… help… I don't… deserve this…"

Drake's eyes glazed over as he heard the mushy sounds of his midsection being emptied by his own son. His head slumped, but Rose caught him by the jaw and raised it back up. She then started to kiss his neck with more passion than she'd ever shown him before.

Under so much pain, stress, and blood loss, Drake could only babble vague notions of speech in confusion as Rose stopped and looked him dead in the eyes.

"I'm hungry, too," she said before arching her neck back and opening her mouth.

Much like their son, Rose's mouth had grown inhumanly large and featured many rows of monstrous teeth. As she snapped her head forward, aiming for his neck, Drake couldn't help but reflect on his bitterness. His would-be queen and heir apparent were feasting upon him, despite his efforts to uplift and enrich them. He hoped they would fail in their conquests, and die worse deaths than him. But more than anything, he prayed that his letter would find Conrad, giving him a chance to destroy that treacherous dog of a Dark Wizard.

The *crunch* of her bite around his neck reminded him of someone chomping into an apple, and for some reason, it made him smile. Drake's head rolled, but something caught him by the hair before he could hit the floor. His eyes fell on Rose's bloody, monstrous face, looking up at him with obvious amusement. At her feet, he caught wind of his headless body, laid out on the floor.

Yet, his air-starved brain stirred one last time, not by a sight, but by a peculiar feeling: the tousling of his hair. Rose was tugging at his strands, and for reasons beyond his current level of comprehension, it horrified him; more than the fact that he was now falling again; more than the gaping hole of a mouth that awaited him below; and even more than the darkness overtaking his eyes, wide open. One more *crunch* overpowered his ears as all fell to black. The king had fallen before his reign could even begin.

THE END

If you enjoyed *A Gathering of Strangers*, join the newsletter and receive free side stories set in the Dark Savior Series world! You'll get all side stories released up to this point, including *Slaying the Beast*, *Ground Into Dust*, and *The Seer's Game*. As more are released, you will receive those for free as well!

https://www.jimclougherty.com/subscribe-fantasy

For more information and updates on the Dark Savior Series, visit https://www.jimclougherty.com/

Amazon Author Page: https://www.amazon.com/Jim-Clougherty/e/B07TXCK9XZ/

Your opinion matters to me. Let me know if you enjoyed this story:

Amazon Review Page: https://www.amazon.com/review/create-review?asin=B0CPT7N9FC

Goodreads Page: https://www.goodreads.com/review/new/203539725-a-gathering-of-strangers

ACKNOWLEDGMENTS

I would like to thank Jean Clougherty, who provided very much helpful feedback in the early stages of this story. And as always, I owe a big thank you to all who have read and supported my novels over the years. These three rewrites have been a long road, but anytime I thought to give up, I only needed to remind myself of the interest and enthusiasm people have shown me over the years. Now that this rewrite is finished, the Dark Savior Series will continue!